Samuel Pepys

Diary and Correspondence of Samuel Pepys F.R.S.

Secretary to the Admiralty in the Reign of Charles II and James II. Vol. II

DIARY AND CORRESPONDENCE

OF

Samuel Pepys, F.R.S.

SECRETARY TO THE ADMIRALTY

IN THE REIGN OF CHARLES II. AND JAMES II.

THE DIARY DECIPHERED BY THE REV. J. SMITH, A. M.,
FROM THE ORIGINAL SHORTHAND MS.

LIFE AND NOTES BY

RICHARD, LORD BRAYBROOKE

WITH FOUR PORTRAITS ON STEEL

IN FOUR VOLUMES
VOL. II

PHILADELPHIA

DAVID McKAY, Publisher

610 So. Washington Square

Samuel Pepys

Diary and Correspondence of Samuel Pepys F.R.S.
Secretary to the Admiralty in the Reign of Charles II and James II. Vol. II

ISBN/EAN: 9783337017309

Printed in Europe, USA, Canada, Australia, Japan

Cover: Foto ©Raphael Reischuk / pixelio.de

More available books at **www.hansebooks.com**

DIARY

OF

SAMUEL PEPYS.

~~~~~~~~~~~~~~~~

1663.

JUNE 1ST. The Duke having been a hunting to-day, and so lately come home and gone to bed, we could not see him, and we walked away. And I with Sir J. Minnes to the Strand May-pole;[1] and there light out of his coach, and walked to the New Theatre,[2] which, since the King's players are gone to the Royal one, is this day begun to be employed by the fencers to play prizes at. And here I come and saw the first prize I ever saw in my life: and it was between one Mathews, who did beat at all weapons, and one Westwicke, who was soundly cut several times both in the head and legs, that he was all over blood: and other deadly blows they did give and take in very good earnest, till Westwicke was in a sad pickle. They fought at eight weapons, three boutes at each weapon. This being upon a private quarrel, they did it in good earnest; and I felt one of their swords, and found it to be very little, if at all, blunter on the edge than the common swords are. Strange to see what a deal of money is flung to them both upon the stage between every boute. So, well pleased for once with this sight, I walked home. This day I hear at Court of the great plot which was lately discovered in Ireland, made among the Presbyters and others, designing to cry up the Covenant,

---

[1] The raising of the Strand Maypole has been assigned to John Clarges, a blacksmith, whose daughter had the good fortune to become the wife of General Monk.—Brayley's *Londiniana*, vol. iii., p. 260.

[2] Opened 8th April, 1663.

and to secure Dublin Castle and other places; and they have debauched a good part of the army there, promising them ready money. Some of the Parliament there, they say, are guilty, and some withdrawn upon it; several persons taken, and among others a son of Scott's, that was executed here for the King's murder. What reason the King hath, I know not; but it seems he is doubtfull of Scotland: and this afternoon, when I was there, the Council was called extraordinary; and they were opening the letters this last post's coming and going between Scotland and us and other places. The King of France is well again.

2d. To St. James's, to Mr. Coventry; where I had an hour's private talk with him concerning his own condition, at present being under the censure of the House, being concerned with others in the Bill for selling of offices. He tells me, that though he thinks himself to suffer much in his fame hereby, yet he values nothing more of evil to hang over him; for that it is against no statute, as is pretended, nor more than what his predecessors time out of mind have taken; and that so soon as he found himself to be in an errour, he did desire to have his fees set, which was done; and since that time he hath not taken a token more. He undertakes to prove, that he did never take a token of any captain to get him employed in his life beforehand, or demanded any thing: and for the other accusation, that the Cavaliers are not employed, he looked over the list of them now in the service, and of the twenty-seven that are employed, thirteen have been heretofore always under the King; two neutralls, and the other twelve men of great courage, and such as had either the King's particular commands, or great recommendation to put them in, and none by himself. Besides that, he sees it is not the King's nor Duke's opinion that the whole party of the late officers should be rendered desperate. And lastly, he confesses that the more of the Cavaliers are put in, the less of discipline hath followed in the fleet; and that, whenever there comes occasion, it must be the old ones that must do any good. He tells me, that he cannot guess whom all this should come from; but he suspects Sir G. Carteret, as I also do, at least that he is pleased with it. But he tells me that he will

bring Sir G. Carteret to be the first adviser and instructor of
him [as to] what is to make his place of benefit to him; telling
him that Smith did make his place worth 5000l., and he believed 7000l. to him the first year; besides something else
greater than all this, which he forbore to tell me. It seems
one Sir Thomas Tomkins,[1] of the House, that makes many
mad motions, did bring it into the House, saying that a letter
was left at his lodgings, subscribed by one Benson, which is a
feigned name, for there is no such in the Navy, telling him
how many places in the Navy have been sold. And in
another letter, left in the same manner since, nobody appearing, he writes him that there is one Hughes, and another,
Butler, both rogues, that have for their roguery been turned
out of their places, that will swear that Mr. Coventry did sell
their places and other things. I offered him my service, and
will with all my heart serve him; but he tells me he do not
think it convenient to meddle, or to any purpose. To Westminster Hall, where I hear more of the plot from Ireland;
which it seems hath been hatching, and known to the Lord
Lieutenant a great while, and kept close till within three days
that it should have taken effect. The terme ended yesterday,
and it seems the Courts rose sooner for want of causes than it
is remembered to have done in the memory of man. To Mr.
Beacham, the goldsmith, he being one of the jury to-morrow,
in Sir W. Batten's case against Field. I have been telling
him our case, and I believe he will do us good service there.
With the vintner's man, who came by my direction to taste
again my tierce of claret, to go down to the cellar with him
to consult about the drawing of it; and there, to my great
vexation, I find that the cellar door hath long been kept un-
locked, and above half the wine drunk.

3d. Sir W. Batten is this morning gone to Guildhall, to his
trial with Field. I to my office, and there read all the
morning in my statute-book, consulting among others the
statute against selling of offices, wherein Mr. Coventry is so
much concerned; and though he tells me that the statute do

---

[1] Burgess for Weobly, and one of the proposed Knights of the Royal Oak,
for Herefordshire.

1 *

not reach him, yet I much fear that it will. At noon, hearing that the trial is done, and Sir W. Batten come to the Sun behind the Exchange, I went thither, where he tells me that he had much ado to carry it on his side, but at the last he did, but the Jury, by the Judge's favour, did give us but 10l. damages, and the charges of the suit, which troubles me, but it is well it went not against us, which would have been much worse.

4th. In the Hall a good while; where I heard that this day the Archbishop of Canterbury, Juxon,[1] a man well spoken of by all for a good man, is dead; and the Bishop of London[2] is to have his seat. Sir J. Minnes do treat my Lord Chancellor and a great deal of guests to-day with a great dinner, which I thank God I do not pay for; and besides, I doubt it is too late for any man to expect any great service from my Lord Chancellor, for which I am sorry, and pray God a worse do not come in his room. The match between Sir J. Cutts[3] and my Lady Jemimah[4] is likely to go on;[5] for which I am glad. In the Hall to-day, Dr. Pierce tells me that the Queen begins to be briske, and play like other ladies, and is quite another woman from what she was. It may be, it may make the King like her the better, and forsake his two mistresses, my Lady Castlemaine and Stewart.

5th. To Paul's Churchyard, where I found several books ready bound for me: among others, the new Concordance of the Bible, which pleases me much, and is a book I hope to make good use of. To Deptford, where Dr. Britton,[6] parson of the town, a fine man and good company, dined with us, and good discourse. To Mrs. Turner's, and there saw Mr. Edward Pepys's lady, who my wife concurs with me to be very pretty,[7] as most women we ever saw.

6th. To York House, where the Russia Embassador do lie;

[1] William Juxon, made Bishop of London, 1633, translated to Canterbury, 1660.

[2] Gilbert Sheldon, who succeeded him.   [3] Of Childerley, near Cambridge.

[4] Montagu.   [5] It went off, and she married Philip Carteret.

[6] Robert Bretton, D.D., vicar of St. Nicholas, Deptford. He was also rector of St. Martin's, Ludgate, and prebendary of Cadington Minor, in the church of St. Paul's. See Evelyn's Diary, Feb. 20, 1672.

[7] Elizabeth, daughter and co-heir of John Walpole of Bransthorp, Norfolk. Ob. s. p. s., 1668.

and there I saw his people go up and down louseing themselves: they are all in a great hurry, being to be gone the
beginning of next week. But that that pleased me best, was
the remains of the noble soul of the late Duke of Buckingham
appearing in his house, in every place, in the door-cases and
the windows. Sir John Hebden,[1] the Russia Resident, did
tell me how he is vexed to see things at Court ordered as they
are by nobody that attends to business, but every man himself or his pleasures. He cries up my Lord Ashley to be
almost the only man that he sees to look after business; and
with the ease and mastery, that he wonders at him. He cries
out against the King's dealing so much with goldsmiths, and
suffering himself to have his purse kept and commanded by
them. He tells me also with what exact care and order the
States of Holland's[2] stores are kept in their Yards, and every
thing managed there by their builders with such husbandry as
is not imaginable; which I will endeavour to understand
further.

7th. (Lord's day.) Mrs. Turner, who is often at Court, do
tell me to-day that for certain the Queen hath much changed
her humour, and is become very pleasant and sociable as any;
and they say is with child, or believed to be so. After church
to Sir W. Batten's; where my Lady Batten inveighed
mightily against the German Princess, and I as high in the
defence of her wit and spirit, and glad that she is cleared at
the Sessions.

10th. To dinner, and thence to the Royal Theatre by
water, and landing, met with Captain Ferrers his friend, the
little man that used to be with him, and he with us, and sat
by us while we saw "Love in a Maze." The play is pretty
good, but the life of the play is Lacy's part, the clown, which
is most admirable; but for the rest, which are counted old
and excellent actors, in my life I never heard both men and
women so ill pronounce their parts. Thence to the whay-
house, and drank a great deal of whay, and so by water home.

12th. To the Royal Theatre; and there saw "The Com-

---

[1] Who had made a fortune in Russia by trade. On the 30th May, 1663, he was
knighted by Charles, at Whitehall.

Hebden had been resident with the States General in 1660.

mittee,"[1] a merry but indifferent play, only Lacy's part, an
Irish footman, is beyond imagination.   Here I saw my Lord
Falconbridge,[2] and his lady, my Lady Mary Cromwell, who
looks as well as I have known her, and well clad: but when
the house began to fill, she put on her vizard,[3] and so kept it
on all the play; which of late is become a great fashion
among the ladies, which hides their whole face.   So to the
Exchange, to buy things with my wife; among others, a
vizard for herself.

13th. To the Royal Theatre; here we saw "The Faithful
Sheepeardesse,"[4] a most simple thing, and yet much thronged
after, and often shown, but it is only for the scenes' sake,
which is very fine indeed, and worth seeing; but I quite out
of opinion of any of their actings but Lacy's, compared with
the other house.   In our way saw my Lady Castlemaine,
who, I fear, is not so handsome as I have taken her for, and
now she begins to decay something.   This is my wife's
opinion also, for which I am sorry.   Thence by coach, with a
mad coachman, that drove like mad, and down byeways,
through Bucklersbury home — everybody through the street
cursing him, being ready to run over them.   Yesterday, upon
conference with the King in the Banqueting House, the Parliament did agree with much ado, it being carried but by
forty-two voices, that they would supply him with a sum of
money; but what, and how, is not yet known, but expected
to be done with great disputes the next week.   But if done
at all, it is well.

---

[1] A comedy, by Sir Robert Howard.

[2] Thomas Belasses, Viscount Falconberg, frequently called Falconbridge, married Mary, third daughter of Oliver Cromwell.   She died 1712.

[3] Vizard masques, probably came into fashion about this time.   On the 1st of
June, 1704, a song was sung at the theatre in Lincoln's Inn Fields, called "The
Misses' Lamentation for want of their Vizard Masques at the Theatre."   Notwithstanding the gross licentiousness of the drama, after the Restoration, numbers of
females of all denominations frequented the theatres, though many of them wore
masks to disguise their features, and this bad habit had a still worse effect, by the
facilities which it afforded to intrigue and assignation.   The custom is pointedly
referred to in Pope's well-known lines:—

> "The fair sat panting at a courtier's play,
> And not a Mask went unimproved away;
> The modest fan was lifted up no more,
> And virgins smiled at what they blushed before."

[4] A pastoral, by John Fletcher.

14th. (Lord's day.) I did give my wife 40s. to carry into
the country to-morrow with her, whereof 15s. is to go for the
coach-hire for her and Ashwell, there being 20s. paid here
already in earnest.　　To Sir W. Pen's, to visit him, and,
finding him alone, sent for my wife, who is in her riding-suit,
to see him, which she hath not done these many months, I
think.　Comes Sir J. Minnes and Sir W. Batten.　So we
sat talking: among other things, Sir J. Minnes brought many
fine expressions of Chaucer, which he doats on mightily, and
without doubt [he] is a very fine poet.

15th. I was forced to go to Thames Street: thence home,
but finding my wife gone, I took coach and after her to her
inn, where I am troubled to see her forced to sit in the back
of the coach, though pleased to see her company none but
women and one parson, and so kissing her often, and Ashwell
once, I bid them adieu.　To the Trinity House; where,
among others, I found my Lords Sandwich and Craven, and
my cousin Roger Pepys, and Sir William Wheeler.　Great
variety of talk.　Mr. Prin, among many, had a pretty talk of
one that brought in a bill in parliament for the impowering
him to dispose his land to such children as he should have
that should bear the name of his wife.　It was in Queen
Elizabeth's time.　One replied, that there are many species
of creatures where the male gives the denomination to both
sexes, as swan and woodcocke, but not above one where the
female do, and that is goose.　Both at and after dinner, we
had great discourses of the nature and power of spirits, and
whether they can animate dead bodies; in all which, as of the
general appearance of spirits, my Lord Sandwich is very
scepticall.　He says the greatest warrants that ever he had
to believe any, is the present appearing of the Devil[1] in

---

[1] "In 1664, there being a generall report all over the kingdom of Mr. Monpesson his house being haunted, which hee himself affirming to the King and
Queene to be true, the King sent the Lord Falmouth, and the Queene sent mee,
to examine the truth of it; but wee could neither see nor heare anything that
was extraordinary; and about a year after, his Majesty told me that bee had
discovered the cheat, and that Mr. Monpesson, upon his Majesty sending for him,
confessed it to him.　And yet Mr. Monpesson, in a printed letter, had afterwards
the confidence to deny that bee had ever made any such confession."—*Letters
of the Second Earl of Chesterfield,* p. 24, 1829, 8vo.　Joseph Glanville pub-

Wiltshire, much of late talked of, who beats a drum up and
down. There are books of it, and, they say, very true ; but
my Lord observes, though he do answer any tune that you
will play to him upon another drum, yet one time he tried to
play and could not ; which makes him suspect the whole ;
and I think it is a good argument. They talked of handsome
women ; and Sir J. Minnes saying that there was no beauty
like what he sees in the country-markets, and specially at
Bury, in which I will agree with him. My Lord replied
thus : Sir John, what do you think of your neighbour's wife ?
looking upon me. Do you not think that he hath a great
beauty to his wife ? Upon my word he hath. Which I was
not a little proud of.

16th. Dined with Sir W. Batten ; who tells me that the
House have voted the supply, intended for the King, shall be
by subsidy.

17th. To White Hall, and in the garden spoke to my Lord
Sandwich, who is in his gold-buttoned suit, as the mode is,
and looks nobly. Captain Ferrers, I see, is come home from
France. He tells me the young gentlemen are well there :
so my Lord went to my Lord Albemarle's to dinner, I by
water home. I sent my cozen Edward Pepys his lady, at my
cozen Turner's, a piece of venison given me yesterday, and
Madam Turner I sent for a dozen bottles of her's, to fill with
wine for her. This day I met with Pierce, the surgeon : who
tells me that the King has made peace between Mr. Edward
Montagu and his father Lord Montagu, and that all is well
again, at which, for the family's sake, I am glad, but do not
think it will hold long.

19th. To Lambeth, expecting to have seen the Archbishop
lie in state ; but it seems he is not laid out yet. At the
Privy Seale Office examined the books, and found the grant of

lished a relation of the famous disturbance at the house of Mr. Monpesson,
at Tedworth, Wilts, occasioned by the beating of an invisible drum every night
for a year. This story, which was believed at the time, furnished the plot for
Addison's play of "The Drummer, or the Haunted House." In the *Mercurius
Publicus*, April 16–23, 1663, there is a curious examination on this subject,
by which it appears that one William Drury, of Uscut, Wilts, was the invisible
drummer.

increase of salary to the principall officers in the year 1639, 300*l.* among the Comptroller, Surveyor, and Clerk to the Shippes.   Met Captain Ferrers; who tells us that the King of France is well again, and that he saw him train his Guards, all brave men, at Paris; and that when he goes to his mistress, Madame La Valière, a pretty little woman, now with child by him, he goes publicly, and his trumpets and kettle-drums with him; and yet he says that, for all this, the Queen do not know of it, for that nobody dares to tell her; but that I dare not believe.   To the Rhenish wine-house, where Mr. Moore showed us the French manner, when a health is drunk, to bow to him that drunk to you, and then apply yourself to him, whose lady's health is drunk, and then to the person that you drink to, which I never knew before; but it seems it is now the fashion.

21st. (Lord's day.) To Mr. Coventry's.   He showed me a list he hath prepared for the Parliament's viewe, if the business of his selling of offices should be brought to further hearing, wherein he reckons up, as I remember, 236 offices of ships which have been disposed of without his taking one farthing. This, of his own accord, he opened his cabinet on purpose to show me; meaning, I suppose, that I should discourse abroad of it, and vindicate him therein, which I shall with all my power do.   To church, and slept all the sermon; the Scot [Creighton], to whose voice I am not to be reconciled, preaching.

22d. To Westminster, where all along I find the shops evening with the sides of the houses, even in the broadest streets; which will make the City very much better than it was.   It seems the House do consent to send to the King to desire that he would be graciously pleased to let them know who it was that did inform him of what words Sir Richard Temple[1] should say, which were to this purpose: "That if the King would side with him, or be guided by him and his party, that he should not lack money:" but, without knowing who told it, they do not think fit to call him to any account for it. The Duke being gone a-hunting, by and by come in and

---

[1] Sir Richard Temple, of Stowe, Bart., M.P. for Buckingham, and K.B. Ob 1694.

shifted himself; he having in his hunting, rather than go about, 'light and led his horse through a river up to his breast, and came so home: and being ready, we had a long discourse with him.

23d. To the office; and, after an hour or two, by water to the Temple, to my cousin Roger; who, I perceive, is a deadly high man in the Parliament business, and against the Court, showing me how they have computed that the King hath spent, at least hath received, above four millions of money since he come in: and in Sir J. Winter's case, in which I spoke to him, he is so high that he says he deserves to be hanged. To the 'Change; and by and by comes the King and the Queen by in great state, and the streets full of people. I stood in Mr. ——'s balcone. They dine all at my Lord Mayor's; but what he do for victualls, or room for them, I know not.

24th. To St. James's, and there an hour's private discourse with Mr. Coventry; he told me one thing to my great joy, that in the business of Captain Cocke's hemp disputed before him the other day, Mr. Coventry absent, the Duke did himself tell him since, that Mr. Pepys and he did stand up and carry it against the rest that were there, which do please me much to see that the Duke do take notice of me. Speaking of Sir G. Carteret slightly, and diminishing of his services for the King in Jersey; that he was well rewarded, and had good lands and rents, and other profits from the King, all the time he was there; and that it was always his humour to have things done his way, he brought an example how he would not let the Castle there be victualled for more than a month, that so he might keep it at his beck, though the people of the town did offer to supply it more often themselves. Another thing he told me, how the Duke of York did give Sir G. Carteret and the Island his profit as Admirall, and other things, towards the building of a pier there; but it was never laid out, nor like to be. So, it falling out that a lady being brought to bed, the Duke was to be desired to be one of the godfathers; and it being objected that that would not be proper, there being no peer of the land to be joyned with him, the lady replied, "Why, let him choose; and if he will not be a godfather without a peer, then let him even stay till he hath made a pier of his own."[1] He tells me too that he hath lately been observed to tack about at Court, and to endeavour to strike in with the persons that are against the Chancellor; but this he says of him, that he do not say nor do any thing to the prejudice of the Chancellor. But he told me that the Chancellor was rising again, and that of late Sir G. Carteret's business and employment hath not been so full as it used to be while the Chancellor stood up. From that, we discoursed of the evil of putting out men of experience in business as the Chancellor, and of the condition of the King's party at present, who, as the Papists, though otherwise fine persons, yet being by law kept for these fourscore years out of employment, they are now wholly incapable of business; and so the Cavaliers for twenty years, who, says he, for the most part, have either given themselves over to look after country and family business, and those the best of them, and the rest to debauchery, &c.; and that it was it that hath made him high against the late Bill brought into the House for the making all men incapable of employment that had served against the King. People, says he, in the sea service, it is impossible to do any thing without them, there being not more than three men of the whole King's side that are fit to command almost; and these were Captain Allen, Smith,[2] and Beech;[3] and, it may be, Holmes, and Utber, and Batts might do something. This day I observed the house, which I took to be the new tennis-court, newly built next my Lord's lodgings, to be fallen down by the badness of the foundation or slight working, which my cozen Roger and his discontented party cry out upon, as an example how the King's work is done. It hath beaten down a good deal of my Lord's lodgings, and had like to have killed Mrs. Sarah, she having but newly gone out of it.

25th. Sir G. Carteret did tell us that upon Tuesday last,

---

[1] In the same spirit, long after this, some question arising as to the best material to be used in building Westminster Bridge, Lord Chesterfield remarked, that there were too many wooden piers (peers) at Westminster already.

[2] Afterwards Sir Thomas Allen, and Sir Jeremy Smith.

[3] Richard Beach, afterwards knighted, and, in 1668, Commissioner at Portsmouth

being with my Lord Treasurer, he showed him a letter from Portugall, speaking of the advance of the Spaniards into their country, and yet that the Portuguese were never more courageous than now: for, by an old prophecy sent thither some years, though not many since, from the French King, it is foretold that the Spaniards should come into their country, and in such a valley they should be all killed, and then their country should be wholly delivered from the Spaniards. This was on Tuesday last, and yesterday come the very first news that in this very valley they had thus routed and killed the Spaniards. This noon I received a letter from the country from my wife, wherein she seems much pleased with the country: God continue, that she may have pleasure while she is there. She, by my Lady's advice, desires a new petticoat of the new silk striped stuff—very pretty. So I went to Pater Noster Row presently, and bought her a very fine rich one—the best I did see there, and much better than she desires or expects.

26th. Mr. Moore and I discoursed of going to Oxford this commencement—Mr. Nathaniel Crewe[1] being proctor, and Mr. Childe commencing Doctor of Musique this year. A sad season. It is said there hath not been one fair day these three months, and I think it is true. The House is upon the King's answer to their message about Temple,[2] which is, that my Lord of Bristoll did tell him that Temple did say those words; so the House are resolved upon sending some of their members to him to know the truth, and to demand satisfaction, if it be not true. Sir W. Batten, Sir J. Minnes, my Lady Batten, and I by coach to Bednal Green, to Sir W. Rider's to dinner, where a fine place,[3] good lady mother, and her daughter, Mrs. Middleton, a fine woman. A noble dinner, and a fine merry walk with the ladies alone after

---

[1] Nathaniel, third Lord Crewe of Stene, successively Bishop of Oxford and Durham. He died in 1701, s. p., when the title became extinct.

[2] See 1st July, postea.

[3] Called Kirby Castle, the property of Sir William Ryder, Knight, who died there in 1669.—Lysons's Environs. The house in which Sir William Ryder resided, was built by John Thorpe, in 1570, for "John Kirby," of whom nothing is known, except that it was called after him. Pepys was evidently misinformed in supposing that it ever could have been inhabited by the blind beggar.

dinner in the garden: the greatest quantity of strawberrys I ever saw, and good. This very house was built by the blind beggar of Bednall Green, so much talked of and sang in ballads; but they say it was only some of the outhouses of it. At table discoursing of thunder and lightning, Sir W. Rider did tell a story of his own knowledge, that a Genoese gally in Leghorne Roads was struck by thunder, so as the mast was broke a-pieces, and the shackle upon one of the slaves was melted clear off his leg without hurting his leg. Sir William went on board the vessel, and would have contributed toward the release of the slave whom Heaven had thus set free; but he could not compass it, and so he was brought to his fetters again.

27th. To the Temple, and so to Lincoln's Inne, and there walked up and down to see the new garden which they are making, and will be very pretty, and so to walk under the Chappell by agreement.

29th. Up and down the streets is cried mightily the great victory got by the Portugalls against the Spaniards, where 10,000 slain, 3 or 4000 taken prisoners, with all the artillery, baggage, money, &c., and Don John[1] of Austria forced to flee with a man or two with him. With my cozen Roger and Mr. Goldsborough to Gray's Inne to his counsel, one Mr. Rawworth, a very fine man, where it being a question whether I as executor should give a warrant to Goldsborough in my reconveying her estate back again, the mortgage being performed against all acts of the testator, but only my own, my cozen said he never heard it asked before; and the other that it was always asked, and that he never heard it denied, or scrupled before, so great a distance was there in their opinions, enough to make a man forswear ever having to do with the law; so they agreed to refer it to Serjeant Maynard.

30th. Yesterday and to-day the sun rising very bright and glorious; and yet yesterday, as it hath been these two months and more, was foul the most part of the day—this being the

---

[1] He was a natural son of Philip IV., King of Spain, who, after his father's death, in 1665, exerted his whole influence to overthrow the Regency appointed during the young King's minority.

only fair day we have had these three or four months. Thus, by God's blessing, ends this book of two years: I being in all points in good health, and a good way to thrive and do well. Some money I do and can lay up, but not much, being worth now above 700*l.*, besides goods of all sorts. My wife in the country with Ashwell, her woman, with my father: myself at home with W. Hewer and my cook-maid Hannah— my boy Waynman being lately run away from me. In my office, my repute and understanding good, specially with the Duke and Mr. Coventry; only the rest of the officers do rather envy than love me, I standing in most of their lights, specially Sir W. Batten, whose cheats I do daily oppose to his great trouble, though he appears mighty kind and willing to keep friendship with me, while Sir J. Minnes, like a dotard, is led by the nose by him. Public matters are in an ill condition: Parliament sitting and raising four subsidys for the King, which is but a little, considering his wants: and yet that parted withal with great hardness. They being offended to see so much money go, and no debts of the public's paid, but all swallowed by a luxurious Court; which the King, it is believed and hoped, will retrench in a little time, when he comes to see the utmost of the revenue which shall be settled on him ; he expecting to have his 1,200,000*l.* made good to him, which is not yet done by above 150,000*l.*, as he himself reports to the House. My differences with my uncle Thomas at a good quiett, blessed be God! and other matters. The town full of the great overthrow lately given to the Spaniards by the Portugall, they being advanced into the very middle of Portugall. The charge of the Navy intended to be limited to 200,000*l.* per annum, the ordinary charge of it, and that to be settled upon the Customes. The King gets greatly taken up with Madam Castlemaine and Mrs. Stewart, which Heaven put an end to! Myself very studious to learne what I can of all things necessary to my place.

July 1st. This morning it rained so hard, though it was fair yesterday, and we therefore in hopes of having some fair weather, which we have wanted these three months, that it wakened Creed, who lay with me last night, and me. Being

in the Parliament Lobby, I there saw my Lord of Bristoll
come to the Commons' House to give his answer to their
question, about some words he should tell the King that were
spoke by Sir Richard Temple. A chair was set at the bar of
the House for him, which he used but little, but made an
harangue of half an hour bareheaded, the House covered.
His speech being done, he come out into a little room till the
House had concluded of an answer to his speech; which they
staying long upon, I went away. And by and by out comes
Sir W. Batten; and he told me that his Lordship had made
a long and a comedian-like speech, and delivered with such
action as was not becoming his Lordship. He confesses he
did tell the King such a thing of Sir Richard Temple, but
that upon his honour the words were not spoke by Sir
Richard, he having taken a liberty of enlarging to the King
upon the discourse which had been between Sir Richard and
himself lately; and so took upon himself the whole blame,
and desired their pardon, it being not to do any wrong to
their fellow-member, but out of zeal to the King. He told
them, among many other things, that as to religion he was a
Roman Catholic, but such a one as thought no man to have
a right to the Crown of England but the Prince that hath it;
and such a one as, if the King should desire counsel as to his
own, he would not advise him to another religion than the
old true reformed religion of this kingdom as it now stands;
and concluded with a submission to what the House shall do
with him, saying, that whatever they shall do,—"thanks be
to God, this head, this heart, and this sword," pointing to
them all, "will find me a being in any place in Europe." The
House hath hereupon voted clearly Sir Richard Temple to
be free from the imputation of saying those words; but when
Sir William Batten come out, had not concluded what to say
to my Lord, it being argued that, to own any satisfaction as
to my Lord from his speech, would be to lay some fault upon
the King, for the message he should upon no better accounts
send to the impeaching of one of their members. Walking
out, I hear that the House of Lords are offended that my
Lord Bristoll should come to this House and make a speech

there without leave first asked of the House of Lords. I hear also of another difficulty now upon him; that my Lord of Sunderland,[1] whom I do not know, was so near to the marriage of his daughter,[2] as that the wedding-clothes were made, and portion and every thing agreed on and ready; and the other day he goes away nobody yet knows whither, sending her the next morning a release of his right or claim to her, and advice to his friends not to enquire into the reason of this doing, for he hath enough for it; and that he gives them liberty to say and think what they will of him, so they do not demand the reason of his leaving her, being resolved never to have her; but the reason desires and resolves not to give. To Sir W. Batten, to the Trinity House; and after dinner we fell a-talking, Mr. Batten telling us of a late trial of Sir Charles Sedley,[3] the other day, before my Lord Chief Justice Foster[4] and the whole bench, for his debauchery[5] a little while since at Oxford Kate's.[6] It seems my Lord and the rest of the Judges did all of them round give him a most high reproofe; my Lord Chief Justice saying, that it was for him, and such wicked wretches as he was, that God's anger and judgments hung over us, calling him sirrah many times. It seems they have bound him to his good behaviour, there being no law against him for it, in 5000*l.* It being told that my Lord Buckhurst was there; my Lord asked whether it was that Buckhurst that was lately tried for robbery;[7] and

---

[1] Robert, second Earl of Sunderland, too well known in the annals of political versatility. Ob. 1702.

[2] For a similar rumour, see in the Appendix a letter from M. de Lionne, July, 1663. The marriage, nevertheless, took place, and the youthful bride, Lady Ann Digby, second daughter, and eventually sole heir of George Digby, Earl of Bristol, became, by the alliance, the ancestress of the Dukes of Marlborough and Earls Spencer.

[3] Sir Charles Sedley, Bart., well known for his wit and profligacy, and author of several plays. He is said to have been fined 500*l.* for this outrage. He was father to James the Second's mistress, created Countess of Dorchester, and died 1701.

[4] Sir Robert Foster, Knt., Chief Justice of the King's Bench. Ob. 1663.

[5] The details in the *Diary* are too gross to print, and may well have disgusted the bench of Judges, accustomed as they were in those times to indecency and profaneness.

[6] In Bow Street. See Shadwell's *Works*, vol. i., p. 45; and art. Bow Street, in Cunningham's *Handbook of London*, ed. 1850.

[7] See an account of this trial, February 22d, 1661-2.

when answered Yes, he asked whether he had so soon forgot his deliverance at that time, and that it would have more become him to have been at his prayers, begging God's forgiveness, than now running into such courses again. This day I hear at dinner that Don John of Austria, since his flight out of Portugall, is dead of his wounds:[1] so there is a great man gone, and a great dispute like to be indeed for the crowne of Spayne, if the King should have died before him. My cousin Roger told us the whole passage of my Lord Bristoll to-day, much as I have said here above; only that he did say that he would draw his sword against the Pope himself, if he should offer any thing against his Majesty, and the good of these nations; and that he never was the man that did either look for a Cardinal's cap for himself, or any body else, meaning Abbot Montagu: and the House upon the whole did vote Sir Richard Temple innocent; and that my Lord Bristoll hath cleared the honour of his Majesty, and Sir Richard Temple's, and given perfect satisfaction of his own respects to the House.

2d. Walking in the garden this evening with Sir G. Carteret and Sir J. Minnes, Sir G. Carteret told us with great content how like a stage-player my Lord Bristoll spoke yesterday, pointing to his head as my Lord did, and saying, "First, for his head," says Sir G. Carteret, "I know when a calfe's head would have done better by half: for his heart and his sword, I have nothing to say to them." He told us that for certain his head cost the late King his, for it was he that broke off the treaty at Uxbridge. He told us also how great a man he [Bristoll] was raised from a private gentleman[2] in France by Monsieur Grandmont,[3] and afterwards by the Cardinal,[4] who raised him to be a Lieutenant-generall, and then higher; and entrusted by the Cardinal, when he was banished out of France, with great matters, and recommended by him to the Queen[5] as a man to be trusted and ruled by: yet, when he

---

[1] It was not true.

[2] He had, however, in June, 1641, been summoned to the House of Peers in his father's barony of Digby.

[3] Antoine, Maréchal-Duc de Grammont.

[4] Cardinal Mazarin.   [5] Anne of Austria, Queen of France.

come to have some power over the Queen, he begun to
dissuade her from her opinion of the Cardinal; which she said
nothing to till the Cardinal was returned, and then she told
him of it; who told my Lord Bristoll, "Eh bien, Monsieur,
vous estes un fort bon amy donc:" but presently put him out
of all; and then, from a certainty of coming in two or three
years to be Mareschall of France, to which all strangers, even
Protestants,[1] and those as often as French themselves, are
capable of coming, though it be one of the greatest places in
France, he was driven to go out of France into Flanders; but
there was not trusted, nor received any kindness from the
Prince of Condé, as one to whom also he had been false, as
he had been to the Cardinal and Grandmont. In fine, he told
us that he is a man of excellent parts, but of no great faith
nor judgment, and one very easy to get up to great height of
preferment, but never able to hold it.

3d. Mr. Moore tells me great news that my Lady
Castlemaine is fallen from Court, and this morning retired.
He gives me no account of the reason, but that it is so; for
which I am sorry; and yet, if the King do it to leave off not
only her, but all other mistresses, I should be heartily glad
of it, that he may fall to look after business. I hear my
Lord Bristoll is condemned at Court for his speech, and that
my Lord Chancellor grows great again. With Mr. Creed
over the water to Lambeth; but could not see the Archbishop's hearse: so over the fields to Southwarke. I spent
half an hour in St. Mary Overy's Church, where are fine
monuments of great antiquity.

4th. Sir Allen Apsley[2] showed the Duke the Lisbon Gazette
in Spanish, where the late victory is set down particularly,
and to the great honour of the English beyond measure.
They have since taken back Evora, which was lost to the
Spaniards, the English making the assault, and lost not more
than three men. Here I learnt that the English foot are

---

[1] Amongst others, Schomberg, who had commanded the Portuguese in the late
fight, obtained this dignity.

[2] Sir Allen Apsley, a faithful adherent to Charles I., after the Restoration
was made Falconer to the King, and Almoner to the Duke of York, in whose
regiment he bore a commission. He was, in 1661, M.P. for Thetford, and died
1683.

highly esteemed all over the world, but the horse not so much,
which yet we count among ourselves the best; but they
abroad have had no great knowledge of our horse, it seems.
With Creed to the King's Head ordinary; but, coming late,
dined at the second table very well for 12*d*.; and a pretty
gentleman in our company, who confirms my Lady Castlemaine's being gone from Court, but knows not the reason;
he told us of one wipe the Queen a little while ago did give
her, when she come in and found the Queen under the
dresser's hands, and had been so long:—"I wonder your
Majesty," says she, "can have the patience to sit so long
a-dressing?"—"I have so much reason to use patience," says
the Queen, "that I can very well bear with it." He thinks
it may be the Queen hath commanded her to retire, though
that is not likely. Thence with Creed to hire a coach to carry
us to Hyde Parke, to-day there being a general muster of the
King's Guards, horse and foot; but they demand so high,
that I, spying Mr. Cutler, the merchant, did take notice of
him, and he going into his coach, and telling me that he
was going to the muster, I asked and went along with him;
where a goodly sight to see so many fine horses and officers,
and the King, Duke, and others come by a-horseback, and
the two Queens in the Queen Mother's coach, my Lady Castlemaine not being there. And after long being there, I
light, and walk to the place where the King, Duke, &c., did
stand to see the horse and foot march by and discharge their
guns, to show a French Marquisse (for whom this muster was
caused) the goodness of our firemen; which indeed was very
good, though not without a slip now and then: and one
broadside close to our coach we had going out of the Park,
even to the nearnesse as to be ready to burn our hairs. Yet
methought all these gay men are not the soldiers that must
do the King's business, it being such as these that lost the
old King all he had, and were beat by the most ordinary
fellows that could be. Thence with much ado out of the
Park, and through St. James's down the water-side over to
Lambeth, to see the Archbishop's corps, who is to be carried
away to Oxford on Monday, but come too late, and so walked

over the fields and bridge home. This day, in the Duke's chamber there being a Roman story in the hangings, and upon the standard written these four letters—S. P. Q. R.; Sir G. Carteret came to me to know what the meaning of those four letters were; which ignorance is not to be borne in a Privy Conncillor, methinks, what a schoolboy should be whipt for not knowing.

5th. (Lord's day.) Lady Batten sent twice to invite me to go with them to Walthamstow to-day—Mrs. Martha[1] being married already this morning to Mr. Castle, at our parish church. I could not rise soon enough to go with them, but got myself ready, and so to Games's, where I got a horse, and rode thither very pleasantly. Being come thither, I was well received, and had two pair of gloves, as the rest, and walked up and down with my Lady in the garden, she mighty kind to me, and I have the way to please her. A good dinner and merry, but methinks none of the kindness nor bridall respect between the bridegroom and bride, that was between my wife and I, but as persons that marry purely for convenience. After dinner to church by coach, and there, my Lady, Mrs. Turner, Mrs. Lemon,[1] and I only, we, in spite to one another, kept one another awake; and sometimes I read in my book of Latin plays, which I kept in my pocket, thinking to have walked it. An old doting parson preached. So home, Sir J. Minnes and I in his coach together, talking all the way of chymistry, wherein he do know something—at least, seems so to me, that cannot correct him.

6th. At my office all the morning, writing out a list of the King's ships in my Navy collections with great pleasure.

7th. In Mr. Pett's garden I eat some of the first cherries I have eat this year, off the tree where the King himself had been gathering some this morning. Deane tells me, what Mr. Pett did to-day, that my Lord Bristoll told the King that he will impeach the Chancellor of High Treason; but I find that my Lord Bristoll hath undone himself already in every body's opinion, and now he endeavours to raise dust to put out other men's eyes as well as his own; but I hope it will not take, in consideration merely that it is hard for a

Prince to spare an experienced old officer, be he never so corrupt; though I hope this man is not so, as some report him to be. He tells me that Don John is yet alive, and not killed, as was said, in the great victory against the Spaniards in Portugall of late.

8th. I hear not what will become of the corn this year, we having had but two fair days these many months.

9th. Sir W. Pen tells me my Lady Castlemaine was at Court, for all this talk this week; but it seems the King is stranger than ordinary to her.

10th. I met Pierce, the chirurgeon, who tells me that for certain the King is grown colder to my Lady Castlemaine than ordinary, and that he believes he begins to love the Queen, and do make much of her, more than he used to do. Mr. Coventry tells me that my Lord Bristoll hath this day impeached my Lord Chancellor in the House of Lords of High Treason. The chief of the articles are these:— 1st. That he should be the occasion of the peace made with Holland lately upon such disadvantageous terms, and that he was bribed to it. 2d. That Dunkirke was also sold by his advice chiefly, so much to the damage of England. 3d. That he had 6000*l.* given him for the drawing-up or promoting of the Irish declaration lately, concerning the division of the lands there. 4th. He did carry on the design of the Portugall match, so much to the prejudice of the Crown of England, notwithstanding that he knew the Queen is not capable of bearing children. 5th. That the Duke's marrying of his daughter was a practice of his, thereby to raise his family; and that it was done by indiscreet courses. 6th. As to the breaking off of the match with Parma, in which he was employed at the very time when the match with Portugall was made up here, which he took as a great slur to him, and so it was; and that indeed is the chief occasion of all this fewde. 7th. That he hath endeavoured to bring in Popery, and wrote to the Pope for a cap for a subject of the King of England's, my Lord Aubigny;[1] and some say that he lays it to the Chancellor, that a good Protestant Secretary.

---

[1] Brother to the Duke of Lennox and Richmond, and Almoner to the King.

Sir Edward Nicholas, was laid aside, and a Papist, Sir H
Bennet, put in his room: which is very strange, when the
last of these two is his own creature, and such an enemy
accounted to the Chancellor, that they never did nor do
agree; and all the world did judge the Chancellor to be
falling from the time that Sir H. Bennet was brought in.
Besides, my Lord Bristoll being a Catholique himself, all this
is very strange.   These are the main of the Articles.   Upon
which my Lord Chancellor desired the noble Lord that brought
in these Articles, would sign to them with his hand; which my
Lord Bristoll did presently.   Then the House did order that
the Judges should, against Monday next, bring in their opinion,
Whether these articles are treason, or no? and next, they
would know, Whether they were brought in regularly or no,
without leave of the Lords' House?

11th. To the docke at Chatham by coach, to see "The
Prince" launched, which hath lain in the docke in repairing
these three years: went into her, and was launched in her.
By barge to St. Mary's Creeke; where Commissioner Pett,
doubtful of the growing greatnesse of Portsmouth by the
finding of those creekes there, do design a wett docke at no
great charge, and yet no little one; he thinks towards 10,000l.
And the place, indeed, is likely to be a very fit place, when
the King hath money to do it with.

12th. (Lord's day.) With Sir J. Minnes to church, where
an indifferent good sermon.   Here I saw Mrs. Becky Allen,
who hath been married, and is this day churched after her
bearing a child.   Coming out of the church I kissed her, and her
sister, and mother-in-law.   Walked to the docke about eleven
at night, and there got a boat and crew, and rowed down to
the guardships, it being a most pleasant moonshine evening
that ever I saw almost.   The guardships were very ready to
hail us, being no doubt commanded thereto by their Captain,
who remembers how I surprised them the last time I was
here.   However, I found him ashore; and so spent the whole
night in visiting all the ships, in which I found, for the most
part, neither an officer aboard, nor any men so much as awake.
which I was grieved to find, specially so soon after a great

alarum as Commissioner Pett brought us word that he provided against, and put all in a posture of defence but a week
ago ; all which I am resolved to represent to the Duke.

13th. I walked to the Temple; and there, from my cousin
Roger, hear that the Judges have this day brought in their
answer to the Lords, That the articles against my Lord
Chancellor are not Treason ; and to-morrow they are to bring
in their arguments to the House for the same. This day
also the King did send by my Lord Chamberlain to the
Lords, to tell them from him, that the most of the articles
against my Lord Chancellor he himself knows to be false. I
met the Queen Mother walking in the Pell Mell, led by my
Lord St. Albans. And finding many coaches at the Gate, I
found upon enquiry that the Duchess is brought to bed of a
boy ;[1] and hearing that the King and Queen are rode abroad
with the Ladies of Honour to the Park ; and, seeing a great
crowd of gallants staying here to see their return, I also staid
walking up and down. By and by the King and Queen, who
looked in this dress, a white laced waistcoate and a crimson
short pettycoate, and her hair dressed *à la négligence*, mighty
pretty : and the King rode hand in hand with her. Here
was also my Lady Castlemaine, who rode among the rest of
the ladies ; but the King took, methought, no notice of her :
nor when she 'light, did any body press, as she seemed to
expect, and staid for it, to take her down, but was taken
down by her own gentleman. She looked mighty out of
humour, and had a yellow plume in her hat, which all took
notice of, and yet is very handsome, but very melancholy ;
nor did any body speak to her, or she so much as smile or
speak to any body. I followed them up into Whitehall, and
into the Queen's presence, where all the ladies walked, talking
and fiddling with their hats and feathers, and changing and
trying one another's by one another's heads, and laughing.
But it was the finest sight to me, considering their great
beautys and dress, that ever I did see in all my life. But,
above all, Mrs. Stewart in this dress, with her hat cocked and
a red plume, with her sweet eye, little Roman nose, and

---

[1] James, Duke of Cambridge. Ob. 20th June, 1667.

excellent taille, is now the greatest beauty I ever saw, I think, in my life; and, if ever woman can, do exceed my Lady Castlemaine, at least in this dress: nor do I wonder if the King changes, which I verily believe is the reason of his coldness to my Lady Castlemaine.

14th. This day I hear the Judges, according to order yesterday, did bring into the Lords' House their reasons of their judgments in the business between my Lord Bristoll and the Chancellor; and the Lords do concur with the Judges that the articles are not Treason, nor regularly brought into the House, and so voted that a Committee should be chosen to examine them; but nothing to be done therein till the next sitting of this Parliament, which is likely to be adjourned in a day or two, and in the mean time the two Lords to remain without prejudice done to either of them.

15th. Captain Grove come and dined with me. He told me of discourse very much to my honour, both as to my care and ability, happening at the Duke of Albemarle's table the other day, both from the Duke and the Duchess themselves: and how I paid so much a year to him whose place it was of right, and that Mr. Coventry did report this of me.

21st. This day the Parliament kept a fast for the present unseasonable weather.

22d. To my Lord Crewe's. My Lord not being come home, I met, and staid below, with Captain Ferrers, who was come to wait upon my Lady Jemimah to St. James's, she being one of the four ladies that hold up the mantle at the christening this afternoon of the Duke's child, a boy. In discourse of the ladies at Court, Captain Ferrers tell me that my Lady Castlemaine is now as great again as ever she was; and that her going away was only a fit of her own upon some slighting words of the King, so that she called for her coach at a quarter of an hour's warning, and went to Richmond; and the King the next morning, under pretence of going a-hunting, went to see her and make friends, and never was a-hunting at all. After which she came back to Court, and commands the King as much as ever, and hath and doth what she will. No longer ago than last night, there was a

private entertainment made for the King and Queen at the
Duke of Buckingham's, and she was not invited: but being
at my Lady Suffolk's, her aunt's,[1] where my Lady Jemimah
and Lord Sandwich dined, yesterday, she was heard to say,
'Well, much good may it do them, and for all that, I will
be as merry as they:" and so she went home, and caused a
great supper to be prepared.　And after the King had been
with the Queen at Wallingford House,[2] he come to my Lady
Castlemaine's, and was there all night, and my Lord Sandwich
with him.　He tells me he believes that, as soon as the King
can get a husband for Mrs. Stewart, however, my Lady
Castlemaine's nose will be out of joynt; for that she comes
to be in great esteem, and is more handsome than she.
Wotton tells me the reason of Harris's[3] going from Sir William Davenant's house is, that he grew very proud, and demanded 20l. for himself extraordinary, more than Betterton
or any body else, upon every new play, and 10l. upon every
revive; which, with other things, Sir W. Davenant would not
give him, and so he swore he would never act there more, in
expectation of being received in the other house; but the
King will not suffer it, upon Sir W. Davenant's desire that
he would not, for then he might shut up house, and that is
true.　He tells me that his going is at present a great loss to
the House, and that he fears he hath a stipend from the other
House privately.　He tells me that the fellow grew very

[1] Barbara Villiers (widow of Philip, son of Viscount Wenman) wife of James
Howard, third Earl of Suffolk. There is a portrait of Lady Suffolk at Audley End.
She died December, 1681, leaving an only child, Elizabeth, who married Sir
Thomas Felton, Bart.　From this match are descended the Earls and Marquis of
Bristol, and Charles Ellis, Baron Howard de Walden.

[2] Wallingford House stood on the site of the present Admiralty. It originally
belonged to the Knollys family, and during the Protectorate, the office for granting
passes to persons going abroad was kept there.

[3] Joseph Harris, a celebrated actor, who first appeared at the Theatre in Lincoln's Inn Fields, in 1662.　He probably died, or left the stage about 1676.
That the Christian name of the actor at Davenant's house, and the friend of Pepys,
was Joseph, rests on the supposition that he was the Joseph Harris author of
several plays produced in the reign of William III., and an actor also. If Pepys's
Harris and the dramatic poet were identical, he lived into Queen Anne's reign.
It seems more probable that they were different persons, and that Pepys's friend
was named Henry.　There is a mezzotint of Joseph Harris, in the character of
Cardinal Wolsey, in the Pepysian Library at Cambridge: only one other impression of this print is known to exist, which belongs to Mr. George Daniel, of
Canonbury.

proud of late, the King and every body else crying him up so
high, and that above Betterton, he being a more ayery man,
as he is indeed.   But yet Betterton, he says, they all say do
act some parts that none but himself can do.   I hear that
the Moores have made some attaques upon the outworks of
Tangier ; but my Lord Teviott,[1] with the loss of about 200
men, did beat them off, and killed many of them.   To-morrow
the King and Queen for certain go down to Tunbridge ; but
the King comes back again against Monday to raise the Parliament.

25th. Having intended this day to go to Banstead Downes
to see a famous race, I sent Will. to get himself ready to go
with me ; but I hear it is put off, because the Lords do sit
in Parliament to-day.[2] After some debate, Creed and I
resolved to go to Clapham, to Mr. Gauden's. When I come
there, the first thing was to show me his house,[3] which is
almost built. I find it very regular and finely contrived, and
the gardens and offices about it as convenient and as full of
good variety as ever I saw in my life. It is true, he hath
been censured for laying out so much money ; but he tells
me that he built it for his brother, who is since dead (the
Bishop),[4] who, when he should come to be Bishop of Winchester,
which he was promised, to which bishopricke at present there
is no house, he did intend to dwell here. By and by to dinner,
and in comes Mr. Creed : I saluted Mr. Gauden's lady, and
the young ladies, and his sister, the Bishop's widow ; who was,
it seems, Sir W. Russel's[5] daughter, the Treasurer of the
Navy ; who I find to be very well-bred, and a woman of
excellent discourse. Towards the evening we bade them
adieu ! and took horse ; being resolved that, instead of the
race which fails us, we would go to Epsom. When we come
there, we could hear of no lodging, the town so full ; but,

[1] See note to 15th December, 1662

[2] The tables are turned : the two Houses now seldom sitting on the "Derby"
day ! In May, 1849, the adjournment of the House of Commons was carried after
a division.

[3] See note to December 12, 1660, ante.

[4] Of Exeter.

[5] Sir William Russell, of Strensham, in Worcestershire, Bart. He advanced
600l. to Sir William Davenant in 1660-1, and had a share in Davenant's
Theatre.

which was better, I went towards Ashted, and there we got a lodging in a little hole we could not stand upright in. While supper was getting, I walked up and down behind my cozen Pepys's house that was, which I find comes little short of what I took it to be, when I was a little boy.

26th. (Lord's day.) Up and to the Wells, where a great store of citizens, which was the greatest part of the company, though there were some others of better quality. Thence I walked to Mr. Minnes's house, and thence to Durdans, and walked within the Court Yard and to the Bowling-green, where I have seen so much mirth in my time; but now no family in it, my Lord Barkeley, whose it is, being with his family at London. Then rode through Epsom, the whole town over, seeing the various companys that were there walking; which was very pleasant to see how they are there, without knowing what to do, but only in the morning to drink waters. But, Lord! to see how many I met there of citizens, that I could not have thought to have seen there; that they had ever had it in their heads or purses to go down thither. We went through None-such Parke¹ to the house, and there viewed as much as we could of the outside, and looked through the great gates, and found a noble court; and altogether believe it to have been a very noble house, and a delicate parke about it, where just now there was a doe killed for the King, to carry up to Court.

27th. We rode hard home, and set up our horses at Fox Hall, and I by water, observing the King's barge attending his going to the House this day, home, it being about one o'clock. By water to Westminster, and there come most luckily to the Lords' House, as the House of Commons were going into the Lords' House, and there I crowded in along with the Speaker, and got to stand close behind him, where he made his speech to the King, who sat with his crown on and robes, and so all the Lords in their robes, a fine sight; wherein he told his Majesty what they have done this Parliament, and now offered for his royall consent. The greatest matters were a bill for the Lord's day, which it seems the

---

¹ See 21st Sept., 1665.

Lords have lost, and so cannot be passed, at which the
Commons are displeased; the bills against Conventicles and
Papists, but it seems the Lords have not passed them; and
giving his Majesty four entire subsidys; which last, with
about twenty smaller Acts, were passed with this form:
The Clerk of the House reads the title of the Bill, and then
looks at the end, and there finds, writ by the King, I suppose,
"Le Roy le veult," and that he reads.   And to others he
reads, "Soit fait comme vous désirez."   And to the Subsidys,
as well that for the Commons, I mean the Layety, as for the
Clergy, the King writes, "Le Roy remerciant les Seigneurs
et Prélats, accepte leur bénévolence."   The Speaker's speech
was far from any oratory, but was as plain, though good
matter, as anything could be, and void of elocution.   After
the bills passed, the King, sitting on his throne, with his
speech writ in a paper which he held in his lap, and scarce
looked off of it all the time, he made his speech to them,
giving them thanks for their subsidys, of which, had he not
need, he would not have asked or received them; and that
need, not from any extravagancys of his, he was sure, in any
thing, but the disorders of the times compelling him to be at
greater charge than he hoped for the future, by their care in
their country, he should be; and that for his family expenses
and others, he would labour, however, to retrench in many
things convenient, and would have all others to do so too.
He desired that nothing of old faults should be remembered,
or severity for the same used to any in the country, it being
his desire to have all forgot, as well as forgiven.   But, however, to use all care in suppressing any tumults, &c.; assuring
them that the restless spirits of his and their adversaries have
great expectations of something to be done this summer.   And
promised, that though the Acts about Conventicles and Papists
were not ripe for passing this Session, yet he would take care
himself that neither of them should in this intervall be
encouraged to the endangering of the peace; and that at
their next meeting he would himself prepare two bills for
them concerning them.   So he concluded that, for the better
proceeding of justice, he did think fit to make this a Session.

and do prorogue them to the 16th of March next. His speech was very plain, nothing at all of spirit in it, nor spoke with any; but rather, on the contrary, imperfectly, repeating many times his words, though he read all: which I am sorry to see, it having not been hard for him to have got all the speech without booke. So they all went away, the King out of the House at the upper end, He being by and by to go to Tunbridge to the Queen; and I in the painted chamber spoke with my Lord Sandwich while he was putting off his robes, who tells me he will now hasten down into the country. By water to White Hall, and walked over the Parke to St. James's, but missed Mr. Coventry; and so out again, and there the Duke was coming along the Pell-Mell. It being a little darkish, I staid not to take notice of him, but went directly back again. And in our walk over the Parke, one of the Duke's footmen come running behind us, and come looking just in our faces to see who we were, and went back again. What his meaning is I know not, but was fearful that I might not go far enough with my hat off.

29th. To Deptford, reading by the way a most ridiculous play, a new one, called "The Politician cheated."[1]

30th. To Woolwich, and there come Sir G. Carteret, and then by water back to Deptford, where we dined with him at his house. I find his little daughter Betty,[2] that was in hanging sleeves but a month or two ago, and is a very little young child, married, and to whom, but to young Scott,[3] son to Madame Catharine Scott,[4] that was so long in law, and at whose trial I was with her husband; he pleading that it was unlawfully got and would not own it; but it seems, a little before his death, he did owne the child, and hath left him his estate not long since. So Sir G. Carteret hath struck up of a sudden a match with him for his little daughter. He hath about 2000l. per annum; and it seems Sir G. C. hath by this

---

[1] A comedy, by Alexander Green, and never acted.

[2] Her name was Caroline. Elizabeth was her younger sister, and died unmarried.

[3] Thomas, eldest son of Sir Thomas Scott, of Scott's Hall, in the parish of Smeeth, Kent.

[4] Prince Rupert was supposed to have intrigued with Mrs. Scott, and was probably the father of the child.

means over-reached Sir H. Bennet, who did endeavour to get
this gentleman for a sister of his. By this means, Sir G.
Carteret hath married two daughters this year, both very well.[1]
The towne talk this day is of nothing but the great foot-race
run this day on Banstead Downes, between Lee, the Duke of
Richmond's footman, and a tyler, a famous runner. And
Lee hath beat him; though the King and Duke of York and
all men almost did bet three or four to one upon the tyler's
head.

31st. To the Exchange, where I met Dr. Pierce, who tells
me of his good luck to get to be groom of the Privy-Chamber
to the Queen, and without my Lord Sandwich's help, but only
by his good fortune, meeting a man that hath let him have
his right for a small matter, about 60*l.*, for which he can every
day have 400*l.* But he tells me my Lord hath lost much
honour in standing so long and so much for that coxcomb
Pickering, and at last not carrying it for him; but hath his
name struck out by the King and Queen themselves, after he
had been in, ever since the Queen's coming. But he tells me
he believes that either Sir H. Bennet, my Lady Castlemaine,
or Sir Charles Barkeley, had received some money for the
place, and so the King could not disappoint them, but was
forced to put out this fool rather than a better man. And I
am sorry to hear what he tells me, that Sir Charles Barkeley
hath still such power over the King, as to be able to fetch him
from the Council-table to my Lady Castlemaine when he
pleases. He tells me also, as a friend, the great injury that
he thinks I do myself by being so severe in the Yards, and
contracting the ill-will of the whole Navy for those offices,
singly upon myself. Now I discharge a good conscience
therein, and I tell him that no man can, nor do he say any say
it, charge me with doing wrong; but rather do as many good
offices as any man. They think, he says, that I have a mind
to get a good name with the King and Duke, who he tells me
do not consider any such thing; but I shall have as good
thanks to let all alone, and do as the rest. But I believe the
contrary; and yet I told him I never go to the Duke alone,

---

[1] The other daughter was Anne, wife of Sir Nicholas Slaning, K.B.

as others do, to talk of my own services.   However, I will
make use of his council, and take some course to prevent
having the single ill-will of the office.   Mr. Grant showed me
letters of Sir William Petty's, wherein he says, that his vessel
which he hath built upon two keeles, a modell whereof, built
for the King, he showed me, hath this month won a wager of
50*l.*, in sailing between Dublin and Holyhead with the
pacquett-boat, the best ship or vessel the King hath there;
and he offers to lay with any vessel in the world.   It is about
thirty ton in burden, and carries thirty men, with good accommodation, as much more as any ship of her burden, and so any
vessel of this figure shall carry more men, with better accommodation by half, than any other ship.   This carries also ten
guns, of about five tons weight.   In their coming back from
Holyhead, they started together, and this vessel come to Dublin
by five at night, and the pacquett-boat not before eight the
next morning; and when they come, they did believe that this
vessel had been drowned, or at least [left] behind, not thinking she could have lived in that sea.   Strange things are told
of this vessel, and he concludes his letter with this position,
"I only affirm that the perfection of sayling lies in my prin-
ciple, finde it out who can."[1]

August 8th.   I with Mr. Coventry down to the water-side,
talking, wherein I see so much goodness and endeavours of
doing the King service, that I do more and more admire him.

9th. (Lord's day.)   To church, and heard Mr. Mills, who is
lately returned out of the country, and it seems was fetched
in by many of the parishioners, with great estate, preach upon
the authority of the ministers, upon these words, "We are

---

[1] Amongst the Sloane MSS. in the British Museum, there is an English satirical
poem on this vessel, the title of which is, "In laudem Navis Geminæ e portu
Dublinii ad Regem Carolum 11^{tum} missæ." It contains three hundred lines, and
is too long and too scurrilous and worthless to print. "Petty," observes Lodge
(*Peerage of Ireland*, vol. ii., p. 352), "in 1663 raised his reputation still higher,
by the success of his invention of the double-bottomed ship, against the judgment of all mankind. Thomas Earl of Ossory, and other persons of honour, embarked on board this ship, which promised to excel all others in sailing, carriage,
and security; but she was at last lost in a dreadful tempest, which overwhelmed
a great fleet the same night. A model of the vessel was deposited by Petty in
Gresham College."

therefore embassadors of Christ." Wherein, among many
other high expressions, he said, that such a learned man used
to say, that if a minister of the word and an angell should
meet him together, he would salute the minister first; which
methought was a little too high. This day I begun to make
use of the silver pen Mr. Coventry did give me, in writing of
this sermon, taking only the heads of it in Latin, which I shall,
I think, continue to do.

10th. To the Committee of Tangier, where my Lord Sandwich, my Lord Peterborough, whom I have not seen before
since his coming back, Sir W. Compton, and Mr. Povy. Our
discourse about supplying my Lord Teviott with money,
wherein I am sorry to see, though they do not care for him,
yet they are willing to let him for civility and compliment
only have money, almost without expecting any account of it;
and he being such a cunning fellow as he is, the King is like
to pay dear for our courtiers' ceremony. Thence by coach
with my Lords Peterborough and Sandwich to my Lord
Peterborough's house; and there, after an hour's looking over
some fine books of the Italian buildings, with fine cuts, and
also my Lord Peterborough's bowes and arrows, of which he
is a great lover, we sat down to dinner, my Lady [1] coming down
to dinner also, and there being Mr. Williamson,[2] that belongs
to Sir H. Bennet, whom I find a pretty understanding and
accomplished man, but a little conceited. Yesterday, I am
told, that Sir J. Lenthall,[3] in Southwarke, did apprehend
about one hundred Quakers, and other such people, and hath
sent some of them to the gaole at Kingston, it being now the
time of the Assizes. Dr. Pierce tells me the Queen is grown
a very debonnaire lady; but my Lady Castlemaine, who rules
the King in matters of state, and do what she list with him,

---

[1] Lady Penelope O'Brien, daughter of Barnabas O'Brien, sixth Earl of Thomond,
wife of the Earl of Peterborough.

[2] Afterwards Sir Joseph Williamson.

[3] Sir John Lenthall was the elder brother of Speaker Lenthall, and uncle of
the person of the same name, mentioned in the *Diary*, May, 21, 1660. He had
been knighted as early as 1616, and was Marshal of the Marshalsea; and, in
1655, was placed in the Commission of the Peace for Surrey, by a special vote
of the House of Commons, which explains his crusade against the Quakers. He
died in 1668.

he believes, is now falling quite out of favour. After the Queen is come back, She goes to Bath, and so to Oxford, where great entertainments are making for her. This day I am told that my Lord Bristoll hath warrants issued out against him, to have carried him to the Tower; but he is fled away, or hid himself. So much the Chancellor hath got the better of him.

13th. Met with Mr. Hoole,[1] my old acquaintance of Magdalene, and walked with him an hour in the Parke, discoursing chiefly of Sir Samuel Morland, whose lady[2] is gone into France. It seems he buys ground and a farm in that country, and lays out money upon building, and God knows what! so that most of the money he sold his pension of 500*l.* per annum for, to Sir Arthur Slingsby,[3] it is believed is gone. It seems he hath very great promises from the King, and Hoole hath seen some of the King's letters, under his own hand, to Morland, promising him great things; and among others, the order of the Garter,[4] as Sir Samuel says, but his lady thought it below her to ask any thing at the King's first coming, believing the King would do it of himself, when, as Hoole do really think, if he had asked to be Secretary of State at the King's first coming, he might have had it. And the other day, at her going into France, she did speak largely to the King herself, how her husband hath failed of what his Majesty had promised, and she was sure intended him; and the King did promise still, as he is a King and a gentleman, to be as good as his word in a little time, to a tittle: but I never believe it.

21st. Meeting with Mr. Creed, he told me how my Lord Teviott hath received another attaque from Guyland at Tangier

---

[1] William, son of Robert Hoole, of Walkeringham, Notts, admitted of Magdalene College, 1648.

[2] Susanne de Milleville, daughter of Daniel de Milleville, Baron of Boessen, in France, naturalized 1662. Sir Samuel Morland survived a second and a third wife, both buried in Westminster Abbey.

[3] A younger son of Sir Guildford Slingsby, Comptroller of the Navy, knighted by Charles II., and afterwards created a Baronet at Brussels, 1657, which title has long been extinct.

[4] Compare Sir Samuel Moreland's own account in his *Autobiography,* printed by Halliwell.

with 10,000 men, and at last, as is said, is come, after a personal treaty with him, to a good understanding and peace with him.

23d. (Lord's day.) To church, and so home to my wife; and with her read "Iter Boreale,"[1] a poem, made first at the King's coming home; but I never read it before, and now like it pretty well, but not so as it was cried up.

24th. At my Lord Sandwich's, where I was a good while alone with my Lord; and I perceive he confides in me, and loves me as he used to do, and tells me his condition, which is now very well: all I fear is that he will not live within compass. There come to him this morning his prints of the river Tagus and the City of Lisbon, which he measured with his own hand, and printed by command of the King. My Lord pleases himself with it, but methinks it ought to have been better done than by Jobing. Besides, I put him upon having some took off upon white satin, which he ordered presently. I offered my Lord my accounts, and did give him up his old bond for 500l., and took a new one of him for 700l., which I am, by lending him more money, to make up; and am glad of it.

25th. This noon, going to the Exchange, I met a fine fellow with trumpets before him in Leadenhall Street, and upon enquiry I find that he is the clerke of the City Market; and three or four men carried each of them an arrow of a pound weight in their hands. It seems this Lord Mayor[2] begins again an old custome, that upon the three first days of Bartholomew Fayre, the first, there is a match of wrestling, which was done, and the Lord Mayor there and the Aldermen in Moorefields yesterday: second day, shooting: and to-morrow hunting. And this officer of course is to perform this ceremony of riding through the city, I think to proclaim or

---

[1] Robert Wild, a Nonconformist Divine, published a poem in 1660, upon Monk's march from Scotland to London, called *Iter Boreale*. It is written in a harsh and barbarous style, filled with clenches and carwickets, as the time called them, which having been in the fashion in the reigns of James I. and his unfortunate son, were revived after the Restoration.—(Scott's *Dryden*, vol. xv., p. 296.) Wood mentions three other works of the same title, by Eades, Corbett, and Marten, it having been a favourite subject at that time.

[2] Sir John Robinson.

challenge any to shoot. It seems that the people of the faire cry out upon it, as a great hindrance to them.

26th. To White Hall, where the Court full of waggons and horses, the King and Court going this day out towards the Bath.[1] Pleased to see Captain Hickes come to me with a list of all the officers of Deptford Yard, wherein he, being a high old Cavalier, do give me an account of every one of them to their reproach in all respects, and discovers many of their knaverys; and tells me, and so I thank God I hear every where, that my name is up for a good husband to the King, and a good man, for which I bless God; and that he did this by particular direction of Mr. Coventry.

28th. At the office betimes. Cold all night and this morn ing, and a very great frost, they say, abroad, which is much, having had no summer at all almost.

September 2d. To dinner with my Lord Mayor and the Aldermen, and a very great dinner and most excellent venison, but it almost made me sick by not daring to drink wine. After dinner, into a withdrawing-room; and there we talked, among other things, of the Lord Mayor's sword. They tell me this sword is at least a hundred or two hundred years old; and another that he hath, which is called the Black Sword, which the Lord Mayor wears when he mournes, but properly is their Lenten sword to wear upon Good Friday and other Lent days, is older than that. Mr. Lewellin, lately come from Ireland, tells me how the English interest falls mightily there, the Irish party being too great, so that most of the old rebells are found innocent, and their lands, which were forfeited and bought, or given to the English, are restored to them; which gives great discontent there among the English. Going through the City, my Lord Mayor told me how the piller set up by Exeter House is only to show where the pipes of water run to the City; and observed that this City is as well watered as any city in the world, and that tho bringing of water to the City hath cost it, first and last, above 300,000l.; but by the

---

[1] The King lay the first night at Maidenhead, and the second near Newbury.

new building, and the building of St. James's,[1] by my Lord
St. Albans, which is now about, and which the City stomach,
I perceive, highly, but dare not oppose it: were it now to be
done, it would not be done for a million of money.

4th. To Westminster Hall, and there bought the first
news-books of L'Estrange's[2] writing, he beginning this week;
and makes, methinks, but a simple beginning. This day I
read a Proclamation[4] for calling in, and commanding every
body to apprehend, my Lord Bristoll.

5th. I did inform myself well in things relating to the East
Indys; both of the country, and the disappointment the King
met with the last voyage, by the knavery of the Portugall
Viceroy, and the inconsiderableness of the place of Bombaim,[5]
if we had had it. But, above all things, it seems strange to
me, that matters should not be understood before they went
out; and also that such a thing as this, which was expected
to be one of the best parts of the Queen's portion, should
not be better understood; it being, if we had it, but a poor
place, and not really so as was described to our King in the
draught of it, but a poor little island; whereas, they made
the King and Lord Chancellor, and other learned men about
the King, believe that that and other islands which are near
it were all one piece; and so the draught was drawn and
presented to the King, and believed by the King, and expected to prove so when our men come thither; but it is quite
otherwise.

7th. To the Black Eagle in Bride Lane, and there had a
chop of veale, and some bread, cheese, and beer, cost me a
shilling to my dinner; and so to Bartholomew Fayre, where
I met with Mr. Pickering, and he and I to see the monkeys

---

[1] St. Albans Street and Market, on the north side of Pall Mall, removed for
the Regent Street improvements. Jermyn Street, St. James's, also takes its
name from him.

[2] Roger L'Estrange, author of numerous pamphlets and periodical papers.
He succeeded Muddyman, who had been put aside as to that employment, and
was Licenser of the Press to Charles II. and his successor, and M.P. for Winchester in James II.'s Parliament. Ob. 1704, aged 88.

[3] The first number of The Intelligencer, dated 31st August, 1663.

[4] Dated 25th August, 1663. A copy of it is in the British Museum

[5] Bombay.

at the Dutch house, which is far beyond the other that my wife and I saw the other day; and thence to see the dancing on the ropes, which was very poor and tedious. But he and I fell in discourse about my Lord Sandwich. He tells me how he is sorry for my Lord at his being at Chelsey; but I could not fish from him, though I knew it, what was the matter; but am very sorry to see that my Lord hath thus much forgot his honour, but am resolved not to meddle with it. The play being done, I stole from him and hied home, buying several things at the ironmonger's; dogs, tongues, and shovells, for my wife's closet, and the rest of my house. By my letters from Tangier to-day, I hear that it grows very strong by land, and the Mole goes on. They have lately killed about two hundred of the Moores, and lost about forty or fifty. I am mightily afraid of laying out too much money in goods upon my house, but it is not money flung away, though I reckon nothing money but what is in the bank, till I have a good sum beforehand in the world.

8th. Dined at home with my wife. It being washing-day, we had a good pie baked of a leg of mutton; and then to Moxon's, and there bought a payre of globes cost me 3*l.* 10*s.*, with which I am well pleased.

9th. I met with Ned Pickering, he telling me the whole business of my Lord's folly with this Mrs. Becke, at Chelsey, of all which I am ashamed to see my Lord so grossly play the fool, to the flinging off of all honour, friends, servants, and every thing and person that is good, with his carrying her abroad, and playing on his lute under her window, and forty other poor sordid things, which I am grieved to hear; but believe it to no purpose for me to meddle with it, but let him go on till God Almighty and his own conscience and thoughts of his lady and family do it.

10th. All the morning making a great contract with Sir W. Warren, for 3000*l.* worth of masts; but, good God! to see what a man might do, were I a knave. Mr. Moore tells me of the good peace that is made at Tangier with the Moores, but to continue but from six months to six months.

11th. This morning, about two or three o'clock, knocked

up in our back yard and rising to the window, being moonshine, I found it was the constable and his watch, who had
found our back yard door open, and so come in to see what
the matter was. So I desired them to shut the door, and bid
them good-night.

12th. Up betimes, and by water to White Hall; and thence
to Sir Philip Warwick, and there had half an hour's private
discourse with him; and did give him some good satisfaction
in our Navy matters, and he also me, as to the money paid
and due to the Navy; so as he makes me assured by particulars, that Sir G. Carteret is paid within 80,000*l.*, every
farthing that we to this day, nay, to Michaelmas day next,
have demanded; and that, I am sure, is above 50,000*l.* more
than truly our expences have been, whatever has become of
the money. Home with great content that I have thus begun
an acquaintance with him, who is a great man, and a man of
as much business as any man in England; which I will endeavour to deserve and keep.

14th. By coach to Bishop's Gate Street, it being a very
promising fair day. There at the Dolphin we met my uncle
Thomas, and his son-in-law, which seems a very sober man,
and Mr. Moore: so Mr. Moore and my wife set out before,
and my uncle and I staid for his son Thomas, who, by a
sudden resolution, is preparing to go with us, which makes
me fear something of mischief which they design to do us.
He staying a great while, the old man and I before, and
about eight miles off, his son comes after us, and about six
miles further, we overtake Mr. Moore and my wife, which
makes me mightily consider what a great deal of ground is
lost in a little time, when it is to be got up again by another,
who is to go his own ground and the others too; and so, after
a little bayte, I paying all the reckonings the whole journey,
at Ware, to Buntingford, where my wife, by drinking some
cold beer, being hot herself, presently after 'lighting, begins
to be sick, and become so pale, and I alone with her in a
great chamber there, that I thought she would have died, and
so in great horror, and having a great trial of my true love
and passion for her, called the maids and mistress of the

house, and so with some strong water, she come to be pretty
well again; and so to bed, and I having put her to bed with
great content, I called in my company, and supped in the
chamber by her, and being very merry in talk, supped and
then parted. This day my cozen Thomas dropped his hanger,
and it was lost.

15th. Up betimes, and rode as far as Godmanchester, Mr.
Moore having two falls—once in water, and another in dirt,
and there 'light and eat and drunk, being all of us very
merry, but especially my uncle and wife. Thence to Brampton, to my father's, and there found all well; and so my father,
cozen Thomas, and I up to Hinchingbroke, where I find my
Lord and his company gone to Boughton; but there I find
my Lady and the young ladies, and there I alone with my
Lady two hours—she carrying me through every part of the
house and gardens, which are, and will be, mighty noble
indeed. Here I saw Mrs. Betty Pickering,[1] who is a very
well-bred and comely lady, but very fat. After supper, my
uncle and son to Stankes's to bed, which troubles me, all my
father's beds being lent to Hinchingbroke.

17th. I was forced to come to a new consideration, whether
it was fit to let my uncle and his son go to Wisbeach about
my uncle Day's estate alone or no, and concluded it unfit;
and so, leaving my wife, I begun a journey with them, and
with much ado through the fenns, along dikes, where sometimes we were ready to have our horses sink to the belly, we
got by night, with a great deal of stir, and hard riding, to
Parson's Drove, a heathen place, where I found my uncle and
aunt Perkins, and their daughters, poor wretches! in a sad,
poor thatched cottage, like a poor barne, or stable, peeling of
hemp, in which I did give myself good content to see their
manner of preparing of hemp; and in a poor condition of
habitt took them to our miserable inne, and there, after long
stay, and hearing of Frank, their son, the miller, play upon
his treble, as he calls it, with which he earnes part of his living,
and singing of a country song, we sat down to supper; the
whole crew, and Spankes's wife and child, a sad company, of

---

[1] Afterwards married to Creed.

which I was ashamed, supped with us. By and by, newes is
brought to us, that one of our horses is stole out of the stable,
which proves my uncle's, at which I am inwardly glad—I
mean, that it was not mine; and at this we were at a great
loss; and they doubting a person that lay at next door, a
Londoner, some lawyer's clerk, we caused him to be secured
in his bed, and other care to be taken to seize the house;
and so, about twelve at night or more, to bed in a sad, cold,
stony chamber; and a little after I was asleep, they waked
me, to tell me that the horse was found, which was good
news, and so to sleep, but was bit cruelly, and nobody else of
our company, which I wonder at, by the gnatts.

18th. Up, and got our people together; and after eating a
dishe of cold creame, which was my supper last night too, we
took leave of our beggarly company, though they seem good
people, too; and over most sad fenns, all the way observing the
sad life which the people of the place—which, if they be born
there, they do call the Breedlings of the place—do live, sometimes rowing from one spot to another, and then wadeing. To
Wisbeach, a pretty town, and a fine church and library,[1] where
sundry very old abbey manuscripts; and a fine house, built
on the church ground, by Secretary Thurlow, and a fine gallery built for him in the church, but now all in the Bishop of
Ely's hands. After visiting the church, &c., we out of the
town, by the help of a stranger, to find out one Blinkehorne,
a miller, of whom we might inquire something of old Day's
disposal of his estate, and in whose hands it now is; and by
great chance we met him, and brought him to our inne to
dinner; and instead of being informed in his estate by this
fellow, we find that he is the next heire to the estate, which
was matter of great sport to my cozen Thomas and me, to
see such a fellow prevent us in our hopes—he being Day's
brother's daughter's son, whereas we are but his sister's sons
and grandsons; so that, after all, we were fain to propose our

---

[1] Watson, in his *History of Wisbeach*, p. 239, names some of the printed books
in the library there, but does not mention any of the MSS. Secretary Thurloe's
gallery had been erected at the expense of the Corporation, out of gratitude to
him for many services rendered to the town. It is now used for the general
accommodation of the inhabitants.

matter to him, and to get him to give us leave to look after
the business, and so he to have one-third part, and we two to
have the other two-third parts, of what should be recovered
of the estate, which he consented to : and, after paying the
reckoning, we mounted again, and rode, being very merry at
our defeate, to Chatteris — my uncle very weary, and after
supper, and my telling of three stories to their good liking
of spirits, we all three in a chamber went to bed.

19th. Up pretty betimes; and I to Brampton, where I find
my father ill in bed still, and Madam Norbery, whom and her
fair daughter and sister I was ashamed to kiss, but did—my
lip being sore with riding in the winde, and bit with the
gnats; and they being gone, I told my father my successe.
My wife and I took horse, and rode with marvellous, and the
first and only hour of, pleasure that ever I had in this estate,
since I had to do with it, to Brampton woods; and through
the wood rode, and gathered nuts in my way, and then at
Graffan, to an old woman's house, to drink, where my wife
used to go; and being in all circumstances highly pleased, and
in my wife's riding and good company at this time, I rode,
and she showed me the river behind my father's house, which
is very pleasant; and so saw her home, and I straight to
Huntingdon; and there a barber come and trimmed me, and
thence walked to Hinchingbroke, where my Lord and ladies
all are just alighted.

20th. (Lord's day.) Walked to Huntingdon Church, where
in my Lord's pew, with the young ladies, by my Lord's own
showing me the place, I stayed the sermon, and so to Hinchingbroke, walking with Mr. Shepley and Dr. King, whom they
account a witty man here, as well as good physician; and
there my Lord singly demanded my opinion, in the walks in
his garden, about the bringing of the crooked wall on the
Mount to a shape; and so to dinner — there being Colonel
Williams and much other company, and a noble dinner. But
having before got my Lord's warrant for travelling to-day,
there being a proclamation read against it at Huntingdon, at
which I am very glad, I took leave, and rode to Bigglesworth,[1] by the help of a couple of countrymen, that led us

---

[1] Biggleswade.

through the very long and dangerous waters, because of the ditches on each side, though it begun to be very dark.

21st. Up very betimes by break of day, and got my wife up, whom the thought of this day's long journey do discourage: and after eating something, and changing a piece of gold to pay the reckoning, we mounted, and through Baldwicke,[1] where the fayre is kept to-day, and a great one for cheese and other such commodities, and to Hatfield; and here we dined, and my wife being very weary, I took the opportunity of an empty coach that was to go to London, and left her to come in it to London, for half a crowne, and so I and the boy home as fast as we could drive, and it was even night before we got home. By and by comes my wife by coach well home, and having got a good fowl ready for supper against her coming, we eat heartily, and so with great content and ease to our own bed, there nothing appearing so to our content as to be at our own home, after being abroad awhile.

22d. This day my wife showed me bills printed, wherein her father, with Sir John Collidon[2] and Sir Edward Ford,[3] have got a patent for curing of smoking chimneys. I wish they may do good thereof. This day the King and Queen are to come to Oxford. I hear my Lady Castlemaine is for certain gone to Oxford to meet him, having lain within here at home this week or two, supposed to have miscarried;[4] but for certain is as great in favour as heretofore; at least, Mrs. Sarah at my Lord's, who hears all from their own family, do

---

[1] Baldock.   [2] Or Colliton: see 18th Oct., 1664.

[3] Sir Edward Ford, of Harting, Sussex, Sheriff for that county, and Governor of Arundel Castle in 1642. Ob. 1670. His only daughter married Ralph Grey, Baron Grey of Werke. He was the author of a tract, entitled, " Experimental Proposals how the King may have money to pay and maintain his Fleets, with ease to his people: London may be rebuilt, and all proprietors satisfied: money to be but at six per cent. on pawns, and the Fishing Trade set up, which alone is able, and sure to enrich us all. And all this without altering, straining, or thwarting, any of our Laws, or Customs, now in use." 4to, 1666.—Repr. Harl. Miscell., iv., 195. Ford was High Sheriff of Sussex, adhered to Charles I., and was knighted in 1643. In 1658, he laid down pipes to supply parts of London with water from the Thames. The second and third Lords Braybrooke descend, in the female line, from his daughter, Catherine Ford, who married Ralph, Lord Grey of Werke, their maternal ancestor.

[4] According to Collins, Henry Fitzroy, Lady Castlemaine's second son by Charles II., was born on the 20th September, 1663. He was the first Duke of Grafton.

say so.   Every day brings news of the Turke's advance into
Germany, to the awakeing of all the Christian Princes thereabouts, and possessing himself of Hungary.   My present care
is fitting my wife's closet and my house, and making her a
velvet coate, and me a new black cloth suit and coat and
cloak.

23d. To my Lord Crewe's, and there dined with him and
Sir Thomas, thinking to have them inquire something about
my Lord's lodgings at Chelsey, but they did not take the
least notice of it.

24th. I went forth by water to Sir Philip Warwick's,
where I was with him a pretty while: and in discourse he
tells me, and made it appear to me, that the King cannot be
in debt to the Navy at this time 5000*l.*; and it is my opinion
that Sir G. Carteret do owe the King money, and yet the
whole Navy debt paid.   Thence I parted, being doubtful of
myself that I have not spoke with the gravity and weight
that I ought to do in so great a business.   But I rather hope
it is my doubtfulness of myself, and the haste which he was
in, some very great personages waiting for him without, while
he was with me, that made him willing to be gone.

28th.   To White Hall, where Sir J. Minnes and I did
spend an hour in the Gallery, looking upon the pictures, in
which he hath some judgement.   And by and by the Commissioners for Tangier met: and there my Lord Teviott,
together with Captain Cuttance, Captain Evans, and Jonas
Moore, sent to that purpose, did bring us a brave draught of
the Mole to be built there; and report that it is likely to be
the most considerable place the King of England hath in the
world; and so I am apt to think it will.   After discourse of
this, and of supplying the garrison with some more horse, we
rose; and Sir J. Minnes and I home again, finding the street
about our house full. Sir R. Ford[1] beginning his shrievalty
to-day; and what with his and our houses being new painted,
the street begins to look a great deal better than it did, and
more gracefull.   News that the King comes to town for certain on Thursday next from his great progress.

---

[1] He lived in Hart Street, and the Navy Board had been in treaty for his
house.

29th. Come Mr. Sympson to set up my wife's chimney-piece in her closet, which pleases me.

30th. In the afternoon by water to White Hall, to the Tangier Committee; where my Lord Teviott; which grieves me to see that his accounts being to be examined by us, there are none of the great men at the Board that in compliment will except against any thing in them, and so none of the little persons dare do it: so the King is abused. Blessed be God, I do find myself 760*l.* creditor, notwithstanding that for clothes for myself and wife, and laying out on her closet, I have spent this month 47*l.* To-morrow the King, Queen, Duke, and his Lady, and the whole court comes to town from their progress. All the common talk for news is, the Turk his advance in Hungary, &c.

October 1st. I am troubled to see that my servants and others should be the greatest trouble I have in the world.

5th. My Lord Sandwich sent a message to know whether the King intends to come to Newmarket, as is talked, that he may be ready to entertain him at Hinchingbroke.

11th. (Lord's day.) At night fell to reading in the Church History of Fuller's, and particularly Cranmer's letter to Queen[1] Elizabeth, which pleases me mightily for its zeal, obedience, and boldness in a cause of religion.

12th. At St. James's we attended the Duke, all of us. And there, after my discourse, Mr. Coventry of his own accord begun to tell the Duke how he found that discourse abroad did run to his prejudice about the fees that he took, and how he sold places and other things; wherein he desired to appeal to his Highness, whether he did any thing more than what his predecessors did, and appealed to us all. So Sir G. Carteret did answer that some fees were heretofore taken, but what he knows not; only that selling of places never was, nor ought to be countenanced. So Mr. Coventry very hotly answered to Sir G. Carteret, and appealed to himself whether he was not one of the first that put him upon looking after this business of fees, and that he told him that Mr. Smith should say that he made 5000*l.* the first year, and he believed

---

[1] *Sic orig.*

he made 7000*l*. This Sir G. Carteret denied, and said, that if he did say so, he told a lie; for he could not, nor did know, that ever he did make that profit of his place; but that he believes he might say 2500*l*. the first year. Mr. Coventry instanced in another thing, particularly wherein Sir G. Carteret did advise with him about the selling of the Auditor's place of the stores, when in the beginning there was an intention of creating such an office. This he confessed, but with some lessening of the tale Mr. Coventry told, it being only for a respect to my Lord FitzHarding. In fine, Mr. Coventry did put into the Duke's hand a list of above 250 places that he did give without receiving one farthing, so much as his ordinary fees for them, upon his life and oath; and that since the Duke's establishment of fees he had never received one token more of any man; and that in his whole life he never conditioned or discoursed of any consideration from any commanders since he come to the Navy. And afterwards, my Lord Barkeley merrily discoursing that he wished his [Mr. Coventry's] profit greater than it was, and that he did believe that he [Mr. Coventry] had got 50,000*l*. since he come in, Mr. Coventry did openly declare that his Lordship, or any of us, should have, not only all he had got, but all that he had in the world, and yet he did not come a beggar into the Navy, nor would yet be thought to speak in any contempt of his Royall Highness's bounty; and should have a year to consider of it too, for 25,000*l*. The Duke's answer was, that he wished we all had made more profit than we had of our places, and that we had all of us got as much as one man below stayres in the Court, which he presently named, and it was Sir George Lane.[1]

13th. I find at Court, that either the King is doubtful of some disturbance, or else would seem so, and I have reason to hope it is no worse, by his commanding little commanders of castles, &c., to repair to their charges; and mustering the Guards the other day himself, where he found reason to dislike their condition to my Lord Gerard, finding so many

---

[1] One of the Clerks of the Privy Council, and Secretary to the Marquis of Ormond. He became Viscount Lanesborough.

absent men, or dead[1] pays.   My Lady Castlemaine, I hear,
is in as great favour as ever, and the King supped with her
the very first night he come from Bath ; and last night and
the night before supped with her ; when there being a chine
of beef to roast, and the tide rising into their kitchen that it
could not be roasted there, and the cook telling her of it, she
answered "Zounds ! she must set the house on fire but it
should be roasted !"   So it was carried to Mrs. Sarah's husband s,[2] and there it was roasted.

14th. After dinner my wife and I, by Mr. Rawlinson's
conduct, to the Jewish Synagogue : where the men and boys
in their vayles, and the women behind a lattice out of sight ;
and some things stand up, which I believe is their Law, in a
press, to which all coming in do bow ; and in the putting on
their vayles do say something, to which others that hear the
Priest do cry, Amen, and the party do kiss his vayle. Their
service all in a singing way, and in Hebrew. And anon their
Laws that they take out of the press are carried by several men,
four or five several burthens in all, and they do relieve one
another : and whether it is that every one desires to have the
carrying of it, thus they carried it round about the room
while such a service is singing. And in the end they had a
prayer for the King, in which they pronounced his name in
Portugall ; but the prayer, like the rest, in Hebrew. But,
Lord ! to see the disorder, laughing, sporting, and no atten-
tion, but confusion in all their service, more like brutes than
people knowing the true God, would make a man forswear
ever seeing them more : and indeed I never did see so much,
or could have imagined there had been any religion in the
whole world, so absurdly performed as this.

17th. Some discourse of the Queen's being very sick,[3] if

---

[1] This is probably an allusion to the practice of not reporting the deaths of
soldiers, that the officers might continue to draw their pay.

[2] Who was a cook.

[3] The Queen's illness was first noticed in *The Intelligencer* on the 13th
October, but Pepys did not hear of it till the 17th. The bulletins of her
Majesty's health continued till 15th November. See in the Appendix to the
last volume some account of the Queen's illness, in M. de Lionne's *Letters* to
Louis XIV.

not dead, the Duke and Duchess of York being sent for
betimes this morning to come to White Hall to her.[1]

18th. (Lord's day.) The parson, Mr. Mills, I perceive, did
not know whether to pray for the Queen or no, and so said
nothing about her; which makes me fear she is dead. But
enquiring of Sir J. Minnes, he told me that he heard she was
better last night. To church again, and there a simple
coxcombe preached worse than the Scot.

19th. Waked with a very high wind, and said to my
wife, "I pray God I hear not of the death of any great
person, this wind is so high!" fearing that the Queen might
be dead. So up; and going by coach with Sir W. Batten
and Sir J. Minnes to St. James's, they tell me that Sir W.
Compton, who it is true had been a little sickly for a week
or fortnight, but was very well upon Friday at night last at
the Tangier Committee with us, was dead,—died yesterday:
at which I was most exceedingly surprised, he being, and so
all the world saying that he was, one of the worthyest men
and best officers of State now in England; and so in my
conscience he was: of the best temper, valour, ability of
mind, integrity, worth, fine person, and diligence of any one
man he hath left behind him in the three kingdoms; and yet
not forty years old, or if so, that is all. I find the sober men
of the Court troubled for him; and yet not so as to hinder
or lessen their mirth, talking, laughing, and eating, drinking,
and doing every thing else, just as if there was no such
thing.

Coming to St. James's, I hear that the Queen did sleep
five hours pretty well to-night, and that she waked and
gargled her mouth, and to sleep again; but that her pulse
beats fast, beating twenty to the King's or my Lady Suffolk's
eleven; but not so strong as it was. It seems she was so

---

[1] "The condition of the Queen is much worse, and the physicians give us but
little hopes of her recovery; by the next you will hear that she is either in a fair
way to it, or dead. To-morrow is a very critical day with her—God's will be done.
The King coming to see her the [this] morning, she told him she willingly left all
the world but him, which hath very much afflicted his Majesty, and all the court
with him."—*Lord Arlington to the Duke of Buckingham*, Whitehall, 17th Oct.,
1663. (Brown's *Miscellanea Aulica*, p. 306.)

ill as to be shaved, and pidgeons put to her feet, and to have the extreme unction given her by the priests, who were so long about it that the doctors were angry.[1] The King, they all say, is most fondly disconsolate for her, and weeps by her, which makes her weep; which one this day told me he reckons a good sign, for that it carries away some rheume from the head. This morning Captain Allen tells me how the famous Ned Mullins, by a slight fall, broke his leg at the ancle, which festered; and he had his leg cut off on Saturday, but so ill done, notwithstanding all the great chyrurgeons about the town at the doing of it, that they fear he will not live with it. Being invited to dinner to my Lord Barkeley's, and so, not knowing how to spend our time till noon, Sir W. Batten and I took coach and to the Coffee-house in Cornhill; where much talk about the Turke's proceedings, and that the plague is got to Amsterdam, brought by a ship from Algiers; and it is also carried to Hambrough. The Duke says the King purposes to forbid any of their ships coming into the river. The Duke also told us of several Christian commanders (French) gone over to the Turkes to serve them; and upon enquiry, I find that the King of France do by this aspire to the Empire, and so to get the Crowne of Spayne also upon the death of the King, which is very probable, it seems. Back to St. James's, and there dined with my Lord Barkeley and his lady, where Sir G. Carteret, Sir W. Batten, and myself, with two gentlemen more: my lady, and one of the ladies of honour to the Duchess —no handsome woman, but a most excellent hand. A fine French dinner. To dinner[2] to my Lord Mayor's, being invited, where was the farmers of the Customes, my Lord Chancellor's three sons, and other great and much company, and a very great noble dinner, as this Mayor is good for nothing else. No extraordinary discourse of any thing, every man being intent upon his dinner.

---

[1] "I have heard they put on the Queen's head, when shee was sick, a nightcap of some sort of precious relick to recover her, and gave her extreme unction; and that my Lord Aubignie told her she must impute her recoverie to these. Shee answered not, but rather to the prayers of her husband."—Ward's *Diary*, p. 98.

[2] Pepys seems to have dined twice in the same day.

20th. This evening, at my Lord's lodgings, Mrs. Sarah talking with my wife and I how the Queen do, and how the King tends her, being so ill. She tells us that the Queen's sickness is the spotted fever; that she was as full of the spots as a leopard: which is very strange that it should be no more known; but perhaps it is not so. And that the King do seem to take it much to heart, for that he hath wept before her;[1] but for all that, that he hath not missed one night, since she was sick, of supping with my Lady Castlemaine; which I believe is true, for she says that her husband hath dressed the suppers every night; and I confess I saw him myself coming through the street dressing up a great supper to-night, which Sarah says is also for the King and her: which is a very strange thing.

21st. Come my brother Tom to me. We did resolve of putting me into a better garbe, and, among other things, to have a good velvet cloak—that is, of cloth, lined with velvet, and other things modish, and a perruque, and so he and my wife out to buy me velvet. This evening I begun to enter my wife in arithmetique, in order to her studying of the globes, and she takes it very well, and I hope I shall bring her to understand many fine things.

22d. This morning, hearing that the Queen grows worse again, I sent to stop the making of my velvet cloak, till I see whether she lives or dies.

23d. The Queen slept pretty well last night, but her fever continues upon her still. It seems she hath never a Portuguese doctor here. To Mr. Holliard, who tells me that Mullins is dead of his leg cut off the other day, and most basely done. To Mr. Rawlinson's, and saw some of my new bottles made, with my crest upon them, filled with wine, about five or six dozen.

24th. Busy all the morning about Mr. Gauden's account,

---

[1] The grief of Charles at the Queen's dangerous condition was thus noticed by Waller:—

"—— when no healing art prevail'd,
When cordials and elixirs fail'd,
On your pale cheek he dropt the shower,
Reviv'd you like a dying flower."

and to dinner with him at the Dolphin, where mighty merry
by pleasant stories of Mr. Coventry's and Sir J. Minnes's,
which I have put down some of in my book of tales.   Called
at Wotton's.[1]   He tells me, that by the Duke of York's
persuasion Harris is come again to Sir W. Davenant upon his
terms that he demanded, which will make him very high and
proud.   The Queen is in a good way of recovery; and Sir
Francis Pridgeon[2] hath got great honour by it, it being all
imputed to his cordiall, which in her despaire did give her
rest, and brought her to some hopes of recovery.   It seems
that, after much talk of troubles and a plot, something is
found in the North that a party was to rise, and some persons
that were to command it, as I find in a letter that Mr.
Coventry read to-day about it from those parts.

26th. Dr. Pierce tells me that the Queen is in a way to be
pretty well again, but that her delirium in her head continues
still; that she talks idle, not by fits, but always, which in
some lasts a week after so high a fever — in some more, and
in some for ever; that this morning she talked mightily that
she was brought to bed, and that she wondered that she
should be delivered without pain and without being sick, and
that she was troubled that her boy was but an ugly boy.   But
the King being by, said, "No, it is a very pretty boy."—
"Nay," says she, "if it be like you, it is a fine boy indeed,
and I would be very well pleased with it."   They say that
the Turkes go on apace, and that my Lord Castlehaven[3] is
going to raise 10,000 men here for to go against him; that
the King of France do offer to assist the Empire upon
condition that he may be their Generalissimo, and the Dolphin
chosen King of the Romans: and it is said that the King of

---

[1] His shoemaker.

[2] Vertue (according to Horace Walpole) had seen a portrait of Dr. Prujean,
painted by Streater, and a print of "Opinion sitting on a tree," thus inscribed:
"Viro clariss. Dno Francisco Prujeano Medico, omnium bonarum artium et ele-
gantiarum fautori et admiratori summo; D.D. D.H Peacham." He was President
of the College of Physicians, 1653.

[3] The eldest son of the infamous Earl of Castlehaven had a new creation to
his father's forfeited titles, in 1634, and died, s. p., 1684. He had served with
distinction under the Marquis of Ormond, and afterwards joined Charles II. at
Paris.

France do occasion this difference among the Christian Princes
of the Empire. which gives the Turke such advantages. They
say also that the King of Spayne is making all imaginable
force against Portugall again. To one or two periwigg shops
about the Temple, having been very much displeased with one
that we saw, a head of greasy and old woman's haire, at
Jervas's, in the morning; and there I think I shall fit myself
of one very handsomely made. To the Globe in Fleet Street,
and talking of the Emperor[1] at table, one young gentleman,
a pretty man, and it seems a Parliament-man, did say that he
was a sot; for he minded nothing of the Government, but was
led by the Jesuites. Several at table took him up.

27th. Mr. Coventry tells me to-day that the Queen had a
very good night last night; but yet it is strange that still she
raves and talks of little more than of her having of children,
and fancys now that she hath three children, and that the
girle is very like the King. And this morning, about five
o'clock, the physician, feeling her pulse, thinking to be better
able to judge, she being still and asleep, waked her, and the
first word she said was, "How do the children?"

29th. Up, it being Lord Mayor's day, Sir Anthony
Bateman.[2] This morning was brought home my new velvet
cloak—that is, lined with velvet, a good cloth the outside—
the first that ever I had in my life, and I pray God it may
not be too soon now that I begin to wear it. I thought it
better to go without it because of the crowde, and so I did
not wear it. At noon I went to Guildhall; and, meeting with
Mr. Proby, Sir R. Ford's son, and Lieutenant-Colonel Baron,
a City commander, we went up and down to see the tables;
where under every salt there was a bill of fare, and at the end
of the table the persons proper for the table. Many were
the tables, but none in the Hall but the Mayor's and the
Lords of the Privy Council that had napkins or knives, which

---

[1] Leopold: ætatis 24.
[2] Second son of Richard Bateman of Hartington, co. Derby, who had been
Chamberlain and M.P. for London. Sir A. Bateman married Elizabeth Russell.
His elder brother was Sir William Bateman, and his younger, Thomas, was
created a Baronet in 1661.

was very strange. We went into the Buttry, and there stayed
and talked, and then into the Hall again, and there wine was
offered, and they drunk, I only drinking some hypocras,[1]
which do not break my vowe, it being, to the best of my
present judgement, only a mixed compound drink, and not
any wine. If I am mistaken, God forgive me! but I do
hope and think I am not. By and by met with Creed: and
we, with the others, went within the several Courts, and there
saw the tables prepared for the Ladies, and Judges, and
Bishops: all great signs of a great dinner to come. By and
by, about one o'clock, before the Lord Mayor come, come
into the Hall, from the room where they were first led into,
the Chancellor, Archbishopp before him, with the Lords of
the Council, and other Bishopps, and they to dinner. Anon
comes the Lord Mayor, who went up to the lords, and then
to the other tables to bid wellcome; and so all to dinner. I
sat near Proby, Baron, and Creed at the Merchant Strangers'
table; where ten good dishes to a messe, with plenty of wine,
of all sorts, of which I drunk none; but it was very
unpleasing that we had no napkins nor change of trenchers,
and drunk out of earthen pitchers, and wooden dishes. It
happened that after the lords had half dined, come the French
Embassador up to the lords' table, where he was to have sat:
he would not sit down nor dine with the Lord Mayor, who
was not yet come, nor have a table to himself, which was
offered; but in a discontent went away again.[2] After I had
dined, I and Creed rose and went up and down the house,
and up to the ladys' room, and there stayed gazing upon
them. But though there were many and fine, both young
and old, yet I could not discern one handsome face there;
which was very strange. I expected musique, but there was
none but only trumpets and drums, which displeased me.
The dinner, it seems, is made by the Mayor and two Sheriffs
for the time being, the Lord Mayor paying one half, and

---

[1] This beverage was taken in France as a morning draught. — Southey's
Common-Place Book.

[2] See, in the Appendix to vol. iv., Monsieur de Lionne's account of the affront
which he received, and the reparation made to him.

they the other. And the whole, Proby says, is reckoned to come to about 7 or 800*l.* at most. Being wearied with looking upon a company of ugly women, Creed and I went away, and took coach, and through Cheapside, and there saw the pageants,[1] which were very silly. The Queen mends apace, they say; but yet talks idle still.

30th. At my periwigg-maker's, and there showed my wife the periwigg made for me, and she likes it very well, and so to my brother's, and to buy a pair of boddice for her.

31st. To my great sorrow find myself 43*l.* worse than I was the last month, which was then 760*l.*, and now it is but 717*l.* But it hath chiefly arisen from my layings-out in clothes for myself and wife; viz., for her about 12*l.*, and for myself 55*l.*, or thereabouts; having made myself a velvet cloak, two new cloth shirts, black, plain both; a new shag gown, trimmed with gold buttons and twist, with a new hat, and silk tops for my legs, and many other things, being resolved henceforward to go like myself. And also two periwiggs, one whereof costs me 3*l.*, and the other 40*s.* I have worn neither yet, but will begin next week, God willing. I having laid out in clothes for myself, and wife, and for her closet and other things without, these two months, this and the last, besides household expenses of victualls, &c., above 110*l.* But I hope I shall with more comfort labour to get more, and with better successe than when, for want of clothes, I was forced to sneak like a beggar. The Queen continues light-headed, but in hopes to recover. The plague is much in Amsterdam, and we in fear of it here, which God defend.[2] The Turke goes on mighty in the Emperor's dominions, and the Princes cannot agree among themselves how to go against him.

November 1st. (Lord's day.) This morning my brother's man brought me a new black baize waiste-coate, faced with silk, which I put on, from this day laying by half-shirts for this winter. He brought me also my new gown of purple

---

[1] The Lord Mayor's "Show" was then *after* dinner.
[2] *Defend* is used in the sense of *forbid.* It is a Gallicism.

shagg: also, as a gift from my brother, a velvet hat,[1] **very** fine to ride in, and the fashion, which pleases me.

2d. Up, and by coach to White Hall, and there in the long Matted Gallery I find Sir G. Carteret, Sir J. Minnes, and Sir W. Batten; and by and by comes the King, to walk there with three or four with him; and, soon as he saw us, says he, "Here is the Navy Office," and there walked twenty turns the length of the gallery, talking, methought, but ordinary talk. By and by come the Duke, and he walked, and at last they went into the Duke's lodgings. The King staid so long, that we could not discourse with the Duke, and so we parted. I heard the Duke say that he was going to wear a perriwigg; and they say the King also will. I never till this day observed that the King is mighty gray.

3d. At noon to the coffee-house, and there heard a long and most passionate discourse between two doctors of physick, of which one was Dr. Allen,[2] whom I knew at Cambridge, and a couple of apothecarys: these maintaining chymistry against their Galenicall physick; and the truth is, one of the apothecarys, whom they charged most, did speak very prettily —that is, his language and sense good, though perhaps he might not be so knowing a physician as to offer to contest with them. At last they come to some cooler terms, and broke up. Home, and by and by comes Chapman, the peri-wigg-maker, and upon my liking it, without more ado I went up, and there he cut off my haire, which went a little to my heart at present to part with it; but, it being over, and my periwigg on, I paid him 3*l.* for it; and away went he, with my own haire, to make up another of; and I, by and by, went abroad, after I had caused all my maids to look upon it; and they conclude it do become me; though Jane was mightily troubled for my parting of my own haire, and so was Besse.

4th. To my office, shewing myself to Sir W. Batten and Sir J. Minnes, and no great matter made of my perriwigg, as I

[1] Which he had probably cribbed from the velvet.

[2] Thomas Allen, M.D., of Caius College, and a member of the College of Physicians.

was afraid there would. The Queen is in a great way to recovery.

6th. To the Coffee-house, and among other things heard Sir John Cutler say, that of his own experience in time of thunder so many barrels of beer as have a piece of iron laid upon them, will not be soured, and the others will. To White Hall, where my Lord met me very fortunately, and wondered first to see me in my perruque, and I am glad it is over. We begun to talk of the court, and he tells me how Mr. Edward Montagu begins to show respect to him again, after his endeavouring to bespatter him all was possible; but he is resolved never to admit him into his friendship again. He tells me how he and Sir H. Bennet, the Duke of Buckingham and his Duchess, was of a committee with somebody else for the getting of Mrs. Stewart for the King; but that she proves a cunning slut, and is advised at Somerset House by the Queen-Mother, and by her mother,[1] and so all the plot is spoiled and the whole committee broke, Mr. Montagu and the Duke of Buckingham fallen a-pieces, the Duchess going to a nunnery; and so Montagu begins to enter friendship with my Lord, and to attend the Chancellor, whom he had deserted. My Lord tells me that Mr. Montagu, among other things, did endeavour to represent him to the Chancellor's sons as one that did desert their father in the business of my Lord of Bristoll; which is most false, being the only man that hath several times dined with him when no soul hath come to him, and went with him that very day home, when the Earl impeached him in the Parliament House, and hath refused ever to pay a visit to my Lord of Bristoll, not so much as in return to a visit of his. So that the Chancellor and my Lord are well known and trusted one by another. But yet my Lord blames the Chancellor for desiring to have it put off to the next Session of Parliament, contrary to my Lord Treasurer's advice, to whom he swore he would not do it : and, perhaps, my Lord Chancellor, for ought I see by my Lord's discourse, may suffer by it when the Parliament comes to sit. My Lord tells me that he observes the Duke of York

---

[1] Mrs. Walter Stuart.

do follow and understand business very well, and is mightily
improved thereby.

7th. This day, Captain Taylor[1] brought me a piece of plate,
a little small state dish, he expecting that I should get him
some allowance for demorage of his ship William, kept long
at Tangier, which I shall, and may justly do.

8th. (Lord's day.) To church, where I found that my coming in a periwigg did not prove so strange as I was afraid it
would, for I thought that all the church would presently have
cast their eyes all upon me, but I found no such thing.[2]

9th. To the Duke, where, when we come into his closet,
he told us that Mr. Pepys was so altered with his new perri
wigg that he did not know him. So to our discourse, and,
among and above other things, we were taken up in talking
upon Sir J. Lawson's coming home, he being come to Portsmouth; and Captain Berkeley[3] is come to town with a letter
from the Duana[4] of Algiers to the King, wherein they do
demand again the searching of our ships and taking out of
strangers and their goods; and that what English ships are
taken without the Duke's pass they will detain, though it be
flat contrary to the words of the peace, as prizes, till they do
hear from our King, which they advise him may be speedy.
And this they did the very next day after they had received
with great joy the Grand Seignor's confirmation of the Peace
from Constantinople by Captain Berkeley; so that there is no
command nor certainty to be had of these people. The King
is resolved to send his will by a fleet of ships; and it is thought

---

[1] Silas Taylor, described by A. Wood as *alias* Domville, was a native of Shrop-
shire, and educated at Oxford, and became a captain in the Parliament forces.
Subsequently to the Restoration, he was appointed Commissary of Ammunition
at Dunkirk, and in 1665 made Keeper of the King's Stores at Harwich. He died
November 4th, 1663. He was an able antiquary, and left materials for a History
of Herefordshire and of Harwich. There is a MS. by Silas Taylor in the British
Museum. (*Addit. MSS.*, 4910.) It formerly belonged to Sir John Hawkins, who
describes Taylor as well skilled in music, and a composer of two anthems, which
pleased the King. See Hawkins's *Hist. of Music*, vol. iv., p. 330, and Wood's
Athenæ. Taylor published in his lifetime a treatise on Gavel-kind.

[2] There is a touch of vanity in this passage that is excessively comic, and the
notice of the slight impression made by the perriwig is admirably descriptive of
the writer.

[3] Afterwards Sir William Berkeley, Governor of Portsmouth, killed in 1666.

[4] Diwan.

best and speediest to send these very ships that are now come
home, five sail of good ships, back again, after cleaning,
victualling, and paying them.   But it is a pleasant thing to
think how their Basha, Shavan Aga, did tear his hair to see
the soldiers order things thus; for, just like his late predecessor, when they see the evil of war with England, then for
certain they complain to the Grand Seignor of him, and cut
his head off: this he is sure of, and knows as certain. Thence
to Westminster Hall, where I met with Mr. Pierce, surgeon;
and, among other things, he asked me seriously whether I
knew any thing of my Lord's being out of favour with the
King; and told me, that for certain the King do take mighty
notice of my Lord's living obscurely in a corner not like himself, and becoming the honour that he is come to.   I was
sorry to hear, and the truth is, from my Lord's discourse
among his people, which I am told of, the uncertainty of
princes' favour, and his melancholy keeping from Court, I am
doubtful of some such thing; but I seemed wholly strange to
him in it, but will make my use of it.   He told me also how
loose the Court is, nobody looking after business, but every
man his lust and gain; and how the King is now become
besotted upon Mrs. Stewart, that he gets into corners, and
will be with her half an hour together, kissing her to the observation of all the world; and she now stays by herself and
expects it, as my Lady Castlemaine did use to do; to whom
the King, he says, is still kind, so as now and then he goes to
her, as he believes; but with no such fondness as he used to
do.   But yet it is thought that this new wench is so subtle,
that it is verily thought, if the Queen had died, he would have
married her.   The Duke of Monmouth is to have part of the
Cockpitt new built for lodgings for him, and they say to be
made Captain of the guards in the room of my Lord Gerard.
Mr. Blackburne[1] and I fell to talk of many things, wherein
he was very open to me: first, in that of religion, he makes
it greater matter of prudence for the King and Council to
suffer liberty of conscience; and imputes the loss of Hungary
to the Turke from the Emperor's denying them this liberty of
their religion   He says that many pious ministers of the

---

[1] A stanch puritan.

word of God, some thousands of them, do now beg their
bread : and told me how highly the present clergy carry themselves every where, so as that they are hated and laughed at
by every body ; among other things, for their excommunica-
tions, which they send upon the least occasions almost that
can be.   And I am convinced in my judgement, not only
from his discourse, but my thoughts in general, that the
present clergy will never heartily go down with the generality
of the commons of England ; they have been so used to
liberty and freedom, and they are so acquainted with the
pride and debauchery of the present clergy.   He did give me
many stories of the affronts which the clergy receive in all
places of England from the gentry and ordinary persons of
the parish.   He do tell me what the City thinks of General
Monk, as of a most perfidious man that hath betrayed every
body, and the King also ; who, as he thinks, and his party, and
so I have heard other good friends of the King say, it might
have been better for the King to have had his hands a little
bound for the present, than be forced to bring such a crew of
poor people about him, and be liable to satisfy the demands of
every one of them.   He told me that, to his knowledge,
being present at every meeting of the Treaty at the Isle of
Wight, the old King did confess himself over-ruled and convinced in his judgement against the Bishopps, and would
have suffered and did agree to exclude the service out of the
churches, nay, his own chapell ; and that he did always say,
that this he did not by force, for that he would never abate
one inch by any violence ; but what he did was out of his
reason and judgement.   He tells me that the King by name,
with all his dignities, is prayed for by them that they call
Fanatiques, as heartily and powerfully as in any of the other
churches that are thought better : and that, let the King
think what he will, it is them that must help him in the day
of warr.   For so generally they are the most substantiall sort
of people, and the soberest ; and did desire me to observe it
to my Lord Sandwich, among other things, that of all the old
army now you cannot see a man begging about the streets ;
but what?   You shall have this captain turned a shoemaker ;

the lieutenant, a baker; this a brewer; that a haberdasher;
this common soldier, a porter; and every man in his apron
and frock, &c., as if they never had done any thing else:
whereas, the others go with their belts and swords, swearing,
and cursing, and stealing; running into people's houses, by
force oftentimes, to carry away something; and this is the
difference between the temper of one and the other; and
concludes, and I think with some reason, that the spirits of
the old parliament soldiers are so quiet and contented with
God's providences, that the King is safer from any evil meant
him by them one thousand times more than from his own
discontented Cavalier. And then to the publick management
of business: it is done, as he observes, so loosely and so care-
lessly, that the kingdom can never be happy with it, every
man looking after himself, and his own lust and luxury; and
that half of what money the Parliament gives the King is not
so much as gathered. And to the purpose, he told me how
the Bellamys, who had some of the Northern counties assigned
them for their debt for the petty warrant victualling, have
often complained to him that they cannot get it collected, for
that nobody minds, or, if they do, they won't pay it in.
Whereas, which is a very remarkable thing, he hath been
told by some of the Treasurers at Warr here of late, to whom
the most of the 120,000*l*. monthly was paid, that for most
months the payments were gathered so duly, that they seldom
had so much or more than 40*s*., or the like, short in the whole
collection, whereas, now the very Commissioners for Assessments and other publick payments are such persons, and
those that they choose in the country so like themselves, that
from top to bottom there is not a man carefull of any thing,
or, if he be, is not solvent; that what between the beggar
and the knave, the King is abused the best part of all his
revenue. We then talked of the Navy, and of Sir W. Pen's
rise to be a general. He told me he was always a conceited
man, and one that would put the best side outward, but that
it was his pretence of sanctity that brought him into play.
Lawson, and Portman, and the fifth-monarchy men, among
whom he was a great brother, importuned that he might be

General; and it was pleasant to see how Blackburne himself
did act it; how, when the Commissioners of the Admiralty
would enquire of the captains and admirals of such and such
men, how they would, with a sigh and casting up the eyes,
say, "such a man fears the Lord," or, "I hope such a man
hath the Spirit of God." But he tells me, that there was a
cruel article against Pen, after one fight, for cowardice, in
putting himself within a coyle of cables, of which he had
much ado to acquit himself: and by great friends did it, not
without remains of guilt, but that his brethren had a mind to
pass it by, and Sir H. Vane did advise him to search his
heart, and see whether this fault or a greater sin was not the
occasion of this so great tryall. And he tells me, that what
Pen gives out about Cromwell's sending and entreating him
to go to Jamaica is very false; he knows the contrary: besides, the Protector never was a man that needed to send for
any man, especially such a one as he, twice. He tells me that
the business of Jamaica did miscarry absolutely by his pride,
and that, when he was in the Tower, he would cry like a
child. And that just upon the turne, when Monk was come
from the North to the City, and did begin to think of bringing in the King, Pen was then turned Quaker. That Lawson
was never counted any thing but only a seaman, and a stout
man, but a false man, and that now he appears the greatest
hypocrite in the world. And Pen the same. He tells me,
that it is much talked of, that the King intends to legitimate
the Duke of Monmouth; and that neither he, nor his friends
of his persuasion, have any hopes of getting their consciences
at liberty but by God Almighty's turning of the King's
heart, which they expect, and are resolved to live and die in
quiet hopes of it; but never to repine, or act any thing more
than by prayers towards it. And that not only himself, but
all of them have, and are willing, at any time, to take the
oaths of Allegiance and Supremacy. Mr. Blackburne observed further to me, some certain notice that he had of the
present plot[1] so much talked of; that he was told by Mr.

---

[1] The plot alluded to is known in Yorkshire by the name of "the Farnley
Plot," of which there are many details in Whitaker's "Loidis and Elmet:"

Rushworth[1] how one Captain Oates, a great Discoverer, did employ several to bring and seduce others into a plot, and that one of his agents met with one that would not listen to him, nor conceal what he had offered him, but so detected the trepan. He did also much insist upon the cowardice and corruption of the King's guards and militia.

10th. The Queen, I hear, is now very well again, and that she hath bespoke herself a new gown.

11th. At noon to the Coffee-house, where, with Dr. Allen, some good discourse about physick and chymistry. And among other things, I telling him what Dribble, the German Doctor, do offer of an instrument to sink ships; he tells me that which is more strange, that something made of gold, which they call in chymistry *Aurum Fulminans*, a grain, I think he said, of it, put into a silver spoon and fired, will give a blow like a musquett, and strike a hole through the silver spoon downward, without the least force upwards; and this he can make a cheaper experiment of, he says, with iron prepared.

13th. After dinner, come my perriwigg-maker, and brings me a second periwigg, made of my own hair, which comes to 21s. 6d. more than the worth of my own hair, so that they both come to 4l. 1s. 6d., which he sayth will serve me two years, but I fear it. He being gone, I to my office, and put on my new shagg purple gown, with gold buttons and loop-lace.

14th. Mr. Moore come to tell me that he had no opportunity of speaking his mind to my Lord yesterday, and so I am resolved to write to him very suddenly.

15th. (Lord's day.) In the afternoon, drew up a letter to my Lord, stating to him what the world talks concerning him,

Captain *Thomas* Oates was a conspicuous person in it, but he was not a Discoverer, as he suffered death for his share in the conspiracy. His son was a Discoverer, and hence the mistake, Pepys writing from the vague rumours of the day. The "great Discoverer who did employ several to bring and seduce others into a plot," was probably Major Greathead, a Commonwealth officer, whom Oliver Heywood, in his *Diaries*, calls "that perfidious wretch, guilty of so much blood in the plot business"—a severity of expression in which he did not often allow himself to indulge.

[1] John Rushworth, Clerk Assistant to the House of Commons, and author of the *Historical Collections*. Ob. 1690

and leaving it to him and myself to be thought of by him as he pleases, but I have done but my duty in it. I wait Mr. Moore's coming, for his advice about sending it. This day being our Queen's birthday, the guns of the Tower went all off; and in the evening the Lord Mayor sent from church to church to order the constables to cause bonfires to be made in every street, which methinks is a poor thing to be forced to be commanded. After a good supper with my wife, and hearing of the maids read in the Bible, to prayers and to bed.

18th. Captain Berkeley, who was lately come from Algiers, did give us a good account of the place, and how the Basha there do live like a prisoner, being at the mercy of the soldiers and officers, so that there is nothing but a great confusion there. I walked home again, reading of a little book of new poems of Cowley's, given me by his brother. Abraham do lie, it seems, very sick, still, but like to recover. Come Mr. Holliard, so full of discourse and Latin, that I think he hath got a cup, but I do not know; but full of talk he is, in defence of Calvin and Luther. This morning I sent Will with my great letter of reproof to Lord Sandwich, who did give it into his own hand. I pray God give a blessing to it; but I confess I am afraid what the consequence may be to me of good or bad, which is according to the ingenuity that he do receive it with. However, I am satisfied that it will do him good, and that he needs it.

[Here follows the letter.]

My Lord,

I do verily hope, that neither the manner nor matter of this advice will be condemned by your Lordship, when, for my defence in the first, I shall alledge my double attempt, since your return from Hinchingbroke, of doing it personally, in both of which your Lordship's occasions, no doubtfulness of mine, prevented me; and that being now fearful of a sudden summons to Portmouth, for the discharge of some ships there, I judge it very unbecoming the duty which every bit of bread I eat tells me I owe to your Lordship to expose the safety of

your honour to the safety of my return. For the matter, my
Lord, it is such as, could I in any measure think safe to conceal from, or likely to be discovered to you by any other hand,
I should not have dared so far to own what from my heart I
believe is false, as to make myself the relater but of others'
discourse ; but, sir, your Lordship's honour being such as I
ought to value it to be, and finding both in city and court
that discourses pass to your prejudice, too generally for mine
or any man's controllings but your Lordship's, I shall, my
Lord, without the least greatening or lessening the matter, do
my duty in laying it shortly before you.

People of all conditions, my Lord, raise matter of wonder
from your Lordship's so little appearance at Court : some concluding thence their disfavour thereby, to which purpose I have
had questions asked me ; and, endeavouring to put off such
insinuations by asserting the contrary, they have replied, that
your Lordship's living so beneath your quality, out of the way,
and declining of Court attendance, hath been more than once
discoursed about the King. Others, my Lord, when the chief
Ministers of State, and those most active of the Council have
been reckoned up, wherein your Lordship never used to want
an eminent place, have said, touching your Lordship, that now
your turn was served, and the King had given you a good
estate, you left him to stand or fall as he would, and, particularly in that of the Navy, have enlarged upon your letting fall
all service there.

Another sort, and those the most, insist upon the bad report
of the house wherein your Lordship, now observed in perfect
health again, continues to sojourne, and by name have charged
one of the daughters for a common courtizan, alledging both
places and persons where and with whom she hath been too
well known, and how much her wantonness occasions, though
unjustly, scandal to your Lordship, and that as well to grati-
fying some enemies, as to the wounding of more friends I am
not able to tell.

Lastly, my Lord, I find a general coldness in all persons
towards your Lordship, such as, from my first dependance on
you, I never knew, wherein I shall not offer to interpose any

thoughts or advice of mine, well knowing your Lordship
needs not any.   But with a most faithful assurance, that no
person nor papers under Heaven is privy to what I here
write, besides myself and this, which I shall be careful to
have put into your own hands, I rest confident of your Lordship's just construction of my dutifull intentions herein, and
in all humility take my leave.   May it please your Lordship,
                    Your Lordship's most obedient Servant.

                                                   S. P.

[The foregoing letter was sealed up and enclosed in the
following.]

          My Lord,

If this find your Lordship either not alone, or not at
leisure, I beg the suspending your opening the enclosed till
you shall have both, the matter very well bearing such a delay,
and in all humility remain, &c.,

November 17th, 1663.   S. P.

My servant hath my directions to put this into your Lordship's own hand, but not to stay for any answer.

19th. With Sir G. Carteret, to my Lord Treasurer,[1] to discourse with him about Mr. Gauden's having of money, and to
offer to him whether it would not be necessary, Mr. Gauden's
credit being so low as it is, to take security of him if he demands any great sum, such as 20,000l., which now ought to
be paid him upon his next year's declaration; which is a sad
thing that, being reduced to this by us, we should be the first
to doubt his credit; but so it is.   However, it will be managed
with great tenderness to him.   My Lord Treasurer we found
in his bed chamber, being laid up of the goute.   I find him
a very ready man, and certainly a brave servant to the King:
he spoke so quick and sensible of the King's charge.   Nothing
displeased me in him but his long nails, which he lets grow
upon a pretty thick white short hand, that it troubled me to
see them.   In our way, Sir G. Carteret told me there is no

----
[1] Earl of Southampton.

such thing likely yet as a Dutch war, neither they nor we being in condition for it, though it will come certainly to that in some time, our interests lying the same way, that is to say, in trade. But not yet. To speak with Mr. Moore, and met him by the way, who tells me, to my great content, that he believes my letter to my Lord Sandwich hath wrought well upon him, and that he will look after himself and his business upon it, for he begins already to do so. But I dare not conclude any thing till I see him, which shall be to-morrow morning, that I may be out of my pain to know how he takes it of me.

20th. To my Lord Sandwich's lodgings, but he was gone out before, and so I am defeated of my expectation of being eased one way or other in the business of my Lord. But I up to Mr. Howe, who I saw this day the first time in a periwigg, which becomes him very well. He tells me, that my Lord is of a sudden much changed, and he do believe that he do take my letter well. However, we both bless God that it hath so good an effect upon him. Thence I home again. A great talk there is to-day of a crush between some of the Fanatiques up in arms, and the King's men in the North; but whether true I know not yet.

21st. At noon, I receive a letter from Mr. Creed, with a token, viz., a very noble parti-coloured Indian gowne for my wife. The letter is oddly writ, over-prizing his present, and little owning any past services of mine. I confess I had expectations of a better account from him of my services about his accounts, and so give his boy 12*d.*, and sent it back again. And this afternoon I went to Ludgate, and, by pricing several there, I guess this gowne may be worth about 12*l.* or 15*l.* But, however, I expect at least 50*l.* of him. My mind being pretty well at ease for my receipt this afternoon of 17*l.* at the Treasury, paid a year since to the carver for his work at my house, which I did intend to have paid myself, but, finding others to do it, I thought it not amisse to get it too.

22d. (Lord's day.) I walked as far as the Temple, and there took coach, and to my Lord's lodgings, whom I found ready to go to Chappell; but I coming, he begun, with a very

serious countenance, to tell me that he had received my late
letter, wherein first he took notice of my care of him and his
honour, and did give me thanks for that part of it where I say,
that from my heart I believe the contrary of what I do there
relate to be the discourse of others; but, since I intended it
not a reproach, but matter of information, and for him to
make a judgement of it for his practice, it was necessary for
me to tell him the persons of whom I have gathered the several
particulars which I there insist on.   I would have made
excuses in it; but, seeing him so earnest in it, I found myself forced to it, and so did tell him Mr. Pierce, the surgeon,
in that of his Lordship's living being discoursed of at Court.
A maid-servant that I kept, that lived at Chelsey school, and
also Mr. Pickering, about the report touching the young
woman, and also Mr. Hunt, in Axe Yard, near whom she
lodged.   I told him the whole city do discourse concerning
his neglect of business; and so I many times asserting my
dutiful intention in all this, and he owning his accepting of it
as such.   That that troubled me most in particular is, that he
did there assert the civility of the people of the house, and the
young gentlewoman, for whose reproach he was sorry.   His
saying that he was resolved how to live, and that though he
was taking a house, meaning to live in another manner, yet it
was not to please any people, or stop report, but to please himself, though this I do believe he might say that he might not
seem to me to be so much wrought upon by what I have
writ; and lastly, and most of all, when I spoke of the tenderness that I have used in declaring this to him, there being
nobody privy to it, he told me that I must give him leave to
except one.   I told him, that possibly somebody might know
of some thoughts of mine — I having borrowed some intelligence in this matter from them, but nobody could say they
knew of the thing itself what I writ.   This, I confess, however, do trouble me, for that he seemed to speak it as a quick
retort, and it must sure be Will. Howe, who did not see any
thing of what I writ, though I told him indeed that I would
write; but in this, methinks, there is no great hurt.   I find
him, though he cannot but own his opinion of my good in-

tention, and so he did again and again profess it, that he is
troubled in his mind at it ; and I confess I think I may have
done myself an injury for his good, which, were it to do again,
and that I believe he would take it no better, I think I
should sit quietly without taking any notice of it ; for I doubt
there is no medium between his taking it very well, or very
ill. I could not forbear weeping before him at the latter end :
which, since, I am ashamed of, though I cannot see what he
can take it to proceed from, but my tenderness and good will
to him. After this discourse was ended, he begun to talk
very cheerfully of other things, and I walked with him to
White Hall, and we discoursed of the pictures in the gallery,
which it may be he might do out of policy, that the boy might
not see any strangeness in him ; but I rather think that his
mind was somewhat eased, and hope that he will be to me as
he was before. At chapel I had room in the Privy Seale pew,
with other gentlemen, and there heard Dr. Killigrew[1] preach.
The anthem was good after sermon, being the fifty-first
psalme, made for five voices by one of Captain Cooke's boys,
a pretty boy. And they say there are four or five of them
that can do as much. And here I first perceived that the
King is a little musicall, and kept good time with his hand all
along the anthem. I met Mr. Povy, who tells me how
Tangier had like to have been betrayed, and that one of the
King's officers is come, to whom 8000 pieces of eight were
offered for his part. To the King's Head ordinary, and there
dined, good and much company and a good dinner : most of
their discourse was about hunting, in a dialect I understand
very little.

23d. To St. Paul's Churchyard, and there bespoke "Rushworth's Collections," and "Scobell's Acts of the Long Parliament," &c., which I will make the King pay for as to the
office, and so I do not break my vowe at all. With Alderman
Backewell, talking of the new money, which he says will never
be counterfeited, he believes ; but it is so deadly incon

---

[1] Henry, youngest son of Sir Robert Killigrew, D.D., Prebendary of Westminster, and Master of the Savoy, and author of some plays and sermons. His
daughter Anne was the well-known poetess.

venient for telling, it is so thick, and the edges are made to turn up.

25th. To my Lord Sandwich, and there I did present him with Mr. Barlow's "Terella,"[1] with which he was very much pleased, and he did show me great kindness, and by other discourse I have reason to think that he is not at all, as I feared he would be, discontented against me.

26th. The plague, it seems, grows more and more at Amsterdam; and we are going upon making of all ships coming from thence and Hambrough, or any other infected places, to perform their Quarantine, for thirty days, as Sir Richard Browne expressed it in the order of the Council, contrary to the import of the word, though, in the general acceptation, it signifies now the thing, not the time spent in doing it, in Holehaven; a thing never done by us before.

27th. My wife mightily pleased with my discourse of getting a trip over to Calis, or some other part of France, the next summer, in one of the yachts, and I believe I shall do it —and it makes good sport that my maid Jane dares not go; and Besse is wild to go, and is mad for joy, but yet will be willing to stay, if Jane hath a mind.

28th. I met with Mr. Pierce, the surgeon, who tells me for good news that my Lord Sandwich is resolved to go no more to Chelsey, and told me he believed that I had been giving my Lord some counsel, which I neither denied nor affirmed. To Paul's Church Yard, and there looked upon the second part of Hudibras, which I buy not, but borrow to read, to see if it be as good as the first, which the world cried so mightily up, though it hath not a good liking in me, though I had tried but twice or three times reading to bring myself to think it witty. To-day, for certain, I am told how in Holland publickly they have pictured our King with reproach: one way is with his pockets turned the wrong side outward, hanging out empty; another, with two courtiers, picking of his pockets;

---

[1] In Grew's *Rarities belonging to the Royal Society*, p. 364, mention is made of a Terella, or Orbicular Loadstone, contrived by Sir Christopher Wren. John Evelyn was shown "a pretty Terella, described with all the circles, and showing all the magnetic deviations."—See his *Diary*, 3d July, 1655.

and a third, leading of two ladies, while others abuse him; which amounts to great contempt.

29th. (Lord's day.) This morning I put on my best black cloth suit, trimmed with scarlett ribbon, very neat, with my cloak lined with velvett, and a new beaver, which altogether is very noble, with my black silk knit canons I bought a month ago.

30th. At White Hall Sir W. Pen and I met the Duke in the Matted Gallery, and there he discoursed with us; and by and by my Lord Sandwich come and stood by, and talked; but, it being St. Andrew's, and a collar-day, he went to the Chapel, and we parted. To the coffee-house, where I heard the best story of a cheat intended by a master of a ship, who had borrowed twice his money upon the bottomary,¹ and as much more insured upon the ship and goods as they were worth, and then would have cast her away upon the coast of France, and there left her, refusing any pilott which was offered him; and so the Governor of the place took her, and sent her over hither to find an owner, and so the ship is come safe, and goods and all: they all worth 500*l.*, and he had, one way or other, taken 3000*l.* The cause is to be tried to-morrow at Guildhall, where I intend to be. Come W. Howe to see me, who tells me that my Lord hath been angry for three or four days with him—would not speak to him: at last did, and charged him with having spoken to me about what he had observed concerning his Lordship, which, W. Howe denying stoutly, he was well at ease, and continues very quiett, and is removing from Chelsey; but, methinks, by my Lord's looks upon me to-day, my Lord is not very well pleased, nor, it may be, will be a good while, which vexes me; but I hope all will [blow] over in time, or else I am but ill rewarded for my good service.

December 1st. After dinner I to Guildhall, to hear a trial at King's Bench before Lord Chief Justice Hide, the same I mention in my yesterday's journall, where every thing was proved how money was so taken up upon bottomary and insurance, and the ship left by the master and seamen upon

¹ The act of borrowing money upon a ship's bottom.

rocks, where, when the sea fell at the ebb, she must perish. The master was offered help, and he did give the pilotts 20 sols to drink, to bid them go about their business, saying that the rocks were old, but his ship was new, and that she was repaired for 6*l.* and less all the damage that she received, and is brought by one sent for on purpose by the insurers, into the Thames, with her cargo, vessels of tallow daubed over with butter, instead of all butter—the whole not worth above 500*l.*, ship and all, and they had took up, as appeared above, 2400*l.* He had given his men money to content them; and yet, for all this, he did bring some of them to swear that it was very stormy weather, and [they] did all they could to save her, and that she was seven feete deep water in hold, and were fain to cut her main and foremast—that the master was the last man that went out, and they were fain to force [him] out when she was ready to sink; and her rudder broke off, and she was drawn into the harbour after they were gone, as wreck, all broken, and goods lost: that she could not be carried out again without new building; and many other things so contrary as is not imaginable more. There was all the great counsel in the kingdom in the cause; but, after one witnesse or two for the plaintiff, it was cried down as a most notorious cheat; and so the jury, without going out, found it for the plaintiff. But it was pleasant to see what mad sort of testimonys the seamen did give, and could not be got to speak in order: and then their terms such as the Judge could not understand; and to hear how sillily the Counsel and Judge would speak as to the terms necessary in the matter, would make one laugh: and, above all, a French-man that was forced to speak in French, and took an English oath he did not understand, and had an interpreter sworn to tell us what he said, which was the best testimony of all. I heard other causes: and the Judge would not suffer Mr. Crow, who hath fined for Alderman, to be called so, but only Mister, and did eight or nine times fret at it, and stop every man that called him so.

3d. This day, Sir G. Carteret did tell us at the table that the Navy, excepting what is due to the Yards upon the quarter now going on, and what few bills he hath not heard of, is quite out of debt: which is extraordinary good news, and upon the 'Change to hear how our creditt goes as good as any merchants' upon the 'Change is a joyfull thing to consider, which God continue! I am sure the King will have the benefit of it, as well as we some peace and creditt.

6th. (Lord's day.) My wife and I all the afternoon at arithmetique, and she is come to do Addition, Subtraction, and Multiplication, very well.

7th. I hear there was the last night the greatest tide that ever was remembered in England to have been in this river: all White Hall having been drowned. I met Dr. Clerke, and fell to discourse of Dr. Knapp, who tells me he is the King's physician, and is become a solicitor for places for people, and I am mightily troubled with him. He tells me that he is the most impudent fellow in the world, that gives himself out to be the King's physician, but is not so. But I may learn what impudence there is in the world, and how a man may be deceived in persons. At White Hall; and anon the King, and Duke, and Duchess come to dinner in the vane-roome, where I never saw them before; but it seems, since the tables are done, he dines there alltogether. The Queen is pretty well, and goes out of her chamber to her little chapel in the house. The King of France, they say, is hiring of sixty sail of ships of the Dutch, but it is not said for what design.

8th. To White Hall, where a great while walked with my Lord Teviott, whom I find a most carefull, thoughtfull, and cunning man, as I also ever took him to be. He is this day bringing in an account where he makes the King debtor to him 10,000*l.* already on the garrison of Tangier account; but yet demands not ready money to pay it, but offers such ways of paying it out of the sale of old decayed provisions as will enrich him finely.

9th. This day, Mrs. Russel did give my wife a very fine St. George in alabaster, which will set out my wife's closet mightily.

10th. To St. Paul's Church Yard, to my bookseller's, and,

having gained this day in the office by my stationer's bill to
the King about 40s. or 3l., calling for twenty books to lay
this money out upon, and found myself at a great loss where
to choose, and do see how my nature would gladly return to
the laying out of money in this trade. Could not tell whether
to lay out my money for books of pleasure, as plays, which my
nature was most earnest in; but at last, after seeing Chaucer,
Dugdale's History of Paul's, Stow's London, Gesner, History
of Trent, besides Shakespeare, Jonson, and Beaumont's plays,
I at last choose Dr. Fuller's Worthys, the Cabbala, or Collections of Letters of State, and a little book, "Delices de
Hollande," with another little book or two, all of good use or
serious pleasure; and Hudibras, both parts, the book now in
greatest fashion for drollery, though I cannot, I confess, see
enough where the wit lies. My mind being thus settled, I
went by link home, and so to my office, and to read in Rushworth; and so home to supper and to bed. Calling at
Wotton's, my shoemaker's, to-day, he tells me that Sir H.
Wright is dying; and that Harris is come to the Duke's
house again; and of a rare play to be acted this week of Sir
William Davenant's: the story of Henry the Eighth, with all
his wives.

11th. At my bookseller's, and I bought at a shop Cardinall
Mazarin's Will in French. At the Coffee-house I went and
sat by Mr. Harrington, and some East country merchants,
and, talking of the country above Quinsborough,[1] and thereabouts, he told us himself that for fish, none there, the
poorest body, will buy a dead fish, but must be alive, unless it
be in the winter: and then they told us the manner of putting
their nets into the water. Through holes made in the thick

---

[1] Quinsborough is Königsberg. It is most probable that Mr. Harrington had
been reading *The Travels of Master George Barkeley, Merchant of London*, as
given by Purchas, ii., 625, 627. Königsberg is there spelled Kinninsburge,
easily corrupted by Pepys into *Quinsborough*. The swallow story is found at p.
626.—"One here in his net drew up a company or heape of swallows, as big as a
bushell, fastened by the leg and bills in one, which being carried to their stoves,
quickened, and flew, and coming again suddenly in the cold air, dyed." It appears to have been generally believed. In the *Advice to a Painter* (1667,) attributed to Sir John Denham, we find the following lines:—
     "So swallows, buried in the sea at Spring,
     Return to land with Summer in their [on the?] wing."

ice, they will spread a net of half a mile long; and he hath
known a hundred and thirty and a hundred and seventy
barrels of fish taken at one draught. And then the people
come with sledges upon the ice with snow at the bottom, and
lay the fish in and cover them with snow, and so carry them
to market. And he hath seen when the said fish have been
frozen in the sledge; so as he hath taken a fish and broke
a-pieces, so hard it hath been; and yet the same fishes taken
out of the snow, and brought into a hot room, will be alive
and leap up and down. Swallows are often brought up in
their nets out of the mud from under water, hanging together
to some twigg, or other, dead in ropes, and brought to the fire
will come to life. Fowl killed in December, Alderman Barker
said, he did buy, and putting into the box under his sledge,
did forget to take them out to eate till Aprill next, and they
then were found there, and were through the frost as sweet
and fresh, and eat as well as at first killed. Young beares
appear there; their flesh sold in market, as ordinarily as beef
here, and is excellent sweet meat. They tell us that beares
there do never hurt any body, but fly away from you, unless
you pursue and set upon them; but wolves do much mischief.
Mr. Harrington told us how they do to get so much honey
as they send abroad. They make hollow a great fir-tree,
leaving only a small slit down straight in one place; and this
they close up again, only leave a little hole, and there the
bees go in and fill the bodys of those trees as full of wax and
honey as they can hold; and the inhabitants at times go and
open the slit, and take what they please without killing the
bees, and so let them live there still and make more. Fir
trees are always planted close together, because of keeping
one another from the violence of the windes; and when a fell
is made, they leave here and there a grown tree to preserve
the young ones coming up. The great entertainment and
sport of the Duke of Corland, and the princes thereabouts, is
hunting; which is not with dogs as we, but he appoints such
a day, and summonses all the country-people as to a cam-
pagnia; and by several companies gives every one their circuit,
and they agree upon a place where the toyle is to be set;

and so, making fires every company as they go, they drive all the wild beasts, whether bears, wolves, foxes, swine, and stags, and roes, into the toyle; and there the great men have their stands in such and such places, and shoot at what they have a mind to, and that is their hunting. They are not very populous there, by reason that people marry, women, seldom till they are towards or above thirty; and, men, thirty or forty years old, or more, oftentimes. Against a public hunting the Duke sends that no wolves be killed by the people; and, whatever harm they do, the Duke makes it good to the person that suffers it: as Mr. Harrington instanced in a house where he lodged, where a wolfe broke into a hog-stye, and bit three or four great pieces off of the back of the hog, before the house could come to help it; and the man of the house told him that there were three or four wolves thereabouts that did them great hurt; but it was no matter, for the Duke was to make it good to him, otherwise he would kill them.

12th. We had this morning a great dispute between Mr. Gauden, Victualler of the Navy, and Sir J. Lawson, and the rest of the Commanders going against Algiers, about their fish and keeping of Lent; which Mr. Gauden so much insists upon to have it observed, as being the only thing that makes up the loss of his dear bargain all the rest of the year. Luellin tells me that W. Symons's wife is dead, for which I am sorry, she being a good woman, and tells me an odde story of her saying before her death, being in good sense, that there stood her uncle Scobell. Home, and there I find that one Abrahall, who strikes in for the serving of the King with ship-chandlery ware, hath sent my wife a Japan gowne, which pleases her very well. This day I heard my Lord Barkeley tell Sir G. Carteret that he hath letters from France that the King hath unduked twelve Dukes, only to show his power and to crush his nobility, who, he said, he did see had heretofore laboured to cross him. And this my Lord Barkeley did mightily magnify, as a sign of a brave and vigorous mind, that what he saw fit to be done he dares do.

14th. To the Duke, where I heard a large discourse

between one that goes over an agent from the King to
Leghorne and thereabouts, to remove the inconveniences his
ships are put to by denial of pratique : which is a thing that
is now-a-days made use of only as a cheat, for a man may
buy a bill of health for a piece of eight, and any enemy may
agree with the Intendent of the Santé for ten pieces of eight
or so, that he shall not give me a bill of health, and so spoil
me in my design, whatever it be.   This the King will not
endure, and so resolves, either to have it removed or to keep
all ships from coming in or going out there, so long as his
ships are stayed for want hereof.   But, among other things,
Lord ! what an account did Sir J. Minnes and Sir W. Batten
make of the pulling down and burning of the head of the
Charles,[1] where Cromwell was placed with people under his
horse, and Peter,[2] as the Duke called him, is praying to him ;
and Sir J. Minnes would needs infer the temper of the people
from their joy at the doing of this and their building a gibbet
for the hanging of his head up, when, God knows, it is even
the flinging away of 100*l.* out of the King's purse, to the
building of another, which it seems must be a Neptune.   To
my Lord Sandwich's lodging, where I and W. Howe talked
a good while.   He tells me that my Lord, it is true, for a
while after my letter, was displeased, and did shew many
slightings of me ; but when I did hear how he is come to
himself, and hath wholly left Chelsey, and the slut, and that
I see he do follow his business, and becomes in better repute
than before, I am rejoiced to see it, though it do cost me
some disfavour for a time.   To the King's Head ordinary,
and there dined among a company of fine gentlemen ; some
of them discoursed of the King of France's greatness, and
how he is come to make the Princes of the Blood to take
place of all foreign Embassadors, which it seems is granted by
them of Venice and other States, and expected from my Lord
Hollis,[3] our King's Embassador there ; and that, either upon

[1] The ship Charles, at Chatham.   [2] Hugh Peters.
[3] Denzil Hollis, second son of John, first Earl of Clare, created, 20th April,
1661, Baron Hollis of Ifield, afterwards Plenipotentiary for the Treaty of Breda.
Ob. 1679-80, aged 82.

that score or something else, he hath not had his entry yet
in Paris, but hath received several affronts, and, among others,
his harness cut, and his gentlemen of his horse killed, which
will breed bad blood, if true.   They say, also, that the King
of France hath hired threescore ships of Holland, and forty
of the Swede, but nobody knows what to do : but some great
designs he hath on foot against the next year.   Then we fell
to talk of Sir J. Minnes's and Sir W. Batten's burning of
Oliver's head while he was there ; which was done with so
much insulting and folly as I never heard of, and had the
trayned band of Rochester to come to the solemnity.   When
all comes to all, Commissioner Pett says it never was made
for him ; but it troubles me the King should suffer 100*l.* loss
in his purse, to make a new one, after it was forgot whose
head it was, or any words spoke of it.

15th. My brother's man come to tell me that my cozen,
Edward Pepys, was dead at Mrs. Turner's, for which my wife
and I are very sorry, and the more for that his wife was the
only handsome woman of our name.

17th. To Mrs. Turner's, where I find her and her sister
Dike very sad for the death of their brother.   After a little
common expression of sorrow, Mrs. Turner told me that the
trouble she would put me to was, to consult about getting an
achievement prepared, scutcheons were done already, to set
over the door.   Come Smith to me, with whom I did agree
for 4*l.* to make a handsome one, all square within the frame.

18th. Among other people, come Mr. Primate, the leather-
seller, in Fleet Street, to see me, he says, coming this way ;
and he tells me that he is upon a proposal to the King,
whereby, by a law already in being, he will supply the King,
without wrong to any man, or charge to the people in general,
so much as it is now, above 200,000*l.* per annum, and God
knows what, and that the King do like the proposal, and hath
directed that the Duke of Monmouth, with their consent, be
made privy, and go along with him and his fellow-proposer in
the business—God knows what it is ; for I neither can guess
nor believe there is any such thing in his head.

19th. To Mrs. Turner's, whom I find busy with Sir W

Turner about advising upon going down to Norfolke with the corps, and I find him in talk a sober, considering man.

21st. To my Lord Sandwich's, and there I had a pretty kind salute from my Lord. To Mrs. Turner's, and there saw the achievement pretty well set up, and it is well done. To Shoe Lane, to see a cocke-fighting[1] at a new pit there, a spot I was never at in my life: but, Lord! to see the strange variety of people, from Parliament man, by name Wildes, that was Deputy Governor of the Tower when Robinson was Lord Mayor, to the poorest 'prentices, bakers, brewers, butchers, draymen, and what not; and all these fellows one with another cursing and betting. I soon had enough of it. It is strange to see how people of this poor rank, that look as if they had not bread to put in their mouths, shall bet three or four pounds at a time, and lose it, and yet bet as much the next battle; so that one of them will lose 10 or 20*l.* at a meeting. Thence to my Lord Sandwich's, where I find him within with Captain Cooke, and his boys, Dr. Childe, Mr. Madge, and Mallard, playing and singing over my Lord's anthem, which he hath made to sing in the King's chapel: my Lord saluted me kindly, and took me into the withdrawing-room to hear it: and indeed it sounds very pretty, and is a good thing, I believe, to be made by him, and they all commend it. My Lord going to White Hall, I went along with him, and made a desire for to have his coach to go along with my cozen Edward Pepys's hearse through the city on Wednesday next, which he granted me presently, though he cannot yet come to speak to me in the familiar stile that he did use to do, nor can I expect it.

22d. A letter from W. Howe, that my Lord hath ordered his coach and six horses for me to-morrow. I hear for certain that my Lady Castlemaine is turned Papist, which the Queen for all do not much like, thinking that she do it not for conscience sake.[2] I heard to-day of a great fray lately

---

[1] See *Handbook of London*, art. Shoe Lane; und Thomas's *Anecdotes and Traditions*, p. 47, for what took place at the cock-fighting in Shoe Lane.

[2] "Le mariage du Chevalier de Grammont," says Monsieur de Lionne, in a letter written to Louis XIV. of this date, "et la conversion de Madame de

between Sir H. Finch's coachman, who struck with his whip
a coachman of the King's, to the loss of one of his eyes; at
which the people of the Exchange seeming to laugh and
make sport, with some words of contempt to him, my Lord
Chamberlain did come from the King to shut up the 'Change,
and by the help of a justice did it; but upon petition to the
King it was opened again.[1] At noon I to Sir R. Ford's,
where Sir Richard Browne and I met upon the freight of a
barge sent to France to the Duchess of Orleans; and here
by discourse I find they greatly cry out against the choice of
Sir John Cutler to be treasurer of Paul's, upon condition that
he gives 1500l. towards it; and it seems he did give it upon
condition that he might be Treasurer for the work, which,
they say, will be worth three times as much money, and talk
as if his being chosen to the office will make people backward
to give; but I think him as likely a man as either of them,
and better.

23d. Up betimes, and my wife; and being in as mourning
a dress as we could, at present, without cost, put ourselves
into, we by Sir W. Pen's coach to Mrs. Turner's, at Salisbury
Court, where I find my Lord's coach and six horses. We
staid till almost eleven o'clock, and much company come, and
anon, the corps being put into the hearse, and the scutcheons
set upon it, we all took coach, and I and my wife and auditor
Beale, in my Lord Sandwich's coach, and went next to Mrs.
Turner's mourning-coach; and so through all the City and
Shoreditch, I believe about twenty coaches, and four or five
with six and four horses. Being come thither, I made up to
the mourners, and bidding them a good journey, I took leave
and back again.

25th. (Christmas-day.) My wife begun, I know not whether
by design or chance, to enquire what she should do, if I should

Castlemaine se sont publiez le même jour: et le Roy d'Angleterre, estant tant
prié par les parents de la Dame d'apporter quelque obstacle à cette action, repondit
galamment que pour l'âme des Dames il ne s'en mêloit point."
[1] Rugge adds, that the Queen was in the carriage when the battle took place,
her coachman striking the first blow; and that the combatants fought a long
time, nobody coming to part them. The Exchange was not re-opened till the
man who injured the royal servant had been given up.

by any accident die, to which I did give her some slight
answer, but shall make good use of it to bring myself to some
settlement for her sake, by making a will as soon as I can.
Late reading Rushworth, which is a most excellent collection
of the beginning of the late quarrels in this kingdom.

26th. Mr. Holliard dined with us, we having a pheasant to
dinner.

28th. Walking through White Hall, I heard the King was
gone to play at Tennis, so I down to the New Tennis Court,
and saw him and Sir Arthur Slingsby play against my Lord
of Suffolke and my Lord Chesterfield. The King beat three,
and lost two sets, they all, and he particularly, playing well,
I thought. Thence went and spoke with the Duke of Albemarle about his wound at Newhall, but I find him a heavy
dull man, methinks, by his answers to me.[1] The Duchess of
York is fallen sick of the meazles.

30th. Up betimes. My Lord Sandwich did ask me how
his cozen, my wife, did, the first time he hath done so since
his being offended, and in my conscience he would be glad to
be free with me again, but he knows not how to begin.

31st. To dinner, my wife and I, a fine turky and a minced
pie, and dined in state, poor wretch, she and I, and have thus
kept our Christmas together all alone almost, having not once
been out. At the Coffee [house], hearing some simple discourse about Quakers being charmed by a string about their
wrists. I bless God I do, after a large expence, even this
month, find that I am worth, in money, besides all my household stuff, or anything of Brampton, above 800l., whereof in my
Lord Sandwich's hand, 700l., and the rest in my hand. I do
live at my lodgings in the Navy Office, my family being,
besides my wife and I, Jane Gentleman, Besse, our excellent,

---

[1] It is a pity that Pepys, instead of hazarding this absurd remark, did not tell
us something more about the Duke of Albemarle's wound, no other allusion to
which has been found; but perhaps he was prejudiced by the hasty and ill-
founded opinion of Lord Sandwich, who, as we have seen, *Diary*, vol. i., p. 55,
termed Monk a thick-sculled fool. In fact, that great man must have possessed
no slight portion of worldly wisdom and common sense. Hallam, whilst differ-
ing from Hume as to Monk's dissimulation, regards his conduct after the King's
return as displaying his accustomed prudence. This is not a feature in the character of a *thick-sculled fool*. Monsieur Guizot takes a similar view of Monk's
good sound sense.

good-natured cook-maid, and Susan, a little girl, having neither man nor boy, nor like to have again a good while, living now in most perfect content and quiet, and very frugally also; my health pretty good. At the office I am well, though envied to the devil by Sir William Batten, who hates me to death, but cannot hurt me. The rest either love me, or at least do not show otherwise, though I know Sir William Pen to be a false knave touching me, though he seems fair. My father and mother well in the country; and at this time the young ladies of Hinchingbroke with them — their house having the smallpox in it. The Queen, after a long and sore sickness, is become well again; and the King minds his mistress a little too much, if it pleased God! but I hope all things will go well, and in the Navy particularly, wherein I shall do my duty, whatever comes of it. The great talk is the design of the King of France, whether against the Pope or King of Spain nobody knows; but a great and a most promising Prince he is, and all the Princes of Europe have their eye upon him. My wife's brother come to great unhappiness by the ill disposition, my wife says, of his wife, and her poverty, which she now professes, after all her husband's pretence of a great portion. At present, I am concerned for my cozen Angier, of Cambridge, lately broke in his trade, and this day am sending his son John, a very rogue, to sea. My brother Tom I know not what to think of; for I cannot hear whether he minds his business or not; and my brother John at Cambridge, with as little hopes of doing good there; for when he was here, he did give me great cause of dissatisfaction with his manner of life. Pall with my father; and God knows what she do there, or what will become of her; for I have not anything yet to spare her, and she grows now old, and must be disposed of, one way or other. The Duchess of York is growing well again. The Turke very far entered into Germany, and all that part of the world at a loss what to expect from his proceedings. Myself, blessed be God! in a good way, and design and resolution of sticking to my business to get a little money with, doing the best service I can to the King also; which God continue! So ends the old year.

1663-64

January 1st. At the Coffee-house, where much talking about a very rich widow, young and handsome, of one Sir Nicholas Gold's,[1] a merchant, lately fallen, and of great courtiers that already look after her: her husband not dead a week yet. She is reckoned worth 80,000*l.* Went to the Duke's house, the first play I have been at these six onths, according to my last vowe, and here saw the so much cried-up play of " Henry the Eighth;' which, though I went with resolution to like it, is so simple a thing, made up of a great many patches, that, besides the shows and processions in it, there is nothing in the world good or well done.

2d. To the King's house, and saw " The Usurper,"[2] which is no good play, though better than what I saw yesterday.

4th. I to my Lord Sandwich's lodgings, but he not being up, I to the Duke's chamber, and there by and by to his closet, where, since his lady was ill, a little red bed of velvet is brought for him to lie alone, which is a very pretty one. After doing business here, I to my Lord's again, and there spoke with him, and he seems now almost friends again, as he used to be. Here meeting Mr. Pierce, the surgeon, he told me, among other Court news, how the Queen is very well again; and that she speaks now very pretty English, and makes her sense out now and then with pretty phrases: as among others this is mightily cried up; that, meaning to say that she did not like such a horse so well as the rest, he being too prancing and full of tricks, she said he did make too much vanity. To the Tennis Court, and there saw the King play at tennis and others: but to see how the King's play was extolled, without any cause at all, was a loathsome sight, though sometimes, indeed, he did play very well, and deserved to be commended: but such open flattery is beastly.' After wards to St. James's Park, seeing people play at Pell Mell;

---

[1] Sir Nicholas Gold, or Gould, created a Baronet in 1660, married Elizabeth daughter of Sir John Garrard, Bart., of Lamers, Herts. She remarried Thomas Neal. See June 20, 1664, *post*.

[2] a tragedy, by the Hon. Edward Howard.

where it pleased me mightily to hear a gallant, lately come from France, swear at one of his companions for suffering his man, a spruce blade, to be so saucy as to strike a ball while his master was playing on the Mall.[1] My wife is mighty sad to think of her father, who is going into Germany against the Turkes; but what will become of her brother I know not. He is so idle, and out of all capacity, I think, to earn his bread.

6th. (Twelfth day.) This morning I began a practice, which I find, by the ease I do it with, that I shall continue, it saving me money and time ; that is, to trimme myself with a razer: which pleases me mightily.

7th. At noon, all of us to dinner to Sir W. Pen's, where a very handsome dinner, Sir J. Lawson among others, and his lady and his daughter ; but to see how Sir W. Pen imitates me in everything, even in having his chimney-piece in his dining-room the same with that in my wife's closet, and in everything else I perceive wherein he can. But to see again how he was out in one compliment: he lets alone drinking any of the ladies' healths that were there, my Lady Batten and Lawson, till he had begun with my Lady Carteret, who was absent, and that was well enough, and then Mr. Coventry's mistress, at which he was ashamed, and would not have had him have drunk it, at least before the ladies present, but his policy, as he thought, was such, that he would do it.

8th. By appointment, took Luellin, Mount, and W. Symons, and Mr. Pierce, the surgeon, home to dinner with me, and were merry. We spent all the afternoon together, and then to cards with my wife, who this day put on her Indian blue gown, which is very pretty. We had great pleasure this afternoon, among other things, to talk of our old passages together in Cromwell's time ; and how W. Symons did make me laugh and wonder to-day when he told me how he had made shift to keep in, in good esteem and employment,

---

[1] When Egerton was Bishop of Durham, he often played at bowls with his guests on the public days. On an occasion of this sort, a visitor happening to cross the lawn, one of the Chaplains exclaimed, "You must not shake the green, for the Bishop is going to bowl."

through eight governments in one year, the year 1659, which were indeed, and he did name them all; and then failed unhappy in the ninth, viz., that of the King's coming in. He made good to me the story which Luellin did tell me the other day, of his wife upon her death-bed; how she dreamt of her uncle Scobell, and did foretell, from some discourse she had with him, that she should die four days thence, and not sooner, and did all along say so, and did so. Upon the 'Change, a great talk there was of one Mr. Tryon, an old man, a merchant in Lyme Streete, robbed last night, his man and maid being gone out after he was a-bed; and gagged and robbed of 1050*l.* in money and about 4000*l.* in jewells, which he had in his house, as security for money. It is believed that his man is guilty of confederacy, by their ready going to his secret till in his desk, wherein the key of his cash-chest lay.

9th. By discourse with my wife, thought upon inviting my Lord Sandwich to a dinner shortly. It will cost me at least ten or twelve pounds; but, however, some arguments of prudence I have, which I shall think again upon before I proceed to that expence. Called at Ludgate, at Ashwell's uncle's, but she was not within, to have spoke to her to have come to dress my wife at the time when my Lord dines here.

10th. (Lord's day.) My brother Tom come to see me, telling me how Mrs. Turner found herself discontented with her late bad journey, and not well taken by them in the country, they not desiring her coming down, nor the burial of Mr. Edward Pepys's corps there.[1] All our discourse to-night was about Mr. Tryon's late being robbed; and that Colonel Turner, a mad, swearing, confident fellow, well known by all, and by me, one much indebted to this man for his very livelihood, was the man that either did or plotted it; and the money and things are found in his hand, and he and his wife now in Newgate for it: of which we are all glad, so very a known rogue he was.

11th. To the Tennis Court till noon, and there saw several great matches played. By invitation to St. James's; where, at Mr. Coventry's chamber, I dined with my Lord Barkeley,

---

[1] He was buried in the church of Taterset, St. Andrew, Norfolk. M. L

Sir G. Carteret, Sir Edward Turner,[1] Sir Ellis Layton,[2] and one Mr. Seymour, a fine gentleman: where admirable good discourse of all sorts, pleasant and serious. This morning I stood by the King, arguing with a pretty Quaker woman, that delivered to him a desire of hers in writing. The King showed her Sir J. Minnes, as a man the fittest for her quaking religion; she modestly saying nothing till he begun seriously to discourse with her, arguing the truth of his spirit against hers; she replying still with these words, "O King!" and thou'd all along. The general talk of the towne still is of Colonel Turner, about the robbery; who, it is thought, will be hanged. I heard the Duke of York tell to-night, how letters are come that fifteen are condemned for the late plot by the Judges at York; and, among others, Captain Oates,[3] against whom it was proved that he drew his sword at his going out, and, flinging away the scabbard, said that he would either return victor or be hanged.

12th. Comes my uncle Wight and my aunt, with their cozens Mary and Robert, and by chance my uncle Thomas Pepys. We had a good dinner — the chief dish, a swan roasted, and that excellent meat.

15th. My wife tells me that my uncle Wight hath been with her, and played at cards with her, and is mightily inquisitive to know whether she is with child or no, which makes me wonder what his meaning is, and after all my thoughts, I cannot think, unless it be in order to the making his will; and I would to God my wife had told him that she was!

17th. (Lord's day.) To the French church, and there heard a good sermon—the first time my wife and I were there ever together. We sat by three sisters, all pretty women. It was

---

[1] Speaker of the House of Commons, and afterwards Solicitor-General, and Lord Chief Baron. Ob. 1675.

[2] The real name of the Knight was Elisha Leighton, whose brother Robert, Bishop of Dumblane, became, soon afterwards, the excellent Archbishop of Glasgow, and as such is more generally known. Their father, Alexander Leighton, was a rank Puritan, author of *Zion's Plea against Prelacy*, for writing which he had his ears cut off, and was exposed in the pillory in that state, with his nose also slit. *Elisha* was apparently euphonized into Ellis by the courtier son, who is described by Le Neve as one of the Duke of York's servants. Pepys speaks of him as Secretary of the Prize Office, and adds, that he had been a mad freaking fellow. See 25th Jan. 1664-5.

[3] See *ante*, Nov. 9, 1863.

pleasant to hear the reader give notice to them, that the children to be catechised next Sunday were them of Houndsditch and Blanche Chapiton.[1]

18th. Abroad to White Hall, where the court all in mourning for the Duchess of Savoy. By coach to the 'Change, after having been at the Coffee-house, where I hear Turner[2] is found guilty of felony and burglary : and strange stories of his confidence at the barr, but yet great indiscretion in his argueing. All desirous of his being hanged.

19th. My eyes began to fail me, and to be in pain, which I never felt to now-a-days.

20th. To my Lord Sandwich's, and I walked with him to the Tennis Court, and there left him, seeing the King play. My Lord Sandwich did also seal a lease for the house he is now taking in Lincoln's Inn Fields, which stands him in 250l. per annum rent. To my brother's, whom I find not well in bed, sick, they say, of a consumption. To Mr. Commander's, in Warwicke Lane, to speak to him about drawing up my will. Sir Richard Ford[3] told me, that Turner is to be hanged to-morrow, and with what impudence he hath carried out his trial; but that last night, when he brought him news of his death, he began to be sober, and shed some tears, and he hopes will die a penitent; he having already confessed all the thing, but says it was partly done for a joke, and partly to get an occasion of obliging the old man by his care in getting him his things again, he having some hopes of being the better by him in his estate at his death. Mr. Pierce tells me, that my Lady Castlemaine is not at all set by, by tho King, but that he do doat upon Mrs. Stewart only, and, that, to the leaving of all business in the world, and to the open slighting of the Queen; that he values not who sees him, or stands by him while he dallies with her openly : and then privately in her chamber below, where the very sentrys observe him going in and out; and that so commonly, that the

---

[1] Blanch Apleton, according to the *Handbook of London*, seems to have been a manor belonging in the reign of Richard II., to Sir Thomas Roos, of Hamelake. It is enumerated (9th Hen. V.) in "The Partition of the inheritance of Humphrey de Bohun, Earl of Hereford and Essex," under the head of "London-Blaunch Appulton." Hall, in his *Chronicle* (ed. 1548) writes it, Blancheebapelton.

[2] See State Trials.   [3] He was one of the sheriffs.

Duke, or any of the Nobles, when they would ask where the King is, they will ordinarily say, "Is the King above or below?" meaning with Mrs. Stewart: that the King do not openly disown my Lady Castlemaine, but that she comes to Court; but that my Lord FitzHarding and the Hambletons,[1] and sometimes my Lord Sandwich, they say, intrigue with her. But he says my Lord Sandwich will lead her from her lodgings in the darkest and obscurest manner, and leave her at the entrance into the Queen's lodgings, that he might be the least observed: that the Duke of Monmouth the King do still doat on beyond measure, insomuch that the King only, the Duke of York, and Prince Rupert, and the Duke of Monmouth, do now wear deep mourning, that is, long cloaks, for the Duchess of Savoy: so that he mourns as a Prince of the Blood, while the Duke of York do no more, and all the Nobles of the land not so much; which gives great offence. But that the Duke of York do give himself up to business, and is like to prove a noble prince; and so indeed I do from my heart think he will. He says that it is believed, as well as hoped, that care is taken to lay up a hidden treasure of money by the King against a bad day. I pray God it be so! but I should be more glad that the King himself would look after business, which it seems he do not in the least. I am resolved to forbear my laying out my money upon a dinner, till I see my Lord in a better posture, and by grave and humble, though high deportment, to make him think I do not want him, and that will make him the readier to admit me to his friendship again—I believe the soonest of anything but downright impudence, and thrusting myself, as others do, upon him, and imposing upon him, which yet I cannot do, nor will not endeavour. To bed, after I had by candle-light shaved myself and cut off all my beard.

21st. Up, and after sending my wife to my aunt Wight's, to get a place to see Turner hanged, I to the 'Change; and seeing people flock in the City, I enquired, and found that Turner was not yet hanged. So I went among them to Leadenhall Street, at the end of Lyme Street, near where the robbery was done; and to St. Mary Axe, where he lived.

---

[1] George Hamilton, and his brother James.

And there I got for a shilling to stand upon the wheel of a cart, in great pain, above an hour before the execution was done : he delaying the time by long discourses and prayers, one after another, in hopes of a reprieve ; but none come, and at last he was flung off the ladder in his cloak.   A comely-looked man he was, and kept his countenance to the end : I was sorry to see him.   It was believed there were at least 12 or 14,000 people in the street.   To the Coffee-house, and heard the full of Turner's discourse[1] on the cart, which was chiefly to clear himself of all things laid to his charge but this fault, for which he now suffers, which he confesses.   He deplored the condition of his family, but his chief design was to lengthen time, believing still a reprieve would come, though the sheriff advised him to expect no such thing, for the King was resolved to grant none.   To my aunt Wight's, where Dr. Burnett[2] did tell me how poorly the sheriffs did endeavour to get one jewell returned by Turner, after he was convicted, as a due to them, and not to give it to Mr. Tryon, the true owner, but ruled against them, to their great dishonour.

22d.   To Deptford, and there viewed Sir W. Petty's vessel; which hath an odd appearance, but not such as people do make of it.

24th.   (Lord's day.)   To my office, and there fell on entering, out of a bye-book, part of my second journall-book, which hath lay these two years and more unentered.   This evening also I drew up a rough draught of my last will.

25th.   Troubled a little in mind, to think that my Lord Sandwich should continue this strangeness to me.

26th.   Tom Killigrew told us of a fire last night in my Lady Castlemaine's lodging, where she bid 40l. for one to adventure the fetching of a cabinet out, which at last was got to be done ; and the fire at last quenched, without doing much wrong.

27th.   At the Coffee-house, where I sat with Sir G. Ascue[3]

---

[1] Turner's speech at his execution has been printed.   London, 8vo., 1663.
[2] The physician.
[3] A distinguished naval officer before and after the Restoration ; he never went to sea subsequently to the action in 1666, in which he had been taken prisoner.

and William Petty, who in discourse is, methinks, one of the
most rational men that ever I heard speak with a tongue,
having all his notions the most distinct and clear, and did,
among other things (saying, that in all his life these three
books were the most esteemed and generally cried up for wit
in the world — "Religio Medici,"[1] Osborne's "Advice to a
Son,"[2] and "Hudibras"), say that in these — the two first
principally—the wit lies, and confirming some pretty sayings,
which are generally like paradoxes, by some argument smartly
and pleasantly urged, which takes with people who do not
trouble themselves to examine the force of an argument,
which pleases them in the delivery, upon a subject which they
like; whereas, as by many particular instances of mine, and
others, out of Osborne, he did really find fault and weaken
the strength of many of Osborne's arguments, so as that in
downright disputation they would not bear weight—at least,
so far but that they might be weakened, and better found in
their rooms to confirm what is there said. He shewed finely
whence it happens that good writers are not admired by the
present age; because there are but few in any age that do
mind any thing that is abstruse and curious; and so longer
before any body do put the true praise, and set it on foot in
the world, the generality of mankind pleasing themselves in
the easy delights of the world, as, eating, drinking, dancing,
hunting, fencing, which we see the meanest men do the best—
those that profess it. A gentleman never dances so well as the
dancing-master; and an ordinary fiddler makes better musick
for a shilling than a gentleman will do after spending forty.
And so in all the delights of the world almost. To Covent
Garden, to buy a maske at the French house, Madame
Charett's,[3] for my wife; in the way observing the street full of
coaches at the new play, at "The Indian Queene;"[4] which

---

[1] By Sir Thomas Browne.

[2] Francis Osborne, an English writer of considerable abilities and popularity,
was the author of *Advice to a Son*, in two parts, Oxford, 1656-8, 8vo. He died in
1659. He is the same person mentioned as "*Father Osborne*," Oct. 19, 1661.

[3] Mrs. Mary Cherrett, called also Madame Cherrett, lived in the Piazza. (Rate
Books of St. Paul's, Covent Garden.) Mr. George Cherret, milliner, and Susan
his wife were living in the Piazza in 1689. (*Ib.*)

[4] "The Indian Queen," a tragedy in heroic verse, by Sir Robert Howard and
Mr. Dryden.

for show, they say, exceeds " Henry the Eighth " Called to see my brother Tom, who was not at home, though they say he is in a deep consumption, and will not live two months.

29th. To the Fleece in Cornhill, by appointment, to meet my Lord Marlborough, a serious and worthy gentleman, who begun to talk of the state of the Dutch in India, which is like to be in a little time without any controll; for we are lost there, and the Portuguese as bad.

30th. The day kept solemnly for the King's murder.   In the evening signed and sealed my last will and testament, which is to my mind, and I hope to the liking of God Almighty.   This evening I tore some old papers; among others, a romance which, under the title of " Love a Cheate," I begun ten years ago at Cambridge: and, reading it over to-night, I liked it very well, and wondered a little at myself, at my vein at that time when I wrote it, doubting that I cannot do so well now if I would try.

31st. (Lord's day.) I did perfectly prepare a state of my estate, and annexed it to my last will and testament, which now is perfect, and find that I am worth 858l. clear, which is the greatest sum I ever yet was master of.   My head very full of thoughts to provide for answering to the Exchequer for my uncle's being Generall-Receiver in the year 1647, which I am at present wholly unable to do.

February 1st. I hear how two men last night, justling for the wall about the new Exchange, did kill one another, each thrusting the other through; one of them of the King's Chapel, one Cave, and the other a retayner of my Lord Generall Middleton's.[1]   I to White Hall; where, in the Duke's chamber, the King come and stayed an hour or two laughing at Sir W. Petty, who was there, about his boat; and at Gresham College in general: at which poor Petty was, I perceive, at some loss; but did argue discreetly, and bear the unreasonacle follies of the King's objections and other bystanders with great discretion; and offered to take oddes against the King's best boates: but the King would not lay, but cried him down with words only. Gresham College[2] he

---

[1] John Middleton, Earl of Middleton, General of the Forces in Scotland.
[2] The Royal Society.

mightily laughed at, for spending time only in weighing of
ayre, and doing nothing else since they sat. Mr. Pierce tells
me how the King, coming the other day to his Theatre to see
"The Indian Queene," which he commends for a very fine
thing, my Lady Castlemaine was in the next box before he
come; and leaning over other ladies awhile to whisper with
the King, she rose out of the box and went into the King's,
and set herself on the King's right hand, between the King
and the Duke of York; which, he swears, put the King himself, as well as every body else, out of countenance; and believes that she did it only to show the world that she is not
out of favour yet, as was believed. To the King's Theatre,
and there saw "The Indian Queene" acted; which indeed is
a most pleasant show, and beyond my expectation; the play
good, but spoiled with the ryme, which breaks the sense.
But above my expectation most, the eldest Marshall[1] did do
her part most excellently well as I ever heard woman in my
life: but her voice is not so sweet as Ianthe's:[2] but, however,
we come home mightily contented. Here we met Mr. Pickering; and he tells me that the business runs high between the
Chancellor and my Lord Bristoll against the Parliament; and
that my Lord Lauderdale and Cowper open high against the
Chancellor; which I am sorry for. This day, W. Bowyer
told me, that his father is dead lately, and died by being
drowned in the river, coming over in the night; but he says
he had not been drinking. He was taken with his stick in
his hand, and cloak over his shoulder, as ruddy as before he

---

[1] Anne Marshall, a celebrated actress at the King's House, and her youngest
sister Becke, so frequently mentioned in the *Diary*, seemed to have been the
daughters of a Presbyterian minister (Oct. 26, 1667); but very little is known
about their history. One of them is erroneously stated, in the notes to the
Mémoires de Grammont, and Davies's *Dramatic Miscellanies*, to have become
Lord Oxford's mistress; for Pepys uniformly calls the Marshalls by their own
name, and only speaks of the other lady as "the first or old Roxalana, who had
quitted the stage." See Feb. 18, 1661-2, and Dec. 27, following; also Oct.
26, 1667.

[2] Malone says, in his *History of the English Stage*, that Mrs. Mary Saun-
derson performed Ianthe in Davenant's play of the "Siege of Rhodes," at the
first opening of his theatre, April, 1662. She married Betterton the following
year, and lived till 1712, having filled almost all the female characters in Shake
speare with great success. She is doubtless the person alluded to here, and frequently mentioned afterwards by the same designation.

died. His horse was taken overnight in the water, hampered in the bridle, but they were so silly as not to look for his master till the next morning that he was found drowned.

2d. To the 'Change, and thence off to the Sun Taverne with Sir W. Warren. He did give me a pair of gloves for my wife wrapt up in a paper, which I would not open, feeling it hard; but did tell him that my wife should thank him, and so went on in discourse. When I come home, Lord! in what pain I was to get my wife out of the room without bidding her go, that I might see what these gloves were; and, by and by, she being gone, it proves a pair of white gloves for her, and forty pieces in good gold, which did so cheer my heart, that I could eat no victuals almost for dinner. I was at a great loss what to do, whether to tell my wife of it or no, for fear of making her think me to be in a better condition, or in a better way of getting money, than yet I am.

3rd. To the Mitre Taverne, and there met with W. Howe come to buy wine for my Lord against his going down to Hinchingbroke, and I private with him, a great while discoursing of my Lord's strangeness to me; but he answers that I have no reason to think any such thing, but that my Lord is only in general a more reserved man than he was before. My wife is full of sad stories of her good-natured father, and roguish brother, who is going for Holland, and his wife, to be a soldier. In Covent Garden to-night, going to fetch home my wife, I stopped at the great Coffee-house[1] there, where I never was before: where Dryden, the poet, I knew at Cambridge, and all the wits of the town, and Harris the player, and Mr. Hoole of our College. And, had I had time then, or could at other times, it will be good coming thither, for there, I perceive, is very witty and pleasant discourse. But I could not tarry, and, as it was late, they were all ready to go away.

4th. To Paul's School, and up to hear the upper form ex-

---

[1] This was Will's Coffee House, where Dryden had a chair reserved for him near the fire-place in winter, and which was carried into the balcony for him in summer. It was on the west side of Bow Street, and at the corner of Russell Street, and took its name from " William Urwin," the landlord.— *Handbook of London*, p 554, edit. 1850

amined; and there was kept, by very many of the Mercers, Clutterbucke,[1] Barker, Harrington, and others; and with great respect used by them all, and had a noble dinner. Here they tell me that, in Dr. Colett's[2] will, he says that he would have a Master found for the School that hath good skill in Latin, and, if it could be, one that had some knowledge of the Greeke; so little was Greeke known here at that time. Dr. Wilkins[3] and one Mr. Smallwood, Posers.

5th. Reading "Faber fortunæ,"[4] which I can never read too often. At home to look after some Brampton papers, and my uncle's accounts as Generall-Receiver of the county for 1647 of our monthly assessement, which, contrary to my expectation, I found in such good order that I did not expect, nor could have thought.

6th. Home, whither come one Father Fogourdy, an Irish priest, of my wife's and her mother's acquaintance in France —a sober and discreet person, but one that I would not have converse with my wife for fear of meddling with her religion. He confirms to me the news that for certain there is peace made between the Pope and King of France.

7th. (Lord's day.) Up and to church, and thence home; and with great mirth read Sir W. Davenant's two speeches in dispraise of London and Paris, by way of reproach one to the other.

8th. Mr. Pierce told me how the King still do doat upon his women, even beyond all shame: and that the good Queen will of herself stop before she goes sometimes into her dressing-room, till she knows whether the King be there, for fear he should be, as she hath sometimes taken him, with Mrs. Stewart; and that some of the best parts of the Queen's joynture are, contrary to faith and against the opinion of my Lord Treasuer and his Council, bestowed or rented, I know

[1] Probably Alderman Clutterbuck, one of the proposed Knights of the Royal Oak for Middlesex. There was a Sir Thomas Clutterbuck, of London, circiter 1670.
[2] Dean of St. Paul's, and founder of the School.
John Wilkins was a learned theologian, and well versed in Mathematics and Natural Philosophy. See Nov. 25, 1660.
[4] By Lord Bacon

not how, to my Lord FitzHarding and Mrs. Stewart, and others of that crew: that the King do doat infinitely upon the Duke of Monmouth, apparently as one that he intends to have succeed him. God knows what will be the end of it!

9th. Great talk of the Dutch proclaiming themselves, in India, Lords of the Southern Seas, and denying traffick there to all ships but their own, upon pain of confiscation; which makes our merchants mad. Great doubt of two ships of ours, the Greyhound and another, very rich, coming from the Streights, for fear of the Turkes. Matters are made up between the Pope and the King of France; so that now all the doubt is, what the French will do with their armies. Mr. Moore told me that my Lord is mightily altered—that is, grown very high and stately, and do not admit of any to come into his chamber to him, as heretofore, and that I must not think of his strangeness to me, for it is the same he do to everybody. I discoursed with him about my money that my Lord hath, and the 1,000*l.* that I stand bound with him in, to my cozen Thomas Pepys, in both which I shall get myself at liberty as soon as I can; for I do not like his being angry and in debt both together to me; and, besides, I do not perceive he looks after paying his debts, but runs farther and farther in.

10th. By coach to my Lord Sandwich, to his new house, a fine house, but deadly dear, in Lincoln's Inne Fields, where I found and spoke a little to him. He is high and strange still, but did ask me how my wife did, and at parting remembering him to his cozen. My wife abroad to buy Lent provisions. I did give my wife's brother 10*s.* and a coat that I had by me, a close-bodied, light-coloured coat, with a gold edgeing in each seam, that was the lace of my wife's best pettycoat, that she had when I married her. He is going into Holland to seek his fortune. My pain do leave me without coming to any great excess; but my cold that I had got I suppose was not very great, it being only the leaving of my wastecoate unbuttoned one morning.

11th. Mr. Falconer come and visited my wife, and brought her a present—a silver state-cup and cover, value about three or 4*l.*, for the courtesy I did him the other day. I am almost sorry for this present, because I would have reserved him for a place to go in summer a-visiting at Woolwich with my wife.

12th. Called at Alderman Backewell's, and there changed Mr. Falconer's state-cup, that he did give us the other day, for a fair tankard. The cup weighed with the fashion 5*l.* 16*s.*, and another little cup that Joyce Norton did give us 17*s.* —both 6*l.* 13*s.* ; for which we had a tankard, which come to 6*l.* 10*s.* at 5*s.* 7*d.* per oz., and 3*s.* in money.

13th. To the African House. Anon down to dinner, to a table which Mr. Coventry keeps here, out of his 300*l.* per annum as one of the Assistants to the Royall Company, a very pretty dinner, and good company, and excellent discourse. Home with my wife, and saw her day's work in ripping the silk standard, which we brought home last night, and it will serve to line a bed, or for twenty uses, to our great content.

14th. (Lord's day.) Up, and to church alone, where a lazy sermon of Mr. Mills, upon a text to introduce catechising in our parish, which I perceive he intends to begin.

15th. To White Hall, to the Duke ; where he first put on a periwigg to-day : but methought his hair cut short in order thereto did look very pretty of itself, before he put on his periwigg. Great news of the arrivall of two rich ships, the Greyhound and another, which they were mightily afraid of, and great insurance given. This afternoon Sir Thomas Chamberlain [1] come to the office to me, and showed me several letters from the East Indys, showing the height that the Dutch are come to there, showing scorn to all the English, even in our only Factory there of Surat,[2] beating several men, and hanging the English standard St. George under the Dutch flag in scorn ; saying that, whatever their masters do or say at home, they will do what they list, and be masters of all the world there ; and have so proclaimed themselves

---

[1] Son of William Chamberlayne, an English Judge, and created a Baronet 1642.

[2] Sir George Oxendon was then the chief factor of the East India Company. In 1686, the English removed to Bombay. Surat is still in our possession.

Soveraignes of all the South Seas: which certainly our King cannot endure, if the Parliament will give him money. But I doubt, and yet do hope, they will not yet, till we are more ready for it.

17th. With my wife, setting her down by her father's in Long Acre, in so ill-looked a place, among all the brothels, that I was troubled at it, to see her go thither. Mr. Pierce tells me of the King's giving of my Lord FitzHarding two leases which belong indeed to the Queen, worth 20,000l. to him; and how people do talk of it! Home, and dined, where I found an excellent mastiffe—his name Towser—sent ne by a surgeon.

19th. Mr. Cutler come, and walked and talked with me a great while: and then to the 'Change together; and it being early, did tell me several excellent examples of men raised upon the 'Change by their great diligence and saving: as also his own fortune, and how credit grew upon him; that, when he was not really worth 1,100l., he had credit for 100,000l.: of Sir W. Rider, how he rose; and others. By and by joyned with us Sir John Bankes;[1] who told us several passages of the East India Company; and how, in every case, when there was due to him and Alderman Mico 64,000l. from the Dutch for injury done to them in the East Indys, Oliver, presently after the peace, they delaying to pay them the money, sent them word, that if they did not pay them by such a day, he would grant letters of mark to those merchants against them; by which they were so fearful of him, they did presently pay the money every farthing. Took my wife, and, taking a coach, went to visit my Ladys Jemimah and Paulina Montagu, and Mrs. Elizabeth Pickering,[2] whom we find at their father's new house in Lincoln's Inn Fields: but the house all in dirt. They received us well enough; but I did not endeavour to carry myself over familiarly with them: and so, after a little stay, there coming in presently after us my Lady Abergueuny and other ladies, we back again by coach.

[1] An opulent merchant, residing in Lincoln's Inn Fields.
[2] Lord Sandwich's niece.
[3] Probably Mary, daughter of Thomas Gifford, of Dunton Walet, Essex, wife to George Nevill, ninth Lord Abergavenny.

21st. (Lord's day.) My wife called up the people to washing by four o'clock in the morning; and our little girl Susan is a most admirable slut, and pleases us mightily, doing more service than both the others, and deserves wages better.

22d. This evening come Mr. Alsopp, the King's brewer, with whom I spent an hour talking and bewailing the posture of things at present; the King led away by half-a-dozen men, that none of his serious servants and friends can come at him. These are Lauderdale, Buckingham, Hamilton, FitzHarding, to whom he hath, it seems, given 12,000*l*. per annum in the best part of the King's estate; and that the old Duke of Buckingham, could never get of the King. Progers[1] is another, and Sir H. Bennett. He loves not the Queen at all, but is rather sullen to her; and she, by all reports, incapable of children. He is so fond of the Duke of Monmouth, that every body admires it; and he says that the Duke hath said, that he would be the death of any man that says the King was not married to his mother: though Alsopp says, it is well known that she was a common strumpet before the King was acquainted with her. But it seems, he says, that the King is mighty kind to these his bastard children; and at this day will go at midnight to my Lady Castlemaine's nurses, and take the child and dance it in his arms: that he is not likely to have his tables[2] up again in his house, for the crew that are about him will not have him come to common view again, but keep him obscurely among themselves. He hath this night, it seems, ordered that the Hall, which there is a ball to be in to-night before the King, be guarded, as the Queen-Mother's is, by his Horse Guards; whereas heretofore they were by the Lord Chamberlain or Steward, and their people. But it is feared they will reduce all to the soldiery, and all other places be taken away; and, what is worst of all, will alter the present militia, and bring all to a flying army. That my Lord Lauderdale, being Middleton's enemy, and one that scorns the Chancellor even to open affronts before the King,

---

[1] Edward Progers, the King's *valet-de-chambre*, and the confidant of his amours. Ob. 1713, aged 96.

[2] At which the King dined in public.

hath got the whole power of Scotland into his hand ; whereas,
the other day, he was in a fair way to have had his whole
estate, and honour, and life, voted away from him. That tho
King hath done himself all imaginable wrong in the business
of my Lord Antrim,[1] in Ireland ; who, though he was the
head of rebels, yet he by his letter owns to have acted by
his father's and mother's, and his commissions : but it seems
the truth is, he hath obliged himself, upon the clearing of his
estate, to settle it upon a daughter of the Queen-Mother's, by
my Lord Jermyn,[2] I suppose, in marriage, be it to whom the
Queen pleases : which is a sad story.   It seems a daughter
of the Duke of Lennox's was, by force, going to be married
the other day, at Somerset House, to Harry Jermyn ; but she
got away and run to the King, and he says he will protect
her.   She is, it seems, very near akin to the King.   Such
mad doings there are every day among them !   There was
a French book in verse, the other day, translated and
presented to the Duke of Monmouth, in such a high stile,
that the Duke of York, he tells me, was mightily offended at
it.   The Duke of Monmouth's mother's brother[3] hath a place
at Court ; and being a Welchman, I think, he told me will
talk very broad of the King's being married to his sister.
The King did the other day, at the Council, commit my Lord
Bristoll's[4] chaplin and steward, and another servant, who went
upon the process begun there against their lord, to swear that
they saw him at church, and receive the Sacrament[5] as a
Protestant, which, the Judges said, was sufficient to prove him
such in the eye of the law ; the King, I say, did commit them
all to the Gate-house, notwithstanding their pleading their
dependence upon him, and the faith they owed him as their
lord, whose bread they eat.   And that the King should say,

[1] Randall Macdonnel, second Earl and first Marquis of Antrim. Ob. 1673
[2] The Earl of St. Albans.
[3] Mr. Justice Waters, said to be " of the Temple," by Thurloe.
[4] The Earl of Bristol, by changing his religion while abroad, at the instigation
of Don John of Austria, had incapacitated himself from holding any office ; and,
in consequence of the disappointment, which he imputed to the interference of
the Lord Chancellor, planned and effected his ruin.   Lord Bristol was installed
L.G. in 1661, and died 1676.
[5] See Monsieur de Lionne's letter in the Appendix to vol. iv., Jan. 25, 1663-4.

that he would soon see whether he was King, or Bristoll.
That the Queen-Mother hath outrun herself in her expences,
and is now come to pay very ill, or run in debt; the money
being spent that she received for leases.   He believes there
is not any money laid up in bank, as I told him some did
hope; but he says, from the best informers, he can assure me
there is no such thing, nor any body that should look after
such a thing, and that there is not now above 80,000*l*. of the
Dunkirke money left in stock.   That Oliver, the year when
he spent 1,400,000*l*. in the Navy, did spend in the whole
expence of the kingdom 2,600,000*l*.   That all the Court are
mad for a Dutch war; but both he and I did concur, that it
was a thing rather to be dreaded than hoped for: unless, by
the French King's falling upon Flanders, they and the Dutch
should be divided.   That our Embassador[1] had, it is true, an
audience; but in the most dishonourable way that could be;
for the Princes of the Blood, though invited by our Embassador, which was the greatest absurdity that ever Embassador
committed these 400 years, were not there; and so were not
said to give place to our King's Embassador.   And that our
King did openly say, the other day in the Privy Chamber, that
he would not be hectored out of his right and pre-eminencys
by the King of France, as great as he was.   That the Pope is
glad to yield to a peace with the French, as the news-book
says, upon the basest terms that ever was.   That the talk
which these people about our King, that I named before, have,
is to tell him how neither priviledge of Parliament nor City
is any thing; but that his will is all, and ought to be so: and
their discourse, it seems, when they are alone, is so base and
sordid, that it makes the cares of the very gentlemen of the
back stairs, I think he called them, to tingle to hear it spoke
in the King's hearing; and that must be very bad indeed.
That my Lord Bristoll did send to Lisbon a couple of priests,
to search out what they could against the Chancellor concerning the match, as to the point of his knowing before-hand that
the Queen was not capable of bearing children; and that
something was given her to make her so.   But, as private as
they were, when they come thither, they were clapped up

---

[1] Denzil Hollis: see 14th Dec. 1663.

prisoners. That my Lord Bristoll endeavours what he can to
bring the business into the House of Commons, hoping there
to master the Chancellor, there being many enemies of his
there: but I hope the contrary. That whereas the late King
did mortgage Clarendon[1] to somebody for 20,000*l.*, and this
King having given it to the Duke of Albemarle, and he sold
it to my Lord Chancellor, whose title of Earldome is fetched
from thence; the King hath this day sent his order to the
Privy Seale for the payment of this 20,000*l.* to my Lord
Chancellor, to clear the mortgage.[2] Ireland in a very distracted condition about the hard usage which the Protestants
meet with, and the too good which the Catholiques. And
from all together, God knows my heart, I expect nothing but
ruin can follow, unless things are better ordered in a little
time.

23d. (Shrove-Tuesday.) This day, by the blessing of God,
I have lived thirty-one years in the world: and, by the grace
of God, I find myself not only in good health in every thing,
and particularly as to the stone, but only pain upon taking
cold, and also in a fair way of coming to a better esteem and
estate in the world, than ever I expected. But I pray God
give me a heart to fear a fall, and to prepare for it!

24th. (Ash-Wednesday.) To the Queen's chapel, where I
staid and saw their masse, till a man come and bid me go out
or kneel down: so I did go out. And thence to Somerset
House; and there into the chapel, where Monsieur d'Espagne[3]
used to preach. But now it is made very fine, and was ten
times more crouded than the Queen's chapel at St. James's;
which I wonder at. Thence down to the garden of Somerset
House, and up and down the new building, which, in every
respect, will be mighty magnificent and costly.

25th. To my Lord's, and saw the young ladies, and thence
to White Hall. Resolved of going to meet my Lord to-
morrow, having got a horse of Mr. Coventry to-day.

---

[1] Clarendon Park, near Salisbury: see 11th July, 1661.   [2] See Aug. 19, 1661.
[3] There is a small volume in the Pepysian Library, called "Shibboleth; ou.
Reformation de quisques Passages de la Bible, par Jean d'Espagne, Ministre du
St Evangile;" printed in 1653, and dedicated to Cromwell.

26th. Up. and, after dressing myself handsomely for riding, I out. and by water to Westminster, to Mr. Creed's chamber, and, after drinking some chocolatte, and playing on the vyall, Mr. Mallard being there, upon Creed's new vyall, which proves, methinks, much worse than mine, we set out from an inne hard by, whither Mr. Coventry's horse was carried; and round about the bush through bad ways to Highgate. Good discourse in the way had between us; and, it being a most admirable pleasant day, stopped at the Cocke, a mile on this side Barnett, being unwilling to put ourselves to the charge or doubtful acceptance of any provision against my Lord's coming by, and there got something and dined, setting a boy to look towards Barnett Hill, against their coming; and, after two or three false alarms, they come, and we met the coach very gracefully, and I had as kind a receipt from both Lord and Lady as I could wish, and some kind discourse, and then rode by the coach a good way, and so fell to discoursing with several of the people, there being a dozen attending the coach, and another coach for the maids and parson. But, when we come to my Lord's house, I went in; and, whether it was my Lord's neglect, or general indifference, I know not, but he made no kind of compliment there; and, methinks, the young ladies look somewhat highly upon me. So I went away, without bidding adieu to any body, being desirous not to be thought too servile.

27th. Sir Martin Noell told us the dispute between him, as farmer of the Additional Duty, and the East India Company, whether callico be linnen or no; which he says it is, having been ever esteemed so: they say it is made of cotton woole, and grows upon trees, not like flax or hemp. But it was carried against the Company, though they stand out against the verdict.

28th. (Lord's day.) Up, and walked to Paul's; and, by chance, it was an extraordinary day for the Readers of the Inns of Court and all the Students to come to church, it being an old ceremony not used these twenty-five years, upon the first Sunday in Lent. Abundance there was of Students, more than there was room to seat but upon forms, and the

Church mighty full. One Hawkins preached, an Oxford man.
A good sermon upon these words: "But the Wisdom from
above is first pure, then peaceable." Both before and after
sermon, I was most impatiently troubled at the Quire, the
worst that ever I heard. But what was extraordinary, the
Bishop of London,[1] who sat there in a pew, made a' purpose
for him, by the pulpitt, do give the last blessing to the con-
gregation : which was, he being a comely old man, a very
decent thing, methought. The Lieutenant of the Tower, Sir
J. Robinson, would needs have me by coach home with him,
where the officers of his regiment dined with him. I did go
and dine with him—his ordinary table being very good, and his
lady a very high-carriaged, but comely big woman :[2] I was
mightily pleased with her. After dinner, to chapel in the
Tower with the Lieutenant, with the keyes carried before us,
and the Warders and Gentleman-porter going before us ; and
I sat with the Lieutenant in his pew, in great state. None,
it seems, of the prisoners in the Tower, that are there now,
though they may, will come to prayers there.

29th. To Sir Philip Warwick, who showed me many excellent collections of the State of the Revenue in former Kings
and the late times, and the present. He showed me how the
very Assessments between 1643 and 1659, which were taxes,
besides Excise, Customes, Sequestrations, Decimations, King
and Queen's and Church Lands, or any thing else but just the
Assessments, come to above fifteen millions. He showed me
a discourse of his concerning the Revenues of this and foreign
States. How that of Spayne was great, but divided with his
kingdoms, and so come to little. How that of France did,
and do much, exceed ours before for quantity ; and that it is
at the will of the Prince to tax what he will upon his people ;
which is not here. That the Hollanders have the best manner
of tax, which is only upon the expence of provisions, by an
excise ; and do conclude that no other tax is proper for England but a pound-rate, or excise upon the expence of provi-

---

[1] Humphrey Henchman, translated from Salisbury, September, 1663. Ob.
1675.

[2] Anne, daughter of Sir George Whitmore, of Barnes, in Surrey.

sions.   He showed me every particular sort of payment away
of money, since the King's coming in, to this day; and told
me, from one to one, how little he hath received of profit from
most of them; and I believe him truly.   That the 1,200,000*l.*,
which the Parliament with so much ado did first vote to the
King, and since hath been re-examined by several committees
of the present Parliament, is yet above 300,000*l.* short of
making up really to the King the 1,200,000*l.*, as by particulars
he showed me.   And in my Lord Treasurer's excellent letter
to the King upon this subject, he tells the King how it was
the spending more than the revenue that did give the first
occasion of his father's ruine, and did since to the rebels; who,
he says, just like Henry the Eighth, had great and sudden increase of wealth, but yet, by overspending both, died poor:
and further tells the King how much of this 1,200,000*l.* depends upon the life of the Prince, and so must be renewed by
Parliament again to his successor; which is seldom done without parting with some of the prerogatives of the Crowne; or,
if denied, and he persists to take it of the people, it gives occasion to a civill war, which did in the late business of tonnage
and poundage prove fatal to the Crowne.   He showed me how
many ways the Lord Treasurer did take before he moved the
King to farme the Customes in the manner he do, and the
reasons that moved him to do it.   He showed me a very excellent argument, to prove, that our importing lesse than we
export do not impoverish the kingdom, according to the received opinion: which, though it be a paradox, and that I do
not remember the argument, yet methought there was a great
deal in what he said.   And, upon the whole, I find him a
most exact and methodicall man, and of great industry: and
very glad that he thought fit to show me all this; though I
cannot easily guess the reason why he should do it to me, unless from the plainness that he sees I use to him in telling him
how much the King may suffer for our want of understanding
the case of our Treasury.   To make up my monthly accounts;
and I find myself worth eight hundred and ninety and odd
pounds, the greatest sum I ever yet knew.   Calling at St.
Paul's Churchyard, looked upon a pretty burlesque poem,

called " Scarronides ; or, Virgile Travesty ;"[1] extraordinary
good. After dinner, my wife cut my hair short, which is
grown pretty long again.

March 2d. This morning, Mr. Burgby, one of the writing
clerks belonging to the Council, a knowing man, complains to
me how most of the Lords of the Council do look after themselves and their own ends, and none the public, unless Sir
Edward Nicholas. Sir G. Carteret is diligent, but for all his
own ends and profit. My Lord Privy Seale, a destroyer of
every body's business, and do no good at all to the public.
The Archbishop of Canterbury[2] speaks very little, nor do
much, being now come to the highest pitch that he can expect.
He tells me, he believes that things will go very high against
the Chancellor by Bristoll, and that bad things will be proved.
Talks much of his neglecting the King ; and making the King
to trot every day to him, when he is well enough to go to
visit his cozen, Chief-Justice Hide, but not to the Council or
King. He commends my Lord of Ormond mightily in Ireland ; but cries out cruelly of Sir G. Lane,[3] for his corruption ;
and that he hath done my Lord great dishonour, by selling of
places here, which are now all taken away, and the poor
wretches ready to starve. But nobody almost understands or
judges of business better than the King, if he would not be
guilty of his father's fault to be doubtfull of himself, and
easily be removed from his own opinion. That my Lord
Lauderdale is never from the King's care nor council, and that
he is a most cunning fellow. Upon the whole, that he finds
things go very bad every where ; and even in the Council nobody minds the public. To my Lord Sandwich, with whom
I spoke, walking a good while with him in his garden, which
and the house is very fine.

4th. There are several people trying a new-fashion gun
brought my Lord Peterborough this morning, to shoot off
often, one after another, without trouble or danger. At
Greenwich I observed the foundation laying of a very great

---

[1] A poem, by Charles Cotton, then just published.
[2] Gilbert Sheldon.
[3] See *ante*, Oct. 12, 1663.

house for the King,[1] which will cost a great deal of money To White Hall; and there being met by the Duke of York, he called me to him. I never had so much discourse with him before, and till now did ever fear to meet him. Home, my mind in great ease, to think of our coming to so good a respect with my Lord again, and my Lady, and that my Lady do so much cry up my father's usage of her children, and the goodness of the ayre there, found in the young ladies' faces at their return thence.

5th. To the office, where, though I had a great cold, I was forced to speak much upon a publick meeting of the East India Company, at our office; where was also my Lord George Barkeley, in behalf of the company of merchants; I suppose he is on that company, who, hearing my name, took notice of me, and condoled my cozen Edward Pepys's death, not knowing whose son I was, nor did demand it of me.

7th. My wife and I by coach to the Duke's house, where we saw "The Unfortunate Lovers;"[2] but I know not whether I am grown more curious than I was or no, but I was not pleased with it, though I know not where to lay the fault, unless it was that the house was very empty, by reason of a new play at the other house. Yet here was my Lady Castlemaine in a box, and it was pleasant to hear an ordinary lady hard by us, that it seems did not know her before, say, being told who she was, that "she was well enough."

8th. Luellin come and dined with me, but we made no long stay at dinner; "Heraclius"[3] being acted, my wife and I have a mighty mind to see it. The play hath one very good passage well managed in it, about two persons pretending, and yet denying themselves, to be son to the tyrant Phocas, and yet heir of Maronicius to the crowne. The garments like Romans very well. The little girl[4] is come to act very prettily,

<hr />

[1] Building by Webb, the kinsman and executor of Inigo Jones; now a part of Greenwich Hospital.

[2] A tragedy, by Sir W. Davenant.

[3] "Heraclius; or, the Emperor of the East," translated from the French of Corneille, by Ludovic Carlell. Pepys saw it again, 4th. Feb. 1666-7, at the Duke's Theatre. Carlell's translation (4to, 1664) was, it is said, never acted. The play which Pepys saw was probably never printed. He saw it at the Duke's Theatre.
[4] See 23rd Feb., 1662-3.

and spoke the epilogue most admirably. But, at the beginning, at the drawing up of the curtain, there was the finest
scene of the Emperor, and his people about him, standing in
their fixed and different postures in their Roman habits, above
all that I ever saw at any of the theatres. Walked home,
calling to see my brother Tom, who is in bed, and I doubt
very ill.

10th. To dinner with my wife, to a good hog's harslet, a
piece of meat I love, but have not eat of I think these seven
years. At the Privy Seale I enquired, and found the Bill
come for the Corporation of the Royall Fishery :[1] whereof the
Duke of York is made present Governor, and several other
very great persons, to the number of thirty-two, made his
assistants for their lives: whereof, by my Lord Sandwich's
favour, I am one ; and take it not only a matter of honour,
but that, that may come to be of profit to me.

14th. To White Hall ; and in the Duke's chamber, while
he was dressing, two persons of quality that were there did tell
his Royal Highness, how, the other night, in Holborne, about
midnight, being at cards, a link-boy come by and run into the
house, and told the people the house was a-falling.[2] Upon
this the whole family was frighted, concluding that the boy
had said that the house was a-fire : so they left their cards
above, and one would have got out of the balcony, but it was
not open ; the other went up to fetch down his children, that
were in bed: so all got clear out of the house. And no
sooner so, but the house fell down indeed, from top to bottom.
It seems my Lord Southampton's canal[3] did come too near their
foundation, and so weakened the house, and down it come:
which, in every respect, is a most extraordinary passage. To
my brother's. The doctors give him over, and so do all that

---

[1] There had been recently established, under the Great Seal of England, a
Corporation for the Royal Fishing, of which the Duke of York was Governor,
Lord Craven Deputy-Governor, and the Lord Mayor and Chamberlain of London,
for the time being, Treasurers, in which body was vested the sole power of
licensing lotteries.—*The News*, Oct. 6, 1664.

[2] *The Intelligencer* of March 12, 1663-64, notices the fall of the house here
mentioned.

[3] Probably the sewer from Lord Southampton's house.

see him. He talks no sense two words together now; and I confess it made me weep to see that he should not be able, when I asked him, to say who I was. The business between my Lords Chancellor and Bristoll, they say, is hushed up; and the latter gone, or going, by the King's license, to France.

15th. My poor brother Tom died. I left my wife to see him laid out, and I by coach home, carrying my brother's papers, all I could find, with me.

16th. Up, and down to my cozen Stradwick's, and uncle Fenner's, about discoursing for the funeral, which I am resolved to put off till Friday next. Then back again to my brother's, to look after things, and saw the coffin brought; and by and by Mrs. Holden come, and saw him nailed up. This day the Parliament met again, after long prorogation, but what they have done I have not been in the way to hear.

17th. To the office, where we sat this afternoon, because of the Parliament, which returned yesterday; but was adjourned till Monday next, upon pretence that many of the members were said to be upon the road: and also the King had other affairs, and so desired them to adjourn till then. But the truth is, the King is offended at my Lord of Bristoll, as they say, whom he hath found to have been all this while, pretending a desire of leave to go into France, and to have all the differences between him and the Chancellor made up, endeavouring to make factions in both Houses to the Chancellor. So the King did this to keep the Houses from meeting; and, in the meanwhile, sent a guard and a herald last night to have taken him at Wimbleton, where he was in the morning, but could not find him: at which the King was and is still mightily concerned, and runs up and down to and from the Chancellor's like a boy: and it seems would make Bristoll's articles against the Chancellor to be treasonable reflections against his Majesty. So that the King is very high, as they say: and God knows what will follow upon it! To my brother's again, preparing things against to-morrow; and I have altered my resolution of burying him in the churchyard among my young brothers and sisters, and bury him in the church, in the middle aisle, as near as I can to my mother's

pew. This cost me 20*s.* more. Home by coach, bringing
my brother's silver tankard, for safety, along with me.

18th. Up betimes, and walked to my brother's, where a
great while putting things in order against anon; and so to
Wotton, my shoemaker, and there got a pair of shoes blacked
on the soles against anon for me : so to my brother's. To
church,[1] and, with the grave-maker, chose a place for my
brother to lie in, just under my mother's pew. But to see
how a man's tombes are at the mercy of such a fellow, that
for sixpence he would, as his own words were, " I will justle
them together but I will make room for him;" speaking of
the fulness of the middle aisle, where he was to lie; and that
he would, for my father's sake, do my brother, that is dead,
all the civility he can ; which was to disturb other corps that
are not quite rotten, to make room for him ; and methought
his manner of speaking it was very remarkable; as of a thing
that now was in his power to do a man a courtesy or not. I
dressed myself, and so did my servant Besse ; and so to my
brother's again : whither, though invited, as the custom is, at
one or two o'clock, they come not till four or five. But, at
last, one after another, they come, many more than I bid :
and my reckoning that I bid was one hundred and twenty ;
but I believe there was nearer one hundred and fifty. Their
service was six biscuits a-piece, and what they pleased of
burnt claret. My cozen Joyce Norton kept the wine and
cakes above ; and did give out to them that served, who had
white gloves given them. But, above all, I am beholden to
Mrs. Holden, who was most kind, and did take mighty pains
not only in getting the house and every thing else ready, but
this day in going up and down to see the house filled and
served, in order to mine and their great content, I think :
the men sitting by themselves in some rooms, and the women
by themselves in others, very close, but yet room enough.
Anon to church, walking out into the street to the conduit,
and so across the street : and had a very good company

---

[1] St. Bride's, of which Richard Pierson, D.D., the vicar, officiated at the funeral
" March 18, 1663-4, Mr. Thomas Pepys."— *Burial Register of St. Bride's, Fleet
Street.*

along with the corps. And, being come to the grave as above, Dr. Pierson, the minister of the parish, did read the service for buriall: and so I saw my poor brother laid into the grave: and so all broke up; and I and my wife, and Madam Turner and her family, to her brother's, and by and by fell to a barrell of oysters, cake, and cheese, of Mr. Honiwood's, with him, in his chamber and below, being too merry for so late a sad work. But, Lord! to see how the world makes nothing of the memory of a man, an hour after he is dead! And, indeed, I must blame myself; for, though at the sight of him dead and dying, I had real grief for a while, while he was in my sight, yet presently after, and ever since, I have had very little grief indeed for him.

19th. My wife and I alone, having a good hen, with eggs, to dinner, with great content. Then to my brother's, where I spent the afternoon in paying some of the charges of the buriall.

21st. This day the Houses of Parliament met; and the King met them, with the Queen with him. And he made a speech to them: among other things, discoursing largely of the plots abroad against him and the peace of the kingdom; and that the dissatisfied party had great hopes upon the effect of the Act for a Triennial Parliament granted by his father, which he desired them to peruse, and, I think, repeal. So the Houses did retire to their own House, and did order the Act to be read to-morrow before them; and I suppose it will be repealed, though I believe much against the will of a good many that sit there.

23d. To the Trinity House, and there dined very well: and good discourse among the old men. Among other things, they observed, that there are but two seamen in the Parliament, viz., Sir W. Batten and Sir W. Pen, and not above twenty or thirty merchants; which is a strange thing in an island. In the evening, my Lady Jemimah, Paulina, and Madame Pickering, come to see us, but my wife would not be seen, being unready. Very merry with them; they mightily talking of their thrifty living for a fortnight before their mother come to town, and other such simple talk, and of their merry life at Brampton, at my father's this winter.

25th. To White Hall, and there to chapel: where it was most infinite full, to hear Dr. Critton.[1] Being not known, some great persons in the pew I pretended to, and went in, did question my coming in. I told them my pretence: so they turned to the orders of the chapel, which hung behind upon the wall, and read it, and were satisfied; but they did not demand whether I was in waiting or no; and so I was in some fear, lest he that was in waiting might come and betray me. The Doctor preached upon the thirty-first of Jeremy, and the twenty-first and twenty-second verses, about a woman compassing a man; meaning the Virgin conceiving and bearing our Saviour. It was the worst sermon I ever heard him make, I must confess; and yet it was good, and in two places very bitter, advising the King to do as the Emperor Severus did, to hang up a Presbyter John, a short coat and a long gowne interchangeably, in all the Courts of England. But the story of Severus was pretty, that he hanged up forty senators before the Senate-house, and then made a speech presently to the Senate in praise of his own lenity; and then decreed that never any senator after that time should suffer in the same manner without consent of the Senate: which he compared to the proceedings of the Long Parliament against my Lord Strafford. He said the greatest part of the lay magistrates in England were Puritans, and would not do justice; and the Bishops' powers were so taken away and lessened, that they could not exercise the power they ought. He told the King and the ladies, plainly speaking of death and of the skulls and bones of dead men and women, how there is no difference; that nobody could tell that of the great Marius or Alexander from a pyoneer; nor, for all the pains the ladies take with their faces, he that should look in a charnel-house could not distinguish which was Cleopatra's, or fair Rosamond's, or Jane Shore's.[2] My father finds Tom's matters very ill, and finds him to have been so negligent, that

---

[1] Creighton.
[2] The preacher had been studying the gravediggers' scene in " Hamlet."

he used to trust his servants with cutting out of clothes,
never hardly cutting out anything himself; and, by the abstract of his accounts, we find him to owe above 290*l.*, and to
be coming to him under 200*l.*

26th. To my office, about my Lord Peterborough's accounts
for Tangier; but, Lord! to see how ridiculous Mr. Povy is
in all he says or do; not like a man more fit to be in such
employments as he is, and particularly that of a treasurer, as
he is, to the King of England. In discourse, Sir W. Rider
said, that he hath kept a journall of his life for almost these
forty years, even to this day, and still do, which pleases me
mightily. So home. This being my solemn feast for my
cutting of the stone, it being now, blessed be God! this day
six years since the time; and I bless God I do in all respects
find myself free from that disease, or any signs of it. Sir W.
Batten told me how Sir Richard Temple hath spoke very dis-
contentful words in the House about the Triennial Bill; but,
it hath been read the second time to-day, and committed:
and, he believes, will go on without more ado, though there are
many in the House are displeased at it, though they dare not
say much. But, above all expectation, Mr. Prin is the man
against it, comparing it to the idoll whose head was of gold,
and his body and legs and feet of different metal. So this
Bill had several degrees of calling of Parliaments, in case the
King, and then the Council, and then the Lord Chancellor,
and then the Sheriffes, should fail to do it. He tells me
also, how, upon occasion of some 'prentices'[1] being put in the
pillory to-day, for beating of their masters, or such like
thing, in Cheapside, a company of 'prentices come and rescued
them, and pulled down the pillory; and they, being set up
again, did the like again. So that the Lord Mayor and
Major-General Browne was fain to come and stay there, to
keep the peace; and drums, all up and down the city, was
beat to raise the trained bands, for to quiet the town; and
by and by, going out, we saw a trained band stand in Cheapside, on their guard. It raining very fast, we met many

---

[1] Two servants of one Ireland, a cooper upon Bread Street Hill.—*The Intelligencer*, March 28, 1664.

brave coaches coming from the Parke; and so we home ourselves, and ended the day with great content. My wife
found her gown come home laced, which is indeed very handsome, but will cost me a great deal of money, more than ever
I intended, but is but for once.

27th. (Lord's day.) It being church-time, walked to St
James's, to try if I could see the belle Butler, but could not;
only saw her sister, who indeed is pretty, with a fine Roman
nose. Thence walked through the ducking-pond fields; but
they are so altered since my father[1] used to carry us to Islington, to the old man's, at the King's Head, to eat cakes and
ale (his name was Pitts), that I did not know which was the
ducking-pond, nor where I was. So home; and in Cheapside, both coming and going, it was full of apprentices, who
have been here all this day, and have done violence, I think,
to the master of the boys that were put in the pillory yesterday. But, Lord! to see how the trained bands are raised
upon this: the drums beating everywhere as if an enemy
were upon them: so much is this city subject to be put into
a disarray upon very small occasions. But it was pleasant to
hear the boys, and particularly one little one, that I demanded
the business of. He told me, that, that had never been done
in the city since it was a city — two 'prentices put in the
pillory! and that it ought not to be so.

28th. To T. Trice, and advised with him about our administering to my brother Tom; but, Lord! what a shame,
methinks, to me, that, in this condition, and at this age, I
should know no better the laws of my own country! Dinner
with Mr. Coventry. The great matter to-day in the House
hath been, that Mr. Vaughan,[2] the great speaker, is this day
come to town, and hath declared himself in a speech of an
hour and a half, with great reason and eloquence, against the

---

[1] In Ben Jonson's "Every Man in his Humour," there is an allusion to the
"Citizens that come a-ducking to Islington Ponds." The piece of ground, long
since built upon, in the Back Road, was called "Ducking-pond Field," from the
pool in which the unfortunate ducks were hunted by dogs, to amuse the Cockneys,
who went to Islington to breathe fresh air and drink cream. The King's Head
tavern stood opposite the church. Islington was classic ground to Pepys, as he
speaks of the house in which he had been nursed at Kingsland.

[2] John Vaughan, afterwards knighted, and made Chief Justice of the Common Pleas.

repealing of the Bill for Triennial Parliaments; but with no
successe: but the House have carried it that there shall be
such Parliaments, but without any coercive power upon the
King, if he will bring in this Act. But, Lord! to see how
the best things are not done without some design; for I perceive all these gentlemen that I was with to-day were against
it, though there was reason enough on their side, yet purely,
I could perceive, because it was the King's mind to have it;
and, should he demand any thing else, I believe they would
give it him. But this the discontented Presbyters, and the
faction of the House, will be highly displeased with; but it
was carried clearly against them in the House. We had excellent good table-talk, some of which I have entered in my
book of stories. Home, and there find, by my wife, that
Father Fogourdy hath been with her to-day, and she is
mightily for our going to hear a famous Roulé preach at the
French Ambassador's house: I pray God he do not tempt
her in any matters of religion, which troubles me. And also,
she had messages from her mother to-day, who sent for her
old morning-gown, which was almost past wearing; and I
used to call it her kingdom, from the ease and content she
used to have in the wearing of it.[1] I am glad I do not hear
of her begging anything of more value.

29th. To Sir G. Carteret's. About noon, Sir W. Batten
come from the House of Parliament, and told us our Bill for
our office was read the second time to-day, with great applause,
and is committed. By and by to dinner, where good cheer,
and Sir G. Carteret in his humour a very good man, and the
most kind father, and pleased father in his children, that ever
I saw. Here is now hung up a picture of my Lady Carteret,
drawn by Lilly, a very fine picture, but yet not so good as I
have seen of his doing.

30th. To Sir G. Carteret's, where my Lady made us drink
our morning draught of several wines: I drank nothing but

---

[1] The piece of poetry beginning —
  "My mind to me a kingdom is,
  Such perfect joy therein I find"—
was set to music by the celebrated W. Byrd, in 1558, in a book called *Psalms,
Sonnets, and Songs of Sadnesse and Pietie*. On the authority of an old MS. in
the Bodleian Library, it has been attributed to Sir Edward Dyer.

some of her coffee, which was poorly made, with a little sugar in it.

31st. To my office, where comes, by and by, Povy, Sir W. Rider, Mr. Bland, Creed, and Vernatty, about my Lord Peterborough's accounts, which we now went through, but with great difficulty, and many high words between Mr. Povy and I; for I could not endure to see so many things extraordinary put in, against truth and reason. He was very angry; but I endeavoured all I could to profess my satisfaction in my Lord's part of the accounts, but not in those foolish idle things, they say I said, that others had put in. To an alehouse, where my cozen Scott was, and my father's new tenant, Langford, a tailor, to whom I have presented my custom, and he seems a very modest carefull young man.

April 1st. To White Hall; and, in the Gallery, met the Duke of York; I also saw the Queen going to the Park, and her Maids of Honour: she herself looks ill, and methinks Mrs. Stewart is grown fatter, and not so fair as she was: and the Duke called me to him, and discoursed a good while with me; and, after he was gone, twice or thrice staid and called me again to him, the whole length of the house: and at last talked of the Dutch; and I perceive do much wish that the Parliament will find reason to fall out with them. To walk in the garden with W. Howe, he telling me, how my Lord is little at home, minds his carding and little else, takes little notice of any body; but that he do not think he is displeased, as I fear, with me, but is strange to all. This day Mrs. Turner did lend me, as a rarity, a manuscript of one Mr. Wallis, writ long ago, teaching the method of building a ship, which pleases me mightily.

3d. (Lord's day.) Called up by W. Joyce,[1] he being summonsed to the House of Lords to-morrow, for endeavouring to arrest my Lady Peters[2] for a debt. In the afternoon, my

---

[1] William Joyce had married Pepys's first cousin, Kate Fenner, "a comely fat woman." See 5th April, 1664.

[2] Elizabeth, daughter of John Savage, second Earl Rivers, and first wife to William, fourth Lord Petre, who was, in 1678, impeached by the Commons of High Treason, and died a prisoner in the Tower, January 5th, 1683, s. p.

wife sent for me home, to see her new laced gown; and indeed it becomes her very nobly, and is well made.

4th. Up, and walked to my Lord Sandwich's; and there spoke with him about W. Joyce, who tells me, he would do what was fit in so tender a point. Thence to Westminster, to the Painted Chamber, and there met the two Joyces. Will in a very melancholy taking. I to the Lords' House, before they sat; and stood within it, while the Duke of York come to me, and spoke to me a good while, about the new ship at Woolwich. Afterwards, I spoke with my Lord Barkeley and my Lord Peterborough about Joyce. And so staid without a good while, and saw my Lady Peters, an impudent jade, soliciting all the Lords on her behalf. And, at last, W. Joyce was called in; and, by the consequences, and what my Lord Peterborough told me, I find that he did speak all he said to his disadvantage, and so was committed to the Black Rod: which is very hard, he doing what he did by the advice of my Lord Peters' own steward. But the Serjeant of the Black Rod did direct one of his messengers to take him in custody, and peaceably conducted him to the Swan with Two Necks, in Tuttil Street, to a handsome dining-room; and there was most civilly used; my uncle Fenner, and his brother Anthony [Joyce], and some other friends, being with him. But who would have thought that the fellow that I should have sworn could have spoken before all the world, should in this be so daunted, as not to know what he said, and now to cry like a child! I protest, it is very strange to observe. So away to Westminster Hall, and, meeting Mr. Coventry, he took me to his chamber, with Sir William Hickman,[1] a member of their House, and a very civill gentleman. Here we dined very plentifully, and thence to White Hall, to the Duke's, where we all met, and, after some discourse of the condition of the Fleet, in order to a Dutch war, for that, I perceive, the Duke hath a mind it should come to, we away to the office. It was a sad sight, methought, to-day to see

---

[1] Only son of Sir Willoughby Hickman, of Gainsborough, who had been created a Baronet in 1643, and whom he succeeded in his title and estates. He was M.P. for East Retford.

my Lord Peters, coming out of the House, fall out with his lady, from whom he is parted, about this business, saying that she disgraced him. But she hath been a handsome woman, and is, it seems, not only a lewd woman, but very high spirited.

5th. Up very betimes, and walked to my cozen Anthony Joyce's, and thence with him to his brother Will, in Tuttil Street, where I find him pretty cheery over what he was yesterday, like a coxcomb, his wife being come to him, and having had his boy with him last night. Thence back, and there spoke to several Lords, and so did his solicitor, one that W. Joyce hath promised 5*l.* to, if he be released. Lord Peterborough presented a petition to the House from W. Joyce: and a great dispute, we hear, there was in the House, for and against it. At last, it was carried that he should be bayled till the House meets again after Easter, he giving bond for his appearance. Anon comes the King, and passed the Bill for repealing the Triennial Act, and another about Writs of Errour. I crowded in, and heard the King's speech to them; but he speaks the worst that ever I heard man in my life: worse than if he read it all, and he had it in writing in his hand. I to W. Joyce, with his brother, and told them all. Here was Kate come, and is a comely fat woman. I went to W. Joyce, where I find the order come, and bayle, his father and brother, given; and he paying his fees, which come to above 12*l.*, besides 5*l.* he is to give one man, and his charges of eating and drinking here, and 10*s.* a day, as many days as he stands under bayle: which, I hope, will teach him hereafter to hold his tongue better than he used to do. This day, great numbers of merchants come to a grand committee of the House, to bring in their claims against the Dutch. I pray God guide the issue for our good!

6th. Come John Noble, my father's old servant, to speak with me. I, smelling the business, took him home; and there, all alone, he told me how he had been serviceable to my brother Tom, in the business of getting his servant, an ugly jade, Margaret, with child. She was brought to bed in St. Sepulchre's parish of two children—one is dead, the other is alive: her name Elizabeth, and goes by the name of Taylor, daughter to John Taylor. It seems, Tom did a great while trust one Cranly with the business, who daily got money of him; and, at last, finding himself abused, he broke the matter to J. Noble, upon a vow of secrecy. Tom's first plot was to go on the other side of the water, and give a beggar-woman something to take the child. They did once go, but did nothing, J. Noble saying that seven years hence the mother might come to demand the child, and force him to produce it, or to be suspected of murder. Then I think it was that they consulted, and got one Cave, a poor pensioner in St. Bride's parish, to take it, giving him 5l., he thereby promising to keep it for ever without more charge to them. The parish hereupon indite the man Cave for bringing this child upon the parish, and by Sir Richard Browne he is sent to the Counter. Cave then writes to Tom to get him out. Tom answers him in a letter of his own hand, which J. Noble shewed me, but not signed by him, wherein he speaks of freeing him and getting security for him, but nothing as to the business of the child, or anything like it: so that, forasmuch as I could guess, there is nothing therein to my brother's prejudice as to the main point, and therefore I did not labour to tear or take away the paper. Cave being released, demands 5l. more to secure my brother for ever against the child; and he was forced to give it him, and took bond of Cave in 100l., made at a scrivener's—one Hudson, I think, in the old Bayly, to secure John Taylor and his assigns, &c., in consideration of 10l. paid him, from all trouble, or charge of meat, drink, clothes, and breeding of Elizabeth Taylor; and it seems, in the doing of it, J. Noble was looked upon as the assignee of this John Taylor. Noble says that he furnished Tom with this money, and is also bound by another bond to pay him 20s. more this next Easter Monday; but nothing for either sum appears under Tom's hand. I told him how I am like to lose a great sum by his death, and would not pay any more myself, but I would speak to my father about it against the afternoon. After dinner took coach, and to Paternoster Row, and there bought a pretty silk for a petticoat for my wife. I heard to-day that the Dutch have begun with us by granting letters of mark against us : but I believe it not.

7th. To the 'Change, where everybody expects a war. Thence to dinner, where my wife got me a pleasant French fricasee of veale.

8th. Sir W. Batten and I to the alms'-house, to see the new building which he, with some ambition, is building of there, during his being Master of Trinity House ; and a good work it is. Home to the only Lenten supper I have had of wiggs[1] and ale.

10th. (Lord's day.) My wife dressed herself, it being Easter-day, but I, not being so well as to go out, she, though much against her will, staid at home with me ; for she had put on her new best gown, which indeed is very fine now with the lace ; and this morning her taylor brought home her other new-laced silk gown with a smaller lace, and new petticoat I bought the other day : both very pretty. We spent the day in pleasant talk and company one with another, reading in Dr. Fuller's book what he says of the family of the Cliffords and Kingsmills.[2]

12th. To my uncle Wight's, where dined my father, poor melancholy man, that used to be as full of life as anybody, and also my aunt's brother, Mr. Sutton, a merchant in Flanders—a very sober, fine man, and Mr. Cole and his lady ; but, Lord ! how I used to adore that man's talk ! and now methinks he is but an ordinary man. To my Lord's. There I found my Lord, and ladies, and my wife at supper. My Lord seems very kind. So home, and find my father come to lie at our house, and so supped, and saw him, poor man, to bed — my heart never being fuller of love to him, nor admiration of his prudence and pains heretofore in the world

---

[1] Bunns, still called wiggs in the West of England.

[2] Pepys had been mistaken in fancying that Fuller's *Worthies* was to be a history of all the families in England (see *ante*, Jan. 22, 1660-1, and Feb. 10, 1661-2), and hence his disappointment when the work came out, some months after the author's decease, at there being no mention in it of his ancesterr. He then looked for the Cliffords, in hopes of finding his wife's lineage ; but with no better success.

than now, to see how Tom hath carried himself in his trade;
and how the poor man hath his thoughts going to provide for
his younger children and my mother. But I hope they shall
never want.

13th. To St. James's, where I found Mr. Coventry, the
Duke being now come thither for the summer, with a gold-
smith, sorting out his old plate to change for new; but,
Lord! what a deal he hath!

14th. Up betimes, and after my father's eating something,
I walked out with him as far as Milk Street, he turning
down to Cripplegate, to take coach; and at the end of the
street I took leave, being much afraid I shall not see him
here any more — he do decay so much every day.

15th. At noon to the 'Change, where I met with Mr. Hill,
the little merchant, with whom, I perceive, I shall contract a
musical acquaintance; but I will make it as little troublesome
as I can.　To the Duke's house, and there saw "The
German Princesse"[1] acted by the woman herself; but never
was anything so well done in earnest, worse performed in jest
upon the stage.　And indeed the whole play, abating the
drollery of him that acts her husband, is very simple, unless,
here and there, a witty sprinkle or two.

16th. With Mr. Coventry to the African House;[2] and,
after a good and pleasant dinner, up with him, Sir W. Rider,
the simple Povy, of all, the most ridiculous fool that ever I
knew to attend to business, and Creed, and Vernatty, about
my Lord Peterborough's accounts; but, the more we look
into them, the more we see of them that makes dispute.

17th. (Lord's day.) Up, and I put on my best cloth
black suit and my velvet cloak, and with my wife in her best
laced suit to church, where we have not been these nine or
ten weeks.　A young simple fellow did preach; slept soundly
all the sermon.　Our parson, Mr. Mills, his own mistake in
reading of the service, was very remarkable—that instead of
saying, "We beseech thee to preserve to our use the kindly
fruits of the earth," he cries, "Preserve to our use our
gracious Queen Katharine!"

---

[1] By Holden. See *ante*, May 29th, 1663.
[2] The African House was in Leadenhall Street.

18th. Up, and by coach to Westminster, and there solicited W. Joyce's business again; and did speak to the Duke of York about it, who did understand it very well. I afterwards did without the House fall in company with my Lady Peters, and endeavoured to mollify her: but she told me she would not, to redeem her from hell, do anything to release him: but would be revenged while she lived, if she lived the age of Methusalem. I made many friends, and so did others. At last, it was ordered by the Lords that it should be referred to the Committee of Privileges to consider. So I away by coach to the 'Change; and there do hear that a Jew hath put in a policy of four per cent. to any man, to insure him against a Dutch war for four months: I could find in my heart to take him at this offer. To Hide Park, where I have not been since last year: where I saw the King with his periwigg, but not altered at all; and my Lady Castlemaine in a coach by herself, in yellow satin and a pinner on; and many brave persons. And myself, being in a hackney and full of people, was ashamed to be seen by the world, many of them knowing me.

19th. To the Physique Garden in St. James's Parke; where I first saw orange trees, and other fine trees.

20th. Mr. Coventry told me how the Committee for Trade have received now all the complaints of the merchants against the Dutch, and were resolved to report very highly the wrongs they have done us, when, God knows! it is only our own negligence and laziness that hath done us the wrong: and this to be made to the House to-morrow.

21st. At the Lords' House heard that it is ordered, that, upon submission upon the knee, both to the House and my Lady Peters, W. Joyce shall be released. I forthwith made him submit, and ask pardon upon his knees; which he did before several Lords. But my Lady would not hear it; but swore she would post the Lords, that the world might know what pitifull Lords the King hath; and that revenge was sweeter to her than milk; and that she would never be satisfied unless he stood in a pillory, and demand pardon there. But I perceive the Lords are ashamed of her. I find that the

House this day have voted that the King be desired to demand right for the wrong done us by the Dutch, and that they will stand by him with their lives and fortunes: which is a very high vote, and more than I expected. What the issue will be, God knows!

22d. I was called up this morning before four o'clock. It was full light enough to dress myself, and so by water against tide, it being a little coole, to Greenwich; and thence, only that it was somewhat foggy till the sun got to some height, walked with great pleasure to Woolwich, in my way staying several times to listen to the nightingales. Thence home, and by coach to Mrs. Turner's, and there, after reading part of a good play, Mrs. The., my wife, and I, in their coach to Hide Parke, where great plenty of gallants, and pleasant it was, only for the dust. Here I saw Mrs. Bendy, my Lady Spillman's fair daughter that was, who continues yet very handsome. Many others I saw with great content, and so home. I did also carry them into St. James's Parke, and showed them the garden.

23d. (Coronation day.) I met with Mr. Coventry, who himself is now full of talk of a Dutch war; for it seems the Lords have concurred in the Commons' vote about it; and so the next week it will be presented to the King, insomuch that he do desire we would look about to see what stores we lack, and buy what we can. Home to dinner, where I and my wife much troubled about my money that is in my Lord Sandwich's hand, for fear of his going to sea, and being killed; but I will get what out of it I can.

25th. The Duke, which gives me great good hopes, do talk of setting up a good discipline in the fleet. In the Duke's chamber there is a bird, given him by Mr. Pierce, the surgeon, come from the East Indys—black the greatest part, with the finest collar of white about the neck; but talks many things, and neyes like the horse and other things, the best almost that ever I heard bird in my life. To my Lord Sandwich's, where by agreement I met my wife, and there dined with the young ladies; my Lady, being not well, kept her chamber. Much simple discourse at table among the young ladies

After dinner walked in the garden, talking with Mr. Moore about my Lord's business. He told me my Lord runs in debt every day more and more, and takes little care how to come out of it. He counted to me how my Lord pays use now for above 9000*l.*, which is a sad thing, especially considering the probability of his going to sea, in great danger of his life, and his children, many of them, to provide for. Thence, the young ladies going out to visit, I took my wife by coach out through the city, discoursing how to spend the afternoon; and conquered, with much ado, a desire of going to the play; but took her out at White Chapel, and took her out to Bednal Green; so to Hackney, where I have not been many a year, since a little child I boarded there. Thence to Kingsland, by my nurse's house, Goody Lawrence, where my brother Tom and I was kept when young. Then to Newington Green, and saw the outside of Mrs. Herbert's house, where she lived, and my aunt Allen with her; but Lord! how in every point I find myself to over-value things when a child. Thence to Islington, and so to St. John's to the Red Bull, and there saw the latter part of a rude prize fought; and thence back to Islington, and at the King's Head, where Pitts lived, we 'light, and eat and drunk for remembrance of the old house sake; and so through Kingsland again, and so to Bishopsgate, and so home with great pleasure. The country mighty pleasant—only a little troubled at the young ladies leaving my wife so to-day, and from some passages fearing my Lady might be offended. But I hope for the best.

29th. Saw W. Joyce; and the late business hath cost the poor man above 40*l.*; besides, he is likely to lose his debt. Lady Peters, Creed says, is a drunken jade, he himself having seen her drunk in the lobby of the House. With my Lord to the Duke. Methought the Duke did not show him any so great fondness as he was wont; and methought my Lord was not pleased that I should see the Duke made no more of him. Creed and I walked round the Parke—a pleasant walk—observing the birds, which is very pleasant; and so walked to the New Exchange, and there had a most delicate dish of curds and cream. Home to the Old Exchange by coach, where great news and true. I saw by written letters, of strange fires seen at Amsterdam in the ayre—and not only there, but in other places thereabout. The talk of a **Dutch war** is not so hot, but yet I fear it will come to it. My wife gone this afternoon to the buriall of my she-cozen Scott, a good woman; **and** it is a sad consideration how the Pepys's decay, and nobody almost that I know in **a** present way of increasing **them.**

27th. Home with Alderman Backewell, whose **opinion is,** that the Dutch will not give over the business without putting **us** to some trouble to set out a fleet; and then, if they see we go on well, will seek **to** salve up the matter. Met **Mr.** Sanchy, of Cambridge, whom I have not met a great **while.** He seems a simple fellow, and tells me their Master,[1] **Dr.** Rainbow, is newly **made** bishop of Carlisle. This day **the** Houses attended the King, and delivered their votes **to** him upon the business **of** the Dutch; **and he** thanks them, and promises **an** answer **in** writing.

29th. To see my Lady Sandwich, where we find all the children, and my **Lord** recovered, and the house so melancholy, that I thought my Lady had been dead, knowing that she was not well; **but** it seems she hath the meazles, and **I** fear the small-pox, **poor** lady. It grieves me mightily; for **it** will be a sad hour to the family should she miscarry.

30th. My Lord Bristoll's business is hushed up, and nothing made of it—he is gone, and the discourse in that ended.

May 2d. By coach to the King's Play-house, to see "The Labyrinth,"[2] but, coming too soon, walked to my Lord's to hear how my Lady do—who is pretty well; at least, past all **fear.** There by Captain Ferrers, meeting with an opportunity of my Lord's coach, to carry us to the Parke anon, we directed it to come to the play-house door; and so we walked, my wife and I and Mademoiselle. I paid for her going in, and there saw "The Labyrinth," the prettiest play, methinks, that ever I saw, there being nothing in **it** but the odd accidents that fell out, by a lady's being bred up in man's apparel, and

---

[1] Of Magdalene College. *See ante,* April 8, 1663.

[2] Or, "The Fatal Embarrassment," taken from Corneille

a man in woman's. Here was Mrs. Stewart, who is indeed
very pretty, but not like my Lady Castlemaine, for all that.
Thence in the coach to the Parke, where no pleasure; there
being much dust, little company, and our horses
almost spoiled by falling down; but all mended presently,
and, after riding up and down, home. Saw Mademoiselle at
home, and we home, and to my office, whither comes Mr.
Bland, and paid me the debt he acknowledged he owed me
for my service in his business of the Tangier merchant—
twenty pieces of new gold, a pleasant sight. It cheered my
heart; and, he being gone, I home to supper, and shewed
them my wife; and she, poor wretch, would fain have kept
them to look on, without any other design but a simple love
to them; but I thought it not convenient, and so took them
into my own hand.

3d. To Mr. Coventry's chamber, and there upon my Lord
Peterborough's account, where I endeavoured to shew the
folly, and punish it as much as I could, of Mr. Povy; for, of
all the men in the world, I never knew any man of his degree
so great a coxcomb in such employments. I see I have lost
him for ever, but I value it not; for he is a coxcomb, and, I
doubt, not over-honest, by some things which I see; and yet,
for all his folly, he hath the good luck, now and then, to speak
his follies in so good words, and with so good a show, as if it
were reason, and to the purpose. To Westminster Hall, and
there, in the Lords' House, did in a great crowd, from ten
o'clock till almost three, hear the cause of Mr. Roberts, my
Lord Privy Seal's, son, against Win, who by false ways did
get the father of Mr. Roberts' wife, Mr. Bodvil, to give him
the estate and disinherit his daughter. The cause was managed
for my Lord Privy Seal's son by Finch, the Solicitor-General;
but I do really think that he is a man of as great eloquence
as ever I heard, or ever hope to hear in all my life. Mr.
Cutler told me how for certain Lawson both proclaimed war
again with Algiers, though they had, at his first coming, given
back the ships which they had taken, and all their men;
though they refused afterwards to make him restitution for

the goods which they had taken out of them. I went with Mr. Norbury, near hand to the Fleece, a mum-house in Leadenhall, and there drunk mum,[1] and by and by broke up.

4th. To my cozen Scott's. There condoled with him the loss of my cozen his wife, and talked about his matters, as attorney to my father, in his administering to my brother Tom. He tells me we are like to receive some shame about the business of his bastarde with Jack Noble; but no matter, so it cost us no money. The plague increases at Amsterdam.

5th. My eyes beginning every day to grow less and less able to bear with long reading or writing, though it be by daylight; which I never observed till now.

8th. (Lord's day.) This day, my new tailor, Mr. Langford, brought me home a new black cloth suit and cloak lined with silk moyre.

9th. To my Lady Sandwich's, who, good Lady, is now, thanks be to God! so well as to sit up, and sent to us, if we were not afraid to come up to her. So we did; but she was mightily against my wife's coming so near her; though, poor wretch! she is as well as ever she was, as to the meazles, and nothing can I see upon her face. There we sat talking with her above three hours, till six o'clock, of several things, with great pleasure, and so away.

13th. Up before three o'clock, and a little after upon the water, it being very light as at noon, and a bright sunrising; but by and by a rainbow appeared, the first that ever in a morning I saw. In the Painted Chamber I heard a fine conference between some of the two Houses upon the Bill for Conventicles. The Lords would be freed from having their houses searched by any but the Lord Lieutenant of the County; and, upon being found guilty, to be tried only by their peers; and, thirdly, would have it added, that whereas the Bill says, "That that, among other things, shall be a conventicle wherein any such meeting is found doing any

---

[1] Mum was a wholesome kind of malt liquor prepared in Germany. The receipt for making it is given in Rees's *Encyclopædia*. One of Andrew Yarranton's wild schemes, at this time, was to bring the mum trade from Brunswick, and fix it at Stratford-on-Avon. See his *England's Improvement*.

thing contrary to the Liturgy of the Church of England,"
they would have it added, " or practice." The Commons to
the Lords said, that they knew not what might hereafter be
found out which might be called the practice of the Church
of England, which were never established by any law, either
common. statute, or canon; as singing of psalms, binding up
prayers at the end of the Bible, and praying extempore before
and after sermon : and though these are things indifferent,
yet things, for aught they at present know, may be started,
which may be said to be the practice .of the Church which
would not be fit to allow.   For the Lords' priviledges, Mr.
Waller told them how tender their predecessors had been of
the priviledges of the Lords; but, however, where the peace
of the kingdom stands in competition with them, they apprehend those priviledges must give place.   He told them that
he thought, if they should own all to be the priviledges of the
Lords which might be demanded, they should be led like the
man, who granted leave to his neighbour to pull off his horse's
tail, meaning that he could not do it at once, that hair by
hair had his horse's tail pulled off indeed : so the Commons,
by granting one thing after another, might be served by the
Lords.   Mr. Vaughan, whom I could not to my grief perfectly hear, did say, if that they should be obliged in this
manner to exempt the Lords from everything, it would in
time come to pass that whatever, be it ever so great, should
be voted by the Commons as a thing penall for a commoner,
the contrary should be thought a priviledge to the Lords :
that also, in this business, the work of an hour, the cause of
a search would be over before a Lord Lieutenant, who may
be many miles off, can be sent for; and that all this dispute
is but about 100l. ; for it is said in the Act, that it shall be
banishment or payment of 100l.   I thereupon heard the
Duke of Lennox say, that there might be Lords who could
not always be ready to lose 100l., or some such thing.   They
broke up without coming to any end in it.   There was also in
the Commons' House a great quarrell about Mr. Prin, and it
was believed that he should have been sent to the Tower, for
adding something to a Bill, after it was ordered to be engrossed,

of his own head — a Bill for measures for wine and other
things of that sort, and a Bill of his own bringing in; but it
appeared he could not mean any hurt in it. But, however,
the King was fain to write in his behalf, and all was passed
over. But it is worth my remembrance, that I saw old Ryly,[1]
the Herald, and his son; and spoke to his son, who told me,
in very bad words concerning Mr. Prin, that the King had
given him an office of keeping the Records: but that he never
comes thither, nor had been there these six months; so that
I perceive they expect to get his employment from him. Thus
every body is liable to be envied and supplanted.

16th. With Mr. Pierce, the surgeon, to see an experiment
of killing a dog, by letting opium into his hind-leg. He and
Dr. Clerke did fail mightily in hitting the vein, and in effect
did not do the business after many trials; but, with the little
they got in, the dog did presently fall asleep, and so lay till
we cut him up, and a little dog also, which they put it down
his throat — he also staggered first, and then fell asleep, and
so continued. Whether he recovered or no, after I was gone,
I know not.

18th. A pretty cabinet sent me by Mr. Shales, which I
give my wife, and very conveniently it comes for her closet.

19th. To a Committee of Tangier; where God forgive how
our Report of my Lord Peterborough's accounts was read
over and agreed to by the Lords, without one of them understanding it! And, had it been what it would, it had gone:
and, besides, not one thing touching the King's profit in it
minded or hit upon.

20th. Mr. Edward Montagu is turned out of the Court,
not to return again. His fault, I perceive, was his pride,

---

[1] At the Restoration, William Ryley had been deprived of all his posts,
including the office of Clerk of the Tower Records, which was given to Prynne.
Ryley was originally made Lancaster Herald by Charles I., but he sided with
the Parliament, and devoted himself to Oliver Cromwell. He was fortunate in
being afterwards restored to the post of Lancaster Herald, which he held till his
death, in 1667, though he failed in getting back Prynne's appointment. By his
wife Elizabeth, daughter of Sir Anthony Chester, Bart., of Chickley, Bucks,
Ryley had a numerous issue. Perhaps the son here mentioned was William
Ryley, described by Prynne as of the Inner Temple, in 1662. See note to Dec. 7.
1661, ante.

and, most of all, his affecting to be great with the Queen;
and it seems indeed he had more of her ear than everybody
else, and would be with her talking alone two or three hours
together; insomuch that the Lords about the King, when he
would be jesting with them about their wives, would tell the
King that he must have a care of his wife too, for she hath
now the gallant: and they say the King himself did once ask
Montagu how his mistress, meaning the Queen, did.[1]   He
grew so proud, and despised every body, besides suffering
nobody, he or she, to get or do anything about the Queen,
that they all laboured to do him a good turn.   They all say
that he did give some affront to the Duke of Monmouth,
which the King himself did speak to him of.   But strange it
is that this man should, from the greatest negligence in the
world, come to be the miracle of attendance: so as to take
all offices from every body, either men or women, about the
Queen.   So he is gone, nobody pitying, but laughing at him;
and he pretends only that he is gone to his father, that is
sick in the country.

22d. (Lord's day.) To White Hall.   Here the Duke of
York called me to him, to ask me whether I did intend to
go with him to Chatham or no.   I told him if he commanded,
but I did believe there would be business here for me, and so
he told me then it would be better to stay.   After staying,
and seeing the throng of people to attend the King to Chapel,
but, Lord! what a company of sad, idle people they are!

23d. The King is gone down with the Duke and a great
crew this morning by break of day to Chatham.

24th. This day I heard that my uncle Fenner is dead,
which makes me a little sad, to see with what speed a great
many of my friends are gone, and more, I fear, for my father's
sake, are going.

25th. This afternoon come Tom and Charles Pepys by my

---

[1] See 23rd Dec. 1662.   Boyer, in his *Life of Queen Anne*, says that he was
dismissed for offending her Majesty by squeezing her hand.   He is mentioned in
the *State Poems*:—

"—— Montagu, by court disaster,
Dwindled into the wooden horse's master."

Advice to a Painter, part I.

sending for, and received of me 40*l.* in part towards their 70*l.* legacy of my uncle's.

26th. Carried my wife to the Old Bayly, and there we were led to the Quest House, by the church, where all the kindred were by themselves at the burial of my uncle Fenner; but, Lord! what a pitiful rout of people there was of them, but very good service, and great company the whole was. And so anon to church, and a good sermon, and so home.

27th. To comfort my heart, Captain Taylor this day brought me 20*l.* he promised me, for my assistance to him about his masts.

29th. (Whit Sunday.) King's birth and Restoration day Mr. Coventry and I did long discourse together of the business of the office, and the war with the Dutch; and he seemed to argue mightily upon the little reason that there is for all this. For, first, as to the wrong, we pretend they have done us: that of the East Indys, for their not delivering of Poleron,[1] it is not yet known whether they have failed or no; that of their hindering the Leopard cannot amount to above 3000*l.*, if true; that of the Guinny Company, all they had done us did not amount to above 2 or 300*l.* he told me truly; and that now, from what Holmes, without any commission, hath done in taking an island and two forts, hath set us much in debt to them; and he believes that Holmes will have been so puffed up with this, that he by this time hath, being reinforced with more strength than he had then, hath, I say, done a great deal more wrong to them. He do, as to the effect of the war, tell me clearly that it is not any skill of the Dutch that can hinder our trade if we will, we having so many advantages over them, of winds, good ports, and men; but it is our pride, and the laziness of the merchant. The main thing he desired to speak with me about was, to understand my Lord Sandwich's intentions as to going to sea with this fleet; saying, that the Duke, if he desires it, is most willing to do it; but, thinking that twelve ships is not a fleet fit for my Lord to be troubled to go out with, he is not willing

---

[1] One of the Banda Islands, which had acknowledged James I. as its sovereign, but was afterwards forcibly seized by the Dutch.

to offer it to him till he hath some intimations of his mind to go or not. He spoke this with very great respect to my Lord, though methinks it is strange they should not understand one another better at this time than to need another's mediation. To the King's closet; whither by and by the King come, my Lord Sandwich carrying the sword. A Bishop preached, but he speaking too low for me to hear. By and by my Lord Sandwich come forth, and called me to him: and we fell into discourse a great while about his business, wherein he seems to be very open with me, and to receive my opinion as he used to do: and I hope I shall become necessary to him again. He desired me to think of the fitness, or not, for him to offer himself to go to sea; and to give him my thoughts in a day or two. Thence after sermon among the ladies in the Queen's side; where I saw Mrs. Stewart, very fine and pretty, but far beneath my Lady Castlemaine. Thence with Mr. Povy[1] home to dinner; where extraordinary cheer. And after dinner up and down to see his house. And in a word, methinks, for his perspective in the little closet; his room floored above with woods of several colours, like but above the best cabinet-work I ever saw; his grotto and vault, with his bottles of wine, and a well therein to keep them cool; his furniture of all sorts; his bath at the top of the house, good pictures, and his manner of eating and drinking; do surpass all that ever I did see of one man in all my life.

31st. To my Lord, and to discourse about his going to sea, and the message I had from Mr. Coventry to him. He wonders, as he well may, that this course should be taken, and he every day with the Duke, who, nevertheless, seems most friendly to him, who hath not yet spoke one word to my Lord of his desire to have him go to sea. My Lord do tell me clearly that were it not that he, as all other men that were of the Parliament side, are obnoxious to reproach, and so is forced to bear what otherwise he would not, he would never suffer everything to be done in the Navy, and he never be consulted; and it seems, in the naming of all these Commanders for this fleet, he hath never been asked one question. But we con-

---

[1] Evelyn, in his *Diary*, July 1, 1664, mentions Povy's house in Lincoln's Inn.

cluded it wholly inconsistent with his honour not to go with
this fleet, nor with the reputation which the world hath of his
interest at Court; and so he did give me commission to tell
Mr. Coventry that he is most willing to receive any commands
from the Duke in this fleet, were it less than it is, and that
particularly in this service. With this message I parted, and
by coach to the office, where I found Mr. Coventry, and told
him this. Methought, I confess, he did not seem so pleased
with it as I expected, or at least could have wished, and asked
me whether I had told my Lord that the Duke do not expect
his going, which I told him I had. To St. James's, to one
Lady Poultny's,[1] where I found my Lord, I doubt, at some
vain pleasure or other. I was told to-day, that, upon Sunday
night last, being the King's birth-day, the King was at my
Lady Castlemaine's lodgings, over the hither-gate at Lambert's
lodgings, dancing with fiddlers all night almost; and all the
world coming by taking notice of it.

June 1st. By water to Woolwich, all the way reading Mr.
Spencer's[2] book of Prodigys, which is most ingeniously writ,
both for matter and stile. Southwell,[3] Sir W. Pen's friend,
tells me the very sad newes of my Lord Teviott's and nineteen
more commission officers being killed at Tangier by the
Moores,[4] by an ambush of the enemy upon them, while they
were surveying their lines: which is very sad, and he says
afflicts the King much. To the King's house, and saw "The
Silent Woman;" but methought not so well done or so good
a play as I formerly thought it to be. Before the play was
done, it fell such a storm of hayle, that we in the middle of
the pit were fain to rise; and all the house in a disorder.[5]

[1] This lady was Grace, youngest daughter of Sir John Corbet, of Stoke, Salop,
who had married Sir William Poulteney, of Mesterton, in Leicestershire, who was
knighted at Whitehall, 4th June, 1660. See more about him, 10th Jan. 1659-60,
note.

[2] John Spencer, D.D., who died in 1695, was also the author of a celebrated
work, De Legibus Hebræorum. His Discourse concerning Prodigies first appeared
in 1663; the 2d edition, of 1665, contains likewise a Discourse concerning Vulgar
Prophecies.

[3] Afterwards Sir Robert Southwell.

[4] The particulars of the loss at Tangiers is given in The Intelligencer, 6th June,
1664.

[5] The Blackfriars Theatre was entirely roofed over, and had a pit, instead of a
mere enclosed yard; whilst the stage portion alone of the public playhouses was
protected from the weather. The house was lighted by a cupola.

2d. To a Committee of Tangier about providing provisions, money, and men; but it is strange to see how poorly and brokenly things are done of the greatest consequence, and how soon the memory of this great man is gone, or, at least, out of mind by the thoughts of who goes next, which is not yet known. My Lord of Oxford, Muskerry, and several others, are discoursed of. It seems my Lord Teviott's design was to go a mile and a half out of the town, to cut down a wood in which the enemy did use to lie in ambush. He had sent several spyes; but all brought word that the way was clear, and so might be for anybody's discovery of an enemy before you are upon them. There they were all snapt, he and all his officers, and about two hundred men, as they say; there being left now in the garrison but four captains. This happened the 3d of May last, being not before that day twelvemonth of his entering into his government there: but, at his going out in the morning, he said to some of his officers, "Gentlemen, let us look to ourselves, for it was this day three years that so many brave Englishmen were knocked on the head by the Moores, when Fines[1] made his sally out."

3d. At the Committee for Tangier all the afternoon — the Duke of York and Mr. Coventry, for ought I see, being the only two that do anything like men; Prince Rupert do nothing but swear and laugh, with an oath or two.

4th. I went forth with J. Noble, who tells me that he will secure us against Cave—that though he knows, and can prove it, yet nobody else can prove it, to be Tom's child; that the bond was made by one Hudson, a scrivener, next to the Fountain taverne, in the Old Bayly; that the children were born, and christened, and entered in the parish-book of St. Sepulchre's, by the name of Anne and Elizabeth Taylor; and he will give us security against Cave if we pay him the money. To the Duke, and was giving him an account how matters go, and of the necessity there is of a power to presse seamen, without which we cannot really raise men for this fleet of twelve sail, besides that it will assert the King's power of pressing, which at present is somewhat doubted, and will make

---

[1] Major Fiennes, whose regiment formed part of the garrison at Tangier.

the Dutch believe that we are in earnest. To the Committee
of Tangier all afternoon, where still the same confused doings,
and my Lord FitzHarding now added to the Committee,
which will signify much. Mr. Coventry discoursing this noon
about Sir W. Batten, what a sad fellow he is, told me how the
King told him the other day how Sir W. Batten, being in the
ship with him and Prince Rupert when they expected to fight
with Warwicke, did walk up and down sweating, with a napkin
under his throat to dry up his sweat : and that Prince Rupert,
being a most jealous man, and particularly of Batten, do walk
up and down swearing bloodily to the King, that Batten had
a mind to betray them to-day, and that the napkin was a
signal : " but, by God," says he, " if things go ill, the first
thing I will do is to shoot him."   He discoursed largely and
bravely to me concerning the different sort of valours, the
active and passive valour.   For the latter, he brought as an
instance General Blake, who, in the defending of Taunton and
Lyme for the Parliament, did, through his sober sort of valour,
defend it the most *opiniastrément* that ever any man did anything ; and yet never was the man that ever made an attaque
by land or sea, but rather avoyded it on all, even fair occasions.
On the other side, Prince Rupert, the boldest attaquer in the
world for personal courage : and yet, in the defending of
Bristol, no man ever did any thing worse, he wanting the
patience and seasoned head to consult and advise for defence,
and to bear with the evils of a siege.   The like he says of my
Lord Teviott, who was the boldest adventurer of his person in
the world : and from a mean man in a few years was come to
this greatness of command and repute only by the death of all
his officers, he many times having the luck of being the only
survivor of them all, by venturing upon services for the King
of France that nobody else would ; and yet no man upon a
defence, he being all fury and of no judgment in a fight.
He tells me, above all, of the Duke of York, that he is more
himself and more of judgment is at hand in him, in the middle
of a desperate service, than at other times, as appeared in the
business of Dunkirke, wherein no man ever did braver things,
or was in hotter service in the close of that day, being sur-

rounded with enemies; and then, contrary to the advice of
all about him, his counsel carried himself and the rest through
them safe, by advising that he might make his passage with
but a dozen with him; "For," says he, "the enemy cannot
move after me so fast with a great body, and with a small one
we shall be enough to deal with them;" and, though he is a
man naturally martiall to the hottest degree, yet a man that
never in his life talks one word of himself or service of his own,
but only that he saw such or such a thing, and lays it down
for a maxime that a Hector can have no courage. He told
me also, as a great instance of some men, that the Prince of
Condé's excellence is, that there not being a more furious man
in the world, danger in fight never disturbs him more than
just to make him civill, and to command in words of great
obligation to his officers and men; but without any the least
disturbance in his judgment or spirit.

6th. By barge with Sir W. Batten to Trinity House.
Here were my Lord Sandwich, Mr. Coventry, my Lord
Craven, and others. A great dinner, and good company.
Mr. Prin, also, who would not drink any health, no, not the
King's, but sat down with his hat on all the while; but nobody
took notice of it to him at all.

8th. With Creed talking of many things, among others of
my Lord's going so often to Chelsey, and he do tell me that
his daughters do perceive all, and do hate the place and the
young woman, Mrs. Betty Becke; for my Lord who sent
them thither only for a disguise for his going thither, will come
under a pretence to see them, and pack them out of doors to
the Parke, and stay behind with her: but now the young
ladies are gone to their mother to Kensington.

11th. With my wife only to take the ayre, it being very
warm and pleasant, to Bowe and Old Ford: and thence to
Hackney. There light, and played at shuffle-board, eat cream
and good cherries: and so with good refreshment home.

13th. Spent the whole morning reading of some old Navy
books; wherein the order that was observed in the Navy then,
above what it is now, is very observable. Mr. Coventry did
talk of a History of the Navy of England, how fit it were to

be writ; and he did say that it hath been in his mind to propose to me the writing of the History of the late Dutch war, which I am glad to hear, it being a thing I much desire, and sorts mightily with my genius; and, if done well, may recommend me much. So he says he will get me an order for making of searches to all records, &c., in order thereto, and I shall take great delight in doing of it.

14th. By coach to Kensington. In the way overtaking Mr. Laxton, the apothecary, with his wife and daughters—very fine young lasses—in a coach; and so both of us to my Lady Sandwich, who hath lain this fortnight here, at Deane Hodges's.[1] Much company come hither to-day—my Lady Carteret, &c., Sir William Wheeler, and his lady, and, above all, Mr. Becke, of Chelsey, and wife and daughter, my Lord's mistress, and one that hath not one good feature in her face, and yet is a fine lady, of a fine taille, and very well carriaged, and mighty discreet. I took all the occasion I could to discourse with the young ladies in her company to give occasion to her to talk, which now and then she did, and that mighty finely, and is, I perceive, a woman of such an ayre, as I wonder the less at my Lord's favour to her, and I dare warrant him she hath brains enough to entangle him. Two or three hours we were in her company, going into Sir H. Finche's garden,[2] and seeing the fountayne, and singing there with the ladies, and a mighty fine cool place it is, with a great laver of water in the middle, and the bravest place for musick I ever heard. After much mirth, discoursing to the ladies in defence of the city against the country or court, and giving them occasion to invite themselves to-morrow to me to dinner to my venison pasty, I got their mother's leave, and so good night, very well pleased with my day's work, and, above all, that I have seen my Lord's mistress.

15th. I got Captain Witham to tell me the whole story of my Lord Teviott's misfortune; for he was upon the guard

[1] Thomas Hodges, vicar of Kensington, and rector of St. Peter's, Cornhill. He had been, in September, 1661, preferred to the Deanery of Hereford, which he held with his two livings till his death, in 1672.

[2] Now Kensington Gardens.

with his horse near the towne, when at a distance he saw the
enemy appear upon a hill, a mile and half off, and made up
to them, and with much ado escaped himself; but what become of my Lord he neither knows nor thinks that anybody
but the enemy can tell.   Our loss was about four hundred.
But he tells me that the greater wonder is, that my Lord
Teviott met no sooner with such a disaster; for every day he
did commit himself to more probable danger than this, for
now he had the assurance of all his scouts that there was no
enemy thereabouts; whereas, he used every day to go out
with two or three with him, to make his discoveries in greater
danger, and yet the man that could not endure to have anybody else to go a step out of order to endanger himself. He
concludes him to be the man of the hardest fate to lose so
much honour at one blow that ever was.   His relation being
done, he parted; and I home.   At home, to look after things
for dinner.   And anon at noon comes Mr. Creed by chance,
and by and by the three young ladies: and very merry we
were with our pasty, very well baked; and a good dish of
roasted chickens; pease, lobsters, strawberries.   And after
dinner to cards: and about five o'clock, by water down to
Greenwich; and up to the top of the hill, and there played
upon the ground at cards.   And so to the Cherry Garden,[1]
and then by water singing finely to the Bridge, and there
landed;[2] and so took boat again, and to Somerset House.
And by this time, the tide being against us, it was past ten
of the clock; and such a troublesome passage, in regard to
my Lady Paulina's fearfullness, that in all my life I never did
see any poor wretch in that condition.   Being come hither,
there waited for them their coach; but, it being so late, I
doubted what to do how to get them home.   After half an
hour's stay in the street, I sent my wife home by coach with
Mr. Creed's boy: and myself and Creed in the coach home
with them.   But, Lord! the fear that my Lady Paulina was
in every step of the way: and indeed, at this time of the

---

[1] The Cherry Garden was at Rotherhithe.
[2] To avoid the danger of what was called "shooting the bridge."   See *ante*
9th Aug. 1662, note.

night, it was no safe thing to go that road; so that I was
even afraid myself, though I appeared otherwise.[1] We come
safe, however, to their house; where we knocked them up, my
Lady and all the family being in bed. So put them into
doors; and, leaving them with the maids, bade them good
night. Then into the town[2]—Creed and I, it being about
twelve o'clock and past: and to several houses—inns, but
could get no lodging, all being in bed. At last, we found
some people drinking and roaring; and, after drinking, got an
ill bed.

16th. I lay in my drawers, and stockings, and waistcoat
till five of the clock, and so up; and, being well pleased with
our frolick, walked to Knightsbridge, and there eat a mess of
cream, and so to St. James's, and I to Whitehall, and took
coach, and found my wife well got home last night, and now
in bed. The talk upon the 'Change is, that De Ruyter is
dead, with fifty men of his own ship, of the plague, at Cales:
that the Holland Embassador here do endeavour to sweeten
us with fair words; and things like to be peaceable. With
my cozen Richard Pepys upon the 'Change, about supplying
us with bewpers[3] from Norwich, which I should be glad of, if
cheap.

20th. I to the Duke, where we did our usual business.
And among other discourse of the Dutch, he was merrily
saying how they print that Prince Rupert, Duke of Albemarle, and my Lord Sandwich, are to be Generalls: and soon
after is to follow them " Vieux Pen:" and so the Duke called
him in mirth Old Pen.[4] They have, it seems, lately wrote to
the King, to assure him that their setting-out ships was only

---

[1] We have here a curious picture of the dreadful state of the streets in London
in 1664. No improvement of what they were a century before, when they were
described as "very foul, full of pits and sloughs, very perilous and noxious,"
('Knight's London, vol. i., p. 26) appears to have taken place. The alarm of
Lady Paulina and Pepys at night was not surprising.

[2] Kensington.

[3] This word is used by Spenser for companions or equals. Mr. Goddard
Johnson, of Norwich, suggests that pieces of cloth, each containing twenty-five
yards, were known by the name of beaupers; but the word has fallen into dis-
use. It appears, from one of the Pepys papers, of a later date, that bewpers
were used as a material for flags.

[4] He was only forty-two years of age.

to defend their fishing-trade, and to stay near home — not to
annoy the King's subjects: and to desire that he would do the
like with his ships: which the King laughs at, but yet is
troubled they should think him such a child, to suffer them to
bring home their fish and East India Company's ships, and
then they will not care for us. Meeting Pickering, he tells
us how my Lady last week went to see Mrs. Becke, the
mother; and by and by the daughter come in, but that my
Lady do say herself, as he says, that she knew not for what
reason, for she never knew they had a daughter, which I do
not believe. She was troubled, and her heart did rise as soon
as she appeared, and seems the most ugly woman that ever
she saw. This, if true, were strange, but I believe it is not.
To my Lord's lodgings; and was merry with the young
ladies, who make a great story of their appearing before their
mother the morning after we carried them, the last week,
home so late; and that their mother took it very well, at
least, without any anger. Here I heard how the rich widow,
my Lady Gold, is married to one Neale,[1] after he had received
a box on the ear by her brother,[2] who was there a sentinel,
in behalf of some courtier, at the door; but made him draw,
and wounded him. She called Neale up to her, and sent for
a priest, married presently, and went to bed. The brother
sent to the Court, and had a serjeant sent for Neale; but
Neale sent for him up to be seen in bed, and she owned
him for her husband: and so all is past. It seems Sir H.
Bennet did look after her. My Lady very pleasant. After
dinner come in Sir Thomas Crewe and Mr. Sidney [Montagu],
lately come from France, who is grown a little, and a pretty
youth he is, but not so improved as they did give him out to
be, but like a child still. But yet I can perceive he hath
good parts and good inclinations.

21st. Meeting Mr. Moore, I perceive by him my Lord's
business of his family and estate goes very ill, and runs in
debt mightily. I would to God I were clear of it, both as to
my own money and the bond of 1000*l.*, which I stand debtor
for him in, to my cozen Thomas Pepys.

---

[1] Thomas Neale.   [2] She had four brothers.

22d. To the 'Change and Coffee House, where great talk of the Dutch preparing of sixty sail of ships. The plague grows mightily among them, both at sea and land.

23d. W. Howe was with me this afternoon, to desire some things to be got ready for my Lord against his going down to his ship, which will be soon; for it seems the King and both the Queens intend to visit him. The Lord knows how my Lord will get out of this charge; for Mr. Moore tells me to-day that he is 10,000*l.* in debt: and this will, with many other things, that daily grow upon him, while he minds his pleasure as he do, set him further backward.

24th. To the City granarys, where, it seems, every company have their granary,[1] and obliged to keep such a quantity of corne always there, or, at a time of scarcity, to issue it at so much a bushell: and a fine thing it is to see their stores of all sorts, for piles for the bridge, and for pipes. To White Hall; and Mr. Pierce showed me the Queen's bed-chamber, and her closet where she had nothing but some pretty pious pictures, and books of devotion; and her holy water at her head as she sleeps, with a clock by her bed-side, wherein a lamp burns that tells her the time of the night at any time. Thence with him to the Park, and there met the Queen coming from chapell, with her Maids of Honour, all in silver-lace gowns again; which is new to me, and that which I did not think would have been brought up again. Thence he carried me to the King's closet: where such variety of pictures, and other things of value and rarity, that I was properly confounded, and enjoyed no pleasure in the sight of them; which is the only time in my life that ever I was so at a loss for pleasure, in the greatest plenty of objects to give it me.

26th. (Lord's day.) At my Lord Sandwich's; where his little daughter, my Lady Katherine, was brought, who is

---

[1] From the commencement of the reign of Henry VIII., or perhaps earlier, it was the custom of the City of London to provide against scarcity, by requiring each of the chartered Companies to keep in store a certain quantity of corn, which was to be renewed from time to time, and when required for that purpose, produced in the market for sale, at such times and prices, and in such quantities, as the Lord Mayor or Common Council should direct: see the report of a case in the Court of Chancery, "Attorney-General *v.* Haberdashers' Company. Mylne and Keen's *Reports*, vol. i., p. 420.

lately come from my father's at Brampton, to have her cheeke
looked after, which is and hath long been sore. But my
Lord will rather have it be as it is, with a scarr in her face,
than endanger it being worse by tampering. I went home,
and with Creed called at several churches, which, God knows,
are supplied with very young men, and the churches very
empty: and at our own church looked in, and there heard one
preach whom Sir William Pen brought, which he desired us
yesterday to hear, that had been his chaplain in Ireland: a
very silly fellow. After dinner, a frolick took us, we would go
this afternoon to the Hope; so my wife dressed herself, and,
with good victuals and drink, we took boat presently, and the
tide with us, got down, but it was night, and the tide spent
by the time we got to Gravesend: so there we stopped, but
went not on shore, only Creed, to get some cherries, and send
a letter to the Hope, where the Fleet lies. And so, it being
rainy, and thundering mightily, and lightning, we returned
with great pleasure home, about twelve o'clock—Creed telling
pretty stories in the boat. He lay with me all night.

27th. To Paul's Churchyard, and there saw Sir Harry
Spillman's book,[1] and I bespoke it and others.

28th. Put on a half shirt first this summer, it being very
hot; and yet so ill-tempered I am grown, that I am afraid
I shall catch cold, while all the world is afraid to melt away.
To the Mitre, and there comes Dr. Burnett to us; and there
I begun to have his advice about my disease, and then invited
him to my house; and I am resolved to put myself into his
hands.

29th. Mr. Shepley tells me how my brave dog I did give
him, going out betimes one morning, to Huntingdon, was set
upon by five other dogs, and worried to pieces, of which I am a
little, and he the most sorry I ever saw man for such a thing.
To Westminster, to see Deane Honiwood,[2] whom I had not
visited a great while. He is a good-natured, but a very weak
man, yet a Deane, and a man in great esteem. My Lady[3] and
I sat two hours alone, talking of the condition of her family's

---

[1] Glossarium Archaiologicum.
[2] See 13th Jan., 1661-2.   [3] Sandwich.

being greatly in debt, and many children now coming up to provide for. I did give her my sense very plainly of it, which she took well, and carried further than myself, to the bemoaning their condition, and remembering how finely things were ordered about six years ago, when I lived there, and my Lord at sea every year.

30th. By water to Woolwich, and walked back from Woolwich to Greenwich all alone; saw a man that had a cudgell in his hand, and, though he told me he laboured in the King's yard, and many other good arguments that he is an honest man, yet, God forgive me! I did doubt he might knock me on the head behind with his club. But I got safe home. Great doubts yet whether the Dutch war go on or no. The Fleet ready in the Hope, of twelve sail. The King and Queens go on board, they say, on Saturday next. Young children of my Lord Sandwich gone with their maids from my mother's, which troubles me — it being, I hear, from Mr. Shepley, with great discontent, saying that, though they buy good meate, yet can never have it before it stinks, which I am ashamed of.

July 1st. Comes Dr. Burnett, who did write me down some direction what to do, but not with the satisfaction I expected. I did give him a piece, with good hopes, however, that his advice will be of use to me. Upon the 'Change, this day, I saw how uncertain the temper of the people is, that, from our discharging about 200 that lay idle, having nothing to do, upon some of our ships, which were ordered to be fitted for service, and their works are now done, the town do talk that the King discharges all his men—200 yesterday, and 800 to-day — and that now he hath got 100,000l. in his hand, he values not a Dutch war. But I undeceived a great many, telling them how it is.

3d. (Lord's day.) At noon, to dinner, where the remains of yesterday's venison, and a couple of brave green geese, which we are fain to eat alone, because they will not keep, which troubled us. Thundering and lightning all the evening, and this year have had the most thunder and lightning, they say, of any in man's memory, and so it is, it seems, in France, and everywhere.

4th. This day the King and the Queen went to visit my Lord Sandwich and the fleet, going forth in the Hope.'

6th. Up very betimes, and my wife also, and got us ready; and, about eight o'clock, having got some bottles of wine and beer, and neat's tongues, we went to our barge at the Tower, where Mr. Pierce and his wife, and a kinswoman and his sister, and Mrs. Clerke and her sister and cozen, were to expect us; and so set out for the Hope, all the way down playing at cards, and other sports, spending our time pretty merry. Come to the Hope about one, and there showed them all the ships, and had a collation of anchovies, gammon, &c., and, after an hour's stay or more, embarked again for home; and so to cards, and other sports, till we come to Greenwich, and there Mrs. Clerke, and my wife and I, on shore, to an alehouse, and so to the barge again, having shown them the King's pleasure-boat: and so home to the Bridge, bringing night home with us: so to the Tower wharf, and home, being very well pleased to-day with the company, especially Mrs. Pierce, who continues her complexion as well as ever, and hath at this day, I think, the best complexion that ever I saw on any woman, young or old, or child either all days of my life. Also, Mrs. Clerke's kinswoman sings very prettily, but is very confident in it—Mrs. Clerke herself witty, but spoils all in being so conceited, and making so great a flutter with a few fine clothes, and some bad tawdry things worn with them. The reason of Dr. Clerke's not being here was, the King being sick last night, and let blood, and so he durst not come away to-day.

7th. To White Hall, and there found the Duke and twenty more reading their commission (of which I am, and was also sent to, to come) for the Royall Fishery, which is very large, and a very serious charter it is; but the Company generally so ill fitted for so serious a work, that I do much fear it will come to little. Home, calling for my new bookes, viz., Sir

---

' Their Majesties were treated at Tilbury Hope by the Earl of Sandwich, returning the same day, abundantly satisfied both with the dutiful respects of that honourable person and with the excellent condition of all matters committed to his charge. — *The Newes*, 7th July, 1664.

II. Spillman's "Whole Glossary," Scapula's "Lexicon," and Shakespeare's plays, which I have got money out of my stationer's bills to pay for. The King is pretty well, to-day.

8th. To the binder's, and directed the doing of my Chaucer, though they were not full neat enough for me, but pretty well it is; and thence to the clasp-maker's, to have it clasped and bossed.

9th. To a Committee for fishing; but the first thing was swearing to be true to the Company; and we were all sworn, but a great dispute we had, which, methought, is very ominous to the Company — some, that we should swear to be true to the best of our power; and others, to the best of our understanding — and carried in the last, though in that we are the least able to serve the Company, because we would not be obliged to attend the business when we can, but when we list.

10th. (Lord's day.) Up, and by water, towards noon, to Somersett House, and walked to my Lord Sandwich's, and there dined with my Lady and the children. After dinner, took our leaves, and my wife her's, in order to her going to the country to-morrow. My Lady showed us my Lady Castlemaine's[1] picture, finely done, given my Lord; and a most beautiful picture it is. Thence with my Lady Jemimah, and Mr. Sidney [Montagu], to St. Gyles's church, and there heard a long, poor sermon. Thence set them down, and in their coach to Kate Joyce's christening, where much company and good service of sweetmeats; and, after an hour's stay, left them, and in my Lord's coach — his noble, rich coach — home.

11th. Betimes up this morning, and, getting ready, we by coach to Holborne, where, at nine o'clock, they set out, and I and my man Will on horseback by my wife to Barnett; a very pleasant day; and there dined with her company, which was very good—a pretty gentlewoman with her, that goes but to Huntingdon, and a neighbour to us in town. Here we staid two hours, and then parted for all together, and my poor wife I shall soon want, I am sure. Thence I and Will to see the

[1] This fine portrait is still at Hinchingbrooke, and in very good preservation.

Wells,[1] half a mile off, and there I drunk three glasses, and walked, and come back and drunk two more: and so we rode home, round by Kingsland, Hackney, and Mile End, till we were quite weary; and not being very well, I betimes to bed.

About eleven o'clock, knowing what money I have in the house, and hearing a noise, I begun to sweat worse and worse, till I melted almost to water. I rung, and could not in half an hour make either of the wenches hear me: and this made me fear the more, lest they might be gag'd; and then I begun to think that there was some design in a stone being flung at the window over our stairs this evening, by which the thiefes meant to try what looking there would be after them, and know our company. These thoughts and fears I had, and do hence apprehend the fears of all rich men that are covetous, and have much money by them. At last, Jane rose, and then I understand it was only the dog wants a lodging, and so made a noyse.

12th. Called up by my Lord Peterborough's gentleman, about getting his Lord's money to-day of Mr. Povy, wherein I took such order, that it was paid, and I had my 50l. brought me, which comforts my heart. Dined alone; sad for want of company, and not being very well, and know not how to eat alone.

14th. I rose a little after four o'clock, and abroad. Walked to my Lord's and nobody up, but the porter rose out of bed to me: so I back again to Fleet Street, and there bought a little book of law; and thence hearing a psalm sung I went into St. Dunstan's, and there heard prayers read, which, it seems, is done there every morning at six o'clock; a thing I never did do at a chapel, but the College chapel, in all my life. Thence to my Lord's again, and my Lord being up, was sent for up, and he and I alone. He did begin with a most solemn profession of the same confidence in and love for me that he ever had, and then told me what a misfortune was fallen upon me and him: on me, by a displeasure which my Lord Chancellor did show to him last night against me, in the highest and most passionate manner that ever any man did speak, even

---

[1] The mineral spring at East Barnet.

to the not hearing of any thing to be said to him: but he
told me, that he did say all that could be said for a man as to
my faithfullnesse and duty to his Lordship, and did me the
greatest right imaginable. And what should the business be,
but that I should be forward to have the trees in Clarendon
Park[1] marked and cut down, which he, it seems, hath bought
of my Lord Albemarle; when, God knows! I am the most
innocent man in the world in it, and did nothing of myself,
nor knew of his concernment therein, but barely obeyed my
Lord Treasurer's warrant for the doing thereof. And said
that I did most ungentlemanly-like with him, and had justified
the rogues in cutting down a tree of his; and that I had sent
the veriest Fanatique [Deane] that is in England to mark them,
on purpose to nose him. All which, I did assure my Lord,
was most properly false, and nothing like it true; and told
my Lord the whole passage. My Lord do seem most nearly
affected with him; partly, I believe, for me, and partly for
himself. So he advised me to wait presently upon my Lord,
and clear myself in the most perfect manner I could, with all
submission and assurance that I am his creature both in this
and all other things; and that I do own that all I have is
derived through my Lord Sandwich from his Lordship. So,
full of horror, I went, and found him busy in trials of law in
his great room; and, it being Sitting-day, durst not stay, but
went to my Lord and told him so: whereupon he directed me
to take him after dinner; and so away I home, leaving my
Lord mightily concerned for me. So I to my Lord Chancellor's; and there, coming out after dinner, I accosted him,
telling him that I was the unhappy Pepys that had fallen into
his high displeasure, and come to desire him to give me leave
to make myself better understood to his Lordship, assuring
him of my duty and service. He answered me very pleas

---

[1] Near Salisbury, granted by Edward VI. to Sir W. Herbert, Earl of Pem
broke, for two lives, which lease determined in 1601, when it reverted to the
Crown, and was conferred on the Duke of Albemarle, whose family got the estate
after Lord Clarendon's fall: for, according to Britton, Clarendon Park was
alienated by Christopher Monk, second Duke of Albemarle, to the Earl of Bath,
from whom it passed, by purchase, to the ancestor of Sir Frederick Hervey
Bathurst, Bart., the present possessor. See 19th Aug., 1661, and 22d Feb.,
1663-4.

ingly, that he was confident upon the score of my Lord Sandwich's character of me, but that he had reason to think what
he did, and desired me to call upon him some evening: I
named to-night, and he accepted of it. To my Lord Chancellor's, and there heard several trials, wherein I perceive my
Lord is a most able and ready man. After all done, he himself called: " Come, Mr. Pepys, you and I will take a turn in
the garden." So he was led down stairs, having the goute,
and there walked with me, I think, above an hour, talking
most friendly, yet cunningly. I told him clearly how things
were: how ignorant I was of his Lordship's concernment in
it; how I did not do, nor say, one word singly, but what was
done, was the act of the whole Board. He told me by name
that he was more angry with Sir G. Carteret than with me,
and also with the whole body of the Board. But, thinking
who it was of the Board that did know him least, he did place
his fear upon me; but he finds that he is indebted to none of
his friends there. I think I did thoroughly appease him, till
he thanked me for my desire and pains to satisfy him; and,
upon my desiring to be directed who I should of his servants
advise with about this business, he told me nobody, but would
be glad to hear from me himself. He told me he would not
direct me in any thing, that it might not be said that the
Lord Chancellor did labour to abuse the King; or, as I offered,
direct the suspending the Report of the Purveyors: but I see
what he means, and will make it my work to do him service
in it. But, Lord! to see how he is incensed against poor Deane,
as a fanatick rogue, and I know not what: and what he did
was done in spite to his Lordship among all his friends and
tenants. He did plainly say, that he would not direct me in
any thing, for he would not put himself into the power of any
man to say that he did so and so; but plainly told me, as if
he would be glad I did something. Lord! to see how we poor
wretches dare not do the King good service for fear of the
greatness of these men. He named Sir G. Carteret, and Sir
J. Minnes, and the rest; and that he was as angry with them
all as with me. But it was pleasant to think that, while he
was talking to me, comes into the garden Sir G. Carteret;

and my Lord avoided speaking with him, and made him and many others stay expecting him, while I walked up and down above an hour, I think; and would have me walk with my hat on. And yet, after all, there has been so little ground for his jealousy of me, that I am sometimes afraid that he do this only in policy to bring me to his side by scaring me; or else, which is worse, to try how faithfull I would be to the King: but I rather think the former of the two. I parted with great assurance how I acknowledged all I had to come from his Lordship; which he did not seem to refuse, but with great kindness and respect parted.

15th. Up, and to my Lord Sandwich's; where he sent for me up, and I did give my Lord an account of what had passed with my Lord Chancellor yesterday: with which he was pleased, and advised me by all means to study in the best manner I could to serve him in this business. After this discourse ended, he begun to tell me that he had now pitched upon his day of going to sea upon Monday next, and that he would now give me an account how matters are with him. He told me that his work now in the world is only to keep up his interest at Court, having little hopes to get more considerably, he saying that he hath now about 8000l. per annum. It is true, he says, he oweth about 10,000l.; but he hath been at great charges in getting things to this pass in his estate; besides his building and good goods that he hath bought. He says that he hath now evened his reckonings at the Wardrobe till Michaelmas last, and hopes to finish it to Lady-day before he goes. He says now there is due, too, 7000l. to him there if he knew how to get paid, besides 2000l. that Mr. Montagu do owe him. As to his interest, he says that he hath had all the injury done him that ever man could have by another bosom friend that knows all his secrets, by Mr. Montagu; but he says that the worst of it all is past, and he gone out and hated, his very person by the King, and he believes the more upon the score of his carriage to him; nay, that the Duke of York did say a little while since in his closet, that he did hate him because of his ungrateful carriage to my Lord of Sandwich. He says that he is as great with the Chancellor, or greater,

than ever in his life. That with the King he is the like; and
he told me an instance, that whereas he formerly was of the
private council to the King before he was last sick, and that
by the sickness an interruption was made in his attendance
upon him; the King did not constantly call him, as he used
to do, to his private council, only in businesses of the sea, and
the like; but of late the King did send a message to him by
Sir Harry Bennet, to excuse the King to my Lord that he had
not of late sent for him as he used to do to his private council,
for it was not out of any distaste, but to avoid giving offence
to some others whom he did not name; but my Lord supposes
it might be Prince Rupert, or it may be only that the King
would rather pass it by an excuse than be thought unkind: but
that now he did desire him to attend him constantly, which of
late he hath done, and the King never more kind to him in his
life than now. The Duke of York as much as is possible; and
in the business of late, when I was to speak to my Lord about
his going to sea, he says that he finds the Duke did it with the
greatest ingenuity and love in the world; "and whereas," says
my Lord, "here is a wise man hard by that thinks himself so,
and, it may be, is in a degree so, naming by and by my Lord
Crewe, would have had me condition with him that neither
Prince Rupert nor any body should come over his head, and I
know not what." The Duke himself hath caused, in his commission, that he be made Admirall of this and what other ships
or fleets shall hereafter be put out after these; which is very
noble. He tells me, in these cases, and that of Mr. Montagu's,
and all others, he finds that bearing of them patiently is the
best way, without noise or trouble, and things wear out of
themselves and come fair again. But says he takes it from me,
never to trust too much to any man in the world, for you put
yourself into his power; and the best seeming friend and real
friend, as to the present, may have or take occasion to fall out
with you, and then out comes all. Then he told me of Sir
Harry Bennet, though they were always kind, yet now it is
become to an acquaintance and familiarity above ordinary, that
for these months he hath done no business but with my Lord's
advice in his chamber, and promises all faithfull love to him and

13 *

service upon all occasions. My Lord says, that he hath the
advantage of being able, by his experience, to help out and
advise him; and he believes that, that chiefly do invite Sir
Harry to this manner of treating him. "Now," says my Lord,
"the only and the greatest embarras that I have in the world
is, how to behave myself to Sir H. Bennet and my Lord Chancellor, in case that there do lie any thing under the embers
about my Lord Bristoll, which nobody can tell; for then," says
he, "I must appear for one or other, and I will lose all I have
in the world rather than desert my Lord Chancellor; so that,"
says he, "I know not, for my life, what to do in that case."
For Sir H. Bennet's love is come to the height, and his confidence, that he hath given my Lord a character,[1] and will
oblige my Lord to correspond with him. "This," says he, "is
the whole condition of my estate and interest; which I tell
you, because I know not whether I shall see you again or no."
Then, as to the voyage, he thinks it will be of charge to him,
and no profit; but that he must not now look after nor think
to encrease, but study to make good what he hath; that what
is due to him from the Wardrobe, or elsewhere, may be paid,
which otherwise would fail, and all a man hath be but small
content to him. So we seemed to take leave one of another;
my Lord of me, desiring me that I would write to him, and
give him information upon all occasions in matters that con-
cern him; which, put together with what he preambled with
yesterday, makes me think that my Lord do truly esteem me
still, and desires to preserve my service to him; which I do
bless God for. In the middle of our discourse, my Lady
Crewe come in, to bring my Lord word that he hath another
son,[2] my Lady being brought to bed just now, for which God
be praised! and send my Lord to study the laying up of something the more! Thence with Creed to St. James's; and,
missing Mr. Coventry, to White Hall; where, staying for him
in one of the galleries, there comes out of the chayre-roome
Mrs. Stewart, in a most lovely forme, with her hair all about
her eares, having her picture taking there. There was the

---

[1] A cipher.
[2] Lord Sandwich's sixth son, James Montagu, who died unmarried.

King and twenty more, I think, standing by all the while, and a lovely creature she in the dress seemed to be.

16th. To the Tangier Committee, and there, above my expectation, got the business of our contract for the victualling carried for my people, viz., Alsop, Lanyon, and Kabsey; and by their promise I do thereby get 300*l.* per annum to myself, which do overjoy me; and the matter is left to me to draw up. Mr. Coventry did also surprise me with a question why Deane did not bring in their report of the timber of Clarendon. What he means thereby I know not, but at present put him off; nor do I know how to steer myself, but I must think of it, and advise with my Lord Sandwich.

17th. (Lord's day.) After dinner walked to my Lord's, and there found him and much other guests at table at dinner, and it seems they have christened his young son to-day — called him James. I got a piece of cake. Dr. Burnett showed me the manner of eating turpentine, which pleases me well, for it is with great ease.

18th. To my Lord's, and there took my leave of him, he seeming very friendly to me in as serious a manner as ever in his life. He sets out this morning for Deale. Sir G. Carteret and I did talk together in the Parke about my Lord Chancellor's business of the timber; he telling me freely that my Lord Chancellor was never so angry with him in all his life as he was for this business, and in a great passion; and that, when he saw me there, he knew what it was about. And plots now with me how we may serve my Lord, which I am mightily glad of; and I hope together we may do it. Thence home, and Creed with me, and there he took occasion to own his obligations to me, and did lay down twenty pieces of gold upon my shelf in my closet, which I did not refuse, but wish and expected should have been more. Now I am out of expectation, and shall henceforward know how to deal with him. After discourse, we went out by coach, and we light at the Temple, and then he took final leave of me, in order to his following my Lord to-morrow. Thence to my Lord Chancellor, and discoursed his business with him. I perceive, and he says plainly, that he will not have any man to have it

in his power to say that my Lord Chancellor did contrive the
wronging the King of his timber; but yet, I perceive, he
would be glad to have service done him therein; and told me
Sir G. Carteret hath told him that he and I would look after
his business, to see it done in the best manner for him.

19th. Coming to the rope-yard at Woolwich, we are told
that Mr. Falconer, who hath been ill of a relapse these two
days, is just now dead. We went up to his widow, who is
sick in bed also. The poor woman in great sorrow, and
entreats our friendship, which we shall, I think, in everything
do for her. I am sure I will.

20th. With Mr. Deane, discoursing upon the business of
my Lord Chancellor's timber, in Clarendon Park, and how to
make a report therein without offending him; which at last
I drew up, and hope it will please him. But I would to God
neither I nor he ever had anything to have done with it! To
White Hall, to the Committee for Fishing; but nothing done,
it being a great day to-day there upon drawing at the Lottery[1]
of Sir Arthur Slingsby. I got in, and stood by the two
Queens and the Duchess of York, and just behind my Lady
Castlemaine, whom I do heartily admire; and good sport to
see how most that did give their ten pounds did go away with
a pair of gloves only for their lot, and one gentlewoman, one
Mrs. Fish, with the only blanke. And one I staid to see
draw a suit of hangings valued at 430l., and they say are well
worth the money, or near it. One other suit there is better
than that; but very many lots of three and fourscore pounds.
I observed the King and Queen did get but as poor lots as
any else. But the wisest man I met with was Mr. Cholmley,
who insured as many as would, from the drawing of the one
blank for 12d.; in which case there was the whole number of
persons to one, which, I think, was three or four hundred.
And so he insured about 200 for 200 shillings, so he could
not have lost if one of them had drawn it, for there was
enough to pay the 10l.; but it happened another drew it, and
so he got all the money he took. I left the lottery, and went
to a play—only a piece of it, which was at the Duke's house,

---

[1] Evelyn says this lottery was a shameful imposition.

"Worse and Worse,"[1] just the same manner of play, and
writ, I believe, by the same man as "The Adventures of Five
Hours;"[2] very pleasant it was, and I begin to admire Harris
more than ever.[3]

21st. This morning to the office. Comes Nicholas Osborne,
Mr. Gauden's clerk, to desire of me what piece of plate I
would choose to have of 100*l.*, or thereabouts, bestowed upon
me, he having order to lay out so much; and, out of his
freedom with me, do of himself come to make this question.
I a great while urged my unwillingness to take any, not
knowing how I could serve Mr. Gauden, but left it wholly to
himself; so at noon I find brought home in fine leather cases
a pair of the noblest flaggons that ever I saw all the days of
my life; whether I shall keep them or no I cannot tell: for
it is to oblige me to him in the business of the Tangier victualling, wherein I doubt I shall not; but glad I am to see
that I shall be sure to get something on one side or other,
have it which will: so, with a merry heart, I looked upon
them, and locked them up. After dinner to give my Lord
Chancellor a good account of his business, and he is very well
pleased therewith, and carries himself with great discretion to
me, without seeming any way glad or beholding to me; and
yet I know that he do think himself so.

22d. To Deptford. Coming too soon, I spent an hour in
looking round the yard, and putting Mr. Shish[4] to measure a
piece or two of timber, which he did most cruelly wrong, and
to the King's loss 12 or 13*s.* in a piece of 28 feet in contents.
Thence to the Clerke of the Cheques, from whose house Mr.
Falconer was buried to-day — Sir J. Minnes and I the only
principall officers that were there. We walked to church
with them, and then I left them without staying the sermon,
and at night home: and there find, as I expected, Mr. Hill,
and Andrews, and one slovenly and ugly fellow, Signor Pedro,
who sings Italian songs to the theorbo most neatly; and they
spent the whole evening in singing the best piece of musique

[1] A comedy, by G. Digby, Earl of Bristol.   [3] Sir Samuel Tuke.
[2] He played Don Antonio, "a soldier haughty and of exact honour."
[4] Jonas Shish, master shipwright at Deptford.

counted of all hands in the world, made by Signor Charissimi,[1] the famous master in Rome. Fine it was indeed, and too fine for me to judge of. Comes Mr. Lanyon, who tells me Mr. Alsop is now become dangerously ill, and fears his recovery, which shakes my expectation of 300*l.* per annum by the business; and, therefore, bless God for what Mr. Gauden hath sent me, which, from some discourse to-day with Mr. Osborne, swearing that he knows not anything of this business of the victualling; but, the contrary, that it is not that that moves Mr. Gauden to me, for he hath had order for it any time these two months. Whether this be true or no, I know not; but I shall hence with the more confidence keep it.

23d. I took occasion to break the business of my Lord Chancellor's timber[2] to Mr. Coventry in the best manner I could. He professed to me, that, till Sir G. Carteret did speak of it at the table, after our officers were gone to survey it, he did not know that my Lord Chancellor had anything to do with it; but now he says that he had been told by the Duke that Sir G. Carteret had spoke to him about it, and that he had told the Duke that, were he in my Lord Chancellor's case, if he were his father, he would rather fling away the gains of two or 3000*l.*, than have it said that the timber, which should have been the King's, if it had continued the Duke of Albemarle's, was concealed by us in favour of my Lord Chanceller; for, says he, he is a great man, and all such as he, and he himself particularly, have a great many enemies that would be very glad of such an advantage against him; and that he would speak to the Duke, that he and Sir G. Carteret might be appointed to attend my Lord Chancellor in it. All this disturbs me mightily. I know not what to say to it, nor how to carry myself therein; for a compliance will discommend me to Mr. Coventry, and a discompliance to my Lord Chancellor. But I think to let it alone, or at least meddle in it as little more as I can.

---

[1] Giacomo Carissimi, maestro di capella of St. Apollinare, in the German College at Rome, one of the most excellent of the Italian musicians. He lived to be ninety years old, composed much, and died very rich. — Hawkins's *Hist. of Music.*

[2] See 18th August, 1662.

25th. Met with a printed copy of the King's commission for the repair of Paul's, which is very large, and large power for collecting money, and recovering of all people that had bought or sold formerly anything belonging to the church. And here I find my Lord Mayor of the city set in order before the Archbishop or any nobleman, though all the greatest officers of the state are there. But yet I do not hear, by my Lord Barkeley, who is one of them, that anything is like to come of it. No news, only the plague is very hot still, and increases among the Dutch.

26th. To Anthony Joyce's, to our gossip's dinner. I had sent a dozen and half of bottles of wine thither, and paid my double share besides, which is 18s. Very merry we were. Great discourse of the fray yesterday in Moorefields, how the butchers at first did beat the weavers, between whom there hath been ever an old competition for mastery, but at last the weavers rallied and beat them. At first, the butchers knocked down all for weavers that had green or blue aprons, till they were fain to pull them off and put them in their breeches. At last the butchers were fain to pull off their sleeves, that they might not be known, and were soundly beaten out of the field, and some deeply wounded and bruised; till at last the weavers went out tryumphing, calling 100l. for a butcher.

27th. To White Hall, where anon the Duke of York came, and a Committee we had of Tangier, where I read over my rough draught for the Tangier victualling, and acquainted them with the death of Mr. Alsopp, which Mr. Lanyon had told me this morning, which is a sad consideration to see how uncertain our lives are, and how little to be presumed of in our greatest undertakings.

28th. Home, and then abroad, and seeing "The Bondman" upon the posts, I went to the Duke's house and saw it acted. It is true, for want of practice, they have many of them forgot their parts a little; but Betterton and my poor Ianthe [Mrs. Betterton?] outdo all the world. There is nothing more taking in the world with me than that play. I am overjoyed in hopes that, upon this month's account, I shall find myself worth 1000l., besides the rich present of two silver and gilt flaggons, which Mr. Gauden did give me the other day. My Lord Sandwich newly gone to sea; and he did, before his going, and by his letter since, show me all manner of respect and confidence.

30th. To the 'Change, where great talk of a rich present brought by an East India ship, from some of the Princes of India, worth to the King 70,000*l.*, in two precious stones, by which, at least, I hope to be 100*l.* or two the better. This afternoon, with great content, I finished the contract for victualling of Tangier, with Mr. Lanyon and the rest; and, to my comfort, got him and Andrews to sign to the giving me 300*l.* per annum.

31st. (Lord's day.) Up, and to church, where I have not been these many weeks.

August 1st. To the Coffee-house, and there all the house full of the victory Generall Soushe,[1] who is a Frenchman, a soldier of fortune, commanding part of the German army, hath had against the Turke; killing 4000 men, and taking most extraordinary spoil. Thence taking up Harman and his wife, carried them to Anthony Joyce's, where he had my venison in a pasty well done; but, Lord! to see how much they made of it, as if they had never eat any before: and very merry we were. Mrs. Harman is a very pretty-humoured wretch, whom I could love with all my heart, being so good and innocent company. Last night I was waked with knocking at Sir W. Pen's door; and what was it but people's running up and down, to bring him word that his brother [Captain Pen], who hath been a good while, it seems, sick, is dead.

2d. To the King's play-house, and there saw "Bartholomew Fayre," which do still please me; and is, as it is acted, the best comedy in the world, I believe. I chanced to sit by Tom Killigrew, who tells me that he is setting up a Nursery [for actors]; that is, is going to build a house in Moorefields, wherein he will have common plays acted. But four operas it shall have in the year, to act six weeks at a time: where

---

[1] General Soushe was Louis Ratuit, Comte de Souches. The battle was fought at Lewentz, in Hungary.

we shall have the best scenes and machines, the best musique, and everything as magnificent as is in Christendome ; and to that end, hath sent for voices and painters and other persons from Italy. Thence homeward called upon my Lord Marlborough.

4th. To a play at the King's house, "The Rivall Ladys,"[1] a very innocent and most pretty witty play. I was much pleased with it, and, it being given me,[2] I look upon it as no breach of my oath. Here we hear that Clun,[3] one of their best actors, was, the last night, going out of towne, after he had acted the Alchymist, wherein was one of his best parts that he acts, to his country-house, set upon and murdered; one of the rogues taken, an Irish fellow. It seems most cruelly butchered and bound. The house will have a great miss of him. Thence visited my Lady Sandwich, who tells me my Lord FitzHarding is to be made a Marquis.

5th. About ten o'clock I dressed myself, and so mounted upon a very pretty mare, sent me by Sir W. Warren, according to his promise yesterday. And so through the City, not a little proud, God knows, to be seen upon so pretty a beast, and to my cozen W. Joyce's, who presently mounted too, and he and I out of towne toward Highgate; in the way, at Kentish Towne, he showing me the place and manner of Clun's being killed and laid in a ditch, and yet was not killed by any wounds, having only one in his arm, but bled to death through his struggling. He told me, also, the manner of it, of his going home so late from drinking with his mistress, and manner of having it found out. Thence forward to Barnett, and so by night to Stevenage, it raining a little, and there, to my great trouble, find that my wife was not come, nor any Stamford coach gone down this week, so that she cannot come. To bed, and, after a little sleep, W. Joyce comes in his shirt into my chamber, with a note, and a mes-

---

[1] A tragedy, by Dryden.　　　[2] His companion paid for him.

[3] A poem upon his death was published at the time, with the following title: —"An Elegy upon the most execrable murder of Mr. Clun, one of the comedians of the Theatre Royal, who was robbed and most inhumanly killed on Tuesday night, being the 2d of August, 1664, near Tatnam Court, as he was riding to his country-house at Kentish Town."

senger from my wife, that she was come by Yorke coach to Bigglesworth, and would be with us to-morrow morning. So, mightily pleased at her discreet action in this business, to sleep again.

6th. Here lay Deane Honiwood last night. I met and talked with him this morning, and a simple priest he is, though a good, well-meaning man. W. Joyce and I to a game at bowles on the green, there till eight o'clock, and then comes my wife, and a coach full of women, only one man riding by. Very joyful, and mounted, and away with them to Welling,[1] and there light, and dined very well and merry, and glad to see my poor wife. After dinner, out again, and to London, all the way the mightiest merry at a couple of young gentlemen, come down to meet the same gentlewoman, that ever I was in my life, and so W. Joyce, too, to see how one of them was horsed upon a hard-trotting sorrell horse, and both of them soundly weary and galled. But it is not to be set down how merry we were all the way. We light in Holborne, and by another coach home, and found all things well, and most mighty neat and clean.

7th. (Lord's day.) My wife telling me sad stories of the ill, improvident, disquiet, and sluttish manner, that my father and mother and Pall do live in the country, which troubles me mightily, and I must seek to remedy it. Showed my wife, to her great admiration and joy, Mr. Gauden's present of plate, the two flaggons, which indeed are so noble that I hardly can think that they are yet mine. I saw several poor creatures carried by, by constables, for being at a conventicle. They go like lambs, without any resistance. I would to God they would either conform, or be more wise, and not be catched!

8th. After dinner, to hang up my five pictures in my dining-room, which makes it very pretty, and so my wife and I abroad to the King's play-house. Here we saw "Flora's Figarys."[2] I never saw it before; and, by the most inge-

---

[1] Welwyn.

[2] "Flora's Vagaries," a comedy, by Richard Rhodes, first acted by the students at Christ Church, Oxford, in 1663. Sir Henry Herbert records its performance in London, on the 3rd Nov. 1663. Flora was afterwards played by Nell Gwynn. See 5th Oct. 1667.

nious performance of the young jade Flora, it seemed as
pretty a pleasant play as ever I saw.

9th. This day comes the newes, that the Emperour hath
beat the Turke;[1] killed the Grand Vizier and several great
Bashas, with an army of 80,000 men killed and routed; with
some considerable loss of his own side, having lost three
generals, and the French forces all cut off almost;[2] which is
thought as good a service to the Emperour as beating the
Turke almost.

10th. Abroad to find out one to engrave my tables upon
my new sliding rule with silver plates, it being so small, that
Browne, that made it, cannot get one to do it. So I got
Cocker,[3] the famous writing-master, to do it, and I set an hour
by him to see him design it all; and strange it is to see him,
with his natural eyes, to cut so small at his first designing it,
and read it all over, without any missing, when for my life
I could not, with my best skill, read one word or letter of it;
but it is use. He says, that the best light for his life to do a
very small thing by, contrary to Chaucer's words to the Sun,
"that he should lend his light to them that small seals
grave,"[4] it should be by an artificial light of a candle, set to
advantage, as he could do it. I find the fellow, by his discourse, very ingenious; and, among other things, a great
admirer of, and well read in, the English poets, and under-

---

[1] This was the battle of St. Gothard, in which the Turks were defeated with
great slaughter by the Imperial forces under Montecuculi, assisted by the con-
federates from the Rhine, and by forty troops of French cavalry under Coligni.
St. Gothard is in Hungary, on the river Raab, near the frontier of Styria: it is
about 120 miles S. of Vienna, and 30 E. of Grätz. The battle took place on the
9th Moharrem, A.H. 1075, or 23d July, A.D. 1664, *old style*, which is that used by
Pepys.

[2] The fact is, the Germans were beaten by the Turks, and the French won the
battle for them.

[3] Edward Cocker, the well-known arithmetician. Ob. circ. 1679.

[4] The words are in *Troilus and Cresside*, book iii., lines 1462 to 1468. — (Chal-
mers's *English Poets*, vol. i., p. 262.)

"Alas, what have these lovers thee agilt?
Dispitious day, thine be the paine of hell,
For many a lover hast thou slain, and wilt,
Thy poring in well nowhere let 'hem dwell;
What profrest thou thy light here for to sell?
Go sell it hem that smale seales 'grave.
We well thee not: us needeth no day have."

takes to judge of them all, and that not impertinently. After dinner, Deane and I had great discourse again about my Lord Chancellor's timber, out of which I wish I may get well.

11th. Comes Cocker, with my rule, which he hath engraved to admiration, for goodness and smallness of work: it cost me 14s. the doing.   This day, for a wager before the King, my Lords of Castlehaven, and Arran, a son of my Lord of Ormond's, they two alone did run down and kill a stoute Bucke in St. James's Parke.

12th. To White Hall, and did much business at a Tangier Committee; where, among other things, speaking about proprietary of the houses there, and how we ought to let the Portuguese have right done them, as many of them as continue, or did sell the houses while they were in possession, and something further in their favour, the Duke, after an anger I never observed in him before, did cry, says he, " All the world rides us, and I think we shall never ride anybody."

13th. Comes Mr. Reeve, with a microscope and scotoscope. For the first I did give him 5l. 10s., a great price, but a most curious bauble it is, and he says, as good, nay, the best he knows in England.   The other he gives me, and is of value; and a curious curiosity it is to discover objects in a dark room with.   Mr. Creed dining with me, I got him to give my wife and me a play this afternoon, lending him money to do it, which is a fallacy that I have found now once, to avoide my vowe with, but never to be more practiced, I swear.   To the new play, at the Duke's house, of " Henry the Fifth;"[1] a most noble play, writ by my Lord Orrery; wherein Betterton, Harris, and Ianthe's parts are most incomparably wrote and done, and the whole play the most full of height and raptures of wit and sense that ever I heard; having but one incongruity, that King Harry promises to plead for Tudor to their mistress, Princess Katharine of France, more than, when it comes to it, he seems to do; and Tudor refused by her with some kind of indignity, not with a

---

[1] Three women played in this piece.   Mrs. Betterton, Mrs. Long, and Mrs. Davis.

difficulty and honour that it ought to have been done in to him.

14th. (Lord's day.) Comes Mr. Herbert, Mr. Honiwood's man, and dined with me—a very honest, plain, and well-meaning man, I think him to be; and, by his discourse and manner of life, the true emblem of an old ordinary serving-man. By and by comes W. Joyce, in his silk suit, and cloak lined with velvett: staid talking with me, and I very merry at it. He supped with me; but a cunning, crafty fellow he is, and dangerous to displease, for his tongue spares nobody.

15th. With Sir J. Minnes; he talking of his cures abroad, while he was with the King as a doctor. And among others, Sir J. Denham, he told me, he had cured to a miracle. At Charing Cross, and there saw the great Dutchman that is come over, under whose arm I went with my hat on, and could not reach higher than his eye-browes with the tip of my fingers. He is a comely and well-made man, and his wife a very little but pretty comely Dutch woman. It is true, he wears pretty high-heeled shoes, but not very high, and do generally wear a turban, which makes him show yet taller than really he is.

16th. Wakened about two o'clock this morning with a noise of thunder, which lasted for an hour, with such continued lightnings, not flashes, but flames, that all the sky and ayre was light; and that for a great while, not a minute's space between new flames all the time: such a thing as I never did see, nor could have believed had ever been in nature. And being put into a great sweat with it, could not sleep till all was over. And that accompanied with such a storm of rain as I never heard in my life. I expected to find my house in the morning overflowed; but I find not one drop of rain in my house, nor any news of hurt done.

17th. Sir W. Batten did give me three bottles of his Essence water, which I drank, and I found myself mightily cooled with them and refreshed. With Sir Thomas Crewe, who told me how Mr. Edward Montagu is for ever blown up, and not quite out with his father again; to whom he pretended that his going down was, not that he was cast out of

14 * L

the Court, but that he had leave to be absent a month; but now he finds the truth. Mr. Pierce tells me, the King do still sup every night with my Lady Castlemaine.

18th. Dined alone at home, my wife going to-day to dine with Mrs. Pierce, and thence with her and Mrs. Clerke to see a new play, "The Court Secret."[1] My wife says, the play is the worst that ever she saw in her life.

19th. To Sir W. Pen's, to see his lady[2] the first time, who is a well looked, fat, short, old Dutchwoman, but one that hath been heretofore pretty handsome, and is now very discreet, and I believe hath more wit than her husband. Here we staid talking a good while, and very well pleased I was with the old woman. The news of the Emperour's victory over the Turkes is by some doubted, but by most confessed to be very small, though great, of what was talked, which was 80,000 men to be killed and taken of the Turke's side.

20th. I walked to Cheapside, to see the effect of a fire there this morning, since four o'clock; which I find in the house of Mr. Bois, that married Dr. Fuller's niece, who are both out of town, leaving only a maid and man in town. It begun in their house, and hath burned much any many houses backward, though none forward; and that in the great uniform pile of buildings in the middle of Cheapside. I am very sorry for them, for the Doctor's sake. Thence to the 'Change, and so home to dinner. And thence to Sir W. Batten's, whither Sir Richard Ford come, the Sheriffe, who hath been at this fire all the while; and he tells me, upon my question, that he and the Mayor were there, as it is their duty to be, not only to keep the peace, but they have power of commanding the pulling down of any house or houses, to defend the City. By and by comes in the Common Cryer of the City to speak with him; and when he was gone, says he, "You may see by this man the constitution of the Magistracy of this City; that this fellow's place, I dare give him, if he

---

[1] A tragi-comedy, by James Shirley "written when the stage was interdicted," and first performed after the Restoration. Before the publication of this notice in Pepys, Langbaine's statement was the only evidence that it had ever been acted.

[2] Margaret, daughter of John Jaspar, a merchant at Rotterdam.

will be true to me. 1000*l.* for his profits every year, and
expect to get 500*l.* more to myself thereby, when," says he.
" I in myself am forced to spend many times as much."

21st. (Lord's day.) Mr. Coventry told us the Duke was
gone ill of a fit of an ague to bed: so we sent this morning
to see how we do.

23d. Talking with my wife, and angry about her desiring
to have a French maid all of a sudden, which I took to arise
from yesterday's being with her mother. But that went over,
and so she be well qualitied, I care not much whether she be
French or no. so a Protestant. I went into New Bridewell, in
my way to Mr. Cole, and there I saw the new model, and it
is very handsome: several at work—among others, one pretty
strumpet brought in last night, which works very lazily. I
did give them 6*d.* to drink. The Dutch East India Fleet are
now come home safe, which we are sorry for. Our Fleets on
both sides are hastening out to Guinny.

24th. To the Wardrobe, and there saw one suit of clothes
made for my boy, and linen set out.

25th. Jacke Noble come to me, to tell me that he had
Cave in prison, and that he would give me and my father
good security, that neither we nor any of our family should
be troubled with the child; for he could prove that he was
fully satisfied for him; and that, if the worst come to the
worst, the parish must keep it: that Cave did bring the child
to his house, but they got it carried back again, and that
thereupon he put him in prison. When he saw that I would
not pay him the money, nor made anything of being secured
against the child. he then said that then he must go to law,
not himself, but come in as a witness for Cave against us. I
could have told him that he could bear witness that Cave is
satisfied, or else there is no money due to himself; but I let
alone any such discourse, only getting as much out of him as
I could. I perceive he is a rogue, and hath inquired into
everything, and consulted with Dr. Pepys.

26th. By water to Deptford Docke Yard, and there saw the
new ship in very great forwardness. To White Hall. There
I could not get into the Park, and so was fain to stay in the

gallery over the gate to look to the passage into the Park, into which the King hath forbid of late anybody's coming. To see some pictures at one Huysman's, a picture-drawer, a Dutchman, which is said to exceed Lilly; and indeed there is both of the Queens and Maids of Honour, particularly Mrs. Stewart's,[1] in a buff doublet like a soldier, as good pictures, I think, as ever I saw. The Queen is drawn in one like a sheperdess, in the other like St. Catherine, most like and most admirably. I was mightily pleased with this sight indeed. Mr. Pen, Sir William's son, is come back from France, and come to visit my wife; a most modish person, grown, she says, a fine gentleman.[2]

27th. To Cutler's house, and there had a very good dinner; and had two or three pretty young ladies of their relations there. Home, and there find my boy, Tom Edwards, come, sent me by Captain Cooke, having been bred in the King's Chapel these four years. I propose to make a clerk of him; and, if he deserves well, to do well by him. Find him a very schoole-boy, that talks innocently and impertinently. All the news this day is, that the Dutch are, with twenty-two sail of ships of war, cruising up and down about Ostend; at which we are alarmed. My Lord Sandwich is come back into the Downes, with only eight sail, which is, or may be, a prey to the Dutch, if they knew our weakness and inability to set out any more speedily.

29th. Mr. Hughes come to speak with me, and told me that, as he come this morning from Deptford, he left the King's yard a-fire. So I presently took a boat, and down, and there found, by God's providence, the fire out; but, if there had been any wind, it must have burned all our stores, which is a most dreadfull consideration. Home, and Creed and I met at my Lady Sandwich's, and there dined; but my Lady is become as handsome, I think, as ever she was; and so good and discreet a woman I know not in the world. I must remember that, never since I was a housekeeper, I ever lived so quietly without any noise, or one angry word almost, as I have done since my present maids Besse, Jane,

[1] Still in the Royal Collection.   [2] He became the celebrated Quaker.

and Susan come, and were together. Now I have taken a boy, and am taking a woman, I pray God we may not be worse!

30th. Comes Mr. Pen to visit me. I perceive something of learning he hath got, but a great deal, if not too much, of the vanity of the French garb, and affected manner of speech and gait. I fear all real profit he hath made of his travel will signify little.

31st. Casting up my monthly accounts, and, blessed be God! find myself worth 1020*l.* Prince Rupert, I hear this day, is to go to command this fleet going to Guinny against the Dutch. I doubt few will be pleased with his going, being accounted an unhappy[1] man. Pretty well in health, since I left off wearing of a gowne within doors all day, and then go back with my legs into the cold, which brought me daily pain.

September 1st. To the 'Change, and thence brought Mr. Pierce, the Surgeon, and Creed, and dined very merry and handsomely; but my wife not being well, she not with us; and we cut up the great cake Moorcocke lately sent us, which is very good.

2d. To Bartholomew fayre, and our boy with us, and there showed them and myself the dancing on the ropes, and several other the best shows; but pretty it is, to see how our boy carries himself so innocently clownish as would make one laugh. Then up and down, to buy combes for my wife to give her maids.

3d. I have had a bad night's rest to-night, not sleeping well, as my wife observed; and I thought myself to be mightily bit with fleas, and in the morning she chid her maids for not looking the fleas a' days. But, when I rose, I found that it is only the change of the weather from hot to cold, which, as I was two winters ago, do stop my pores, and so my blood tingles and itches all day, all over my body.

4th. (Lord's day.) All the morning looking over my old wardrobe, and laying by things for my brother John and my father, by which I shall leave myself very bare in clothes, but yet as much as I need, and the rest could but spoil in the keeping. Mr. Hill come to tell me, that he had got a gentle-

---

i. e. unlucky, or unfortunate, infelix, now obsolete in this sense woman for my wife — one Mrs. Ferrabosco, that sings most admirably. I seemed glad of it; but I hear she is too gallant for me, and I am not sorry that I misse her.

5th. With the Duke; where all our discourse of war in the highest measure. Prince Rupert was with us; who is fitting himself to go to sea in the Heneretta. And afterwards I met him and Mr. Gray, and says he, "I can answer but for one ship, and in that I will do my part; for it is not in that as in an army, where a man can command every thing." Come W. Bowyer, and dined with us; but strange to see how he could not endure onyons in sauce to lamb, but was overcome with the sight of it, and so was forced to make his dinner of an egg or two. To Woolwich, with a gally, all the way reading Sir J. Suckling's "Aglaura," which, methinks, is but a mean play: nothing of design in it.

6th. Called upon Doll, our pretty 'Change woman, for a pair of gloves trimmed with yellow ribbon, to [match] the petticoat my wife bought yesterday, which cost me 20s.; but she is so pretty, that, God forgive me! I could not think it too much, which is a strange slavery that I stand in to beauty, that I value nothing near it. This day Mr. Coventry did tell us how the Duke did receive the Dutch Embassador the other day; by telling him that, whereas they think us in jest, he believes that the Prince Rupert, which goes in this fleet to Guinny, will soon tell them that we are in earnest, and that he himself will do the like here, in the head of the fleet here at home; and that he did not doubt to live to see the Dutch as fearfull of provoking the English, under the government of a King, as he remembers them to have been under that of a Coquin.

7th. With Creed walked to Bartholomew fayre—this being the last day, and there I saw the best dancing on the ropes that I think I ever saw in my life.

8th. All haste made in setting out this Guinny fleet, but yet not such as will ever do the King's business, if we come to a war. My wife this afternoon being very well dressed by her new woman, Mary Mercer, a decayed merchant's daughter that our Will helps us to, did go to the christening of Mrs. Mills the parson's wife's child, where she never was before.

9th. Up, and put things in order against dinner. I out and bought some things; among others, a dozen of silver salts; and at noon comes my company, namely, Anthony and Will Joyce and their wives; my aunt James, newly come out of Wales, and my cozen Sarah Gyles.[1] Her husband did not come; and by her I did understand, afterwards, that it was because he was not able to pay me the 40s. she had borrowed a year ago of me. I was as merry as I could, giving them a good dinner; but W. Joyce did so talk, that he made everybody else dumb, but only laugh at him. I forgot there was Mr. Harman and his wife, my aunt, a very good harmless woman. All their talk is of her and my two she-cozen Joyces, and Will's little boy Will, who was also here to-day. They eyed mightily my great cupboard of plate— I this day putting my two flaggons upon my table; and indeed it is a fine sight, and better than ever I did hope to see of my own. Mercer dined with us at table, this being her first dinner in my house. After dinner, my wife and Mercer, and Tom and I, sat till eleven at night, singing and fiddling, and a great joy it is to see me master of so much pleasure in my house. The girle plays pretty well upon the harpsichon, but only ordinary tunes, but hath a good hand; sings a little, but hath a good voyce and eare. My boy, a brave boy, sings finely, and is the most pleasant boy at present, while his ignorant boy's tricks last, that ever I saw.

10th. All the morning much troubled to think what the end of our great sluggishness will be; for we do nothing in this office like people able to carry on a war. We must be put out, or other people put in. My wife and I, and Mercer, to the Duke's house, and there saw " The Rivall's,"[2] which is no excellent play, but good acting in it; especially Gosnell comes and sings and dances finely; but, for all that, fell out of the key, so that the musique could not play to her

---

[1] Pepys would have been more proud of his cousin had he anticipated her husband's becoming a Knight, for she was probably the same person whose burial is recorded in the register of St. Helen's, Bishopgate, September 4, 1704— " Dame Sarah Gyles, widow, relict of Sir John Gyles."

[2] A comedy; an alteration of " The Two Noble Kinsmen," &c., but ascribed to Davenant by Downes, p. 23, and by Langbaine, p. 547. Harris played Theocles. Gosnell is not mentioned in the cast by Downes.

afterwards; and so did Harris also go out of the time to agree with her. This night I received, by Will, 105*l.*, the first fruits of my endeavours in the late contract for victualling of Tangier, for which God be praised! for I can, with a safe conscience, say that I have therein saved the King 5,000*l.* per annum, and yet got myself a hope of 300*l.* per annum, without the least wrong to the King.

11th. (Lord's day.) Up, and to church in the best manner I have gone a good while—that is to say, with my wife, and her woman, Mercer, along with us, and Tom, my boy, waiting on us. A dull sermon. With Mr. Blagrave, walking in the Abbey, he telling me the whole government and discipline of White Hall Chapel, and the caution now used against admitting any debauched persons. This afternoon, it seems, Sir J. Minnes fell sick at church, and, going down the gallery stairs, fell down dead,[1] but come to himself again, and is pretty well.

12th. Up, and to my cozen Anthony Joyce's, and there took leave of my Aunt James, and both cozens, their wives, who are this day going down to my father's by coach. I did give my aunt 20*s.*, to carry as a token to my mother, and 10*s.* to Pall.[2] With the Duke; and saw him with great pleasure play with his little girle,[3] like an ordinary private father of a child. To Mr. Creed's lodgings, talking mightily of the convenience and necessity of a man's wearing good clothes, after eating a mess of creame.

13th. To Fishmongers' Hall, where we met the first time upon the Fishery Committee, and many good things discoursed of, concerning making of farthings, which was proposed as a way of raising money for this business, and then that of lotterys, but with great confusion; but I hope we shall fall into greater order.

15th. After dinner, many people come in, and kept me all the afternoon: among other, the Master and Wardens of Chyrurgeons' Hall, who staid arguing their cause with me.

16th. Mr. Gauden coming to me, I had a good opportunity to speak to him about his present, which hitherto hath been a burden to me, because I was doubtfull that he meant it as a

[1] Hibernice, *kilt.*   [2] His sister Paulina.   [3] Afterwards Queen Mary.

temptation to me, to stand by him in the business of Tangier
victualling; but he clears me it was not, and that what he
did was for my old kindnesses to him, and dispatching of his
business. Met Sir W. Warren, and afterwards to the Sun
taverne, where he brought to me, being all alone, a 100l. in
a bag, which I offered him to give him my receipt for, but he
told me no, it was my owne, which he had a little while since
promised me; and so most kindly he did give it me, and I
as joyfully, even out of myself, carried it home in a coach —
he himself expressly taking care that nobody might see this
business done, though I was willing enough to have carried a
servant with me to have received it, but he advised me to do
it myself. Met Mr. Partiger, and he would needs have me
drink a cup of horse-radish ale, which he and a friend of his,
troubled with the stone, have been drinking of, which we did,
and then walked into the fields as far almost as Sir G.
Whitmore's,[1] all the way talking of Russia, which, he says, is
a sad place; and, though Moscow is a very great city, yet it
is from the distance between house and house, and few people
compared with this, and poor, sorry houses, the Emperor
himself living in a wooden house; his exercise only flying a
hawke at pigeons, and carrying pigeons ten or twelve miles
off, and then laying wagers which pigeon shall come soonest
home to her house. All the winter within doors, some few
playing at chesse, but most drinking their time away.
Women live very slavishly there, and, it seems, in the
Emperor's court, no room hath above two or three windows,
and those the greatest not a yard wide or high, for warmth in
winter time, and that the general cure for all diseases there is
their sweating-houses; or, people that are poor, they get into
their ovens, being heated, and there lie. Little learning
among them of any sort. Not a man that speaks Latin,
unless the Secretary of State by chance. Old Hardwicke

---

[1] Baulmes, at Hoxton, situate in the parish of Hackney, near the Islington
boundary, belonged to Sir George Whitmore, of Barnes, in Surrey, who was Lord
Mayor in 1631, and a great sufferer for the Royal Cause. His daughter Anne,
mentioned by Pepys, Feb, 12, 1663–4, *ante*, married Sir John Robinson, Lieutenant of the Tower. Baulmes is described as an old square mansion, with two
stories in the roof: it was afterwards converted into a madhouse, and demolished
in the year 1852.

come, and redeemed a watch he had left with me in pawn for 40s. seven years ago, and I let him have it.

18th. (Lord's day.) Last night, my aunt Wight did send my wife a new scarfe, laced, as a token for her many givings to her: but my aime is to get myself something more from my uncle's favour than this.

19th. My wife having put on to-day, her winter new suit of moyre, which is handsome, after dinner I did give her 15l., to lay out in linen and necessaries for the house, and to buy a suit for Pall. Dr. Pierce tells me, when I was wondering that Fraizer[1] should order things with the Prince in that confident manner, that Fraizer is so great with my Lady Castlemaine, and Stewart, and all the ladies at Court, in helping to slip their calfes when there is occasion, and with the great men in curing of them, that he can do what he please with the King, in spite of any man, and upon the same score with the Prince; they all having more or less occasion to make use of him. Colonel Reames[2] did this day tell me how it is clear that, if my Lord Teviott had lived, he would have quite undone Tangier, or designed himself to be master of it. He did put the King upon most great, chargeable, and unnecessary works there: and took the course industriously to deter all other merchants but himself to deal there, and to make both King and all others to pay what he pleased for all that was brought thither.

20th. Met Captain Poyntz, who hath some place, or title to a place, belonging to gameing. I discoursed with him about our business of improving of the Lotterys, for the King's benefit, and that of the Fishery, and had some light from him in the business. I find, with great delight, that I am come to my good temper of business again. God continue me in it!

21st. To Huysman's,[3] the great picture-drawer, and saw

[1] Sir William Fraizer, one of the King's Physicians. Sir John Denham refers to him very unceremoniously in "A Dialogue between Sir John Pooley and Mr. Thomas Killigrew."

[2] Bullen Reymes, M.P. for Melcombe Regis, in 1664, was appointed one of the Commissioners for sick and wounded prisoners of war. — Evelyn's *Diary*, Oct 27, 1664.

[3] James Huysman, a native of Antwerp, who settled in London, and attained considerable eminence as a painter. His portraits are still highly valued. He died in 1696.

again very fine pictures, and have his promise, for Mr. Povy's sake, to take pains in what picture I shall set him about, and I think to have my wife's. To Povy's, to dinner, where great and good company; among others, Sir John Skeffington,[1] whom I knew at Magdalene College, a fellow-commoner, my fellow-pupil, but one with whom I had no great acquaintance, he being then, God knows! much above me.

22d. My wife not well, and she tells me she thinks she is with child, but I neither believe nor desire it. But God's will be done! Home to bed; having got a strange cold in my head, by flinging off my hat[2] at a dinner, and sitting with the wind in my neck.

23d. Comes Mr. Fuller, that was the wit of Cambridge, and Prevaricator[3] in my time, and staid all the morning with me, discoursing, and his business to get a man discharged, which I did do for him. To the office, where Sir G. Carteret, and we met about an order of the Council for the hiring him a house, giving him 1000l. fine, and 70l. per annum for it. Here Sir J. Minnes took occasion, in the most childish and most unbecoming manner, to reproach us all, but most himself, that he was not valued as Comptroller among us, nor did anything but only set his hand to paper, which is but too true, and everybody had a palace, and he no house to lie in, and wished he had but as much to build him a house with, as we have laid out in carved work. It was to no end to oppose, but all bore it, and, after, laughed at him for it.

---

[1] Described in the Magdalene College Register-book as John Skeffington, son of Sir Richard Skeffington, Knt., of Coventry, admitted as a Pensioner, Sept. 19, 1649, and in April, 1651, made a Fellow-Commoner. Sir John Skeffington married Mary, only daughter and heir of Sir John Clotworthy, who was, in 1660, created Viscount Massareene, of Ireland, with remainder to his son-in-law, Sir John Skeffington, who succeeded as second Viscount in 1665, and died in 1695.

[2] In Lord Clarendon's Essay "On the Decay of Respect paid to Age," he says, that in his younger days he never kept his hat on before those older than himself, except at dinner.

[3] In Dean Peacock's work on the Statutes of the University of Cambridge, Appendix A., p. xxvi., there is an interesting account of the Varier or Prevaricator, who was appointed at the commencement of the year preceding, and made an oration, in which he was authorized by custom, like the Tripos at the lesser Comitia, to use considerable freedom of language, a privilege the abuse of which led by degrees to the abolition of the office. The functionary was named from varying the question, which he proposed either by a play on the words, or by the transposition of the terms in which it was expressed.

24th. Comes one Philips, who is concerned in the Lottery, and from whom I collected much concerning that business. He told me that Monsieur du Puy, that is so great a man at the Duke of York's, and this man's great opponent, is a knave, and by quality but a tailor. We were told to-day of a Dutch ship of 3 or 400 tons, where all the men were dead of the plague, and the ship cast ashore at Gottenburgh.

25th. (Lord's day.) My throat being yet very sore, and my head out of order, went not to church, but spent all the morning reading of "The Madd Lovers,"[1] a very good play. Read another play, "The Custome of the Country,"[1] which is a very poor one, methinks.

26th. I have looked a little too much after Tangier and the Fishery, and that in the sight of Mr. Coventry; but I have good reason to love myself for serving Tangier, for it is one of the best flowers in my garden.

28th. My Lord Rutherford would needs carry me and another Scotch Lord to a play, and so we saw, coming late, part of "The Generall;"[2] my Lord Orrery, Broghill's, second play; but, Lord! to see how no more either in words, sense, or design, it is to his "Harry the 5th," is not imaginable, and so poorly acted, though in finer clothes, is strange. My mind at a great loss how to go down to Brampton this week, to satisfy Pigott; but, what with the fears of my house, my money, my wife, and my office, I know not how in the world to think of it; Tom Hater being out of town, and I having near 1000*l.* in my house.

29th. After dinner, to Sir G. Carteret, and with him to his new house he is taking in Broad Street, and there surveyed all the rooms and bounds, in order to the drawing up a lease thereof; and that done, Mr. Cutler, his landlord, took me up and down, and shewed me all his ground and house, which is extraordinary great, he having bought all the Augustine Fryers, and many, many a 1000*l.* he hath, and will bury there. Fresh newes comes of our beating the Dutch at

---

[1] Both these plays were by Beaumont and Fletcher.

[2] Shirley has a Prologue "To a play in Ireland called The Generall," which, Mr. Dyce observes, "was probably never printed. A tragi-comedy under this title was in the library of Dr. Farmer, and afterwards in that of Mr. Reed."—Shirley's *Works*, vi., 495.

Guinny quite out of all their castles almost, which will make them quite mad here at home sure. And Sir G. Carteret did tell me, that the King do joy mightily at it; but asked him, laughing, "But," says he, "how shall I do to answer this to the Embassador, when he comes?" Nay, they say that we have beat them out of the New Netherlands,[1] too; so that we have been doing them mischief for a great while in several parts of the world, without publick knowledge or reason. Their fleete for Guinny is now, they say, ready, and abroad, and will be going this week.

30th. At my accounts, it being a great month, both for profit and layings out—the last being 89*l.* for kitchen, and clothes for myself and wife, and a few extraordinaries for the house; and my profits, besides salary, 239*l.*; so that I have this week, not-withstanding great layings out, and preparations for laying out, which I make as paid this month, my balance to come to 1203*l.*

October 1st. We go now on with vigour in preparing against the Dutch; who, they say, will now fall upon us without doubt upon this high news come of our beating them so wholly in Guinny.[3]

2d. (Lord's day.) Walked with my boy through the city, putting in at several churches, among others at Bishopsgate, and there saw the picture[1] usually put before the King's book,

---

[1] Captain (afterwards Sir Robert) Holmes' expedition to attack the Dutch settlements in Africa eventuated in an important exploit. Holmes suddenly left the coast of Africa, sailed across the Atlantic, and reduced the Dutch settlement of *New Netherlands* to English rule. under the title of NEW YORK.—"The short and true state of the matter is this: the country mentioned was part of the province of Virginia; and, as there is no settling an extensive country at once, a few Swedes crept in there, who surrendered the plantations they could not defend to the Dutch, who having bought the charts and papers of one Hudson, a seaman, who, by commission from the crown of England, discovered a river, to which he gave his name, conceited they had purchased a province. Sometimes, when we had strength in those parts, they were English subjects: at others, when that strength declined, they were subjects of the United Provinces. However, upon King Charles's claim the States disowned the title, but resumed it during our confusions. On March 12th, 1663–4, Charles II. granted it to the Duke of York. . . . . The King sent Holmes, when he returned, to the Tower, and did not discharge him, till he made it evidently appear that he had not infringed the law of nations."—Campbell's *Naval Hist.*, ii., 89. How little did the King or Holmes himself foresee the effects of the capture!

[2] ce *Poems on State Affairs*, vol. i., p. 32.

[3] Of Charles I.; still to be seen in several churches, and engraved before the Eikon Basilike.—See *Notes and Queries*, vol. i., p. 137.

put up in the church, but very ill painted, though it were a
pretty piece to set up in a church. I intended to have seen
the Quakers, who, they say, do meet every Lord's day at the
Mouth, at Bishopsgate; but I could see none stirring, nor was
it fit to ask for the place; so I walked over Moorefields, and
thence to Clerkenwell Church, and there, as I wished, sat next
pew to the fair Butler, who indeed is a most perfect beauty
still; and one I do very much admire myself for my choice of
her, for a beauty, having the best lower part of her face that
ever I saw all days of my life. After church, I walked to my
Lady Sandwich's, through my Lord Southampton's new buildings in the fields behind Gray's Inn;[1] and, indeed, they are a
very great and a noble work. My Lady asked me my opinion
about Creed, whether he would have a wife or no, and proposed Mrs. Wright for him, which, she says, she heard he was
once inquiring after. She desired I would take a good time
and manner of proposing it, and I said I would, though I believed he would love nothing but money, and much was not to
be expected there, she said. So away back to Clerkenwell
Church, and so we walked all over the fields home, and there
my wife was angry with me for not coming home, and for
gadding abroad to look after beauties.

3d. With Sir J. Minnes, by coach, to St. James's; and
there all the news now of very hot preparations for the Dutch:
and, being with the Duke, he told us he was resolved to take
a tripp himself, and that Sir W. Pen should go in the same
ship with him. Which honour, God forgive me! I could
grudge him, for his knavery and dissimulation, though I do not
envy much the having the same place myself. Talk also of
great haste in the getting out another fleet, and building some
ships; and now it is likely we have put one another's dalliance
past a retreate.

4th. This morning Sir W. Pen went to Chatham to look
after the ships now going out thence, and particularly that
wherein the Duke and himself go. He took Sir G. Ascue
with him, whom, I believe, he hath brought into play. After
dinner, to a play, to see "The Generall;" which is so dull and
so ill acted, that I think it is the worst I ever saw or heard in

---

[1] Gray's Inn Square.

all my days. I happened to sit near to Sir Charles Sedley; who I find a very witty man, and he did at every line take notice of the dullness of the poet and badness of the action, and that most pertinently; which I was mightily taken with.

5th. To New Bridewell, and there I did with great pleasure see the many pretty works, and the little children employed, every one, to do something, which was a very fine sight, and worthy encouragement. Fell in discourse with the Secretary of the Virtuosi[1] of Gresham College. He tells me of a new-invented instrument to be tried before the College anon, and I intend to see it. So to Trinity House, and there I dined among the old dull fellows. Comes Mr. Cocker to see me, and I discoursed with him about his writing and ability of sight, and how I shall do to get some glass or other to help my eyes by candlelight; and he tells me he will bring me the helps he hath, within a day or two, and show me what he do. To the Musique-meeting at the Post-office, where I was once before. And thither anon come all the Gresham College, and a great deal of noble company: and the new instrument was brought called the Arched Viall, where, being tuned with lute-strings, and played on with keys like an organ, a piece of parchment is always kept moving; and the strings, which, by the keys, are pressed down upon it, are grated in imitation of a bow, by the parchment; and so it is intended to resemble several vialls played on with one bow, but so basely and so harshly, that it will never do. But, after three hours' stay, it could not be fixed in tune; and so they were fain to go to some other musique of instruments. This morning, by three o'clock, the Prince,[2] and King, and Duke, with him, went down the River, and the Prince under sail the next tide after, and so is gone from the Hope. God give him better success than he used to have!

7th. Come Mr. Cocker, and brought me a globe of glasse and a frame of oyled paper, as I desired, to show me the manner of his gaining light to grave by, and to lessen the glaringness of it at pleasure by an oyled paper. This I bought of him, giving him a crowne for it; and so, well satis-fied, he went away.

---

[1] Henry Oldenborough.   [2] Rupert.

9th. (Lord's day.) Mr. Fuller, my Cambridge acquaint
ance coming, he told me he was to preach at Barking Church,[1]
and so I to hear him, and he preached well and neatly.   To
bed without prayers, it being cold, and to-morrow washing-day.

10th. Sir W. Pen do grow every day more and more regarded
by the Duke, because of his service heretofore in the Dutch
war, which I am confident is by some strong obligations he
hath laid upon Mr. Coventry ; for Mr. Coventry must needs
know that he is a man of very mean parts, but only a bred
seaman.   Sat up till past twelve at night, to look over the
account of the collections for the Fishery, and to the loose
and base manner that monies so collected are disposed of in,
would make a man never part with a penny in that manner ;
and, above all, the inconvenience of having a great man,
though never so seeming pious as my Lord Pembroke[2] is.
He is too great to be called to an account, and is abused by
his servants, and yet obliged to defend them for his own sake.
This day, by the blessing of God, my wife and I have been
married nine years ; but my head being full of business, I did
not think of it to keep it in any extraordinary manner.   But
bless God for our long lives, and loves, and health together,
which the same God long continue, I wish from my very heart !

11th. Luellin tells me what an obscene, loose play this
" Parson's Wedding "[3] is, that is acted by nothing but women
at the King's house.   To the Fishery in Thames Street, and
there several good discourses about the letting of the Lotterys, and, among others, one Sir Thomas Clifford, whom yet
I knew not, do speak very well and neatly.   My wife tells
me the sad news of my Lady Castlemaine's being now become
so decayed that one would not know her ; at least far from a
beauty, which I am sorry for.   This day, with great joy,
Captain Titus told us the particulars of the French's expedition against Gigery upon the Barbary Coast. in the Streights,
with 6000 chosen men.[4]   They have taken the Fort of Gigery,

[1] Allhallows.

[2] Philip Herbert, fifth Earl. Ob. 1669.

[3] A comedy, by Thomas Killigrew.

[4] Colbert, in his desire to establish French colonies, wished to found one on
the Mediterranean coast of Africa.   For this purpose the Duc de Beaufort,
High Admiral of France, took possession, on the 22d July, 1664, of Gigeri, in

wherein were five men and three guns, which makes the whole story of the King of France's policy and power to be laughed at.

12th. For news, all say De Ruyter is gone to Guinny before us. Sir J. Lawson is come to Portsmouth, and our fleet is hastening all speed; I mean, this new fleet. Prince Rupert with his is got into the Downes.

13th. Taking leave of my wife, I by coach to the Red Lyon in Aldersgate Street, and there, by agreement, met W. Joyce and Tom Trice, and mounted — I upon a very fine mare that Sir W. Warren helps me to — and so very merrily rode till it was very dark, I leading the way through the dark to Welling, and there to supper and to bed: but very bad accommodation at the Swan. In my way to Brampton, in this day's journey, I met with Mr. White, Cromwell's chaplain that was, and had a great deal of discourse with him. Among others, he tells me that Richard is, and hath long been, in France, and is now going into Italy. He owns publickly that he do correspond with him, and return him all his money. That Richard hath been in some straits in the beginning; but relieved by his friends. That he goes by another name, but do not disguse himself, nor deny himself to any man that challenges him. He tells me, for certain, that offers had been made to the old man[1] of marriage between the King and his daughter to have obliged him, but he would not. He thinks, with me, that it never was in his power to bring in the King with the consent of any of his officers about him; and that he scorned to bring him in as Monk did, to secure himself and deliver every body else. When I told him of what I found writ in a French book of one Monsieur Sorbière,[2] that gives an account of his observations here in

the province of Bugia, and be placed a garrison there under the command of Lieut.-General Guadagni. The Duke had scarcely retired before the Moors attacked the place in great force and with such success, that Guadagni thought himself happy in evacuating it with safety. He embarked on the night of the 29th Oct., abandoning his artillery and stores. The regiment of Picardy perished by shipwreck.

[1] Oliver Cromwell.

[2] Samuel Sorbière, who, after studying divinity and medicine at Paris, travelled in different parts of Europe, and published his voyage into England, described by Voltaire as a dull, scurrilous satire upon a nation of which the author knew

England; among other things, he says, that it is reported
that Cromwell did, in his life-time, transpose many of the
bodies of the kings of England from one grave to another,
and that, by that means, it is not known certainly whether
the head that is now set up upon a post be that of Cromwell,
or of one of the kings; Mr. White tells me that he believes
he never had so poor a low thought in him to trouble himself
about it.   He says the hand of God is much to be seen;
that all his children are in good condition enough as to estate,
and that their relations that betrayed their family are all now
either hanged or very miserable.

14th. Up by break of day, and got to Brampton by three
o'clock, where my father and mother overjoyed to see me,
my mother ready to weep every time she looked upon me.
To the [Manorial] Court, and there did all our business to
my mind.   So home, and after supper I to bed.

15th. My father and I up, and walked alone to Hinchingbroke; and among the late chargeable works that my Lord
hath done there, we saw his water-works, which are very fine;
and so is the house all over, but I am sorry to think of the
money at this time spent therein.   Taking leave, W. Joyce
and I set out, calling T. Trice at Bugden, and got by night
to Stevenage, and there mighty merry, though I in bed, more
weary than the other two days, which I think, proceeded from
our galloping so much; but I find that a coney skin in my
breeches preserves me perfectly from galling.

16th. (Lord's day.) It raining, we set out betimes, and
about nine o'clock got to Hatfield in church-time, and I
'light, and saw my simple Lord Salisbury[1] sit there in the
gallery.   To Barnett, and there dined at the Red Lyon;[2]
thence home by four o'clock, weary, but very well.

nothing. Ob. 1670. It is not clear whether he invented or only repeated the story
here related, which has been disposed of by the discovery of Charles the First's
coffin in 1813; and, indeed, how any doubt upon this subject could have arisen,
seems extraordinary, considering that several persons were present at the inter
ment; and that we have Sir T. Herbert's testimony as to the fact in his published
Memoirs. See also Diary, 26th February, 1665-6, when Pepys was shown the
place where the late king was buried in St. George's chapel, and Fuller's Church
History, book xi., p. 327.

[1] See his character in Clarendon: he was at this time seventy-four years of age
[2] Still existing

18th. We made a very great contract with Sir W. Warren for 3000 load of timber. In the afternoon to the Fishery, where, very confused and very ridiculous, my Lord Craven's proceedings, especially his finding fault with Sir J. Collaton[1] and Colonel Griffin's[2] report in the accounts of the lottery-men. Thence I with Mr. Gray in his coach to White Hall; but the King and Duke being abroad, we returned to Somerset House. I find him a very worthy and studious gentleman in the business of trade. He says that it is concluded, among merchants, that, where a trade hath once been and do decay, it never recovers again; and, therefore, that the manufacture of cloth of England will never come to esteem again: that, among other faults, Sir Richard Ford cannot keep a secret: that Sir Ellis Layton is, for a speech of forty words, the wittiest man that ever he knew in his life, but longer he is nothing. At Somerset House I saw the Queen Dowager's new rooms, which are most stately and nobly furnished; and there I saw her and the Duke of York and Duchess. The Duke espied me, and come to me, and talked with me a very great while.

19th. Weighed my two silver flaggons at Steven's. They weigh 212 oz., 27 dwt., which is about 50*l.*, at 5*s.* per oz.; and then they judge the fashion to be worth about 5*s.* per oz. more; nay, some say 10*s.* an ounce the fashion. Sorry to see that the fashion is worth so much, and the silver come to no more.

20th. Took two silver tumblers home, which I have bought.

21st. To Sir W. Turner's, and there bought my cloth,

[1] Sir John Collaton, or Colladon, of St. Martin-in-the-Fields, Physician in ordinary to the King, was knighted at Somerset House, 8th of August, 1664.

[2] Edward Griffin, of Braybrooke, in Northamptonshire, at this time Lieut.-Colonel in the Duke of York's Regiment of Foot-Guards, now called the Coldstream; he was raised to the peerage in 1688, by the title of Lord Griffin, and followed the fortunes of his Royal Master after the Revolution, and was outlawed, Being taken prisoner in the attempted invasion of Scotland in 1708, he was committed to the Tower, and died there, in confinement, in November, 1710. He married Lady Essex Howard, eldest daughter, and one of the two co-heirs of James Howard, third Earl of Suffolk. Their grandson, Edward, third Lord Griffin, dying s. p. m., in 1742, the barony became extinct.

coloured, for a suit and cloak, to line with plush. I find
that I must go handsomely, whatever it costs me, and the
charge will be made up in the fruits it brings. Comes Mr.
Martin, to trouble me again to get him a Lieutenant's place,
for which he is as fit as a fool can be. But I put him off like
an asse, as he is.

23d. (Lord's day.) To church. At noon comes unex-
pected Mr. Fuller, and dines with me. At night to the office,
doing business, and then home to supper. Then a psalm, to
prayers, and to bed.

24th. Into the galleries at White Hall, to talk with my
Lord Sandwich; among other things, about the Prince's
writing up to tell us of the danger he and his fleet lie in at
Portsmouth, of receiving affronts from the Dutch; which, my
Lord said, he would never have done, had he lain there with
one ship alone; nor is there any great reason for it, because
of the sands. However, the fleet will be ordered to go and
lay themselves up at the Cowes. Much beneath the prowesse
of the Prince, I think, and the honour of the nation, at the
first to be found to secure themselves. My Lord is well
pleased to think that, if the Duke and the Prince go, all the
blame of any miscarriage will not light on him; and that, if
any thing goes well, he hopes he shall have the share of the
glory, for the Prince is by no means well esteemed of by any
body. This day the great O'Neale[1] died; I believe, to the
content of all the Protestant pretenders in Ireland.

25th. Taking care of a piece of plate for Mr. Commissioner
Pett, against the launching of his new great ship to-morrow
at Woolwich, which I singly did move to His Royal Highness
yesterday, and did obtain it for him, to the value of twenty
pieces. And he, under his hand, do acknowledge to me that
he did never receive so great a kindness in the world as from
me herein.

26th. My people rising mighty betimes, to fit themselves
to go by water; and my boy, he could not sleep, but wakes

<hr>

[1] Daniel O'Neale, husband of the Countess of Chesterfield. "Mr. O'Neale, of
the Bedchamber, dyed yesterday, very rich, and left his old lady all" Ed. Savage
to Dr. Sancroft, 25th Oct., 1664.—*Harl. MS.*, 3785, fol. 19.

about four o'clock, and in bed lay playing on his lute till daylight, and, it seems, did the like last night till twelve o'clock.
About eight o'clock, my wife and her woman, and Bessy and
Jane, and W. Hewer and the boy, to the water-side, and
there took boat, and by and by I out of doors, to look after
the flaggon, to get it ready to carry to Woolwich. By and
by, the flaggon being finished at the burnisher's, I home, and
there fitted myself, and took a hackney-coach I hired, it being
a very cold and foule day, to Woolwich, all the way reading
in a good book touching the fishery, and that being done, in
the book upon the statute of charitable uses, mightily to my
satisfaction. At Woolwich; I there up to the King and
Duke. Here I staid above with them while the ship was
launched,[1] which was done with great success; and the King
did very much like the ship, saying, she had the best bow
that ever he saw. But, Lord! the sorry talk and discourse
among the great courtiers round about him, without any
reverence in the world, but with so much disorder. By and
by the Queen comes and her Maids of Honour; one whereof,
Mrs. Boynton,[2] and the Duchess of Buckingham had been
very sick coming by water in the barge, the water being very
rough: but what silly sport they made with them in very
common terms, methought, was very poor, and below what
people think these great people say and do. The launching
being done, the King and company went down to take barge;
and I sent for Mr. Pett, and put the flaggon into the Duke's
hand, and he, in the presence of the King, did give it Mr.
Pett, taking it upon his knee. This Mr. Pett is wholly beholding to me for, and he do know, and I believe will acknowledge it. Going out of the gate, an ordinary woman prayed
me to give her room to London, which I did, but spoke not
to her all the way, but read as long as I could see my book

---

[1] The Royal Catharine, of 82 guns. It was observed, that just upon her
launching there appeared a fair rainbow, once the sign of a covenant betwixt God
and the world, that it should never perish by water: and we hope it will prove
as auspicious to this vessel.—*The Newes*, 27th Oct., 1664. See also Appendix,
vol. iv., for the French Ambassador's letter describing the launch.

[2] Daughter of Matthew, second son to Sir Matthew Boynton, Bart., of Barn-
ston, Yorkshire. She became the first wife of Richard Talbot, afterwards Duke
of Tyrconnel.

again. Dark when we come to London, and a stop of coaches
in Southwarke. Into the Beare, at the Bridge-foot, to Sir
W. Batten. Presently the stop is removed, and there going
out to find my coach, I could not find it: so I fain to go
through the dark and dirt over the bridge, and my leg fell in
a hole broke on the bridge, but, the constable standing there
to keep people from it, I was catched up, otherwise I had
broke my leg: for which mercy the Lord be praised! So
home, where the little girl hath looked to the house well, but
no wife come home, which made me begin to fear for her,
the water being very rough, and cold and dark. But by and
by she and her company come in all well, at which I was glad,
though angry. The City did last night very freely lend the
King 100,000l., without any security but the King's word,
which was very noble.

27th. At noon, Sir G. Carteret, Sir J. Minnes, Sir W.
Batten, Sir W. Pen, and myself, were treated at the Dolphin,
by Mr. Foly,[1] the ironmonger, where a good plain dinner, but
I expected musique, the missing of which spoiled my dinner,
only very good merry discourse at dinner.

28th. My tailor brings me home my fine, new, coloured-
cloth suit, my cloak lined with plush—as good a suit as ever
I wore in my life, and mighty neat, to my great content.

29th. Up, and it being my Lord Mayor's show,[2] my boy
and three maids went out; but, it being a very foul, rainy
day, from morning till night, I was sorry my wife let them
go out. All the talk is that De Ruyter is come over land
home with six or eight of his captains to command here at
home, and their ships kept abroad in the Streights: which
sounds as if they had a mind to do something with us.

30th. (Lord's day.) Put on my new, fine, coloured cloth
suit, with my cloak lined with plush, which is a dear and
noble suit, costing me about 17l.

---

[1] Thomas Foley, afterwards of Witley Court. He was the grandfather of the
first Lord Foley, and died on the 1st October, 1677, aged 59. His portrait is
engraved in Nash's *History of Worcestershire.*

[2] Sir John Lawrence. The King and Queen were present at the banquet—
The Intelligencer, 31st Oct. 1664.

31st. To a Committee of Tangier, when Mr. Coventry proposed the retrenching some of the charge of the horse The first word asked by the Duke of Albemarle was, " let us see who commands them," there being three troops. One of them he calls to mind was by Sir Toby Bridges.[1] Says he, " there is a very good man. If you must reform[2] two of them, be sure let him command the troop that is left." This day, I hear young Mr. Stanly, a brave young gentleman, that went out with young Jermin, with Prince Rupert, is already dead of the small-pox, at Portsmouth. All preparations against the Dutch; and the Duke of York fitting himself with all speed to go to the fleet which is hastening for him; being now resolved to go in the Charles.

November 3d. To the office, where strange to see how Sir W. Pen is flocked to by people of all sorts against his going to sea. This night, Sir W. Batten did tell me strange news, which troubles me, that my Lord Sandwich will be sent Governor to Tangier, which, in some respects, indeed, I should be glad of, for the good of the place and the safety of his person, but I think his honour will suffer, and, it may be, his interest fail by his distance.

4th. To St. James's, where I find Mr. Coventry full of business, packing up for his going to sea with the Duke. Walked with him, talking, to White Hall, where to the Duke's lodgings, who is gone thither to lodge lately. Talking about the management of our office, Mr. Coventry tells me the weight of dispatch will lie most upon me, and told me freely his mind touching Sir W. Batten and Sir J. Minnes, the latter of whom, he most aptly said, was like a lapwing, that all he did was to keep a flutter, to keep others from the nest that they would find. He told me an old story of the former about the light-houses, how just before he had certified to the Duke against the use of them, and what a burden they are to trade, and presently after, at his being at Harwich, comes to desire that he might have the setting one up there,

---

[1] Perhaps we should read Sir Thomas Bridges, made a K.B., at the Restoration.—Kennet's *Chronicle.*

[2] Reform—*i. e.*, reduce or abolish.

and gets the usefulness of it certified also by the Trinity-House. After discoursing as how the King hath resolved upon Captain [Silas] Taylor and Colonell Middleton, the first to be commissioner for Harwich, and the latter for Portsmouth, home, and Mr. Duke, our Secretary for the Fishery, dined with me.

5th. To the Duke's house, to see "Macbeth,"[1] a pretty good play, but admirably acted. Thence home; the coach being forced to go round by London Wall home, because of the bonfires; the day being mightily observed in the City.

6th. (Lord's day.) Up, and with my wife to church. Dined at home. At night, to supper with my uncle Wight, where very merry, and so home. To prayers and to bed.

7th. To White Hall, where mighty thrusting about the Duke now upon his going. We were with him long. He advised us to follow our business close, and to be directed in his absence by the Committee of the Councell for the Navy. By and by a meeting of the Fishery, where the Duke was; but I see the greatest businesses are done so superficially, that I wonder anything succeeds at all among us, that is publick. To my Lady Sandwich's, and there met my wife and dined, but I find that I dine as well myself—that is, as neatly, and my meat as good and well-dressed, as my good Lady do, in the absence of my Lord.

8th. To the office, where by and by Mr. Coventry come, and after doing a little business, took his leave of us, being to go to sea with the Duke to-morrow. At noon, I and Sir J. Minnes and Lord Barkeley, who with Sir J. Duncum[2] and Mr. Chichly are made Masters of the Ordnance, to the office of the Ordnance, to discourse about wadding for guns. Thence to dinner, all of us to the Lieutenant's of the Tower; where a good dinner, but disturbed in the middle of it by the King's coming into the Tower; and so we broke up, and to him, and went up and down the store-houses and magazines; which are, with the addition of the new great store-house, a noble sight. This day, Mr. Lever sent my wife a pair of silver candlesticks, very pretty ones. The first man

---

[1] As altered by Davenant.   [2] M.P. for Bury St. Edmunds.

that ever presented me, to whom I have not only done little service, but apparently did him the greatest disservice in his business of accounts, as Purser-Generall, of any man at the board.

9th. Called up, as I had appointed, between two and three o'clock. I and my boy Tom by water with a gally down to the Hope, it being a fine starry night. Got thither by eight o'clock, and there, as expected, found the Charles, her mainmast setting. Commissioner Pett aboard. I up and down to see the ship I was so well acquainted with, and a great work it is, the setting so great a mast. Thence the Commissioner and I on board Sir G. Ascue, in the Henry, who lacks men mightily, which makes me think that there is more believed to be in a man that hath heretofore been employed than truly there is; for one would never have thought, a month ago, that he would have wanted 1000 men at his heels. Nor do I think he hath much of a seaman in him: for he told me, says he, "Heretofore, we used to find our ships clear and ready, everything to our hands in the Downes. Now I come, and must look to see things done like a slave —things that I never minded, nor cannot look after." And by his discourse I find that he hath not minded anything in her at all. To White Hall, and there the King being in his Cabinet Council, I desiring to speak with Sir G. Carteret, I was called in, and demanded by the King himself many questions, to which I did give him full answers. There were at this Council my Lord Chancellor, Archbishop of Canterbury, Lord Treasurer, the two Secretarys, and Sir G. Carteret. Not a little contented at this chance of being made known to these persons, and called often by my name by the King. The Duke of York is this day gone away to Portsmouth.

10th. Abroad, intending to have spoke with my Lord Chancellor about the old business of his wood at Clarendon, but could not. My little girle Susan is fallen sick of the meazles, we fear, or, at least, of a scarlett fevour.

11th. To the Council-chamber at White Hall, where, looking upon some books of heraldry of Sir Edward Walker's making, which are very fine, I observed the Duke of Mon-

16 *

mouth's armes are neatly done, and his title, "The most noble
and high-born Prince, James Scott, Duke Monmouth," &c.;
nor could Sir J. Minnes, nor anybody there, tell whence
he should take the name of Scott.[1] And then I found my
Lord Sandwich, his title under his armes is, "The most noble
and mighty Lord, Edward Earl of Sandwich," &c. Sir
Edward Walker, afterwards coming in, in discourse did say
that there was none of the families of princes in Christendom
that do derive themselves so high as Julius Cæsar, nor so far,
by 1000 years, that can directly prove their rise; only some
in Germany do derive themselves from the patrician families of
Rome, but that uncertainly; and, among other things, did much
inveigh against the writing of romances, that 500 years hence
being wrote of matters in general true, as the romance of
Cleopatra, the world will not know which is true and which is
false. A gentleman told us he saw, the other day, and did
bring the draught of it to Sir Francis Pridgeon, a monster
born of an hostler's wife at Salisbury, two women children
perfectly made, joyned at the lower part of their bellies, and
every part as perfect as two bodies, and only one payre of
legs coming forth on one side from the middle where they
were joined. It was alive 24 hours, and cried, and did as all
hopefull children do; but, being showed too much to people,
was killed. To the Council at White Hall, where a great
many lords: Anglesey in the chair. But, Lord! to see what
work they will make us, and what trouble we shall have to inform men in a business they are to begin to know, when the
greatest of our hurry is, is a thing to be lamented; and I
fear the consequence will be bad to us. Put on my new
shaggy purple gown with gold buttons and loop lace.

13th. (Lord's day.) This morning to church, where mighty
sport, to hear our clerke sing out of tune, though his master
sits by him, that begins and keeps the time aloud for the
parish. With my wife within doors, and getting a speech out
of Hamlett, "to bee or not to bee," without book. In the
evening to sing psalms, and so to prayers and to bed.

---

[1] He had married Anne Scot, heiress of Buccleuch. They were created joint
Duke and Duchess. The present Duke inherits *her* Dukedom.

14th. Up, and with Sir W. Batten to White Hall, to the
Lords of the Admiralty, and there did our business betimes.
Thence to Sir Philip Warwick about Navy business: and my
Lord Ashly; and afterwards to my Lord Chancellor, who is
very well pleased with me, and my carrying of his business.[1]
And so to the 'Change, where mighty busy; and so home to
dinner, where Mr. Creed and Moore: and after dinner I to
my Lord Treasurer's, to Sir Philip Warwick there, and then
to White Hall to the Duke of Albemarle, about Tangier;
and then homeward to the Coffee-house, to hear news. And
it seems, the Dutch, as I afterwards found by Mr. Coventry's
letters, have stopped a ship of masts of Sir W. Warren's,
coming for us in a Swede's ship, which they will not release
upon Sir G. Downing's claiming her: which appears as the
first act of hostility; and is looked upon as so, by Mr.
Coventry. The Elias, coming from New England, Captain
Hill, commander, is sunk: only the captain and a few men
saved. She foundered at sea.

15th. To a Committee of Tangier, where, and everywhere
else, thank God, I find myself growing in repute; and so
home, and late, very late, at business, nobody minding it but
myself, and so home to bed, weary and full of thoughts.

16th. This day my wife went to the burial of a little boy
of W. Joyce's.

17th. This day I received from Mr. Foley, but for me to
pay for if I like it, an iron chest, having now received back
some money I had laid out for the King, and I hope to have
a good sum of money by me, thereby, in a few days—I think
above 800l. But, when I come home at night, I could not
find the way to open it; but, which is a strange thing, my
little girl Susan could carry it alone from one table clear
from the ground, and set upon another, when neither I nor
any one in my house but Jane, the cook-maid, could do it.

18th. To the Committee of the Fishery, where so poor
simple doings about the business of the Lottery, that I was
ashamed to see it, that a thing so low and base should have
anything to do with so noble an undertaking. But I had

---

[1] About the timber in Clarendon Park.

the advantage this day to hear Mr. Williamson discourse, who come to be a contractor with others for the Lotterys, and indeed I find he is a very logicall man and a good speaker. I had a letter from Mr. Coventry, who tells me that my Lord Bouncker is to be one of our Commissioners, of which I am very glad, if any more must be.

20th. (Lord's day.) Up, and with my wife to church, where Pegg Penn very fine in her new coloured silk suit laced with silver lace.

21st. This day, for certain, news is come that Teddiman hath brought in eighteen or twenty Dutchmen, merchants, their Bourdeaux fleet, and two men of war to Portsmouth. And I had letters this afternoon, that three are brought into the Downes and Dover; so that the war is begun: God give a good end to it!

22d. To my Lord Treasurer's; where with Sir Philip Warwick, studying all we could to make the last year swell as high as we could. And it is much to see how he do study for the King, to do it to get all the money from the Parliament he can: and I shall be serviceable to him therein, to help him to heads upon which to enlarge the report of the expense. He did observe to me how obedient this Parliament was for awhile, and the last Session how they begin to differ, and to carp at the King's officers; and what they will do now, he says, is to make agreement for the money, for there is no guess to be made of it. He told me he was prepared to convince the Parliament that the Subsidys are a most ridiculous tax, the four last not rising to 40,000l., and unequall. He talks of a tax of Assessment of 70,000l. for five years; the people to be secured that it shall continue no longer than there is really a war; and the charges thereof to be paid. He told me, that one year of the late Dutch war cost 1,623,000l. Thence to my Lord Chancellor's, and there staid long with Sir W. Batten and Sir J. Minnes, to speak with my lord about our Prize Office business; but, being sick and full of visitants, we could not speak with him, and so away home, where Sir Richard Ford did meet us with letters from Holland this day, that it is likely the Dutch fleet will not come out this year; they have not victuals to keep them out, and it is likely they will be frozen before they can get back.' Captain Cocke is made Steward for sick and wounded seamen.

23d. Sir G. Carteret was here this afternoon; and strange to see how we plot to make the charge of this war to appear greater than it is, because of getting money.

24th. To a coffee-house, to drink Jocolatte — very good, and so by coach to Westminster, being the first day of the Parliament's meeting. After the House had received the King's speech, and what more he had to say, delivered in writing, the Chancellor being sick, it rose.

25th. At my office all the morning, to prepare an account of the charge we have been put to extraordinary by the Dutch already; and I have brought it to appear 852,700*l.*: but God knows this is only a scare to the Parliament, to make them give the more money. Thence to the Parliament House, and there did give it to Sir Philip Warwick; the House being hot upon giving the King a supply of money. Mr. Jennings tells me the mean manner that Sir Samuel Morland lives near him, in a house that he hath bought and laid out money upon, in all to the value of 1200*l.*; but is believed to be a beggar. At Sir W. Batten's, I hear that the House have given the King 2,500,000*l.* to be paid for this war, only for the Navy, in three years' time: which is a joyful thing to all the King's party, I see; but was much opposed by Mr. Vaughan and others, that it should be so much.

27th. (Lord's day.) To church in the morning, then dined at home, and to my office, and there all the afternoon setting right my business of flaggs. In the evening come Mr. Andrews and Hill,[2] and we sung, with my boy, Ravenscroft's 4-part psalms — most admirable musick. After supper, fell into the rarest discourse with Mr. Hill about Rome and Italy; but most pleasant that ever I had in my life.

---

[1] If they made the attempt to put to sea.

[2] Thomas Hill, a merchant, whom Pepys describes, in his *Collection of Signs Manual*, as "my friend, who died at Lisbon in 1675."

28th. Certain newes of our peace made by Captain Allen with Algiers; and that the Dutch have sent part of their fleet round by Scotland; and resolve to pay off the rest half-pay, promising the rest in the Spring, hereby keeping their men. But how true this, I know not.

29th. Sir G. Carteret told us how the King inclines to our request making us Commissioners of the Prize Office.

30th. To the Committee of the Lords, and there did our business; but, Lord! what a sorry despatch these great persons give to business. My heart glad to see my accounts fall so right in this time of missing monies and confusion. Home and to bed.

December 2d. After dinner with my wife and Mercer to the Duke's house, and there saw "The Rivalls," which I had seen before; but the play not good, nor any thing but the good actings of Betterton, and his wife, and Harris. Thence homewards, and the coach broke with us in Lincoln's Inn Fields. We all to Sir J. Minnes, where good discourse of the late troubles, they knowing things, all of them, very well; and Cocke, from the King's own mouth, being then intrusted himself much, do know particularly that the King's credulity to Cromwell's promises, private to him, against the advice of his friends, and the certain discovery of the practices and discourses of Cromwell in councill, by Major Huntington,[1] did take away his life, and nothing else. To my office, to fit up an account for Povy. At it till almost two o'clock, then to supper and to bed.

3d. To a Committee of the Fishery; there only to hear Sir Edward Ford's proposal about farthings, wherein, O God! to see almost every body interested for him; only my Lord Anglesey, who is a grave, serious man. My Lord Barkeley was there, but is the most hot, fiery man in discourse, without

[1] According to Clarendon, the officer here alluded to was a major in Cromwell's own regiment of horse, and employed by him to treat with Charles I. whilst at Hampton Court; but being convinced of the insincerity of the proceeding, communicated his suspicions to that monarch, and immediately gave up his commission. We hear no more of Huntington till the Restoration, when his name occurs with those of many other officers, who tendered their services to the King. His reasons for laying down his commission are printed in Thurloe's *State Papers*, and Maseres's *Tracts*.

any cause, that ever I saw, even to breach of civility to my Lord Anglesey, in his discourse, opposing to my Lord's. At last, though without much satisfaction to me, it was voted that it should be requested of the King, and that Sir Edward Ford's proposal is the best yet made. The Duke of York is expected to-night with great joy from Portsmouth, after his having been abroad at sea three or four days with the fleet: and the Dutch are all drawn into their harbours. But it seems like a victory; and a matter of some reputation to us it is, and blemish to them; but in no degree like what it is esteemed at, the weather requiring them to do so.

4th. (Lord's day.) This day I hear the Duke of York is come to town, though expected last night, as I observed, but by what hindrance stopped, I can't tell.

5th. Up, and to White Hall with Sir J. Minnes; and there, among an infinite crowd of great persons, did kiss the Duke's hand; but had no time to discourse. By appointment comes my cozen Roger Pepys and Mrs. Turner, and dined with me, and very merry we were. To White Hall, and there saw Mr. Coventry come to town, and, with all my heart, am glad to see him.

6th. To the Old Exchange, and there hear that the Dutch are fitting their ships out again, which puts us to new discourse, and to alter our thoughts of the Dutch, as to their want of courage or force. Povy tells me how he believes, and in part knows, Creed to be worth 10,000*l*.—nay, that now and then he hath three or 4000*l*. in his hands, for which he gives [Creed] the interest the King gives, which is ten per cent., and that Creed do come and demand it every three months the interest to be paid him, which Povy looks upon as a cunning and mean trick of him; but, for all that, he will do, and is very rich.

7th. By coach to my Lady Sandwich's, and there dined with her, and found all well and merry. Thence to White Hall, and we waited on the Duke, who looks better than he did, methinks, before his voyage; and, I think, a little more stern than he used to do. Povy and Creed staid and eat with me, but I was sorry I had no better cheer for Povy; for the fool may be useful, and is a cunning fellow in his way, though a strange one, and that, that I meet not in any other man, nor can describe in him.

9th. This day I had several letters from several places, of our bringing in great numbers of Dutch ships.

10th. At the office, where comes my Lord Brouncker with his patent in his hand; and I in his coach with him to the 'Change, where he set me down: a modish, civil person he seems to be, but wholly ignorant in the business of the Navy as possible, but I hope to make a friend of him, being a worthy man. Major Holmes is come from Guinny, and is now at Plymouth with great wealth, they say.

11th. (Lord's day.) To church alone in the morning. In the afternoon to the French church, where much pleased with the three sisters of the parson—very handsome, especially in their noses, and sing prettily. I heard a good sermon of the old man, touching duty to parents. Here was Sir Samuel Morland and his lady very fine, with two footmen in new liverys, the church taking much notice of them, and going into their coach after sermon with great gazing. So I home: my cozen, Mary Pepys's husband, comes after me, and told me that out of the money he received some months since he did receive 18_d._ too much, and did now come and give it me, which was very pretty.

12th. To White Hall, where all of us, with the Duke, Mr. Coventry did privately tell me the reason of his advice against our pretences to the Prize Office, in his letter from Portsmouth, because he knew that the King and the Duke had resolved to put in some Parliament men that deserved well, and that would be obliged, by putting them in. Comes Cutler to tell us that the King of France hath forbid any canvass to be carried out of his kingdom. This day, to see how things are ordered in the world, I had a command from the Earl of Sandwich, at Portsmouth, not to be forward with Mr. Chomly and Sir J. Lawson about the Mole at Tangier, because that what I do therein will, because of his friendship to me known, redound against him, as if I had done it upon his score. So I wrote to my Lord my mistake, and am contented to promise never to pursue it more, which goes against my mind with all my heart.

14th. To my bookseller's, and there spoke for several books against new year's day, I resolving to lay out about 7*l.* or 8*l.*: and bespoke also some plate spoons and forks.

15th. It seems, of all mankind, there is no man so led by another as the Duke is by my Lord Muskerry[1] and this Fitz-Harding. Insomuch, as when the King would have him to be Privy Purse, the Duke wept, and said, " But, Sir, I must have your promise, if you will have my dear Charles from me, that if ever you have occasion for an army again, I may have him with me ; believing him to be the best commander of an army in the world." But Mr. Chomly thinks, as all other men I meet do, that he is a very ordinary fellow. It is strange how the Duke also do love naturally, and affect the Irish, above the English.[2] He, of the company he carried with him to sea, took above two-thirds Irish and French. He tells me the King do hate my Lord Chancellor ; and that they, that is, the King and Lord FitzHarding, do laugh at him for a dull fellow ; and in all this business of the Dutch war do nothing by his advice, hardly consulting him. Only he is a good minister in other respects, and the King cannot be without him ; but, above all, being the Duke's father-in-law, he is kept in ; otherwise FitzHarding were able to fling down two of him. This all the wise and grave Lords see, and cannot help it ; but yield to it. But he bemoans what the end of it may be, the King being ruled by these men, as he hath been all along since his coming ; to the razing all the strongholds in Scotland, and giving liberty to the Irish in Ireland, whom Cromwell had settled all in one corner ; who are now able, and it is feared every day a massacre beginning among them. To the coffee-house, where great talk of the Comet seen in several places ; and, among our men at sea, and by my Lord Sandwich, to whom I intend to write about it to-night. This night

---

[1] **Eldest son of the Earl of Clancarty. He had served with distinction in Flanders, as colonel of an infantry regiment, and was killed on board the Duke of York's ship, in the sea-fight, 1665.**

[2] **Because so many of the Irish were Roman Catholics.**

I begun to burn wax candles in my closet at the office, to try the charge, and to see whether the smoke offends like that of tallow candles.

16th. Bought a looking-glass by the Old Exchange, which cost me 5*l.* 5*s.*, and 6*s.* for the hooks. A very fair glass.

17th. To the 'Change, and there, among others, had my first meeting with Mr. L'Estrange, who hath endeavoured several times to speak with me. It is to get, now and then, some news of me, which I shall, as I see cause, give him. He is a man of fine conversation, I think, but I am sure most courtly, and full of compliments. Mighty talk there is of this Comet that is seen a'nights : and the King and Queen did sit up last night to see it, and did, it seems. And to-night I thought to have done so too : but it is cloudy, and so no stars appear. But I will endeavour it. Mr. Gray did tell me to-night, for certain, that the Dutch, as high as they seem, do begin to buckle ; and that one man in this Kingdom did tell the King that he is offered 40,000*l.* to make a peace, and others have been offered money also. It seems the taking of their Bourdeaux fleet thus, arose from a printed Gazette of the Dutch's boasting of fighting, and having beaten the English : in confidence whereof, it coming to Bourdeaux, all the fleet comes out, and so falls into our hands.

18th. (Lord's day.) After supper, Mr. Fuller, the parson, and I, told many stories of apparitions and delusions thereby, and I out with my storys of Tom Mallard ; and then to prayers and to bed.

19th. With Sir J. Minnes to White Hall, and there we waited on the Duke ; and, among other things, Mr. Coventry took occasion to vindicate himself before the Duke and us, being all there, about the choosing of Taylor[1] for Harwich. Upon which the Duke did clear him, and did tell us that he did expect that, after he had named a man, none of us shall then oppose or find fault with the man ; but, if we had any thing to say, we ought to say it before he had chose him. Sir G. Carteret thought himself concerned, and endeavoured to clear himself : and by and by Sir W. Batten did speak,

---

[1] Silas Taylor, storekeeper there.

knowing himself guilty, and did confess, that, being pressed
by the Council, he did say what he did, that he was accounted
a fanatique; but did not know that at that time he had been
appointed by his Royal Highness. To which the Duke
replied, that it was impossible but he must know that he had
appointed him: and so it did appear that the Duke did mean
all this while Sir W. Batten.

21st. To Mrs. Turner, to Salisbury Court, and with her a
little; and carried her, the porter staying for me, our eagle,
which she desired the other day, and we were glad to be rid
of her. They are much pleased with her. My Lord Sandwich this day writes me word that he hath seen, at Portsmouth, the Comet, and says it is the most extraordinary thing
he ever saw.

22d. Met with a copy of verses, mightily commended by
some gentlemen there, of my Lord Mordaunt's,[1] in excuse of
his going to sea this late expedition, with the Duke of York.
But, Lord! they are sorry things; only a Lord made them.
Thence, to the 'Change; and there, among the merchants, I
hear fully the news of our being beaten to dirt at Guinny, by
De Ruyter, with his fleete. The particulars, as much as by
Sir G. Carteret afterwards I heard, I have said in a letter to
my Lord Sandwich this day at Portsmouth; it being most
wholly to the utter ruine of our Royall Company, and
reproach and shame to the whole nation, as well as justifica-
tion to them, in their doing wrong to no man as to his private
property, only taking whatever is found to belong to the
Company and nothing else. Dined at the Dolphin — Sir G.
Carteret, Sir J. Minnes, Sir W. Batten, and I, with Sir
William Boreman, and Sir Theophilus Biddulph[2] and others,
Commissioners of the Sewers, about our place below to lay
masts in. But coming a little too soon, I out again, and
took boat down to Redriffe; and just in time within two
minutes, and saw the new vessel of Sir William Petty's
launched, the King and Duke being there. It swims and
looks finely, and I believe will do well. Coming away back

---

[1] See note, November 26th, 1666.
[2] Sir Theophilus Biddulph, of Westcombe, Kent, who had been previously
knighted, was made a Baronet, 2nd November, 1664. He was then serving in
Parliament for Litchfield.

immediately to dinner, where a great deal of good discourse, and Sir G. Carteret's discourse of this Guinny business, with great displeasure at the loss of our honour there, and do now confess that the trade brought all these troubles upon us between the Dutch and us.

24th. Having sat up all night till past two o'clock this morning, our porter, being appointed, comes and tells us that the bellman tells him that the Star is seen upon Tower Hill; so I, that had been all night setting in order all my old papers in my chamber, did leave off all, and my boy and I to Tower Hill, it being a most fine, bright, moonshine night, and a great frost, but no Comet to be seen. At noon to the 'Change, to the Coffee-house; and there heard Sir Richard Ford tell the whole story of our defeat at Guinny, wherein our men are guilty of the most horrid cowardice and perfidiousness, as he says and tells it, that ever Englishmen were. Captain Raynolds, that was the only commander of any of the King's ships there, was shot at by De Ruyter, with a bloody flag flying. He, instead of opposing, which, indeed, had been to no purpose, but only to maintain honour, did poorly go on board himself, to ask what De Ruyter would have, and so yield to whatever Ruyter would desire. The King and Duke are highly vexed at it, it seems, and the business deserves it. I saw the Comet,[1] which now, whether worn away or no, I know not, appears not with a tail, but only is larger and duller than any other star, and is come to rise betimes, and to make a great arch, and is gone quite to a new place in the heavens than it was before; but I hope, in a clearer night, something more will be seen.

25th. (Lord's day.) To Mr. Rawlinson's church,[2] where I heard a good sermon of one that I remember was at Paul's with me — his name Maggett; and very great store of fine women there is in this church, more than I know anywhere else about us.

26th. To Sir W. Batten's, where Mr. Coventry and all our families here, and Sir R. Ford and his, and a great feast, and good discourse and merry, and so home to bed, where my wife

---

[1] It is one of the twenty-four comets of which the observations have been collected in Halley's *Astronomia Cometicæ Synopsis*.

[2] St. Dionis Backchurch.

and people innocently at cards, very merry. I to bed, leaving them to their sport and blindman's buff.

27th. Up at seven, and to Deptford and Woolwich in a gally; the Duke calling me out of a barge in which the King was with him, to know whither I was going. I told him to Woolwich, but was troubled afterwards I should say no further, being in a gally, lest he should think me too profuse in my journeys. The Comet appeared again to-night, but duskishly. I went to bed, leaving my wife, and all her folks, and Will also, to come to make Christmas gambols to-night.

28th. My wife to bed at eight o'clock in the morning, which vexed me a little, but I believe there was no hurt in it at all, but only mirth. Visited my Lady Sandwich, and was there, with her and the young ladies, playing at cards till night. Then home to bed, leaving my wife and people up to more sports, but without any great satisfaction to myself.

30th. To several places to pay away money, to clear myself in all the world, and, among others, paid my bookseller 6*l.* for books I had from him this day, and the silversmith 22*l.* 18*s.* for spoons, forks, and sugar-box.

31st. To my accounts of the whole year till past twelve at night, it being bitter cold, but yet I was well satisfied with my work; and, above all, to find myself, by the great blessing of God, worth 1349*l.*, by which, as I have spent very largely, so I have laid up above 500*l.* this year above what I was worth this day twelve month. The Lord make me for ever thankful to his holy name for it! Soon as ever the clock struck one, I kissed my wife in the kitchen by the fireside, wishing her a merry new year.

So ends the old year, I bless God, with great joy to me, not only from my having made so good a year of profit, as having spent 420*l.* and laid up 540*l.* and upwards; but I bless God I never have been in so good plight as to my health in so very cold weather as this is, nor indeed in any hot weather, these ten years, as I am at this day, and have been these four or five months. But I am at a great loss to know whether it be my hare's foote,[1] or taking every morning of a pill of

---

[1] As a charm against the colic.

turpentine, or my having left off the wearing of a gowne. My
family is my wife, in good health, and happy with her; her
woman Mercer, a pretty, modest, quiet maid; her chamber-
maid Besse, her cook-maid Jane, the little girl Susan, and my
boy, which I have had about half a year, Tom Edwards, which
I took from the King's Chapel; and as pretty and loving quiet
a family I have as any man in England. My credit in the
world and my office grows daily, and I am in good esteem
with everybody, I think. My troubles of my uncle's estate
pretty well over; but it comes to be of little profit to us, my
father being much supported by my purse. But great vexa-
tions remain upon my father and me from my brother Tom's
death and ill condition, both to our disgrace and discontent,
though no great reason for either. Public matters are all in
a hurry about a Dutch war. Our preparations great; our
provocations against them great; and, after all our presumption, we are now afraid as much of them as we lately con-
temned them. Every thing else in the State quiet, blessed
be God! My Lord Sandwich at sea with the fleete, at Portsmouth; sending some about to cruise for taking of ships,
which we have done to a great number. This Christmas I
judged it fit to look over all my papers and books, and to tear
all that I found either boyish or not to be worth keeping, or
fit to be seen, if it should please God to take me away suddenly. Among others, I found these two or three notes,
which I thought fit to keep.

AGE OF MY GRANDFATHER'S CHILDREN.

Thomas,	1595.	Edith, October 11, 1599.	
Mary, March 16, 1597.		John (my Father), January 14, 1601.	

My father and mother marryed at Newington, in Surry, Oct. 15, 1626.

THEYR CHILDREN'S AGES.

Mary, July 24, 1627,	*mort.*[1]	Sarah, August 25, 1635.	*mort.*
Paulina, Sept 18, 1628.	*mort.*	Jacob, May 1, 1637.	*mort.*
Esther, March 27, 1630.	*mort.*	Robert, Nov. 18, 1638.	*mort.*
John, January 10, 1631.	*mort.*	Paulina, Oct. 18, 1640.	
Samuel,[2] Feb. 23, 1632.		John, Nov. 26, 1641.	*mort.*
Thomas, June 18, 1634.	*mort.*	December 31, 1664.	

[1] The word "*mort*" must have been in some instances added long after the entry
was first made.

[2] To this name is affixed the following note: — "Went to reside in Magd. Coll.
Camb. and did put on my gown first, March 5, 1650–1."

CHARMES.

FOR STENCHING OF BLOOD

Sanguis mane in te,
Sicut Christus fuit in se;
Sanguis mane in tuâ venâ

Sicut Christus in suâ pœnâ;
Sanguis mane fixus,
Sicut Christus quando fuit crucifixus.

2. A THORNE.

Jesus, that was of a Virgin born,
Was pricked both with nail and thorn;
It neither wealed nor belled, rankled nor boned;
In the name of Jesus no more shall this.

Or, thus:—

Christ was of a Virgin born,
And he was pricked with a thorn;
And it did neither bell, nor swell;
And I trust in Jesus this never will.

3. A CRAMP.

Cramp be thou faintless,
As our Lady was sinless,
When she bare Jesus.

4. A BURNING.

There came three Angells out of the East;
The one brought fire, the other brought frost—
Out fire; in frost,
In the name of the Father, and Son, and Holy Ghost.

AMEN.

1664-5.

January 1st. (Lord's day.) This day I was dividing my expense, to see what my clothes and every particular hath stood me in: I mean all the branches of my expense. At noon a good venison-pasty and a turkey to ourselves, without any body so much as wished by us, a thing unusuall for so small a family of my condition: but we did it, and were very merry.

2d. To my Lord Brouncker's, by appointment, in the Piazza, in Covent Garden; where I occasioned much mirth with a ballet[1] I brought with me, made from the seamen at

---

[1] The Earl of Dorset's song. "To all ye ladies now on land," &c. It is stated by Prior, in the Dedication of his Poems to Lionel Earl of Dorset and Middlesex that the Earl's father wrote the celebrated sea-song. "The night before the Engagement with the Dutch, in 1665;" but this assertion seems very questionable. Dr. Johnson, indeed, after remarking that seldom any splendid story is wholly true, mentions his having heard from the Earl of Orrery, who was

sea to their ladies in town; saying Sir W. Pen, Sir G. Ascue, and Sir J. Lawson, made them. Here a most noble French dinner and banquet. The street full of footballs, it being a great frost.

3d. Up, and found Mr. Coventry walking in St. James's Park. I did my errand to him about the felling of the King's timber in the forests, and then to my Lord of Oxford, Justice in Eyre, for his consent thereto, for want whereof my Lord Privy Seale[1] stops the whole business. I found him in his lodgings, in but an ordinary furnished house, and room where he was, but I find him to be a man of good discreete replys. Certain news that the Dutch have taken some of our colliers to the North: some say four, some say seven. To Sir W. Batten's who is going out of town to Harwich to-morrow to set up a light-house there, which he hath lately got a patent for the King to set up, that will turn much to his profit.

4th. To my Lord of Oxford's, but his Lordship was in bed at past ten o'clock: and Lord help us! so rude a dirty family I never saw in my life. To the 'Change, where I hear of some more of our ships lost to the Northward. Mr. Moore and I to "Love in a Tubb,"[2] which is very merry, but only

---

likely to have good hereditary intelligence, that Lord Buckhurst had been a week employed upon the performance, and only retouched, or finished, it on the memorable evening. "But even this," adds the Doctor, "whatever it may subtract from his facility, leaves him his courage." In Johnson's *Poets*, 1790, the song is described as "written at sea in the first Dutch war, the night before an engagement." T. Durfey, in his *Wit and Drollery*, vol. v., speaks of the composition as "a ballad written by the late Lord Dorset, *when at sea;*" and in the fifth stanza he substitutes "Count Thoulouse" for "foggy Opdam," and "French" for "Dutch;" but the original words have been restored in more recent versions. In the absence of certain evidence, we cannot decide upon the fact; but all accounts agree in representing Buckhurst as having served as a volunteer under the Duke of York, whose *first cruize took place* in *November*, 1664. Perhaps, then, the ballad was written at this time, when an action between the two fleets was only delayed by the Dutch retiring to port. Thus Pepys might well have seen the song in January, 1664-5; and it still may have been retouched, and brought out with *éclat* during the excitement consequent upon the victory of June 3, following. Nor is it, indeed, easy to imagine that any one ever wrote a ballad when about to take part in a great naval conflict; or that, if two songs had been contemporaneously composed on the same subject, with titles so nearly identical, one only should be known to exist.

[1] Lord Robartes, mentioned Aug. 21, 1660.

[2] "The Comical Revenge; or, Love in a tub;" a comedy, by Sir George Etherege.

so by gesture, not wit at all, which methinks is beneath the house.

6th. At night home, being twelfth-night, and there chose my piece of cake, but went up to my viall, and then to bed, leaving my wife and people at their sports, which they continue till morning, not coming to bed at all.

8th. (Lord's day.) To White Hall Chapel, where one Dr. Beaumont[1] preached a good sermon, and afterwards a brave anthem upon the 150 Psalm, where upon the word "trumpet" very good musique was made.

9th. Walked to White Hall. In my way saw a woman that broke her thigh, by her heels slipping up upon the frosty street. I saw the Royal Society bring their new book, wherein is nobly writ their charter and laws, and comes to be signed by the Duke as a Fellow; and all the Fellows are to be entered there, and lie as a monument; and the King hath put his, with the word Founder.[2] Holmes was this day sent to the Tower, but I perceive it is made matter of jest only; but if the Dutch should be our masters, it may come to be of earnest to him, to be given over to them for a sacrifice, as Sir W. Ralegh was. To a Tangier committee, where I was accosted and most highly complimented by my Lord Bellasses,[3] our new governor, beyond my expectation; and I may make good use of it. Our patent is renewed, and he and my Lord Barkeley and Sir Thomas Ingram[4] put in as commissioners.

11th. This evening, by a letter from Plymouth, I hear that two of our ships, the Leopard and another, in the Streights, are lost by running aground; and that three more had like to have been so, but got off, whereof Captain Allen one: and that a Dutch fleete are gone thither; and if

---

[1] Joseph Beaumont, D.D., Prebendary of Ely, and Master of Jesus College, Cambridge.

[2] The book is still in use, containing the autograph of every Fellow from the institution of the Society to the present time.

[3] John Lord Bellasis, second son of Thomas Viscount Falconberg, an officer of distinction on the King's side, during the Civil War. He was afterwards Governor of Tangier, and Captain of the Band of Gentlemen Pensioners. Being a Catholic, the Test Act deprived him of all his appointments in 1672; but James II., in 1684, made him first Commissioner of the Treasury. Ob. 1689.

[4] Chancellor of the Duchy of Lancaster, and a Privy Councillor. Ob. 1671.

they should meet with our lame ships, God knows what
would become of them. This I reckon most sad news; God
make us sensible of it! When I come home, I was much
troubled to hear my poor canary-bird, that I have kept these
three or four years, was dead.

12th. Spoke with a Frenchman, who was taken, but released, by a Dutch man-of-war of thirty-six guns, with seven
more of the King's, or greater ships, off the North Foreland,
by Margett, which is a strange attempt, that they should
come to our teeth; but the wind being easterly, the wind
that should bring our force from Portsmouth will carry them
away home.

13th. Walked to my Lord Bellasses's lodgings, in Lincoln's Inne Fields, and there he received and discoursed with
me, in the most respectfull manner that could be; telling
me what a character of my judgment, and care and love to
Tangier, he had received of me; that he desired my advice
and my constant correspondence, which he much valued, and
my courtship, in which, though I understand his design very
well, and that it is only a piece of courtship, yet it is a comfort to me, that I am become so considerable, as to have him
need say that to me, which, if I did not do something in the
world, would never have been. Yesterday's news confirmed,
though a little different; but a couple of ships in the Streights
we have lost, and the Dutch have been in the Margett Road.
To the King's house, to a play, "The Traytor," where, unfortunately, I met with Sir W. Pen, so that I must be forced to
confess it to my wife, which troubles me. Thence walked
home, being ill satisfied with the present actings of the house,
and prefer the other house before this. To my Lady Batten's,
where I find Pegg Pen, the first time that ever I saw her to
wear spots.

14th. Our late ill news confirmed, in loss of two ships in
the Streights, but are now the Phœnix and Nonsuch. To
the King's house, there to see Vulpone,[1] a most excellent
play; the best I think I ever saw, and well acted.

15th. (Lord's day.) To church, where a most insipid young

---

[1] A comedy, by Ben Jonson.

coxcomb preached. After dinner, to read in " Rushworth's Collections," about the charge against the late Duke of Buckingham,[1] in order to the fitting me to speak and understand the discourse anon, before the King, about the suffering the Turkey merchants to send out the fleete at this dangerous time, when we can neither spare them ships to go, nor men, nor King's ships to convey them. With Sir W. Pen in his coach to my Lord Chancellor's, where, by and by, Mr. Coventry; Sir W. Pen, Sir J. Lawson, Sir G. Ascue and myself were called in to the King, there being several of the Privy Council, and my Lord Chancellor lying at length upon a couch, of the goute, I suppose; and there Sir W. Pen spoke pretty well to dissuade the King from letting the Turkey ships go out: saying, in short, the King having resolved to have 130 ships out by the spring, he must have above 20 of them merchantmen, towards which, he in the whole River could find but 12 or 14, and of them, the five ships taken up by these merchants were a part, and so could not be spared. That we should need 30,000 sailors to man these 130 ships, and of them in service we have not above 16,000; so that we shall need 14,000 more. That these ships will, with their convoys, carry about 2000 men, and those the best men that could be got; it being the men used to the Southward that are the best men for war, though those bred in the North, among the colliers, are good for labour. That it will not be safe for the merchants, nor honourable for the King, to expose these rich ships with his convoy of six ships to go, it not being enough to secure them against the Dutch, who, without doubt, will have a great fleet in the Streights. This Sir J. Lawson enlarged upon. Sir G. Ascue chiefly spoke that the war and trade could not be supported together. Mr. Coventry showed how the medium of the men the King hath one year with another employed in the Navy since his coming, hath not been above 3000 men, or at most 4000 men; and now, having occasion of 30,000, the remaining 26,000 must be found out of the trade of the nation. He showed how the cloaths, sending by these merchants to Turkey, are already

[1] On the expedition to the Isle of Rhé.

bought and paid for to the workmen, and are as many as they would send these twelve months or more; so the poor do not suffer by their not going, but only the merchant, upon whose hands they lie dead; and so the inconvenience is the less. And yet for them he propounded, either the King should, if his Treasurer would suffer it, buy them, and showed the loss would not be so great to him: or, dispense with the Act of Navigation, and let them be carried out by strangers; and ending that he doubted not but when the merchants saw there was no remedy, they would and could find ways of sending them abroad to their profit. All ended with a conviction, unless future discourse with the merchants should alter it, that it was not fit for them to go out, though the ships be loaded. So we withdrew, and the merchants were called in. Staying without, my Lord FitzHarding come thither, and fell to discourse of Prince Rupert's disease,[1] telling the horrible degree of its breaking out on his head. He observed, also, from the Prince, that courage is not what men take it to be, a contempt of death; for, says he, how chagrined the Prince was, the other day, when he thought he should die, having no more mind to it than another man. But, says he, some men are more apt to think they shall escape than another man in fight, while another is doubtfull he shall be hit. But, when the first man is sure he shall die, as now the Prince is, he is as much troubled and apprehensive of it as any man else; for, says he, since we told him that we believe he would overcome his disease, he is as merry, and swears and laughs and curses, and do all the things of a man in health, as ever he did in his life; which, methought, was a most extraordinary saying, before a great many persons there of quality.

16th. Ned Pickering met me, and told me how active my Lord is at sea; and that my Lord Hinchingbroke is now at Rome; and, by all report, a very noble and hopefull gentleman. Thence to Mr. Povy's, and dined well, after his old manner of plenty and curiosity. To a Tangier Committee, where my Lord Barkeley was very violent against Povy. My Lord Ashly, I observe, is a most clear man in matters of accounts, and most ingeniously did discourse and explain all matters.

---

[1] Morbus, scil. Gallicus.

17th. To my Lord Ashly's, where to see how simply, beyond all patience, Povy did again, by his many words and non-understanding, confound himself and his business, to his disgrace, and rendering every body doubtfull of his being either a fool or a knave, is very wonderfull. We broke up all dissatisfied. Here it was mighty strange to find myself sit here in committee with my hat on, while Mr. Sherwin stood bare as a clerk, with his hat off to his Lord Ashly and the rest; but I thank God I think myself never a whit the better man for all that. A brave dinner, by having a brace of pheasants, and very merry about Povy's folly.

18th. To my bookseller's, and there did give thorough direction for the new binding of a great many of my old books, to make my whole study of the same binding, within very few.

19th. To Exeter House,[1] and there was a witness of most base language against Mr. Povy, from my Lord Peterborough, who is most furiously angry with him, because the other, as a fool, would needs say that the 26,000*l.* was my Lord Peterborough's account, and that he had nothing to do with it. Home, by coach, with my Lord Barkeley, who, by his discourse, I find do look upon Mr. Coventry as an enemy, but yet professes great justice and pains. This day was buried, but I could not be there, my cozen Percivall Angier; and yesterday I received the news that Dr. Tom Pepys is dead, at Impington, for which I am but little sorry, not only because he would have been troublesome to us, but a shame to his family and profession—he was such a coxcomb.

20th. To my bookseller's, and there took home Hook's book of Microscopy, a most excellent piece, and of which I am very proud. Homeward, in my way buying a hare, and taking it home, which arose upon my discourse to-day with Mr. Batten, in Westminster Hall, who showed me my mistake that my hare's foot hath not the joynt to it; and assures me he never had his cholique since he carried it about him: and it is a strange thing how fancy works, for I no sooner handled his foot, but I become very well, and so continue.

---

[1] Where Lord Ashley then lived.

21st. Mr. Povy carried me to Somerset House, and there showed me the Queen-Mother's chamber and closet, most beautiful places for furniture and pictures; and so down the great stone stairs to the garden, and tried the brave echo upon the stairs; which continues a voice so long as the singing three notes, concords, one after another, they all three shall sound in consort together a good while most pleasantly. To a Tangier Committee, where I saw nothing ordered by judgement, but great heat and passion and faction now in behalf of my Lord Bellasses, and to the reproach of my Lord Teviott. So away with Mr. Povy—a simple fellow I now find him, to his utter shame, in this business of accounts, as none but a sorry fool would have discovered himself; and yet, in little, light, sorry things, very cunning; yet, in the principal, the most ignorant man I ever met with in so great trust as he is. Now mighty well, and truly I can but impute it to my fresh hare's foote.

22d. (Lord's day.) To church. Thence home, discoursing, among other things, of a design I have of making a match between Mrs. Betty Pickering and Mr. Hill, my friend the merchant, that loves musique, and comes to me a'Sundays, a most ingenious and sweet-natured and highly accomplished person. I know not how their fortunes may agree, but their disposition and merits are much of a sort, and persons, though different, yet equally, I think, acceptable.

23d. Up, and with Sir W. Batten and Sir W. Pen to White Hall; but, there finding the Duke gone to his lodgings in St. James's for altogether, his Duchess being ready to lie in, we to him, and there did our usual business. And here I met the great news confirmed by the Duke's own relation, by a letter from Captain Allen. First, of our own loss of two ships, the Phœnix and Nonsuch, in the Bay of Gibraltar: then of his and his seven ships with him, in the Bay of Cales, or thereabouts, fighting with the 34 Dutch Smyrna fleete; sinking the King Salamon, a ship worth a 150,000l. or more; some say 200,000l. and another; and taking of three merchant-ships. Two of our ships were disabled, by the Dutch unfortunately falling against their will against them; the Advice, Captain W. Poole, and Antelope, Captain Clerke. The Dutch men-of-war did little service. Captain Allen, before he would fire one gun, come within pistol-shot of the enemy. The Spaniards, at Cales, did stand laughing at the Dutch, to see them run away and flee to the shore, 34 or thereabouts, against eight Englishmen at most. I do purpose to get the whole relation, if I live, of Captain Allen himself. In our loss of the two ships in the Bay of Gibraltar, the world do comment upon the misfortune of Captain Moone of the Nonsuch, who did lose, in the same manner, the Satisfaction, as a person that hath ill-luck attending him; without considering that the whole fleete was ashore. Captain Allen led the way, and himself writes, that all the masters of the fleete, old and young, were mistaken, and did carry their ships aground. But I think I heard the Duke say, that Moone, being put into the Oxford, had in this conflict regained his credit, by sinking one and taking another. Captain Seale, of the Milford, hath done his part very well, in boarding the King Salamon, which held out half an hour after she was boarded; and his men kept her an hour after they did master her, and then she sunk, and drowned about 17 of her men.

24th. The Dutch have, by consent of all the Provinces, voted no trade to be suffered for eighteen months, but that they apply themselves wholly to the war.[1] Home to supper, having a great cold, got on Sunday last, by sitting too long with my head bare, for Mercer to comb and wash my eares.

25th. Dined upon a hare pye, very good meat. Mr. Hill tells me, that he is to be Assistant to the Secretary of the Prize Office, Sir Ellis Layton, which, methinks, is but some-

---

[1] This statement of a total prohibition of all trade, and for so long a period as eighteen months, by a government so essentially commercial as that of the United Provinces, seems extraordinary. The fact was, that when, in the beginning of the year 1665, the States-General saw that the war with England was become inevitable, they took several vigorous measures, and determined to equip a formidable fleet; and, with a view to obtain a sufficient number of men to man it, prohibited all navigation, especially in the great and small fisheries, as they were then called, and in the Whale fishery. This measure appears to have resembled the embargoes so commonly resorted to in this country on similar occasions, rather than a total prohibition of trade.

thing low, but perhaps may bring him something considerable;
but it makes me alter my opinion of his being so rich as to
make a fortune for Mrs. Pickering. Visited Sir J. Minnes,
who continues ill, but he told me what a mad, freaking fellow
Sir Ellis Layton hath been, and is, and once at Antwerp was
really mad.

27th. To my Lord Bellasses's, and so with my Lord in his
coach to White Hall, and with him to my Lord Duke of
Albemarle, finding him at cards. After a few dull words or
two, I away to White Hall again, and there walked up and
down, talking with Mr. Slingsby, who is a very ingenious
person, about the Mint. He argues, that there being
700,000l. coined in the Rump time, and by all the Treasurers
of that time, it being their opinion that the Rump money was
in all payments, one with another, about a tenth part of all
their money; then, says he, the nearest guess we can make
is, that the money passing up and down in business is
700,000l. He also made me fully understand that the old
law of prohibiting bullion to be exported is, and ever was, a
folly and injury, rather than good. Arguing thus, that if
the exportations exceed the importations, then the balance
must be brought home in money, which, when our merchants
know cannot be carried out again, they will forbear to bring
home in money, but let it lie abroad for trade, or keep in
foreign banks: or, if our importations exceed our exportations,
then, to keep credit, the merchants will and must find ways
of carrying out money by stealth, which is a most easy thing
to do, and is everywhere done; and, therefore, the law against
it signifies nothing in the world. Besides, that it is seen,
that where money is free, there is great plenty: where it is
restrained, as here, there is great want, as in Spain.

28th. To clear all my matters about Colours,' and I find
myself to have got clear, by that commodity, 50l., and
something more; and earned it with due pains and care, and
issuing of my own money, and saved the King near 100l.
in it.

30th. This is solemnly kept as a fast all over the City,

' Flags.

but I kept my house, putting my closet to rights again. To my office, and, being late at it, comes Mercer to me, to tell me that my wife was in bed, and desired me to come home; for they hear, and have, night upon night, lately heard noises over their head upon the leads. Now, knowing that I have a great sum of money in my house, this puts me into a most mighty affright, that for more than two hours, I could not almost tell what to do or say, but feared this night, and remembered that this morning I saw a woman and two men stand suspiciously in the entry, in the dark; I calling to them, they made me only this answer, the woman saying that the men come to see her; but who she was I could not tell. The truth is, my house is mighty dangerous, having so many ways to be come to; and at my windows, over the stairs, to see who goes up and down; but, if I escape to-night, I will remedy it. God preserve us this night safe! So, at almost two o'clock, I home to my house, and, in great fear, to bed, thinking every running of a mouse really a thief; and so to sleep, very brokenly, all night long, and found all safe in the morning.

February 1st. After being in bed, my people come and say there is a great stink of burning, but no smoke. We called upon Sir J. Minnes's and Sir W. Batten's people, and Griffin, and the people at the madhouse, but nothing could be found to give occasion to it. At this trouble we were till past three o'clock, and then the stink ceasing, I to sleep, and my people to bed.

3d. To Mrs. Turner's, who, I perceive, is vexed, because I did not serve her in something against the great feasting for her husband's reading, in helping her to some good penn'eths, but I care not. She was dressing herself by the fire in her chamber, and there took occasion to show me her leg, which, indeed, is the finest I ever saw, and she not a little proud of it. My bill for the rebinding of some old books to make them suit with my study, cost me, besides other new books in the same bill, 3l.; but it will be very handsome. News is come from Deale, that the same day my Lord Sandwich sailed thence with the Fleet, that evening some Dutch men-of-war

were seen on the back side of the Goodwin, and, by all
conjecture, must be seen by my Lord's fleete; which, if so,
they must engage.   To my uncle Wight's, where the Wights
all dined; and, among the others, pretty Mrs. Margaret, who
indeed is a very pretty lady; and, though by my vow it costs
me 12*d*. a kiss after the first, yet I did adventure upon a
couple.   To visit my Lady Sandwich, and she discoursed
largely to me her opinion of a match, if it could be thought
fit by my Lord, for my lady Jemimah, with Sir G. Carteret's
eldest son; but I doubt he hath yet no settled estate in land.
But I will inform myself, and give her my opinion.   Then
Mrs. Pickering, after private discourse ended, we going into
the other room, did, at my Lady's command, tell me the
manner of a masquerade before the King and Court the other
day,[1] where six women, my Lady Castlemaine and Duchess of
Monmouth being two of them, and six men, the Duke of
Monmouth and Lord Arran,[2] and Monsieur Blanfort,[3] being
three of them, in vizards, but most rich and antique dresses,
did dance admirably and most gloriously.   God give us cause
to continue the mirth!

4th. I to the Sun behind the 'Change, to dinner to my
Lord Bellasses.   He told us a very handsome passage of the
King's sending him his message about holding out the town
of Newarke, of which he was then governor for the King.
This message he sent in a slugg-bullet, being writ in cypher,
and wrapped up in lead and sealed.   So the messenger come
to my Lord, and told him he had a message from the King,
but it was yet in his belly; so they did give him some physick,
and out it come.   This was a month before the King's flying
to the Scots; and therein he told him that, at such a day,
the 3d or 6th of May, he should hear of his being come to

---

[1] *i. e.* yesterday. See Evelyn's *Diary*, and De Grammont.

[2] Richard Butler, second son of James, first Duke of Ormond, created Earl of
Arran, in Ireland, in 1662; and, in 1674, made Baron Butler, of Weston, co. Huntingdon, which honours became extinct at his death, s. p. m. in 1685.

[3] Lewis Duras, Marquis de Blanquefort, naturalized 17th Charles II., and created
Baron Duras, 1672, and in 1677 succeeded to the Earldom of Feversham, under
the limitation in the patent by which his father-in-law, who died without issue,
had been raised to that title. He was afterwards made K.G. by James II., whom
he had attended in the sea-fight of 1665, as Captain of the Guard.

the Scots, being assured by the King of France, that in
coming to them he should be used with all the liberty,
honour, and safety, that could be desired. And at the just
day he did come to the Scots. He told us another odd
passage : how the King having newly put out Prince Rupert
of his generalship, upon some miscarriage at Bristol, and Sir
Richard Willis of his governorship of Newarke, at the
entreaty of the gentry of the County, and put in my Lord
Bellasses; the great officers of the King's army mutinied,
and come in that manner with swords drawn, into the market-
place of the town where the King was ; which the King hearing,
says, " I must horse." And there himself personally, when
every body expected they should have been opposed, the King
come, and cried to the head of the mutineers, which was
Prince Rupert, " Nephew, I command you to be gone." So
the Prince, in all his fury and discontent, withdrew, and his
company scattered.

5th. (Lord's day.) Up and down to my chamber, among
my new books, which is now a pleasant sight to me to see
my whole study almost of one binding.

6th. One of the coldest days, all say, they ever felt in
England.

7th. At home at dinner. It being Shrove Tuesday, had
some very good fritters. This day, Sir W. Batten, who hath
been sick four or five days, is now very bad, so as the people
begin to fear his death ; and I at a loss whether it will be
better for me to have him die, because he is a bad man, or
live, for fear a worse should come.

9th. Sir William Petty tells me, that Mr. Barlow[1] is dead ;
for which, God knows my heart, I could be as sorry as is
possible for one to be for a strangier, by whose death he gets
100l. per annum.

10th. To Paul's Churchyard, there to see the last of my
books new bound : among others, my " Court of King James,"
and " The Rise and Fall of the Family of the Stewarts ;"

<hr>

[1] Thomas Barlow, Pepys's predecessor as Clerk of the Acts, to whom he paid
part of the salary. Barlow had previously been Secretary to Algernon, Earl of
Northumberland, when High Admiral.

and much pleased I am now with my study; it being, me-thinks, a beautiful sight. In Mr. Grey's coach to West-minster, where I heard that yesterday the King met the Houses to pass the great bill for 2,500,000*l*.

12th. (Lords day.) To church, to St. Lawrence's in the Jewry, to hear Dr. Wilkins, the great scholar, for curiosity, I having never heard him: but was not satisfied with him at all. I was well pleased with the church—it being a very fine church.

13th. On board Sir W. Petty's "Experiment," which is a fine roomy vessel, and I hope may do well. Light upon some Dutchmen, with whom we had good discourse, touching stoveing,[1] and making of cables. But to see how despicably they speak of us for using so many hands more to do any-thing than they do—they closing a cable with 20, that we use 60 men upon. Captain Stokes, it seems, is dead at Portsmouth.

14th. (St. Valentine.) This morning comes betimes Dicke Pen, to be my wife's Valentine, and come to our bedside. By the same token, I had him brought to my side, thinking to have made him kiss me: but he perceived me, and would not; so went to his Valentine: a notable, stout, witty boy. My Lord Sandwich is, it seems, with his fleet at Aldborough Bay.

15th. Busy all the morning. At noon, with Creed to the Trinity-house, where a very good dinner among the old jokers, and an extraordinary discourse of the manner of the loss of The Royall Oake coming home from Bantam, upon the rocks of Scilly. Thence with Creed to Gresham College, where I had been by Mr. Povy the last week proposed to be admitted a member; and was this day admitted, by signing a book and being taken by the hand of the President, my Lord Brouncker, and some words of admittance said to me.[2] But it is a most acceptable thing to hear their discourse, and see

[1] Stoveing, in sail-making, is the heating of the bolt-ropes, so as to make them pliable.

[2] Pepys was afterwards President. His portrait, by Kneller, presented by himself, is still to be seen in the Great Room of the Society.

their experiments; which were this day on fire, and how it goes out in a place where the ayre is not free, and sooner out where the ayre is exhausted, which they showed by an engine on purpose. After this being done, they to the Crown Tavern, behind the 'Change, and there my Lord and most of the company to a club supper; Sir P. Neale, Sir R. Murray,[1] Dr. Clerke, Dr. Whistler, Dr. Goddard,[2] and others, of the most eminent worth. Above all, Mr. Boyle was at the meeting, and above him Mr. Hooke,[3] who is the most, and promises the least, of any man in the world that ever I saw. Here excellent discourse till ten at night, and then home.

16th. To White Hall, where a Committee of Tangier, but, Lord! to see what a degree of contempt — nay, scorn, Mr. Povy, through his prodigious folly, hath brought on himself in his accounts, that if he be not a man of a great interest, he will be kicked out of his employment for a fool. Mrs. Hunt dined with me. and poor Mrs. Batters, who brought her little daughter with her, and a letter from her husband, wherein, as a token, the fool presents me very seriously with his daughter for me to take the charge of bringing up for him and to make my owne. But I took no notice to her at all of the substance of the letter.

17th. Povy tells me how he was hunted the other day, and is still, by my Lord Barkeley; and, among other things, tells me, what I did not know, that my Lord will say openly that he hath fought more set fields than any man in England hath done.

18th. At noon, to the Royall Oak taverne in Lombard Street; where Sir William Petty and the owners of the double-bottomed boat, the Experiment, did entertain my Lord Brouncker, Sir R. Murray, myself, and others, with

[1] One of the Founders of the Royal Society, made a Privy Councillor for Scotland after the Restoration.

[2] Jonathan Goddard, M.D., F.R.S. He had been Physician to Cromwell, and was M.P. for Oxfordshire in 1653.

[3] D. Robert Hooke, Professor of Geometry at Gresham College, and Curator of the Experiments to the Royal Society, of which he was one of the earliest and most distinguished members. Ob. March 3, 1702-3.

marrow-bones, and a chine of beef, of the victuals they have
made for this ship: and excellent company and good discourse:
but, above all, I do value Sir William Petty. Thence home:
and took my Lord Sandwich's draught of the harbour of
Portsmouth down to Ratcliffe, to one Burston, to make a
plate for the King, and another for the Duke, and another
for himself; which will be very neat. My Lord Sandwich,
and his fleete of twenty-five ships in the Downes, returned
from cruising, but could not meet with any Dutchmen.

19th. (Lord's day.) Hearing by accident of my maid's
letting in a roguing Scotch woman that haunts the office, to
help them to wash and scour in our house, and that very
lately, I fell mightily out, and made my wife, to the disturbance of the house and neighbours, to beat our little girle,
and then we shut her down into the cellar, and there she lay
all night.

20th. Rode into the beginning of my Lord Chancellor's
new house,[1] near St. James's: which common people have
already called Dunkirke-house, from their opinion of his
having a good bribe for the selling of that towne. And very
noble I believe it will be. Near that is my Lord Barkeley
beginning another on one side, and Sir J. Denham on the
other. To the Sun taverne, where we dined merry, but my
club and the rest come to 7s. 6d., which was too much.

21st. My wife busy in going with her woman to the hot-
house to bathe herself, after her long being within doors in the
dirt, so that she now pretends to a resolution of being hereafter very clean. How long it will hold I can guess. I
dined with Sir W. Batten and my Lady, they being nowa'days
very fond of me. My Lady Sandwich tells me how my Lord
Castlemaine is coming over from France, and it is believed
will soon be made friends with his Lady again. What mad
freaks the Mayds of Honour at Court have: that Mrs.

---

[1] " Oct. 8, 1667. The Lord Chancellor's House, called 'Clarendon House,' is
now almost finished. The chapel is quite completed, and was consecrated, when
His Honour gave a rich Bible, the cover of which was of silver, and the Book of
Common Prayer with the same covering, together with bowls and other vessels
for the Sacrament, to the value of 1000l. A Sermon was preached that day by a
Bishop."—Rugge's *Diurnal*.

Jenings,[1] one of the Duchess's maids, the other day dressed herself like an orange wench, and went up and down and cried oranges: till, falling down, or by some accident, her fine shoes were discerned, and she put to a great deal of shame; that such as these tricks, being ordinary, and worse among them, thereby few will venture upon them for wives: my Lady Castlemaine will in merriment say, that her daughter, not above a year old or two, will be the first mayd in the Court that will be married. This day my Lord Sandwich writ me word from the Downes, that he is like to be in town this week.

22d. At noon to the 'Change, busy; where great talk of a Dutch ship in the North put on shore, and taken by a troop of horse.

23d. This day, by the blessing of Almighty God, I have lived thirty-two years in the world, and am in the best degree of health at this minute that I have been almost in my life time, and at this time in the best condition of estate that ever I was in — the Lord make me thankful!

25th. At noon to the 'Change; where, just before I come, the Swede that had told the King and the Duke so boldly a great lie of the Dutch flinging our men back to back into the sea at Guinny, so particularly, and readily, and confidently, was whipt round the 'Change: he confessing it a lie, and that he did it in hopes to get something. It is said the Judges, upon demand, did give it their opinion that the law would judge him to be whipt, to lose his cares, or to have his nose slit: but I do not hear that any thing more is to be done to him. They say he is delivered over to the Dutch Embassador to do what he pleased with him. To the Sun taverne, and there dined with Sir W. Batten and Mr. Gifford, the merchant: and I hear how Nick Colborne, that lately lived and got a great estate there, is gone to live like a prince in the country, and that this Wadlow, that did the like at the Devil[2]

---

[1] Frances, daughter of Richard Jennings, Esq., of Sundridge, near St. Albans, and eldest sister of Sarah, Duchess of Marlborough, married, 1st, George Hamilton, afterwards knighted, and in the French service: 2dly, Richard Talbot, created Duke of Tyrconnel. She died in Ireland, 1730. The anecdote here related is told in the *Mémoires de Grammont.*

[2] The Devil Tavern stood between Temple Bar and the Middle Temple Gate.

by St. Dunstan's, did go into the country, and there spent
almost all he had got, and hath now choused this Colborne
out of his house, that he might come to his old trade again.
But, Lord! to see how full the house is, no room for any
company almost to come into it.   Late home, and to clean
myself with warm water; my wife will have me, because she
do use it herself.

27th. We to a Committee of the Council, to discourse concerning pressing of men; but, Lord! how they meet, never
sit down: one comes, now another goes, then comes another;
one complaining that nothing is done, another swearing that
he hath been there these two hours, and nobody come.   At
last my Lord Anglesey says, "I think we must be forced to
get the King to come to every Committee; for I do not see
that we do any thing at any time but when he is here."   And
I believe he said the truth: and very constant he is on coun-
cil-days: which his predecessors, it seems, very rarely were.
To Sir Philip Warwick's; and there he did contract with me
a kind of friendship and freedom of communication, wherein
he assures me to make me understand the whole business of
the Treasurer of the Navy, that I shall know, as well as Sir
G. Carteret, what money he hath; and will needs have me
come to him sometimes, or he meet me, to discourse of things
tending to the serving the King; and I am mighty proud and
happy in becoming so known to such a man.   And I hope
shall pursue it.

March 1st. Being the day that by a promise, a great
while ago, made to my wife, I was to give her 20*l.* to lay out
in clothes against Easter, I did give it her, and then she
abroad to buy her things.   To Gresham College, where Mr.
Hooke read a second very curious lecture about the late
Comet; among other things, proving very probably that this
is the very same Comet that appeared before in the year 1618,
and that in such a time probably it will appear again, which
is a very new opinion; but all will be in print.   Then to the

nearly opposite to St. Dunstan's Church.   Child's Place, so called from the
Banking-house adjoining, was built in 1788, on the site of the tavern.   See *Handbook of London.*

meeting, where Sir G. Carteret's two sons, his own, and Sir N. Slaning,[1] were admitted of the society: and this day I did pay my admission money, 40s., to the Society. Here was very fine discourses and experiments, but I do lack philosophy enough to understand them, and so cannot remember them. Among others, a very particular account of the making of the several sorts of bread in France, which is accounted the best place for bread in the world.

2d. Begun this day to rise betimes before six o'clock, and, going down to call my people, found Besse and the girle with their clothes on, lying within their bedding upon the ground close by the fireside, and a candle burning all night, pretending they would rise to scoure. But Besse is going, and so she will not trouble me long.

3d. To see Mrs. Turner, who takes it mightily ill I did not come to dine with the Reader in Law, her husband, which, she says, was the greatest feast that ever was yet kept by a Reader, and I believe it was well. But I am glad I did not go, which confirms her in an opinion that I am grown proud.

4th. William Howe come to see me, being come up with my Lord from sea: he is grown a discreet but very conceited fellow. He tells me how little respectfully Sir W. Pen did carry it to my Lord on board the Duke's ship at sea: and that Captain Minnes, a favourite of Prince Rupert's, do show my Lord little respect; but that every body else esteems my Lord as they ought. This day was proclaimed at the 'Change the war with Holland.

5th. (Lord's day.) To my Lord Sandwich's, and dined with my Lord; it being the first time he hath dined at home since his coming from sea: and a pretty odd demand it was of my Lord to my Lady before me: "How do you, sweetheart? How have you done all this week?" himself taking notice of it to me, that he had hardly seen her the week before. At dinner he did use me with the greatest solemnity in the world, in carving for me, and nobody else, and calling often to my Lady to cut for me; and all the respect possible.

---

[1] Sir Nicholas Slaning, K.B., married a daughter of Sir George Carteret.

6th. With Sir J. Minnes to St. James's, and there did our
business with the Duke. Great preparations for his speedy
return to sea. I saw him try on his buff coat and hat-piece
covered with black velvet. It troubles me more to think of
his venture than of any thing else in the whole war. I saw
Besse go away; she having, of all wenches that ever lived with
us, received the greatest love and kindness, and good clothes
besides wages, and gone away with the greatest ingratitude.

8th. This morning is brought me to the office the sad news
of The London, in which Sir J. Lawson's men were all bringing her from Chatham to the Hope, and thence he was to go
to sea in her; but a little on this side the buoy of the Nore,
she suddenly blew up. About twenty-four men and a woman
that were in the round-house and coach saved; the rest, being
above 300, drowned: the ship breaking all in pieces, with 80
pieces of brass ordnance. She lies sunk, with her round-
house above water. Sir J. Lawson hath a great loss in this
of so many good chosen men, and many relations among them.
I went to the 'Change, where the news taken very much to
heart. To Gresham College, and there saw several pretty
experiments.

9th. At Paule's school, where I visited Mr. Crumlum at his
house; and, Lord! to see how ridiculous a conceited peda-
gogue he is, though a learned man, he being so dogmaticall in
all he do and says. But, among other discourse, we fell to
the old discourse of Paule's Schoole; and he did, upon my
declaring my value of it, give me one of Lilly's grammars of a
very old impression, as it was in the Catholique times, which
I shall much set by. This night my wife had a new suit of
flowered ash-coloured silk, very noble.

10th. At noon to the 'Change, where very hot, people's
proposal of the City giving the King another ship for The
London, that is lately blown up. It would be very handsome,
and, if well managed, might be done; but, I fear, if it be put
into ill hands, or that the courtiers do solicit it, it will never
be done. To the Committee of Tangier at White Hall,
where my Lord Barkeley, and Craven, and others; but, Lord!
to see how superficially things are done in the business of the

Lottery, which will be the disgrace of the Fishery and without profit.

11th. Sir J. Minnes from Lee Roade, where they have been to see the wrecke of "The London," out of which, they say, the guns may be got, but the hull of her will be wholly lost, as not being capable of being weighed.

12th. (Lord's day.) Borrowing Sir J. Minnes's coach, to my Lord Sandwich's, but he was gone abroad. I sent the coach back for my wife, my Lord a second time dining at home, on purpose to meet me, he having not dined once at home, but those times, since his coming from sea. I sat down, and read over the Bishop of Chichester's' sermon upon the anniversary of the King's death—much cried up, but methinks but a mean sermon. Down to dinner, where my wife in her new lace whiske, which indeed is very noble, and I am much pleased with it, and so my Lady also. Here very pleasant my Lord was at dinner; and after dinner did look over his plate,[2] which Burston hath brought him to-day, and is the last of the three that he will have made. After much discourse with my Lady about Sir G. Carteret's son, of whom she hath some thoughts for a husband for my Lady Jemimah, we away home by coach again.

13th. To St. James's, and there much business, the King also being with us a great while. This day my wife began to wear light-coloured locks, quite white almost, which, though it makes her look very pretty, yet, not being natural, vexes me, that I will not have her wear them. This day I saw my Lord Castlemaine at St. James's, lately come from France.

14th. Dined with Sir W. Batten and Sir J. Minnes, at the Tower, with Sir J. Robinson, at a farewell dinner which he gives Major Holmes at his going out of the Tower, where he hath for some time, since his coming from Guinny, been a prisoner,[3] and, it seems, had presented the Lieutenant with fifty pieces yesterday. Here a great deal of good victuals and company.

---

[1] See note to July 8, 1660.　　　　　[2] See Feb. 18, 1664-5.

[3] For taking New York from the Dutch. See 29th Sept., 1664, *ante*.

15th. To dinner, where my wife being gone down upon a
sudden warning from my Lord Sandwich's daughters, to the
Hope with them, to see the Prince, I dined alone. Anon to
Gresham College, where, among other good discourse, there
was tried the great poyson of Macassa[1] upon a dogg, but it
had no effect all the time we sat there.

16th. At noon, home to dinner, where my wife told me the
unpleasant journey she had yesterday among the children,
whose fear upon the water and folly made it very unpleasing
to her. This afternoon, Mr. Harris, the sayle-maker, sent
me a noble present of two large silver candlesticks and
snuffers, and a slice to keep them upon, which indeed is very
handsome.

17th. This night, my Lady Wood died of the small-pox,
and is much lamented among the great persons for a good-
natured woman and a good wife. The Duke did give us
some commands, and so broke up, not taking leave of him.
But the best piece of newes is, that, instead of a great many
troublesome Lords, the whole business is to be left with the
Duke of Albemarle to act as Admirall in his stead; which is
a thing that do cheer my heart; for the other would have
vexed us with attendance, and never done the business. Povy
and I by water to London together. In the way, of his own
accord, he proposed to me that he would surrender his
place of Treasurer[2] to me to have half the profit. The thing
is new to me; but, the more I think, the more I like it, and
do put him upon getting it done by the Duke.

19th. (Lord's day.) Mr. Povy sent his coach for me betimes, and I to him, and there, to our great trouble, do find
that my Lord FitzHarding do appear for Mr. Brouncker[3] to
be Paymaster on Povy's going out, by a former promise of
the Duke's, and offering to give as much as any for it. This
put us all into a great damp; and so we went to Creed's new
lodging in the Mewes, and there we found Creed with his
parrot upon his shoulder, which struck Mr. Povy coming by just
by the eye, very deep, which had it hit his eye, had put it out.

[1] The Upas-tree.   [2] For Tangier.
[3] See note to March 24, 1667, postea.

At last, I t) Mr. Coventry, and there had his most friendly
and ingenuous advice, advising me not to decline the thing, it
being that, that will bring me to be known to great persons,
while now I am buried among three or four of us, says he, in
the Navy; but do not make a declared opposition to my
Lord FitzHarding. Then to my Lord Sandwich's to dinner,
and after dinner to Mr. Povy's, who hath been with the Duke
of York, and, by the mediation of Mr. Coventry, the Duke
told him that the business shall go on, and he will take off
Brouncker, and my Lord FitzHarding is quiett, too. Mr. Povy
and I in his coach to Hyde Parke, being the first day of the
tour there; where many brave ladies: among others, Castlemaine lay impudently upon her back in her coach, asleep,
with her mouth open. There was also my Lady Kerneguy,[1]
once my Lady Anne Hambleton. Here I saw Sir J. Lawson's daughter and husband, a fine couple, and also Mr.
Southwell and his new lady, very pretty. Thence back,
putting in at Dr. Where's, where I saw his lady, a very fine
woman.

20th. Creed and I had Mr. Povy's coach sent for us, and
we to his house; where we did some business, in order to the
work of this day. Povy and I to my Lord Sandwich, who
tells me that the Duke is not only a friend to the business,
but to me, in terms of the greatest love and respect and
value of me that can be thought, which overjoys me. Thence
to St. James's, and there was in great doubt of Brouncker;
but at last I hear that Brouncker desists. The Duke did
direct Secretary Bennet to declare his mind to the Tangier
Committee, that he approves of me for Treasurer; and with a
character of me to be a man whose industry and discretion he
would trust as soon as any man's in England: and did the like
to my Lord Sandwich. So to White Hall, to the Committee
of Tangier, where there were present, my Lord of Albemarle,
my Lord Peterborough, Sandwich, Barkeley, FitzHarding,
Secretary Bennet, Sir Thomas Ingram, Sir John Lawson,

---

[1] Daughter of William Duke of Hamilton, wife of Lord Carnegy, who became
Earl of Southesk on his father's death. She is frequently mentioned in the
Mémoires de Grammont, and in the Letters of the second Earl of Chesterfield.

Povy, and I; where, after other business. Povy did declare
his business very handsomely; that he was sorry he had been
so unhappy in his accounts, as not to give their Lordships the
satisfaction he intended, and that he was sure his accounts
were right, and continues to submit them to examination, and
is ready to lay down in ready money the fault of his account;
and that for the future, that the work might be better done,
and with more quiet to him, he desired, by approbation of the
Duke, he might resign his place to Mr. Pepys. Whereupon,
Secretary Bennet did deliver the Duke's command, which was
received with great content and allowance beyond expectation; the Secretary repeating also the Duke's character of me.
And I could discern my Lord FitzHarding was well pleased
with me, and signified full satisfaction, and whispered something seriously of me to the Secretary. And there I received
their constitution under all their hands presently; so that I
am already confirmed their Treasurer, and put into a condition of striking of tallys: and all without one harsh word of
dislike, but quite the contrary; which is a good fortune beyond
all imagination. Here we rose, and Povy and Creed and I,
all full of joy, thence to dinner, they setting me down at Sir
J. Winter's, by promise, and dined with him, and a worthy
fine man he seems to be, and of good discourse; and a fine
thing it is to see myself come to the condition of being
received by persons of this rank, he being, and having long
been, Secretary to the Queen-Mother. News is this day
come of Captain Allen's being come home from the Streights,
as far as Portland, with eleven of the King's ships, and
about twenty-two of merchantmen.

21st. My taylor coming to me, did consult all my wardrobe,
how to order my clothes against next summer. Received a
couple of state-caps, very large, coming, I suppose, to about
6l. a-piece, from Burrows, the slop-seller.

22d. To Mr. Houblon's,¹ the merchant, where Sir William

---

¹ James Houblon, an eminent London merchant, remarkable for his piety and
plainness. Two of his sons rose to great wealth, and became Knights and Aldermen.
Sir James Houblon served in Parliament for his native city. Sir John was Lord
Mayor in 1695, and at the same time a Lord of the Admiralty and Governor of

Petty, and abundance of most ingenious men, owners and
freighters of "The Experiment," now going with her two
bodies to sea. Most excellent discourse. Sir William Petty
did tell me that in good earnest he hath in his will[1] left some
parts of his estate to him that could invent such and such
things. As among others, that could discover truly the way
of milk coming into the breasts of a woman; and he that
could invent proper characters to express to another the mixture of relishes and tastes. And says, that to him that
invents gold, he gives nothing for the philosopher's stone;
for, says he, they that find out that, will be able to pay themselves. But, says he, by this means it is better than to go
to a lecture; for here my executors, that must part with this,
will be sure to be well convinced of the invention, before they
do part with their money. After dinner, Mr. Hill took me
with Mrs. Houblon,[2] who is a fine gentlewoman, into another
room, and there made her sing, which she do very well, to
my great content. Thence to Gresham College, and there
did see a kitling killed almost quite, but that we could not
quite kill her, with such a way: the ayre out of a receiver,
wherein she was put, and then the ayre being let in upon her,
revives her immediately—nay, and this ayre is to be made by
putting together a liquor and some body that ferments — the
steam of that do do the work. I saw the Duke, kissed his
hand, and had his most kind expressions of his value and

---

the Bank. The best account of the father is to be found in the subjoined epitaph
said to be written by Pepys. Mr. John Archer Houblon, of Hallingbury, Essex,
is the present representative of this very respectable family.

Jacobus Houblon,
Londin: Petri filius,
Ob fidem Flandriâ exulantis:
Ex C. Nepotibus habuit LXX superstites:
Filios V. videns mercatores florentissimos;
Ipse Londinensis Bursæ Pater.
Piissimâ obiit Nonagenarius,
A.D. MDCLXXXII.
See Pennant's *London*, 4to. ed., p. 305.

[1] A copy of Sir William Petty's will, dated 1685, is in the British Museum
Addit. MSS., No. 15,858, fol. 109. See also Lodge's *Irish Peerage*, vol. ii.,
p. 60.

[2] The wife of James Houblon, Mary Ducane. They were married 11th November, 1620, and had twelve children.

opinion of me, which comforted me above all things in the world: the like from Mr. Coventry most heartily and affectionately. Saw, among other fine ladies, Mrs. Middleton,[1] a very great beauty; and I saw Waller,[2] the poet, whom I never saw before.

23d. To my Lord Sandwich, who follows the Duke this day by water down to the Hope, where the Prince lies. He received me, busy as he was, with mighty kindness and joy at my promotions; telling me most largely how the Duke hath expressed on all occasions his good opinion of my service, and love for me. I paid my thanks and acknowledgement to him; and so back home, where at the office all the morning.

24th. To Povy's, and there delivered him his letters of greatest import to him that is possible, yet dropped by young Bland, just come from Tangier, upon the road by Sittingburne, taken up, and sent to Mr. Pett, at Chatham. Thus everything done by Povy is done with a fatal folly and neglect. To my Lady Sandwich's, where my wife all this day, having kept Good Friday very strict with fasting. Here we supped, and talked very merry. My Lady alone with me, very earnest about Sir G. Carteret's son, with whom I perceive they do desire my Lady Jemimah may be matched.

25th. This afternoon of a sudden is come home Sir W. Pen from the fleet, upon what score I know not.

26th. (Lord's day and Easter day.) With my wife to church. Home to dinner, my wife and I, Mercer staying the Sacrament, alone. This is the day seven years which, by the blessing of God, I have survived of my being cut of the stone, and am now in very perfect good health, and have long been; and though the last winter hath been as hard a winter as any have been these many years, yet I never was better in my life, nor have not, these ten years, gone colder in the summer than I have done all this winter, wearing only a doublet, and a

---

[1] Jane, daughter of Sir Robert Needham, is frequently mentioned in *Mémoires de Grammont*. Her portrait is in the Royal Collection at Hampton Court amongst the beauties of Charles II.'s Court. See *postea*, Feb. 17, 1668-9. Sir Robert Needham was related to John Evelyn: *Diary*, Aug. 2, 1683.

[2] Edmund Waller.

waistcoat cut open on the back; abroad, a cloak, and within
doors a coat I slipped on. Now I am at a loss to know
whether it be my hare's foot which is my preservation; for I
never had a fit of the collique since I wore it, or whether it be
my taking of a pill of turpentine every morning.

27th. Up betimes to Mr. Povy's, and there did sign and
seal my agreement with him about my place of being Treasurer for Tangier. Thence to the Duke of Albemarle, the first
time that we officers of the Navy have waited upon him since
the Duke of York's going, who hath deputed him to be
Admirall in his absence;[1] and I find him a quiet heavy man,
that will help business when he can, and hinder nothing. I
did afterwards alone give him thanks for his favour to me about
my Tangier business, which he received kindly, and did speak
much of his esteem of me. Thence, and did the same to Sir
H. Bennet, who did the like to me very fully. To my Lord
Peterborough's; where Povy, Creed, Williamson, Auditor
Beale, and myself, and mighty merry to see how plainly my
Lord and Povy do abuse one another about their accounts,
each thinking the other a fool, and I thinking they were not
either of them, in that point, much in the wrong, though in
everything, and even in this manner of reproaching one another, very witty and pleasant. Among other things, we had
here the genteelest dinner and the neatest house that I have
seen many a day, and the latter beyond anything I ever saw
in a nobleman's house. Thence visited my Lord Barkeley,
and he mighty friendly to me about the same business of
Tangier. He said that the Parliament must be called again
soon, and more money raised, not by tax, for he said he believed the people could not pay it, but he would have either a
general excise upon everything, or else that every city incorporate should pay a toll into the King's revenue, as he says it
is in all the cities in the world; for here a citizen hath no
more laid on than their neighbours in the country, whereas,

[1] In a letter of 22 March, 1664–5, from the Duke of York to the Duke,
Albemarle, on the power he assigns to him in his absence, printed in *Memoirs
of Naval Affairs*, &c., 8vo, 1729, p. 51. On the 23d, the Duke of York
assumed the command of the fleet against the Dutch.

as a city, it ought to pay considerably to the King, for their charter; but I fear this will breed ill blood.

29th. Drawing up a proposal for Captain Taylor, for him to deliver to the City about his building the new ship, which I have done well, and I hope will do the business.

31st. To visit my Lord of Falmouth, who did also receive me pretty civilly, but not as I expected; he, I perceive, believing that I had undertaken to justify Povy's accounts, taking them upon myself; but I rectified him therein. I find Creed mightily transported by my Lord of Falmouth's kind words to him, and saying that he hath a place in his intention for him, which he believes will be considerable. A witty man he is in every respect, but of no good nature, nor a man ordinarily to be dealt with. My Lady Castlemaine is sick again—people think, slipping her filly.[2]

April 1st. Dining at Captain Cocke's, in Broad Streete, very merry. Among other tricks, there did come a blind fiddler to the door, and Sir G. Carteret did go to the door, and lead the blind fiddler by the hand in. With Sir G. Carteret, Sir W. Batten, and Sir J. Minnes, to my Lord Treasurer, and there did lay open the expence for the six months past, and an estimate of the seven months to come, to November next; the first arising to above 500,000l., and the latter will, as we judge, come to above 1,000,000l. But to see how my Lord Treasurer did bless himself, crying he would do no more than he could, nor give more money than he had, if the occasion and expence were never so great, which is but a bad story.

3d. To a play at the Duke's, of my Lord Orrery's, called "Mustapha,"[3] which, being not good, made Betterton's part and Ianthe's but ordinary too. All the pleasure of the play was, the King and my Lady Castlemaine were there; and pretty witty Nell Gwynn, at the King's house, and the younger Marshall sat next us; which pleased me mightily.

---

[1] Lord Fitzharding had just been advanced to the Earldom of Falmouth.

[2] This did not occur, for George Fitzroy, created Duke of Northumberland, was born 28th September following.

[3] There was another tragedy of this name, by Fulke Greville, Lord Brook.

5th. This day was kept publicly, by the King's command, as a fast day against the Dutch war. To Woolwich and Deptford, where did a very great deal of business, and then home, and there by promise find Creed, and he and my wife, and Mercer and I, by coach to take the ayre; and where we had formerly been, at Hackney, did there eat some pullets we carried with us, and some things of the house; and after a game or two at shuffle-board, home, and Creed lay with me; but, being sleepy, he had no mind to talk about business, which indeed I intended, by inviting him to lie with me, so to bed, he and I to sleep, being the first time I have been so much at my ease, and taken so much fresh ayre, these many weeks or months.

6th. Attended the Duke of Albemarle about the business of money. I also went to Jervas's, my barber, for my periwigg that was mending there. Great talk of a new Comet: and it is certain do appear as bright as the late one at the best; but I have not seen it myself.

7th. Sir Philip Warwick did show me nakedly the King's condition for money for the Navy; and he do assure me, unless the King can get some nobleman or rich money-gentlemen to lend him money, or to get the City to do it, it is impossible to find money: we having already, as he says, spent one year's share of the three-years' tax, which comes to 2,500,000*l*.

8th. To the Old Exchange, and there, of my pretty seamstress, bought four bands. The French Embassadors[1] are come incognito before their train, which will, hereafter, be very pompous. It is thought they come to get our King to joyne with the King of France, in helping him against Flanders, and they to do the like to us against Holland. We have lain a good while with a good fleete at Harwich. The Dutch not said yet to be out. We, as high as we make our shew, I am sure, are unable to set out another small fleete, if this should be worsted. Wherefore, God send us peace! I cry.

9th. (Lord's day.) To church with my wife, in the morning,

---

[1] The French Ambassadors were Henri de Bourbon, Duc de Verneuil, natural son of Henry IV. and brother of Henrietta Maria; and M. de Courtin.

in her new light-coloured silk gown, which is, with her new point, very noble. In the afternoon, to Fenchurch, the little church in the middle of Fenchurch Street, where a very few people, and few of any rank.

10th. My Lord Brouncker took me and Sir Thomas Harvy in his coach to the Park, which is very troublesome with the dust; and ne'er a great beauty there to-day but Mrs. Middleton.

11th. At noon dined at the Sun, behind the 'Change, with Sir Edward Deering,[1] and his brother and Commissioner Pett, we having made a contract with Sir Edward this day about timber.

12th. To a Committee of Tangier, where, contrary to all expectation, my Lord Ashly, being vexed with Povy's accounts, did propose it as necessary that Povy should be still continued Treasurer of Tangier till he had made up his accounts; and with such arguments as, I confess, I was not prepared to answer, but by putting off of the discourse, and so, I think, brought it right again, but it troubled me. Sir G. Carteret, my Lord Brouncker, Sir Thomas Harvy, and myself, down to my Lord Treasurer's chamber to him and the Chancellor, and the Duke of Albemarle; and there I did give them a large account of the charge of the Navy, and want of money. But strange to see how they hold up their hands, crying, "What shall we do?" Says my Lord Treasurer, "Why, what means all this, Mr. Pepys? This is all true, you say; but what would you have me to do? I have given all I can for my life. Why will not people lend their money? Why will they not trust the King as well as Oliver? Why do our prizes come to nothing, that yielded so much heretofore?" And this was all we could get, and went away without other answer, which is one of the saddest things that, at such a time as this, with the greatest action on foot that ever was in England, nothing should be minded, but let things go on of themselves, and do as well as they can. So home, vexed, and going to

[1] Sir Edward Dering, of Surrenden Dering, Kent, which county he represented frequently in Parliament. He was the second Baronet of his family, and some time one of the Lords of the Treasury. He died in 1684.

my Lady Batten's, there found a great many women with her, in her chamber merry—my Lady Pen and her daughter, among others, where my Lady Pen flung me down upon the bed, and herself and others, one after another, upon me, and very merry we were.

13th. To Sheriff Waterman's[1] to dinner, all of us men of the office in town, and our wives, my Lady Carteret and daughters, and Ladies Batten, Pen, and my wife, &c. Very good cheer we had, and merry musique at and after dinner, and a fellow danced a jigg; but, when the company begun to dance, I come away, lest I should be taken out; and God knows how my wife carried herself, but I left her to try her fortune.

14th. Up, and betimes to Mr. Povy, being desirous to have an end of my trouble of mind touching my Tangier business, whether he hath any desire of accepting what my Lord Ashly offered, of his becoming Treasurer again: and there I did, with a seeming most generous spirit, offer him to take it back again upon his own terms; but he did answer me, that he would not, above all things in the world, at which I was for the present satisfied; but, going away thence, and speaking with Creed, he puts me in doubt that the very nature of the thing will require that he be put in again; and did give me the reasons of the auditors, which, I confess, are so plain, that I know not how to withstand them. But he did give me most ingenious advice what to do in it, and anon, my Lord Barkeley and some of the Commissioners coming together, though not in a meeting, I did procure that they should order Povy's payment of his remain of accounts to me; which order, if it do pass, will put a good stop to the fastening of the thing upon me. Called my wife, and with her through the city, to Mile-End Greene, and eat some creame and cakes, and so back home. This morning, I was saluted with news that the fleetes, our's and the Dutch, were engaged, and that the guns were heard at Walthamstow to play all yesterday, and that Captain Teddiman's legs were shot off in the Royall

---

[1] George Waterman, Sheriff of London, afterwards knighted, and Lord Mayor, 672.

Catherine. But, before night, I heard the contrary, both by letters of my own, and messengers thence, that they were all well of our side, and no enemy appears yet, and that the Royall Catherine is come to the fleete, and likely to prove as good a ship as any the King hath, of which I am heartily glad, both for Christopher Pett's sake, and Captain Teddiman, that is in her.

16th. (Lord's day.) I walked to the Rolls' Chapel, expecting to hear the great Stillingfleet[1] preach, but he did not; but a very sorry fellow, which vexed me. Captain [Silas] Taylor,[2] my old acquaintance at Westminster, supped with me, and a good understanding man he is, and a good schollar; and, among other things, a great antiquary. He can, as he says, show the very originall Charter to Worcester, of King Edgar's,[3] wherein he stiles himself, Rex Marium Britanniæ, &c.; which is the great text that Mr. Selden and others do quote, but imperfectly and upon trust. But he hath the very originall, which, he says, he will show me. This night news is come of our taking three Dutch men-of-war, with the loss of one of our Captains.

17th. To the Duke of Albemarle's, where he showed me Mr. Coventry's letters, how three Dutch privateers are taken, in one whereof Everson's son is captaine. But they have killed poor Captain Golding in the Diamond. Two of them, one of 32, and the other of 20 odd guns, did stand stoutly up against her, which hath 46, and the Yarmouth, that hath 52 guns, and as many more men as they. So that they did

---

[1] Edward Stillingfleet, the learned Divine, consecrated Bishop of Worcester in 1689. Ob. 1699.

[2] See *ante*, Nov. 7, 1663.

[3] This is the celebrated *Charta Eadgari R. de Oswaldeslawe*, dat. Gloucester. 28th Dec., 964, mentioning not only the Dominion of the Sea, but also that Edgar had subdued the greatest part of Ireland, a piece of history which rests solely on the authority of this instrument. It is cited by Coke, Selden, Ussher, Dugdale, and Spelman, not to mention inferior names. Three copies existed; the finest and most complete, and probably the same which is here mentioned by Taylor, is now in the Harleian Collection in the British Museum. It is fully described in the *Dissertatio Epistolaris* (p. 86) prefixed by Hickes to his *Thesaurus Linguarum Septentrionalium*, and an engraved fac-simile of the whole is given by him at the end. It is right to say, that the charter is now generally considered to be a forgery executed in later times.

more than we could expect, not yielding till many of their men were killed. And Everson, when he was brought before the Duke of York, and was observed to be shot through the hat, answered, that he wished it had gone through his head, rather than been taken. One thing more is written; that two of our ships the other day appearing upon the coast of Holland, they presently fired their beacons round the country to give them notice. And news is brought the King, that the Dutch Smyrna fleete is seen upon the back of Scotland; and thereupon the King hath wrote to the Duke, that he do appoint a fleete to go to the Northward, to try to meet them coming home round: which God send! Thence to White Hall; where the King, seeing me, did come to me, and, calling me by name, did discourse with me about the ships in the River: and this is the first time that ever I knew the King did know me personally; so that hereafter I must not go thither, but with expectation to be questioned, and to be ready to give good answers. Thence with Creed, who come to dine with me, to the Old James, where we dined with Sir W. Rider and Cutler, and, by and by, being called by my wife, we all to a play, "The Ghosts,"[1] at the Duke's house, but a very simple play. This day was left at my house a very neat silver watch, by one Briggs, a scrivener and solicitor, which I was angry with my wife for receiving, or, at least, for opening the box wherein it was, and so far witnessing our receipt of it, as to give the messenger 5s. for bringing it; but it can't be helped, and I will endeavour to do the man a kindness, he being a friend of my uncle Wight's.

18th. To Sir Philip Warwick, and with him to my Lord Treasurer, who signed my commission for Tangier Treasurer, and the docquet of my Privy Scale, for the monies to be paid to me.

19th. Up by five o'clock, and by water to White Hall; and there took coach, and with Mr. Moore to Chelsey: where, after all my fears what doubts and difficulties my Lord Privy Seale would make at my Tangier Privy Seale, he did pass it

---

[1] A comedy, on the authority of Downes (p. 26), attributed to a Mr. Holden, and probably never printed.

at first reading, without my speaking with him: and then called me in, and was very civil to me. I passed my time in contemplating, before I was called in, the picture of my Lord's son's lady,[1] a most beautiful woman, and most like to Mrs. Butler. Thence very much joyed to London back again, and found out Mr. Povy; told him this, and then went and left my Privy Seale at my Lord Treasurer's: and so to the 'Change, and thence to Trinity-house; where a great dinner of Captain Crisp, who is made an Elder Brother. And so, being very pleasant at dinner, away home, Creed with me, and there met Povy; and we to Gresham College, where we saw some experiments upon a hen, a dog, and a cat, of the Florence poyson. The first it made for a time drunk, but it come to itself again quickly; the second it made vomit mightily, but no other hurt. The third I did not stay to see the effect of it.

20th. This night I am told the first play is played in White Hall noon-hall, which is now turned to a house of playing.

21st. This day we hear that the Duke and the fleete are sailed yesterday. Pray God go along with them, that they have good speed in the beginning of their work.

22d. My wife making great preparations to go to Court to Chapel to-morrow.

23d. (Lord's day.) Mr. Povy, according to promise, sent his coach betimes, and I carried my wife and her woman to White Hall Chapel, and heard the famous young Stillingfleet, whom I knew at Cambridge, and he is now newly admitted one of the King's chaplains; and was presented, they say, to my Lord Treasurer for St. Andrew's, Holborn, where he is now minister, with these words: that they, the Bishops of Canterbury, London, and another, believed he is the ablest young man to preach the Gospel of any since the Apostles. He did make a most plain, honest, good, grave sermon, in the most unconcerned and easy yet substantial manner, that ever I heard in my life, upon the words of Samuel to the people: "Fear the Lord in truth with all your heart, and remember

---

[1] Sarah Bodvill. See 3d May, 1664.

the great things that he hath done for you;" it being proper to this day, the day of the King's Coronation. After dinner, Creed and we by coach took the ayre in the fields beyond St. Pancras, it raining now and then, which it seems is most welcome weather. After supper, Creed and I together to bed, in Mercer's bed; and so to sleep.

24th. To the Duke of Albemarle, where very busy. To my Lady Sandwich's to dinner, where my wife by agreement. My Lady told me, with the prettiest kind of doubtfullness, whether it would be fit for her with respect to Creed to do it, that is in the world, that Creed had broke his desire to her of being a servant to Mrs. Betty Pickering, and placed it upon encouragement which he had from some discourse of her ladyship, commending of her virtues to him, which, poor lady, she meant most innocently. She did give him a cold answer, but not so severe as it ought to have been; and, it seems, as the lady since to my Lady confesses, he had wrote a letter to her, which she answered slightly, and was resolved to contemn any notion of his therein. My Lady takes the thing very ill, as it is fit she should; but I advise her to stop all future occasions of the world's taking notice of his coming thither so often, as of late he hath done. But to think that he should have this devilish presumption to aim at a lady so near to my Lord is strange, both for his modesty and discretion. Thence to the Cocke-pitt, and there walked an hour with my Lord Duke of Albemarle alone in his garden, where he expressed in great words his opinion of me; that I was the right hand of the Navy here, nobody but I taking any care of anything therein; so that he should not know what could be done without me. At which I was, from him, not a little proud. So by coach with my wife and Mercer to the Parke; but the King being there, and I now-a-days being doubtfull of being seen in any pleasure, did part from the tour, and away out of the Park to Knightsbridge, and there eat and drank in the coach, and so home.

25th. This afternoon, W. Pen, lately come from his father in the fleete, did give me an account how the fleete did sail, about 103 in all, besides small catches, they being in

20 *

sight of six or seven Dutch scouts, and sent ships in chase of them.

26th. Away to White Hall, talking with Povy alone, about my opinion of Creed's indiscretion in looking after Mrs. Pickering, desiring him to make no more a sport of it, but to correct him, if he finds that he continues to own any such thing. This I did by my Lady's desire, and do intend to pursue the stop of it. To my Lady Sandwich's, and with her talking again about Creed's folly; but strange it is that he should dare to propose this business himself of Mrs. Pickering to my Lady, and to tell my Lady that he did it for her virtue sake, not minding her money, for he could have a wife with more, but, for all that, he did intend to depend upon her Ladyship to get as much of her father and mother for her as she could. But I do very much fear that Mrs. Pickering's honour, if the world comes to take notice of it, may be wronged by it.

27th. Creed dined with me; and, after dinner, walked in the garden, he telling me that my Lord Treasurer now begins to be scrupulous, and will know what becomes of the 26,000l. saved by my Lord Peterborough, before he parts with any more money, which puts us into new doubts, and me into a great fear, that all my cake will be doe[1] still. This night, William Hewer is returned from Harwich, where he hath been paying off some ships this fortnight, and went to sea a good way with the fleete, which was 96 in company then, men of war, besides some come in, and following them since, which makes now above 100 — whom God bless!

28th. Down the River, to visit the victualling-ships, where I find all out of order. And come home to dinner, and then to write a letter to the Duke of Albemarle about them, and carried it myself to the Council-chamber; and, when they rose, my Lord Chancellor, passing by, stroked me on the head, and told me that the Board had read my letter, and taken order for the punishing of the watermen for not appearing on board the ships. And so did the King afterwards, who do now know me so well, that he never sees me but he speaks to me about our Navy business.

---

[1] Dough.

29th. Troubled in my mind to hear that Sir W. Batten and Sir J. Minnes do take notice that I am now-a-days much from the office, upon no office business : but what troubles me more is, that I do omit to write, as I should do, to Mr. Coventry, which I must not do, though this night I minded it so little as to sleep in the middle of my letter to him, and committed forty blotts and blurrs, but of this I hope never more to be guilty.

30th. (Lord's day.) I with great joy find myself to have gained, this month, above 100*l.* clear, and in the whole to be worth 1400*l.* Thus I end this month in great content as to my estate and gettings : in much trouble as to the pains I have taken, and the rubs I expect to meet with, about the business of Tangier. The fleete, with about 106 ships upon the coast of Holland, in sight of the Dutch, within the Texel. Great fears of the sicknesse here in the City, it being said that two or three houses are already shut up. God preserve us all !

May 1st. I met my Lord Brouncker, Sir Robert Murray, Dean Wilkins, and Mr. Hooke, going by coach to Colonel Blunt's[1] to dinner. So they stopped, and took me with them. Landed at the Tower-wharf, and thence by water to Greenwich ; and there coaches met us : and to his house, a very stately site for situation and brave plantations ; and among others, a vine-yard, the first that ever I did see. No extraordinary dinner, nor any other entertainment good ; but afterwards to the tryal of some experiments about making of coaches easy. And several we tried ; but one did prove mighty easy, not here for me to describe, but the whole body of the coach lies upon one long spring, and we all, one after another, rid in it ; and it is very fine and likely to take. Thence to Deptford, and in to Mr. Evelyn's,[2] which is a most beautiful place ; but, it being dark, and late, I staid not ; but Dean Wilkins, and

---

[1] At Wricklesmarsh, in the parish of Charlton, which belonged, in 1617, to Edward Blount, whose family alienated it towards the end of the seventeenth century. The old mansion was pulled down by Sir Gregory Page, Bart., who erected a magnificent stone structure on the site ; which, devolving to his great nephew, Sir Gregory Page Turner, shared the same fate as the former house, having been sold in lots in 1784. The site of Colonel Blount's house is now covered with villas, and is called Blackheath Park.

[2] Sayes Court, the well-known residence of John Evelyn.

Mr. Hooke and I, walked to Redriffe; and noble discourse all day long did please me.

3d. To the Inn by Cripplegate, expecting my mother's coming to town, but she is not come this week, the coach being too full. My Lord Chief-Justice Hide did die suddenly this week, a day or two ago, of an apoplexy.

5th. After dinner, to Mr. Evelyn's; he being abroad, we walked in his garden, and a lovely noble ground he hath indeed. And, among other rarities, a hive of bees, so as, being hived in glass, you may see the bees making their honey and combs mighty pleasantly. This day, after I had suffered my own hayre to grow long, in order to wearing it, I find the convenience of periwiggs is so great, that I have cut off all short again, and will keep to periwiggs.

7th. (Lord's day.) Up, and to church with my wife. Yesterday begun my wife to learn to limn of one Browne, which Mr. Hill helps her to, and by her beginning, upon some eyes, I think she will do very fine things, and I shall take great delight in it.

9th. At noon comes Mrs. The. Turner, and dines with us, and my wife's painting-master staid and dined. This day we have news of eight ships being taken by some of ours, going into the Texel—their two men-of-war, that convoyed, running in. They come from about Ireland, round to the North.

10th. To the Cocke-pitt, where the Duke of Albemarle did give Sir W. Batten and me an account of the late taking of eight ships, and of his intent to come back to the Gunfleete with the fleete presently; which creates us much work and haste therein, against the fleete comes. And thence to the Guard in Southwarke, there to get some soldiers, by the Duke's order, to go keep pressmen on board our ships.

12th. By water to the Exchequer, and strike my tallys[1] fo-

---

[1] The use of tallies, so frequently alluded to in the Diary, having been discontinued, some explanation of the term may not be considered unacceptable. Formerly, accounts were kept, and large sums of money paid and received, by the King's Exchequer, with little other form than the exchange or delivery of tallies, pieces of wood notched or scored, corresponding blocks being kept by the parties to the account: and from this usage one of the head officers of the Exchequer was called the Tallier, or Teller. These tallies were often negotiable

17,500*l*., which methinks is so great a testimony of the goodness of God to me, that I, from a mean clerk there, should come to strike tallys myself for that sum, and in the authority that I do now, is a very stupendous mercy to me. But to see how every little fellow looks after his fees, and to get what he can for everything, is a strange consideration. The King's fees that he must pay himself for this 17,500*l*. coming to above 100*l*. After dinner comes my cozen, Thomas Pepys, of Hatcham,[1] to receive some money of my Lord Sandwich's, and then I paid him what was due to him, upon my uncle's score, but, contrary to my expectation, did get him to sign and seal to any sale of lands for payment of debts.

13th. To the 'Change, after office, and received my watch from the watch-maker, and a very fine one it is, given me by Briggs, the scrivener. But, Lord, to see how much of my old folly and childishnesse hangs upon me still, that I cannot forbear carrying my watch in my hand, in the coach, all this afternoon, and seeing what o'clock it is one hundred times, and am apt to think with myself, how could I be so long without one; though I remember, since, I had one, and found it a trouble, and resolved to carry one no more about me while I lived. Troubled at a letter from Mr. Cholmly from Tangier, wherein he do advise me how people are at work to overthrow our Victualling business, by which I shall lose 300*l*. per annum. I am much obliged to him for this secret kindness, and look after this.

14th. (Lord's day.) To church, it being Whit-Sunday; my wife very fine in a new yellow bird's-eye hood, as the fashion is now; my mother having her new suit brought home, which

---

Adam Smith, in his *Wealth of Nations*, book 11, ch. xi. says, that "in 1696 *tallies* had been at forty, and fifty and sixty per cent. discount, and bank-notes at twenty per cent." The system of tallies was discontinued about twenty years ago; and the destruction of the old Houses of Parliament, in the night of Oct. 16, 1834, is thought to have been occasioned by the overheating of the flues, when the furnaces were employed to consume the tallies, rendered useless by the alteration in the mode of keeping the Exchequer accounts. In the *Times* newspaper of the 1st November following appeared an article on *Tallies*, which embraces all that can be said on the subject: but although well worthy of being read, it is too long for insertion in these pages. It ends with the words, "yet one word more—Tally-ho!" It was written by Wm. Hone.

[1] Thomas Pepys, of Hatcham Barnes, Surrey, Master of the Jewell Office to Charles II., and in the next reign.

makes her very fine. My wife and she and Mercer to Thomas
Pepys's wife's christening of his first child. I took a coach,
and to Wanstead, the house where Sir H. Mildmay died, and
now Sir Robert Brookes lives, having bought it of the Duke
of York, it being forfeited to him: a fine seat, but an old-
fashioned house, and, being not full of people, looks flatly. I
all the afternoon in the coach, reading the treasonous book
of the Court of King James, printed a great while ago, and
worth reading, though ill intended.[1]

15th. After dinner to the King's playhouse, all alone, and
saw "Love's Maistresse"—some pretty things, and good variety
in it, but no or little fancy. Letters from Sir G. Downing,
of four days' date, that the Dutch are come out and joyned,
well manned, and resolved to board our best ships, and fight,
for certain, they will.

17th. To Langford's, where I never was since my brother
died there. I find my wife and Mercer, having with him
agreed upon two rich silk suits for me, which is fit for me to
have, but yet the money is too much, I doubt, to lay out
altogether; but it is done, and so let it be, it being the
expense of the world that I can the best bear with, and the
worst spare. The Duchess of York went down yesterday to
meet the Duke.

18th. To the Duke of Albemarle, where we did examine
Nixon and Stanesby, about their late running from two
Dutchmen; for which they were committed to a vessel to
carry them to the fleete to be tried. A most fowle unhand-
some thing as ever was heard, for plain cowardice on Nixon's
part. Thence with the Duke of Albemarle in his coach to my
Lord Treasurer, and there was before the King, who ever now
calls me by my name, and Lord Chancellor, and many other
great Lords, discoursing about insuring some of the King's
goods, wherein the King accepted of my motion that we should;
and so away, well pleased.

19th. To the Exchequer, and there got my tallys for
17,500l., the first payment I ever had out of the Exchequer,
and at the Legg spent 14s. upon my old acquaintance, some

---

[1] The work alluded to is Sir Anthony Weldon's.

of them the clerks, and away home with my tallys in a coach, fearful every moment of having one of them fall out, or snatched from me. Sir W. Warren did give me several good hints and principles not to do anything suddenly, but consult my pillow upon my Treasurership of Tangier, and every great thing in my life, before I resolve anything in it.

21st. (Lord's day.) This day is brought home one of my new silk suits—the plain one, but very rich camelott and noble. Tried it, and pleases me, but did not wear it, being I would not go out to-day to church.

22d. To Deptford, it being Trinity-Monday, and so the day of choosing the Master of Trinity House for the next year, where, to my great content, I find that, contrary to the practice and design of Sir W. Batten, to break the rule and custom of the Company in choosing their Masters by succession, he would have brought in Sir W. Rider or Sir W. Pen, over the head of Hurleston, who is a knave, too; besides, I believe, the younger brothers did all oppose it against the elder, and with great heat did carry it for Hurleston, which I know will vex him to the heart. Thence, the election being over, to church, where an idle sermon from that conceited fellow, Dr. Britton, saving that his advice to unity, and laying aside all envy and enmity among them, was very apposite. To the Trinity House, and a great dinner, as is usual.

23d. Late comes Sir Arthur Ingram[1] to my office, to tell me, that, by letters from Amsterdam, of the 18th of this month, the Dutch fleete, being about 100 men-of-war, besides fire-ships, &c., did set out upon the 13th and 14th inst. Being divided into seven squadrons, viz. 1. General Opdam. 2. Cottenar,[2] of Rotterdam. 3. Trump. 4. Schram, of Horne. 5. Stillingworth, of Freezland. 6. Everson. 7. One other, not named, of Zealand.

24th. To the Coffee-house, where all the news is of the Dutch being gone out, and of the plague growing upon us in this town; and of remedies against it: some saying one thing, and some another.

---

[1] Sir Arthur Ingram, of Knottingley, Surveyor of the Customs at Hull.
[2] Who died of his wounds after the sea-fight in 1665.

26th. In the evening by water to the Duke of Albemarle, whom I found mightily off the hooks, that the ships are not gone out of the River; which vexed me to see.

28th. (Lord's day.) I hear that Nixon is condemned to be shot to death, for his cowardice, by a Council of War. To Sir Philip Warwick's to dinner, where abundance of company come in unexpectedly; and here I saw one pretty piece of household stuff, as the company increaseth, to put a larger leaf upon an ovall table. After dinner, much good discourse with Sir Philip, who, I find, I think a most pious good man, and a professor of a philosophicall manner of life, and principles like Epictetus. Thence to my Lady Sandwich's, where, to my shame, I had not been a great while. Here, upon my telling her a story of my Lord Rochester's[1] running away on Friday night last with Mrs. Mallet, the great beauty and fortune of the North,[2] who had supped at White Hall with Mrs. Stewart, and was going home to her lodgings with her grandfather, my Lord Haly,[3] by coach; and was at Charing Cross seized on by both horse and foot-men, and forcibly taken from him, and put into a coach with six horses, and two women provided to receive her, and carried away. Upon immediate pursuit, my Lord of Rochester, for whom the King had spoke to the lady often, but with no success, was taken at Uxbridge; but the lady is not yet heard of, and the King mighty angry, and the Lord sent to the Tower. Hereupon my Lady did confess to me, as a great secret, her being concerned in this story; for if this match breaks between my Lord Rochester and her, then, by the consent of all her friends, my Lord Hinchingbroke stands fair, and is invited for her. She is worth, and will be at her mother's death, who keeps but a little from her, 2500l. per annum. Pray God give a good success to it! But my poor Lady,

---

[1] John Wilmot, second Earl of Rochester, notorious for his wit and profligacy. Ob. 1680. He married the lady alluded to, Elizabeth, daughter of John Mallett, of Enmore, co. Somerset. See 25th November, 1666.

[2] South?

[3] Mrs. Mallett's mother was Elizabeth, daughter of Lord Hawley, of Buckland House, Somersetshire, created a Baronet 1642, and in 1646 an Irish peer, by the title of Baron Hawley of Donamore; in 1671 he was chosen M.P. for St. Michael's, and in 1673 became a Gentleman of the Bedchamber to the Duke of York. Ob. 1684, aged 76.

who is afraid of the sickness, and resolved to be gone into
the country, is forced to stay in town a day or two, or three,
about it, to see the event of it. Thence to see my Lady Pen,
where my wife and I were shown a fine rarity: of fishes kept
in a glass of water, that will live so for ever; and finely
marked they are, being foreign.[1]

29th. To the Swan, and there drank at Herbert's, and so
by coach home — it being kept a great holyday through the
city, for the birth and restoration of the King. Home to
dinner, and then, with my wife, mother, and Mercer in one
boat, and I in another, down to Woolwich. We have everywhere taken some prizes. Our merchants had good luck to
come home safe—colliers from the North, and some Streights'
men, just now. And our Hambrough ships, of whom we
were so much afraid, are safe in Hambrough. Our fleete
resolve to sail out again from Harwich in a day or two.

30th. To dinner to Sir G. Carteret's. Here a very fine,
neat, French dinner, without much cost, we being all alone
with my Lady, and one of the house with her: and then, in
the evening, by coach, with my wife, and mother, and Mercer,
our usual tour by coach, and at the old house at Islington:
but, Lord! to see how my mother found herself talk upon
every object to think of old stories. Here I met with one
that tells me that Jack Cole, my old schoole-fellow, is dead
and buried lately of a consumption, who was a great chrony
of mine.

31st. To the 'Change, where great the noise and trouble of
having our Hambrough ships lost; and that very much placed
upon Mr. Coventry's forgetting to give notice to them of the
going away of our fleete from the coast of Holland. But all
without reason, for he did; but the merchants, not being
ready, staid longer than the time ordered for the convoy to
stay, which was ten days. To Huysman's, the painter, who,
I intend, shall draw my wife. He was not within, but I saw
several good pictures.

June 1st. After dinner, I put on my new camelott suit;
the best that ever I wore in my life, the suit costing me

---

[1] They were gold fish, brought from China.

above 24*l*. In this I went with Creed to Goldsmiths' Hall,
to the burial of Sir Thomas Viner;[1] which Hall, and Haberdashers' also, was so full of people, that we were fain for ease
and coolness to go forth to Pater Noster Row, to choose a
silk to make me a plain ordinary suit. That done, we walked
to Corne-hill, and there, at Mr. Cade's stood in the balcon,
and saw all the funeral, which was with the blue-coat boys
and old men, all the Aldermen, and Lord Mayor, &c., and
the number of the company very great : the greatest I ever
did see for a taverne.

2d. Met an express from Sir W. Batten at Harwich, that
the fleete is all sailed from Solebay, having spied the Dutch
Fleete at sea, and that, if the calms hinder not, they must
needs now be engaged with them. A letter also come to me
from Mr. Hater, committed by the Council this afternoon to
the Gate House, upon the misfortune of having his name
used by one, without his knowledge or privity, for the
receiving of some powder that he had bought. Up to Court
about these two, and for the former was led up to my Lady
Castlemaine's lodgings, where the King, and she, and others
were at supper, and there I read the letter and returned: and
to Sir G. Carteret about T. Hater, and shall have him released
to-morrow, upon my giving bail for his appearance. Sir G.
Carteret did go on purpose to the King to ask this, and it is
granted.

3d. To White Hall, and, upon entering into recognizances,
T. Hater was released. Home, vexed to be kept from the
office all the morning, which I had not been in many months
before, if not some years. All this day, by all people upon
the River, and almost everywhere else hereabout, were heard
the guns, our two fleets for certain being engaged; which was
confirmed by letters from Harwich, but nothing particular,
and all our hearts full of concernment for the Duke, and I
particularly for my Lord Sandwich and Mr. Coventry, after
his Royall Highness.

[1] Sheriff of London, 1648; when Lord Mayor in 1654, he was knighted by
Cromwell (Ludlow's *Memoirs*), and made Baronet, 1660. He was a goldsmith,
and dying 11th May, 1665, was buried in St. Mary Woolnoth, in Lombard
Street.

4th. (Lord's day.) News come that our fleete is pursuing the Dutch, who, either by cunning or by being worsted, do give ground, but nothing more for certain.

5th. Great talk of the Dutch being fled, and we in pursuit of them, and that our ship Charity is lost upon our Captain's, Wilkinson, and Lieutenant's yielding, but of this there is no certainty, save the report of some of the sick men of the Charity, turned adrift in a boat, and taken up and brought on shore yesterday to Sole Bay, and the news hereof brought by Sir Henry Felton.[1] Certain news come that our fleete is in sight of the Dutch ships.

6th. To my Lady Sandwich's; who, poor lady, expects every hour to hear of my Lord; but in the best temper, neither confident nor troubled with fear, that I ever did see in my life. She tells me my Lord Rochester is now declaredly out of hopes of Mrs. Mallett, and now she is to receive notice in a day or two how the King stands inclined to the giving leave for my Lord Hinchingbroke to look after her, and, that being done, to bring it to an end shortly.

7th. This morning my wife and mother rose about two o'clock; and with Mercer, Mary, the boy, and W. Hewer, as they had designed, took boat, and down to refresh themselves on the water to Gravesend. To the Dolphin taverne, where Sir J. Minnes, Lord Brouncker, Sir Thomas Harvy, and myself dined, upon Sir G. Carteret's charge, and very merry we were, Sir Thomas Harry being a very drolle. To the New Exchange, and there drunk whey, with much entreaty getting it for our money, and they would not be entreated to let us have one glasse more. So took water to Fox-Hall, to the Spring garden, and there walked an hour or two with great pleasure, saving our minds ill at ease concerning the fleete and my Lord Sandwich : but we have no news of them, and ill reports run up and down of his being killed, but without ground. Here staid, pleasantly walking, and spending

---

[1] Sir Henry Felton, of Playford, Suffolk, Bart., who married Susanne, daughter of Sir Lionel Talmash, of Helmingham, Bart. Their second son, Sir Thomas Felton, married Lady Elizabeth Howard, daughter and co-heir of James Lord Howard de Walden, and third Earl of Suffolk.

but 6d. till nine at night. The hottest day that ever I felt in my life. This day, much against my will, I did in Drury Lane see two or three houses marked with a red cross upon the doors, and "Lord have mercy upon us!" writ there; which was a sad sight to me, being the first of the kind that, to my remembrance, I ever saw. It put me into an ill conception of myself and my smell, so that I was forced to buy some roll-tobacco to smell to and chaw, which took away the apprehension. By water home, where weary with walking, and with the mighty heat of the weather, and for my wife's not coming home, I staying walking in the garden till twelve at night, when it begun to lighten exceedingly, through the greatness of the heat. Then, despairing of her coming home, I to bed.

8th. About five o'clock my wife come home, it having lightened all night hard, and one great shower of rain. She come and lay upon the bed: I up, and to the office all the morning. At one at home to dinner—my wife, mother, and Mercer dining at W. Joyce's; I giving her a caution to go round by the Half Moone to his house, because of the plague. I to my Lord Treasurer's by appointment of Sir Thomas Ingram's, to meet the Goldsmiths; where I met with the great news at last newly come, brought by Bab May[1] from

---

[1] Although the two Mays are so frequently mentioned in these pages, and by almost every contemporary annalist, no authentic account of their parentage has been traced; nor is it clear whether they were brothers, or in any way related. There is, however, a strong presumption that they sprung from a family of the same name, seated at Rawmere, in Sussex, one of whom, Jeffrey May, acquired property at Sutton Cheynell, in Leicestershire, in 1574, which was sold by the representatives of Baptist May, in 1712, under an Act passed for the payment of his debts. But though Nichols (*Hist. of Leicestershire*, vol. iv., part. ii., p. 548) gives a detailed pedigree of the Mays, he could not ascertain whose son Baptist May was, who held the office of Privy Purse to Charles II.; and he does not even allude to Hugh May. It is stated in Collins's *Peerage*, vol. ii., p. 560, edit. 1741, that during their flight after the battle of Worcester, James Duke of York delivered his George, which had been a present from the Queen his mother, to Mr. Hugh May, who preserved it through all difficulties, and afterwards returned it to his Royal Highness in Holland. Soon after 1662, Hugh May was established as an architect, and employed at Windsor, and in erecting stables at Cornbury, and in building Berkeley House, Piccadilly, and Cassiobury. (Evelyn's *Diary*.) He also held a place under Sir John Denham, the Surveyor of the Works, whom he expected to succeed; but the office becoming vacant, by the knight's death in 1667, was given to Sir Christopher Wren, and May was

the Duke of York, that we have totally routed the Dutch: that the Duke himself, the Prince, my Lord Sandwich, and Mr. Coventry are all well: which did put me into such joy, that I forgot almost all other thoughts. With great joy to the Cocke-pitt, where the Duke of Albemarle, like a man out of himself with content, new-told me all; and by and by comes a letter from Mr. Coventry's own hand to him, which he never opened, which was a strange thing, but did give it me to open and read, and consider what was fit for our office to do in it, and leave the matter with Sir W. Clerke; which, upon such a time and occasion, was a strange piece of indifference, hardly possible. I copied out the letter, and did also take minutes out of Sir W. Clerke's other letters; and the sum of the news is :—

VICTORY OVER THE DUTCH, JUNE 3, 1665.

This day they engaged: the Dutch neglecting greatly the opportunity of the wind they had of us; by which they lost the benefit of their fire-ships. The Earl of Falmouth, Muskerry, and Mr. Richard Boyle[2] killed on board the Duke's ship, the Royall Charles, with one shot: their blood and brains flying in the Duke's face; and the head of Mr. Boyle striking down the Duke, as some say. Earl of Marlborough, Portland,[3]

promised an annuity of 300l. out of the Works, to make up for his disappointment. Whatever may have been his professional merits, he is not even named in Horace Walpole's list of Architects: and we know nothing more of his career, except that in 1683 he was busy in building a house at Chiswick, for Sir Stephen Fox. Baptist May's history is soon told:—He was born about 1627, and after the Restoration belonged to the Duke of York's household: but he was promoted by the King to the office of Keeper of the Privy Purse, and became the confidant of Charles's amours. He was also made a Page of the Bed-chamber, which place he lost, having contrived to offend his Royal Master. In 1689-90, we find him returned at the general election as Burgess for Windsor, with Sir Christopher Wren: they were, however, both unseated by petition. Baptist died the 2d of May, 1693, and lies buried in St. George's Chapel, where the slab inscribed to his memory is still to be seen.

[1] See Sir John Denham's *Advice to a Painter* concerning the Dutch War, in *Poems on State Affairs*, vol. i., p. 24.

[2] Second son to the Earl of Burlington.

[3] Charles Weston, third Earl of Portland.

21 *

Rear Admirall Sansum,[1] to Prince Rupert, killed, and Captain
Kirby and Ableson. Sir John Lawson wounded on the
knee:[2] hath had some bones taken out, and is likely to be
well again. Upon receiving the hurt, he sent to the Duke
for another to command the Royall Oake. The Duke sent
Jordan[3] out of the St. George, who did brave things to her.
Captain Jeremiah Smith, of the Mary, was second to the
Duke, and stepped between him and Captain Seaton, of the
Urania, 76 guns and 400 men, who had sworn to board the
Duke; killed him 200 men, and took the ship; himself losing
99 men, and never an officer saved, but himself and lieutenant. His master indeed is saved, with his leg cut off. Admirall Opdam blown up, Trump killed, and said by Holmes;
all the rest of their admiralls, as they say, but Everson, whom
they dare not trust for his affection to the Prince of Orange,
are killed: we have taken and sunk, as is believed, about
twenty-four of their best ships; killed and taken near 8 or
10,000 men, and lost, we think, not above 700. A greater
victory never known in the world. They are all fled; some
43 got into the Texell, and others elsewhere, and we in pursuit of the rest. Thence, with my heart full of joy, home:

---

[1] "Robert Sansum, Commander of ye Resolution, being Rear Ad¹ of ye White."
—Pepys's *Collection of Signs Manual.*

[2] When Opdam's ship blew up, a shot from it mortally wounded Sir John
Lawson, which is thus alluded to in the *Poems on State Affairs*, vol. i. p. 28 :—

> "————— Destiny allowed
> Him his revenge, to make his death more proud.
> A fatal bullet from his side did range,
> And battered *Lawson*; oh. too dear exchange!
> He led our fleet that day too short a space,
> But lost his knee: since died, in glorious race:
> *Lawson*, whose valour beyond Fate did go,
> And still fights *Opdam* in the lake below."

In the same poem, Lord Falmouth's death is thus noticed :—

> "Falmouth was there, I know not what to act;
> Some say 'twas to grow Duke, too, by contract
> An untaught bullet, in its wanton scope,
> Dashes him all to pieces, and his *Hope.*
> Such was his rise, such was his fall, unpraised;
> A chance-shot sooner took him than chance raised:
> His shattered head the fearless Duke distains,
> And gave the last first proof that he had brains."

[3] Afterwards Sir Joseph Jordan, Commander of the Royal Sovereign, and Vice
Admiral of the Red, 1672. He was knighted on the 1st July, 1665.

then to my Lady Pen's, where they are all joyed, and not a little puffed up at the good success of their father; and good service indeed is said to have been done by him. Had a great bonfire at the gate; and I, with my Lady Pen's people, and others, to Mrs. Turner's great room, and there down into the street. I did give the boys 4s. among them, and mighty merry: so home to bed, with my heart at great rest and quiet, saving that the consideration of the victory is too great for me presently to comprehend.

9th. To White Hall, and in my way met with Mr. Moore, who eases me in one point wherein I was troubled; which was, that I heard of nothing said or done by my Lord Sandwich: but he tells me that Mr. Cooling, my Lord Chamberlain's secretary, did hear the King say that my Lord Sandwich had done nobly and worthily.[1] The King, it seems, is much troubled at the fall of my Lord Falmouth; but I do not meet with any man else that so much as wishes him alive again, the world conceiving him a man of too much pleasure to do the King any good, or offer any good office to him. But I hear, of all hands, he is confessed to be a man of great honour, that did show it in this his going with the Duke, the most that ever any man did. Home, where my people busy to make ready a supper against night for some guests, in lieu of my stone-feasts.[2] With my taylor to buy a silk suit, which though I had one lately, yet I do, for joy of the good news we have lately had of our victory over the Dutch, which makes me willing to spare myself something extraordinary in clothes; and, after long resolution of having nothing but black, I did buy a coloured silk ferrandin.

10th. In the evening home to supper; and there, to my great trouble, hear that the plague is come into the City, though it hath, these three or four weeks since its beginning, been wholly out of the City; but where should it begin but in my good friend and neighbour's, Dr. Burnett, in Fenchurch Street: which, in both points, troubles me mightily.

---

[1] See Charles II.'s letter of thanks to Lord Sandwich, in Ellis's *Letters*, vol. iii, p. 327, First Series.
[2] See *Life*, vol. i.

11th. (Lord's day.) Up, and expected long a new suit; but, coming not, dressed myself in my new black silk camelott suit; and, when fully ready, comes my new one of coloured ferrandin, which my wife puts me out of love with, which vexes me. At noon, by invitation, comes my two cozen Joyces and their wives — my aunt James and he-cozen Harman — his wife being ill. Had a good dinner for them, and as merry as I could be in such company. They being gone, I out of doors a little, to show, forsooth, my new suit. I saw poor Dr. Burnett's door shut; but he hath, I hear, gained great good-will among his neighbours: for he discovered it himself first, and caused himself to be shut up of his own accord: which was very handsome.

12th. Up, and in my yesterday's new suit to the Duke of Albemarle, and thence returned; and, with my taylor, bought some good lace for my sleeve bands in Pater Noster Row. The Duke of York is sent for last night, and expected to be here to-morrow.

13th. At noon with Sir G. Carteret to my Lord Mayor's to dinner, where much company in a little room. His name, Sir John Lawrence. Here were at table three Sir Richard Brownes, viz.: he of the Councill, a clerk, and the Alderman,[1] and his son; and there was a little grandson, also Richard, who will hereafter be Sir Richard Browne. The alderman did here openly tell in boasting how he had, only upon suspicion of disturbances, if there had been any bad news from sea, clapped up several persons that he was afraid of; and that he had several times done the like, and would do, and take no bail where he saw it unsafe for the King. But by and by he said that he was now sued in the Exchequer for false imprisonment, that he had, upon the same score, imprisoned while he was Mayor four years ago, and asked advice about it. I told him I believed there was none, and

---

[1] Alderman Sir Richard Browne, Bart., was Lord Mayor in 1621, and Major-General of the Trained-bands: see ante, Feb. 22, 1659–60. His son was Sir Richard Browne, Knight. Sir Richard Browne, the Clerk of the Councill, noticed Jan. 25, 1661–62, was of a different family. The Lord Mayor was seated at Debden Hall, in Essex, which he had purchased soon after 1660, and the estate was alienated by his son, the second Baronet.

told my story of Field, at which he was troubled, and said
that it was then unsafe for any man to serve the King; and,
I believed, knew not what to do therein; but that Sir
Richard Browne, of the Council, advised him to speak with
my Lord Chancellor about it. My Lord Mayor very
respectful to me; and so I after dinner away, and found Sir
J. Minnes ready with his coach and four horses at our office
gate, for him and me to go out of town to meet the Duke of
York coming from Harwich to town, and so as far as Ilford,
and there 'light. By and by comes to us Sir John Shaw
and Mr. Neale, that married the rich widow Gold, upon the
same errand. After eating a dish of creame, we took coach
again, hearing nothing of the Duke, and away home—a most
pleasant evening and road.

14th. I met with Mr. Cooling, who observed to me how
he finds every body silent in the praise of my Lord Sandwich,
to set up the Duke and the Prince; but that the Duke did,
both to the King and my Lord Chancellor, write abundantly
of my Lord's courage and service. And I this day met with
a letter of Captain Ferrers, wherein he tells how my Lord was
with his ship in all the heat of the day, and did most worthily.
To Westminster: and there saw my Lord Marlborough
brought to be buried,[1] several Lords of the Council carrying
him, and with the Heralds in some state.

15th. Up, and put on my new stuff suit with close knees,
which becomes me most nobly, as my wife says. At noon,
put on my first laced band, all lace; and to Kate Joyce's to
dinner, where my mother, wife, and abundance of their friends,
and good usage. At Woolwich, discoursed with Mr. Sheldon
about my bringing my wife down for a month or two to his
house, which he approves of, and, I think, will be very convenient. This day, the News-book,[2] upon Mr. Moore's showing L'Estrange Captain Ferrers's letter, did do my Lord
Sandwich great right as to the late victory. The Duke of
York not yet come to town. The town grows very sickly,
and people to be afraid of it: there dying this last week of
the plague 112, from 43 the week before: whereof but one in

---

[1] He was buried in Westminster Abbey.   [2] L'Estrange's *Intelligencer*.

Fenchurch Streete, and one in Broad Streete, by the Treasurer's office.

16th. After dinner, and doing some business at the office, I to White Hall, where the Court is full of the Duke and his courtiers returned from sea. All fat and lusty, and ruddy by being in the sun. I kissed his hands, and we waited all the afternoon. By and by saw Mr. Coventry, which rejoiced my very heart. Anon he and I, from all the rest of the company, walked into the Matted Gallery; where, after many expressions of love, we fell to talk of business; among other things, how my Lord Sandwich, both in his councils and personal service, hath done most honourably and serviceably. Sir J. Lawson is come to Greenwich; but his wound in his knee yet very bad. Jonas Poole, in the Vantguard, did basely, so as to be, or will be, turned out of his ship. Captain Holmes expecting, upon Sansum's death, to be made Rear-admirall to the Prince — but Harman[1] is put in — hath delivered up to the Duke his commission, which the Duke took and tore. He, it seems, had bid the Prince, who first told him of Holmes's intention, that he should dissuade him from it; for that he was resolved to take it if he offered it. Yet Holmes would do it, like a rash, proud coxcombe. But he is rich, and hath, it seems, sought an occasion of leaving the service. Several of our captains have done ill. The great ships are the ships to do the business, they quite deadening the enemy. They run away upon sight of the Prince. It is strange to see how people do already slight Sir William Barkeley,[2] my Lord FitzHarding's [Earl of Falmouth's]

---

[1] John Harman, afterwards knighted. He had served with great reputation in several naval fights, and was desperately wounded in 1673, while engaged with a Dutch man-of-war, which he captured. He survived the action some years, but never recovered his health.

[2] Commander of the Swiftsure in this action, and killed in the sea-fight the following year, when Vice-Admiral of the Blue. See June 16th, 1666. Sir William Berkeley received the honour of knighthood Oct. 12, 1664. His behaviour, after the death of his brother, Lord Falmouth, is severely commented upon, in *Poems on State Affairs*, vol. i. p. 29: —

     "*Berkeley* had heard it soon, and thought not good
     To venture more of Royal *Harding's* blood;
     To be immortal he was not of age,
     And did e'en now the *Indian Prize* presage;

brother, who, three months since, was the delight of the
Court. Captain [Jeremiah] Smith, of the Mary, the Duke
talks mightily of; and some great thing will be done for him.
Strange to hear how the Dutch do relate, as the Duke says,
that they are the conquerors; and bonfires are made in
Dunkirke in their behalf; though a clearer victory can never
be expected. Mr. Coventry thinks they cannot have lost less
than 6000 men, and we not dead above 200, and wounded
about 400; in all about 600. Captain Grove, the Duke told
us this day, hath done the basest thing at Lowestoffe, in
hearing of the guns, and could not, as others, be got out,
but staid there; for which he will be tried; and is reckoned
a prating coxcombe, and of no courage.

17th. At the office find Sir W. Pen come home, who looks
very well; and I am gladder to see him than otherwise I
should be because of my hearing so well of him for his
serviceableness in this late great action. It struck me very
deep this afternoon going with a hackney-coach from Lord
Treasurer's down Holborne,[1] the coachman I found to drive
easily and easily, at last stood still, and come down hardly
able to stand, and told me that he was suddenly struck very
sick, and almost blind—he could not see; so I 'light, and
went into another coach, with a sad heart for the poor man
and for myself also, lest he should have been struck with the
plague. Sir John Lawson, I hear, is worse than yesterday:
the King went to see him to-day most kindly. It seems his
wound is not very bad; but he hath a fever, a thrush, and a
hickup, all three together, which are, it seems, very bad
symptoms.

18th. (Lord's day.) Up, and to church, where Sir W.
Pen was the first time since he come from sea, after the
battle. Mr. Mills made a sorry sermon. Sir W. Batten and
my Lady are returned from Harwich. I went to see them,

　　　　And judged it safe and decent, cost what cost,
　　　　To lose the day, since his dear brothers lost.
　　　　With his whole squadron straight away he bore,
　　　　And, like good boy, promised to fight no more."

　Lord Southampton lived on the north side of Bloomsbury Square. His
house was afterwards Bedford House.

and it is pretty to see how we appear kind one to another, though neither of us care 2d. for another.

19th. To my little new goldsmith's [Colvill], whose wife, indeed, is one of the prettiest, modest black women that ever I saw. I paid for a dozen of silver salts 6l. 14s. 6d. Thence to see Sir J. Lawson, who is better, but continues ill—his hickup not being yet gone, could have little discourse with him.

20th. Thankes-giving-day for victory over the Dutch. To the Dolphin Taverne, where all we officers of the Navy met with the Commissioners of the Ordnance by agreement, and dined: where good musique at my direction. Our club come to 34s. a man, nine of us. By water to Fox-hall, and there walked an hour alone, observing the several humours of the citizens that were there this holiday, pulling off cherries,[1] and God knows what. This day I informed myself that there died four or five at Westminster of the plague, in several houses, upon Sunday last, in Bell Alley, over against the Palace-gate: yet people do think that the number will be fewer in the town than it was the last week. The Dutch are come out again with 20 sail under Bankert: supposed gone to the Northward, to meet their East India fleete.

21st. I find our talleys will not be money in less than sixteen months, which is a sad thing for the King to pay all that interest for every penny he spends; and, which is strange, the goldsmiths with whom I spoke do declare that they will not be moved to part with money upon the increase of their consideration of ten per cent. which they have. I find all the town almost going out of town, the coaches and waggons being all full of people going into the ccuntry.

22d. In great pain whether to send my mother into the country to-day or no; I hearing, by my people, that the poor wretch hath a mind to stay a little longer, and I cannot blame her. At last, I resolved to put it to her, and she agreed to go, because of the sickness in town, and my intentions of removing my wife. She was to the last unwilling to go, but would not say so, but put it off till she lost her place in the coach, and was fain to ride in the waggon part.

23d. To a Committee for Tangier, where, unknown to me,

---

[1] The game of bob-cherry.

comes my Lord Sandwich, who, it seems, come to town last
night.   After the Committee was up, my Lord Sandwich did
take me aside in the robe-chamber, telling me how much the
Duke and Mr. Coventry did, both in the fleete and here, make
of him, and that in some opposition to the Prince; and, as a
more private passage, he told me that he hath been with them
both when they have made sport of the Prince, and laughed
at him: yet that all the discourse of the town, and the printed
relation, should not give him one word of honour, my Lord
thinks very strange; he assuring me, that, though by accident
the Prince was in the van in the beginning of the fight for
the first pass, yet, all the rest of the day, my Lord was in
the van, and continued so.   That, notwithstanding all this
noise of the Prince, he had hardly a shot in his side, nor a
man killed, whereas he [Lord Sandwich] above 30 in her
hull, and not one mast whole nor yard; but the most battered
ship of the fleet, and lost most men, saving Captain Smith of
the Mary.   That the most the Duke did was almost out of
gun-shot; but that, indeed, the Duke did come up to my
Lord's rescue, after he had a great while fought with four of
them.   How poorly Sir John Lawson performed, notwithstanding all that was said of him; and how his ship turned
out of the way, while Sir J. Lawson himself was upon the
deck, to the endangering of the whole fleete.   It therefore
troubles my Lord, that Mr. Coventry should not mention a
word of him in his relation.   I did, in answer, offer that I
was sure the relation was not compiled by Mr. Coventry, but
by L'Estrange, out of several letters, as I could witness, and
that Mr. Coventry's letter that he did give the Duke of
Albemarle he as much writ as the Prince; for I myself
read it first, and then copied it out, which I promised to show
my Lord, with which he was something satisfied.   From that
discourse my Lord did begin to tell me how much he was
concerned to dispose of his children, and would have my
advice and help; and propounded to match my Lady
Jemimah to Sir G. Carteret's eldest son,[1] which I approved

---

[1] Philip Carteret, afterwards knighted. He perished on board his father-in-law,
Lord Sandwich's flag-ship, at the battle of Solebay.

of, and did undertake the speaking with him about it as from myself, which my Lord liked. To one Mr. Finch, one of the Commissioners of the Excise, to be informed about some things of the Excise, in order to our settling matters therein better. I find him a very discreet, grave person. Creed and I took boat, and to Fox Hall, where we spent two or three hours talking of several matters very soberly and contentfully to me, which, with the ayre and pleasure of the garden, was a great refreshment to me, and methinks that which we ought to joy ourselves in. Home, by hackney-coach, which is become a very dangerous passage now-a-days, the sickness encreasing mightily.

24th. (Midsummer-day.) To Dr. Clerke's, and there I, in the best manner I could, broke my errand about a match between Sir G. Carteret's eldest son and my Lord Sandwich's eldest daughter, which he, as I knew he would, took with great content; and we both agreed that my Lord and he, being both men relating to the sea, under a kind respect of His Majesty, already good friends, and both virtuous and good familys, their alliance might be of good use to us; and he did undertake to find out Sir George this morning, and put the business in execution. So I to White Hall, where I, with Creed and Povy, attended my Lord Treasurer, and did prevail with him to let us have an assignment for 15 or 20,000l., which, I hope, will do our business for Tangier. To Sir G. Carteret, and, in the best manner I could, moved the business: he received it with great respect and content, and thanks to me, and promised that he would do what he possibly could for his son, to render him fit for my Lord's daughter, and showed great kindness to me, and sense of my kindness to him herein. Sir William Pen told me this day that Mr. Coventry is to be sworn a Privy Counsellor, at which my soul is glad.

25th. (Lord's day.) To White Hall, where, after I again visited Sir G. Carteret, and received his and now his lady's full content in my proposal, my Lord Sandwich did direct me to return to Sir G. Carteret, and give him thanks for his kind acceptation of this offer, and that he would the next day

---

' Daniel Finch.

be willing to enter discourse with him about the business. My Lord, I perceive, intends to give 5000*l.* with her, and expects about 800*l.* per annum joynture. To Greenwich, by water, thinking to have visited Sir J. Lawson, where when I come, I find that he died this morning, at which I was much surprized, and indeed the nation hath a great loss: though I cannot, without dissembling, say that I am sorry for it; for he was a man never kind to me at all. Mr. Coventry, among other talk, entered upon the great question now in the House about the Duke's going to sea again; about which the whole House is divided. He did concur with me that, for the Duke's honour and safety, it were best, after so great a service and victory and danger, not to go again; and, above all, that the life of the Duke cannot but be a security to the Crowne—if he were away, it being more easy to attempt anything upon the King—but how the fleete will be governed without him, the Prince [Rupert] being a man of no government, and severe in council, that no ordinary man can offer any advice against his—saying, truly, that it had been better he had gone to Guinny; and that, were he away, it were easy to see how things might be ordered — my Lord Sandwich being a man of temper and judgement, as much as any man he ever knew, and that upon good observation he said this, and that his temper must correct the Prince's. But I perceive he is much troubled what will be the event of the question.

26th. To the Committee of Tangier, where my Lord Treasurer was, the first and only time he ever was there, and did promise us 15,000*l.* for Tangier, and no more, which will be short. With Creed to the King's Head[1] ordinary, and good sport with one Mr. Nicholls, a prating coxcombe, that would be thought a poet, but would not be got to repeat any of his verses. Home, and there find my wife's brother, and his wife, a pretty little modest woman, where they come to dine with my wife. He did come to desire my assistance for a living, and. upon his good promises of care, and that it should be no burden to me, I did say and promise I would

---

[1] At the corner of Chancery Lane.

think of finding something for him, and the rather because his wife seems a pretty discreet young thing, and humble, and he, above all things, desirous to do something to maintain her, telling me sad stories of what she endured in Holland and I hope it will not be burdensome. The plague encreases mightily, I this day seeing a house, at a bitt-maker's, over against St. Clement's Church, in the open street, shut up; which is a sad sight.

28th. I did take my leave of Sir William Coventry, who, it seems, was knighted, and sworn a Privy Counsellor two days since: who with his old kindness treated me, and I believe I shall ever find him a noble friend. Sir G. Carteret tells me how all things proceed between my Lord Sandwich and himself to full content, and both sides depend upon having the match finished presently, and professed great kindness to me, and said that now we were something akin. In my way to Westminster Hall, I observed several plague-houses in King's Street and near the Palace. My Lord Sandwich is gone towards the sea to-day. It being a sudden resolution, I have taken no leave of him.

29th. By water to White Hall, where the Court full of waggons and people ready to go out of town. This end of the town every day grows very bad of the plague. The Mortality Bill is come to 267; which is about ninety more than the last; and of these but four in the City, which is a great blessing to us. Took leave again of Mr. Coventry; though I hope the Duke is not gone to stay, and so do others too. Home; calling at Somerset House, where all were packing up too: the Queen-Mother setting out for France this day, to drink Bourbon waters this year, she being in a consumption; and intends not to come till winter come twelve-months.

30th. To White Hall, to the Duke of Albemarle, who I find at Secretary Bennet's, there being now no other great statesman, I think, but my Lord Chancellor, in town. At night, back by water, and in the dark and against the tide, shot the bridge,¹ groping with their pole for the way, which

¹ See note, 8th Aug. 1662.

troubled me before I got through.   So home, about one or two o'clock in the morning, my family at a great loss what was become of me.   Thus this book of two years ends. Myself and family in good health, consisting of myself and wife, Mercer, her woman, Mary, Alce, and Susan, our maids, and Tom, my boy.   In a sickly time of the plague growing on.   Having upon my hands the troublesome care of the Treasury of Tangier, with great sums drawn upon me, and nothing to pay them with : also the business of the office great.   Considering of removing my wife to Woolwich ; she lately busy in learning to paint, with great pleasure and successe.   All other things well ; especially a new interest I am making, by a match in hand between the eldest son of Sir G. Carteret, and my Lady Jemimah Montagu.   The Duke of York gone down to the fleete ; but all suppose not with intent to stay there, as it is not fit, all men conceive, he should.

July 1st. To the Duke of Albemarle's, by appointment, to give him an account of some disorder in the Yard at Portsmouth, by workmen's going away of their own accord, for lack of money, to get work of haymaking, or anything else, to earn themselves bread.   To Westminster, where, I hear, the sickness encreases greatly.   Sad at the news, that seven or eight houses in Burying Hall[1] Street are shut up of the plague.

2d. (Lord's day.) Sir G. Carteret did send me word that the business between my Lord and him is fully agreed on, and is mightily liked of the King and the Duke of York. Sir J. Lawson[2] was buried late last night at St. Dunstan's by us, without any company at all.   The condition of his family is but very poor.

3d. The season growing so sickly, that it is much to be feared how a man can escape having a share with others in it, for which the good Lord God bless me! or make me fitted to receive it.

4th. I hear this day the Duke and Prince Rupert are both

---

[1] Probably Basinghall.

[2] In the register of the Old Church at Greenwich, is the following entry :— "Sir John Lawson carried away, June 27, 1665."

come back from sea, and neither of them go back again.
Bankert is come home with the little fleete he has been
abroad with, without doing anything, so that there is nobody
of an enemy at sea.   We are in great hopes of meeting with
the Dutch East India fleet, which is mighty rich, or with De
Ruyter, who is so also.   Sir Richard Ford told me this day,
at table, a fine account, how the Dutch were like to have
been mastered by the present Prince of Orange his father to
be besieged in Amsterdam [1]—having drawn an army of foot
into the town, and horse near to the town by night, within
three miles, and they never knew of it; but by chance the
Hamburgh post in the night fell among the horse, and heard
their design, and knowing the way, it being very dark and
rainy, better than they, went from them, and did give notice
to the town before the others could reach the town, and so
were saved.   It seems this De Witt and another family, the
Beckarts, were among the chief of the familys that were
enemies to the Prince, and were afterwards suppressed by the
Prince, and continued so till he was, as they say, poisoned ;
and then they turned all again, as it was, against the young
Prince, and have so carried it to this day, it being about 12
and 14 years, and De Witt in the head of them.

5th. Advised about sending my wife's bedding and things
to- lay to Woolwich, in order to her removal thither.   Mr.
Coventry tells me how matters are ordered in the fleete : my
Lord Sandwich goes Admiral; under him Sir G. Ascue, and
Sir T. Teddiman: Vice-Admiral, Sir W. Pen ; and under
him Sir W. Barkeley, and Sir Jos. Jordan :[2] Rear-Admiral
Sir Thomas Allen; and under him Sir Christopher Mings,[3]
and Captain Harman.   Walked round to White Hall, the

---

[1] *Sic orig.*   The period alluded to is 1650, when the States-General dis-
banded part of the forces which the Prince of Orange (William) wished to retain.
The Prince attempted, but unsuccessfully, to possess himself of Amsterdam.   In
the same year he died, at the early age of 24 ; some say of the small-pox ;
others, with Sir Richard Ford, say of poison.

[2] Commanded the Royal Sovereign as Vice-Admiral of the Red, in 1672 ; and
distinguished himself in the battle of Solebay, and on other occasions.   He had
just been knighted.

[3] The son of a shoemaker, bred to the sea-service: he rose to the rank of an
Admiral.   He was killed in the fight with the Dutch, June, 1666.

Park being quite locked up; and I observed a house shut up
this day in the Pell Mell, where heretofore, in Cromwell's
time, we young men used to keep our weekly clubs. Sir G.
Carteret do now take all my Lord Sandwich's business to
heart, and makes it the same with his own. He tells me
how at Chatham it was proposed to my Lord Sandwich to be
joined with the Prince in the command of the fleete, which he
was most willing to; but, when it come to the Prince, he was
quite against it; saying, there could be no government, but
that it would be better to have two fleetes, and neither under
the command of the other, which he would not agree to. So
the King was not pleased; but, without any unkindness, did
order the fleete to be ordered as above, as to the Admirals and
commands: so the Prince is come up; and Sir G. Carteret, I
remember, had this word thence, that, says he, by this means,
though the King told him that it would be but for this expedition, yet I believe we shall keep him out for altogether.
He tells me how my Lord was much troubled at Sir W. Pen's
being ordered forth, as it seems he is to go to Solebay, and
with the best fleete he can, to go forth, and no notice taken of
my Lord Sandwich going after him, and having the command
over him. By water to Woolwich, where I found my wife
come, and her two maids, and very prettily accommodated
they will be; and I left them going to supper, grieved in my
heart to part with my wife, being worse by much without her,
though some trouble there is in having the care of a family
at home this plague time.

6th. Alderman Backewell is ordered abroad upon some
private score with a great sum of money; wherein I was in-
strumental the other day in shipping him away. It seems
some of his creditors have taken notice of it, and he was like
to be broke yesterday in his absence: Sir G. Carteret telling
me that the King and the kingdom must as good as fall with
that man at this time; and that he was forced to get 4000*l.*
himself to answer Backewell's people's occasions, or he must
have broke; but committed this to me as a great secret. I
could not see Lord Brouncker, nor had much mind, one of the
two great houses within two doors of him being shut up: and,

Lord! the number of houses visited, which this day I observed through the town, quite round in my way, by Long Lane and London Wall. To Sir W. Batten, and spent the evening at supper; and, among other discourse, the rashness of Sir John Lawson, for breeding up his daughter so high and proud, refusing a man of great interest, Sir W. Barkeley, to match her with a melancholy fellow, Colonel Norton's son,[1] of no interest nor good-nature nor generosity at all, giving her 6000*l.*, when the other would have taken her with two — when he himself knew that he was not worth the money himself in all the world, he did give her that portion, and is since dead, and left his wife and two daughters beggars, and the other gone away with 6000*l.*, and no content in it, through the ill qualities of her father-in-law and husband, who, it seems, though a pretty woman, contracted for her as if he had been buying a horse; and, worst of all, is now of no use to serve the mother and two little sisters in any stead at Court, whereas, the other might have done what he would for her: so here is an end of this family's pride, which, with good care, might have been what they would, and done well. Sir W. Pen, it seems, sailed last night from Solebay, with about sixty sail of ships, and my Lord Sandwich in the Prince and some others, it seems, going after them to overtake them.

7th. At this time I have two tierces of Claret, two quarter casks of Canary, and a smaller vessel of Sack; a vessel of Tent, another of Malaga, and another of white wine, all in my wine-cellar together; which, I believe, none of my friends of my name now alive ever had of his own at one time.

9th. (Lord's day.) To Sir G. Carteret, and there find my Lady in her chamber, not very well, but looks the worst almost that ever I did see her in my life. It seems her drinking of the water at Tunbridge did almost kill her. Received with most extraordinary kindness by my Lady Carteret and her children, and dined most nobly. I took occasion to have much discourse with Mr. Ph. Carteret, and find him a very modest man; and I think verily of mighty good nature, and pretty understanding. He did give me a good

---

[1] Whose death is mentioned, 29th August, 1666.

account of the fight with the Dutch. Took boat and home, and there shifted myself into my black silk suit; and, having promised Harman yesterday, I to his house, which I find very mean, and mean company. His wife very ill: I could not see her. Here I, with her father and Kate Joyce, who was also very ill, were godfathers and godmother to his boy, and was christened Will. Mr. Meriton [1] christened him. The most observable thing I found there to my content, was to hear him and his clerk tell me, that in this parish of Michell's Cornhill, one of the middlemost parishes, and a great one of the town, there hath, notwithstanding this sickliness, been buried of any disease, man, woman, or child, not one for thirteen months last past; which is very strange. And the like, in a good degree, in most other parishes, I hear, saving only of the plague in them. Down to my Lady Carteret's. It is mighty pretty to think how my poor Lady Sandwich, between her and me, is doubtfull whether her daughter will like of the match or no, and how troubled she is for fear of it, which I do not fear at all, and desire her not to do it, but her fear is the most discreet and pretty that ever I did see.

10th. Having a coach of Mr. Povy's attending me, by appointment, in order to my coming to dine at his country-house, at Branford, where he and his family is, I went, and Mr. Tasbrough with me therein, it being a pretty chariot, but most inconvenient as to the horses throwing dust and dirt into one's eyes, and upon one's clothes. Creed rode before, and Mr. Povy and I after him in the chariot; and I was set down by him at the Parke pale, where one of his saddle-horses was ready for me, he himself not daring to come into the house or be seen, because that a servant of his, out of his house, happened to be sick, but is not yet dead, but was never suffered to come into the house after he was ill. But this opportunity was taken to injure Povy, and most horribly he is abused by some persons hereupon, and his fortune, I believe, quite broke; but that he hath a good heart to bear, or a cunning one to conceal his evil. It is, I perceive, an unpleasing

[1] Joseph Meriton, instituted to the rectory of St. Michael, Cornhill, 1663, of which he continued incumbent nearly forty years.

thing to be at Court, everybody being fearful one of another, and all so sad enquiring after the plague, so that I stole away by my horse to Kingston, and there, with much trouble, was forced to press two sturdy rogues to carry me to London, and met at the water-side with Mr. Charnocke, Sir Philip Warwick's clerk, who had been with company, and was quite foxed.¹ I took him with me in my boat, and so away to Richmond, and there, by night, walked with him to Mortlake, a very pretty walk, and there staid a good while.

11th. All night down by water, a most pleasant passage, and come thither by two o'clock, and so walked from the Old Swan home, and there to bed to my Will—he lodging at my desire in my house.

12th. After doing what business I could in the morning, it being a solemn fast-day for the plague growing upon us, I took boat, and down to Deptford, where I stood with great pleasure an hour or two by my Lady Sandwich's bedside, talking to her, she lying prettily in bed, of my Lady Jemimah's being from my Lady Pickering's when our letters come to that place; she being at my Lord Montagu's, at Boughton. The truth is, I had received letters of it two days ago, but had dropped them, and was in a very extraordinary strait what to do for them, or what account to give my Lady: but sent to Mortlake, where I had been the night before, and there they were found, which with mighty joy come safe to me; but all ending with satisfaction to my Lady and me, though I find my Lady Carteret not much pleased with this delay, and principally because of the plague, which renders it unsafe to stay long at Deptford. I eat a bit, my Lady Carteret being the most kind lady in the world, and so took boat, and a fresh boat at the Tower, and so up the river, against tide all the way, I having lost it by staying prating to and with my Lady; and, from before one, made it seven before we got to Hampton-Court; and, when I come there, all business was over, saving my finding Mr. Coventry at his chamber; and so away to my boat, and all night upon the water, and come home by two o'clock, shooting the bridge at that time of night. Heard

---

¹ Drunk.

Mr. Williamson repeat at Hampton-Court, to-day, how the King of France hath lately set out a most high arrest[1] against the Pope, which is reckoned very lofty and high.

13th. By water, at night late, to Sir G. Carteret's,[2] but, there being no oars to carry me, I was fain to call a skuller that had a gentleman already in it, and he proved a man of love to musique, and he and I sung together the way down with great pleasure. Above 700 died of the plague this week.

14th. I by water to Sir G. Carteret's, and there find my Lady Sandwich buying things for my Lady Jem.'s wedding: and my Lady Jem. is, beyond expectation, come to Dagenhams,[3] where Mr. Carteret is to go to visit her to-morrow; and my proposal of waiting on him, he being to go alone to all persons strangers to him, was well accepted, and so I go with him. But, Lord! to see how kind my Lady Carteret is to her! Sends her most rich jewells, and provides bedding and things of all sorts most richly for her, which makes my Lady

---

[1] *Arrêt.* The rupture between Alexander VII. and Louis XIV. was healed in 1664, by the treaty signed at Pisa, on the 12th Feb. On the 9th of August, the Pope's nephew, Cardinal Chigi, made his entry into Paris, as Legate, to give the King satisfaction for the insult offered at Rome by the Corsican guard to the Duc de Créqui, the French Ambassador: see vol. i., p. 376. Cardinal Imperiali, Governor of Rome, asked pardon of the King in person, and all the hard conditions of the treaty were fulfilled. But no *arrêt* against the Pope was set forth in 1665. On the contrary, Alexander, now wishing to please the King, issued a Constitution on the 2d of Feb., 1665, ordering all the clergy of France, without any exception, to sign a formulary condemning the famous five propositions extracted from the works of Jansenius; and on the 29th of April, the King in person ordered the Parliament to register the bull. The Jansenist party, of course, demurred to this proceeding: the Bishops of Alais, Angers, Beauvais, and Pamiers, issuing mandates calling upon their clergy to refuse. It was against these mandates, as being contrary to the King's declaration and the Pope's intentions, that the *arrêt* was directed.

[2] At the Treasurer's house at Deptford, Sir G. Carteret's official residence.

[3] Dagenhams, near Romford, the seat of Lady Wright, widow of Sir Henry Wright, and sister of Lady Sandwich. (See 27th March, 1660.) This estate was devised by Anne, daughter of Sir Henry and Lady Wright, widow first of Sir Robert Pye, of Berkshire, and afterwards of William Rider, Esq., only surviving child of Sir Henry Wright, to her first cousin, Edward Carteret, Postmaster-General, third son of Sir Philip Carteret and Lady Jemimah Montagu; whose daughters, in 1749, sold it to Henry Muilman; in 1772 it was again disposed of to Mr. Neave, grandfather of the present proprietor (Sir Richard Digby Neave, Bart.), who pulled down the old house built by Sir Henry Wright, and erected the present mansion on a different site. — See Lysons's *Environs*, vol. iv., p. 191.

and me out of our wits almost to see the kindness she treats us all with, as if they would buy the young lady.

15th. Mr. Carteret and I to the ferry-place at Greenwich, and there staid an hour crossing the water to and again to get our coach and horses over; and by and by set out, and so toward Dagenhams. But, Lord! what silly discourse we had as to love-matters, he being the most awkward man ever I met with in my life as to that business. Thither we come, and by that time it began to be dark, and were kindly received by Lady Wright and my Lord Crewe. And to discourse they went, my Lord discoursing with him, asking of him questions of travell, which he answered well enough in a few words; but nothing to the lady from him at all. To supper, and after supper to talk again, he yet taking no notice of the lady. My Lord would have had me have consented to leaving the young people together to-night, to begin their amours, his staying being but to be little. But I advised against it, lest the lady might be too much surprised. So they led him up to his chamber, where I staid a little, to know how he liked the lady, which he told me he did mightily; but, Lord! in the dullest insipid manner that ever lover did. So I bid him good night, and down to prayers with my Lord Crewe's family; and, after prayers, my Lord, and Lady Wright, and I, to consult what to do; and it was agreed, at last, to have them go to church together, as the family used to do, though his lameness was a great objection against it. But, at last, my Lady Jem. sent me word by my Lady Wright, that it would be better to do just as they used to do before his coming; and therefore she desired to go to church, which was yielded to them.

16th. (Lord's day.) I up, having lain with Mr. Moore in the chaplain's chamber. And, having trimmed myself, down to Mr. Carteret; and we walked in the gallery an hour or two, it being a most noble and pretty house that ever, for the bigness, I saw. Here I taught him what to do: to take the lady always by the hand to lead her, and telling him that I would find opportunity to leave them together, he should make these and these compliments, and also take a time to do the like to Lord Crewe and Lady Wright. After I had instructed him, which he thanked me for, owning that he needed my teaching him, my Lord Crewe come down and family, the young lady among the rest; and so by coaches to church four miles off: where a pretty good sermon, and a declaration of penitence of a man that had undergone the Churche's censure for his wicked life. Thence back again by coach, Mr. Carteret having not had the confidence to take his lady once by the hand, coming or going, which I told him of when we come home, and he will hereafter do it. So to dinner. My Lord excellent discourse. Then to walk in the gallery, and to sit down. By and by my Lady Wright and I go out, and then my Lord Crewe, he not by design, and lastly my Lady Crewe come out, and left the young people together. And a little pretty daughter of my Lady Wright's most innocently come out afterwards, and shut the door to, as if she had done it, poor child, by inspiration: which made us without have good sport to laugh at. They together an hour, and by and by church-time, whither he led her into the coach and into the church, where several handsome ladies. But it was most extraordinary hot that ever I knew it. So home again, and to walk in the gardens, where we left the young couple a second time; and my Lady Wright and I to walk together, who tells me that some new clothes must of necessity be made for Lady Jemimah, which and other things I took care of. Anon to supper, and excellent discourse and dispute between my Lord Crewe and the chaplain, who is a good scholler, but a nonconformist. Here this evening I spoke with Mrs. Carter, my old acquaintance, that hath lived with my Lady these twelve or thirteen years, the sum of all whose discourse and others for her is, that I would get her a good husband; which I have promised, but know not when I shall perform. After Mr. Carteret was carried to his chamber, we to prayers, and then to bed.

17th. Up all of us, and to billiards; my Lady Wright, Mr. Carteret, myself, and every body. By and by, the young couple left together. Anon to dinner; and after dinner Mr. Carteret took my advice about giving to the servants 10*l.* among them, which he did, by leaving it to the chief man-servant, Mr. Medows, to do for him. Before we went, I took my Lady Jem. apart, and would know how she liked this gentleman, and whether she was under any difficulty concerning him. She blushed, and hid her face awhile; but at last I forced her to tell me. She answered, that she could readily obey what her father and mother had done; which was all she could say, or I expect. But, Lord! to see, among other things, how all these great people here are afraid of London, being doubtful of anything that comes from thence, or that hath lately been there, that I was forced to say that I lived wholly at Woolwich. So anon took leave, and for London. In our way, Mr. Carteret did give me mighty thanks for my care and pains for him, and is mightily pleased, though the truth is, my Lady Jem. hath carried herself with mighty discretion and gravity, not being forward at all in any degree, but mighty serious in her answers to him, as by what he says and I observed, I collect. To Deptford, where mighty welcome, and brought the good news of all being pleased. Mighty mirth of my giving them an account of all; but the young man could not be got to say one word before me or my Lady Sandwich of his adventures; but, by what he afterwards related to his father and mother and sisters, he gives an account that pleases them mightily. Here Sir G. Carteret would have me lie all night, which I did most nobly, better than ever I did in my life; Sir G. Carteret being mighty kind to me, leading me to my chamber; and all their care now is, to have the business ended, and they have reason, because the sickness puts all out of order, and they cannot safely stay where they are.

18th. To the 'Change, where a little business, and a very thin Exchange; and so walked through London to the Temple, where I took water for Westminster to the Duke of Albemarle, to wait on him, and so to Westminster Hall, and there paid for my news-books, and did give Mrs. Michell, who is going out of town because of the sickness, and her husband, a pint of wine. I was much troubled this day to hear, at Westminster, how the officers do bury the dead in the open Tuttle-fields, pretending want of room elsewhere; whereas

the New Chapel church-yard was walled-in at the publick
charge in the last plague-time, merely for want of room; and
now none, but such as are able to pay dear for it, can be
buried there.

19th. To Deptford, where I find all[1] full of joy, and preparing to go to Dagenhams to-morrow.

20th. To Deptford, and after dinner saw my Lady Sandwich
and Mr. Carteret and his two sisters over the water, going to
Dagenhams, and my Lady Carteret towards Cranburne.[2]
Walked to Redriffe, where I hear the sickness is, and indeed
is scattered almost everywhere, there dying 1089 of the
plague this week. My Lady Carteret did this day give me
a bottle of plague-water home with me. I received yesterday
a letter from my Lord Sandwich, giving me thanks for my
care about their marriage business, and desiring it to be dispatched, that no disappointment may happen therein. Lord!
to see how the plague spreads! it being now all over King's
Streete, at the Axe, and next door to it, and in other places.

21st. To Anthony Joyce's, and there broke to him my
desire to have Pall married to Harman, whose wife, poor
woman, is lately dead, to my trouble, I loving her very much,
and he will consider it. Late in my chamber, setting some
papers in order; the plague growing very raging; and my
apprehensions of it great.

22d. The Duke of Albemarle being gone to dinner to my
Lord of Canterbury's, I thither, and there walked and viewed
the new hall, a new old-fashioned hall,[3] as much as possible
— begun, and means left for the ending of it, by Bishop
Juxon. To Fox-hall, where to the Spring garden; but I do
not see one guest there, the town being so empty of any
body to come thither. Only, while I was there, a poor
woman come to scold with the master of the house that a
kinswoman, I think, of her's, that was nearly dead of the
plague, might be buried in the church-yard; for, for her

---

[1] The Carterets.

[2] The Royal Lodge of that name in Windsor Forest, occupied by Sir George
Carteret, as Vice-Chamberlain to the King.

[3] The hall here spoken of was converted into the archiepiscopal library by the
late Archbishop Howley.

part, she should not be buried in the commons, as they said
she should. I by coach home, not meeting with but two
coaches and but two carts from White Hall to my own
house, that I could observe, and the streets mighty thin of
people. I met this noon with Dr. Burnett, who told me, and
I find in the news-book this week that he posted upon the
'Change, that whoever did spread the report that, instead of
dying of the plague, his servant was by him killed, it was
forgery, and shewed me the acknowledgment of the Master of
the pest-house, that his servant died of a bubo on his right
groine, and two spots on his right thigh, which is the plague.
All the news is great: that we must of necessity fall out
with France, for He will side with the Dutch against us.
That Alderman Backewell is gone over, which indeed he is,
with money, and that Ostend is in our present possession.
But it is strange to see how poor Alderman Backewell is like
to be put to it in his absence, Mr. Shaw, his right hand,
being ill. And the Alderman's absence gives doubts to
people, and I perceive they are in great straits for money,
besides what Sir G. Carteret told me about fourteen days
ago. Our fleete, under my Lord Sandwich, being about the
latitude 55½, which is a great secret, to the northward of the
Texel.

23d. (Lord's day.) Called by Mr. Cutler, by appointment,
and with him, in his coach and four horses, over London
Bridge to Kingston, a very pleasant journey, and to Hampton
Court, where I followed the King to chapel, and there heard
a good sermon; and after sermon with my Lord Arlington,
Sir Thomas Ingram, and others, spoke to the Duke about
Tangier, but not to much purpose. I was not invited any
where to dinner, though a stranger, which did also trouble
me; but yet I must remember it is a Court, and indeed
where most are strangers: but, however, Cutler carried me to
Mrs. Marriott's, the house-keeper, and there we had a very
good dinner and good company, among others Lilly, the
painter. Thence to the councill-chamber, but the council
begun late to sit; so that when I got free, and come back to
look for Cutler, he was gone with his coach, without leaving

any word with anybody to tell me so; so that I was forced
with great trouble to walk up and down, looking of him, and
at last forced to get a boat to carry me to Kingston, and
there, after eating a bit at a neat inne, which pleased me well,
I took boat, and slept all the way, without intermission, from
thence to Queenhithe, where, it being about two o'clock, too
late and too soon to go home to bed, I lay and slept till
about four.

24th. Up and home, and there dressed myself, and by
appointment to Deptford, to Sir G. Carteret's, between six
and seven o'clock, where I found him and my Lady almost
ready, and by and by went over to the ferry, and took coach
and six horses nobly for Dagenhams, himself and lady, and
their little daughter Louisonne[1] and myself in the coach,
where, when we come, we were bravely entertained, and spent
the day most pleasantly with the young ladies, and I so
merry as never before. With great content all the day, as I
think I ever passed a day in my life, because of the content-
fulness of our errand, and the nobleness of the company, and
our manner of going. But I find Mr. Carteret as backward
almost in his caresses as he was the first day. At night,
about seven o'clock, took coach again: but, Lord! to see in
what a pleasant humour Sir G. Carteret hath been both
coming and going—so light, so fond, so merry, so boyish, so
much content he takes in this business—it is one of tho
greatest wonders I ever saw in my mind. In serious discourse he did say that, if he knew his son to be a debauchee,
as many and most are now-a-days about the Court, he would
tell it, and my Lady Jem. should not have him; and so enlarged both he and she about the baseness and looseness of
the Court, and told several stories of the Duke of Monmouth,
and Richmond, and some great person, my Lord of Ormond's
second son,[2] married to a lady[3] of extraordinary quality, fit,
and that might have been made a wife for the King himself,

---

[1] Louisa Marguerite Carteret, afterwards married to Sir Robert Atkins, of
Seperton, Gloucestershire.
[2] See note 4th February, 1664–5.
[3] Lady Mary Stuart, only surviving child of James Duke of Richmond and
Lennox, who died in 1655, and heir to her brother Esme, who deceased in 1666.
She survived till 1683.

about six months since; and discoursed how much this would
oblige the kingdom, if the King would banish some of these
great persons publickly from the Court. We set out so late,
that it grew dark, so as we doubted the losing of our way:
and a long time it was, or seemed, before we could get to the
water-side, and that about eleven at night, where, when we
come, all merry, we found no ferry-boat was there, nor no
oares to carry us to Deptford. However, afterwardes oares
was called from the other side at Greenwich; but, when it
come, a frolick, being mighty merry, took us, and there we
would sleep all night in the coach in the Isle of Doggs: so we
did, there being now with us my Lady Scott;[1] and with great
pleasure drew up the glasses, and slept till daylight, and then
some victuals and wine being brought us, we ate a bit, and so
up and took boat, merry as might be; and, when come to
Sir G. Carteret's, there all to bed.

25th. Our good humour in everybody continuing, I slept
till seven o'clock. Sad the story of the plague in the City,
it growing mightily. This day my Lord Brouncker did give
me Grant's book upon the Bills of Mortality, new printed and
enlarged.[2] To my office: thence by coach to the Duke of
Albemarle's, not meeting one coach, going nor coming. This
day come a letter to me from Paris, from my Lord Hinchming-
broke, about his coming over; and I have sent this night an
order from the Duke of Albemarle for a ship of 36 guns to
go to Calais to fetch him.[3]

26th. To Greenwich, to the Park, where I heard the King
and Duke are come by water this morn from Hampton Court.
They asked me several questions. The King mightily pleased
with his new buildings there. I followed them to Castle's
ship, in building, and there met Sir W. Batten, and thence
to Sir G. Carteret's, where all the morning with them; they
not having any but the Duke of Monmouth, and Sir W.
Killigrew,[4] and one gentleman, and a page more. Great

---

[1] Caroline, second daughter of Sir George Carteret, wife of Sir Thomas Scott
of Scott's Hall, Kent. See ante, July 30, 1663.
[2] See note, p. 266, vol. i.
[3] For the letter, see the *Correspondence*.
[4] Vice-Chamberlain to the Queen, and elder brother of Tom Killigrew.

variety of talk, and was often led to speak to the King and
Duke. By and by they to dinner, and all to dinner and sat
down to the King, saving myself, which, though I could not
in modesty expect, yet, God forgive my pride! I was sorry I
was there, that Sir W. Batten should say that he could sit
down where I could not. The King having dined, he came
down, and I went in the barge with him, I sitting at the
door. Down to Woolwich, and there I just saw and kissed
my wife, and saw some of her painting, which is very curious;
and away again to the King, and back again with him in the
barge, hearing him and the Duke talk, and seeing and observing their manner of discourse. And, God forgive me!
though I admire them with all the duty possible, yet the
more a man considers and observes them, the less he finds of
difference between them and other men, though, blessed be
God! they are both princes of great nobleness and spirits.
The Duke of Monmouth is the most skittish leaping gallant
that ever I saw, always in action, vaulting or leaping, or
clambering. Sad news of the death of so many in the parish
of the plague, forty last night. The bell always going. To
the Exchange, where I went up and sat talking with my
beauty, Mrs. Batelier, a great while, who is indeed one of the
finest women I ever saw in my life. This day poor Robin
Shaw at Backewell's died, and Backewell himself now in
Flanders. The King himself asked about Shaw, and being
told he was dead, said he was very sorry for it. The sickness is got into our parish this week, and is got, indeed,
every where; so that I begin to think of setting things in
order, which I pray God enable me to put, both as to soul
and body.

27th. With Mr. Gauden to Hampton Court, where I saw
the King and Queen set out towards Salisbury, and after
them the Duke and Duchess, whose hands I did kiss. And
it was the first time I did ever, or did see anybody else, kiss
her hand, and it was a most fine white and fat hand. But
it was pretty to see the young, pretty ladies dressed like men,
in velvet coats, caps with ribbands, and with laced bands,
just like men. Only the Duchess herself it did not become.

They gone, we, with great content, took coach again; and, hungry, come to Clapham about one o'clock, and Creed there, too, before us, where a good dinner, the house having dined, and so to walk up and down in the gardens, mighty pleasant. By and by comes, by promise to me, Sir G. Carteret, and viewed the house above and below, and sat and drank there, and I had a little opportunity to kiss and spend some time with the ladies above — his[1] daughter, a buxom lass, and his sister Fissant, a serious lady, and a little daughter of hers, that begins to sing prettily. Thence, with mighty pleasure, with Sir G. Carteret by coach, with great discourse of kindness with him to my Lord Sandwich, and to me also; and I every day see more good by the alliance—to Half-way House, and so home, in my way being shown my cozen Patience's house, which seems, at distance, a pretty house. At home met the weekly Bill, where above 100 encreased in the Bill; and of them, in all, about 1700 of the plague, which hath made the officers this day resolve of sitting at Deptford, which puts me to some consideration what to do.

28th. Set out with my Lady Sandwich all alone with her with six horses to Dagenhams; going by water to the Ferry. And a pleasant going, and a good discourse; and, when there, very merry, and the young couple now well acquainted. But, Lord! to see in what fear all the people here do live. How they are afraid of us that come to them, insomuch that I am troubled at it, and wish myself away. But some cause they have; for the chaplain, with whom, but a week or two ago, we were here mighty high disputing, is since fallen into a fever, and dead, being gone hence to a friend's a good way off. A sober and a healthful man. These considerations make us all hasten the marriage, and resolve it upon Monday next, which is three days before we intended it.

29th. Up betimes, and, after viewing some of my wife's pictures, which now she is come to do very finely, to the office. At noon to dinner, where I hear that my Will is come in thither, and laid down upon my bed, ill of the headache, which put me into extraordinary fear; and I

---

[1] Mr. Gauden's.

studied all I could to get him out of the house, and set my people to work to do it without discouraging him, and myself went forth to the Old Exchange to pay my fair Batelier for some linnen, and took leave of her, they breaking up shop for a while : and so by coach to Kate Joyce's, and there used all the vehemence and rhetorique I could to get her husband to let her go down to Brampton, but I could not prevail with him ; he urging some simple reasons, but most that of profit, minding the house, and the distance, if either of them should be ill. However, I did my best, and more than I had a mind to do, but that I saw him so resolved against it, while she was mightily troubled at it. At last, he yielded she should go to Windsor, to some friends there : so I took my leave of them, believing it is great odds that we ever all see one another again ; for I dare not go any more to that end of the town. Will is gone to his lodging, and is likely to do well, it being only the headache.

30th. (Lord's day.) Up, and in my night-gown, cap, and neckcloth, undressed, all day long—lost not a minute, but in my chamber, setting my Tangier accounts to rights. Will is very well again. It was a sad noise to hear our bell to toll and ring so often to-day, either for deaths or burials ; I think, five or six times.

31st. Up, and very betimes by six o'clock at Deptford, and there find Sir G. Carteret, and my Lady ready to go : I being in my new-coloured silk suit, and coat trimmed with gold buttons and gold broad lace round my hands, very rich and fine. By water to the Ferry, where, when we come, no coach there ; and tide of ebb so far spent as the horse-boat could not get off on the other side the river to bring away the coach. So we were fain to stay there in the unlucky Isle of Doggs, in a chill place, the morning cool, and wind fresh, above two if not three hours, to our great discontent. Yet, being upon a pleasant errand, and seeing that it could not be helped, we did bear it very patiently ; and it was worth my observing to see how, upon these two scores, Sir G. Carteret, the most passionate man in the world, and that was in greatest haste to be gone, did bear with it, and very pleasant all the while,

at least, not troubled so much as to fret and storm at it.
Anon the coach comes: in the mean time, there coming a
News thither with his horse to go over, that told us he did
come from Islington this morning; and that Proctor,[1] the
vintner, of the Miter, in Wood Street, and his son, are dead
this morning there, of the plague: he having laid out
abundance of money there, and was the greatest vintner for
some time in London for great entertainments. We, fearing
the canonicall hour would be past before we got thither, did,
with a great deal of unwillingness, send away the licence and
wedding-ring. So that when we come, though we drove hard
with six horses, yet we found them gone from home; and,
going towards the church, met them coming from church,
which troubled us.   But, however, that trouble was soon
over; hearing it was well done: they being both in their old
clothes: my Lord Crewe giving her, there being three coach-
fulls of them.   The young lady mighty sad, which troubled
me; but yet I think it was only her gravity in a little greater
degree than usual.   All saluted her, but I did not, till my
Lady Sandwich did ask me whether I saluted her or no.   So
to dinner, and very merry we were; but in such a sober way
as never almost any thing was in so great families: but it
was much better.   After dinner company divided, some to
cards, others to talk.   My Lady Sandwich and I up to settle
accounts, and pay her some money.   And mighty kind she
is to me, and would fain have had me gone down for company
with her to Hinchingbroke; but for my life I cannot.   At
night to supper, and so to talk; and which, methought, was
the most extraordinary thing, all of us to prayers as usual,
and the young bride and bridegroom too: and so, after
prayers, soberly to bed; only I got into the bridegroom's
chamber while he undressed himself, and there was very
merry, till he was called to the bride's chamber, and into bed
they went.   I kissed the bride in bed, and so the curtains
drawne with the greatest gravity that could be, and so good

---

[1] 1665, Aug. 1.   Mr. Wm. Proctor, vintner, at y⁰ Mitre, in Wood Street,
with his young son, died at Islington (insolvent). *Ex peste.* Smith's *Obituary,*
p. 64.

night.   But the modesty and gravity of this business was so
decent, that it was to me indeed ten times more delightful
than if it had been twenty times more merry and jovial.
Whereas, I feared we must have sat up all night, we did here
all get good beds, and I lay in the same I did before, with
Mr. Brisband, who is a good scholar and sober man; and we
lay in bed, getting him to give me an account of Rome,
which is the most delightful talk a man can have of any
traveller: and so to sleep.   Thus, I ended this month with
the greatest joy that ever I did any in my life, because I have
spent the greatest part of it with abundance of joy, and
honour, and pleasant journeys, and brave entertainments, and
without cost of money; and at last live to see the business
ended with great content on all sides.   This evening with
Mr. Brisband, speaking of enchantments and spells, I telling
him some of my charmes; he told me this, of his own
knowledge, at Bourdeaux, in France.   The words were
these : —

> Voyci un Corps mort,
> Royde comme un Baston,
> Froid comme Marbre,
> Leger comme un Esprit,
> Levons le au nom de Jesus Christ.

He saw four little girls, very young ones — all kneeling each
of them, upon one knee; and one begun the first line,
whispering in the eare of the next, and the second to the
third, and the third to the fourth, and she to the first.   Then
the first begun the second line, and so round quite through;
and, putting each one finger only to a boy that lay flat upon
his back on the ground, as if he was dead; at the end of the
words, they did with their four fingers raise this boy as high
as they could reach; and Mr. Brisband, being there, and
wondering at it, as also being afraid to see it, for they would
have had him to have bore a part in saying the words, in the
room of one of the little girls that was so young that they
could hardly make her learn to repeat the words, did, for fear
there might be some slight used in it by the boy, or that the

boy might be light, call the cook of the house, a very lusty
fellow, as Sir G. Carteret's cook, who is very big: and they
did raise him just in the same manner.[1] This is one of the
strangest things I ever heard, but he tells it me of his own
knowledge, and I do heartily believe it to be true. I enquired
of him whether they were Protestant or Catholique girles; and
he told me they were Protestant, which made it the more
strange to me. Thus we end this month, as I said, after the
greatest glut of content that ever I had; only under some
difficulty because of the plague, which grows mightily upon
us, the last week being about 1700 or 1800 of the plague.

---

[1] The secret is now well known, and is described by Sir David Brewster, in his
Natural Magic, p. 256:—"One of the most remarkable and inexplicable experiments, relative to the strength of the human frame, is that in which a heavy man
is raised up the instant that his own lungs and those of the persons who lift him
are inflated with air. This experiment was, I believe, first shown in England a
few years ago by Major H., who saw it performed in a large party at Venice, under
the direction of an officer of the American Navy. As Major H. performed it more
than once in my presence, I shall describe as nearly as possible the method which
he prescribed. The heaviest person in the party lies down upon two chairs, his
legs being supported by the one, and his back by the other. Four persons, one
at each leg, and one at each shoulder, then try to raise him, and they find his
dead weight to be very great, from the difficulty they experience in supporting
him. When he is replaced in the chair, each of the four persons takes hold of the
body, as before, and the person to be lifted gives two signals, by clapping his
hands. At the first signal, he himself and the four lifters begin to draw a long
and full breath: and when the inhalation is completed, or the lungs filled, the
second signal is given for raising the person from the chair. To his own surprise,
and that of his bearers, he rises with the greatest facility, as if he were no heavier
than a feather. On several occasions, I have observed, that when one of the
bearers performs his part ill, by making the inhalation out of time, the part of the
body which he tries to raise is left as it were behind. As you have repeatedly
seen this experiment, and have performed the part both of the load and of the
bearer, you can testify how remarkable the effect appears to all parties, and how
complete is the conviction, either that the load has been lightened, or the bearer
strengthened, by the prescribed process. At Venice, the experiment was performed in a much more imposing manner. The heaviest man in the party was
raised and sustained upon the points of the fore-fingers of six persons. Major H.
declared that the experiment would not succeed, if the person lifted were placed
upon a board, and the strength of the individuals applied to the board. He conceived it necessary that the bearers should communicate directly with the body to
be raised. I have not had an opportunity of making any experiments relative to
these curious facts: but, whether the general effect is an illusion, or the result of
known or new principles, the subject merits a careful investigation." I learn, on
the authority of Dr. Maitland, that a similar experiment was once tried in Gloucestershire, upon a very stout gentleman; and that the lifters were so astonished
at their success, that they permitted him to fall to the ground, to his sore discomfiture. Ex. infor. W. J. Thoms. It would be very serious, if these experiments
were frequent, to find one-self the *heaviest* person in a party.

My Lord Sandwich at sea with a fleet of about 100 sail, to the Northward, expecting De Ruyter, or the Dutch East India fleet. My Lord Hinchingbroke coming over from France, and will meet his sister at Scott's-hall. Myself having obliged both these families in this business very much; as both my Lady and Sir G. Carteret and his Lady do confess exceedingly, and the latter do also now call me cozen, which I am glad of. So God preserve us all friends long, and continue health among us!

August 1st. Lay long; then up, and my Lord Crewe and Sir G. Carteret being gone abroad, I first to see the bride-groom and bride, and found them both up, and he gone to dress himself. Thence down, and Mr. Brisband and I to billiards: anon come my Lord and Sir G. Carteret in, who have been looking abroad and visiting some farms that Sir G. Carteret hath thereabouts, and, among other things, report the greatest stories of the bigness of the calfes they find there, ready to sell to the butchers—as big, they say, as little cowes, and that they do give them a piece of chalke to licke, which they hold makes them white in the flesh within. About five o'clock, Sir G. Carteret, and his lady, and I, took coach with the greatest joy: drove hard, and it was night ere we got to Deptford, where, with much kindness from them to me, I left them, and home to the office, where I find all well.

2d. Up, it being a public fast, as being the first Wednesday of the month, for the plague; within doors all day, and upon my monthly accounts late. I did find myself really worth 1900*l.*, for which the great God of Heaven and Earth be praised!

3d. Up, and betimes to Deptford to Sir G. Carteret's, where, not knowing the horse which had been hired by Mr. Unthwayt for me, I did desire Sir G. Carteret to let me ride his new 40*l.* horse; and so to the ferry, where I was forced to stay a great while before I could get my horse brought over, and then mounted, and rode very finely to Dagenhams; all the way, people, citizens, walking to and fro, enquire how the plague is in the City this week by the Bill; which, by chance, at Greenwich, I had heard was 2020 of the plague, and 3000 and odd, of all diseases; but methought it was a sad question to be so often asked me. Coming to Dagenhams, I there met our company coming out of the house, having staid as long as they could for me; so I let them go a little way before, and went and took leave of my Lady Sandwich, good woman, who seems very sensible of my service, in this late business, and having her directions in some things —among others, to get Sir G. Carteret and my Lord to settle the portion, and what Sir G. Carteret is to settle, into land, soon as may be, she not liking it should lie long undone, for fear of death on either side. So took leave of her, and down to the buttery, and eat a piece of cold venison pie, and drank, and took some bread and cheese in my hand; and so mounted after them, Mr. Marr very kindly staying to lead me the way. By and by met my Lord Crewe returning; Mr. Marr telling me, by the way, how a maid servant of Mr. John Wright's, who lives thereabouts, falling sick of the plague, she was removed to an out-house, and a nurse appointed to look to her; who, being once absent, the maid got out of the house at the window, and run away. The nurse coming and knocking, and, having no answer, believed she was dead, and went and told Mr. Wright so; who and his lady were in a great straight what to do to get her buried. At last, resolved to go to Burntwood,[1] hard by, being in the parish, and there get people to do it. But they would not: so he went home full of trouble, and in the way met the wench walking over the common, which frighted him worse than before; and was forced to send people to take her, which he did; and they got one of the pest-coaches, and put her into it, to carry her to a pest-house. And, passing in a narrow lane, Sir Anthony Browne,[2] with his brother and some friends in the coach, met this coach with the curtains drawn close. The brother, being a young man, and believing there might be some lady in it that would not be seen, and the way being narrow, he thrust his head out of his own into her coach, and to look, and there saw somebody looking very ill,

---

[1] Brentwood.
[2] He commanded a troop of horse in the Train-bands, 1662.

and in a silk dress, and stunk mightily; which the coachman also cried out upon. And presently they come up to some people that stood looking after it, and told our gallants that it was a maid of Mr. Wright's carried away sick of the plague; which put the young gentleman into a fright had almost cost him his life, but is now well again. I, overtaking our young people, 'light, and into the coach to them, where mighty merry all the way; and anon come to the Blockehouse,[1] over against Gravesend, where we staid a great while, in a little drinking-house. Sent back our coaches to Dagenhams. I, by and by, by boat to Gravesend, where no news of Sir G. Carteret come yet: so back again, and fetched them all over, but the two saddle-horses that were to go with us, which could not be brought over in the horse-boat, the wind and tide being against us, without towing; so we had some difference with some watermen, who would not tow them over under 20s., whereupon I swore to send one of them to sea, and will do it. Anon some others did it for 10s. By and by comes Sir G. Carteret, and so we set out for Chatham: in my way overtaking some company, wherein was a lady, very pretty, riding singly, her husband in company with her. We fell into talk, and I read a copy of verses, which her husband showed me, and he discommended; but the lady commended: and I read them, so as to make the husband turn and commend them. By and by he and I fell into acquaintance, having known me formerly at the Exchequer. His name is Nokes, over-against Bow Church. He was servant to Alderman Dashwood. We promised to meet, if ever we come both to London again; and, at parting, I had a fair salute on horseback, in Rochester streets, of the lady. My Lady Carteret come to Chatham in a coach, by herself, before us. Great mind they have to buy a little hacquenee that I rode on from Greenwich, for a woman's horse.

4th. Up by five o'clock, and by six walked out alone, with my Lady Slaning,[2] to the Docke Yard, where walked up and

---

[1] Tilbury Fort.

[2] Sir George Carteret's eldest daughter Anne, married to Sir Nicholas Slaning, K.B.

down, and so to Mr. Pett's, who led us into his garden, and
there the lady, the best-humoured woman in the world, and a
devout woman, I having spied her on her knees half an hour
this morning in her chamber, clambered up to the top of the
banquetting-house, to gather nuts; and so to the Hill-house,
to breakfast, and mighty merry. Then they took coach, and
Sir G. Carteret kissed me himself heartily, and my Lady
several times, with great kindness, and then the young ladies,
and so, with much joy, bade "God be with you!" and an
end, I think, it will be to my mirth for a great while, it
having been the passage of my whole life the most pleasing
for the time, considering the quality and nature of the business, and my noble usage in the doing of it, and very many
fine journys, entertainments, and great company. So home,
and found all things well, and letters that my Lord Hinchingbroke is arrived at Dover, and would be at Scott's hall[1] this
night, where the whole company will meet. I wish myself
with them.

5th. In the morning up, and my wife showed me several
things of her doing, especially one fine woman's Persian head,
mighty finely done; beyond what I could expect of her: and
so away by water, having ordered in the yard six or eight
bargemen to be whipped, who had last night stolen some of
the King's cordage from out of the yard. De Ruyter is
come home, with all his fleet, which is very ill news. I am
told of a great ryott upon Thursday last in Cheapside; Colonel Danvers, a delinquent, having been taken, and in his way
to the Tower was rescued from the captain of the guard, and
carried away; one only of the rescuers being taken.

7th. Talking with Mrs. Pegg Pen, and looking over her
pictures, and commended them; but, Lord! so far short of

---

[1] Scott's Hall was in the parish of Smeeth, near Ashford, in Kent: it was long
the residence of William Baliol *le Scot*, a brother of John Baliol, King of Scotland.
At this time it belonged to Sir Thomas Scott, son-in-law to Sir George Carteret:
see July 30, 1663, and July 24, 1665. The property was sold in 1784 to John
Honywood, and afterwards alienated to the late Sir Edward Knatchbull, Bart.,
who pulled down the house. Hasted says it was of the time of Henry VIII.;
but from rough sketches of the building, in the possession of one of the Scott
family, who lived to be nearly ninety, it was conjectured to have been much more
ancient.

my wife's as no comparison. Comes Rayner, the boat-maker, about some business, and brings a piece of plate with him, which I refused. He gone, then comes Luellin, about Mr Deering's business of planke, to have the contract perfected, and offers me twenty pieces in gold, but I refused it.

8th. To my office a little, and then to the Duke of Albemarle's about some business. The streets empty all the way, now, even in London, which is a sad sight. And to Westminster Hall, where talking, hearing very sad stories from Mrs. Mumford; among others, of Mr. Mitchell's son's family. And poor Will, that used to sell us ale at the Hall-door, his wife and three children died, all, I think, in a day. So home, through the City again, wishing I may have taken no ill in going; but I will go, I think, no more thither. The news of De Ruyter's coming home is certain; and told to the great disadvantage of our fleete, and the praise of De Ruyter; but it cannot be helped.

10th. My she-cozen Porter, the turner's wife, to tell me that her husband was carried to the Tower, for buying of some of the King's powder, and would have my help, but I could give her none, not daring to appear in the business. By and by to the office, where we sat all the morning; in great trouble to see the Bill this week rise so high, to above 4000 in all, and of them above 3000 of the plague. Home, to draw over anew my will, which I had bound myself by oath to dispatch by to-morrow night; the town growing so unhealthy, that a man cannot depend upon living two days.

11th. To the Exchequer, about striking new tallys, and I find the Exchequer, by proclamation, removing to Nonsuch.[1] Setting my house, and all things, in the best order I can, lest it should please God to take me away, or force me to leave my house.

12th. Sent for by Sir G. Carteret, to meet him and my Lord Hinchingbroke at Deptford, but my Lord did not come thither, he having crossed the river at Gravesend to Dagenhams, whither I dare not follow him, they being afraid of me; but Sir G. Carteret says, he is a most sweet youth in

---

[1] Nonsuch House, near Epsom.

every circumstance. Sir G. Carteret being in haste of going
to the Duke of Albemarle and the Archbishop, he was pettish
The people die so, that now it seems they are fain to carry
the dead to be buried by daylight, the nights not sufficing to
do it in. And my Lord Mayor commands people to be within
at nine at night all, as they say, that the sick may have
liberty to go abroad for ayre. There is one also dead out of
one of our ships at Deptford, which troubles us mightily—
the Providence, fire-ship, which was just fitted to go to sea;
but they tell me, to-day, no more sick on board. And this
day W. Bodham tells me that one is dead at Woolwich, not
far from the Rope-yard. I am told, too, that a wife of one
of the groomes at Court is dead at Salisbury; so that the
King and Queen are speedily to be all gone to Wilton.[1] So
God preserve us!

13th. (Lord's day.) It being very wet all day, clearing all
matters, and giving instructions in writing to my executors,
thereby perfecting the whole business of my will, to my very
great joy; so that I shall be in much better state of soul, I
hope, if it should please the Lord to call me away this sickly
time. I find myself worth, besides Brampton estates, the
sum of 2165*l*., for which the Lord be praised!

14th. To Sir G. Carteret; and, among other things, he
told me, that he was not for the fanfaroone,[2] to make a show
with a great title, as he might have had long since, but the
main thing, to get an estate; and another thing, speaking of
minding of business — " By G—d," says he, " I will, and
have already almost brought it to that pass, that the King
shall not be able to whip a cat, but I mean to be at the tayle
of it !" meaning, so necessary he is, and the King and my
Lord Treasurer all do confess it, which, while I mind my
business, is my own case in this office of the Navy. After
dinner, beat Captain Cocke at billiards; won about 8*s.* of
him and my Lord Brouncker. This night I did present my

[1] Near Salisbury, then the seat of Philip, fifth Earl of Pembroke, who married
Katharine, daughter of Sir Wm. Villiers, of Brookesby, cousin of the Duke of
Buckingham.
[2] To make a great flourish or bravado.—*Cotgrave.*

wife, with a dyamond ring, awhile since given me by Mr.
Vines's brother, for helping him to be a purser, valued at
about 10*l*., the first thing of that nature I did give her.
Great fears we have that the plague will be a great Bill this
week.

15th. It was dark before I could get home, and so land at
Church-yard stairs, where, to my great trouble, I met a dead
corps of the plague, in the narrow ally, just bringing down
a little pair of stairs. But I thank God I was not much disturbed at it. However, I shall beware of being late abroad
again.

16th. To the Exchange, where I have not been a great
while. But, Lord! how sad a sight it is to see the streets
empty of people, and very few upon the 'Change! Jealous of
every door that one sees shut up, lest it should be the plague;
and about us two shops in three, if not more, generally shut
up. This day, I had the ill news from Dagenhams, that my
poor Lord of Hinchingbroke his indisposition is turned to the
small-pox. Poor gentleman! that he should be come from
France so soon to fall sick, and of that disease too, when he
should be gone to see a fine lady, his mistress! I am most
heartily sorry for it.

18th. To Sheernesse, where we walked up and down, laying
out the ground[1] to be taken in for a yard to lay provisions
for cleaning and repairing of ships, and a most proper place
it is for the purpose. Late in the dark to Gravesend, where
great is the plague, and I troubled to stay there so long for
the tide.

19th. Come letters from the King and Lord Arlington, for
the removal of our office to Greenwich. I also wrote letters,
and made myself ready to go to Sir G. Carteret, at Windsor;
and, having borrowed a horse of Mr. Blackbrough, sent him
to wait for me at the Duke of Albemarle's door: when, on a
sudden, a letter comes to us from the Duke of Albemarle, to

---

[1] The yard and fortifications of Sheerness were designed and first "staked
out" by Sir Bernard de Gomme (see 24th March, 1667). The original plan is
in the British Museum.

tell us that the fleete is all come back to Solebay, and are presently to be dispatched back again.   Whereupon I presently
by water to the Duke of Albemarle, to know what news; and
there I saw a letter from my Lord Sandwich to the Duke of
Albemarle, and also from Sir W. Coventry and Captain Teddiman; how my Lord having commanded Teddiman, with
twenty-two ships, of which but fifteen could get thither, and
of those fifteen but eight or nine could come up to play, to go
to Bergen;[1] where, after several messages to and from the

---

[1] A view of this attack on Bergen, "described from the life in Aug., 1665, by
C. H.," being a contemporary coloured drawing, on vellum, showing the range
of the ships engaged, as in the British Museum. See Sir Gilbert Talbot's narrative of this action, Harleian MS., No. 6859, and Lord Rochester's account of it
in a letter to his mother.—Wordsworth's *Eccl. Biog.*, 4th ed., vol. iv., p. 611.
The affair of Bergen did not escape Denham's satiric lash :

> " ———— all our navy 'scaped so sound of limb,
> That a short space served to refresh and trim :
> And a tame fleet of theirs'[1] doth convoy want,
> Laden with both the Indies and Levant:
> Paint but this one scene more, the world's our own,
> And Halcyon *Sandwich* doth command alone :
> To *Bergen* we with confidence make haste,
> And secret spoils by hope already taste ;
> Tho' *Clifford* in the character appear
> Of supra-cargo to our fleet, and there
> Wearing a signet ready to clap on,
> And seize all for his master *Arlington,*
> *Ruyter,* whose little squadron skimmed the seas,
> And wasted our remotest colonies,
> With ships all foul, returned upon our way ;
> *Sandwich* would not disperse nor yet delay ;
> And therefore like commander grave and wise,
> To 'scape his sight and fight, shut both his eyes :
> And for more state and sureness, *Cuttance,* true,
> The left eye closeth the right *Montagu ;*
> And even *Clifford* proffered in his zeal,
> To make all safe, to apply to both his seal.
> Ulysses so, till Syrens he had past,
> Would by his mates be pinioned to the mast.
> Now can our navy view the wished port,
> But there (to see the fortune!) was a fort :
> *Sandwich* would not be beaten, nor yet beat :
> *Fools only fight, the prudent use to treat.*
> His cousin Montagu, by court-disaster,
> Dwindled into the wooden-horse's master,
> To speak of peace seemed amongst all most proper,
> Had *Talbot* then treated of nought but copper:

---

[1] The Dutch.

Governor of the Castle, urging that Teddiman ought not to come thither with more than five ships, and desiring time to think of it, all the while he suffering the Dutch ships to land their guns to the best advantage, Teddiman, on the second pretence, began to play at the Dutch ships, whereof ten East India-men, and in three hours' time, the town and castle, without any provocation, playing on our ships, they did cut all our cables, so as the wind being off the land, did force us to go out, and rendered our fire-ships useless, without doing any thing, but what hurt of course our guns must have done them: we having lost five commanders, besides Mr. Edward Montagu[1] and Mr. Windham.[2]   Our fleete is come home, to our great grief, with not above five weeks' dry and six days' wet provisions: however, must go out again; and the Duke hath ordered the Soveraigne,[3] and all other ships ready, to go out

Or, what are forts, when void of ammunition?
With friends or foes what would we more condition?
Yet we three days, till the Dutch furnished all,
Men, powder, money, cannon, treat with wall!
Then *Tydiman*, finding the Danes would not,
Sent in six captains bravely to be shot.
And Montagu, though drest like any bride,
And aboard him too, yet was reached and died.
Sad was the chance, and yet a deeper care
Wrinkled his membranes under forehead fair,
The Dutch armado yet hath th' impudence
To put to sea, to waft their merchants thence,
For, as if all their ships of walnut were,
The more we beat them, still the more they bear:
But a good pilot, and a favouring wind,
Brings *Sandwich* back, and once again did blind."

Advice to a Painter.

[1] Mr. Edward Montagu was killed in the action at Bergen, and is much lamented by his friends.—Earl of Arlington's *Letters*, vol. ii., p. 87.

[2] This Mr. Windham had entered into a formal engagement, with the Earl of Rochester, "not without ceremonies of religion, that if either of them died, he should appear, and give the other notice of the future state, if there was any." He was probably one of the brothers of Sir Wm. Wyndham, Bart. See Wordsworth's *Ecclesiastical Biography*, 4th edit., vol. iv., p. 615.

[3] "The Sovereign of the Seas" was built at Woolwich, in 1637, of timber which had been stripped of its bark, while growing in the spring, and not felled till the second autumn afterwards; and it is observed by Dr. Plot (*Phil. Trans.* for 1691) in his discourse on the most seasonable time for felling timber, written by the advice of Pepys, that after forty-seven years, "all the ancient timber then remaining in her, it was no easy matter to drive a nail into it."—*Quarterly Review*, vol. viii., p. 35.

to the fleet and strengthen them.   This news troubles us all,
but cannot be helped.   Having read all this news, and received
commands of the Duke with great content, he giving me the
words which, to my great joy, he hath several times said to me,
that his greatest reliance is upon me ; and my Lord Craven
also did come out to talk with me, and told me that I am in
mighty esteem with the Duke, for which I bless God.   Home ;
and having given my fellow-officers an account hereof at
Chatham, and wrote other letters, I by water to Charing-Cross,
to the post-house, and there the people tell me they are shut
up; and so I went to the new post-house, and there got a
guide and horses to Hounslow.   So to Staines, and there, by
this time, it was dark night, and got a guide, who lost his way
in the forest, till, by help of the moone, which recompences
me for all the pains I ever took about studying of her motions,
I led my guide into the way back again ; and so we made a
man rise that kept a gate, and so he carried us to Cranborne,[1]
where, in the dark, I perceive an old house new building, with
a great deal of rubbish, and was fain to go up a ladder to Sir
G. Carteret's chamber.   And there, in his bed, I sat down,
and told him all my bad news, which troubled him mightily ;
but yet we were very merry, and made the best of it ; and
being myself weary, did take leave; and, after having spoken
with Mr. Fenn[2] in bed, I to bed in my Lady's chamber that
she uses to lie in, where the Duchess of York, that now is,
was born.   So to sleep; being very well, but weary, and the
better by having carried with me a bottle of strong water ;
whereof, now and then, a sip did me good.

20th. (Lord's day.)   Sir G. Carteret come and walked by
my bedside half an hour, talking, and telling how my Lord is
unblameable in all this ill success, he having followed orders ;
and that all ought to be imputed to the falseness of the King
of Denmark, who, he told me as a secret, had promised to
deliver up the Dutch ships to us ; and we expected no less ;
and swears it will, and will easily, be the ruin of him and his

[1] One of the Lodges belonging to the Crown, in Windsor Forest.   See 20th
July, ante.
[2] Probably John Fenne of the Navy Office ; of whom see more afterwards.

kingdom, if we fall out with him, as we must in honour do; but that all that can be, must be to get the fleete out again, to intercept De Witt, who certainly will be coming home with the East India fleete, he being gone thither. I up, and to walk forth to see the place; and I find it to be a very noble seat in a noble forest, with the noblest prospect towards Windsor, and round about over many countys, that can be desired: but otherwise a very melancholy place, and little variety, save only trees. So took horse for Staines, and thence to Branford, to Mr. Povy's. Mr. Povy not being at home, I lost my labour—only eat and drank there with his lady, and told my bad news, and hear the plague is round about them there. So away to Branford; and there, at the inn that goes down to the water-side, I 'light and paid off my post-horses, and so slipped on my shoes, and laid my things by, the tide not serving, and to church, where a dull sermon, and many Londoners. After church, to my inn, and eat and drank, and so about seven o'clock by water, and got, between nine and ten, to Queenhive,[1] very dark; and I could not get my waterman to go elsewhere, for fear of the plague. Thence with a lanthorn, in great fear of meeting of dead corpses, carrying to be buried; but, blessed be God! met none, but did see now and then a link, which is the mark of them, at a distance.

21st. Called up, by message from my Lord Brouncker, and the rest of my fellows, that they will meet me at the Duke of Albemarle's this morning; so I up, and weary, however, got thither before them, and spoke with my Lord, and with him and other gentlemen to walk in the Parke, where, I perceive, he spends much of his time, having no whither else to go: and here I heard him speak of some Presbyter people that he caused to be apprehended yesterday, at a private meeting in Covent Garden, which he would have released upon paying 5*l.* per man for the poor, but it was answered, they would not pay anything: so he ordered them to another prison from the guard. By and by comes my fellow-officers, and the Duke walked in, and to council with us; and that being done, we parted, and Sir W. Batten and I to the office, where, after

---

business, I to his house to dinner, whither comes Captain Cocke, for whose epicurism a dish of partridges was sent for. Thence to my Lord Brouncker, at Greenwich, to look after the lodgings appointed for us there for our office, which do by no means please us; they being in the heart of all the labourers and workmen there, which makes it as unsafe as to be, I think, at London. Mr. Hugh May,[1] who is a most ingenuous man, did show us the lodgings, and his acquaintance I am desirous of. Messengers went to get a boat for me, to carry me to Woolwich, but all to no purpose; so I was forced to walk it in the dark, at ten o'clock at night, with Sir J. Minnes's George with me, being mightily troubled for fear of the doggs at Coome farme, and more for fear of rogues by the way, and yet more because of the plague which is there, which is very strange, it being a single house, all alone from the town, but it seems they use to admit beggars, for their own safety, to lie in their barns, and they brought it to them. To my wife, and having first viewed her last piece of drawing since I saw her, which is seven or eight days, which pleases me beyond anything in the world, to bed, with great content, but weary.

22d. Up, and being importuned by my wife and her two maids, which are both good wenches, for me to buy a necklace of pearl for her, and I promising to give her one of 60*l*. in two years at furthest, and less if she pleases me in her painting. I went away, and walked to Greenwich, in my way seeing a coffin with a dead body therein, dead of the plague, lying in an open close belonging to Coome farme, which was carried out last night, and the parish have not appointed any body to bury it; but only set a watch there all day and night, that nobody should go thither or come thence: this disease making us more cruel to one another than we are to dogs. Walked to Redriffe, troubled to go through the little lane, where the plague is, but did, and took water and home, where all well.

23d. Busy writing letters, and received a very kind and good one from my Lord Sandwich, of his arrival with the fleete at Solebay, and the joy he had of my late news he met with,

---

[1] See note to June 8, 1665, *ante*.

of the marriage of my Lady Jemimah, and he tells me more, the good news that all our ships, which were in such danger that nobody would insure upon them, from the Eastland,[1] were all safe arrived.

25th. This day I am told that Dr. Burnett,[2] my physician, is this morning dead of the plague; which is strange, his man dying so long ago, and his house this month open again. Now himself dead.   Poor unfortunate man!

26th. With Mr. Andrews and Mr. Yeabsly, talking about their business. We parted at my Lord Brouncker's door, where I went in, having never been there before, and there he made a noble entertainment for Sir J. Minnes, myself, and Captain Cocke, none else, saving some painted lady that dined there: I know not who she is.[3] But very merry we were, and after dinner into the garden, and to see his and her chamber, where some good pictures, and a very handsome young woman for my Lady's woman.   By water home, in my way seeing a man taken up dead, out of the hold of a small catch that lay at Deptford. I doubt it might be the plague, which, with the thought of Dr. Burnett, did something disturb me. So home, sooner than ordinary, and, after supper, to read melancholy alone, and then to bed.

28th. To Mr. Colvill, the goldsmith's, having not for some days been in the streets; but now how few people I see, and those looking like people that had taken leave of the world. To the Exchange, and there was not fifty people upon it, and but few more like to be, as they told me. I think to take adieu to-day of the London streets. In much the best posture I ever was in, in my life, both as to the quantity and the certainty I have of the money I am worth; having most of it

---

[1] Baltic Sea.

[2] See *ante*, August 24th, 1662.   He was reported to have fallen a victim to his zeal. "Dr. Burnett, Dr. Glover, and one or two more of the College of Physicians, with Dr. O'Dowd, which was licensed by my Lord's Grace of Canterbury, some surgeons, apothecaries, and Johnson, the chemist, died all very suddenly.   Some say (but God forbid that I should report it for truth) that these, in a consultation together, if not all, yet the greatest part of them, attempted to open a dead corpse which was full of the tokens; and being in hand with the dissected body, some fell down dead immediately, and others did not outlive the next day at noon."—J. Tillison to Dr. Sancroft, 14th Sept. 1665, in 2 *Ellis*, iv., 37.

[3] Mrs. Williams, frequently mentioned afterwards.

in my hand.   But then this is a trouble to me what to do
with it, being myself this day going to be wholly at Woolwich ; but, for the present, I am resolved to venture it in an
iron chest—at least, for a while.   Just now comes news
that the fleete is gone, or going this day, out again, for which
God be praised! and my Lord Sandwich hath done himself
great right in it, in getting so soon out again.   I met my
wife walking to the water-side, with her painter, Mr. Browne,
and her maids.   There I met Commissioner Pett, and my Lord
Brouncker, and the lady at his house had been there to-day,
to see her.

29th. To Greenwich, and called at Sir Theophilus Biddulph's, a sober, discreet man, to discourse of the preventing
of the plague in Greenwich, and Woolwich, and Deptford,
where in every place it begins to grow very great.

30th. Abroad, and met with Hadley, our clerke, who, upon
my asking how the plague goes, told me it encreases much,
and much in our parish; for, says he, there died nine this
week, though I have returned but six: which is a very ill
practice, and makes me think it is so in other places; and
therefore the plague much greater than people take it to be.
I went forth, and walked towards Moorefields to see, God forgive my presumption! whether I could see any dead corpse
going to the grave; but, as God would have it, did not.   But,
Lord! how every body's looks, and discourse in the street, is
of death, and nothing else; and few people going up and down,
that the town is like a place distressed and forsaken.

31st. Up: and, after putting several things in order to my
removal, to Woolwich; the plague having a great encrease
this week, beyond all expectation, of almost 2000, making the
general Bill 7000, odd 100; and the plague above 6000.
Thus this month ends with great sadness upon the publick,
through the greatness of the plague every where through the
kingdom almost.   Every day sadder and sadder news of its
encrease.   In the City died this week 7496, and of them
6102 of the plague.   But it is feared that the true number
of the dead this week is near 10,000; partly from the poor
that cannot be taken notice of, through the greatness of the

number, and partly from the Quakers and others that will not have any bell ring for them.   Our fleete gone out to find the Dutch, we having about 100 sail in our fleete, and in them the Soveraigne one; so that it is a better fleete than the former with which the Duke was.   All our fear is, that the Dutch should be got in before them; which would be a very great sorrow to the publick, and to me particularly, for my Lord Sandwich's sake: a great deal of money being spent, and the kingdom not in a condition to spare, nor a parliament, without much difficulty to meet, to give more.   And to that; to have it said, what hath been done by our late fleetes?   As to myself, I am very well, only in fear of the plague, and as much of an ague, by being forced to go early and late to Woolwich, and my family to lie there continually.   My late greetings have been very great, to my great content, and am likely to have yet a few more profitable jobbs in a little while; for which Tangier and Sir W. Warren I am wholly obliged to.

September 1st. At the Duke of Albemarle's I overheard some examinations of the late plot that is discoursed of, and a great deal of do there is about it.   Among other discourses, I heard read an examination and discourse of Sir Philip Howard's,[1] with one of the plotting party.   These words being, "Then said Sir P. Howard, 'If you so come over to the King, and be faithful to him, you shall be maintained, and be set up with a horse and armes,'" and I know not what.   And then said such a one, "Yes, I will be true to the King."   And thus I believe twelve times Sir P. Howard answered him a damn me, which was a fine way of rhetorique to persuade a Quaker or Anabaptist from his persuasion.   And this was read in the hearing of Sir P. Howard, before the Duke and twenty more officers, and they made sport of it, only without any reproach, or he being anything ashamed of it.   But the plotter did at last bid them remember that he had not told them what King he would be faithful to.

3d. (Lord's day.)   Up, and put on my coloured silk suit

---

[1] Seventh son of Thomas Howard, first Earl of Berkshire; he was the direct ancestor of the present Earl of Suffolk, to whom both the titles descended.

very fine, and my new periwigg, bought a good while since, but durst not wear, because the plague was in Westminster when I bought it; and it is a wonder what will be the fashion after the plague is done, as to periwiggs, for nobody will dare to buy any haire, for fear of the infection, that it had been cut off the heads of people dead of the plague. I took my Lady Pen home, and her daughter Pegg; and, after dinner, I made my wife show them her pictures, which did mad Pegg Pen, who learns of the same man.[1] My Lord Brouncker, Sir J. Minnes, and I, up to the Vestry at the desire of the Justices of the Peace, in order to the doing something for the keeping of the plague from growing; but, Lord! to consider the madness of people of the town, who will, because they are forbid, come in crowds along with the dead corpses to see them buried; but we agreed on some orders for the prevention thereof. Among other stories, one was very passionate, methought, of a complaint brought against a man in the town, for taking a child from London from an infected house. Alderman Hooker told us it was the child of a very able citizen in Gracious Street, a saddler, who had buried all the rest of his children of the plague, and himself and wife now being shut up in despair of escaping, did desire only to save the life of this little child; and so prevailed to have it received stark-naked into the arms of a friend, who brought it, having put it into new fresh clothes, to Greenwich; where, upon hearing the story, we did agree it should be permitted to be received and kept in the town. By water to Woolwich, in great apprehensions of an ague. Here was my Lord Brouncker's lady of pleasure,[2] who, I perceive, goes everywhere with him; and he, I find, is obliged to carry her, and make all the courtship to her that can be.

4th. Walked home, my Lord Brouncker giving me a very neat cane to walk with; but it troubled me to pass by Coome farme, where about twenty-one people have died of the plague.

5th. After dinner, comes Colonel Blunt,[3] in his new chariot made with springs; as that was of wicker, wherein a while

---

¹ Brown.   ² Mrs. Williams.   ³ Of Wricklesmarsh.

since we rode at his house. And he hath rode, he says, now his journey, many miles in it with one horse, and out-drives any coach, and out-goes any horse, and so easy, he says. So, for curiosity, I went into it to try it, and up the hill¹ to the heath,² and over the cart-ruts, and found it pretty well, but not so easy as he pretends.

6th. To London, to pack up more things; and there I saw fires burning in the street, as it is through the whole City, by the Lord Mayor's order. Thence by water to the Duke of Albemarle's: all the way fires on each side of the Thames, and strange to see in broad daylight two or three burials upon the bankside, one at the very heels of another: doubtless, all of the plague; and yet at least forty or fifty people going along with every one of them. The Duke mighty pleasant with me; telling me that he is certainly informed that the Dutch were not come home upon the 1st instant, and so he hopes our fleete may meet with them.

7th. To the Tower, and there sent for the Weekly Bill, and find 8252 dead in all, and of them 6978 of the plague; which is a most dreadful number, and shows reason to fear that the plague hath got that hold that it will yet continue among us. Thence to Branford, reading "The Villaine," a pretty good play, all the way. There a coach of Mr. Povy's³ stood ready for me, and he at his house ready to come in, and so we together merrily to Swakeley,⁴ to Sir R. Viner's: a very

---

¹ Shooter's Hill.   ² Blackheath.
³ Aug. 6, 1666.   Dined with Mr. Povy, and then went with him to see a country-house he had brought near Brentford. — *Evelyn's Diary*.
⁴ Swakeley House, in the parish of Ickenham, Middlesex, was built in 1638, by Sir Edmund Wright, whose daughter marrying Sir James Harrington, one of Charles I.'s judges, he became possessed of it, *jure uxoris*. Sir Robert Vyner, Bart., to whom the property was sold in 1665, entertained Charles II. at Guild-hall, when Lord Mayor. The house was lately the residence of Thomas Clarke, Esq., whose father, in 1750, bought the estate of Mr. Lethieullier, to whom it had been alienated by the Vyner family. — *Lysons's Environs*. Sir Robert Vyner was ruined by the shutting of the Exchequer. The crown owed him on 1st January, 1676, no less a sum than 416,724*l*. 13*s*. 1*d*., to pay which, the King granted him 25,000*l*. 9*s*. 4*d*. per annum, out of the duty of Excise. These particulars are stated by Lord Keeper Somers, in his judgment, delivered in the Exchequer Chamber. In the *Spectator* (No. 462) is told the story of Sir Robert's successfully urging the King, at an entertainment given by him, "to return and take t'other bottle." Vyner afterwards erected a statue of the Merry Monarch in Stock's Market, and rendered the Crown many great services.

pleasant place, bought by him of Sir James Harrington's
lady. He tock us up and down with great respect, and
showed us all his house and grounds; and it is a place not
very moderne in the garden nor house, but the most uniforme
in all that ever I saw; and some things to excess. Pretty to
see over the screene of the hall, put up by Sir J. Harrington,
a long Parliament-man, the King's head, and my Lord of
Essex[1] on one side, and Fairfax on the other; and, upon the
other side of the screene, the parson of the parish, and the
lord of the manor and his sisters. The window-cases, door-
cases, and chimnys of all the house are marble. He showed
me a black boy that he had, that died of a consumption;
and, being dead, he caused him to be dried in an oven, and
lies there entire in a box. By and by to dinner, where his
lady[2] I find yet handsome, but hath been a very handsome
woman: now is old. Hath brought him near 100,000l., and
now he lives, no man in England in greater plenty, and commands both King and Council with his credit he gives them.
After dinner, Sir Robert led us up to his long gallery, very
fine, above stairs, and better, or such, furniture I never did
see. A most pleasant journey we had back. Povy tells me,
by a letter he showed me, that the King is not, nor hath been
of late, very well, but quite out of humour; and, as some
think, in a consumption, and weary of every thing. He
showed me my Lord Arlington's house[3] that he was born in,
in a towne called Harlington: and so carried me through a
most pleasant country to Branford, and there put me into my
boat, and good night. So I wrapped myself warm, and by
water got to Woolwich, about one in the morning.

9th. To my Lord Brouncker's, all of us, to dinner, where
a good venison pasty, and mighty merry. Here was Sir

---

[1] The Parliament General.

[2] Mary, daughter of John Whitchurch, Esq., and widow of Sir Thomas Hyde,
Bart., of Albury, Herts.

[3] Dawley House, near Hounslow, long the seat of the Bennet family. Harling-
ton, in which parish it is situated, gave the title of Baron and Earl to Sir Henry
Bennet; the aspirate being dropped (it may be said, "according to the custom of
London"). The mansion was alienated by Ford Grey, Earl of Tankerville, to
Viscount Bolingbroke, since which it has often changed owners.

W. Doyly, lately come from Ipswich about the sick and
wounded, and Mr. Evelyn and Captain Cocke. My wife
also was sent for by my Lord Brouncker, and was here.
After dinner, my Lord and his mistress would see her home
again, it being a most rainy afternoon, and I, forced to go to
the office on foot, was almost wet to the skin, and spoiled my
silk breeches almost. I was forced to get a bed at Captain
Cocke's, where I find Sir W. Doyly, and he, and Evelyn at
supper; and I with them full of discourse of the neglect of
our masters, the great officers of State, about all business, and
especially that of money: having now some thousand prisoners,
kept to no purpose at a great charge, and no money provided almost for the doing of it. We fell to talk largely of
the want of some persons understanding to look after businesses, but all goes to rack. "For," says Captain Cocke,
"my Lord Treasurer, he minds his ease, and lets things go
how they will: if he can have his 8000*l*. per annum, and a
game at l'Ombre, he is well. My Lord Chancellor he minds
getting of money and nothing else; and my Lord Ashly will
rob the devil and the Altar, but he will get money if it be to
be got." But that which puts us into this great melancholy,
was news brought to-day, which Captain Cocke reports as a
certain truth, that all the Dutch fleete, men-of-war and
merchant East India ships, are got every one in from Bergen
the 3d of this month, Sunday last; which will make us all
ridiculous. Full of these melancholy thoughts, to bed;
where, though I lay the softest I ever did in my life, with a
down bed, after the Danish manner, upon me, yet I slept
very ill, chiefly through the thoughts of my Lord Sandwich's
concernment in all this ill success at sea.

10th. (Lord's day.) Walked home; being forced thereto
by one of my watermen falling sick yesterday, and it was
God's great mercy I did not go by water with them yesterday, for he fell sick on Saturday night, and it is to be feared
of the plague. So I sent him away to London, with his

---

¹ Sir William Doyly, of Shottisham, Norfolk, knighted 1642; created a
Baronet 1663; M.P. for Yarmouth. Ob. 1677. He and Evelyn were at this
time appointed Commissioners for the care of the sick and wounded seamen and
prisoners of war.

family; but another boat come to me this morning. My wife, before I come out, telling me the ill news that she hears, that her father is very ill, and then I told her I feared of the plague, for that the house is shut up. And so she much troubled, and did desire me to send them something, and I said I would, and will do so. But, before I come out, there happened news to come to me by an expresse from Mr. Coventry, telling me the most happy news of my Lord Sandwich's meeting with part of the Dutch; his taking two of their East India ships, and six or seven others, and very good prizes:[1] and that he is in search of the rest of the fleete, which he hopes to find upon the Wellbancke, with the loss only of the Hector, poor Captain Cuttle. To Greenwich, and there sending away Mr. Andrews, I to Captain Cocke's, where I find my Lord Brouncker and his mistress, and Sir J. Minnes, where we supped; there was also Sir W. Doyly and Mr. Evelyn; but the receipt of this news did put us all into such an extasy of joy, that it inspired into Sir J. Minnes and Mr. Evelyn such a spirit of mirth, that in all my life I never met with so merry a two hours as our company this night was. Among other humours, Mr. Evelyn's repeating of some verses made up of nothing but the various acceptations of *may* and *can*, and doing it so aptly upon occasion of something of that nature, and so fast, did make us all die almost with laughing, and did so stop the mouth of Sir J. Minnes in the middle of all his mirth, and in a thing agreeing with his own manner of genius, that I never saw any man so out-done in all my life; and Sir J. Minnes's mirth, too, to see himself out-done, was the crown of all our mirth. In this humour we sat till about ten at night, and so my Lord and his mistress home, and we to bed.

11th. Over to the ferry, where Sir W. Batten's coach was ready for us, and to Walthamstow drove merrily, and there a good plain venison dinner. After dinner, to billiards, where I won an angel. Sir W. Hickes[2] was there, and my Lady

---

[1] These prizes, it will be seen, caused great trouble.

[2] Sir William Hickes, created a Baronet 1619. Ob. 1680, aged 84. His country-seat was called Ruckholts, or Rookwood, at Layton, in Essex, where he entertained King Charles II. after hunting.

Batten invited herself to dine with him this week, and she invited us all to dine with her there, which we agreed to, only to vex him, he being the most niggardly fellow, it seems, in the world. So to Greenwich, where my Lord Rutherford and Creed come from Court, and have brought me several orders for money to pay for Tangier; and, among the rest, 7000*l.* and more, to this Lord, which is an excellent thing to consider, that, though they can do nothing else, they can give away the King's money upon their progresse. I did give him the best answer I could to pay him with tallys, and that is all they could get from me.

13th. My Lord Brouncker, Sir J. Minnes, and I, took boat, and in my Lord's coach to Sir W. Hickes's, whither, by and by, my Lady Batten and Sir William comes. It is a good seat, with a fair grove of trees by it, and the remains of a good garden; but so let to run to ruine, both house and every thing in and about it, so ill furnished and miserably looked after, I never did see in all my life. Not so much as a latch to his dining-room door, which saved him nothing, for the wind, blowing into the room for want thereof, flung down a great bow-pott that stood upon the side-table, and that fell upon some Venice glasses, and did him a crown's worth of hurt. He did give us the meanest dinner, of beef, shoulder and umbles of venison,[1] which he takes away from the keeper of the Forest,[2] and a few pigeons, and all in the meanest manner, that ever I did see, to the basest degree. I was only pleased at a very fine picture of the Queen-Mother, when she was young, by Vandike; a very good picture, and a lovely face.

14th. To London, where I have not been now a pretty while. To the Duke of Albemarle, where I find a letter of the 12th, from Solebay, from my Lord Sandwich, of the fleete's

---

[1] Dr. Johnson was puzzled by the following passage in "The Merry Wives of Windsor," act. v., sc. 3.—"Divide me like a bribe-buck, each a haunch. I will keep the sides to myself; *my shoulders for the fellow of this walk.*" If he could have read the account of Sir William Hickes's dinner, he would at once have understood the allusion to the keeper's perquisites of the shoulders of all deer killed in his walk. The matter, however, is rightly explained in the modern editions of Shakspeare.

[2] Epping Forest, of which he was Ranger.

meeting with about eighteen more of the Dutch fleete, and his taking of most of them: and the messenger says, they had taken three after the letter was wrote and sealed; which being twenty-one, and the fourteen took the other day, is forty-five[1] sail; some of which are good, and others rich ships.   And, having taken a copy of my Lord's letter, I away toward the 'Change, the plague being all thereabouts.   Here my news was highly welcome, and I did wonder to see the 'Change so full; I believe 200 people; but not a man or merchant of any fashion, but plain men all.   And, Lord! to see how I did endeavour all I could to talk with as few as I could, there being now no observation of shutting up of houses infected, that to be sure we do converse and meet with people that have the plague upon them.   I spent some thoughts upon the occurrences of this day, giving matter for as much content on one hand, and melancholy on another, as any day in all my life.   For the first; the finding of my money and plate, and all safe at London, and speeding in my business this day The hearing of this good news to such excess, after so great a despair of my Lord's doing any thing this year; adding to that, the decrease of 500 and more, which is the first decrease we have yet had in the sickness since it begun; and great hopes that the next week it will be greater.   Then, on the other side, my finding that though the Bill in general is abated, yet the City, within the walls, is encreased, and likely to continue so, and is close to our house there.   My meeting dead corpses of the plague, carried to be buried close to me at noonday through the City in Fenchurch Street.   To see a person sick of the sores carried close by me by Grace-church in a hackney-coach.   My finding the Angel Tavern, at the lower end of Tower Hill, shut up; and more than that, the alehouse at the Tower Stairs; and more than that, that the person was then dying of the plague when I was last there, a little while ago, at night.   To hear that poor Payne, my waiter, hath buried a child, and is dying himself.   To hear that a labourer I sent but the other day to Dagenhams, to know how they did there, is dead of the plague; and that one of my own

---

[1] Thirty-five?

watermen, that carried me daily, fell sick as s on as he had
landed me on Friday morning last, when I had been all night
upon the water, and I believe he did get his infection that
day at Branford, and is now dead of the plague.　To hear
that Captain Lambert and Cuttle are killed in the taking these
ships; and that Mr. Sidney Montagu is sick of a desperate
fever at my Lady Carteret's, at Scott's Hall.　To hear that
Mr. Lewis hath another daughter sick.　And, lastly, that
both my servants, W. Hewer, and Tom Edwards, have lost
their fathers, both in St. Sepulchre's parish, of the plague
this week, do put me into great apprehensions of melancholy,
and with good reason.　But I put off my thoughts of sadness
as much as I can, and the rather to keep my wife in good
heart, and family also.

15th. With Captain Cocke, and there drank a cup of good
drink, which I am fain to allow myself during this plague time,
by advice of all, and not contrary to my oath, my physician
being dead, and chyrurgeon out of the way, whose advice I am
obliged to take.　In much pain to think what I shall do this
winter time; for going every day to Woolwich I cannot,
without endangering my life; and staying from my wife at
Greenwich is not handsome.

16th. To the office; where I find Sir J. Minnes gone to
the fleete, like a doating fool, to do no good, but proclaim
himself an asse; for no service he can do here, nor inform
my Lord, who is come in thither to the buoy of the Nore,
in any thing worth his knowledge.　The likelihood of the
increase of the plague this week makes us a little sad.　To
Captain Cocke's, meaning to lie there, it being late, and he
not being at home, I walked to him to my Lord Brouncker's,
and there staid a while, they being at Tables;[1] and so by and
by parted, and walked to his house; and, after a mess of
good broth, to bed, in great pleasure, his company being most
excellent.

17th. (Lord's day.) To church, where a company of fine
people, and a fine church, and very good sermon, Mr. Plume[2]

---

[1] Tables, better known, at present, by the name of backgammon.

[2] Thomas Plume, D.D., Vicar of Greenwich, 1662, and installed Archdeacon of
Rochester, 1679.　Ob. 1704.

being a very excellent scholler and preacher. To Gravesend
in the Bezan Yacht, and there come to anchor for all night,
and supped and talked, and with much pleasure at last settled
ourselves to sleep, having very good lodgings upon cushions
in the cabbin.

18th. By break of day we come to within sight of the fleete,
which was a very fine thing to behold, being above 100 ships,
great and small; with the flag-ships of each squadron, distinguished by their several flags on their main, fore, or mizen-
masts. Among others, the Soveraigne, Charles, and Prince;
in the last of which my Lord Sandwich was. And so we come
on board, and we find my Lord Sandwich newly up in his
nightgown very well. He received us kindly; telling us the
state of the fleete, lacking provisions, having no beer at all,
nor have had, most of them, these three weeks or month, and
but few days' dry provisions. And, indeed, he tells us that he
believes no fleete was ever set to sea in so ill condition of provision, as this was when it went out last. He did inform us
in the business of Bergen, so as to let us see how the judgment of the world is not to be depended on in things they
know not; it being a place just wide enough, and not so much
hardly, for ships to go through to it, the yard-armes sticking
in the very rocks. He do not, upon his best enquiry, find
reason to except against any part of the management of the
business by Teddiman; he having staid treating no longer
than during the night, while he was fitting himself to fight,
bringing his ship a-breast, and not a quarter of an hour longer,
as it is said; nor could more ships have been brought to play,
as is thought. Nor could men be landed, there being 10,000
men effectively always in armes of the Danes; nor, says he,
could we expect more from the Danes than he did, it being
impossible to set fire on the ships but it must burn the towne.
But that wherein the Dane did amisse is, that he did assist
them, the Dutch, all the time, while he was treating with us,
when he should have been neutrall to us both. But, however, he did demand but the treaty of us; which is, that we
should not come with more than five ships. A flag of truce
is said, and confessed by my Lord, that he believes it, was

hung out; but, while they did hang it out, they did shoot at us; so that it was not seen, or perhaps they would not cease upon sight of it, while they continued actually in action against us. But the main thing my Lord wonders at and condemns the Dane for is, that the blockhead, who is so much in debt to the Hollander, having now a treasure more by much than all his crowne was worth, and that, which would for ever have beggared the Hollander, should not take this time to break with the Hollander, and thereby pay his debt, which must have been forgiven him, and have got the greatest treasure into his hands that ever was together in the world. By and by my Lord took me aside to discourse of his private matters, and was very free with me touching the ill condition of the fleete that it hath been in, and the good fortune that he hath had, and nothing else, that these prizes are to be imputed to. He also talked with me about Mr. Coventry's dealing with him in sending Sir W. Pen away before him, which was not fair nor kind; but that he hath mastered and cajoled Sir W. Pen, that he hath been able to do nothing in the fleete, but been obedient to him; but withal tells me he is a man that is but of very mean parts, and a fellow not to be lived with, so false and base he is; which I knew well enough to be true; and did, as I had formerly done, give my Lord my knowledge of him. By and by was called a Council of War on board, when comes Sir W. Pen there, and Sir Christopher Mings, Sir Edward Spragg, Sir Joseph Jordan, Sir Thomas Teddiman, and Sir Roger Cuttance. Great spoil, I hear, there hath been of the two East India ships, and that yet they will come into the King very rich; so that I hope this journey will be worth a 100*l.* to me. So to our yacht again, having seen many of my friends there, and continued till we come into Chatham river. Among others, I hear that W. Howe will grow very rich by this late business, and grows very proud and insolent by it; but it is what I ever expected. I hear by everybody how much my poor Lord Sandwich was concerned for me during my silence a while, lest I had been dead of the plague in this sickly time.

19th. To Sir John Minnes's, where I find my Lady Batten

come, and she and my Lord Brouncker and his mistress, and
the whole house-full there at cards.

20th. Up, and, after being trimmed, the first time I have
been touched by a barber these twelve months, I think, and
more, by and by Sir J. Minnes and Sir W. Batten met, to
go into my Lord Brouncker's coach, and so we four to
Lambeth, and thence to the Duke of Albemarle, to inform
him what we have done as to the fleete, which is very little,
and to receive his direction.   But, Lord! what a sad time it
is to see no boats upon the river; and grass grows all up and
down White Hall court, and nobody but poor wretches in the
streets!   And, which is worst of all, the Duke showed us the
number of the plague this week, brought in the last night
from the Lord Mayor; that it is increased about 600 more
than the last, which is quite contrary to our hopes and
expectations, from the coldness of the late season.   For the
whole general number is 8297, and of them the plague 7165;
which is more in the whole, by above 50, than the biggest
Bill yet: which is very grievous to us all.   I find Sir W.
Batten and his lady gone home to Walthamstow, with some
necessity, hearing that a maid-servant of their's is taken ill.

21st. Up between five and six o'clock; and, by the time I
was ready, my Lord Brouncker's coach comes for me; and
taking Will Hewer with me, who is all in mourning for his
father, who is lately dead of the plague, as my boy Tom's is
also, I set out, and took about 100l. with me to pay the fees
at the Exchequer at Nonsuch, and so I rode in some fear of
robbing.   When I come thither, I find only Mr. Ward, who
led me to Burges's bedside, and Spicer's, who, watching of
the house, as it is their turns every night, did lie long in bed
to-day, and I find nothing at all done in my business, which
vexed me.   But, not seeing how to help it, I did walk up
and down with Mr. Ward to see the House.   Walked up and
down the house and park; and a fine place it hath heretofore
been, and a fine prospect about the house.   A great walk of
an elme and a walnutt set one after another in order.   And
all the house on the outside filled with figures of stories, and
good painting of Rubens' or Holbein's doing.   And one

great thing is, that most of the house is covered— mean,
the posts and quarters in the walls, with lead, and gilded. I
walked, also, into the ruined garden. Strange to see how
young W. Bowyer looks at 41 years: one would not take him
for 24 or more, and is one of the greatest wonders I ever did
see. I got to my Lord Brouncker's before night, and there
I sat and supped with him, and his mistress, and Cocke,
whose boy is yet ill. Thence, after losing a crowne betting at
Tables, we walked home. Cocke seeing me to my new lodging.

22d. At Blackwall. Here is observable what Johnson
tells us, that, in digging the late Docke, they did, 12 feet
under ground, find perfect trees over-covered with earth.
Nut-trees, with the branches and the very nuts upon them;
some of whose nuts he showed us. Their shells black with
age; and their kernell, upon opening, decayed, but their shell
perfectly hard as ever. And a yew-tree, upon which the very
ivy was taken up whole about it, which, upon cutting with
an addes,[1] we found it to be rather harder than the living
tree usually is. The armes, they say, were taken up at first
whole, about the body, which is very strange. To Woolwich,
and my Lord Sandwich, not being come, we took a boat, and
about a mile off, met him in his Catch, and boarded him, and
come up with him; and, after making a little halt at my
house, which I ordered, to have my wife see him, we altogether by coach to Mr. Boreman's,[2] where Sir J. Minnes did
receive him very handsomely, and there he is to lie; and Sir
J. Minnes did give him, on the sudden, a very handsome
supper and brave discourse, my Lord Brouncker, and Captain
Cocke, and Captain Herbert being there, with myself. Here
my Lord did witness great respect to me, and very kind
expressions, and did take notice how I was overjoyed at first
to see the King's letter to his Lordship, and told them how I
did kiss it, and that, whatever he was, I did always love the
King. Among other discourse concerning long life, Sir J.
Minnes saying that his great-grandfather was alive in Edward
the Vth's time; my Lord Sandwich did tell us how few there
have been of his family since King Harry the VIIIth; that

---

[1] Adze.

[2] Afterwards Sir William Boreman, Clerk of the Green Cloth.

is to say, the then Chiefe Justice,[1] and his son and the Lord
Montagu, who was father to Sir Sidney,[2] who was his father.
And yet, what is more wonderfull, he did assure us, from the
mouth of my Lord Montagu himself, that, in King James's
time, when he had a mind to get the King to cut off the
entayle of some land which was given in Harry the VIIIth's
time to the family, with the remainder in the Crowne; he did
answer the King in showing how unlikely it was that ever it
could revert to the Crown, but that it would be a present
convenience to him; and did show that, at that time, there
were 4000 persons derived from the very body of the Chiefe
Justice.[3]   It seems the number of daughters in the family
having been very great, and they too had, most of them,
many children, and grandchildren, and great-grandchildren.
This he tells as a most known and certain truth.   After
supper, my Lord Brouncker took his leave, and I also did
mine, taking Captain Herbert home to my lodging to lie with
me, who did mighty seriously inquire after who was that in
the black dress with my wife yesterday, and would not believe
that it was my wife's maid Mercer, but it was she.

23d. To my Lord Sandwich, who did advise alone with me
how far he might trust Captain Cocke in the business of the
prize-goods,[1] my Lord telling me that he hath taken into his

---

[1] Sir Edward Montagu.   Ob. 1556.

[2] Master of the Requests to Charles I.

[3] Lord Sandwich speaks of five generations, in which the number of descendants
might have multiplied ad infinitum.   "When King James came into England,"
observes Ward, in his Diary, p. 170, "he was fleasted at Boughton, by Sir
Edward Montagu, and his six sonnes brought upp the six first dishes; three of
them after were lords, and three more knights—Sir Walter Montagu, Sir Sydney,
and Sir Charles, whose daughter Lady Hatton is."   Fuller, also, in his Worthies,
records that "Hester Sandys, the wife of Sir Thomas Temple, of Stowe, Bart.,
had four sons and nine daughters, which lived to be married, and so exceedingly
multiplied, that she saw seven hundred extracted from her body.   Besides, there
was a new generation of marringeable females just at her death."—See Collins's
Peerage, vol. ii., p. 411.   When Charles, thirteenth Duke of Norfolk, had completed his restoration of Arundel Castle, he proposed to entertain all the descendants of his ancestor, Jock of Norfolk, who fell at Bosworth Field; but gave up
his intention on finding that he should have to invite upwards of six thousand
persons.

[4] In the British Museum, Egerton, MS., 861, is an account showing the value
of all prizes taken during the war with the Dutch; distinguishing the vessels,
their goods, the ports at which they were condemned, and the parties to whose
accounts the amounts were debited.

hands 2 or 3000*l.* value of them : it being a good way, he
says, to get money, and afterwards to get the King's allowance
thereof, it being easier, he observes, to keep money when got
of the King than to get it when it is too late.   I advised him
not to trust Cocke too far.   Thence to Lambeth — his Lordship, and all our office, and Mr. Evelyn, to the Duke of
Albemarle, where we sat down to consult of the disposing and
supporting of the fleete with victuals, and money, and for the
sick men and prisoners; and I did propose the taking out
some goods out of the prizes, to the value of 10,000*l.* which
was accorded to ; but what inconveniences may arise from it,
I do not yet see, but fear there may be many.   Here we
dined, and I did hear my Lord Craven whisper, as he is
mightily possessed with a good opinion of me, much to my
advantage, which my good Lord did second, and anon my
Lord Craven did speak publickly of me to the Duke, in the
hearing of all the rest; and the Duke did say something of
the like advantage to me — I believe, not much to the satisfaction of my brethren ; but I was mightily joyed at it.
Thence took leave, leaving my Lord Sandwich to go visit
the Bishop of Canterbury.   With Captain Cocke set out in
the yacht for the fleete about ten o'clock at night.

24th. (Lord's day.) Waked, and up, and drank; and
then, being about Grayes, and a very calm, curious morning,
we took our wherry, and to the fisherman, and bought a great
deal of fine fish, and to Gravesend to White's, and had part
of it dressed; and, in the mean time, we to walk about a mile
from the town, and so back again ; and there one of our
watermen told us he had heard of a bargain of cloves for us,
and we went to a blind alehouse at the further end :f the
town, to a couple of wretched, dirty seamen, who, poor
wretches ! had got together about 37lb. of cloves, and 10lb.
of nutmeggs, and we bought them of them — the first at
5*s.* 6*d.* per lb., and the latter at 4*s.*, and paid them in gold ;
but, Lord ! to see how silly these men are in the selling of
it, and easy to be persuaded almost to anything.   But it
would never have been allowed by my conscience to have
wronged the poor wretches, who told us how dangerously

they had got some, and dearly paid for the rest of these goods.'

25th. Found ourselves come to the fleete, and so aboard the Prince: and there, after a good while in discourse, we did agree to a bargain of 5000*l.* for my Lord Sandwich, for silk, cinnamon, nutmegs, and indigo. And I was near signing to an undertaking for the payment of the whole sum, but I did by chance escape it; having since, upon second thoughts, great cause to be glad of it, reflecting upon the craft and not good condition, it may be, of Captain Cocke. I could get no trifles for my wife, and so away to the Prince, and presently comes my Lord on board from Greenwich, with whom, after a little discourse about his trusting of Cocke, we parted, and to our yacht; but, it being calm, we, to make haste, took our wherry towards Chatham; but, it growing dark, we were put to great difficultys — our simple, but confident waterman, not knowing a step of the way; and we found ourselves to go backward and forward, which, in the dark night and a wild place, did vex us mightily. At last, we got a fisher boy by chance, and took him into the boat, and, being an odd kind of boy, did vex us too; for he would not answer us aloud when we spoke to him, but did carry us safe thither, though with a mistake or two; but I wonder they were not more. In our way, I was astonished, and so were we all, at the strange nature of the sea-water in a dark night, that it seemed like fire upon every stroke of the oare, and, they say, is a sign of winde. We went to the Crowne Inn, at Rochester, and there to supper, and made ourselves merry with the poor fisher-boy, who told us he had not been in bed the whole seven years he come to 'prentice, and hath two or three more years to serve. We, in our clothes, to bed.

27th. Up and saw and admired my wife's picture of Our Saviour, now finished, which is very pretty. By water to Greenwich, where to the King's Head, the great musique-house, the first time I was ever there. Much troubled to hear from Creed, that he was told at Salisbury,[2] that I am

---

' Stolen from the prizes.

[2] To which place the Court had retired, on account of the plague. See 20th Aug., *ante.*

come to be a great swearer and drunkard; but, Lord! to see how my late little drinking of wine is taken notice of by envious men, to my disadvantage. To Captain Cocke's, and he not yet come from town, to Mr. Evelyn, where much company; and thence in his coach with him to the Duke of Albemarle, by Lambeth, who was in a mighty pleasant humour; and tells us that the Dutch do stay abroad, and our fleete must go out again. or be ready to do so. Here we got several things ordered, as we desired, for the relief of the prisoners, and sick and wounded men. Here I saw this week's Bill of Mortality, wherein, blessed be God! there is above 1800 decrease, being the first considerable decrease we have had. Most excellent discourse with Mr. Evelyn touching all manner of learning, wherein I find him a very fine gentleman, and particularly of paynting, in which he tells me the beautifull Mrs. Middleton is rare, and his own wife do brave things. Captain Cocke brought one parcel of our goods by waggons, and I first resolved to have lodged them at our office; but the thoughts of its being the King's house altered our resolution, and so put them at his friend's, Mr. Glanville's, and there they are safe. Would the rest of them were so, too! In discourse, we come to mention my profit, and he offers me 500*l.* clear, and I demand 600*l.* We part to night, and I lie at Mr. Glanville's house, there being none there but a mayd-servant and a young man, being in some pain, partly from not knowing what to do in this business, having a mind to be at a certainty in my profit, and partly through his having Jacke sick still, and his blackemore now also fallen sick. So he being gone, I to bed.

29th. I had my horse I borrowed of Mr. Gilethropp, Sir W Batten's clerke, brought to me at Greenwich, and so set out and rode hard, and was at Nonsuch[1] by about eight o'clock, a very fine journey, and a fine day. There I come just about chappell-time, and so I went to chappell with them, and thence to the severall offices about my tallies, which I find done, but strung for sums not to my purpose. But. Lord! what ado I had to persuade the dull fellows to it.

---

[1] Nonsuch House, near Epsom.

especially Mr. Warder, Master of the Pells, and yet without any manner of reason for their scruple. But, at last, I did, and so walked to Ewell, and to horse again, and come to Greenwich before night. Sir Martin Noell is this day dead of the plague, in London, where he hath lain sick of it these eight days.

30th. The great burden we have upon us at this time at the office, is the providing for prisoners and sick men that are recovered, they lying before our office doors all night and all day, poor wretches. Having been on shore, the Captains won't receive them on board, and other ships we have not to put them on, nor money to pay them off, or provide for them. God remove this difficulty! Hither come Luellin to me, and would force me to take Mr. Deering's 20 pieces in gold he did offer me a good while since, which I did, yet really and sincerely against my will and content, being not likely to reap any comfort in having to do with, and be beholden to, a man that minds more his pleasure and company than his business. Was set upon by the poor wretches, whom I did give words and some little money to, and the poor people went away like lambs, and, in good earnest, are not to be censured, if their necessities drive them to bad courses. Thence to the office, and then to Captain Cocke's, where I find Mr. Temple, the fat blade, Sir Robert Viner's chief man. I do end this month with the greatest content, and may say that these last three months, for joy, health, and profit, have been much the greatest that ever I received all my life in any twelve months, having nothing upon me but the consideration of the sickliness of the season to mortify me.

October 1st. (Lord's day.) Embarked on board the Bezan, and come to the fleete about two of the clock. My Lord received me mighty kindly; and, among other things, to my great joy, he did assure me that he had wrote to the King and Duke about these prize-goods, and told me that they did approve what he had done, and that he would own what he had done, and would have me tell all the world so, and did, under his hand, give Cocke and me his certificate of our bargains, and giving us full power of disposal of what we

have so bought. This do ease my mind of all my fear. He
did discourse to us of the Dutch fleete being abroad, eighty-
five of them still. After supper, Captain Cocke and I, and
Temple, on board the Bezan, and there to cards for a while,
and so to sleep. But, Lord! the mirth which it caused to
me, to be waked in the night by their snoring round about
me: I did laugh till I was ready to burst, and waked one of
the two companions of Temple, who could not a good while
tell where he was, that he heard one laugh so, till he recol-
lected himself, and I told him what it was at, and so to sleep
again, they still snoring.

2d. Having sailed all night, and I do wonder how they in
the dark could find the way, we got by morning to Gilling-
ham, and thence all walked to Chatham; and there, with
Commissioner Pett, viewed the Yard; and, among other
things, a team of four horses come close by us, he being with
me, drawing a piece of timber, that I am confident one man
could easily have carried upon his back. I made the horses
be taken away, and a man or two to take the timber away
with their hands. To Rochester, to visit the old Castle ruins,
which hath been a noble place; but, Lord! to see what a
dreadful thing it is to look upon the precipices, for it did
fright me mightily. The place hath been great and strong
in former ages. So to walk up and down the Cathedral, and
thence to the Crowne, whither Mr. Fowler, the Mayor of the
towne, was come in his gowne, and is a very reverend magis-
trate. Took horses to Gravesend, and there staid not, but
got a boat, the sickness being very much in the town still,
and so called on board my Lord Brouncker and Sir John
Minnes, on board one of the East Indiamen at Erith, and
there do find them full of envious complaints for the pillaging
of the ships, but I did pacify them.

3d. Sir W. Batten is gone this day to meet to adjourne
the Parliament to Oxford. Comes one to tell me my Lord
Rutherford is come; so I to the King's Head to him, where
I find his lady—a fine young Scotch lady,[1] pretty handsome,
and plain. My wife also, and Mercer, by and by comes,

---

[1] Christian, daughter of Sir Alexander Urquhart, of Cromarty.

Creed bringing them; and so presently to dinner, and very merry. That being done, and some music and other diversions, at last, away goes my Lord and Lady. This night, I hear that, of our two watermen that used to carry our letters, and were well on Saturday last, one is dead, and the other dying sick of the plague; the plague, though decreasing elsewhere, yet being greater about the Tower and thereabouts.

4th. This night comes Sir George Smith[1] to see me at the office, and tells me how the plague is decreased this week 740, for which God be praised! but that it encreases at our end of the town still. All the town is full of Captain Cocke's being in some ill condition about prize-goods, his goods being taken from him, and I know not what. Being come to my wife, at our lodging, I did go to bed, and left my wife with her people, to laugh and dance, and I to sleep.

5th. Among other things, talking of my sister Pall, and my wife of herself is very willing that I should give her 400l. to her portion, and would have her married soon as we could; but this great sickness time do make it unfit to send for her up. Read a book of Mr. Evelyn's translating,[2] and sending me as a present, about directions for gathering a library; but the book is above my reach, but his epistle to my Lord Chancellor is a very fine piece. Then to Mr. Evelyn's, to discourse of our confounded business of prisoners, and sick and wounded seamen, wherein he and we are so much put out of order. And here he showed me his gardens, which are, for variety of evergreens, and hedge of holly, the finest things I ever saw in my life. Thence in his coach to Greenwich, and there to my office, all the way having fine discourse of trees and the nature of vegetables. Renewed my promises of observing my vowes as I used to do; for I find that, since I left them off, my mind is run a wool-gathering and my business neglected.

7th. Did business, though not much, at the office, because

[1] Sir George Smith, of St. Bartholomew, by the Exchange. He married Martha, daughter of John Swift of London, merchant.
[2] Gabriel Naudé's Instructions concerning the erecting of a Library; translated by Evelyn in 1661. See his *Diary*, Nov. 16, 1661.

of the horrible crowd and lamentable moan of the poor seamen, that lie starving in the streets for lack of money, which do trouble and perplex me to the heart; and more at noon, when we were to go through them, for then above a whole hundred of them followed us; some cursing, some swearing, and some praying to us. A letter come this afternoon from the Duke of Albemarle, signifying the Dutch to be in sight, with 80 sail, yesterday morning, off Solebay, coming right into the bay. God knows what they will and may do to us, we having no force abroad able to oppose them, but to be sacrificed to them. At night come two waggons from Rochester, with more goods from Captain Cocke; and in housing them come two of the Custom-house, and did seize them: but I showed them my *Transire*. However, after some angry words, we locked them up, and sealed up the key, and did give it to the constable to keep until Monday, and so parted. But, Lord! to think how the poor constable come to me in the dark, going home; "Sir," says he, "I have the key, and, if you would have me do any service for you, send for me betimes to-morrow morning, and I will do what you would have me." Whether the fellow do this out of kindness or knavery, I cannot tell; but it is pretty to observe. Talking with him in the high way, come close by the bearers with a dead corpse of the plague; but, Lord! to see what custom is, that I am come almost to think nothing of it.

8th. (Lord's day.) A letter from the Duke of Albemarle to me, to order as many ships forth out of the river as I can presently, to joyne to meet the Dutch; having ordered all the Captains of the ships in the river to come to me, I did some business with them, and so to Captain Cocke's to dinner — he being in the country. But here his brother Solomon was, and, for guests, myself, Sir G. Smith, and a very fine lady, Mrs. Penington, and two more gentlemen. But, both before and after dinner, most excellent witty discourse with this lady, who is a very fine witty lady, one of the best I ever heard speak, and indifferent handsome. To the office, where ended the business with the Captains; and I think, of twenty-two ships, we shall make shift to get out

seven, God help us! men being sick, or provisions lacking.
This day. I hear the Pope is dead;[1] and one said, that the news
is, that the King of France is stabbed, but that the former
is very true, which will do great things sure, as to the
troubling of that part of the world, the King of Spain
[Philip IV.] being so lately dead. And one thing more —
Sir Martin Noell's lady is dead with grief, for the death of
her husband; but it seems nobody can make anything of his
estate, whether he be dead worth anything or no, he having
dealt in so many things, publick and private, as nobody can
understand whereabouts his estate is, which is the fate of
these great dealers at everything.

9th. Called upon Sir John Shaw, to whom I did give a
civil answer about our prize goods, that all his dues, as one
of the Farmers of the Customes, are paid, and showed him
our *Transire;* with which he was satisfied, and parted. To
the Duke of Albemarle, and what should it be, but to tell me,
that if my Lord Sandwich do not come to town, he do resolve to go with the fleete to sea himself, the Dutch, as he
thinks, being in the Downes, and so desired me to get a pleasure-boat for to take him in to-morrow morning, and do
many other things, and with a great liking of me, and my
management especially, as that coxcombe Lord Craven do
tell me, and I perceive it, and I am sure take pains enough
to deserve it.

10th. Up, and receive a stop from the Duke of Albemarle
of setting out any more ships, or providing a pleasure-boat for
himself, which I am glad of, and do think, what I thought
yesterday, that this resolution of his was a sudden one and
silly. Sir G. Ascue says, that he did, from the beginning,
declare against these [prize] goods, and would not receive his
dividend; and that he and Sir W. Pen are at odds about it,
and that he fears Mings hath been doing ill offices to my
Lord. I did to-night give my Lord an account of all this.

11th. Comes up my landlady, Mrs. Clerke, to make an
agreement for the time to come; and I, for the having room
enough, and to keep out strangers, and to have a place to

---

[1] A false report.

retreat to for my wife, if the sicknesse should come to Woolwich, am to pay dear: so, for three rooms, and a dining-
room, and for dinner, and bread and beer and butter, at nights
and mornings, I am to give her 5*l.* 10*s.* per month. To
Erith, and there we met Mr. Seymour, one of the Commissioners for Prizes, and a Parliament-man, and he was mighty
high, and had now seized our goods on their behalf; and he
mighty imperiously would have all forfeited. But I could
not but think it odd that a Parliament-man, in a serious discourse before such persons as we and my Lord Brouncker,
and Sir John Minnes, should quote " Hudibras," as being
the book I doubt he hath read most. To Woolwich, where
we had appointed to keep the night merrily; and so, by Captain Cocke's coach, had brought a very pretty child, a
daughter of one Mrs. Tooker's, next door to my lodging, and
so she, and a daughter and kinsman of Mrs. Pett's, made up
a fine company at my lodgings at Woolwich, where my wife,
and Mercer, and Mrs. Barbara Sheldon,[1] danced, and mighty
merry we were, but especially at Mercer's dancing a jigg,
which she does the best I ever did see, having the most
natural way of it, and keeps time the most perfectly I ever
did see. This night is kept in lieu of yesterday, for my
wedding-day[2] of ten years; for which God be praised! being
now in an extreme good condition of health and estate and
honour, and a way of getting more money, though at this
hour under some discomfiture, rather than damage, about
some prize-goods that I have bought off the fleete, in partner-
ship with Captain Cocke, and for the discourse about the
world concerning my Lord Sandwich, that he hath done a
thing so bad: and indeed it must needs have been a very rash
act; and the rather because of a Parliament now newly met
to give money, and will have some account of what hath
already been spent, besides the precedent for a General to
take what prizes he pleases, and the giving a pretence to take
away much more than he intended, and all will lie upon him;

---

[1] Daughter of his Woolwich landlord.
[2] The date of the registry of Pepys's marriage, given in the *Life*, vol. i., does not
accord with this statement, or with that in the *Diary*, Oct. 10, 1664.

VOL. II. — 27

and not giving to all the Commanders, as well as the Flags, he displeases all them, and offends even some of the Flags, thinking others to be better served than themselves; and lastly, puts himself out of a power of begging anything again a great while of the King. Having danced my people as long as I saw fit to sit up, I to bed, and left them to do what they would. I forgot that we had W. Hewer there, and Tom, and Golding, my barber at Greenwich, for our fiddler, to whom I did give 10s.

12th. About the prize-goods, and do find that extreme ill use was made of my Lord Sandwich's order. Having learned as much as I could, which was, that the King and Duke were very severe in this point, whatever order they before had given my Lord in approbation of what he had done, and that all will come out, and the King see, by the entries at the Custome House, what all do amount to that had been taken, and so I took leave. So to Cocke, and he tells me that he hath cajolled with Seymour, who will be our friend; but that, above all, Seymour tells him that my Lord Duke did shew him to-day an order from Court, for having all respect paid to the Earl of Sandwich, and what goods had been delivered by his order. Good news this week that there are about 600 less dead of the plague than the last.

13th. Sir Jeremiah Smith¹ to see me in his way to Court, and a good man he is, and one that I must keep fair with. To the Duke of Albemarle, where I find him with Lord Craven and Lieutenant of the Tower about him — among other things, talking of ships to get of the King to fetch coles for the poor of the city, which is a good work. But, Lord! to hear the silly talk between these three great people! Yet I have no reason to find fault, the Duke and my Lord Craven being my very great friends.

14th. My heart and head to-night is full of the Victualling business, being overjoyed and proud at my success in my proposal about it, it being read before the King, Duke, and the Caball with complete applause and satisfaction; this Sir G.

---

¹ A distinguished naval officer, made a Commissioner of the Navy, vice Sir W Penn, 1669.

Carteret and Sir W. Coventry both writ me. My own proper accounts are in great disorder, having been neglected about a month. This, and the fear of the sickness, and providing for my family, do fill my head very full, besides the infinite business of the office, and nobody here to look after it but myself.

15th. (Lord's day.) Up, and while I staid for the barber, tried to compose a duo of counter-point; and I think it will do very well, it being by Mr. Berkenshaw's rule. Comes Mr. Povy's coach, and, more than I expected, him himself, to fetch me to Branford: so he and I immediately to set out, having drunk a draught of mulled sacke; and so rode most nobly, in his most pretty and best-contrived chariott in the world, with many new conveniences, his never having till now, within a day or two, been yet finished. Anon we come to his house, and so, with fresh horses, his noble, fine horses, the best confessedly in England, the King having none such, he sent me to Sir Robert Viner's,[1] whom I met coming just from church; and he and I into his garden to discourse of money, but none is to be had. The Parliament, it seems, have voted the King 1,250,000*l.* at 50,000*l.* per month tax for the war; and voted to assist the King against the Dutch, and all that shall adhere to them; and thanks to be given him for his care of the Duke of York, which last is a very popular vote on the Duke's behalf. The taxes of the last assessment, which should have been in good part gathered, are not yet laid, and that even in part of the City of London; and the Chimny-money comes almost to nothing, nor any thing else looked after.

16th. Up about seven o'clock; and, after drinking, and I observing Mr. Povy's being mightily mortified in his eating and drinking, and coaches and horses, he desiring to sell his best, and everything else, his furniture of his house, he walked with me to Syon,[2] and there I took water, in our way he discoursing of the wantonness of the Court, and how it minds nothing else. Upon the Exchange, which is very empty, God knows! and but mean people there. The news for

---

[1] At Swakeley.
[2] Now the seat of the Duke of Northumberland.

certain that the Dutch are come with their fleete before
Margett. and some men were endeavouring to come on shore
when the post come away — perhaps to steal some sheep.   I
walked to the Tower ; but, Lord ! how empty the streets are,
and melancholy, so many poor, sick people in the streets full
of sores ; and so many sad stories overheard as I walk, everybody talking of this dead, and that man sick, and so many in
this place, and so many in that.   And they tell me that, in
Westminster, there is never a physician and but one apothecary
left, all being dead ; but that there are great hopes of a great
decrease this week : God send it !   At the Tower found my
Lord Duke [of Albemarle] and Duchess at dinner ; so I sat
down ; and much good cheer. the Lieutenant and his lady,
and several officers with the Duke.   But, Lord ! to hear the
silly talk was there would make one mad ; the Duke having
none almost but fools about him.   Much talk about the
Dutch, in reproach of them in whose hands the fleete is ; but,
Lord help him ! there is something will hinder him and all
the world in going to sea, which is want of victuals ; for we
have not wherewith to answer our service ; and how much
better it would have been if the Duke's advice had been taken,
for the fleete to have gone presently out ; but, God help the
King ! while no better counsels are given, and what is given
no better taken.   I have received letters from my Lord Sandwich to-day, speaking very high about the prize-goods, that
he would have us to fear nobody, but be very confident in
what we have done, and not to confess any fault or doubt of
what he hath done ; for the King hath allowed it, and do
now confirm it, and do send orders, as he says, for nothing to
be disturbed that his Lordship hath ordered therein as to the
division of the goods to the fleete ; which do comfort us.   To
the Still Yard,¹ which place, however, is now shut up of the
plague ; but I was there, and we now make no bones of it.
Much talk there is of the Chancellor's speech and the King's
at the Parliament's meeting, which are very well liked ; and
that we shall certainly, by their speeches, fall out with France

---

¹ The Still Yard was formerly the resort of the Hans Town merchants. It was
destroyed in the Great Fire.

at this time, together with the Dutch, which will find us work.

18th. Making up my accounts of Tangier, which I did with great difficulty, and after eating something, to-bed, my mind eased of a great deal of figures and castings.

19th. Come to an agreement yesterday with my landlady for 6l. per month, for so many rooms for myself, them, and my wife, and maid, when she shall come, and to pay, besides, for my dyett. To the Duke of Albemarle this evening; and, among other things, spoke to him for my wife's brother Balty to be of his guard, which he kindly answered that he should. My business of the Victualling goes on as I would have it; and now my head is full how to make some profit of it to myself or people. To that end, when I come home, I wrote a letter to Mr. Coventry, offering myself to be the Surveyor-Generall, and am apt to think he will assist me in it, but I do not set my heart much on it, though it would be a good help.

20th. Up, and had my last night's letters brought back to me, which troubles me, because of my accounts, lest they should be asked for before they come, which I abhor, being more ready to give than they can be to demand them: so I sent away an express to Oxford with them, and another to Portsmouth, with a copy of my letter to Mr. Coventry.

22d. (Lord's day.) Met some letters, which made me resolve to go after church to my Lord Duke of Albemarle's: so, after dinner, I took Cocke's chariott, and to Lambeth; but, in going and getting over the water and through White Hall, I spent so much time, the Duke had almost dined. However, fresh meat was brought for me to his table, and there I dined, and full of discourse and very kind. There they are again talking of the prizes, and my Lord Duke did speak very broad that my Lord Sandwich and Pen should do what they would, and answer for themselves. For his part, he would lay all before the King.

23d. On board the East India ship, where my Lord Brouncker had provided a great dinner. But I am troubled with the much talk and conceitedness of Mrs. Williams, in

27 *

case she be not married to my Lord. Captain Taylor with me to the office, and there he and I reckoned ; and I perceive I shall get 100*l.* profit by my services of late to him, which is a very good thing.

24th. My Lord Sandwich is come to town: so I presently to Boreman's, where he is, and there found him; he mighty kind to me, but no opportunity of discourse private yet, which he tells me he must have with me ; only his business is sudden to go to the fleete to get out a few ships to drive away the Dutch.   To him again to Captain Cocke's, where he supped, and lies, and never saw him more merry: and here is Charles Harbord, who the King hath lately knighted. My Lord, to my great content, did tell me before them, that never anything was read to the King and Council, all the chief Ministers of State being there, as my letter about the victualling was, and no more said upon it than a most thorough consent to every word was said.

25th. My Lord tells me that Mr. Coventry and he are not reconciled, but declared enemies—the only occasion of it being, he tells me, his ill usage from him about the first Fight, wherein he had no right done him, which, methinks, is a poor occasion, for, in my conscience, that was no design of Coventry's.   He tells me, as very private, that there are great factions at the Court between the King's party and the Duke of York's, and that the King, which is a strange difficulty, do favour my Lord in opposition to the Duke's party—that my Lord Chancellor, being now, to be sure, the patron of the Duke's, it is a mystery whence it should be that Mr. Coventry is looked upon by him [Clarendon] as an enemy to him [Clarendon]; that if he had a mind himself to be out of this employment, as Mr. Coventry, he believes, wishes, and himself and I do incline to wish it also, in many respects, yet he believes he shall not be able, because of the King, who will keep him in on purpose, in opposition to the other party ; that Prince Rupert and he are all possible friends in the world ; that Coventry hath aggravated this business of the prizes, though never so great plundering in the world us while the Duke and he were at sea ; and in Sir John

Lawson's time he could take and pillage, and then sink a
whole ship in the Streights, and Coventry say nothing to
it ; that my Lord Arlington is his fast friend ; that the Chancellor is cold to him, and, though I told him that I and
the world do take my Lord Chancellor, in his speech the
other day, to have said as much as could be wished, yet
he thinks he did not.   That my Lord Chancellor do from
hence begin to be cold to him, because of his seeing him
and Arlington so great : that nothing at Court is minded but
faction and pleasure, and nothing intended of general good
to the Kingdom by anybody heartily ; so that he believes
with me, that in a little time confusion will certainly come
over all the nation.   He told me how a design was carried
on a while ago, for the Duke of York to raise an army in
the North. and to be the Generall of it, and all this without
the knowledge or advice of the Duke of Albemarle, which,
when he come to know, he was so vexed, they were fain to
let it fall to content him : that his matching with the family
of Sir G. Carteret do make the difference greater between
Coventry and him—they being enemies ; that the Chancellor
did, as every body else, speak well of me the other day, but
yet was, at the Committee for Tangier, angry that I should
offer to suffer a bill of exchange to be protested.

26th. Sir Christopher Mings and I together by water to
the Tower ; and I find him a very witty, well-spoken fellow,
and mighty free to tell his parentage, being a shoemaker's
son.   I to the 'Change, where I hear how the French have
taken two, and sunk one, of our merchant-men in the Streights,
and carried the ships to Toulon ; so that there is no expectation but we must fall out with them.   The 'Change pretty
full, and the town begins to be lively again, though the streets
very empty, and most shops shut.

27th. To the Duke of Albemarle's, and there much company, but I staid and dined, and he makes mighty much of
me ; and here he tells us the Dutch are gone, and have lost
above 150 cables and anchors, through the late foul weather.
He proposed to me from Mr. Coventry that I should be Surveyor-Generall of the Victualling business, which I accepted.

But, indeed, the terms in which Mr. Coventry proposes it for me are the most obliging that ever I could expect from any man, and more; he saying that I am the fittest man in England; and that he is sure, if I will undertake, I will perform it; and that it will be also a very desirable thing that I might have this encouragement, my encouragement in the Navy alone being in no wise proportionable to my pains or deserts. This, added to the letter I had three days since, from Mr. Southerne,[1] signifying that the Duke of York had, in his master's absence, opened my letters, and commanded him to tell me that he did approve of my being the Surveyor-General, do make me joyful beyond myself that I cannot express it, to see, that as I do take pains, so God blesses me, and hath sent me masters that do observe that I take pains.

28th. Sir W. Clerke tells me the Parliament hath given the Duke of York 120,000*l.*,[2] to be paid him after 1,250,000*l.* is gathered upon the tax which they have now given the King; also that the Dutch have lately launched sixteen new ships; all which is great news. The King and Court, they say, have now finally resolved to spend nothing upon clothes, but what is of the growth of England; which, if observed, will be very pleasing to the people, and very good for them.

29th. (Lord's day.) In the street, at Woolwich, did overtake and almost run upon two women crying and carrying a man's coffin between them; I suppose the husband of one of them, which, methinks, is a sad thing.

31st. Meeting yesterday the Searchers, with their rods in their hands, coming from Captain Cocke's house, I did overhear them say that his Black did not die of the plague. About nine at night I come home, and there find Mrs. Pierce come, and little Frank Tooker, and Mr. Hill, and other people, a great many dancing; and anon comes Mrs. Coleman[3] and

---

[1] Secretary to Sir W. Coventry.

[2] This sum was granted by the Commons to Charles, with a request that he would bestow it on his brother.

[3] Doubtless the person mentioned in Malone's *Account of the English Stage.*— "In 1659 or 60, in imitation of foreign theatres, women were first introduced on the scene. In 1656, indeed, Mrs. Coleman, wife to Mr. Edward Coleman, represented Ianthe, in the first part of the *Siege of Rhodes*; but the little she had to say was spoken in recitative." Sir W. Davenant's patent contained a clause permitting all women's parts to be acted by females.

her husband, and she sung very finely; though her voice is
decayed as to strength, but mighty sweet though soft, and a
pleasant, jolly woman, and in mighty good humour. Among
other things, Laneare[1] did, at the request of Mr. Hill, bring
two or three the finest prints for my wife to see that ever I
did see in all my life. But, for singing, among other things,
we got Mrs. Coleman to sing part of the Opera, though she
would not own she did get any of it without book in order to
the stage; but, above all, her counterfeiting of Captain Cooke's
part, in his reproaching his man with cowardice—"Baso
slave," &c.—she do it most excellently. Thus we end the
month merrily; and the more that, after some fears that the
plague would have increased again this week, I hear for certain that there is above 400 less; the whole number of deaths
being 1388, and of them of the plague 1031. Want of money
in the Navy puts every thing out of order. Men grow
mutinous; and nobody here to mind the business of the Navy
but myself. I in great hopes of my place of Surveyor-General
of the Victualling, which will bring me 300*l.* per annum.

November 1st. Lay very long in bed, discoursing with Mr.
Hill of most things of a man's life, and how little merit do
prevail in the world, but only favour; and that, for myself,
chance without merit brought me in; and that diligence only
keeps me so, and will, living as I do among so many lazy
people that the diligent man becomes necessary, that they
cannot do anything without him. My Lord Brouncker with
us to Mrs. Williams's lodgings, and Sir W. Batten, Sir
Edmund Pooly,[2] and others; and there, it being my Lord's
birthday, had every one a green riband tied in our hats very
foolishly; and, methinks, mighty disgracefully for my Lord
to have his folly so open to all the world with this woman.

---

[1] Nicholas Lanier, composer of the Symphonies to several of the Masques
written by Ben Jonson, and performed at Court, had died, æt. 78, Nov. 4th,
1646, and was buried at St. Martin's-in-the-Fields.—*Somerset House Gazette*,
vol. i., p. 57. The Letters-Patent under which the Society of Musicians was
incorporated at the Restoration, mention a Lanier, possibly a son of Nicholas, as
first Marshal, and four others of his name as Wardens or Assistants of the Company. There is an engraved portrait of him in the British Museum (*Addit. MS.*,
15,858, fol. 55), and a letter to his niece, Mrs. Richards, "at her house in the
Old Aumery, Westminster."

[2] M.P. for Bury St. Edmunds, and in the list of proposed Knights of the Royal
Oak for Suffolk.

4th. I hear that one of the little boys at my lodging is not
well; and they suspect, by their sending for plaister and fume,
that it may be the plague; so I sent Mr. Hater and W.
Hewer to speak with the mother; but they returned to me,
satisfied that there is no hurt nor danger, but the boy is well,
and offers to be searched. After dinner, to the office, and
much troubled to have 100 seamen all the afternoon there,
swearing below, and cursing us, and breaking the glasse
windows, and swear they will pull the house down on Tuesday
next. I send word of this to Court, but nothing will help it
but money and a rope.

5th. (Lord's day.) To the Cocke-pitt, where I heard the
Duke of Albemarle's chaplain make a simple sermon: among
other things, reproaching the imperfection of humane learning,
he cried—"All our physicians cannot tell what an ague is,
and all our arithmetique is not able to number the days of a
man"—which, God knows, is not the fault of arithmetique,
but that our understandings reach not the thing. I hear that
the plague increases much at Lambeth, St. Martin's, and
Westminster, and fear it will all over the city. By water to
Deptford, and there made a visit to Mr. Evelyn, who, among
other things, showed me most excellent painting in little; in
distemper, in Indian incke, water colours: graveing; and,
above all, the whole secret of mezzo-tinto,[1] and the manner of
it, which is very pretty, and good things done with it. He
read to me very much also of his discourse, he hath been
many years and now is about, about Gardenage; which will
be a most noble and pleasant piece. He read me part of a
play or two of his making, very good, but not as he conceits
them, I think, to be. He showed me his "Hortus Hye-
malis;" leaves laid up in a book of several plants kept dry,
which preserve colour, however, and look very finely, better
than an Herball. In fine, a most excellent person he is, and
must be allowed a little for a little conceitedness; but he may
well be so, being a man so much above others. He read me,
though with too much gusto, some little poems of his own,
that were not transcendant, yet one or two very pretty epi-

---

[1] Not long before invented by Prince Rupert.

grams; among others, of a lady looking in at a grate, and being pecked at by an eagle that was there.

6th. Sir G. Carteret and I did walk an hour in the garden before the house, talking of my Lord Sandwich's business: what enemies he hath, and how they have endeavoured to bespatter him: and particularly about his leaving of 30 ships of the enemy, when Pen would have gone, and my Lord called him back again: which is most false. However, he says it was purposed by some hot-heads in the House of Commons, at the same time when they voted a present to the Duke of York, to have voted 10,000*l.* to the Prince, and half-a-crowne to my Lord of Sandwich; but nothing come of it. But, for all this, the King is most firme to my Lord, and so is my Lord Chancellor, and my Lord Arlington: the Prince, in appearance, kind; the Duke of York silent, says no hurt; but admits others to say it in his hearing: Sir W. Pen, the falsest rascal that ever was in the world; and that this afternoon the Duke of Albemarle did tell him that Pen was a very cowardly rogue, and one that hath brought all these rogueish fanatick Captains into the fleete, and swears he should never go out with the fleete again: that Sir W. Coventry is most kind to Pen still; and says nothing, nor do any thing openly, to the prejudice of my Lord. He agrees with me, that it is impossible for the King to set out a fleete again the next year; and that he fears all will come to ruine, there being no money in prospect but these prizes, which will bring, it may be, 20,000*l.*, but that will signify nothing in the world for it.

7th. To Sir G. Carteret, and I with him by water: and, among other things, Lord! to see how he wondered to see the river so empty of boats—nobody working at the Custome-house keys, and how fearful he is: and vexed that his man, holding a wine-glass in his hand for him to drink out of, did cover his hands, it being a cold, windy, rainy morning, under the waterman's coat, though he brought the waterman from six or seven miles up the river, too. Nay, he carried his glass with him for his man to let him drink out of at the Duke of Albemarle's, where he intended to dine, though this he did to prevent sluttery: for the same reason, he carried a napkin with him to Captain Cocke's, making him believe that he should not eat with foul linnen.

8th. It being a fast-day, all people were at church, and the office quiet: so I did much business, and at noon adventured to my old lodging. By water to Deptford, and, about eight o'clock at night, did take water, being glad I was out of the town: for the plague, it seems, rages there more than ever.

9th. At noon, by water, to the King's Head at Deptford, where Captain Taylor invites Sir W. Batten and Sir John Robinson, who come in with a great deal of company from hunting, and brought in a hare alive, and a great many silly stories they tell of their sport, which pleases them mightily, and me not at all, such is the different sense of pleasure in mankind; and strange to see how a good dinner and feasting reconciles everybody. The Bill of Mortality, to all our griefs, is encreased 399 this week, and the encrease generally through the whole City and suburbs, which makes us all sad.

10th. In the evening, news is brought me my wife is come: so I to her; and she told me, having herself been this day at my house at London, which was boldly done, that a neighbour of our's, Mr. Hollworthy, a very able man, is dead by a fall in the country from his horse — his foot hanging in the stirrup, and his brains beat out.

12th. (Lord's day.) They hope here the plague will be less this week. Reading over part of Mr. Stillingfleet's "Origines Sacræ," wherein many things are very good, and some frivolous.

14th. Captain Cocke and I in his coach through Kent Streete, a sad place through the plague, people sitting sick and with plaisters about them in the street begging. To the Duke of Albemarle by water, late, where I find he had remembered that I had appointed to come to him this day about money, which I excused not doing sooner; but I see, a dull fellow as he is, he do sometimes remember what another thinks he mindeth not. My business was about getting money of the East India Company; but, Lord! to see how the Duke himself magnifies himself in that he had done with the Company; and my Lord Craven what the King could have done without my Lord Duke, and a great deal of stir; but most mightily what a brave fellow I am. Back by water, it raining hard, and so to the office, and stopped my going, as I intended, to the buoy of the Nore, and great reason I had to rejoice at it, for it proved the night of as great a storm as was almost ever remembered. This day I hear that my pretty grocer's wife, Mrs. Beverham, over the way there, her husband is lately dead of the plague at Bow, which I am sorry for, for fear of losing her neighbourhood.

15th. To the King's Head taverne,[1] where all the Trinity House dined to-day, to choose a new Master in the room of Hurlestone, that is dead, and Captain Crispe is chosen. After dinner, who comes in but my Lady Batten, and a troop of a dozen women almost, and expected, as I found afterwards, to be made mighty much of, but nobody minded them: but the best jest was, that when they saw themselves not regarded, they would go away, and it was horrible foul weather; and my Lady Batten walking through the dirty lane with new spick and span white shoes, she dropped one of her galoshes in the dirt, where it stuck, and she forced to go home without one, at which she was horribly vexed, and I led her; and, vexing her a little more in mirth, I parted, and to Glanville's, where I knew Sir John Robinson, Sir G. Smith, and Captain Cocke were gone, and then, with the company of Mrs. Penington, whose father,[2] I hear, was one of the Court of Justice, and died prisoner, of the stone, in the Tower, I made them, against their resolutions, to stay from hour to hour, till it was almost midnight, and a furious, dark, and rainy, and windy, stormy night, and, which was best, I, with drinking small beer, made them all drunk drinking wine, at which Sir John Robinson made great sport. But, they being gone, the lady and I very civilly sat an hour by the fireside, showing the folly of this Robinson, that makes it his work to praise himself; and all he says and do, like a heavy-headed coxcomb.

---

[1] At the corner of Chancery Lane.—*Handbook of London.*

[2] Isaac Pennington, an Alderman of London, convicted as one of the King's judges. His sentence was probably changed to imprisonment. His death, on 17th December, 1661, is recorded in Smyth's *Obituary*, p. 55.

The plague, blessed be God! is decreased 400; making the whole this week but 1300 and odd: for which the Lord be praised!

16th. To Erith; where, after making a little visit to Madam Williams, she did give me information of W. Howe's having bought eight bags of precious stones taken from about the Dutch Vice-Admirall's neck, of which there were eight diamonds, which cost him 4000*l.* sterling in India, and hoped to have made 12,000*l.* here for them. And that is told by one that sold him one of the bags, which hath nothing but rubys in it, which he had for 35*s.*; and that it will be proved he hath made 125*l.* of one stone that he bought. This she desired, and I resolved, I would give my Lord Sandwich notice of. So I on board my Lord Brouncker; and there he and Sir Edmund Pooly carried me down into the hold of the India shipp, and there did show me the greatest wealth lie in confusion that a man can see in the world. Pepper scattered through every chink, you trod upon it; and in cloves and nutmegs I walked above the knees: whole rooms full. And silk in bales, and boxes of copper-plate, one of which I saw opened. Having seen this, which was as noble a sight as ever I saw in my life, I away on board the other ship in despair to get the pleasure-boat of the gentlemen there to carry me to the fleete. They were Mr. Ashburnham,[1] and Colonell Wyndham;[2] but, pleading the King's business, they did presently agree I should have it. So I presently on board, and got under sail, and had a good bedd by the shift, of Wyndham's.

17th. Sailed all night, and got down to Quinborough water, where all the great ships are now come, and there on board my Lord, and was soon received with great content. And, after some little discourse, he and I on board Sir W.

[1] John Ashburnham, a Groom of the Bedchamber to Charles I., whom he attended during the whole of the Rebellion, and afterwards filled the same post under Charles II. He was, in 1661, M.P. for Sussex. Ob. 1671. The late Earl of Ashburnham, who was lineally descended from him, wrote an excellent vindication of his ancestor, against the insinuations of Clarendon and others.

[2] Colonel Francis Wyndham, a distinguished loyalist, Governor of Dunster Castle, Somersetshire. He was created a Baronet 18th November, 1673.

Pen; and there held a Council of War about many wants of
the fleete; and so followed my Lord Sandwich, who was gone
a little before me on board the Royall James. And there
spent an hour, my Lord playing upon the gittarr, which he now
commends above all musique in the world. As an infinite
secret, my Lord tells me the factions are high between the
King and the Duke, and all the Court are in an uproar with
their loose amours; the Duke of York being in love desperately with Mrs. Stewart. Nay, that the Duchess herself is
fallen in love with her new Master of the Horse, one Harry
Sidney,[1] and another, Harry Savill.[2] So that God knows
what will be the end of it. And that the Duke is not so
obsequious as he used to be, but very high of late; and would
be glad to be in the head of an army as Generall; and that
it is said that he do propose to go and command under the
King of Spayne, in Flanders. That his amours to Mrs.
Stewart are told the King; so that all is like to be nought
among them. Away to my Bezan[3] again, and there to read
in a pretty French book, "*La Nouvelle Allegorique*," upon
the strife between rhetorique and its enemies—very pleasant.
So, after supper, to sleep, and sailed all night, and come to
Erith before break of day.

18th. About nine of the clock, I went on shore, and hired
an ill-favoured horse, and away to Greenwich, to my lodgings,
where I hear how rude the soldiers have been in my absence,
swearing what they would do with me.

19th. (Lord's day.) Alone by water to Erith. Being come
there, on board my Lord Brouncker, I find Captain Cocke
and other company, the lady not well, and mighty merry we
were — Sir Edmund Pooly being very merry, and a right
English gentleman, and one of the discontented cavaliers, that
think their loyalty is not considered. After dinner, all on
shore to my Lady Williams, and there drank and talked; but,

---

[1] Younger son of Robert Sidney, Earl of Leicester, created Earl of Romney,
1694. He was Lord-Lieutenant of Ireland, Master of the Ordnance, and Warden
of the Cinque Ports, in the reign of King William. Ob. 1704, unmarried.

[2] Henry Saville, some time one of the Grooms of the Bedchamber to the Duke
of York.

[3] The yacht.

Lord! the most impertinent bold woman with my Lord that ever I did see.

20th. Up before day, and so took horse for Nonesuch, with two men with me, and the ways very bad, and the weather worse, for wind and rain. Thither, and I did get my tallys, and thence took horse, but it rained hard and blew, but got home very well. Here I find Mr. Deering come to trouble me about business, which I soon despatched, he telling me that Luellin hath been dead this fortnight, of the plague, in St. Martin's Lane, which much surprised me.

22d. I was very glad to hear that the plague is come very low; that is, the whole under 1000, and the plague 600 and odd: and great hopes of a further decrease, because of this day's being a very exceeding hard frost, and continues freezing. This day the first of the Oxford Gazettes come out, which is very pretty, full of news, and no folly in it, wrote by Williamson.[1] It pleased me to have it demonstrated, that a Purser without professed cheating is a professed loser, twice as much as he gets.

23d. Up betimes, and so, being trimmed, I to get papers ready against Sir H. Cholmly come to me by appointment, he being newly come over from Tangier. He did by and by come, and we settled all matters about his money, and he is a most satisfied man in me, and do declare his resolution to give me 200l. per annum. It continuing to be a great frost, which gives us hopes for a perfect cure of the plague, he and I to walk in the park, and there discoursed with grief of the calamity of the times. I brought him home, and had a good dinner for him. Captain Cuttance tells me how W. Howe is laid by the heels, and confined to the Royall Katharine, and his things all seized: and how, also, for a quarrell, which indeed my Lord the other night told me, Captain Ferrers having cut all over the back of another of my Lord's servants, is parted from my Lord. We in extraordinary lack of money and everything else to go to sea next year. My Lord Sandwich is gone from the fleete yesterday towards Oxford.

---

[1] No. xxiv. of the *Oxford Gazette* was the first London Gazette. The Williamson who "wrote" it was afterwards Sir Joseph Williamson.

24th. To London, and there, in my way, at my old oyster shop in Gracious Streete, bought two barrels of my fine woman of the shop, who is alive after all the plague, which now is the first observation or inquiry we make at London concerning everybody we know. To the 'Change, where very busy with several people, and mightily glad to see the 'Change so full, and hopes of another abatement still the next week. I went home with Sir G. Smith to dinner, sending for one of my barrels of oysters, which were good, though come from Colchester, where the plague hath been so much. Here a very brave dinner, though no invitation; and, Lord! to see how I am treated, that come from so mean a beginning, is matter of wonder to me. But it is God's mercy to me, and his blessing upon my taking pains, and being punctual in my dealings. Visited Mr. Evelyn, where most excellent discourse with him; among other things, he showed me a ledger[1] of a Treasurer of the Navy, his great-grandfather, just 100 years old; which I seemed mighty fond of, and he did present me with it, which I take as a great rarity; and he hopes to find me more, older than it. He also showed us several letters of the old Lord of Leicester's,[2] in Queen Elizabeth's time, under the very handwriting of Queen Elizabeth, and Queen Mary, Queen of Scots; and others, very venerable names. But, Lord! how poorly, methinks, they wrote in those days, and in what plain uncut paper.

26th. (Lord's day.) Up before day to dress myself to go towards Erith, which I would do by land, it being a horrible cold frost to go by water: so borrowed two horses of Mr. Howell and his friend, and with much ado set out, after my horses being frosted,[3] which I know not what it means to this day, and my boy having lost one of my spurs and stockings, carrying them to the smith's, and I borrowed a stocking, and so got up, and Mr. Tooker with me, and rode to Erith, and

---

[1] This ledger is now in the British Museum, amongst some of Pepys's Papers, in the Ducket Collection.

[2] Amongst these documents, still in the Pepysian Library—for Evelyn complains (*Correspondence*, vol. iii., p. 381, edit. 1852) that he lent them to Pepys, who omitted to return them—are some letters relating to the death of Amy Robsart, Lady Robert Dudley, for which see the *Appendix* to vol. iv.

[3] Frosting means, having the horses shoes turned up by the smith.

there on board my Lord Brouncker met with Sir W. Warren upon his business, among others, and did a great deal; Sir J. Minnes, as God would have it, not being there to hinder us with his impertinences. To my wife at Woolwich, where I found, as I had directed, a good dinner to be made against to-morrow, and invited guests in the yard, meaning to be merry, in order to her taking leave, for she intends to come in a day or two to me for altogether. But here, they tell me, one of the houses behind them is infected, and I was fain to stand there a great while, to have their back-doors opened, but they could not, having locked them fast, against any passing through, so was forced to pass by them again, close to their sick beds, which they were removing out of the house, which troubled me : so I made them uninvite their guests, and to resolve of coming all away to me to-morrow.

27th. To the Duke of Albemarle, who is visited by everybody against his going to Oxford; and mighty kind to me; and upon my desiring his grace to give me his kind word to the Duke of York, if any occasion there were of speaking of me, he told me he had reason to do so; for there had been nothing done in the Navy without me. He is agog to go to sea himself the next year. To dinner, he most exceeding kind to me, to the observation of all that are there. With Sir G. Carteret, who tells me that my Lord hath received still worse and worse usage from some base people about the Court. But the King is very kind, and the Duke do not appear the contrary; and my Lord Chancellor swore to him, "by —— I will not forsake my Lord of Sandwich." I into London, t being dark night, by a hackney-coach; the first I have durst to go in many a day, and with great pain now, for fear. But it being unsafe to go by water in the dark, and frosty cold, and I unable, being weary with my morning walk, to go on foot, this was my only way. Few people yet in the streets, nor shops open, here and there twenty in a place almost; though not above five or six o'clock at night. The Goldsmiths do decry the new Act, for money to be all brought into the Exchequer, and paid out thence, saying they will not advance one farthing upon it; and indeed it is their interest to say and do so. To Sir G. Smith's, it being now night, and there up to his chamber, and sat talking, and I barbing[1] against to-morrow; and anon, at nine at night, comes to us Sir G. Smith and the Lieutenant of the Tower, and there they sat talking and drinking till past midnight, and mighty merry we were — the Lieutenant of the Tower being in a mighty vein of singing, and he hath a very good care and strong voice, but no manner of skill. Sir G. Smith showed me his lady's closet, which is very fine; and after being very merry, here I lay in a noble chamber, and mighty highly treated, the first night I have lain in London a long time.

28th. Up before day, and Cocke and I took a hackney-coach appointed with four horses to take us up, and so carried us over London Bridge. But there, thinking of some business, I did light at the foot of the bridge, and by help of a candle at a stall, where some pavers were at work, I wrote a letter to Mr. Hater, and never knew so great an instance of the usefulness of carrying pen and ink and wax about one: so we, the way being very bad, to Nonsuch, and thence to Sir Robert Long's house[2]—a fine place, and dinner-time ere we got thither; but we had breakfasted a little at Mr. Gauden's, he being out of town though, and there borrowed Dr. [Jeremy] Taylor's sermons, and is a most excellent book, and worth my buying, where had a very good dinner, and curiously dressed, and here a couple of ladies, kinswomen of his, not handsome though, but rich, that knew me by report of The. Turner, and mighty merry we were. After dinner to talk of our business, and we parted. Captain Cocke and I through Wandsworth. Drunk at Sir Allen Broderick's,[3] a great friend and comrade of Cocke's, whom he values above the world for a witty companion, and I believe he is so. So

---

[1] An old word for shaving.

[2] Nonsuch, afterwards called Worcester Park, co. Surrey. Sir Robert Long was Auditor of the Exchequer, which office was removed from Westminster to His Majesty's honour of Nonsuch, 15th August, 1665. On the 22d Sept. 1670, the King demised the Great Park, Great Park Meadow, and the mansion house called Worcester Park, to Sir Robert Long, Bart., for ninety-nine years—Manning and Bray's *Surrey*, vol. ii., p. 606.

[3] Son of Sir Thomas Broderick, of Richmond, Yorkshire, and Wandsworth Surrey, knighted by Charles II., and Surveyor-general in Ireland to that King.

to Fox-hall, and there took boat, and down to the Old Swan, and thence to Lumbard Street — it being dark night, and thence to the Tower. Took boat, and down to Greenwich. Cocke home, and I to the office, and then to my lodgings, where my wife is come, and I am well pleased with it, only much trouble in those lodgings we have, the mistress of the house being so deadly dear in everything we have; so that we do resolve to remove home soon as we know how the plague goes this week, which we hope will be a good decrease. So to bed.

29th. Home to my house, calling my wife, where the poor wretch is putting things in a way to be ready for our coming home, and so by water together to Greenwich.

30th. At noon comes Sir Thomas Allen, and I made him dine with me, and very friendly he is, and a good man, I think, but one that professes he loves to get and to save. Great joy we have this week in the weekly Bill, it being come to 544 in all, and but 333 of the plague; so that we are encouraged to get to London soon as we can. And my father writes as great news of joy to them, that he saw York's waggon go again this week to London, and full of passengers; and tells me that my aunt Bell hath been dead of the plague these seven weeks.

December 1st. All the day long shut up in my little closet at my office. Then home by promise to my wife, to have mirth there. So we had our neighbours, little Miss Tooker and Mrs. Daniels, to dance, and after supper I to bed, and left them merry below, which they did not part from till two or three in the morning.

2d. Dined with my wife at noon, and took leave of her, she being to go to London for altogether.

3d. (Lord's day.) It being Lord's day, up and dressed, and to church, thinking to have sat with Sir James Bunce [1] to hear his daughter [2] and her husband sing, that are so much commended, but was prevented by being invited into Colonel Cleggat's pew. However, there I sat, near Mr. Laneare,

---

[1] James Bunce, an Alderman of London, 1660.
[2] Mrs. Chamberlain.

with whom I spoke, and my fat brown beauty of our Parish,
the rich merchant's lady, a very noble woman, and Madame
Pierce. A good sermon of Mr. Plume's. To Captain Cocke's,
and there dined with him and Colonel Wyndham, a worthy
gentleman, whose wife[1] was nurse to the present King, and
one that, while she lived, governed him and every thing else,
as Cocke says, as a minister of state ; the old King putting
mighty weight and trust upon her. They talked much of
matters of State and persons, and particularly how my Lord
Barkeley hath all along been a fortunate, though a passionate,
and but weak man as to policy; but as a kinsman, brought
in and promoted by my Lord of St. Albans, and one that is
the greatest vapourer in the world, this Colonell Wyndham
says ; and to whom only, with Jacke Ashburnham[2] and
Colonel Legg,[3] the King's removal to the Isle of Wight from
Hampton Court was communicated ; and, though betrayed by
their knavery, or at best by their ignorance, insomuch that
they have all solemnly charged one another with their failures
therein, and have been at daggers drawing, publickly about
it, yet now none greater friends in the world.

4th. Home to my house at the office, where my wife hath
got a dinner for me: and it was a joyful thing for us to meet
here, for which God be praised! Here was her brother
come to see her, and speak with me about business. It seems
that my recommendation of him hath not only obtained his
presently being admitted into the Duke of Albemarle's guards,
and present pay, but also by the Duke's and Sir Philip
Howard's direction, to be put as a right-hand man, and other
marks of special respect, at which I am very glad—partly for
him, and partly to see that I am reckoned something in my
recommendations. Upon the 'Change to-day, Colvill tells
me, from Oxford, that the King in person hath justified my

[1] Colonel Wyndham's wife was Anne, daughter and co-heir of Thomas Gerard,
of Trent, Somersetshire. As to Mrs. Wyndham's influence over Charles II.,
when Prince of Wales, see Clarendon, vol. v., p. 153, ed. 1826.

[2] See Sir John Ashburnham's *Vindication*, and note to 16th November,
ante.

[3] William Legge, Groom of the Bedchamber to Charles I., and father to the
first Lord Dartmouth He was M.P. for Southampton. Ob. 1672.

Lord Sandwich to the highest degree; and is right in his favour to the uttermost.

6th. Up betimes, it being fast-day; and by water to the Duke of Albemarle,[1] who come down to town from Oxford last night. He is mighty brisk, and very kind to me, and asks my advice principally in every thing. He surprises me with the news that my Lord Sandwich goes Embassador to Spain speedily; though I know not whence this arises, yet I am heartily glad of it. I spent the afternoon upon a song of Solyman's words to Roxalana,[2] that I have set, and so with my wife walked and Mercer to Mrs. Pierce's, where Captain Rolt and Mrs. Knipp,[3] Mr. Coleman and his wife, and Laneare, Mrs. Worshipp[4] and her singing daughter, met; and by and by, unexpectedly comes Mr. Pierce from Oxford. Here the best company for musique I ever was in, in my life, and wish I could live and die in it, both for musique and the face of Mrs. Pierce, and my wife, and Knipp, who is pretty enough; but the most excellent, mad-humoured thing, and sings the noblest that ever I heard in my life, and Rolt, with her, some things together, most excellently. I spent the night in an

---

[1] At the Cockpit.

[2] These are Solyman's words to Roxalana, *The Siege of Rhodes*, part ii, act iv., sc. 2:—

> "Beauty, retire! thou dost my pity move,
> Relieve my pity, and then trust my love. [*Exit* ROXALANA.
> At first I thought her by our Prophet sent,
>   As a reward for valour's toils,
>   More worth than all my father's spoils.
> And now she is become my punishment.
> But thou art just, O Power Divine!
>   With new and painful arts,
>   Of studied war, I break the hearts
> Of half the world, and she breaks mine."

[3] Genest, in his *History of the British Stage*, vol. i., enumerates sixteen characters filled by Mrs. Knipp, at the King's House, between 1664 and 1678, when she disappears from the playbills, in which her name is spelt in six different ways. The details in the *Diary* respecting this lively actress and "her brute of a husband," whom Pepys describes as a "horse jockey," are so amusing, that any particulars of their subsequent history would have been interesting. Those readers who may wish to know what performers spoke or acted in any plays, prologues, or epilogues, mentioned by Pepys, will find information in Genest's work, above quoted; but it was not thought necessary to transplant all the particulars into these pages.

[4] Sister of Mrs. Clerke, wife of Dr. Clerke. See 13th Feb., 1666-7.

extasy almost; and, having invited them to my house a day
or two hence, we broke up, Pierce having told me how the
King hath done my Lord Sandwich all the right imaginable,
by showing him his countenance before all the world on every
occasion, to remove thoughts of discontent; and he is to go
Embassador, and the Duke of York is made Generall of all
forces by land and sea, and the Duke of Albemarle Lieutenant-Generall.

8th. To give order to my maid to buy things to send down
to Greenwich for supper to-night; and I also to buy other
things, as oysters, and lemons, 6d. per piece, and oranges, 3d.
To White Hall, where we found Sir G. Carteret with the
Duke, and also Sir G. Downing, whom I had not seen in
many years before. He greeted me very kindly, and I him;
though methinks I am touched that it should be said that he
was my master heretofore, as doubtless he will. Sir G.
Carteret tells me that he is glad of my Lord's being made
Embassador, and that it is the greatest courtesy his enemies
could do him; yet I find that he is not heartily merry upon
it, and that it is no design of my Lord's friends, but the
prevalence of his enemies, and that the Duke of Albemarle
and Prince Rupert are like to go to sea together the next
year. I pray God, when my Lord is gone, they do not fall
hard upon the Vice-Chamberlain, being alone, and in so
envious a place. By water down to Greenwich, and there
found all my company come—that is, Mrs. Knipp, and an ill,
melancholy, jealous-looking fellow, her husband, that spoke
not a word to us all the night, Pierce and his wife, and Rolt,
Mrs. Worshipp and her daughter, Coleman and his wife, and
Lancare, and to make us perfectly happy, there comes by
chance to town Mr. Hill to see us. Most excellent musique
we had in abundance, and a good supper, dancing, and a
pleasant scene of Mrs. Knipp's rising sick from table, but
whispered me it was for some hard word or other her husband
give her just now when she laughed, and was more merry
than ordinary. But we got her in humour again, and mighty
merry; spending the night, till two in the morning, with most
complete content as ever in my life. And we to bed—
Mr. Hill and I, whom I love more and more, and he us.

9th. My Lord Brouncker and I dined with the Duke of Albemarle. At table, the Duchess, a very ill-looked woman, complaining of her Lord's going to sea the next year, said these cursed words: "If my Lord had been a coward, he had gone to sea no more: it may be then he might have been excused, and made an Embassador:" meaning my Lord Sandwich. This made me mad, and I believe she perceived my countenance change, and blushed herself very much. I was in hopes others had not minded it, but my Lord Brouncker, after we were come away, took notice of the words to me with displeasure. To Mr. Hill, and sang, among other things, my song of "Beauty, retire," which he likes, only excepts against two notes in the base, but likes the whole very well.

11th. That I may remember it the more particularly, I thought fit to insert this memorandum of Temple's' discourse this night with me, which I took in writing from his mouth. Before the Harp and Crosse money was cried down, he and his fellow goldsmiths did make some particular trials what proportion that money bore to the old King's money, and they found that it generally come to, one with another, about 25*l.* in every 100*l.* Of this money there was, upon the calling of it in, 650,000*l.* at least brought into the Tower; and from thence he computes that the whole money of England must be full 16,250,000*l.*, but, for all this, believes that there is about 30,000,000*l.*: he supposing that about the King's coming in, when he began to observe the quantity of the new money, people begun to be fearfull of this money's being cried down, and so picked it out and set it a-going as fast as they could to be rid of it; and he thinks 30,000,000*l.* the rather, because, if there were but 16,250,000*l.*, the King having 2.000,000*l.* every year, would have the whole money of the Kingdom in his hands in eight years. He tells me, about 350,000*l.* sterling was coined out of the French money, the proceeds of Dunkirke: so that, with what was coined of the Cross money, there is new coined about 1,000,000*l.* besides

---

' John Temple and John Seale were goldsmiths, at the Three Tuns, in Lombard Street. See " A Collection of the Names of the Merchants living in and about the City of London, 1677." 12mo.

the gold, which is guessed at 500,000*l.* He tells me, that, though the King did deposit the French money in pawn all the while for the 350,000*l.*, he was forced to borrow thereupon till the tools could be made for the new Minting in the present form. Yet the interest he paid for that time come to 35,000*l.*: Viner having to his knowledge 10,000*l.* for the use of 100,000*l.* of it.

13th. Invited by Sheriff Hooker,[1] who keeps the poorest, mean, dirty table in a dirty house that ever I did see any Sheriff of London; and a plain, ordinary, silly man I think he is, but rich — only his son, Mr. Lethulier, I like, for a pretty, civil, understanding merchant; and the more by much, because he happens to be husband to our noble, fat, brave lady in our parish, that I and my wife admire so.[2] Thence away to the Pope's Head tavern, and called to see my wife, who is well; though my great trouble is that my poor little parish is the greatest number this week in all the city within the walls, having six, from one the last week, and so by water to Greenwich. To Mr. Pierce's, where he and his wife made me drink some tea. Away to the 'Change, and there hear the ill news, to my great and all our great trouble, that the plague is encreased again this week, notwithstanding there hath been a long day or two great frosts; but we hope it is only the effects of the late close, warm weather, and, if the frost continue the next week, may fall again; but the town do thicken so much with people, that it is much if the plague do not grow again upon us.

15th. Met with Sir James Bunce. "This is the time for you," says he, "that were for Oliver heretofore; you are full of employment, and we, poor Cavaliers, sit still and can get nothing;" which was a pretty reproach, I thought; but answered nothing to it, for fear of making it worse.

16th. News is come to-day of our Sound fleete being come.

17th. (Lord's day.) Word brought me that Cutler's

---

[1] Afterwards Sir William Hooker.

[2] Mr. Lethieulier's lady was Anne, daughter of Sir William Hooker. See Oct. 14, 1666.

coach is, by appointment, come to the Isle of Doggs for me, and so I over the water; and in his coach to Hackney, a very fine, cold, clear, frosty day. At his house, I find him with a plain little dinner, good wine, and welcome. He is still a prating man; and, the more I know him, the less I find in him. A pretty house he hath here indeed, of his own building. His old mother was an object at dinner that made me not like it; and, after dinner, to visit his sick wife I did not also take much joy in.

18th. To the 'Change, and walked as low as Ducke Lane, and enquired for some Spanish books. Home by water to Greenwich, the river beginning to be very full of ice, so as I was a little frighted, but got home well, it being darke.

20th. Took Sir Ellis Layton to Captain Cocke's, where my Lord Brouncker and Lady Williams dine, and we all mighty merry; but Sir Ellis Layton one of the best companions at a meal in the world.

21st. At noon, all of us dined at Captain Cocke's at a good chine of beef, and other good meat; but, being all frost-bitten, was most of it unroast; but very merry, and a good dish of fowl we dressed ourselves. Mr. Evelyn there, in very good humour.

22d. I to my Lord Brouncker's, and there spent the evening by my desire in seeing his Lordship open to pieces and make up again his watch, thereby being taught what I never knew before; and it is a thing very well worth my having seen, and am mightily pleased and satisfied with it. Somewhat vexed at a snappish answer Madam Williams did give me to herself, upon my speaking a free word to her in mirth, calling her a mad jade. She answered, we were not so well acquainted yet. But I was more at a letter from my Lord Duke Albemarle to-day, pressing us to continue our meetings for all Christmas, which, though everybody intended not to have done, yet I am concluded in it, who intended nothing less. The weather hath been frosty these eight or nine days, and so we hope for an abatement of the plague the next week, or else God have mercy upon us! for the plague will certainly continue the next year, if it do not.

23d. This day one come to me with four great turkies, as a present from Mr. Deane, at Harwich, three of which my wife carried in the evening home with her to London in her coach.

24th. (Sunday.) To dinner, my landlady and her daughters with me, and had mince-pies, and very merry at a mischance her young son had, in the tearing of his new coat quite down the outside of his sleeve in the whole cloth. Then to church, and placed myself in the parson's pew under the pulpit, to hear Mrs. Chamberlain in the next pew sing, who is daughter to Sir James Bunce,[1] of whom I have heard much, and indeed she sings very finely.

25th. (Christmas day.) To church in the morning, and there saw a wedding in the church, which I have not seen many a day; and the young people so merry one with another! and strange to see what delight we married people have to see these poor fools decoyed into our condition, every man and woman gazing and smiling at them. Here I saw again my beauty Lethulier. Home to look over and settle my papers, both of my accounts private, and those of Tangier, which I have let go so long that it were impossible for any soul, had I died, to understand them, or ever come to good end in them. I hope God will never suffer me to come to that disorder again.

26th. To the office, where Sir John Minnes and my Lord Brouncker and I met, to give our directions to the Commanders of all the ships in the river to bring in lists of their ships' companies, where young Seymour, among 20 that stood bare, stood with his hat on—a proud, saucy young man. To Mr. Cuttle's, being invited, and dined nobly and neatly; with a very pretty house and a fine turret at top, with winding stairs, and the first prospect I know about all Greenwich, save the top of the hill. Saw some fine writing-work and flourishing of Mr. Hoare, with one that I knew long ago, an acquaintance of Mr. Tomson's at Westminster, that is this man's clerk. It is the story of the several Archbishops of

---

[1] He had married Mary, daughter of Thomas Gipps, or Gibbs, of London.

Canterbury, engrossed in vellum, to hang up in Canterbury Cathedrall in tables, in lieu of the old ones, which are almost worn out.

27th. Home to my wife, and angry about her desiring a maid yet, before the plague is quite over. It seems Mercer is troubled that she hath not one under her, but I will not venture my family by encreasing it, before it is safe.

30th. All the afternoon to my accounts; and there find myself, to my great joy, a great deal worth, above 4000*l*., for which the Lord be praised! and is principally occasioned by my getting 500*l*. of Cocke, for my profit in his bargains of prize goods, and from Mr. Gauden's making me a present of 500*l*. more, when I paid him 800*l*. for Tangier.

31st. (Lord's day.) Thus ends this year, to my great joy, in this manner. I have raised my estate from 1300*l*. in this year to 4400*l*. I have got myself greater interest, I think, by my diligence, and my imployments encreased by that of Treasurer for Tangier and Surveyor of the Victualls. It is true we have gone through great melancholy because of the great plague, and I put to great charges by it, by keeping my family long at Woolwich; and myself and another part of my family, my clerks, at my charge, at Greenwich, and a maid at London; but I hope the King will give us some satisfaction for that. But now the plague is abated almost to nothing, and I intending to get to London as fast as I can. The Dutch war goes on very ill, by reason of lack of money; having none to hope for, all being put into disorder by a new Act that is made as an experiment to bring credit to the Exchequer, for goods and money to be advanced upon the credit of that Act. The great evil of this year, and the only one, indeed, is the fall of my Lord Sandwich, whose mistake about the prizes hath undone him, I believe, as to interest at Court; though sent, for a little palliating it, Embassador into Spain, which he is now fitting himself for. But the Duke of Albemarle goes with the Prince to sea this next year, and my Lord is very meanly spoken of; and, indeed, his miscarriage about the prize goods is not to be excused, to suffer a company of rogues to go away with ten times as much as

himself, and the blame of all to be deservedly laid upon him.
My whole family hath been well all this while, and all my
friends I know of, saving my aunt Bell, who is dead, and
some children of my cozen Sarah's, of the plague. But many
of such as I know very well, dead; yet, to our great joy, the
town fills apace, and shops begin to be open again. Pray
God continue the plague's decrease! for that keeps the Court
away from the place of business, and so all goes to rack as to
publick matters, they at this distance not thinking of it.

1665–6.

January 1st. Called up by five o'clock by Mr. Tooker,
who wrote, while I dictated to him, my business of the Pursers; and so, without eating or drinking, till three in the
afternoon, to my great content, finished it.[1]

2d. Up by candle-light again, and my business being
done, to my Lord Brouncker's, and there find Sir J. Minnes
and all his company, and Mr. Boreman and Mrs. Turner,
but, above all, my dear Mrs. Knipp, with whom I sang, and
in perfect pleasure I was to hear her sing, and especially her
little Scotch song of "Barbary Allen;" and to make our
mirth the completer, Sir J. Minnes was in the highest pitch
of mirth, and his mimicall tricks, that ever I saw, and most
excellent pleasant company he is, and the best musique that
ever I saw, and certainly would have made an excellent
actor, and now would be an excellent teacher of actors.
Then, it being past night, against my will, took leave.

3d. I to the Duke of Albemarle and back again: and,
at the Duke's, with great joy, I received the good news of the
decrease of the plague this week to 70, and but 253 in all;
which is the least Bill hath been known these twenty years in
the City, though the want of people in London is it, that

---

[1] This document is in the British Museum (*Harleian MS.*, 6287), and is entitled, "A Letter from Mr. Pepys, dated at Greenwich, 1 Jan. 1665–6, which he
calls his New Year's Gift to his hon. friend, Sir Wm. Coventry, wherein he lays
down a Method for securing his Majesty in husbandly execution of the Victualling Part of the Naval Expence." It consists of nineteen closely written
folio pages, and is a remarkable specimen of Pepys's business habits.

must make it so low, below the ordinary number for Bills.
So home, and find all my good company I had bespoke, as
Coleman and his wife, and Laneare, Knipp and her surly husband; and good musick we had, and among other things, Mr.
Coleman sang my words I set, of "Beauty, retire," and they
praise it mightily. Then to dancing and supper, and mighty
merry till Mr. Rolt come in, whose pain of the toothache made
him no company, and spoilt ours; so he away, and then my
wife's teeth fell of aching, and she to bed. So forced to break
up all with a good song, and so to bed.

5th. I with my Lord Brouncker and Mrs. Williams by
coach with four horses to London, to my Lord's house in
Covent Garden.[1] But, Lord! what staring to see a nobleman's coach come to town! And porters every where bow
to us; and such begging of beggars! And delightful it is to
see the town full of people again; and shops begin to open,
though in many places seven or eight together, and more, all
shut; but yet the town is full, compared to what it used to
be. I mean the City end: for Covent Garden and Westminster are yet very empty of people, no Court, nor gentry
being there. Home, thinking to get Mrs. Knipp, but could
not, she being busy with company, but sent me a pleasant
letter, writing herself "Barbary Allen." Reading a discourse
about the river of Thames, the reason of its being choked up
in several places with shelfes: which is plain is, by the en-
croachments made upon the River, and running out of cause-
ways into the River, at every wood-wharfe: which was not
heretofore, when Westminster Hall and White Hall were
built, and Redriffe Church, which now are sometimes over-
flown with water.

6th. To a great dinner and much company. Mr. Cuttle
and his lady and I went, hoping to get Mrs. Knipp to us,
having wrote a letter to her in the morning, calling myself
"Dapper Dicky,"[2] in answer to her's of "Barbary Allen," but

---

[1] In the Piazza; and one of the largest houses in what was then the most
fashionable part of London.

[2] A song called "Dapper Dicky," is in the British Museum; it begins, "In
a barren tree." It was printed in 1710.

could not, and am told by the boy that carried my letter, that he found her crying; and I fear she lives a sad life with that ill-natured fellow her husband: so we had a great, but I a melancholy dinner. After dinner to cards, and then comes notice that my wife is come unexpectedly to me to town: so I to her. It is only to see what I do, and why I come not home; and she is in the right that I would have a little more of Mrs. Knipp's company before I go away. My wife to fetch away my things from Woolwich, and I back to cards, and after cards to choose King and Queene, and a good cake there was, but no marks found; but I privately found the clove, the mark of the knave, and privately put it into Captain Cocke's piece, which made some mirth, because of his lately being known by his buying of clove and mace of the East India prizes. At night home to my lodging, where I find my wife returned with my things. It being Twelfth-Night, they had got the fiddler, and mighty merry they were; and I above, come not to them, leaving them dancing, and choosing King and Queene.

7th. (Lord's day.) The town talks of my Lord Craven being to come into Sir G. Carteret's place; but sure it cannot be true. But I do now fear those two families, his and my Lord Sandwich's, are quite broken; and I must now stand upon my own legs. With my wife and Mercer took boat and away home; but in the evening, before I went, comes Mrs. Knipp, just to speak with me privately, to excuse her not coming to see me yesterday, complaining how like a devil her husband treats her, but will be with us in town a week hence.

8th. To Bennett's, in Paternoster Row, few shops there being yet open, and there bought velvett for a coat, and camelott for a cloak for myself; and thence to a place to look over some fine counterfeit damasks to hang my wife's closet, and pitched upon one.

9th. To the office, where we met first since the plague, which God preserve us in! Pierce tells me how great a difference hath been between the Duke and Duchesse, he suspecting her to be naught with Mr. Sidney. But some way or other the matter is made up; but he [Sidney] was banished the Court, and the Duke for many days did not speak to the Duchess at all. He tells me that my Lord Sandwich is lost there at Court, though the King is particularly his friend. But people do speak every where slightly of him; which is a sad story to me, but I hope it may be better again. And that Sir G. Carteret is neglected, and hath great enemies at work against him. That matters must needs go bad, while all the town, and every boy in the street, openly cries, "The King cannot go away till my Lady Castlemaine be ready to come along with him;" she being lately put to bed.[1] And that he visits her and Mrs. Stewart every morning before he eats his breakfast.

10th. I do find Sir G. Downing to be a mighty talker, more than is true, which I now know to be so, and suspected it before. To my Lord Brouncker's house in Covent Garden. The plague is encreased this week from seventy to eighty-nine. We have also great fear of our Hambrough fleete, of their meeting with the Dutch; as also have certain news, that by storms Sir Jer. Smith's[2] fleete is scattered, and three of them come without masts back to Plymouth. Seeing and saluting Mrs. Stokes, my little goldsmith's wife in Paternoster Row, and there bespoke a silver chafing-dish for warming plates. To the Duke of Albemarle. Here I saw Sir W. Coventry's kind letter to him concerning my paper,[3] and among other of his letters, which I saw all, and that is a strange thing, that whatever is writ to this Duke Albemarle, all the world may see; for this very night he did give me Mr. Coventry's letter to read soon as it come to his hand, before he had read it himself, and bid me take out of it what concerned the Navy, and many things there was in it, which I should not have thought fit for him to have let anybody so suddenly see; but, among other things, find him profess himself to the Duke a friend into the inquiring further into the

---

[1] 28th Dec., 1665. In a fellow's chamber in Merton College, Oxford, of George Fitzroy, afterwards Duke of Northumberland.

[2] Admiral Sir Jeremy Smith, mentioned Oct. 13, 1665, *ante*, commanded a fleet in the Streights at this time, and another in the Channel, in 1668.

[3] Pepys's request to the Surveyor-General.

business of prizes, and advises that it may be publick, for the righting the King, and satisfying the people—the blame to be rightly laid where it should be, which strikes very hard upon my Lord Sandwich, and troubles me to read it. Besides, the Duchess cried mightily out against the having of gentlemen captains with feathers and ribbands, and wished the King would send her husband to sea with the old plain sea Captains that he served with formerly, that would make their ships swim with blood, though they could not make leagues as Captains now-a-days can.

11th. At noon to dinner all of us by invitation to Sir W. Pen's, and much company. Among others, Lieutenant of the Tower, and Broome, his poet, and Dr. Whistler, and his [Sir William Pen's] son-in-law Lowther,[1] servant to Mrs. Margaret Pen, and Sir Edward Spragg, a merry man, that sang a pleasant song pleasantly.

12th. I and my Lord Brouncker by coach a little way, for discourse sake, till our coach broke, and tumbled me over him quite down the side of the coach, falling on the ground about the stockes, but up again. To my poor wife, who works all day at home like a horse, at the making of her hangings for our chamber and the bed.

13th. Home with his Lordship to Mrs. Williams's, in Covent Garden, to dinner, the first time I ever was there, and there met Captain Cocke ; and pretty merry, though not perfectly so, because of the fear that there is of a great encrease again of the plague this week. And again my Lord Brouncker do tell us, that he hath it from Sir John Baber,[2] who is related to my Lord Craven, that my Lord Craven do look after Sir G. Carteret's place, and do reckon himself sure of it.

14th. (Lord's day.) Long in bed, till raised by my new

---

[1] Anthony Lowther, of Marske, in Yorkshire, who shortly afterwards married Margaret Penn, was M.P. for Appleby in 1678 and 1679. He was buried at Walthamstow in 1692. William, his son by Margaret Penn, created a Baronet in 1697, married the heir of Thomas Preston, of Holker, Lancashire. The second Baronet married Elizabeth, daughter of William, Duke of Devonshire, and their son, dying unmarried, bequeathed Holker and other estates to his cousin, Lord George Cavendish, whence the Earl of Burlington enjoys them.

[2] Physician in Ordinary to the King, who had knighted him in 1660-61.

taylor. Mr. Penny, who comes and brings me my new velvet coat, very handsome, but plain. At noon eat the second of the two cygnets Mr. Shepley sent us for a new year's gift. This afternoon, after sermon, comes my dear fair beauty of the Exchange, Mrs. Batelier, brought by her sister, an acquaintance of Mercer's, to see my wife. I saluted her with as much pleasure as I had done any a great while. We sat and talked together an hour, with infinite pleasure to me, and so the fair creature went away, and proves one of the modestest women and pretty, that ever I saw in my life, and my wife judges her so, too.

15th. To Mrs. Pierce, to her new house in Covent Garden, a very fine place and fine house. Took her thence home to my house, and so by water to Boreman's by night, where the greatest disappointment that ever I saw in my life — much company, a good supper provided, and all come with expectation of excess of mirth, but all blank through the wayward-nesse of Mrs. Knipp, who, though she had appointed the night, could not be got to come. Not so much as her husband could get her to come; but, which was a pleasant thing in all my anger, I asking him, while we were in expectation what answer one of our many messengers would bring, what he thought, whether she would come or no, he answered that, for his part, he could not so much as think. At last, very late, and supper done, she come undressed, but it brought me no mirth at all; only, after all being done, without singing, or very little, and no dancing, Pierce and I to bed together, and he and I very merry to find how little and thin clothes they give us to cover us, so that we were fain to lie in our stockings and drawers, and lay all our coats and clothes upon the bed.

16th. Mightily troubled at the news of the plague's being encreased, and was much the saddest news that the plague hath brought me from the beginning of it; because of the lateness of the year, and the fear we may with reason have of its continuing with us the next summer. The total being now 375, and the plague 158.

17th. After dinner, late took horse, and I rode to Dagen

hams in the dark. It was my Lord Crewe's desire that I should come, and chiefly to discourse with me of my Lord Sandwich's matters; and therein to persuade, what I had done already, that my Lord should sue out a pardon for his business of the prizes, as also for Bergen, and all he hath done this year past, before he begins his Embassy to Spain; for it is to be feared that the Parliament will fly out against him, and particular men, the next Session. He is glad also that my Lord is clear of his sea-imployment, though sorry, as I am, only in the manner of its bringing about. After supper, up to wait on my Lady Crewe, who is the same weak silly lady as ever, asking such saintly questions.

18th. To Captain Cocke's, where Mrs. Williams was, and Mrs. Knipp. I was not heartily merry, though a glass of wine did a little cheer me. After dinner to the office. Anon comes to me thither my Lord Brouncker, Mrs. Williams, and Knipp. I brought down my wife in her night-gown, she not being indeed very well, to the office to them. My wife and I anon and Mercer, by coach, to Pierce's, where mighty merry, and sing and dance with great pleasure; and I danced, who never did in company in my life.

19th. It is a remarkable thing how infinitely naked all that end of the town, Covent Garden, is, at this day, of people, while the City is almost as full again of people as ever it was.

20th. I sent my boy home for some papers, where, he staying longer than I would have him, I become angry, and boxed my boy when he come, that I do hurt my thumb so much, that I was not able to stir all the day after, and in great pain.

22d. At noon my Lord Brouncker did come, but left the keys of the chest we should open, at Sir G. Carteret's lodgings, of my Lord Sandwich's, wherein Howe's supposed jewels[1] are; so we could not, according to my Lord Arlington's order, see them to-day: but we parted, resolving to meet here at night; my Lord Brouncker being going with Dr.

---

[1] The jewels were stolen from the Dutch Vice-Admiral. See Nov. 16, 1665 ante.

Wilkins, Mr. Hooke,[1] and others, to Colonel Blunt's, to consider again of the business of chariots, and to try their new
invention, which I saw here my Lord Brouncker ride in; where
the coachman sits astride upon a pole over the horse, but do
not touch the horse, which is a pretty odde thing; but it
seems it is most easy for the horse, and, as they say, for the
man also.   The first meeting of Gresham College since the
plague.   Dr. Goddard did fill us with talk, in defence of his
and his fellow physicians going out of town in the plague-
time; saying, that their particular patients were most gone
out of town, and they left at liberty; and a great deal more.
But what, among other fine discourse, pleased me most,
was Sir G. Ent,[2] about respiration; that it is not to this day
known, or concluded on, among physicians, nor to be done
either, how the action is managed by nature, or for what use
it is.

23d. Good news beyond all expectation of the decrease
of the plague, being now but 79, and the whole but 272.
So home with comfort to bed.   A most furious storme all
night and morning.

24th. My Lord [Brouncker] and I, the weather being a
little fairer, by water to Deptford, to Sir G. Carteret's house,
where W. Howe met us, and there we opened the chests and
saw the poor sorry rubys which have caused all this ado to
the undoing of W. Howe; though I am not much sorry for
it, because of his pride and ill nature.   About 200 of these
very small stones, and a cod of muske, which it is strange I
was not able to smell, is all we could find; so locked them up
again, and my Lord and I, the wind being again very furious,
so as we durst not go by water, walked to London quite
round the bridge, no boat being able to stirre; and, Lord!
what a dirty walk we had, and so strong the wind, that in
the fields we many times could not carry our bodies against
it, but were driven backwards.   We went through Horsly-
downe, where I never was since a boy, that I went to enquire

[1] See Feb. 15, 1664-5.
[2] Sir George Ent, F.R.S., President of the College of Pysicians.   Ob. 1689.

after my father, whom we did give over for lost coming from
Holland. It was dangerous to walk the streets, the bricks
and tiles falling from the houses, that the whole streets were
covered with them; and whole chimneys, nay, whole houses,
in two or three places, blowed down. But, above all, the
pales of London Bridge, on both sides, were blown away, so
that we were fain to stoop very low for fear of blowing off of
the bridge. We could see no boats in the Thames afloat,
but what were broke loose, and carried through the bridge, it
being ebbing water. And the greatest sight of all was,
among other parcels of ships driven here and there in clusters
together; one was quite overset, and lay with her masts all
along in the water, and keel above water.

25th. It is now certain that the King of France hath publickly declared war against us, and God knows how little fit
we are for it.

26th. Pleased mightily with what my poor wife hath been
doing these eight or ten days with her own hands, like a
drudge, in fitting the new hangings of our bed-chamber of
blue, and putting the old red ones into my dressing-room.

28th. (Lord's day.) Took coach, and to Hampton Court,
where we find the King, and Duke, and Lords, all in council;
so we walked up and down: there being none of the ladies
come, and so much the more business I hope will be done.
The Council being up, out comes the King, and I kissed his
hand, and he grasped me very kindly by the hand. The
Duke also, I kissed his, and he mighty kind, and Sir W.
Coventry. I found my Lord Sandwich there, poor man! I
see with a melancholy face, and suffers his beard to grow on
his upper lip more than usual. I took him a little aside, to
know when I should wait on him, and where: he told me,
that it would be best to meet at his lodgings, without being
seen to walk together, which I liked very well; and, Lord!
to see in what difficulty I stand, that I dare not walk with
Sir W. Coventry, for fear my Lord or Sir G. Carteret should
see me; nor with either of them, for fear Sir W. Coventry
should. I went down into one of the Courts, and there met
the King and Duke: and the Duke called me to him. And

the King come to me of himself, and told me, "Mr. Pepys," says he, "I do give you thanks for your good service all this year, and I assure you I am very sensible of it' And the Duke of York did tell me with pleasure, that he had read over my discourse about pursers, and would have it ordered in my way, and so fell from one discourse to another. I walked with them quite out of the Court into the fields, and then back, and to my Lord Sandwich's chamber, where I find him very melancholy, and not well satisfied, I perceive, with my carriage to Sir G. Carteret, but I did satisfy him that I have a very hard game to play; and he told me that he was sorry to see it, and the inconveniences which likely may fall upon me with him; but, for all that, I am not much afraid, if I can but keep out of harm's way. He hath got over the business of the prizes, so far as to have a privy seal passed for all that was in his distribution to the officers, which I am heartily glad of; and, for the rest, he must be answerable for what he is proved to have. But for his pardon for anything else, he thinks it not seasonable to ask it, and not useful to him; because that will not stop a Parliament's mouth, and for the King, he is not sure of him. Took boat, and by water to Kingston, and so to our lodgings.

29th. Up, and to Court by coach, where to council before the Duke of York, the Duke of Albemarle with us. My Lord Sandwich come in, in the middle of the business, and, poor man, very melancholy, methought, and said little at all, or to the business, and sat at the lower end, just as he come, no room being made for him, only I did give him my stool, and another was reached me. Mr. Evelyn and I into my Lord Brouncker's coach, and rode together with excellent discourse till we come to Clapham, talking of the vanity and vices of the Court, which makes it a most contemptible thing; and, indeed, in all his discourse, I find him a most worthy person. Particularly he entertained me with discourse of an Infirmary, which he hath projected for the sick and wounded seamen against the next year, which I mightily approve of; and will endeavour to promote it, being a worthy thing, and of use, and will save money. He set me down at Mr.

Gauden's, where I took a book and into the gardens, and there walked and read till dark. Anon come in Creed and Mr. Gauden, and his sons, and then they bring in three ladies, who were in the house, but I do not know them — his [Gauden's] daughter and two nieces, daughters of Dr. Whistler's, with whom and Creed mighty sport at supper, the ladies very pretty and mirthfull. After supper, I made the ladies sing, yet it was the saddest stuff I ever heard. However, we sat up late, and then I, in the best chamber, like a prince, to bed, and Creed with me, and, being sleepy, talked but little.

30th. Home, finding the town keeping the day solemnly, it being the day of the King's murther; and they being at church, I presently into the church. This is the first time I have been in the church since I left London for the plague, and it frighted me indeed to go through the church more than I thought it could have done, to see so many graves lie so high upon the churchyards, where people have been buried of the plague. I was much troubled at it, and do not think to go through it again a good while.[1]

31st. I find many about the City that live near the churchyards solicitous to have the churchyards covered with lime, and I think it is needful, and ours, I hope, will be done. To my Lord Chancellor's new house which he is building, only to view it, hearing so much from Mr. Evelyn of it; and, indeed, it is the finest pile I ever did see in my life, and will be a glorious house. To White Hall, and, to my great joy, people begin to bustle up and down there, the King holding his resolution to be in town to-morrow, and hath good encouragement, blessed be God! to do so, the plague being decreased this week to 56, and the total to 227.

February 2d. My Lord Sandwich is come to town with the

---

[1] The following summary of the deaths from the plague of 1665, in the parish of St. Olave's, Hart Street, was extracted from the Register, by the Rev. C. Murray, and printed in *The Gentleman's Magazine*, October, 1815:— In July, 4; August, 22; September, 63; October, 54; November, 18; December, 5. Of these, there were buried in the churchyard, 98; in the new churchyard, 12; in vaults, 12; in the church, 7; in the chancel, 1. Buried, places of interment not specified, 166. Total, 326. No wonder that Pepys felt nervous on first entering the church after the sickness abated.

King and Duke. To London, and there, among other things, did look over some pictures at Cade's for my house, and did carry home a silver drudger[1] for my cupboard of plate, and did call [at Stokes's] for my silver chafing-dishes; and, with my wife, looked over our plate, and picked out 40*l.* worth, I believe, to change for more useful plate, to our great content, and then we shall have a very handsome cupboard of plate.

4th. (Lord's day.) My wife and I the first time together at church since the plague, and now only because of Mr. Mills his coming home to preach his first sermon; expecting a great excuse for his leaving the parish before any body went, and now staying till all are come home; but he made but a very poor and short excuse, and a bad sermon. It was a frost, and had snowed last night, which covered the graves in the churchyard, so as I was the less afraid for going through. My wife tells me my aunt James is lately dead of the stone.

5th. To the Sun, behind the Exchange, about seven o'clock, where I find all the five brothers Houblons, and mighty fine gentlemen they are all, and used me mighty respectfully. We were mighty civilly merry, and their discourses, having been all abroad, very fine.

7th. It being fast-day, I staid at home all day long, putting my chamber in the same condition it was before the plague.

8th. Lord Brouncker with the King and Duke upon the water to-day, to see Greenwich house, and the yacht Castle is building of.

9th. To Westminster, to the Exchequer, about my Tangier

---

[1] The dredger was probably the *drageoir* of France: in low Latin, *dragerium*, or *drageria*, in which comfits (*dragées*) were kept. Roquefort says, "The ladies wore a little spice-box, in shape like a watch, to carry *dragées*, and it was called a *drageoir*." The custom continued certainly till the middle of the last century. Old Palsgrave, in his *Éclaircissement de la Langue Françayse*, gives "dradge" as spice, rendering it by the French word *dragée*. Chaucer says, of his Doctor of Physic, —

> "Full ready hadde he his Apothecaries
> To send him dragges, and his lattuaries."

The word sometimes may have signified the pounded condiments in which our forefathers delighted. It is worth notice, that *dragge* was applied to a grain in the eastern counties, though not exclusively there, appearing to denote mixed grain. Bishop Kennett tells us, that "dredge mault is mault made up of oats, mixed with barley, of which they make an excellent, freshe, quiete sort of drinke, in Staffordshire." The dredger is still commonly used in our kitchen.

business, and so to Westminster Hall, where the first day of
the Terme, and the hall very full of people, and much more
than was expected, considering the plague that hath been.
Anon the five brothers Houblons come, and Mr. Hill, and a
very good supper we had, and good company and discourse,
with great pleasure. My new plate sets off my cupboard very
nobly. A fine sight it is to see these five brothers thus loving
one to another, and all industrious merchants. Mr. Hill's
going for them to Portugall was the occasion of this entertainment.

10th. To the office. This day comes first Sir Thomas
Harvey after the plague, having been out of town all this
while. He was coldly received by us, and he went away before we rose also, to make himself appear a man less necessary. To supper, and to bed, being now-a-days, for these
four or five months, mightily troubled with my snoring in my
sleep, and know not how to remedy it.

11th. (Lord's day.) Up, and put on a new black cloth suit
to an old coat, that I make to be in mourning at Court, where
they are all, for the King of Spain.[1] I to the Park, and
walked two or three turnes of the Pell Mell with the company
about the King and Duke; the Duke speaking to me a good
deal. There met Lord Brouncker and Mr. Coventry, and discoursed about the Navy business; and all of us much at a loss
that we yet can hear nothing of Sir Jeremy Smith's fleete, that
went away to the Streights the middle of December, through
all the storms that we have had since, that have driven back
three or four of them, with their masts by the board. Yesterday came out the King's Declaration of War against the
French,[2] but with such mild invitations of both them and the
Dutch, to come over here, with promise of their protection,
that every body wonders at it.

12th. Comes Mr. Cæsar, my boy's lute-master, whom I

---

[1] Philip IV. died 17th Sept., 1665.
[2] It was proclaimed by the Herald-at-Arms, and two of his brethren, His
Majesty's Sergeants-at-Arms, with other usual officers (with his Majesty's Trum-
peters attending), before his Royal palace at Whitehall; and afterwards (the
Lord Mayor and his brethren assisting) at Temple Bar, and other the usual parts
of the city.—*The London Gazette*, Feb. 8-12, 1665-6.

have not seen since the plague before, but he hath been in
Westminster all this while, very well; and tells me, in the
height of it, how bold people there were, to go in sport to one
another's burials; and in spite, too, ill people would breathe
in the faces, out of their windows, of well people going by.

13th. Ill news this night, that the plague is encreased this
week, and in many places else about the town, and at Chatham
and elsewhere.

14th. (St. Valentine's day.) This morning called up by Mr.
Hill, who, my wife thought, had come to be her Valentine—
she, it seems, having drawn him, but it proved not. However, calling him up to our bed-side, my wife challenged him.
I took Mr. Hill to my Lord Chancellor's new house[1] that is
building, and went, with trouble, up to the top of it; and
there is the noblest prospect that ever I saw in my life, Greenwich being nothing to it; and in every thing is a beautiful
house, and most strongly built in every respect; and as if, as
it hath, it had the Chancellor for its master.[2] I staid a meeting of the Duke of York's, and the officers of the Navy and
Ordnance. My Lord Treasurer lying in bed of the gowte.

15tn. Mr. Hales[3] begun my wife's portrait in the posture
we saw one of my Lady Peters, like a St. Catharine.[4] While
he painted, Knipp, and Mercer, and I, sang; and by and by
comes Mrs. Pierce, with my name in her bosom for her Valentine, which will cost me money. We hear this night of Sir
Jeremy Smith, that he and his fleete have been seen at Malaga;
which is good news.

16th. To my Lord Sandwich, to talk of his affairs, and particularly of his prize goods, wherein I find he is weary of being
troubled, and gives over the care of it to let it come to what
it will, having the King's release for the dividend made, and for
the rest he thinks himself safe from being proved to have anything more. To the Coffee-House, the first time I have been

[1] See 18th Feb., 1665, and 9th May, 1667.

[2] Two years after he was in exile.

[3] John Hayls, or Hales, a portrait-painter, "remarkable for copying Vandyke
well, and for being a rival of Lely," though very inferior to him.

[4] It was at this time the fashion to be painted as St. Catherine, in compliment
to the Queen. The so-called Lady Bellasys, among the beauties of Charles II,
now at Hampton Court, is thus represented.

there, where very full, and company, it seems, hath been there all the plague time. The Queen comes to Hampton Court to-night. With Mr. Hater in the garden, talking about a husband for my sister, and reckoning up all our clerks about us, none of which he thinks fit for her and her portion.

17th. News of Sir Jeremy Smith's being very well with his fleete at Cales.

18th. (Lord's day.) It being a brave day, I walked to White Hall, where the Queen and ladies are all come: I saw some few of them, but not the Queen, nor any of the great beauties. Thence took coach, and home, calling by the way at my book-seller's for a book writ about twenty years ago in prophecy of this year coming on, 1666, explaining it to be the mark of the beast.[1]

19th. To see my Lord Hinchingbroke, which I did, and I am mightily out of countenance in my great expectation of him by others' report, though he is indeed a pretty gentleman, yet nothing what I took him for, methinks, either as to person or discourse. I am told for certain, what I have heard once or twice already, of a Jew in town, that in the name of the rest do offer to give any man 10*l.* to be paid 100*l.* if a certain person now at Smyrna be within these two years owned by all the Princes of the East, and particularly the grand Signor, as the King of the world, in the same manner we do the King of England here, and that this man is the true Messiah. One named a friend of his that had received ten pieces in gold upon this score, and says that the Jew hath disposed of 1100*l.* in this manner, which is very strange; and certainly this year of 1666 will be a year of great action; but what the conse-quences of it will be, God knows! To the 'Change, and from

[1] The book purchased by Pepys is entitled, "An Interpretation of the Number 666, wherein not only the manner how this Number ought to be interpreted is clearly proved and demonstrated; but it is also shewed that this number is an exquisite and perfect character, truly, exactly, and essentially describing that state of Government to which all other notes of Antichrist doe agree. With all knowne objections solidly and fully answered, that can be mate-rially made against it." By Francis Potter, B.D., Oxford, 1642, 4to. A copy of this work in the British Museum contains the book-plate of "William Hewer, of Clapham, in the county of Surrey, Esq., 1699." See 4th and 10th Nov., 1666, post.

my stationer's thereabouts carried home by coach two books of Ogilby's, his Æsop and Coronation, which fell to my lot at his lottery.[1] Cost me 4*l.* besides the binding. To my Lord Treasurer's, where the state of our Navy debts was laid open, there being but 1,500,000*l.* to answer a certain expence and debt of 2,300,000*l.* To White Hall, and there saw the Queen at cards with many ladies, but none of our beauties were there But glad I was to see the Queen so well, who looks prettily and methinks hath more life than before, since it is confessed of all that she miscarried lately; Dr. Clerke telling me yester day of it at White Hall.[2]

20th. Up, and to the office; where, among other businesses, Mr. Evelyn's proposition about publick Infirmarys was read and agreed on, he being there: and at noon I took him home to dinner, being desirous of keeping my acquaintance with him; and a most excellent humoured man I still find him, and mighty knowing. To my Lord Sandwich's, where, bolting into the dining-room, I there found Captain Ferrers going to christen a child of his, born yesterday, and I come just pat to be a godfather, along with my Lord Hinchingbroke and Madam Pierce, my Valentine. A little vexed to see myself so beset with people to spend me money. After that done, and gone and kissed my mother in bed, I away to Westminster Hall, and thence home, where little Mrs. Tooker staid all night with us, and a pretty child she is, and happens to be niece to my beauty that is dead, that lived at the Jackanapes, in Cheapside.

21st. My brother John is shortly to be Master in Arts, and writes me this week a Latin letter that he is to go into orders this Lent. To the Duke's chamber, and here the Duke did bring out a book of great antiquity, of some of the customs of the Navy, about 100 years since, which he did lend us to read, and deliver him back again. To Trinity-house, being invited to an Elder Brother's feast; and there met and sat by Mr. Prin, and had good discourse about the privileges of Parlia-

---

[1] At the old Theatre, between Lincoln's Inn Fields and Vere Street.
[2] The details in the original are very coarsely expressed, but leave no doubt of the fact, exculpating the Chancellor from the charge of having selected the Queen as incapable of bearing children.

ment, which, he says, are few to the Commons' House, and
those not examinable by them, but only by the House of
Lords. Thence with my Lord Brouncker to Gresham College, the first time after the sickness that I was there, and the
second time any met. And here a good lecture of Mr. Hooke's
about the trade of felt-making, very pretty; and anon he alone
with me about the art of drawing pictures by Prince Rupert's
rule and machine, and another of Dr. Wren's;[1] but he says
nothing do like squares, or, which is the best in the world,
like a dark roome.[2]

22d. We are much troubled that the sickness in general,
the town being so full of people, should be but three, and yet
of the particular disease of the plague there should be ten
encrease.

23d. To my Lord Sandwich's, who did lie the last night at
his house in Lincoln's Inne Fields. It being fine walking in
the morning, and the streets full of people again. There I
staid, and the house full of people come to take leave of my
Lord, who this day goes out of towne upon his embassy
towards Spain; and I was glad to find Sir W. Coventry to
come, though I know it is only a piece of courtship. To Mr.
Hales's, and my wife's picture pleases me well, and I begin to
doubt the picture of my Lady Peters my wife takes her posture from, and which is an excellent picture, is not of his
making—it is so master-like. Comes Mrs. Knipp to see my
wife, and I spent all the night talking with this baggage, and
teaching her my song of "Beauty, retire," which she sings
and makes go most rarely, and a very fine song it seems to be.
She also entertained me with repeating many of her own and
others' parts of the play-house, which she do most excellently;
and tells me the whole practices of the play-house and players,
and is in every respect most excellent company. So I supped,
and was merry at home all the evening, and the rather it being
my birthday 33 years, for which God be praised that I am in
so good a condition of health and estate, and everything else
as I am, beyond expectation, in all.

24th. At the office till past three o'clock. At that hour

---

[1] Sir Christopher Wren.   [2] The camera obscura.

home, and eat a bit alone, my wife being gone out. So
abroad by coach with Mr. Hill, who staid for me to speak
about business, and he and I to Hales's, where I find my
wife, and her woman, and Pierce and Knipp. There sung,
and was mighty merry, and I joyed myself in it; but vexed
at first to find my wife's picture not so like as I expected;
but it was only his having finished one part, and not another,
of the face; but, before I went, I was satisfied it will be an
excellent picture. Here we had ale and cakes, and mighty
merry, and sung my song, which she [Knipp] now sings
bravely, and makes me proud of myself. Thence left my
wife to go home with Mrs. Pierce, while I home to the office,
and there pretty late, and to bed, after fitting myself for to-
morrow's journey.

25th. (Lord's day.) My wife up between three and four
of the o'clock in the morning to dress herself, and I about
five, and were all ready to take coach, she and I and Mercer,
a little past five, but, to our trouble, the coach did not come
till six. I hired it on purpose, and Lechmere to ride by,
through the city, it being clear day, to Branford, and so with
our coach of four horses to Windsor, and so to Cranborne,[1]
about eleven o'clock, and found my Lord[2] and the ladies at
a sermon in the house; which being ended, we to them, and
all the company glad to see us, and mighty merry to dinner.
Here was my Lord, and Lord Hinchingbroke, and Mr.
Sidney,[3] Sir Charles Herbert [Harbord],[4] and Mr. Carteret,

---

[1] Cranbourne Lodge. Sir G. Carteret's official residence, as Vice-Chamberlain.
See 20th July, 1665.

[2] Sandwich.   [3] Sidney Montagu, Lord Sandwich's second son.

[4] This person, erroneously called by Pepys Sir C. Herbert, will be best defined
by subjoining the inscription on his monument in Westminster Abbey: — "Sir
Charles Harbord, Knight, third son of Sir Charles Harbord, Knight, Surveyor-
General, and First Lieutenant of the Royall James, under the most noble and
illustrious Captaine, Edward, Earle of Sandwich, Vice-Admirall of England,
which, after a terrible fight, maintained to admiration against a squadron of the
Holland fleet, above six hours, neere the Suffolk coast, having put off two fire-
ships; at last, being utterly disabled, and few of her men remaining unhurt, was,
by a third, unfortunately set on fire. But he (though he swoine well) neglected to
save himselfe, as some did, and out of perfect love to that worthy Lord, whom, for
many yeares, he had constantly accompanyed, in all his honourable employments,
and in all the engagements of the former warre, dyed with him, at the age
of xxxii., much bewailed by his father, whom he never offended; and much
beloved by all for his knowne piety, vertue, loyalty, fortitude, and fidelity."

my Lady Carteret, my Lady Jemimah, and Lady Slaning.[1]
After dinner to walk in the Park, my Lord and I alone; and
he tells me my Lord of Suffolk, Lord Arlington, Archbishop
of Canterbury, Lord Treasurer, Mr. Atturny Montagu, Sir
Thomas Clifford in the House of Commons, Sir G. Carteret,
and some others I cannot presently remember, are friends
that I may rely on for him. He dreads the issue of this
year, and fears there will be some very great revolutions
before his coming back again. He doubts it is needful for
him to have a pardon for his last year's actions, all which he
did without commission, and at most but the King's private
single word for that of Bergen; but he dares not ask it at
this time, lest it should make them think that there is something more in it than yet they know; and if it should be
denied, it would be of very ill consequence. He says, also,
if it should in Parliament be enquired into the selling of
Dunkirke, though the Chancellor was the man that would
have sold it to France, saying the King of Spain had no
money to give for it, yet he will be found to have been the
greatest adviser of it, which he is a little apprehensive may
be called upon by this Parliament. He told me it would not
be necessary for him to tell me his debts, because he thinks
I know them so well. He tells me, that for the match propounded of Mrs. Mallet for my Lord Hinchingbroke, it hath
been lately off, and now her friends bring it on again, and an
overture hath been made to him by a servant of hers, to
compass the thing without consent of friends, she herself
having a respect to my Lord's family, but my Lord will not
listen to it but in a way of honour.[2] Then I with the young
ladies and gentlemen, who played on the guittar, and mighty
merry, and anon to supper; and then my Lord going away
to write, the young gentlemen to flinging of cushions, and
other mad sports, till towards twelve at night, and then,
being sleepy, I and my wife in a passage-room to bed, and
slept not very well, because of noise.

26th. Called up about five in the morning, and my Lord

---

[1] Sir G. Carteret's daughter Caroline.
[2] She afterwards married Lord Rochester.

up, and took leave, a little after six, very kindly of me and
the whole company. So took coach and to Windsor, to the
Garter, and thither sent for Dr. Childe,[1] who come to us and
carried us to St. George's Chapel, and there placed us among
the Knight's stalls; and pretty the observation, that no man,
but a woman, may sit in a Knight's place, where any brass
plates are set, and hither come cushions to us, and a young
singing-boy to bring us a copy of the anthem to be sung.
And here, for our sakes, had this anthem and the great
service sung extraordinary, only to entertain us. It is a
noble place indeed, and a good Quire of voices. Great
bowing by all the people, the poor Knights in particularly, to
the Altar. After prayers, we to see the plate of the chapel,
and the robes of Knights, and a man to show us the banners
of the several Knights in being, which hang up over the
stalls. And so to other discourse very pretty, about the
Order. Was shown where the late King is buried, and King
Henry the Eighth, and my Lady Seymour.[2] This being
done, to the King's house, and to observe the neatness and
contrivance of the house and gates: it is the most romantique
castle that is in the world. But, Lord! the prospect that is
in the balcone in the Queen's lodgings, and the terrace and
walk, are strange things to consider, being the best in the
world, sure; and so, giving a great deal of money to this and
that man and woman, we to our tavern, and there dined, the
Doctor with us; and so took coach and away to Eton, the
Doctor with me. Before we went to Chapel this morning,
Kate Joyce, in a stage-coach going towards London, called to
me. I went to her and saluted her, but could not get her to
stay with us, having company. At Eton I left my wife in
the coach, and he and I to the College, and there find all
mighty fine. The school good, and the custom pretty of boys
cutting their names in the shuts of the window when they go
to Cambridge, by which many a one hath lived to see himself
a Provost and Fellow, that hath his name in the window
standing. To the Hall, and there find the boys' verses, "De

---

[1] William Child, Doctor of Music, Organist of St. George's Chapel, at Windsor
Ob. 1696, aged 91.   [2] Queen Jane Seymour.

Peste :" it being their custom to make verses at Shrove-tide.
I read several, and very good they were; better, I think,
than ever I made when I was a boy, and in rolls as long and
longer than the whole Hall, by much.   Here is a picture of
Venice hung up, and a monument made of Sir H. Wotton's
giving it to the College.   Thence to the porter's, in the
absence of the butler, and did drink of the College beer, which
is very good; and went into the back fields to see the scholars
play.   And so to the chapel, and there saw, among other
things, Sir H. Wotton's stone with this Epitaph:

Hic jacet primus hujus sententiæ Author: —
Disputandi pruritus fit ecclesiæ scabies.

But unfortunately the word "Author" was wrong writ, and
now so basely altered that it disgraces the stone.   Thence
took leave of the Doctor, and so took coach, and finely, but
sleepy, away home, and got thither about eight at night, and
after a little at my office, I to bed; and an hour after, was
raked with my wife's quarrelling with Mercer, at which I was
angry, and my wife and I fell out.   But with much ado to
sleep again, I beginning to practice more temper, and to give
her her way.

28th. Mrs. Knipp and we dined together, she the plea-
santest company in the world.   After dinner, I did give my
wife money to lay out on Knipp, 20s.

March 1st. Blessed be God! a good Bill this week we
have; being but 237 in all, and 42 of the plague, and of them
but six in the City: though my Lord Brouncker says, that
these six are most of them in new parishes, where they were
not the last week.

2d. To Sir Philip Warwick's by appointment.   He shewed
me his house, which is yet all unhung, but will be a very
noble house indeed.   Mr. James Houblon told me in my care
this night that he and his brothers have resolved to give me
200l. for helping them out with two or three ships.   A good
sum, and I did expect little less.

3d. To Hales's, and there saw my wife sit; and I do like
her picture mightily, and very like it will be, and a brave
piece of work; but he do complain that her nose hath cost

him as much work as another's face, and he hath done it finely indeed.

4th. (Lord's day.) All day at my Tangier and private accounts, having neglected them since Christmas, which I hope I shall never do again; for I find the inconvenience of it, it being ten times the labour to remember and settle things. But I thank God I did it at last, and brought them all fine and right; and I am, I think, by all appears to me — and I am sure I cannot be 10*l*. wrong — worth about 4600*l*., for which the Lord be praised, being the biggest sum I ever was worth yet.

5th. I was at it till past two o'clock on Monday morning, and then read my vows, and to bed with great joy. News for certain of the King of Denmark's declaring for the Dutch, and resolution to assist them.

6th. In the evening, being at Sir W. Batten's, I find my Lord Brouncker and Mrs. Williams, and they would of their own accord, though I had never obliged them, nor my wife neither, with one visit for many of theirs, go see my house and my wife; which I showed them, and made them welcome with wine and China oranges, now a great rarity since the war, none to be had. My house happened to be mighty clean, and did me great honour, and they mightily pleased with it.

7th. Up betimes, and to St. James's, thinking Mr. Coventry had lain there; but he do not, but at White Hall; so thither I went to him. We walked an hour in the Matted Gallery: he of himself begun to discourse of the unhappy differences between him and my Lord of Sandwich; and, from the beginning to the end, did run through all passages wherein my Lord hath, at any time, gathered any dissatisfaction, and cleared himself to me most honourably; and, in truth, I do believe he do as he says. I did afterwards purge myself of all partiality in the business of Sir G. Carteret, whose story Sir W. Coventry did also run over—that I do mind the King's interest, notwithstanding my relation to him; all which he declares he firmly believes, and assures me he hath the same kindness and opinion of me as ever. And, when I said I was jealous of myself, that, having now come to such an income as I am, by his favour, I should not be found to do as much service as might deserve it; he did assure me, he thinks it not too much for me, but thinks I deserve it as much as any man in England. All this discourse did cheer my heart, and sets me right again, after a good deal of melancholy, out of fears of his disinclination to me, upon the difference with my Lord Sandwich and Sir G. Carteret; but I am satisfied thoroughly, and so went away quite another man, and, by the grace of God, will never lose it again by my folly in not visiting and writing to him, as I used heretofore to do. It being a holyday, a fast-day, I to Greenwich, to Captain Cocke's, where dined, he, and Lord Brouncker, and Matt. Wren,[1] Boltele, and Major Cooper, who is also a very pretty companion; but they all drink hard, and, after dinner, to gaming at cards. The King and Duke are to go to-morrow to Audley End, in order to the seeing and buying of it of my Lord Suffolk.[2]

8th. To Hales's, where my wife is sitting; and, indeed, her face and neck, which are now finished, do so please me, that I am not myself almost in consideration of the fine picture that I shall be master of.

9th. Made a visit to the Duke of Albemarle, and, to my great joy, find him the same man to me he has been heretofore, which I was in great doubt of, through my negligence in not visiting of him a great while; and, having now set all to rights there, I shall never suffer matters to run so far backwards again as I have done of late, with reference to my neglecting him and Sir W. Coventry.

---

[1] Matthew Wren, eldest son of the Bishop of Ely, of both his names, M.P. for St. Michael's, 1661, and made Secretary to Lord Clarendon, after whose fall he filled a similar office under the Duke of York, till his death, in 1672. According to Pepys's *Signs Manual*, Wren was mortally wounded in the battle of Solebay. He was one of the earliest members of the Royal Society, and published two tracts in answer to Harrington's *Oceana*.

[2] The King took possession of Audley End the following autumn, but the conveyance of the estate was not executed till May 8th, 1699; of the purchase-money, which was 50,000*l.*, 20,000*l.* remained on mortgage of the Hearth Tax in Ireland; and, in 1701, Henry Howard, fifth Earl of Suffolk, was allowed by the Crown, upon the debt being cancelled, to re-establish himself in the seat of his ancestors. It seems very doubtful whether the interest of the mortgage was ever received by the Suffolk family.

10th. I find at home Mrs. Pierce and Knipp come to dine with me. We were mighty merry; and, after dinner, I carried them and my wife out by coach to the New Exchange, and there I did give my Valentine, Mrs. Pierce, a dozen pair of gloves, and a pair of silk stockings, and Knipp for company, though my wife had, by my consent, laid out 20s. on her the other day, six pair of gloves. The truth is, I do indulge myself a little the more in pleasure, knowing that this is the proper age of my life to do it; and, out of my observation that most men that do thrive in the world do forget to take pleasure during the time that they are getting their estate, but reserve that till they have got one, and then it is too late for them to enjoy it.

12th. My uncle Talbot Pepys died the last week. All the news now is, that Sir Jeremy Smith is at Cales with his fleete; and Mings in the Elbe. The King is come this noon to town from Audley End, with the Duke of York and a fine train of gentlemen.

13th. The plague encreased this week 29 from 28, though the totall fallen from 238 to 207.

14th. With my Lord Brouncker towards London, in our way called in Covent Garden, and took in Sir John, formerly Dr., Baber; who hath this humour, that he will not enter into discourse while any stranger is in company, till he be told who he is that seems a stranger to him. This he did declare openly to me, and asked my Lord who I was. Thence to Guildhall, in our way taking in Dr. Wilkins, and there my Lord and I had full and large discourse with Sir Thomas Player,[1] the Chamberlain of the City, a man I have much heard of, about the credit of our tallys, which are lodged there for security to such as should lend money thereon to the use of the Navy. I had great satisfaction therein: and, the truth is, I find all our matters of credit to be in an ill condition. To walk all alone in the fields behind Grayes Inne, making an end of reading over my dear " Faber for-

---

[1] One of the City Members in the Oxford and Westminster Parliaments. See more of him in the *Notes*, by Scott, to Absalom and Achitophel; in which poem he is introduced under the designation of "railing Rabsheka."

tunæ," of my Lord Bacon's.   To Mrs. Pierce's, where I find
her, my wife, Mrs. Worshipp and her daughter, and Harris
the player, and Knipp, and Mercer, and Mrs. Barbary
Shelden, who is come this day to spend a week with my wife:
and here with musick we danced, and sung, and supped, till
past one in the morning: and much mirth with Sir Anthony
Apsley and one Colonel Sidney, who lodge in the house; and,
above all, they are mightily taken with Mrs. Knipp.

15th. To Hales's, where I met my wife and people; and do
find the picture, above all things, a most pretty picture, and
mighty like my wife; and I asked him his price: he says
14*l.*; and, the truth is, I think he do deserve it.

17th. To Hales's, and paid him 14*l.* for the picture, and
1*l.* 5*s.* for the frame.   This day I began to sit, and he will
make me, I think, a very fine picture.   He promises it shall
be as good as my wife's, and I to sit to have it full of shadows,
and do almost break my neck looking over my shoulder to
make the posture for him to work by.   Home, having a great
cold: so to bed, drinking butter-ale.

19th. After dinner, we walked to the King's playhouse, all
in dirt, they being altering of the stage to make it wider.
But God knows when they will begin to act again; but my
business here was to see the inside of the stage and all the
tiring-rooms and machines; and, indeed, it was a sight worthy
seeing.   But to see their clothes, and the various sorts, and
what a mixture of things there was; here a wooden leg,[1]
there a ruff, here a hobby-horse, there a crown, would make
a man split himself to see with laughing: and particularly
Lacy's wardrobe, and Shotrell's.[2]   But then again to think
how fine they show on the stage by candle-light, and how
poor things they are to look at too near hand, is not pleasant
at all.   The machines are fine, and the paintings very pretty.

---

[1] Compare 5th October, 1667.

[2] Robert and William Shotterel both belonged to the King's Company at the
opening of their new theatre in 1664.   One of them, called by Downes a good
actor, had been Quarter-master to the troop of horse in which Hart was serving
as Lieutenant, and Burt as Cornet, under Charles the First's standard; but
nothing further is recorded of his merits and career.   Pepys refers to Robert
Shotterel, who, it appears, was living in Playhouse Yard, Drury Lane, 1681-4.

With Sir W. Warren, talking of many things belonging to
us particularly, and I hope to get something considerably by
him before the year be over.   He gives me good advice of
circumspection in my place, which I am now in great mind to
improve ; for I think our office stands on very ticklish terms,
the Parliament likely to sit shortly, and likely to be asked
more money, and we be able to give a very bad account of
the expence and of what we have done with what they did
give before.   Besides, the turning out the prize officers may
be an example for the King's giving us up to Parliament's
pleasure as easily, for we deserve it as much.   Besides, Sir
G. Carteret did tell me to-night how my Lord Brouncker,
whose good-will I could have depended as much on as any,
did himself to him take notice of the many places I have ;
and, though I was a painful man, yet the Navy was enough
for any man to go through with in his own single place there,
which much troubles me, and yet shall provoke me to more
and more care and diligence than ever.   My father propounds
a match in the country for Pall, which pleased me well, of
one that hath seven score and odd pounds land per annum in
possession ; and expects 1000*l.* in money, by the death of an
old aunt.   He hath neither father, mother, sister, nor brother,
but demands 600*l.* down, and 100*l.* on the birth of first child,
which I had some inclination to stretch to.   He is kinsman
to, and lives with, Mr. Phillips ; but my wife tells me he is a
drunken, ill-favoured, ill-bred country fellow.

21st. To the Duke of York, and did our usual business
with him ; but, Lord ! how anything is yielded presently,
even by Sir W. Coventry, that is propounded by the Duke,
as now to have Troutbecke,[1] his old surgeon, intended to go
Surgeon-General to the fleete, to go Physician-General of the
fleete, of which there never was any precedent in the world,
and he for that to have 20*l.* per month.   Sir Robert Long
told us of the plenty of partridges in France, where he says
the King of France and his company killed with their guns,
in the plain de Versailles, 300 and odd partridges at one bout.

---

[1] John Troutbecke, in 1661, was surgeon to the Life-Guards, commanded by
the Duke of Albemarle.

With Sir W. Warren, who tells me, that at the Committee of the Lords for the prizes to-day, there passed very high words between my Lord Ashly and Sir W. Coventry, about our business of the prize ships; and that my Lord Ashly did snuff and talk as high to him as he used to do to any ordinary man; and that Sir W. Coventry did take it very quietly; but yet, for all, did speak his mind soberly, and with reason; and went away, saying, that he had done his duty therein.

24th. After the Committee up, I had occasion to follow the Duke into his lodgings, into a chamber where the Duchess was sitting to have her picture drawn by Lilly, who was then at work. But I was well pleased to see that there was nothing near so much resemblance of her face in his work, which is now the second, if not the third time, as there was of my wife's at the very first time. Nor do I think at last it can be like, the lines not being in proportion to those of her face.

26th. My Lord Brouncker and I to the Tower, to see the famous Engraver,[1] to get him to grave a seal for the office. And did see some of the finest pieces of work, in embossed work, that ever I did see in my life, for fineness and smallness of the images thereon. Here I also did see bars of gold melting, which was a fine sight.

28th. With Sir W. Clerke into St. James's Park, and met with Mr. Hayes, Prince Rupert's Secretary, who are mighty, both, brisk blades; but I fear they promise themselves more than they expect. To the Cockpitt, and dined with a great deal of company at the Duke of Albemarle's, and a bad and dirty, nasty dinner. This night, I am told, the Queen of Portugall,[2] the mother to our Queen, is lately dead, and news brought of it hither this day.

29th. This day, poor Jane, my old, little Jane, come to us again, to my wife's and my great content, and we hope to take mighty pleasure in her, she having all the marks and qualities of a good and loving and honest servant, she coming by force away from the other place, where she hath lived

---

[1] One of the Roetiers. Simon was dead.

[2] The celebrated Donna Luiza, widow of Juan IV., and daughter of the Duke do Medina Sidonia.

ever since she went from us, and at our desire, her late mistress having used all the stratagems she could to keep her.

30th. Up, and away goes Alce, our cook-maid, a good servant, whom we loved and did well by her, and she an excellent servant, but would not bear being told of any fault in the fewest and kindest words, and would go away of her own accord, after having given her mistress warning fickly. I out to Lombard Streete, and there received 2200*l.*, and brought it home ; and, contrary to expectation, received 35*l.* for the use of 2000*l.* of it for a quarter of a year, where it hath produced me this profit, and hath been a convenience to me, as to care and security, at my house, and demandable at two days' warning, as this hath been. To Hales's, and there sat till almost quite dark upon working my gowne, which I hired to be drawn in ; an Indian gowne.

31st. To my accounts, but, Lord! what a deal of do I have to understand any part of them ; for I have sat up these four nights till past twelve at night to master them, but cannot. However, I do see that I must be grown richer than I was by a good deal last month.

April 1st. (Lord's day.) To Charing Cross, to wait on Sir Philip Howard, whom I find in bed : and he do receive me very civilly. My request was about suffering my wife's brother to go to sea, and to save his pay in the Duke's guards ; which, after a little difficulty, he did with great respect agree to. I find him a very fine-spoken gentleman, and one of great parts, and very courteous. Meeting Dr. Allen, the physician, he, and I, and another walked in the Park, a most pleasant, warm day, and to the Queen's chapel ; where I do not so dislike the musick. Here I saw on a post an invitation to all good Catholicks to pray for the soul of such a one departed this life. The Queen, I hear, do not yet hear of the death of her mother, she being in a course of physick, that they dare not tell it her. Up and down my Lord St. Albans his new building and market-house,[1] looking to and

---

[1] Jermyn Street and St. Albans, from his name and title. The market was afterwards called St. James's Market ; a portion of which still remains, south of that part of Jermyn Street that lies between Regent Street and the Haymarket.

again into every place building. I this afternoon made a visit to my Lady Carteret, whom I understood newly come to towne ; and she took it mighty kindly, but I see her face and heart are dejected from the condition her husband's matters stand in. But I hope they will do all well enough ; and I do comfort her as much as I can, for she is a noble lady.

2d. Walking with Mr. Gauden in Westminster Hall, to talk of his son Benjamin ; and I propounded a match for him, and at last named my sister, which he embraces heartily ; and, full of it, did go with him to London to the 'Change ; and there, with Sir W. Warren, who very wisely did shew me that my matching my sister with Mr. Gauden would undo me in all my places, everybody suspecting me in all I do ; and I shall neither be able to serve him, nor free myself from imputation of being of his faction, while I am placed for his severest check. I was convinced that it would be for neither of our interests to make this alliance. To Westminster Hall, where I purposely took my wife well-dressed into the Hall to see and be seen ; and, among others, met Howlet's daughter, who is newly married, and is she I call wife, and one I love mightily.

4th. Home, and, being washing-day, dined upon cold meat.

5th. At Viner's was shown the silver plates made for Captain Cocke, to present to my Lord Brouncker ; and I chose a dozen of the same weight to be bespoke for myself, which he told me yesterday he would give me. The plague is, to our great grief, encreased nine this week, though decreased a few in the total. And this encrease runs through many parishes, which makes us much fear the next year.

6th. Up mighty betimes upon my wife's going this day towards Brampton. I could not go, but W. Hewer hath leave from me to go the whole day's journey with her. Met by agreement with Sir Stephen Fox and Mr. [William] Ashburnbam, and discoursed the business of our Excise tallys ; the former being Treasurer of the Guards, and the other Cofferer of the King's household. This day great news of the Swedes declaring for us against the Dutch, and, so far as that, I believe it.

7th. To Hales's, and there find Mrs. Pierce. She had done sitting the first time, and indeed her face is mighty like at first dash. About ten of the clock, W. Hewer comes to me to tell me that he left my wife well this morning at Bugden, which was great riding, and brings me a letter from her.

8th. (Lord's day.) To the Duke of York, where we all met to hear the debate between Sir Thomas Allen and Mr. Wayth, the former complaining of the latter's ill usage of him at the late pay of his ship; but a very sorry, poor occasion he had for it. The Duke did determine it with great judgment, chiding both, but encouraging Wayth to continue to be a check to all captains in anything to the King's right. And, indeed, I never did see the Duke do any thing more in order, nor with more judgement than he did pass the verdict in this business. The Court full this morning of the news of Tom Cheffin's[1] death, the King's closet-keeper. He was as well last night as ever, playing at tables in the house, and not very ill this morning at six o'clock, yet dead before seven: they think, of an imposthume in his breast. But it looks fearfully among people now-a-days, the plague, as we hear, encreasing everywhere again. To the Chapel, but could not get in to hear well. But I had the pleasure, once in my life, to see an Archbishop,[2] this was of York, in a pulpit. Then at a loss how to get home to dinner, having promised to carry Mrs. Hunt thither. At last, got my Lord Hinchingbroke's coach, he staying at Court; and so took her up to Axe-yard, and home and dined; and good discourse of the old matters of the Protector and his family, she having a relation to them. The Protector[3] lives in France: spends about 500l. per annum. To St. James's Chapel, thinking to have heard a Jesuit preach, but come too late.

---

[1] Sir E. Walker, Garter King-at-Arms, in 1664, gave a grant of arms gratis to Thomas Chiffinch, one of the pages of his Majesty's Bedchamber, Keeper of his Private Closet, and Comptroller of the Excise. His brother William (whose daughter Barbara married Edward Villiers, first Earl of Jersey) appears to have succeeded to the two first-named appointments, and became a great favourite with the King, whom he survived. He died 6th April, 1666, and was buried on the 10th, in Westminster Abbey. There is a portrait of William Chiffinch at Gorhambury.

[2] Richard Sterne, Bishop of Carlisle, elected Archbishop of York, 1664. Ob. 1683.   [3] Richard Cromwell.

9th. By coach to Mrs. Pierce's, and with her and Knipp, and Mrs. Pierce's boy and girl, abroad, thinking to have been merry at Chelsey; but being come almost to the house by coach near the water-side, a house alone—I think the Swan, a gentleman walking by called to us to tell us that the house was shut up of the sickness. So we, with great affright, turned back, being holden to the gentleman; and went away, I, for my part, in great disorder, for Kensington.

10th. To the office, and again all the afternoon, the first time of our resolution to sit both forenoons and afternoons.

11th. My people to work about setting rails upon the leads of my wife's closet, a thing I have long designed. To Hales's, where there was nothing found to be done more to my picture,[1] but the musique, which now pleases me mightily, it being painted true. To Gresham College, where a great deal of do and formality in choosing of the Council and officers. I had three votes to be of the Council, who am but a stranger, nor expected any, my Lord Brouncker being confirmed President.

12th. My Lady Pen comes to me, and takes me into her house, where I find her daughter and a pretty lady of her acquaintance, one Mrs. Lowther,[2] sister, I suppose, of her servant Lowther's, with whom I, notwithstanding all my resolution to follow business close this afternoon, did stay talking, and playing the fool almost all the afternoon. Mrs. Margaret Pen grows mighty homely, and looks old. Thence to the office, where my Lord Brouncker come: and he and I had a little fray, he being, I find, a very peevish man, if he be denied what he expects, and very simple in his arguments.

13th. Called up by my wife's brother, for whom I have got a commission from the Duke of York for Muster-Master of one of the divisions, of which Harman[1] is Rere Admirall. To

---

[1] A picture without any name, but described in the catalogue as "*Portrait of a Musician*," was bought by Mr. Peter Cunningham at the sale of the Cockerell Collection, in May, 1845, who supposes it to be the painting here mentioned, in which the music was introduced. The person represented seems, however, to have been much older than our journalist; nor do the features accord with the recognised likenesses of him. The Editor's impression is, that the picture is the copy of the portrait of Mr. Hill, the merchant, Pepys's *musical* friend, mentioned 16th May following.

[2] Margaret Lowther, subsequently married to John Holmes, afterwards knighted

the Queen's chapel—it being Good-Friday—where people were all upon their knees very silent; but, it seems, no masse this day. To Mr. Hales's, where he and I presently resolved of going to White Hall, to spend an hour in the galleries there, among the pictures, and we did so, to my extraordinary satisfaction, he shewing me the difference in the paintings, and I do not find so many good things as I thought there was.

15th. (Lord's day.) Walked into the Park to the Queen's chapel, and there heard a good deal of their mass, and some of their musique, which is not so contemptible, I think, as our people would make it, it pleasing me very well; and, indeed, better than the anthem I heard afterwards at White Hall, at my coming back. I staid till the King went down to receive the Sacrament, and stood in his closet with a great many others, and there saw him receive it, which I never did see the manner of before. But I do see very little difference between the degree of the ceremonies used by our people in the administration thereof, and that in the Roman church, saving that, methought, our Chapel was not so fine, nor the manner of doing it so glorious, as it was in the Queen's chapel. Thence walked to Mr. Pierce's, and there dined: very good company and good discourse, they being able to tell me all the businesses of the Court; the amours and the mad doings that are there: how for certain Mrs. Stewart is become the King's mistress; and that the King hath many bastard children that are known and owned, besides the Duke of Monmouth. To the Park, and thence home to Mr. Pierce again; and he being gone forth, she, and I, and the children, out by coach to Kensington, to where we were the other day, and, with great pleasure, staid till night; and were mighty late getting home, the horses tiring and stopping. The horses at Ludgate Hill made a final stop; so there I lighted, and with a link walked home.

16th. Comes Mrs. Mercer, and fair Mrs. Turner, a neighbour of hers, to visit me. I staid a great while with them, being taken with this pretty woman, though a mighty silly, affected, citizen woman she is.

17th. To the office, but, Lord! what a conflict I had with myself, my heart tempting me 1000 times to go abroad about some pleasure or other, notwithstanding the weather foul. However, I did not budge; and, to my great content, did a great deal of business.

18th. To Mr. Lilly's, the painter's; and there saw the heads, some finished, and all begun, of the Flaggmen[1] in the late great fight with the Duke of York against the Dutch. The Duke of York hath them done to hang in his chamber, and very finely they are done indeed. Here are the Prince's, Sir G. Ascue's, Sir Thomas Teddiman's,[2] Sir Christopher Mings's, Sir Joseph Jordan's, Sir William Barkeley's, Sir Thomas Allen's,[3] and Captain Harman's, as also the Duke of Albemarle's; and will be my Lord Sandwich's, Sir W. Pen's, and Sir Jeremy Smith's.[4] I was very well satisfied with this sight, and other good pictures hanging in the house. To the Exchange, and there did see great plenty of fine prints; but did buy only a print of an old pillar in Rome made for a Naval triumph,[5] which, for the antiquity of the shape of the ships, I buy and keep.[6]

21st. I down to walk in the garden at Whitehall, it being a mighty hot and pleasant day; and there was the King, who, among others, talked to us a little; and, among other pretty things, he swore merrily that he believed the ketch that Sir W. Batten bought the last year at Colchester was of his own getting, it was so thick to its length. Another pleasant thing he said of Christopher Pett, commanding him that he will not alter his moulds upon any man's advice; "as," says he, "Commissioner Taylor, I fear, do of his New London, that he makes it differ, in hopes of mending the old London, built by him." "For," says he, "he finds that God hath put him

---

[1] Admirals.   [2] Then Vice-Admiral of the White.
[3] He became Comptroller of the Navy.
[4] Pepys omits Sir John Lawson. The pictures (Prince Rupert excepted) are now in the Naval Hall at Greenwich.
[5] The *columna rostrata* erected in the Forum to C. Duilius, who obtained a triumph for the first naval victory over the Carthaginians, B.C. 261. Part of the column was discovered in the ruins of the Forum near the Arch of Septimius, and transferred to the Capitol.
[6] This is the first mention of Pepys's buying prints.

into the right, and so will keep in it while he is in." "And," says the King, "I am sure it must be God put him in, for no art of his own ever could have done it;" for it seems he cannot give a good account of what he do as an artist. Thence with my Lord Brouncker in his coach to Hide Parke, the first time I have been there this year. There the King was; but I was sorry to see my Lady Castlemaine; for the mourning forcing all the ladies to go in black, with their hair plain and without spots, I find her to be a much more ordinary woman than ever I durst have thought she was; and, indeed, is not so pretty as Mrs. Stewart.

22d. (Lord's day.) Up, and put on my new black coate long down to my knees. To White Hall, where all in deep mourning for the Queen's mother. To the Queen's Chapel at St. James's, and there saw a little mayd baptized: many parts and words whereof are the same with that of our Liturgy, and little that is more ceremonious than ours. To Worcester House, and there staid and saw the Council up. Back to the Cockepitt, and there took my leave of the Duke of Albemarle, who is going to-morrow to sea. He seems mightily pleased with me, which I am glad of; but I do find infinitely my concernment in being careful to appear to the King and Duke to continue my care of his business, and to be found diligent as I used to be. Sat a great while with Will Joyce, who come to see me the first time since the plague, and find him the same impertinent, prating coxcomb that ever he was.

23d. To White Hall, where I had the opportunity to take leave of the Prince, and again of the Duke of Albemarle; and saw them kiss the King's hand and the Duke's; and much content, indeed, there seems to be in all people at their going to sea, and they promise themselves much good from them. This morning the House of Parliament do meet, only to adjourne again till winter. The plague, I hear, encreases in the town much, and exceedingly in the country everywhere. Bonfires in the street, for being St. George's day, and the King's Coronation, and the day of the Prince and Duke's going to sea.

24th. Comes Mr. Bland to me, the first time since his

coming from Tangier; and tells me, in short, how all things are out of order there, and like to be; and the place never likely to come to any thing while the soldiers govern all, and do not encourage trade.

25th. I to the office, where Mr. Prin come to meet about the Chest-business;[1] and till company come, did discourse with me a good while in the garden about the laws of England, telling me the main faults in them; and, among others, their obscurity through multitude of long statutes, which he is about to abstract out of all of a sort;[2] and, as he lives and Parliaments come, get them put into laws, and the other statutes repealed, and then it will be a short work to know the law. Having supped upon the leads, to bed. The plague, blessed be God! is decreased sixteen this week.

28th. My wife to her father's, to carry him some ruling work,[3] which I have advised her to let him do. It will get him some money. She was also to look after a necklace of pearl, which she is mighty busy about, I being contented to lay out 80l. in one for her. Balty took leave of us, going to sea, and upon very good terms, to be Muster-Master of a squadron, which will be worth 100l. this year to him, besides keeping him the benefit of his pay in the Guards.

29th. (Lord's day.) To Church, where Mr. Mills, a lazy sermon upon the Devil's having no right to anything in this world. To Mr. Evelyn's, where I walked in his garden till he come from Church, with great pleasure reading Ridly's Discourse,[4] all my way going and coming, upon the Civill and Ecclesiastical Law. He being come home, he and I walked together in the garden with mighty pleasure, he being a very ingenious man; and the more I know him, the more I love him. Weary to bed, after having my hair of my head cut shorter, even close to my skull, for coolness, it being mighty hot weather.

---

[1] At Chatham.

[2] Early in the session of 1852-3, Lord Cranworth, Lord High Chancellor, intimated the appointment of a Commission to prepare the way for a general *Code Victoria* to emulate the *Code Napoleon*.

[3] Apparently preparing paper for accounts.

[4] Sir Thomas Ridley, a Master in Chancery; ob. 1629. His work was first printed in 1607.

30th. I after dinner to even all my accounts of this month; and, bless God! I find myself, notwithstanding great expences of late; viz., 80*l.* now to pay for a necklace; near 40*l.* for a set of chairs and couch; near 40*l.* for my three pictures: yet I do gather, and am worth 5200*l.* My wife comes home by and by, and hath pitched upon a necklace with three rows, which is a very good one, and 80*l.* is the price. So ends this month with great layings-out. Good health and gettings, and advanced well in the whole of my estate, for which God make me thankful!

May 1st. At noon, my cozen Thomas Pepys did come to me, to consult about the business of his being a Justice of the Peace, which he is much against; and, among other reasons, tells me, as a confidant, that he is not free to exercise punishment according to the Act against Quakers and other people, for religion. Nor do he understand Latin, and so is not capable of the place as formerly, now all warrants do run in Latin. Nor he in Kent, though he be of Deptford parish, his house standing in Surry.[1] However, I did bring him to incline towards it, if he be pressed to take it. I do think it may be some repute to me to have my kinsman in Commission there, specially if he behave himself to content in the country. To Redriffe, reading a new French book my Lord Brouncker did give me to-day, "L'Histoire Amoureuse des Gaules,"[2] being a pretty libel against the amours of the Court of France. My wife tells me the ill news, that our Susan is sick, and gone to bed, with great pain in her head and back, which troubles us all.

2d. With Captain Cocke to my office, to consult about serving him in getting him some money, he being already tired of his slavery to my Lord Brouncker, and the charge it costs him, and gets no manner of courtesy from him for it.

3d. Up, and to send up and down for a nurse to take the girle home, and would have given anything. I offered, to the only one that we could get, 20*s.* per week, and we to find

---

[1] Hatcham, near New Cross, on the Deptford Road. A house there still preserves the name.

[2] This was the scandalous work by the Comte de Bussy Rabutin, which gave such just offence to his cousin, Madame de Sévigné, and procured him a long imprisonment in the Bastille.

clothes, and bedding, and physick, and would have given 30s., as demanded, but desired an hour or two's time. Sent for the girl's mother; she come, and undertakes to get her daughter a lodging and nurse at next door to her, though she dare not for the parish' sake, whose sexton her husband is, to have her into her own house.

4th. To Mr. Hales, to see what he had done to Mrs. Pierce's picture, and whatever he pretends, I do not think it will ever be so good a picture as my wife's. Thence home to dinner, and had a great fray with my wife about Browne's coming to teach her to paint, and sitting with me at table, which I will not yield to. I do thoroughly believe she means no hurt in it; but very angry we were, and I resolved all into my having my will done, without disputing, be the reason what it will; and so I will have it. This evening, being weary of my late idle courses, I bound myself to very strict rules till Whitsunday next.

5th. It being a very fine moonshine, my wife and Mercer come into the garden, and, my business being done, we sang till about twelve at night, with mighty pleasure to ourselves and neighbours, by their casements opening.

8th. Comes Mr. Downing, the anchor-smith, who had given me 50 pieces in gold the last month, to speak for him to Sir W. Coventry, for his being smith at Deptford; but, after I had got it granted to him, he finds himself not fit to go on with it, so lets it fall. I, therefore, in honour and conscience, took him home, and forced him to take the money again, and glad to have given him so much cause to speak well of me.

9th. To White Hall, and heard the Duke commend Deane's ship, "The Rupert," before "The Defyance," built by Castle, in hearing of Sir W. Batten, which pleased me mightily. To Pierce's, where I find Knipp. Thence with them to Cornhill, to call and choose a chimneypiece for Pierce's closet. My wife mightily vexed at my being abroad with these women; and, when they were gone, called them I know not what, which vexed me, having been so innocent with them.

10th. Going out towards Hackney by coach for the ayre, the silly coachman carries us to Shoreditch, which way so pleasant a piece of simplicity in him and us, that made us mighty merry.

11th To the 'Change, to speak with Captain Cocke, among other things, about the getting of the silver plates[1] of him, which he promises to do; but in discourse he tells me that I should beware of my fellow-officers; and by name told me that my Lord Brouncker should say in his hearing, before Sir W. Batten, of me, that he could undo the man, if he would; wherein I think he is a foole; but, however, it is requisite I be prepared against the man's friendship. Thence home to dinner alone, my wife being abroad. After dinner to the setting some things in order, in my dining-room; and by and by comes my wife home, and Mrs. Pierce with her, so I lost most of this afternoon with them, and in the evening abroad with them—our long tour, by coach, to Hackney, so to Kingsland, and then to Islington, there entertaining them by candlelight very well, and so home with her, set her down, and so home, and to bed.

12th. I find my wife troubled at my checking her last night in a coach, in her long stories out of Grand Cyrus, which she would tell, though nothing to the purpose, nor in any good manner.[2] This she took unkindly, and I think I was to blame indeed; but she do find with reason, that, in the company of Pierce, Knipp, or other women that I love, I do not value her, or mind her as I ought. However, very good friends by and by. Met Sir G. Downing on White Hall bridge, and there walked half an hour, talking of the success of the late new Act; and, indeed, it is very much, that hath stood really in the room of 800,000*l.*,[3] now since

---

[1] See 5th April, *ante*.

[2] Sir Walter Scott observes, in his *Life of Dryden*, that the romances of Calprenede and Scuderi, those ponderous and unmerciful folios, now consigned to oblivion, were, in their day, not only universally read and admired, but supposed to furnish the most perfect models of gallantry and heroism. Dr. Johnson read them all. "I have," says Mrs. Chapone, 'and yet I am still alive, dragged through 'Le Grand Cyrus,' in twelve huge volumes; 'Cleopatra,' in eight or ten; 'Ibrahim,' 'Clelie,' and some others, whose names, as well as all the rest of them, I have forgotten."— *Letters to Mrs. Carter*. No wonder that Pepys sat on thorns, when his wife began to recite "Le Grand Cyrus," in the coach "and trembled at the impending tale."

[3] There appears to be some error in these figures. Pepys's financial details are, in fact, seldom to be relied on.

Christmas, being itself but 1,250,000*l.* And so I do really take it to be a very considerable thing done by him; for the beginning, end, and every part of it, is to be imputed to him. This day come home again my little girle Susan, her sickness proving an ague, and she had a fit soon almost as she come home. The fleete is not yet gone from the Nore. The plague encreases in many places, and is 53 this week with us.

13th. (Lord's day.) To Westminster, and into St. Margett's[1] Church, where I heard a young man play the fool upon the doctrine of Purgatory.

14th. To the Exchequer, and there met Sir G. Downing, and my Lord of Oxford coming by, also took him, and shewed him his whole method of keeping his books, and everything of it, which indeed is very pretty. In the evening, out with my wife and my aunt Wight, to take the ayre, and happened to have a pleasant race between our hackney-coach and a gentleman's.

15th. I to my Lord Crewe's, who is very lately come to town, and he talked for half an hour of the business of the war, wherein he is very doubtful, from our want of money, that we shall fail; and I do concur with him therein. After some little discourse of ordinary matters, I away to Sir Philip Warwick's again, and he was come in, and gone out to my Lord Treasurer's; whither I followed him, and there my business was, to be told that my Lord Treasurer hath got 10,000*l.* for us in the Navy, to answer great necessities, which I did thank him for; but the sum is not considerable. The five brothers Houblons came, and Mr. Hill, to my house; and here they were till about eleven at night.

16th. To the Exchequer, where the lazy rogues have not yet done my tallys, which vexes me. To Mr. Hales, and paid him for my picture, and Mr. Hill's, for the first 14*l.* for the picture, and 25*s.* for the frame, and for the other 7*l.* for the picture, it being a copy of his only, and 5*s.* for the frame: in all, 22*l.* 10*s.* I am very well satisfied in my pictures, and so took them in another coach home : with great pleasure my wife and I hung them.

19th. Mr. Deane and I did discourse about his ship Rupert,

built by him, which succeeds so well as he hath got great
honour by it, and I some, by recommending him; the King,
Duke, and everybody, saying it is the best ship that was ever
built. And then he fell to explain to me his manner of
casting the draught of water which a ship will draw beforehand: which is a secret the King and all admire in him; and
he is the first that hath come to any certainty beforehand, of
foretelling the draught of water of a ship before she be
launched.

20th. (Lord's day.) With my wife to church. At noon
dined mighty nobly, ourselves alone. After dinner, my wife
and Mercer by coach to Greenwich, to be gossip to Mrs.
Daniel's child. I discoursed awhile with Mr. Yeabsly, whom
I met and took up in my coach with me, and who hath this
day presented my Lord Ashly with 100*l.* to bespeak his
friendship to him in his accounts now before us: and my
Lord hath received it, and so I believe is as bad, as to bribes,
as what the world says of him. My wife much pleased with
the reception she had, and she was god-mother, and did hold
the child at the Font, and it is called John.

21st. I away, in some haste, to my Lord Ashly, where it
is stupendous to see how favourably, and yet closely, my Lord
Ashly carries himself to Mr. Yeabsly in his business, so as I
think we shall do his business for him in very good manner.
But it is a most extraordinary thing to observe, and that
which I would not but have had the observation of, for a
great deal of money.

23d. Towards White Hall, calling in my way on my Lord
Bellasses, where I come to his bed-side, and he did give me
a full and long account of his matters, how he kept them at
Tangier. Declares himself fully satisfied with my care:
seems cunningly to argue for encreasing the number of men
there. Told me the whole story of his gains by the Turky
prizes, which he owns he hath got about 5000*l.* by. Promised me the same profits Povy was to have had; and, in
fine, I find him a pretty subtle man; and so I left him.
Staid at Sir G. Carteret's chamber till the Council rose, and
then he and I, by agreement this morning, went forth in his

coach by Tiburne, to the Park; discoursing of the state of
the Navy as to money, and the state of the kingdom too,
how ill able to raise more: and of our office, as to the condition of the officers; he giving me caution as to myself,
that there are those that are my enemies as well as his,
and by name by Lord Brouncker, who hath said some odd
speeches against me. So that he advises me to stand on
my guard; which I shall do, and, unless my too-much ad-
diction to pleasure undo me, will be acute enough for any
of them. My right eye sore, and full of humour of late,
I think, by my late change of my brewer, and having of
8s. beer.

24th. Mr. Shepley is newly come out of the country, and
come to see us. He left all well there; but I perceive
under some discontent in my Lord's behalfe, thinking that
he is under disgrace with the King; but he is not so, as Sir
G. Carteret assures me.

25th. Captain Cocke tells me my silver plates are ready
for me, and shall be sent me speedily; and proposes another
proposition of serving us with a thousand tons of hemp, and
tells me it shall bring me 500*l.* if the bargain go forward,
which is a good word. A gentleman arrived here this day,
Mr. Brown, of St. Maloes, among other things, tells me the
meaning of the setting out of dogs every night out of the town
walls, which are said to secure the city; but it is not so, but
only to secure the anchors, cables, and ships that lie dry,
which might otherwise in the night be liable to be robbed.
And these dogs are set out every night, and called together
in, every morning, by a man with a horne, and they go in very
orderly.

27th. (Lord's day.) To church, my wife with me. Home
to dinner, whither come my uncle Wight, and aunt and uncle
Norbury.

28th. Mr. Lovett and his wife come to see us. They are
a pretty couple, and she a fine bred woman. They dined
with us, and Browne, the painter, and she plays finely on the
lute. My wife and I were well pleased with her company.
To bed, my wife telling me where she hath been to-day with

my aunt Wight, and seen Mrs. Margaret Wight, and says that she is one of the beautifullest women that ever she saw in her life — the most excellent nose and mouth. They have been also to see pretty Mrs. Batelier, and conclude her to be a prettier woman than Mrs. Pierce, whom my wife led my aunt to see also this day.

29th. King's birth-day, and Restoration day. Waked with the ringing of bells all over the town: so up before five o'clock, and to the office. At noon I did, upon a small invitation of Sir W. Pen's, go and dine with Sir W. Coventry at his office, where very good cheer, and many pleasant stories of Sir W. Coventry. After dinner, to the Victualling Office; and there, beyond belief, did acquit myself very well to full content; so that, beyond expectation, I got over that second rub in this business; and if ever I fall on it again, I deserve to be undone. My wife comes to me, to tell me, that if I would see the handsomest woman in England, I shall come home presently; and who should it be but the pretty lady of our parish, that did heretofore sit on the other side of our church, over against our gallery, that is since married — she with Mrs. Anne Jones, one of this parish, that dances finely. And so I home; and indeed she is a pretty black woman — her name Mrs. Horsely. But, Lord! to see how my nature could not refrain from the temptation; but I must invite them to go to Foxhall, to Spring Gardens, though I had freshly received minutes of a great deal of extraordinary business. However, I sent them before with Creed, and I did some of my business; and so after them, and find them there, in an arbour, and had met with Mrs. Pierce, and some company with her. So here I spent 20s. upon them, and were pretty merry. Among other things, had a fellow that imitated all manner of birds, and dogs, and hogs, with his voice, which was mighty pleasant. Staid here till night: then set Mrs. Pierce in at the New Exchange; and ourselves took coach, and so set Mrs. Horsely home, and then home ourselves, but with great trouble in the streets, by bonfires, it being the King's birth-day and day of Restoration; but, Lord! to see the difference how many there were on the

other side, and so few on ours, the City side of the Temple,
would make one wonder the difference between the temper of
one sort of people and the other : and the difference among all
between what they do now, and what it was the night when
Monk come into the City. Such a night as that I never
think to see again, nor think it can be.

30th. I find the Duke gone out with the King to-day on
hunting. Word is brought me that my father and my sister
are come ; he, poor man, looks very well, and hath rode up
this journey on horseback very well, only his eyesight and
hearing is very bad. I staid and dined with them, my wife
being gone by coach to Barnett, with W. Hewer and Mercer,
to meet them, and they did come Ware way. To Lord
Ashly, who, it is strange to see, how prettily he dissembles
his favour to Yeabsly's business, which none in the world
could mistrust, only I, that am privy to his being bribed.
My wife tells me, that Balty's wife is brought to bed, by
some fall, or fit, before her time, of a great child but dead.
If the woman do well, we have no reason to be sorry, because
his staying a little longer without a child will be better for
him and her.

31st. Saw all my family up, and my father and sister, who
is a pretty good-bodied woman, and not over thicke, as I
thought she would have been, but full of freckles, and not
handsome in face. To dinner with my father and sister and
family, mighty pleasant all of us ; and among other things,
with a sparrow that our Mercer hath brought up now for
three weeks, which is so tame, that it flies up and down, and
upon the table, and eats and pecks, and do everything so
pleasantly, that we are mightily pleased with it. A public,
Fast-day, appointed to pray for the good success of the fleete.
But it is a pretty thing to consider how little a matter they
make of this keeping of a fast, that it was not so much as
declared time enough to be read in the churches, the last
Sunday ; but ordered by proclamation since : I suppose upon
some sudden news of the Dutch being come out. Thus ends
this month, with my mind oppressed by my defect in my
duty of the Victualling, which lies upon me as a burden, till

I get myself into a better posture therein. As to public business; by late tidings of the French fleete being come to Rochelle, how true, though, I know not, our fleete is divided; Prince Rupert being gone with about thirty ships to the Westward, as is conceived, to meet the French, to hinder their coming to join with the Dutch. My Lord Duke of Albemarle lies in the Downes with the rest, and intends presently to sail to the Gunfleete.

June 1st. Dined at aunt Wight's. Here dined the fair Mrs. Margaret Wight, who is a very fine lady, but the cast of her eye, got only by an ill habit, do her much wrong, and her hands are bad; but she hath the face of a noble Roman lady. My uncle and Wooly and I out into their yard, to talk about what may be done hereafter to all our profits, by prize-goods, which did give us reason to lament the loss of the opportunity of the last year, which, if we were as wise as we are now, and at the peaceable end of all those troubles that we met with, all might have been such a hit as will never come again in this age.

2d. Up, and to the office, where certain news is brought us of a letter come to the King this morning from the Duke of Albemarle, dated yesterday at eleven o'clock, as they were sailing to the Gunfleete, that they were in sight of the Dutch fleete, and were fitting themselves to fight them; so that they are, ere this, certainly engaged: besides, several do averr that they heard the guns yesterday in the afternoon. This put us at the Board into a tosse. Presently come orders for our sending away to the fleete a recruit of 200 soldiers. So I rose from the table, and to the Victualling-office, and thence upon the river among several vessels, to consider of the sending them away; and, lastly, down to Greenwich, and there appointed two yachts to be ready for them; and did order the soldiers to march to Blackewall. Having set all things in order against the next flood, I went on shore with Captain Erwin at Greenwich, and into the Parke, and there we could hear the guns from the fleete most plainly. We walked to the water-side, and there, seeing the King and Duke come down in their barge to Greenwich-

house, I to them, and did give them an account what I was
doing. They went up to the Park to hear the guns of the
fleete go off. All our hopes now are, that Prince Rupert with
his fleete is coming back, and will be with the fleete this even:
a message being sent to him for that purpose, on Wednesday
last; and a return is come from him this morning, that he
did intend to sail from St. Ellen's point about four in the
afternoon yesterday; which gives us great hopes, the wind
being very fair, that he is with them this even, and the fresh
going off of the guns makes us believe the same. Down to
Blackewall, and there saw the soldiers, who were by this time
gotten most of them drunk, shipped off. But, Lord! to see
how the poor fellows kissed their wives and sweethearts in
that simple manner at their going off, and shouted, and let
off their guns, was strange sport. In the evening come up
the river the Catharine yacht, Captain Fazeby, who hath
brought over my Lord of Aylesbury,[1] and Sir Thomas
Liddall,[2] with a very pretty daughter, and in a pretty travel-
ling-dress, from Flanders, who saw the Dutch fleete on Thursday, and ran from them; but from that hour to this hath not
heard one gun, nor any news of any fight. Having put the
soldiers on board, I home.

3d. (Lord's day; Whit-sunday.) Up, and by water to
White Hall, and there met with Mr. Coventry, who tells me
the only news from the fleete is brought by Captain Elliott,
of the Portland, which, by being run on board by the
Guernsey, was disabled from staying abroad; so is come in to
Aldbrough. That he saw one of the Dutch great ships blown
up, and three on fire. That they begun to fight on Friday;
and, at his coming into port, he could make another ship of
the King's coming in, which he judged to be the Rupert:
that he knows of no other hurt to our ships. With this
good news, I home by water again, and to church in the
sermon-time, and with great joy told it my fellows in the

---

[1] Robert Bruce, second Earl of Elgin and first Earl of Ailesbury, who died in
1685.

[2] Of Ravensworth Castle, Durham, succeeded his grandfather, the first Baronet,
1650. He had three daughters. Ob. 1697.

pew. After church time, to the Exchange, as full of people, and hath been all this noon, as of any other day, only for news. To White Hall, and there met with this bad news farther, that the Prince come to Dover but at ten o'clock last night, and there heard nothing of a fight; so that we are defeated of all our hopes of his help to the fleete. It is also reported by some Victuallers, that the Duke of Albemarle and Holmes their flags were shot down, and both fain to come to anchor to renew their rigging and sails. A letter is also come this afternoon, from Harman in the Henery; which states, that she was taken by Elliott for the Rupert; that being fallen into the body of the Dutch fleete, he made his way through them, was set on by three fire-ships, one after another, got two of them off, and disabled the third; was set on fire himself; upon which many of his men leapt into the sea and perished; among others, the parson first. Have lost above 100 men, and a good many women (God knows what is become of Balty), and at last quenched his own fire, and got to Aldbrough; being, as all say, the greatest hazard that ever any ship escaped, and so bravely managed by him. The mast of the third fire-ship fell into their ship on fire, and hurt Harman's leg, which makes him lame now, but not dangerous. I to Sir G. Carteret, who told me there hath been great bad management in all this; that the King's orders that went on Friday for calling back the Prince were sent but by the ordinary post on Wednesday; and come to the Prince his hands but on Friday; and then, instead of sailing presently, he stays till four in the evening. And that which is worst of all, the Hampshire, laden with merchants' money, come from the Streights, set out with or but just before the fleete, and was in the Downes by five in the clock yesterday morning; and the Prince with his fleete come to Dover but at ten of the clock at night. This is hard to answer, if it be true. This puts great astonishment into the King, and Duke, and Court, every body being out of countenance. Home by the 'Change, which is full of people still, and all talk highly of the failure of the Prince, in not making more haste after his instructions did come, and of our managements here in not giving it sooner, and with more care, and oftener.

4th. To White Hall, where, when we come, we find the Duke at St. James's, whither he is lately gone to lodge. So walking through the Park, we saw hundreds of people listening at the Gravel-pits, and to and again in the Park, to hear the guns. I saw a letter, dated last night, from Strowd, Governor of Dover Castle, which says that the Prince come thither the night before with his fleete; but that for the guns which we writ that we heard, it is only a mistake for thunder; and, so far as to yesterday, it is a miraculous thing that we all Friday, and Saturday, and yesterday, did hear every where most plainly the guns go off, and yet at Deale and Dover, to last night, they did not hear one word of a fight, nor think they heard one gun. This, added to what I have set down before, the other day, about the Catharine, makes room for a great dispute in philosophy, how we should hear it and they not, the same wind that brought it to us being the same that should bring it to them: but so it is. Major Halsey, however, who was sent down on purpose to hear the news, did bring news this morning that he did see the Prince and his fleete at nine of the clock yesterday morning, four or five leagues to sea behind the Goodwin, so that, by the hearing of the guns this morning, we conclude he is come to the fleete. After waiting upon the Duke with Sir W. Pen, who was commanded to go to-night, by water, down to Harwich, to dispatch away all the ships he can, I home; where no sooner come, but news is brought me of a couple of men come to speak with me from the fleete; so I down, and who should it be but Mr. Daniel, all muffled up, and his face as black as the chimney, and covered with dirt, pitch, and tar, and powder, and muffled with dirty clouts, and his right eye stopped with oakum. He is come last night, at five o'clock, from the fleete, with a comrade of his that hath endangered another eye. They were set on shore at Harwich this morning, and at two o'clock, in a catch, with about twenty more wounded men from the Royall Charles. They being able to ride, took post about three this morning, and were here between eleven and twelve. I went presently into the coach with them, and carried them to Somerset-House stairs, and there took water, all the world gazing upon us, and concluding it to be news from the fleete, and every body's face appeared expecting of news, to the Privy-stairs, and left them at Mr. Coventry's lodging, he, though, not being there; and so I into the Park to the King, and told him my Lord Generall was well the last night at five o'clock, and the Prince come with his fleete and joyned with his about seven. The King was mightily pleased with this news, and so took me by the hand and talked a little of it, I giving him the best account I could; and then he bid me to fetch the two seamen to him, he walking into the house. So I went and fetched the seamen into the Vane Room to him, and there he heard the whole account.

THE FIGHT.

How we found the Dutch fleete at anchor on Friday, half seas over, between Dunkirke and Ostend, and made them let slip their anchors. They about ninety, and we less than sixty. We fought them, and put them to the run, till they met with about sixteen sail of fresh ships, and so bore up again. The fight continued till night, and then again the next morning, from five till seven at night. And so, too, yesterday morning they begun again, and continued till about four o'clock, they chasing us for the most part of Saturday, and yesterday we flying from them. The Duke himself, and then those people who were put into the catch, by and by spied the Prince's fleete coming, upon which De Ruyter called a little council, being in chase at this time of us, and thereupon their fleete divided into two squadrons; forty in one, and about thirty in the other, the fleete being at first about ninety, but, by one accident or other, supposed to be lessened to about seventy; the bigger to follow the Duke, the less to meet the Prince. But the Prince come up with the Generall's fleete, and the Dutch come together again, and bore towards their own coast, and we with them; and now what the consequence of this day will be, we know not. The Duke was forced to come to anchor on Friday, having lost his sails and rigging. No particular person spoken of to be hurt but Sir W. Clerke, who hath lost his leg, and bore it bravely. The Duke himself had a little hurt in his thigh, but signified little. The King did pull out of his pocket about twenty pieces in gold, and did give it Daniel for himself and his companion; and so parted, mightily pleased with the account he did give him of the fight, and the success it ended with, of the Prince's coming, though it seems the Duke did give way again and again. The King did give order for care to be had of Mr. Daniel and his companion; and so we parted from him, and then met the Duke of York, and gave him the same account: and so broke up, and I left them going to the surgeon's. So home, about four o'clock, to dinner, and was followed by several people to be told the news, and good news it is. God send we may hear a good issue of this day's business! To the Crown, behind the 'Change, and there supped at the club with my Lord Brouncker, Sir G. Ent and others of Gresham College; and all our discourse is of this fight at sea, and all are doubtful of the success, and conclude all had been lost if the Prince had not come in, they having chased us the greatest part of Saturday and Sunday. Thence with my Lord Brouncker and Creed by coach to White Hall, where fresh letters are come from Harwich, where the Gloucester, Captain Clerke, is come in, and says that, on Sunday night, upon the coming in of the Prince, the Duke did fly; but all this day they have been fighting; therefore they did face again, to be sure. Captain Bacon of the Bristoll is killed. They cry up Jennings of the Ruby, and Saunders of the Sweepstakes. They condemn mightily Sir Thomas Teddiman for a coward, but with what reason time must show.

5th. At noon, though I should have dined with my Lord Mayor[1] and Aldermen at an entertainment of Commissioner Taylor's, yet, it being a time of expectation of the success of the fleete, I did not go. No manner of news this day, but of the Rainbow's being put in from the fleete, maimed as the other ships are.

---

[1] Sir Thomas Bludworth.

33 *

6th. By water to St. James's, it being a monthly fast-day
for the plague. There we all met, and did our business as
usual with the Duke. By and by walking a little further,
Sir Philip Frowde[1] did meet the Duke with an express to Sir
W. Coventry, who was by, from Captain Taylor, the Storekeeper at Harwich, being the narration of Captain Hayward
of the Dunkirke; who gives a very serious account, how upon
Monday the two fleetes fought all day, till seven at night, and
then the whole fleete of Dutch did betake themselves to a very
plain flight, and never looked back again. That Sir Christopher Mings is wounded in the leg; that the Generall is
well. That it is conceived reasonably, that of all the Dutch
fleete, which, with what recruits they had, come to one hundred sail, there is not above fifty got home: and of them, few,
if any, of their flags. And that little Captain Bell, in one of
the fire-ships, did at the end of the day fire a ship of 70 guns.
We were also so overtaken with this good news, that the Duke
ran with it to the King, who was gone to chapel, and there all
the Court was in a hubbub, being rejoiced over head and ears
in this good news. Away I go by coach to the new Exchange,
and there did spread this good news a little, though I find it
had broke out before. And so home to our own church, it
being the common Fast-day, and it was just before sermon;
but, Lord! how all the people in the church stared upon me
to see me whisper to Sir John Minnes and my Lady Pen.
Anon I saw people stirring and whispering below, and by and
by comes up the sexton from my Lady Ford to tell me the
news, which I had brought, being now sent into the church
by Sir W. Batten in writing, and passed from pew to pew.
But that which pleased me as much as the news, was, to have
the fair Mrs. Middleton at our church, who indeed is a very
beautiful lady. My father to Hales's, where my father is to
begin to sit to-day for his picture, which I have a desire to
have. At home, drawing up my vows for the rest of the year,
to Christmas; but, Lord! to see in what a condition of hap-

---

[1] A loyal officer in the army of Charles I., afterwards Secretary to Anne Hyde,
Duchess of York. His grandson, of the same name, was author of some plays
and poems, and died in 1738.

piness I am, if I would but keep myself so; but my love of pleasure is such, that my very soul is angry with itself for its vanity in so doing. Home, and my father and wife not coming in, I proceeded with my coach to take a little ayre as far as Bow all alone, and there turned back; but, before I got home, the bonfires were lighted all the town over, and I going through Crouched Friars, seeing Mercer at her mother's gate, stopped, and light, and into her mother's, the first time I ever was there, and find all my people, father and all, at a very fine supper at W. Hewer's lodging, very neatly, and to my great pleasure. After supper, into his chamber, which is mighty fine, with pictures and everything else, very curious. Thence to the gate, with all the women about me, and Mrs. Mercer's son had provided a great many serpents, and so I made the women all fire some serpents. By and by comes in our fair neighbour, Mrs. Turner, and two neighbours' daughters, Mrs. Tite — the eldest of which, a long red-nosed silly jade; the other, a pretty black girl, and the merriest sprightly jade that ever I saw. Idled away the whole night, till twelve at night, at the bonfire in the streets. Some of the people thereabouts going about with musquets, and did give me two or three vollies of their musquets, I giving them a crown to drink; and so home. Mightily pleased with this happy day's news, and the more, because confirmed by Sir Daniel Harvy,[1] who was in the whole fight with the Generall, and tells me that there appear but thirty-six in all of the Dutch fleete left at the end of the voyage when they run home. The joy of the City was this night exceeding great.

7th. Up betimes, and to my office about business, Sir W. Coventry having sent me word that he is gone down to the fleete to see how matters stand, and to be back again speedily; and with the same expectation of congratulating ourselves with the victory that I had yesterday. But my Lord Brouncker and Sir T. H.[2] that come from Court, tell me the contrary news, which astonishes me: that is to say, that we are beaten,

---

[1] Ranger of Richmond Park. He was brother-in-law to the Edward Montagu killed at Bergen.

[2] Sir Thomas Harvey.

lost many ships and good commanders; have not taken one
ship of the enemy's; and so can only report ourselves a
victory; nor is it certain that we were left masters of the
field.　But, above all, that the Prince run on shore upon the
Galloper, and there stuck; was endeavoured to be fetched off
by the Dutch, but could not; and so they burned her; and Sir
G. Ascue is taken prisoner, and carried into Holland.　Thi
news do much trouble me, and the thoughts of the ill consequences of it, and the pride and presumption that brought
us to it.　At noon to the 'Change, and there find the discourse
of town, and their countenances much changed; but yet not
very plain.　By and by comes Mr. Wayth to me; and discoursing of our ill success, he tells me plainly, from Captain
Page's own mouth, who hath lost his arm in the fight, that
the Dutch did pursue us two hours before they left us, and
then they suffered us to go on homewards, and they retreated
towards their coast: which is very sad news.　The Duke much
damped in his discourse, touching the late fight, and all the
Court talk sadly of it.　The Duke did give me several letters
he had received from the fleete, and Sir W. Coventry and Sir
W. Pen, who are gone down thither, for me to pick out some
works to be done for the setting out the fleete again; and so
I took them home with me, and was drawing out an abstract
of them till midnight.　And, as to news, I do find great
reason to think that we are beaten in every respect, and that
we are the losers.　The Prince upon the Galloper, where both
the Royall Charles and Royall Catharine had come twice
aground, but got off.　The Essex carried into Holland; the
Swiftsure missing, Sir W. Barkeley,[1] ever since the beginning
of the fight.　Captains Bacon, Tearne, Wood, Mootham,
Whitty, and Coppin, slayne.　The Duke of Albemarle writes,
that he never fought with worse officers in his life, not above
twenty of them behaving themselves like men.　Sir William
Clerke lost his leg; and in two days died.　The Loyall George,
Seven Oakes, and Swiftsure, are still missing, and have never, as
the Generall writes himself, engaged with them.　It was as great

---

[1] Governor of Portsmouth; one of the younger brothers of the Earl of
Falmouth.

an alteration to find myself required to write a sad letter instead of a triumphant one, to my Lady Sandwich this night,
as ever on any occasion I had in my life.

8th. To my very great joy, I find Balty come home without
any hurt, after the utmost imaginable danger he hath gone
through in the Henery, being upon the quarter-deck with
Harman all the time ; and for which service, Harman I heard
this day commended most seriously and most eminently by
the Duke of York.   As also the Duke did do most utmost
right to Sir Thomas Teddiman, of whom a scandal was raised,
but without cause, he having behaved himself most eminently
brave all the whole fight, and to extraordinary great service
and purpose, having given Trump himself such a broadside as
was hardly ever given to any ship.   Mings is shot through
the face, and into the shoulder, where the bullet is lodged.
Young Holmes[1] is also ill wounded, and Atber in the Rupert.
Balty tells me the case of the Henery ; and it was, indeed,
most extraordinary sad and desperate.   After dinner, Balty
and I to my office, and there talked a great deal of this fight ;
and I am mightily pleased in him, and have great content in,
and hopes of, his doing well.   Thence out to White Hall to a
Committee for Tangier, but it met not.   But, Lord ! to see
how melancholy the Court is, under the thoughts of this last
overthrow, for so it is, instead of a victory, so much and so
unreasonably expected.   We hear the Swiftsure, Sir W.
Barkeley, is come in safe to the Nore, after her being absent
ever since the beginning of the fight, wherein she did not
appear at all from beginning to end.

9th. The Court is divided about the Swiftsure and the
Essex's being safe ; and wagers and odds laid on both sides.
Sir W. Coventry is come to town ; so I to his chamber.   But
I do not hear that he is at all pleased or satisfied with the late
fight ; but he tells me more news of our suffering, by the death
of one or two captains, more than I knew before.   But he do
give over the thoughts of the safety of the Swiftsure or
Essex.

---

[1] Afterwards Sir John Holmes, who married Margaret Lowther.

10th. (Lord's day.) I met with Pierce, the surgeon, who is lately come from the fleete, and tells me that all the commanders, officers, and even the common seamen, do condemn every part of the late conduct of the Duke of Albemarle: both in his fighting at all, running among them in his retreat, and running the ships on ground; so as nothing can be worse spoken of. That Holmes, Spragg, and Smith do all the business, and the old and wiser commanders nothing: so as Sir Thomas Teddiman, whom the King and all the world speak well of, is mightily discontented, as being wholly slighted. He says we lost more after the Prince came than before, too. The Prince was so maimed, as to be forced to be towed home. He says all the fleete confess their being chased home by the Dutch; and yet the body of the Dutch that did it was not above forty sail at most; and yet this put us into the fright, as to bring all our ships on ground. He says, however, that the Duke of Albemarle is as high almost as ever, and pleases himself to think that he hath given the Dutch their bellies full, without sense of what he hath lost us; and talks how he knows now the way to beat them. But he says, that even Smith himself, one of his creatures, did himself condemn the late conduct from the beginning to the end. He tells me further, how the Duke of York is wholly given up to his new mistress, my Lady Denham,[1] going at noonday with all his gentlemen with him to visit her in Scotland Yard; she de-

---

[1] Margaret Brook, married to Sir John Denham, May 25, 1665. George Brook, third son of William Brook, Lord Cobham, was attainted and executed for his share in Ralegh's plot. He left a son, William Brook, who, having been restored in blood, and made a Knight of the Bath, espoused Penelope, third daughter of Sir Moyses Hill, of Hillsborough Castle, in Ireland, the ancestor of the Marquises of Downshire, by whom he had issue three daughters:— *First*, Hill, who became the wife of Sir William Boothby; the *second*, Frances, described, on the lettering of her engraved portrait, as "Lady Whitmore." She was the wife of Sir Thomas Whitmore, of Bridgenorth, second son of Sir Thomas Whitmore, of Apley, Bart. Her daughter Francis, married William, grandson of Sir George Whitmore, of Balmes, mentioned by Pepys. See Dryden's epitaph on her in his *Works* (Scott's edit., vol. xi., p. 150): the *third*, was Lady Denham.

Their mother, Lady Brook, surviving her husband, re-married Edward Russell, youngest son of Francis, fifth Earl of Bedford, whose sister was Countess of Bristol. Hence the relationship, or rather the connexion, between the two families; for Hamilton (*Mém. de Grammont*), mentioning that "*les Demoiselles Brook*" assisted at all Lord Bristol's fêtes, calls them "*ses parents*."

claring she will not be his mistress, as Mrs. Price.[1] to go up
and down the Privy Stairs, but will be owned publickly; and
so she is. Mr. Brouncker, it seems, was the pimp to bring it
about; and my Lady Castlemaine, who designs thereby to
fortify herself by the Duke; there being a falling-out the other
day between the King and her: on this occasion, the Queen,
in ordinary talk before the ladies in her drawing-room, did say
to my Lady Castlemaine that she feared the King did take
cold by staying so late abroad at her house. She answered,
before them all, that he did not stay so late abroad with her,
for he went betimes thence, though he do not before one, two,
or three in the morning, but must stay somewhere else. The
King then coming in, and overhearing, did whisper in the eare
aside, and told her she was a bold, impertinent woman, and
bid her to be gone out of the Court, and not come again till
he sent for her; which she did presently, and went to a
lodging in the Pell Mell, and kept there two or three days,
and then sent to the King to know whether she might send
for her things away out of her house. The King sent to her,
she must first come and view them: and so she come, and the
King went to her, and all friends again. He tells me she did,
in her anger, say she would be even with the King, and print
his letters to her; so, putting all together, we are, and are like
to be, in a sad condition; we are endeavouring to raise money
by borrowing it of the City; but I do not think the City will
lend a farthing. Sir G. Carteret and I walked an hour in the
church-yard, under Henry the Seventh's Chapel, he being
lately come from the fleete; and tells me, as I hear from
every body else, that the management in the late fight was
bad, from top to bottom. That several said that this would
not have been, if my Lord Sandwich had had the ordering of
it. Nay, he tells me that certainly, had my Lord Sandwich
had the misfortune to have done as they have done, the King
could not have saved him. There is, too, nothing but discontent among the officers; and all the old, experienced men are
slighted. He tells me, to my question, but as a great secret,
that the dividing of the fleete did proceed first from a propo-

---

[1] The Maid of Honour.

sition from the fleete, though agreed to hence; but he confesses it arose from want of due intelligence. He do, however, call the fleete's retreat on Sunday a very honourable one,
and that the Duke of Albemarle did do well in it, and it
would have been well if he had done it sooner, rather than
venture the loss of the fleete and crown, as he must have done,
if the Prince had not come. He was surprised when I told
him I heard that the King did intend to borrow some
money of the City, and would know who had spoke of it
to me; I told him Sir Ellis Layton this afternoon. He
says it is a dangerous discourse, for that the City certainly
will not be invited to do it; and then, for the King to
ask it and be denied, will be the beginning of our sorrow.
He seems to fear we shall all fall to pieces among ourselves.
This evening we hear that Sir Christopher Mings is dead
of his late wounds; and Sir W. Coventry did commend him
to me in a most extraordinary manner. But this day,
after three days' trial in vain, and the hazard of the spoiling
of the ship in lying till next spring, besides the disgrace
of it, news is brought that the Loyall London is launched at
Deptford.

11th. I, with my Lady Pen and her daughter, to see
Harman, whom we find lame in bed. His bones of his
ancle are broke, but he hopes to do well soon; and a fine
person, by his discourse, he seems to be; and he did plainly
tell me that at the Council of war before the fight, it was
against his reason to begin the fight then, and the reasons of
most sober men there, the wind being such, and we to wind-
ward, that they could not use their lower tier of guns, which
was a sad thing for us to have the honour and weal of the
nation ventured so foolishly. Late comes Sir J. Bankes, to
see me, who tells me that, coming up from Rochester, he
overtook three or four hundred seamen; and he believes every
day they come flocking from the fleete in like numbers;
which is a sad neglect there, when it will be impossible to
get others; and we have little reason to think these will
return presently again. Walking in the galleries at White
Hall, I find the Ladies of Honour dressed in their riding

garbs, with coats and doublets with deep skirts, just, for all
the world, like mine; and buttoned their doublets up the
breast, with perriwigs and with hats; so that, only for a long
petticoat dragging under their men's coats, nobody could take
them for women in any point whatever; which was an odde
sight, and a sight did not please me. It was Mrs. Wells and
another fine lady that I saw thus.

13th. Sir H. Cholmley tells me there are great jars between the Duke of York and the Duke of Albemarle, about
the latter's turning out one or two of the commanders put in
by the Duke of York. Among others, Captain du Tell, a
Frenchman,[1] put in by the Duke of York, and mightily
defended by him; and is therein led by Monsieur Blancford,
that it seems hath the same command over the Duke of York
as Sir W. Coventry hath; which raises ill blood between
them. And I do, in several little things, observe that Sir W.
Coventry hath of late, by the by, reflected on the Duke of
Albemarle and his captains, particularly in that of old Teddiman, who did deserve to be turned out this fight, and was so;
but I heard Sir W. Coventry say that the Duke of Albemarle
put in one as bad as he is in his room, and one that did as
little. With Balty to Hales's by coach. Here I find my
father's picture begun, and so much to my content, that it
joys my very heart to think that I should have his picture so
well done; who, besides that he is my father, and a man that
loves me, and hath ever done so, is also, at this day, one of
the most careful and innocent men in the world. Invited to
Sir Christopher Mings's funeral, but find them gone to
church. However, I into the church, which is a fair, large
church, and a great chapel, and there heard the service, and
staid till they buried him, and then out; and there met with
Sir W. Coventry, who was there out of great generosity, and
no person of quality there but he, and went with him into his
coach; and, being in it with him, there happened this extraordinary case—one of the most romantique that ever I heard of
in my life, and could not have believed, but that I did see it;
which was this:—About a dozen able, lusty, proper men

---

[1] See July 27, 1666, postea.

come to the coach-side with tears in their eyes, and one of them that spoke for the rest begun, and said to Sir W. Coventry, " We are here a dozen of us, that have long known and loved, and served our dead commander, Sir Christopher Mings, and have now done the last office of laying him in the ground. We would be glad we had any other to offer after him, and in revenge of him. All we have is our lives; if you will please to get his Royal Highness to give us a fire-ship among us all, here are a dozen of us, out of all which, choose you one to be commander; and the rest of us, whoever he is, will serve him; and, if possible, do that which shall show our memory of our dead commander, and our revenge." Sir W. Coventry was herewith much moved, as well as I, who could hardly abstain from weeping, and took their names, and so parted; telling me that he would move his Royal Highness as in a thing very extraordinary, which was done. The truth is, Sir Christopher Mings was a very stout man, and a man of great parts, and most excellent tongue among ordinary men; and, as Sir W. Coventry says, could have been the most useful man at such a pinch of time as this. He was come into great renowne here at home, and more abroad, in the West Indys. He had brought his family into a way of being great; but, dying at this time, his memory and name, his father being always, and at this day, a shoemaker, and his mother a hoyman's daughter, of which he was used frequently to boast, will be quite forgot in a few months as if he had never been, nor any of his name be the better by it; he having not had time to will any estate, but is dead poor, rather than rich. So we left the church and crowd. Walked to Mrs. Bagwell's, and went into her house; but I was not a little fearful of what she told me but now, which is, that her servant was dead of the plague, and that she had new-whitened the house all below stairs, but that above stairs they are not so fit for me to go up to, they being not so. So I parted thence, with a very good will, but very civilly, and away to the water-side, and sent for a pint of sack, and drank what I would, and give the waterman the rest.

14th. With my wife and father to Hales's, and there

looked only on my father's picture, which is mighty like; and so away to White Hall to a Committee for Tangier, where the Duke of York was, and Sir W. Coventry, and a very full committee; and, instead of having a very prejudiced meeting, they did, though inclined against Yeabsly, yield to the greatest part of his account, so as to allow of his demands to the value of 7000*l.* and more, and only give time for him to make good his pretence to the rest; which was mighty joy to me: and so we rose up. But I must observe the force of money, which did make my Lord Ashly to argue and behave himself in the business with the greatest friendship, and yet with all the discretion imaginable; and it will be a business of admonition and instruction to me concerning him, and other men, too, for aught I know, as long as I live.

15th. Mr. Bland presented me yesterday with a very fine African mat, to lay upon the ground under a bed of state, being the first-fruits of our peace with Guyland. To the Exchequer, but could not persuade the blockheaded fellows to do what I desire, of breaking my great tallies into less, notwithstanding my Lord Treasurer's order, which vexed me so much that I would not bestow more time and trouble among a company of dunces. Creed come and dined with me; but, Lord! to hear how he pleases himself in behalf of my Lord Sandwich, in the miscarriage of the Duke of Albemarle.

16th. The King, Duke of York, and Sir W. Coventry are gone down to the fleete. To Woolwich and Deptford, all the way down and up, reading of "The Mayor of Quinborough,"[1] a simple play. Comes Mr. Williamson, Sir Arther Ingram, and Jacke Fen, to see the new ships, and a very fine gentleman Mr. Williamson is. It seems, the Dutch do mightily insult of their victory, and they have great reason. Sir W. Barkeley was killed before his ship taken; and there he lies dead in a sugar-chest,[2] for everybody to see, with his flag

<hr>

[1] A comedy, by Thomas Middleton.
[2] "Whitehall, July 15. This day arrived a trumpet from the States of Holland, who came over from Calais in the Dover packet-boat, with a letter to his Majesty, that the States have taken order for the embalming the body of Sir William Berkeley, which they have placed in the chapel of the great church at the Hague, a civility they profess to owe to his corpse, in respect to the quality

standing up by him; and Sir George Ascue is carried up and
down the Hague for people to see.

17th. (Lord's day.) To Christ Church, and there heard a
silly sermon. To Joyce's, where William Joyce and his wife
were, and had a good dinner; but, Lord! how sick was I of
the company, only hope I shall have no more of it a good
while; but am invited to Will's this week; and his wife,
poor, unhappy woman! cried to hear me say that I could not
be there, she thinking that I slight her: so they got me to
promise to come. Down to the milke-house, and drank three
glasses of whey, and then up into the Strand again.

18th. To the office, and so to Lumbard Streete, to borrow
a little money upon a tally, but cannot. To my Lord Bellassis,
by invitation, and there dined with him, and his lady and
daughter; and at dinner there played to us a young boy,
lately come from France, where he had been learning a year
or two on the viallin, and plays finely. But it was pretty to
see how passionately my Lord's daughter loves musick. Sir
W. Coventry is returned this night from the fleete; he being
the activest man in the world, and we all, myself particularly,
more afraid of him than of the King, or his service, for aught
I see; God forgive us! This day the great news is come of
the French, their taking the island of St. Christopher's from
us; and it is to be feared they have done the like of all those
islands thereabouts: this makes me mad.

19th. I to Sir G. Carteret's by appointment; where, I
perceive by him, the King is going to borrow some money of
the City; but I fear it will do no good, but hurt. He tells
me how the Generall[1] is displeased, and there have been some

---

of his person, the greatness of his command, and of the high courage and valour
he showed in the late engagement; desiring his Majesty to signify his pleasure
about the further disposal of it." — *The London Gazette*, No. 69. "Frederick
Ruysch, the celebrated Dutch anatomist, undertook, by order of the States-General, to inject the body of the English Admiral Berkeley, killed in the sea-fight of
1666; and the body, already somewhat decomposed, was sent over to England as
well prepared as if it had been the fresh corpse of a child. This produced to
Ruysch, on the part of the States-General, a recompence worthy of their liberality,
and the merit of the anatomist."—James's *Medical Dictionary*, quoted in the *Gent.
Mag.*, vol. lvii., p. 211. Sir William Berkeley was buried the following August in
Westminster Abbey.

[1] Duke of Albemarle.

high words between the General and Sir W. Coventry. And
it may be so: for I do not find Sir W. Coventry so highly
commending the Duke as he used to be, but letting fall, now
and then, some little jerkes: as this day, speaking of news
from Holland, he says, "I find their victory begins to shrinke
there, as well as ours here." Here I met with Captain
Cocke, and he tells me, that the first thing the Prince said to
the King, upon his coming, was complaining of the Commissioners of the Navy; that they could have been abroad in
three or four days but for us; that we do not take care of
them: which I am troubled at, and do fear may, in violence,
break out upon this office some time or other; for we shall
not be able to carry on the business.

20th. Up, but in some pain of the collique. I have of
late taken too much cold by washing my feet, and going in a
thin silk waistcoat, without any other coat over it, and open-
breasted. I did this morning give my father some money to
buy him a horse, and for other things to himself and my
mother and sister, among them 20*l.*, which the poor man
takes with infinite kindness.

21st. Up, and at the office all the morning; where, by
several circumstances, I find Sir W. Coventry and the Duke
of Albemarle do not agree as they used to do; Sir W.
Coventry commending Aylett, in some reproach to the Duke,
whom the Duke hath put out for want of courage; and
found fault with Steward, whom the Duke keeps in, though
as much in fault as any commander in the fleete. At noon
home to dinner—my father, sister, and wife dining at Sarah
Giles's, poor woman! where I should have been; but my
pride would not suffer me. At Mr. Debasty's I saw, in a
gold frame, a picture of a fluter playing on his flute, which,
for a good while, I took for painting, but at last observed it
was a piece of tapestry, and is the finest that ever I saw in
my life for figures, and good natural colours, and a very fine
thing it is indeed. Sir George Smith tells me that this day
my Lord Chancellor, and some of the Court, have been with
the City, and that the City have voted to lend the King
100,000*l.*; which, if soon paid, as he says he believes it will,

will be a greater service than I did ever expect at this time from the City.

22d. Up, and before I went out Mr. Peter Barr sent me a tierce of claret, which is very welcome. All day upon my Tangier accounts; my father, wife, and sister, late abroad on the water.

23d. My father and sister very betimes took their leave; and my wife, with all possible kindness, went with them to the coach, I being mightily pleased with their company so long, and my father with his being here, and it rejoices my heart that I am in a condition to do anything to comfort him, he is such innocent company. To Tower Wharfe, but could get no watermen; they being now so scarce, by reason of the great press; so to the Custome House, and there, with great threats, got a couple to ferry me down to Deptford — all the way reading Pompey the Great,¹ a play translated from the French by several noble persons; among others, my Lord Buckhurst, that to me is but a mean play, and the words and sense not very extraordinary. From Deptford, I walked to Redriffe, and in my way was overtaken by Bagwell, lately come from sea in the Providence, who did give me an account of several particulars in the late fight, and how his ship was deserted basely by the York, Captain Swanly, commander.

24th. (Lord's day.) To White Hall. There I hear that Sir Francis Prujean is dead, after being married to a widow about a year, or thereabouts. He died very rich, and had, for the last year, lived very handsomely — his lady bringing him to it. He was no great pains-taker in person, yet died very rich; and, as Dr. Clerke says, was of a very great judgment, but hath writ nothing to leave his name to posterity. In the gallery, among others, met with Major Halsey, a great creature of the Duke of Albemarle's; who tells me that the Duke, by name, hath said that he expected to have the work here up in the River done, having left Sir W. Batten and Mr. Phipps there. He says that the Duke of Albemarle do say that this is a victory we have had, having, as he was sure,

---

¹ Corneille's play, one act of which had been translated by Edmund Waller, and the rest by Lord Buckhurst, Sir C. Sedley, and Mr. Godolphin.

killed them 8000 men, and sunk about fourteen of their ships; but nothing like this appears true. He lays much of the little success we have had, however, upon the fleete's being divided by order from above, and the want of spirit in the commanders; and that he was commanded, by order, to go out of the Downes to the Gun-fleete, and in the way meeting the Dutch fleete, what should he do? should he not fight them? especially having beat them heretofore at a great disadvantage. He tells me further, that, having been downe with the Duke of Albemarle, he finds that Holmes and Spragge do govern most business of the Navy; and by others I understand that Sir Thomas Allen is offended thereat, that he is not so much advised with as he ought to be. He tells me, also, as he says, of his own knowledge, that several people, before the Duke went out, did offer to supply the King with 100,000*l.*, provided he would be treasurer of it, to see it laid out for the Navy; which he refused, and so it died; but I believe none of this. This day I saw my Lady Falmouth,[1] with whom I remember now I have dined at my Lord Barkeley's heretofore, a pretty woman; she was now in her second or third mourning, and pretty pleasant in her looks. By and by the Council rises, and Sir W. Coventry come out; and he and I went aside, and discoursed of much business of the Navy; and afterwards took his coach, and to Hide Parke he and I alone: there we had much talk. First, he started a discourse of a talk he hears about the town, which, says he, is a very bad one, and fit to be suppressed, if we knew how: which is, the comparing of the success of the last year with that of this; saying that, that was good, and that bad. I was as sparing in speaking as I could, being jealous of him and myself also, but wished it could be stopped; but said I doubted it could not otherwise than by the fleete's being abroad again, and so finding other work for men's minds and discourse. Then to discourse of himself, saying, that he

---

[1] Elizabeth, daughter of Hervey Bagot, and widow of Charles Berkeley, Earl of Falmouth, for whom she still wore mourning, married secondly, Charles, sixth Earl of Dorset, and died in childbed, in 1679, leaving an only daughter. She had been Maid of Honour to the Duchess of York.

heard that he was under the lash of people's discourse about the Prince's not having notice of the Dutch being out, and for him to come back again, nor the Duke of Albemarle notice, that the Prince was sent for back again : to which he told me very particularly how careful he was the very same night that it was resolved to send for the Prince back, to cause orders to be writ, and waked the Duke, who was then in bed, to sign them; and that they went by express that very night, being the Wednesday night before the fight, which begun on the Friday; and that for sending them by the post express, and not by gentlemen on purpose, he made a sport of it, and said, I knew of none to send it with, but would at least have lost more time in fitting themselves out, than any diligence of theirs beyond that of the ordinary post would have recovered.   I told him that this was not so much the towne talk, as the reason of dividing the fleete.   To this he told me he ought not to say much; but did assure me, in general, that the proposition did first come from the fleete;[1] and the resolution, not being prosecuted with orders so soon as the General thought fit, the General did send Sir Edward Spragge up on purpose for them; and that there was nothing in the whole business which was not done with the full consent and advice of the Duke of Albemarle.   But he did adde, as the Catholiques call *le secret de la Messe*, that Sir Edward Spragge, who had, even in Sir Christopher Mings's time, put in to be the great favourite of the Prince; but much more now had a mind to be the great man with him, and to that end had a mind to have the Prince at a distance from the Duke of Albemarle, that they might be doing something alone — did, as he believed, put on this business of dividing the fleete, and that thence it came.   He tells me, as to the business of intelligence, the want whereof the world did complain much of, that for that it was not his business ; and, as he was, therefore, to have no share in the blame, so he would not meddle to lay it any where else.   That De Ruyter was ordered by the States not to make it his business to come into much danger, but to preserve himself, as much

as was fit, out of harm's way, to be able to direct the fleete.
He do, I perceive, with some violence, forbear saying any
thing to the reproach of the Duke of Albemarle; but, contrarily, speaks much of his courage; but I do as plainly see
that he do not like the Duke of Albemarle's proceedings;
but, contrarily, is displeased therewith. And he do plainly
diminish the commanders put in by the Duke, and do lessen
the miscarriages of any that have been removed by him. He
concurs with me, that the next bout will be a fatal one to one
side or other; because, if we be beaten, we shall not be able
to set out our fleete again. He do confess with me, that the
hearts of our seamen are much saddened; and for that reason,
among others, wishes Sir Christopher Mings was alive, who
might inspire courage and spirit into them. Speaking of
Holmes, how great a man he is, and that he do for the present, and hath done all the voyage, kept himself in good order
and within bounds; but, says he, a cat will be a cat still, and,
some time or other, out his humours must break again. He
do not disowne but that the dividing of the fleete, upon the
presumptions that were then had, which, I suppose, was the
French fleete being come this way, was a good resolution.
Having had all this discourse, he and I back to Whitehall;
and there I left him, being in a little doubt whether I had
behaved myself in my discourse with the policy and circumspection which ought to be used to so great a courtier as he
is, and so wise and factious a man, and by water home, and
so, after supper, to bed.

25th. News from Sir W. Coventry, that the Dutch are
certainly come out. All this day on the water entertained
myself with the play of Commenius.[1] Mrs. Pen carried us to
two gardens at Hackny, which I every day grow more and
more in love with, Mr. Drake's, one, where the garden is
good, and house and the prospect admirable; the other my

[1] John Amos Comenius, a learned grammarian, born in Moravia, in 1592.
Amongst other works, he published the play here mentioned, entitled "Schola
Ludus seu Encyclopædia Viva (hoc est) Januæ Linguarum Praxis Scenica." This
curious book contains the details of eight dramatic pieces, represented at the
author's school, at Patak, in 1654. Comenius died at Amsterdam, in 1671.

Lord Brooke's,[1] where the gardens are much better, but the house not so good, nor the prospect good at all. But the gardens are excellent; and here I first saw oranges grow: some green, some half, some a quarter, and some full ripe, on the same tree; and one fruit of the same tree do come a year or two after the other. I pulled off a little one by stealth, the man being mightily curious of them, and eat it, and it was just as other little green small oranges are; as big as half the end of my little finger. Here were also great variety of other exotique plants, and several labyrinths, and a pretty aviary. This being the first day of my putting on my black stuff bombazin suit.

26th. In the morning come Mr. Chichly[2] to Sir W. Coventry, to tell him the ill success of the guns made for the Loyall London; which is, that in the trial every one of the great guns, the whole cannon of seven, as I take it, broke in pieces.

27th. To Sir W. Coventry's chamber, where I saw his father my Lord Coventry's picture hung up, done by Stone,[3] who then brought it home. It is a good picture, drawn in his judge's robes, and the great seal by him. And, while it was hanging up, "This," says Sir W. Coventry, merrily, "is the use we make of our fathers." But what I observed most from the discourse, was this of Sir W. Coventry, that he do look upon ourselves in a desperate condition. The issue of all standing upon this one point, that, by the next fight, if we beat, the Dutch will certainly be content to take eggs for their money, that was his expression; or, if we be beaten, we must be contented to make peace, and glad if we can have it without paying too dear for it. And withall we do

---

[1] Robert Greville, Lord Brooke, ob. 1676. Evelyn (*Diary*, May 8, 1654) mentions this garden as Lady Brooke's. Brooke House, at Clapton, was lately a private madhouse.

[2] Thomas Chicheley, afterwards knighted, and made a Privy Councillor, and Commissioner of the Ordnance.

[3] This portrait, if an original, must have been finished long before, for the Lord Keeper died in 1639, and Henry Stone, the painter, better known as Old Stone, in 1657; or possibly it was a copy made for Sir W. Coventry by Henry's brother, John Stone, who, according to Walpole, survived the Restoration, and was the last of his race.

rely wholly upon the Parliament's giving us more money
the next sitting, or else we are undone. To Mr. Hales's,
to pay for my father's picture, which cost me 10*l.* the picture,
and 25*s.* the frame. I did this afternoon visit my Lord
Bellassis, who professes all imaginable satisfaction in me. My
Lord is going down to his garrison to Hull, by the King's
command, to put it in order for fear of an invasion: which
course, I perceive, is taken upon the seacoasts round; for
we have a real apprehension of the King of France's in-
vading us.

28th. The Dutch are now known to be out, and we may
expect them every hour upon our coast. But our fleete is in
pretty good readiness for them.

29th. To the office; where I met with a letter from Dover,
which tells me, and it come by express, that news is brought
over by a gentleman from Callice, that the Dutch fleete, 130
sail, are come upon the French coast; and that the country
is bringing in picke-axes, and shovells, and wheel-barrows
into Callice; that there are 6000 men armed on head, back,
and breast, Frenchmen, ready to go on board the Dutch fleete,
and will be followed by 1200 more. That they pretend they
are to come to Dover; and that thereupon the Governor of
Dover Castle is getting the victuallers' provisions out of the
town into the Castle to secure it. But I do think this a
ridiculous conceit; but a little time will show.

30th. Mightily troubled all this morning with going to my
Lord Mayor, Sir Thomas Bludworth, a silly¹ man, I think,
and other places, about getting shipped some men that they
have these two last night pressed in the City out of the
houses: the persons wholly unfit for sea, and many of them
people of very good fashion, which is a shame to think of,
and carried to Bridewell they are, yet without being impressed
with money legally as they ought to be. But to see how the
King's business is done; my Lord Mayor himself did scruple,
at this time of extremity, to do this thing, because he had
not money to pay the pressed-money to the men; he told

¹ As his conduct during the Great Fire fully proved, when he is said to have
boasted, that he would extinguish the flames by the same means to which Swift
tells us Gulliver had recourse at Lilliput.

me so himself; nor to take up boats to carry them down
through bridge to the ships I had prepared to carry them
down in : insomuch that I was forced to promise to be his
paymaster, and he did send his City Remembrancer afterwards to the office, and at the table, in the face of the
officers, I did out of my own purse disburse 15*l.* to pay for
their pressing, and diet last night and this morning; which
is a thing worth record of my Lord Mayor. Busy about
this all the morning, and about the getting off men pressed
by our officers of the fleete into the service; even our own
men that are at the office, and the boats that carry us. So
that it is now become impossible to have so much as a letter
carried from place to place, or any message done for us; nay,
out of Victualling ships full loaden to go down to the fleete,
and out of the vessels of the officers of the Ordnance, they
press men, so that for want of discipline in this respect, I
do fear all will be undone. Late to bed; and, while I was
undressing myself, our new ugly maid, Luce, had like to have
broke her neck in the dark, going down our upper stairs;
but, which I was glad of, the poor girle did only bruise her
head, but at first did lie on the ground groaning, and drawing
her breath, like one a-dying.

July 1st. (Lord's day.) Comes Sir W. Pen to town, which
I little expected, having invited my Lady and her daughter
Pegg to dine with me to-day; which at noon they did, and
Sir W. Pen with them; and pretty merry we were. And
though I do not love him, yet I find it necessary to keep in
with him; his good service at Shearnesse, in getting out the
fleete, being much taken notice of, and reported to the King
and Duke, even from the Prince and Duke of Albemarle
themselves, and made the most of to me and them by Sir W.
Coventry; therefore, I think it discretion, great and necessary
discretion, to keep in with him. To the Tower several times,
about the business of the pressed men, and late at it till
twelve at night, shipping them. But, Lord! how some poor
women did cry; and in my life I never did see such natural
expression of passion as I did here, in some women's bewailing themselves, and running to every parcel of men that were
brought, one after another, to look for their husbands, and

wept over every vessel that went off, thinking they might be
there, and looking after the ship as far as ever they could by
moone-light, that it grieved me to the heart to hear them.
Besides, to see poor, patient, labouring men and house-
keepers, leaving poor wives and families, taken up on a
sudden by strangers, was very hard, and that without press-
money, but forced against all law to be gone.   It is a great
tyranny.

2d. Up betimes, and forced to go to my Lord Mayor's,
about the business of the pressed men; and, indeed, I find
him a mean man of understanding and despatch of any
publick business.   Thence, out of curiosity, to Bridewell, to
see the pressed men, where there are about 300; but so
unruly, that I durst not go among them: and they have
reason to be so, having been kept these three days prisoners,
with little or no victuals, and pressed out, and, contrary to
all course of law, without press-money, and men that are not
liable to it.   Here I met with prating Colonel Cox, one of
the City colonels, heretofore a great presbyter: but to hear
how the fellow did commend himself, and the service he do
the King; and, like an asse, at Paul's did take me out of my
way on purpose to show me the gate, the little north gate,
where he had two men shot close by him on each side, and
his own hair burnt by a bullet-shot, in the insurrection of
Venner, and himself escaped.   Called by Pegg Pen to her
house, where her father and mother, and Mrs. Norton, the
second Roxalana,[1] a fine woman, indifferent handsome, good
body, and hand, and good mind, and pretends to sing, but
do it not excellently.   I found one of the vessels loaden with
the Bridewell birds in a great mutiny, and they would not
sail, not they; but with good words, and cajoling the ring-
leader into the Tower, where, when he was come, he was
clapped up in the hole, they were got very quietly; but I
think it is much if they do not run the vessel on ground.

3d. Mr. Finch, one of the Commissioners of Excise, and
I walked two hours together in the garden, talking of many
things; sometimes of Mr. Povy, whose vanity, prodigality,

[1] The first having been Mrs. Davenport.

neglect of his business, and committing it to unfit hands,
hath undone him, and outed him of all his public employ
ments, and the thing set on foot by a revivall of a business,
wherein he had three or four years ago, by surprize, got the
Duke of York to sign to having a sum of money paid out of
the Excise, before some that was due to him, and now the
money is fallen short, and the Duke never likely to be paid.
This being revived hath undone Povy.   Then we fell to discourse of the Parliament, and the great men there; and,
among others, Mr. Vaughan,[1] whom he reports as a man of
excellent judgement and learning, but most passionate and
opiniastre.   He had done himself the most wrong, though
he values it not, that is, the displeasure of the King, in his
standing so long against the breaking of the Act for a trien-
niall parliament; but yet do believe him to be a most loyall
gentleman.   He told me Mr. Prin's character; that he is a
man of mighty labour and reading, and memory, but the
worst judge of matters, or layer together of what he hath
read, in the world; which I do not, however, believe him in;
that he believes him very true to the King in his heart, but
can never be reconciled to episcopacy; that the House do
not lay much weight upon him, or anything he says.   Settling
my last month's accounts, and, to my great joy, find myself
worth about 5600*l*.   News come yesterday from Harwich,
that the Dutch had appeared on our coast with their fleete,
and, we believe, did go to the Gun-fleete, and they are supposed to be there now; but I have heard nothing of them
to-day.   Yesterday, Dr. Whistler, at Sir W. Pen's, told
me that Alexander Broome, the great song-maker, is lately
dead.[2]

    4th. Thanks be to God! the plague is, as I hear, increased
but two this week; but in the country, in several places, it
rages mightily, and particularly in Colchester, where it hath
long been, and is believed will quite depopulate the place.
With the Duke, all of us, discoursing about the places where

---

[1] See 25th March, 1664.

[2] He died 30th June, 1666, and was buried, by his own desire, under Lincoln's
Inn Chapel, by the side of Prynne.

to build ten great ships: the King and Council have resolved
on none to be under third-rates; but it is impossible to do
it, unless we have more money towards the doing it than yet
we have in any view. But, however, the show must be made
to the world. In the evening, Sir W. Pen came to me, and
we walked together, and talked of the late fight. I find him
very plain, that the whole conduct of the late fight was ill;
that two-thirds of the commanders of the whole fleete have
told him so: they all saying, that they durst not oppose it at
the Council of War, for fear of being called cowards, though
it was wholly against their judgement to fight that day, with
the disproportion of force; and then, we not being able to
use one gun of our lower tier, which was a greater disproportion than the other. Besides, we might very well have
staid in the Downs without fighting, or any where else, till
the Prince could have come up to them; or, at least, till the
weather was fair, that we might have the benefit of our whole
force in the ships that we had. He says, three things must be
remedied, or else we shall be undone by this fleete. 1. That
we must fight in a line, whereas we fight promiscuously, to
our utter and demonstrable ruine: the Dutch fighting otherwise; and we, whenever we beat them.—2. We must not
desert ships of our own in distress, as we did, for that makes
a captain desperate, and he will fling away his ship, when
there are no hopes left him of succour.—3. That ships, when
they are a little shattered, must not take the liberty to come
in of themselves, but refit themselves the best they can, and
stay out—many of our ships coming in with very small dis-
ableness. He told me that our very commanders, nay, our
very flag-officers, do stand in need of exercising among themselves, and discoursing the business of commanding a fleete;
he telling me, that even one of our flag-men in the fleete did
not know which tacke lost the wind, or kept it, in the last
engagement. He says, it was pure dismaying and fear that
made them all run upon the Galloper, not having their wits
about them; and that it was a miracle they were not all lost.
He much inveighs upon my discoursing of Sir John Lawson's
saying heretofore, that sixty sail would do as much as one

hundred: and says that he was a man of no counsel at all, but had got the confidence to say as the gallants did, and did propose to himself to make himself great by them, and saying as they did; but was no man of judgement in his business, but hath been out in the greatest points that have come before them. And then, in the business of fore-castles, which he did oppose, all the world sees now the use of them for shelter of men. He did talk very rationally to me, insomuch that I took more pleasure this night in hearing him discourse, than I ever did in my life in any thing that he had said.

5th. At noon dined, and Mr. Shepley with me, who come to town the other day. I lent him 30l. in silver upon 30 pieces in gold. But to see how apt every body is to neglect old kindnesses! I must charge myself with the ingratitude of being unwilling to lend him so much money without pawn, if he should have asked it, but he did not.

6th. To the Tower about shipping of some more pressed men, and that done, away to Bread Street, to Sir G. Carteret, who is at a pay of tickets all alone; and I believe not less than one thousand people in the streets. But it is a pretty thing to observe that, both there and every where else, a man shall see many women now-a-days of mean sort in the streets, but no men; men being so afraid of the press. I dined with Sir G. Carteret, and, after dinner, had much discourse about our public business; and he do seem to fear every day more and more what I do; which is, a general confusion in the State; plainly answering me to the question, who is it that the weight of the war depends upon? that it is only Sir W. Coventry. He tells me, too, the Duke of Albemarle is dissatisfied, and that the Duchess do curse Coventry as the man that betrayed her husband to the sea: though I believe that it is not so. Thence to Lumbard Streete, and received 2000l.. and carried it home: whereof 1000l. in gold. This I do for security sake, and convenience of carriage; though it costs me above 70l. the change of it, at 18½d. per piece. Being at home, I there met with a letter from Bab. Allen,[1]

---

to invite me to be god-father to her boy, with Mrs. Williams, which I consented to, but know not the time when it is to be.

7th. Creed tells me, he finds all things mighty dull at Court; and that they now begin to lie long in bed; it being, as we suppose, not seemly for them to be found playing and gaming as they used to be; nor that their minds are at ease enough to follow those sports, and yet not knowing how to employ themselves, though there be work enough for their thoughts and councils and pains, they keep long in bed. But he thinks with me, that there is nothing in the world can help us but the King's personal looking after his business and his officers, and that, with that, we may yet do well; but otherwise must be undone; nobody at this day taking care of any thing, nor hath any body to call him to account for it.˙ To bed; and it proved the hottest night that ever I was in in my life, and thundered and lightened all night long, and rained hard. But, Lord! to see in what fear I lay a good while, hearing of a little noise of somebody walking in the house: so rung the bell, and it was my maids going to bed about one o'clock in the morning. But the fear of being robbed, having so much money in the house, was very great, and is still so, and do much disquiet me.

8th. (Lord's day.) To church—wife and Mercer and I, in expectation of hearing some mighty preacher to-day, Mrs. Mary Batelier sending us word to; but it proved an ordinary silly lecturer, which made me merry, and she laughed upon us to see her mistake. I expected to have had news sent me of Knipp's christening to day; but, hearing nothing of it, I did not go, though I fear it is but their forgetfulness, and s. I may disappoint them. To church, after dinner, again —a thing I have not done a good while before, go twice in one day.

9th. To my office, where busy till come to by Lovett and his wife. Home with them, and there find my aunt Wight with my wife, come to take her leave of her, being going for the summer into the country; and there was also Mrs. Mary Batelier and her sister, newly come out of France—a black, very black woman, but mighty goodnatured people both, as

35 *

ever I saw. Here I made the black one sing a French song, which she did mighty innocently; and then Mrs. Lovett play on the lute, which she do very well; and then Mercer and I sang; and so, with great pleasure, I left them, having showed them my chamber and 1000*l.* in gold, which they wondered at, and given them sweetmeats, and shewn my aunt Wight my father's picture, which she admires.

10th. To the office; the yard being very full of women, I believe above three hundred, coming to get money for their husbands and friends that are prisoners in Holland; and they lay clamouring, and swearing, and cursing us, that my wife and I were afraid to send a venison-pasty that we have for supper to-night to the cook's to be baked, for fear of their offering violence to it: but it went, and no hurt done. To the Tower, to speak with Sir John Robinson about the bad condition of the pressed men for want of clothes. Home, and there find my wife and the two Mrs. Bateliers walking in the garden; and then they and we and Mrs. Mercer, the mother, and her daughter Anne, and our Mercer, to supper to a good venison-pasty and other good things, and had a good supper, and very merry—Mistress Bateliers being both very good-humoured. We sang and talked, and then led them home, and there they made us drink; and, among other things, did show us, in cages, some birds brought from Bordeaux, that are all fat, and, examining one of them, they are so, almost all fat. Their name is Ortolans, which are brought over to the King for him to eat, and indeed are excellent things.

11th. I away by coach to St. James's, and there hear that the Duchess is lately [1] brought to bed of a boy. By and by called to wait on the Duke, the King being present; and there agreed, among other things, on the places to build the ten new great ships ordered to be built; and as to the relief of prisoners in Holland. And then about several stories of the basenesse of the King of Spain's being served with officers: they in Flanders having as good common men as any Prince in the world, but the veriest cowards for the officers, nay, for the general officers, as the General and Lieu-

<hr>

[1] On the 4th. Charles Duke of Kendall, died 22 . ..y, 1667

tenant-general, in the whole world. But, above all things, the King did speak most in contempt of the ceremoniousnesse of the King of Spain, that he do nothing but under some ridiculous form or other. I shall get in near 2000*l.* into my own hands, which is in the King's, upon tallies; which will be a pleasure to me, and satisfaction to have a good sum in my own hands, whatever evil disturbances should be in the State; though it troubles me to lose so great a profit as the King's interest of ten per cent. for that money. To the office. I there met with a command from my Lord Arlington, to go down to a galliott at Greenwich, by the King's particular command, that is going to carry the Savoy Envoye over, and we fear there may be many Frenchmen then on board; and so I have a power and command to search for, and seize, all that have not passes from one of the Secretaries of State, and to bring them and their papers in custody. So I to the Tower, and got a couple of musquetiers with me, and Griffen and my boy Tom, and so down; and, being come, found none on board but two or three servants, looking to horses and doggs, there on board. On shore at Greenwich, the night being late, and the tide against us: so, having sent before, to Mrs. Clerke's, and there had a good bed, and well received, the whole people rising to see me.

12th. Up again by five o'clock, and away to the Tower, and thence, having shifted myself, to St. James's, to Goring House, there to wait on my Lord Arlington, to give him an account of my night's work, but he was not up, being not long since married:[1] so, after walking up and down the house below, being the house I was once at Hartlib's[2] sister's wedding, and is a very fine house, and finely furnished; and then I away to St. James's, and with Sir W. Coventry into London, to the office. And all the way I observed him mightily to make mirth of the Duke of Albemarle and his people about him, saying, that he was the happiest man in the world for doing of great things by sorry instruments;

---

[1] To Isabella, daughter of Louis de Nassau, Lord of Beverweert, and Count of Nassau, natural son of Prince Maurice. She was sister of the Countess of Ossory; her daughter by Lord Arlington was afterwards first Duchess of Grafton. See 15th Nov. 1666.

[2] See July 10, 1660.

and so particularized in Sir W. Clerke, and Riggs, and Halsey, and others; and then, again, said that the only quality eminent in him was, that he did persevere; and indeed he is a very drudge, and stands by the King's business. And this he said, that one thing he was good at, that he never would receive an excuse if the thing was not done; listening to no reasoning for it, be it good or bad. And then he begun to say what a great man Warcupp was, and something else, and what was that but a great lyer; and told me a story, how at table he did, they speaking about antipathys, say, that a rose touching his skin anywhere would make it rise and pimple; and, by and by the dessert coming, with roses upon it, the Duchess[1] bid him try, and they did; but they rubbed and rubbed, but nothing would do in the world, by which his lie was found. He spoke contemptibly of Holmes and his mermidons, that come to take down the ships from hence, and have carried them without any necessaries, or anything almost, that they will certainly be longer getting ready than if they had staid here. In fine, I do observe he hath no esteem nor kindness for the Duke's matters, but, contrarily, do slight him and them; and I pray God the kingdom do not pay too dear by this jarring; though this blockheaded Duke I did never expect better from.

14th. Up betimes to the office, to write fair a laborious letter I wrote as from the Board, to the Duke of York, laying out our want of money again; and particularly the business of Captain Cocke's tender[2] of hemp, which my Lord Brouncker brought in, under an unknown hand, without name, wherein his Lordship will have no great success, I doubt. That being done, I down to Thames Streete, and there agreed for four or five tons of corke, to send this day to the fleete, being a new device to make barricados with, instead of junke. After a song in the garden, which is now the greatest pleasure I take, and indeed do please me mightily, to bed. This evening I had Davila[3] brought home to me, and find it a most excellent history as ever I read.

---

[1] Of Albemarle.　　　　[2] For which Pepys was to receive 500*l*.
[3] The work referred to is *Storia delle guerre civili di Francia*, by Arrigo Caterino Davila. It is still a very popular book.

15th. (Lord's day.) To church, where our lecturer made a
sorry silly sermon, upon the great point of proving the truth
of the Christian religion. Walked to the Park, and there, it
being mighty hot and I weary, lay down by the canalle, upon
the grass, and slept awhile, and was thinking of a lampoon
which hath run in my head this week, to make up the late
fight at sea, and the miscarriages there; but other businesses
put it out of my head, and so home, and there drank a great
deal of small beer; and so took up my wife and Betty
Mitchell and her husband, and away into the fields, to take
the ayre, as far as beyond Hackney, and so back again, in
our way drinking a great deal of milke, which I drank to
take away my heart-burne. Home, and to bed in some pain,
and fear of more. In mighty pain all night long, which I
impute to the milk that I drank upon so much beer, and the
cold, to my washing my feet the night before.

16th. A wonderful dark sky, and shower of rain this morning. At Harwich a shower of hail as big as walnuts. Passed
the day with Balty, who is come from sea for a day or two
before the fight, and I perceive could be willing fairly to be
out of the next fight, and I cannot much blame him, he
having no reason by his place to be there; however, would
not have him to be absent manifestly to avoid being there.

17th. I went and bought a common riding-cloak for
myself, to save my best. It cost me but 30s., and will do my
turn mighty well. This day I did bid Balty to agree with
——, the Dutch painter, which he once led me to, to see
landscapes, for a winter-piece of snow, which indeed is a good
piece, and costs me but 40s., which I would not take the
money again for, it being, I think, mighty good.

18th. To St. James's after my fellows; and here, among
other things, before us all, the Duke of York did say, that
now at length he is come to a sure knowledge that the
Dutch did lose in the late engagements twenty-nine captains
and thirteen ships. Upon which Sir W. Coventry did publicly move that, if his Royall Highness had this of a certainty,
it would be of use to send this down to the fleete, and to
cause it to be spread about the fleete, for the recovering of

the spirits of the officers and seamen; who are under great dejectedness, for want of knowing that they did do anything against the enemy, notwithstanding all that they did to us, which, though it be true, yet methought was one of the most dishonourable motions to our countrymen that ever was made; and is worth remembering. Thence with Sir W. Pen home, calling at Lilly's, to have a time appointed when to be drawn among the other Commanders of Flags in the last year's fight; and so full of work Lilly is, that he was fain to take his table-book out to see how his time is appointed, and appointed six days hence for him (Sir W. Pen), to come between seven and eight in the morning. Thence with him home; and there by appointment I find Dr. Fuller, now Bishop of Limericke, in Ireland; whom I knew in his low condition at Twittenham,[1] and find the Bishop the same good man as ever; and, in a word, kind to us, and, methinks, one of the comeliest and most becoming prelates in all respects that ever I saw in my life. During dinner, comes an acquaintance of his, Sir Thomas Littleton;[2] whom I knew not while he was in my house, but liked his discourse: and afterwards, by Sir W. Pen, do come to know that he is one of the greatest speakers in the House of Commons, and the usual second to the great Vaughan: so was sorry I did observe him no more, and gain no more of his acquaintance. Walked to Woolwich, reading "the Rivall Ladys" all the way, and find it a most pleasant and fine writ play.

19th. Full of wants of money, and much stores to buy, for to replenish the stores, and no money to do it with. Balty takes his leave of us, he going towards the fleete, where he will pass through one great engagement more before he be two days older, I believe. The fleete is sailed this morning; God send us good news of them!

---

[1] Twickenham, where he kept a school.

[2] Afterwards made Treasurer of the Navy, in conjunction with Sir Thomas Osborne. He was the eldest son of Sir Adam Littleton, of Stoke Milburgh, Salop, who had been created a Baronet in 1642. He married Anne, daughter and heir of Edward Lord Littleton, the Lord Keeper, and died in 1681, aged 57. Sir Thomas Littleton, the only son of this match, became Speaker of the House of Commons, and deceased, s.p., in 1709.

20th. To Lovett's, there to see how my picture goes on to be varnished, a fine Crucifix[1] which will be very fine; and here I saw some fine prints, brought from France by Sir Thomas Crewe. Lovett did present me with a varnished staff, very fine and light to walk with. Come Mrs. Daniel and her sister Sarah, and dined with us; and old Mr. Hawly, whose condition pities me, he being forced to turn under parish-clerk at St. Giles's — I think at the other end of the town.

21st. At noon walked in the garden with Commissioner Pett, newly come to town, who tells me how infinite the disorders are among the commanders and all officers of the fleete. No discipline: nothing but swearing and cursing, and everybody doing what they please; and the Generals, understanding no better, suffer it, to the reproaching of this Board, or whoever it will be. He himself hath been challenged twice to the field, or something as good, by Sir Edward Spragge and Captain Seamons.[2] He tells me that Captains carry, for all the late orders, what men they please. So that he fears, and I do no less, that God Almighty cannot bless us while we keep in this disorder that we are in: he observing to me, too, that there is no man of council or advice in the fleete; and, the truth is, that the gentlemen-captains will undo us, for they are not to be kept in order, their friends about the King and Duke, and their own houses, are so free, that it is not for any person but the Duke himself to have any command over them.

22d. (Lord's day.) Walked to White Hall, where saw nobody almost, but walked up and down with Hugh May, who is a very ingenious man. Among other things, discoursing of the present fashion of gardens to make them plain, that we have the best walks of gravell in the world, France having none, nor Italy; and our green of our bowling allies is better than any they have. So our business here being ayre, this is the best way, only with a little mixture of

---

[1] This crucifix occasioned Pepys trouble long afterwards, having been brought as evidence that he was a Papist. See *Life*, vol. i.

Query, Seymour

statues, or pots, which may be handsome, and so filled with
another pot of such or such a flower or greene, as the season
of the year will bear. And then for flowers, they are best
seen in a little plat by themselves : besides, their borders spoil
the walks of another garden : and then for fruit, the best
way is to have walls built circularly one within another, to
the South, on purpose for fruit, and leave the walking garden
only for that use. Thence walked through the House, where
most people mighty hush, and, methinks, melancholy. I see
not a smiling face through the whole Court: and, in my
conscience, they are doubtfull of the conduct again of the
Generals, and I pray God they may not make their fears
reasonable. Sir Richard Fanshaw is lately dead[1] at Madrid.
The fleete cannot get clear of the River, but expect the first
wind to be out, and then to be sure to fight. The Queen and
Maids of Honour are at Tunbridge.

23d. Comes Simpson, the Joyner ; and he and I with great
pains, contriving presses to put my books up in : they now
growing numerous, and lying one upon another on my chairs,
I lose the use to avoid the trouble of removing them, when I
would open a book. All full of expectation of the fleete's
engagement, but it is not yet. Sir W. Coventry says they
are eighty-nine men-of-war ; but one fifth-rate, and that, the
Sweepstakes, which carries forty guns. They are most infinitely manned. He tells me the Loyall London, Sir J.
Smith, which, by the by, he commends to be the best ship in
the world, large and small, hath above eight hundred men ;
and, moreover, takes notice, which is worth notice, that the
fleete hath lain now near fourteen days without any demand
for a farthing-worth of any thing of any kind, but only to get
men. He also observes, that, with this excess of men, nevertheless, they have thought fit to leave behind them sixteen
ships, which they have robbed of their men, which certainly
might have been manned, and they have been serviceable in
the fight, and yet the fleete well manned, according to the
excess of supernumeraries, which we hear they have. At
least, two or three of them might have been left manned, and

---

[1] He died 16th June, 1666.

sent away with the Gottenburgh ships.   They conclude this
to be much the best fleete, for force of guns, greatness and
number of ships and men, that ever England did see; being,
as Sir W. Coventry reckons, besides those left behind, eighty-
nine men-of-war, and twenty fire-ships, though we cannot hear
that they have with them above eighteen.   The French are
not yet joined with the Dutch, which do dissatisfy the Hollanders; and, if they should have a defeat, will undo De
Witt;[1] the people generally of Holland do hate this league
with France.

24th. Busy very late, till midnight, drawing up a repre-
sentation of the state of my victualling business to the Duke
in writing, I now having had the advantage of having had
two fleetes despatched in better condition than ever any fleetes
were yet, I believe—at least, with less complaint; and by this
means I shall with the better confidence get my bills out for
my salary.

25th. At White Hall; we find the Court gone to Chapel,
it being St. James's-day. And, by and by, while they are at
chapel, and we waiting chapel being done, come people out of
the Park, telling us that the guns are heard plainly. And so
every body to the Park, and by and by the chapel done; and
the King and Duke into the bowling-green, and upon the
leads, whither I went, and there the guns were plain to be
heard; though it was pretty to hear how confident some
would be in the loudnesse of the guns, which it was as much
as ever I could do to hear them. By and by the King to
dinner, and I waited there his dining; but, Lord! how little
I should be pleased, I think, to have so many people crowd-
ing about me; and, among other things, it astonished me to
see my Lord Barkeshire[2] waiting at table, and serving the
King drink, in that dirty pickle as I never saw man in my
life.   Here I met Mr. Williams, who would have me to dine
where he was invited to dine, at the Backe-stayres. So, after
the King's meat was taken away, we thither; but he could

---

[1] Pepys seems to have foreseen the fate of De Witt.
[2] Thomas Howard, second son of Thomas, first Earl of Suffolk, created Earl of
Barkshire, 1625-6, K.G.   Ob. 1669, aged nearly 90.

not stay, but left me there among two or three of the King's
servants, where we dined with the meat that come from his
table; which was most excellent, with most brave drink
cooled in ice, which, at this hot time, was welcome; and I
drinking no wine, had metheglin for the King's own drinking,
which did please me mightily.

26th. Dined at home: Mr. Hunt and his wife, who is very
gallant, and newly come from Cambridge, because of the sickness, with us. With my wife and Mercer to my Lord Chancellor's new house, and there carried them up to the leads,
where I find my Lord Chamberlain, Lauderdale, Sir Robert
Murray, and others, and do find it the most delightful place
for prospect there ever was in the world, it even abashing me;
and that is all, in short, I can say of it. To the office, but
no news at all from the fleete.

27th. To White Hall. The waterman tells me that news
is come that our ship Resolution is burnt, and that we had
sunk four or five of the enemy's ships. To Sir W. Coventry's
lodging, and there he showed me Captain Talbot's letter,
wherein he says that the fight begun on the 25th: that our
White Squadron begun with one of the Dutch squadrons, and
then the Red with another—so hot, that we put them both to
giving way; and so they continued in pursuit all the day, and
as long as he stayed with them: that the blow fell to the
Zealand squadron; and, after a long dispute, he against two
or three great ships, received eight or nine dangerous shots,
and so come away; and says, he saw the Resolution burned
by one of their fire-ships, and four or five of the enemy's; but
says that two or three of our great ships were in danger of
being fired by our fire-ships, which Sir W. Coventry and I
cannot understand. But, upon the whole, he and I walked
two or three turns in the Park under the great trees; and do
doubt that this Gallant is come away a little too soon, having
lost never a mast nor sail. And then we did begin to discourse of the young genteel captains, which he was very free
with me in speaking his mind of the unruliness of them; and
what a loss the King hath of his old men; and now of this
Hannam, of the Resolution, if he be dead. He told me how

he is disturbed to hear the commanders at sea called cowards here on shore, and that he was yesterday concerned publickly at a dinner to defend them, against somebody that said that not above twenty of them fought as they should do, and indeed it is derived from the Duke of Albemarle himself, who wrote so to the King and Duke, and that he told them how they fought four days—two of them with great disadvantage. The Count de Guiche,[1] who was on board De Ruyter, writing his narrative home in French of the fight, do lay all the honour that may be upon the English courage above the Dutch, and that he himself[2] was sent down from the King and Duke of York after the fight, to pray them to spare none that they thought had not done their parts, and that they had removed but four, whereof Du Tell is one, of whom he would say nothing; but, it seems, the Duke of York hath been much displeased at his removal, and hath now taken him into his service,[3] which is a plain affront to the Duke of Albemarle; and two of the others, Sir W. Coventry did speak very slenderly of their faults. Only the last, which was old Teddiman, he says, is in fault, and hath little to excuse himself with; and that, therefore, we should not be forward in condemning men of want of courage, when the Generals, who are both men of metal, and hate cowards, and had the sense of our ill success upon them, thought fit to remove no more of them, when desired by the King and Duke of York to do it, without respect to any favour any of them can pretend to in either of them.

28th. To the Pope's Head, where my Lord Brouncker and his mistress dined, and Commissioner Pett, Dr. Charleton,[4]

---

[1] Eldest son of the Duke de Grammont.

[2] Sir W. Coventry.

[3] As Yeoman of the Cellar and Cup-bearer. This most improper step of the Duke of York is alluded to in the *Poems on State Affairs*, vol. i., p. 36, ed. 1703:—

> "Cashier the memory of Dutell, raised up
> To taste, instead of death, his Highness' cup."

[4] Walter Charleton, a native of Somersetshire, Physician in Ordinary to Charles II. during his exile and after the Restoration. He was a learned and voluminous author, and died in 1707

and myself, were entertained with a venison pasty by Sir
W. Warren. Here very pretty discourse of Dr. Charleton's,
concerning Nature's fashioning every creature's teeth according to the food she intends them; and that men's, it is plain,
was not for flesh, but fruit, and that he can at any time tell
the food of a beast unknown by the teeth; and that all children love fruit, and none brought to flesh, but against their
wills, at first. Thence with my Lord to his coach-house, and
there put in six horses into his coach, and he and I alone to
Highgate. Being come thither, we went to my Lord Lauderdale's house ¹ to speak with him, and find him and his lady,
and some Scotch people, at supper: pretty odd company,
though, my Lord Brouncker tells me, my Lord Lauderdale is
a man of mighty good reason and judgement. But at supper
there played one of their servants upon the viallin some Scotch
tunes only; several, and the best of their country, as they
seemed to esteem them, by their praising and admiring them:
but, Lord! the strangest ayre that ever I heard in my life,
and all of one cast. But strange to hear my Lord Lauderdale say himself that he had rather hear a cat mew, than the
best musique in the world; and the better the musique, the
more sick it makes him; and that of all instruments, he hates
the lute most, and, next to that, the baggpipe.

29th. (Lord's day.) Before sermon was done at Church,
comes news by a letter to Sir W. Batten, to my hand, of the
late fight, which I sent to his house, he at Church. But,
Lord! with what impatience I staid till sermon was done, to
know the issue of the fight, with a thousand hopes and fears
and thoughts about the consequences of either. At last
sermon is done, and he come home, and the bells immediately
rung soon as the church was done. But coming to Sir W.
Batten to know the news, his letter said nothing of it; but
all the town is full of a victory. By and by, a letter from
Sir W. Coventry tells me that we have the victory. Beat
them into the Weelings; had taken two of their great ships;

¹ Lord Lauderdale's house was on the eastern part of Highgate Hill, and is
still known by that name. It was lately inhabited by Sir Richard Bethell
Solicitor-General; it is now the residence of James Yates, Esq., of Liverpool

but, by the orders of the Generals, they are burned. This being, methought, but a poor result after the fighting of two so great fleetes, and four days having no tidings of them, I was still impatient: but could know no more. I to Sir W. Batten, where the Lieutenant of the Tower' was, and Sir John Minnes, and the news I find is what I had heard before; only that our Blue squadron, it seems, was pursued the most of the time, having more ships, a great many, than its number, allotted to its share. Young Seymour is killed, the only captain slain. The Resolution burned; but, as they say, most of her crew and commander saved. This is all, only we keep the sea, which denotes a victory, or, at least, that we are not beaten; but no great matters to brag of, God knows.

30th. To Sir W. Coventry, at St. James's, where I find him in his new closet, which is very fine, and well supplied with handsome books. I find him speak very slightly of the late victory: dislikes their staying with the fleete up their coast, believing that the Dutch will come out in fourteen days, and then we, with our unready fleete, by reason of some of the ships being maymed, shall be in bad condition to fight them upon their coast: is much dissatisfied with the great number of men, and their fresh demands of twenty-four victualling-ships, they going out the other day as full as they could stow. He spoke slightly of the Duke of Albemarle, saying, when De Ruyter come to give him a broadside—"Now," says he, chewing of tobacco the while, "will this fellow come and give me two broadsides, and then he shall run;" but it seems he held him to it two hours, till the Duke himself was forced to retreat, to refit, and was towed off, and De Ruyter staid for him till he come back again to fight. One in the ship saying to the Duke, "Sir, methinks De Ruyter hath given us more than two broadsides;"—"Well," says the Duke, "but you shall find him run by and by;" and so he did, says Sir W. Coventry; but after the Duke himself had been first made to fall off. The Resolution had all brass guns, being the same that Sir J. Lawson had in her in the Streights. It is

' Sir John Robinson.

observed, that the two fleetes were even in number to one ship.

Thence home; and to sing with my wife and Mercer in the garden; and coming in, I find my wife plainly dissatisfied with me, that I can spend so much time with Mercer, teaching her to sing, and could never take the pains with her, which I acknowledge; but it is because that the girl do take musick mighty readily, and she do not, and musick is the thing of the world that I love most, and all the pleasure almost that I can now take. So to bed, in some little discontent, but no words from me.

31st. The Court empty, the King being gone to Tunbridge, and the Duke of York a-hunting. I had some discourse with Pevy, who is mightily discontented, I find, about his disappointments at Court; and says, of all places, if there be hell, it is here: no faith, no truth, no love, nor any agreement between man and wife, nor friends. He would have spoke broader, but I put it off to another time; and so parted. Povy discoursed with me about my Lord Peterborough's 50*l.*, which his man did give me from him, the last year's salary I paid him, which he would have Povy pay him again; but I have not taken it to myself yet, and therefore will most heartily return him, and mark him out as a coxcomb. Povy went down to Mr. Williamson's, and brought me up this extract out of the Flanders' letters to-day come:—That Admiral Everson, and the Admiral and Vice-Admiral of Freezeland, with many captains and men, are slain; that De Ruyter is safe, but lost 250 men out of his own ship; but that he is in great disgrace, and Trump in better favour; that Bankert's ship is burned, himself hardly escaping with a few men on board De Haes; that fifteen captains are to be tried the seventh of August; and that the hangman was sent from Flushing to assist the Council of War. How much of this is true, time will show. Mighty well, and end this month in content of mind and body. The public matters looking more safe for the present than they did, and we having a victory of the Dutch just such as I could have wished, and as the kingdom was fit to bear—enough to give us the name of con

querors, and leave us masters of the sea, but without any
such great matters done as should give the Duke of Albemarle any honour at all, or give him cause to rise to his former
insolence.

August 1st. Walked over the Park with Sir W. Coventry,
who I clearly see is not thoroughly pleased with the late
management of the fight, nor with any thing that the Generals
do; only is glad to hear that De Ruyter is out of favour, and
that this fight hath cost them 5000 men, as they themselves
do report. And it is a strange thing, as he observes, how
now and then the slaughter runs on one hand; there being
5000 killed on theirs, and not above 400 or 500 killed and
wounded on ours, and as many flag-officers on theirs as ordinary captains on ours; there being Everson, and the Admiral
and Vice-Admiral of Freezeland on theirs, and Seymour,
Martin, and ——, on ours.

2d. To the office, where we sat, and in discourse at the
table with Sir W. Batten, I was obliged to tell him it was
an untruth, which did displease him mightily, and parted at
noon very angry with me. Balty's wife is in great pain for
her husband, not hearing of him since the fight; but I understand he was not in it, going hence too late.

3d. The death of Everson, and the report of our success,
beyond expectation, in the killing of so great a number of
men, hath raised the estimation of the late victory considerably; but is only among fools; for all that was but acci-
dental. But this morning, getting Sir W. Pen to read over
the Narrative with me, he did sparingly, yet plainly, say that
we might have intercepted their Zealand squadron coming
home, if we had done our parts; and more, that we might
have spooned¹ before the wind as well as they, and have overtaken their ships in the pursuit, in all the while.

4th. Mr. Cooke dined with us, who is lately come from
Hinchingbroke. The family all well. This evening Sir
W. Pen come into the garden, and walked with me, and told
me that he had certain notice that at Flushing they are in

¹ To spoom, or spoon, is to go right before the wind, without any sail. — *Sea
Dictionary*, 1708.

great distraction. De Ruyter dares not come on shore for
fear of the people; nor any body open their houses or shops
for fear of the tumult; which is a very good hearing.

5th. (Lord's day.) To the church, where, I believe, Mrs.
Horsely goes, by Merchant-tailors' hall, and there I find in the
pulpit, Elborough, my old schoolfellow and a simple rogue,[1]
and yet I find preaching a very good sermon, and in as right
a parson-like manner, and in as good a manner, as I have
heard anybody; and the church very full, which is a surprising consideration. After dinner, with my wife and Mercer
and Jane, by water up as high as Mortlake with great pleasure, and a fine day, reading over the second part of the Siege
of Rhodes, with great delight. We landed, and walked at
Barne-elmes, and then at the net-houses I landed, and bought
a millon, and we did also land and eat and drink at Wandsworth, and so to the Old Swan, and thence walked home.
It being a mighty fine cool evening, my wife and I spent an
hour in the garden talking of our living in the country, when
I shall be turned out of the office, as I fear the Parliament
may find faults enough to remove us all. Nan, at Sir W.
Pen's, lately married to one Markeham, a kinsman of Sir
W. Pen's — a pretty wench she is.

6th. To my Lady Montagu's, at Westminster, and there
visited my Lord Hinchingbroke, newly come from Hinchingbroke, and find him a mighty sober gentleman, to my great
content. In Fenchurch Street met with Mr. Battersby;
says he, "Do you see Dan Rawlinson's[2] door shut up?"
which I did, and wondered. "Why," says he, "after all
this sickness, and himself spending all the last year in the

---

[1] See Sept. 2, 1666, post.

[2] In the church of St. Dionis Backchurch, amongst other memorials of different
members of his family, is a monument on a pillar for Daniel Rawlinson, the person
mentioned in the text. He was a London wine-merchant, descended from the
Grasdales of Lancashire, born in this parish, and died in 1679, aged 65. He was
the father of Sir Thomas Rawlinson, President of Bridewell Hospital, and Lord
Mayor in 1706; two of whose sons, Thomas and Richard, LL.D., were well known
in the literary world as eminent antiquaries and book collectors, though their
extensive libraries were ultimately consigned to the hammer. Richard, who had
been educated at St. John's College, Oxford, will long be remembered as a magnificent benefactor to that university. — See Malcolm's *London*, vol iii., p. 438, edit.
1803.

country, one of his men is now dead of the plague, and his
wife and one of his maids sick, and himself shut up;" which
troubles me mightily. So home; and there do hear also
from Mrs. Sarah Daniel, that Greenwich is at this time much
worse than ever it was, and Deptford too: and she told us
that they believed all the town would leave the town, and
come to London; which is now the receptacle of all the
people from all infected places. God preserve us! After
dinner, in comes Mrs. Knipp, and I sat and talked with her,
it being the first time of her being here since her being
brought to bed. I very pleasant to her; but perceive my
wife hath no great pleasure in her being here. However, we
talked and sang, and were very pleasant. By and by comes
Mr. Pierce and his wife, the first time she also hath been
here since her lying-in, both having been brought to bed of
boys, and both of them dead. Knipp and I sang, and then
I offered to carry them home, and to take my wife with me,
but she would not go: so I with them, leaving my wife in a
very ill humour. However, I would not be removed from
my civility to them, but sent for a coach, and went with
them; and in our way, Knipp saying that she come out of
doors without a dinner to us, I took them to Old Fish Street,
to the very house and woman where I kept my wedding
dinner,[1] where I never was since, and there I did give them
a jole of salmon, and what else was to be had. And here we
talked of the ill-humour of my wife, which I did excuse as
much as I could, and they seemed to admit of it, but did
both confess they wondered at it; but from thence to other
discourse of my Lord Brouncker. They told me how poorly
my Lord carried himself the other day to his kinswoman,
Mrs. Howard, and was displeased because she called him
uncle to a little gentlewoman that is there with him, which
he will not admit of; for no relation is to be challenged from
others to a lord, and did treat her thereupon very rudely and
ungenteely. Knipp tells me, also, that my Lord keeps

---

[1] The tavern was evidently selected to mark Pepys's disgust at his wife's ill-
humour; but he probably did not venture to mention the circumstance on his
return home.

another woman besides Mrs. Williams; and that, when I was
there the other day, there was a great hubbub in the house,
Mrs. Williams being fallen sick, because my Lord was gone
to his other mistress, making her wait for him till his return
from the other mistress; and a great deal of do there was
about it; and Mrs. Williams swounded at it, at the very time
when I wondered at the reason of my being received so
negligently. I set them both at home—Knipp at her house,
her husband being at the doore; and glad she was to be
found to have staid out so long with me and Mrs. Pierce,
and none else. Home, and there find my wife mightily out
of order, and reproaching Mrs. Pierce and Knipp as wenches,
and I know not what. But I did give her no words to offend
her, and quietly let all pass.

7th. Comes Mr. Reeve, with a twelve-foote glasse. Up
to the top of the house, and there we endeavoured to see the
moon, and Saturn and Jupiter, but the heavens proved
cloudy, and so we lost our labour, having taken pains to get
things together, in order to the managing of our new glass.
I receive fresh intelligence that Deptford and Greenwich are
now afresh exceedingly afflicted with the sickness more than
ever.

8th. Discoursed with Mr. Hooke about the nature of
sounds, and he did make me understand the nature of
musicall sounds made by strings, mighty prettily; and told
me that having come to a certain number of vibrations
proper to make any tone, he is able to tell how many strokes
a fly makes with her wings, those flies that hum in their
flying, by the note that it answers to in musique, during
their flying. That, I suppose, is a little too much refined;
but his discourse in general of sound was mighty fine. To
St. James's, where we attended with the rest of my fellows
on the Duke, whom I found with two or three patches upon
his nose and about his right eye, which came from his being
struck with the bough of a tree the other day in his hunting;
and it is a wonder it did not strike out his eye. After we
had done our business with him, which is now but little, the
want of money being such as leaves us but little to do but to

answer complaints of the want thereof; the representing of
our want of money being now become uselesse.   To Bow, to
my Lady Pooly's,[1] where my wife was with Mr. Batelier and
his sisters; and there I found a noble supper.   About ten
o'clock we rose from table, and sang a song; and so home in
two coaches, Mr. Batelier and his sister Mary, and my wife
and I in one, and Mercer alone in the other; and, after being
examined at Allgate whether we were husbands and wives,
home.   I find Reeves there, it being a mighty fine bright
night, and so upon my leads, though very sleepy, till one in
the morning, looking on the moon and Jupiter, with his
twelve-foot glass, and another of six foot, that he hath
brought with him to-night, and the sights mighty pleasant,
and one of the glasses I will buy.   So to bed mighty sleepy,
but with much pleasure, Reeves lying at my house; and
mighty proud I am, and ought to be thankful to God Almighty
that I am able to have a spare bed for my friends.

9th.   Mightily pleased with a Virgin's head that my wife
is now drawing of.   In the evening to Lumbard Street, about
money, to enable me to pay Sir G. Carteret's 3000*l.* which
he hath lodged in my hands, in behalf of his son and my
Lady Jemimah, towards their portion.   Mrs. Rawlinson is
dead of the sickness, and her maid continues mighty ill.   He[2]
himself is got out of the house.   I met with Mr. Evelyn in
the street, who tells me the sad condition at this very day at
Deptford, for the plague, and more at Deale, within his
precinct, as one of the Commissioners for sick and wounded
seamen, that the towne is almost quite depopulated.

10th.   Homeward, and hear in Fenchurch Street, that now
the maid is also dead at Mr. Rawlinson's; so that there are
three dead in all—the wife, a man-servant, and maid-servant.
Pleased to hear of Mrs. Barbara Sheldon's good fortune, who
is like to have Mr. Wood's son, the mast-maker, a very rich
man, and to be married speedily, she being already mighty
fine upon it.

12th.   (Lord's day.)   I and my wife up to her closet, to

---

[1] Wife of Sir Edmund Pooly, mentioned before.
[2] Her husband, Daniel Rawlinson.

examine her kitchen accounts, and there I took occasion to
fall out with her, for her buying a laced handkercher and
pinner without my leave. From this we began both to be
angry, and so continued till bed.

13th. Up, without being friends with my wife, nor great
enemies, being both quiet and silent. To Paul's church-
yard, to treat with a bookbinder to come and gild the backs
of all my books, to make them handsome, to stand in my
new presses.

14th. (Thanksgiving day.)[1] Comes Mr. Foley and his man,
with a box of great variety of carpenter's and joyner's tooles,
which I had bespoke, which please me mightily, but I will
have more. Povy tells me how mad my letter makes my
Lord Peterborough, and what a furious letter he hath writ to
me in answer, though it is not come yet. This did trouble
me; for, though there be no reason, yet to have a nobleman's
mouth open against a man, may do a man hurt; so I endeavoured to have found him out and spoke with him, but could
not. So to the chapel, and heard a piece of the Dean of
Westminster's[2] sermon, and a speciall good anthemne before
the King, after sermon. After dinner, with my wife and
Mercer to the Beare Garden;[3] where I have not been, I
think, of many years, and saw some good sport of the bull's
tossing the dogs—one into the very boxes. But it is a very
rude and nasty pleasure. We had a great many hectors in
the same box with us, and one very fine went into the pit,
and played his dog for a wager; which was a strange sport
for a gentleman; where they drank wine, and drank Mercer's
health first; which I pledged with my hat off. We supped
at home, and very merry. And then about nine to Mrs.
Mercer's gate, where the fire and boys expected us, and her
son had provided abundance of serpents and rockets; and

---

[1] In honour of the naval success.

[2] John Dolben, afterwards Archbishop of York. The sermon was printed.

[3] The Bear-Garden was situated on Bankside, close to the precinct of the Clinke
Liberty, and very near to the old Palace of the Bishops of Winchester. The
name still exists in a street or lane at the foot of Southwark Bridge. This old
English, but barbarous sport, which had been suppressed by the Puritans, was
revived at the Restoration. There are many particulars about the Bear-Garden
in the *Gentleman's Mag.* for 1833, part i., p. 483; part ii., p. 507.

there mighty merry, my Lady Pen and Pegg going thither with us, and Nan Wright, till about twelve at night, flinging our fireworks, and burning one another, and the people over the way. And, at last, our business being most spent, we went into Mrs. Mercer's, and there mighty merry, smutting one another with candle grease and soot, till most of us were like devils. And that being done, then we broke up, and to my house; and there I made them drink, and upstairs we went, and then fell into dancing, W. Batelier dancing well; and dressing, him and I, and one Mr. Banister, who, with my wife, come over also with us, like women; and Mercer put on a suit of Tom's, like a boy, and mighty mirth we had, and Mercer danced a jigg; and Nan Wright and my wife and Pegg Pen put on perriwigs. Thus we spent till three or four in the morning, mighty merry; and then parted, and to bed.

15th. Mighty sleepy; slept till past eight of the clock, and was called up by a letter from Sir W. Coventry; which, among other things, tells me how we have burned one hundred and sixty ships of the enemy within the Fly. I up, and with all possible haste, and in pain for fear of coming late, it being our day of attending the Duke of York, to St. James's, where they are full of the particulars; how they are generally good merchant-ships, some of them laden and supposed rich ships. We spent five fire-ships upon them. We landed on the Schelling, Sir Philip Howard with some men, and Holmes, I think, with others, about 1000 in all, and burned a town; and so come away. By and by the Duke of York, with his books, showed us the very place and manner: and that it was not our design and expectation to have done this, but only to have landed on the Fly, and burned some of their stores; but, being come in, we spied those ships, and with our long boats, one by one, fired them, our ships running all a-ground, it being so shoal water. We were led to this by, it seems, a renegado captain of the Hollanders, who found himself ill used by De Ruyter for his good service, and so come over to us, and hath done us good service; so that now we trust him, and he himself did go on this expedition. The service is very

great, and our joys as great for it.   All this will make the
Duke of Albemarle in repute again, I doubt.   Down the
river, reading "The Adventures of Five Houres," which, the
more I read, the more I admire.   The guns of the Tower
going off, and there being bonfires also in the street for this
late good successe.

16th. This day Sir W. Batten did show us at the Table a
.etter from Sir T. Allen, which says, that we have taken ten
or twelve ships, since the late great expedition of burning
their ships and town, laden with hemp, flax, tar, deals, &c.
This was good news; but by and by comes in Sir G. Carteret,
and he asked us with full mouth what we would give for good
news.   Says Sir W. Batten, "I have better than you, for a
wager."   They laid sixpence, and we that were by were to
give sixpence to him that told the best news.   So Sir W.
Batten told his of the ten or twelve ships.   Sir G. Carteret
did then tell us that, upon the news of the burning of the
ships and town, the common people of Amsterdam did besiege
De Witt's house, and he was forced to flee to the Prince of
Orange, who is gone to Cleve, to the marriage of his sister.
This we concluded all the best news, and my Lord Brouncker
and myself did give Sir G. Carteret our sixpence a-piece,
which he did give Mr. Smith to give to the poor.   Thus we
made ourselves mighty merry.

17th. Down by water to Woolwich, and had a piece of
bridecake sent me by Mrs. Barbary [1] into the boate after me,
she being here at her uncle's, with her husband, Mr. Wood's
son, and mighty nobly married.   They say she was very fine,
and he very rich—a strange fortune for so odd a looked maid,
though her hands and body be good, and nature very good, I
think.   With Captain Erwin, discoursing about the East
Indys, where he hath often been.   And, among other things,
he tells me how the King of Syam seldom goes out without
thirty or forty thousand people with him, and not a word
spoke, nor a hum or cough in the whole company to be
heard.   He tells me, the punishment frequently there for
malefactors, is cutting off the crowne of their head, which

---

[1] Sheldon.

they do very dexterously, leaving their brains bare, which kills them presently. He told me, what I remember he hath once done heretofore; that every body is to lie flat down at the coming by of the King, and nobody to look upon him upon pain of death. And that he and his fellows, being strangers, were invited to see the sport of taking a wild elephant; and they did only kneel, and look towards the King. Their druggerman[1] did desire them to fall down, for otherwise he should suffer for their contempt of the King. The sport being ended, a messenger comes from the King, which the druggerman thought had been to take away his life; but it was to enquire how the strangers liked the sport. The druggerman answered, that they did cry it up to be the best that ever they saw, and that they never heard of any Prince so great in every thing as this King. The messenger being gone back, Erwin and his company asked their druggerman what he had said, which he told them. "But why," they say, "would you say that without our leave, it being not true?"—"It makes no matter for that,' says he; "I must have said it, or have been hanged; for our King do not live by meat, nor drink, but by having great lyes told him." In our way back, we come by a little vessel that come into the river this morning, and says she left the fleete in Sole Bay, and that she hath not heard, she belonging to Sir W. Jennings in the fleete, of any such prizes taken as the ten or twelve I enquired about, and said by Sir W. Batten yesterday to be taken, so I fear it is not true. I had the good fortune to see Mrs. Stewart, who is grown a little too tall, but is a woman of most excellent features. The narrative of the late expedition in burning the ships is in print,[2] and makes it a great thing; and I hope it is so. Sir Richard Ford did, very understandingly, methought, give us an account of the originall of the Hollands Bank, and the nature of it, and how they do never give any interest at all to any person that brings in their money, though what is brought 'n upon the public faith, interest is given by the State for. The unsafe condition of a Bank under a Monarch, and the little safety to a Monarch

---

[1] Dragoman.   [2] See 15th August, ante.

to have any ; or Corporation alone, as London in answer to
Amsterdam, to have so great a wealth or credit, it is, that
makes it hard to have a Bank here.   And, as to the former,
he did tell us how it sticks in the memory of most merchants
how the late King, when, by the war between Holland and
France and Spain, all the bullion of Spain was brought
hither, one third of it to be coyned ; and indeed it was found
advantageous to the merchant to coyne most of it, was persuaded in a strait, by my Lord Cottington,[1] to seize upon the
money in the Tower : which, though in a few days the merchants concerned did prevail to get it released, yet the thing
will never be forgot.   Sir John Minnes come home to-night,
not well, from Chatham, where he hath been at a pay, holding it at Upnor Castle, because of the plague so much in the
towne of Chatham.   He hath, they say, got an ague, being
so much on the water.

18th.   At my little mercer's, in Lumbard Street, who hath
the pretty wench, like the old Queen, and there cheapened
some stuffs to hang my room.

19th.   (Lord's day.)   Comes by agreement Mr. Reeves,
bringing me a lanthorn, with pictures in glass, to make strange
things appear on a wall, very pretty.   We did also at night
see Jupiter and his girdle and satellites, very fine, with my
twelve-foot glass, but could not Saturne, he being very dark.
Spong and I had also several fine discourses upon the globes,
this afternoon, particularly why the fixed stars do not rise and
set at the same hour all the year long, which he could not
demonstrate, nor I neither.

20th.   Waked this morning, about six o'clock, with a violent knocking at Sir J. Minnes's door, to call up Mrs. Ham-
mon, crying out that Sir J. Minnes is a-dying.   I saw him on
Saturday, after his fit of the ague, and then he was pretty
lusty, which troubles me mightily ; for he is a very good,

---

[1] Sir Francis Cottington, a younger son of Philip Cottington, of Godmanston,
Somerset, was created, by Charles I., Lord Cottington, of Hanworth.   He be-
came successively one of the Clerks of the Council, Chancellor of the Exchequer,
Ambassador into Spain, and Lord Treasurer of England, under the two elder
Stuarts.   He died at Valladolid in 1653, s. p., and his body was brought to
England, and interred under a stately monument in Westminster Abbey, erected
by Charles Cottington, his nephew and heir.   See 6th Dec. 1667, for an account
of his disinheriting a nephew for a foolish speech.

harmless, honest, gentleman, though not fit for business. To Deptford by water, reading "Othello, Moor of Venice," which I ever heretofore esteemed a mighty good play; but, having so lately read "The Adventures of Five Houres," it seems a mean thing. All the afternoon upon my Tangier accounts, getting Tom Wilson to help me in writing as I read; and I find myself right to a farthing, in an account of 127,000*l*. I visited Sir J. Minnes, who is much impatient by this few days' sickness, and I fear indeed it will kill him.

21st. Mr. Batelier told me how, being with some others at Bourdeaux, making a bargain with another man at a taverne for some clarets, they did hire a fellow to thunder, which he had the art of doing, upon a deale board, and to rain and hail, that is, make the noise of, so as did give them a pretence of undervaluing their merchants' wines, by saying this thunder would spoil and turn them, which was so reasonable to the merchant, that he did abate two pistolls per ton for the wine, in belief of that.

22d. I to St. James's, and there with the Duke of York. I had opportunity of much talk with Sir W. Pen to-day, he being newly come from the fleete; and he do much undervalue the honour that is given to the conduct of Holmes in burning the ships and town,[1] saying it was a great thing indeed, and of great profit to us in being of great loss to the enemy, but that it was wholly a business of chance. Mrs. Knipp tells me, my song of "Beauty Retire" is mightily cried up, which I am not a little proud of; and do think I have done "It is Decreed" better, but I have not finished it. My closet is doing by an upholsterer, which I am pleased with, but fear my purple will be too sad for that melancholy room. My wife, Knipp, and Mercer, by coach to Moorfields, and there saw Polichinello, which pleases me mightily.

23d. Sir W. Coventry sent me word that the Dutch fleete is certainly abroad; and so we are to hasten all we have to send to our fleete with all speed. But, Lord! to see how my

[1] The town burned (see 15th Aug., *ante*) was Brandaris, a place of 1000 houses, on the isle of Schelling: the ships lay between that island and the Fly (*i. e.* Vlieland), the adjoining island. This attack probably provoked that by the Dutch on Chatham: see Pepys' remarks, 30th June, 1667, *post*.

Lord Brouncker undertakes the despatch of the fire-ships, when he is no more fit for it than a porter; and all the while Sir W. Pen, who is the most fit, is unwilling to displease him, and do not look after it; and so the King's work is like to be well done.

24th. Comes Sympson, to set up my other new presses for my books, to my most extraordinary satisfaction; so that I think it will be as noble a closet as any man hath; though, indeed, it would have been better to have had a little more light. This afternoon comes Mrs. Barbary Sheldon, now Mrs. Wood, to see my wife: I was so busy, I would not see her. But she come, it seems, mighty rich in rings and fine clothes, and like a lady, and says she is matched mighty well, at which I am very glad, but wonder at her good fortune, and the folly of her husband.

26th. (Lord's day.) I was a little disturbed with news my Lord Brouncker brought me, that we are to attend the King at White Hall this afternoon, and that it is about a complaint from the Generals against us. Sir W. Pen and I by coach to White Hall, and there staid till the King and Cabinet met in the Green Chamber, and then we were called in; and there the King begun with me, to hear how the victualls of the fleete stood. I did, in a long discourse, tell him and the rest, the Duke of York, Lord Chancellor, Lord Treasurer, both the Secretarys, Sir G. Carteret, and Sir W. Coventry, how it stood, wherein they seemed satisfied, but press mightily for more supplies; and the letter of the Generals, which was read, did lay their not going, or too soon returning from the Dutch coast, this next bout, to the want of victuals. They then proceeded to the enquiry after the fire-ships; and did all very superficially, and without any severity at all. But, however, I was in pain, after we come out, to know how I had done, and hear, well enough; but, however, it shall be a caution to me to prepare myself against a day of inquisition. Being come out, I met with Mr. Moore; and he and I an hour together in the Gallery, telling me how far they are gone in getting my Lord Sandwich's pardon, so as the Chancellor is prepared in it; and Sir H. Bennet do promote it, and the warrant for the King's signing is drawn. The business between my Lord

Hinchingbroke and Mrs. Mallet is quite broke off; he attended her at Tunbridge, and she declaring her affections to be settled; and he not being fully pleased with the vanity and liberty of her carriage. Thence to discourse of the times; and he tells me he believes both my Lord Arlington and Sir W. Coventry, as we'l as my Lord Sandwich and Sir G. Carteret, have reason to fear, and are afraid, of this Parliament now coming on. He tells me that Bristoll's faction is getting ground apace against my Lord Chancellor. He told me that my Lord Coventry[1] was a cunning, crafty man, and did make as many bad decrees in Chancery as any man; and that, in one case, that occasioned many years' dispute, at last when the King come in, it was hoped, by the party grieved, to get my Lord Chancellor to reverse a decree of his. Sir W. Coventry took the opportunity of the business between the Duke of York and the Duchess, and said to my Lord Chancellor that he had rather be drawn up Holborne to be hanged, than live to see any decree of his father's reversed; and so the Chancellor did not think fit to do it. But it still stands, to the undoing of one Norton, a printer, about his right to the printing of the Bible,[2] and Grammar, &c. Sir J. Minnes had a very bad fit this day, and a hickup do take him, which is a very bad sign.

27th. Up, and to my new closet. Then to break open a window to the leads' side in my old closet, which will enlighten the room mightily, and make it mighty pleasant. Sir G. Carteret tells me what is done about my Lord's pardon, and is not for letting the Duke of York know any thing of it beforehand, but to carry it as speedily and quietly as we can. He seems to be very apprehensive that the Parliament will be troublesome and inquisitive into faults; but seems not to value them as to himself.

28th. At noon I, with my wife and Mercer, to Philpott

---

[1] The Lord Keeper. Ob. 1639–40.

[2] Roger Norton, of Little Britain, Printer of Latin, Greek, and Hebrew, to His Majesty, and one of the Patentees in the office of King's Printer, in whom, as well as in the universities of Oxford and Cambridge, is still vested the exclusive right of printing the authorized English Version of the Scriptures. He was Master of the Stationers' Company in 1684. Ob. 26th October, 1723.

Lane, a great cook's shop, to the wedding of Mr. Longracke, our purveyor, a civil man, and hath married a sober, serious mayde. Here I met much ordinary company, I going thither at his great request; but there was Mr. Madden and his lady, a fine, noble, pretty lady, and he a fine gentleman seems to be. We four were most together, but the whole company was very simple and innocent. After dinner, the young women went to dance; among others, Mr. Christopher Pett his daughter, who is a very pretty, modest girl: I am mightily taken with her. That being done, we broke up mighty civilly, the bride and bridegroom going to Greenwich. They keeping their dinner here only for my sake. To the office, and anon, on a sudden, called to meet Sir W. Pen and Sir W. Coventry, who did read me a letter from the Generals to the King, a most scurvy letter, reflecting most upon him, and then upon me for my accounts, not that they are not true, but that we do not consider the expence of the fleete; and then upon the whole office, in neglecting them and the King's service, and this in very plain, and sharp, and menacing terms. But a great supply must be made, and shall be, in grace of God!

29th. Found Sir W. Pen talking to Orange Moll, of the King's house, who, to our great comfort, told us that they begun to act on the 18th of this month. So on to St. James's, in the way Sir W. Pen telling me that Mr. Norton that married Sir J. Lawson's daughter [1] is dead—she left 800*l.* a year joynture, a son to inherit the whole estates. She freed from her father-in-law's tyranny, and is in condition to help her mother, who needs it; of which I am glad — the young lady being very pretty. To St. James's, and there Sir W. Coventry took Sir W. Pen and me apart, and read to us his answer to the General's letter to the King, that he read last night; wherein he is very plain, and states the matter in full defence of himself, and of me with him, which he could not avoid; which is a good comfort to me, that I happened to be involved with him in the same cause. And then, speaking of the supplies which have been made to this fleete, more than ever in all kinds to any, even that wherein the Duke of York himself

---

[1] See 6th July, 1665, *ante.*

was, "Well," says he, "if this will not do, I will say, as Sir J. Falstaffe did to the Prince, 'Tell your father, that if he do not like this, let him kill the next Piercy himself.'"

31st. Much pleased to-day with thoughts of gilding the backs of all my books alike, in all my new presses.

September 1st. My wife and I to Polichinello, but were there horribly frighted to see Young Killigrew come in, with a great many more young sparks: but we hid ourselves, so as we think they did not see us.

2d. (Lord's day.) Some of our maids sitting up late last night to get things ready against our feast to-day, Jane called us up about three in the morning, to tell us of a great fire they saw in the City. So I rose, and slipped on my night-gown, and went to her window; and thought it to be on the back-side of Marke-lane at the farthest; but, being unused to such fires as followed, I thought it far enough off; and so went to bed again, and to sleep. About seven rose again to dress myself, and there looked out at the window, and saw the fire not so much as it was, and further off. So to my closet to set things to rights, after yesterday's cleaning. By and by Jane comes and tells me that she hears that above 300 houses have been burned down to-night by the fire we saw, and that it is now burning down all Fish Street, by London Bridge. So I made myself ready presently, and walked to the Tower; and there got up upon one of the high places, Sir J. Robinson's little son going up with me; and there I did see the houses at that end of the bridge all on fire, and an infinite great fire on this and the other side the end of the bridge; which, among other people, did trouble me for poor little Michell and our Sarah on the bridge. So down, with my heart full of trouble, to the Lieutenant of the Tower, who tells me that it begun this morning in the King's baker's [1] house in Pudding-lane, and that it hath burned down St. Magnus's Church and most part of Fish Street already. So I down to the water-side, and there got a boat, and through bridge, and there saw a lamentable fire. Poor Michell's house, as far as the Old Swan, already burned that way, and

---

[1] His name was Faryner.

the fire running further, that, in a very little time, it got as
far as the Steele-yard, while I was there.   Every body endeavouring to remove their goods, and flinging into the river,
or bringing them into lighters that lay off; poor people staying in their houses as long as till the very fire touched them,
and then running into boats, or clambering from one pair of
stairs, by the waterside, to another.   And, among other
things, the poor pigeons, I perceive, were loth to leave their
houses, but hovered about the windows and balconys, till
they burned their wings, and fell down.   Having staid, and
in an hour's time seen the fire rage every way; and nobody,
to my sight, endeavouring to quench it, but to remove their
goods, and leave all to the fire; and, having seen it get as far
as the Steele-yard, and the wind mighty high, and driving it
into the City; and everything, after so long a drought, proving combustible, even the very stones of churches; and, among
other things, the poor steeple[1] by which pretty Mrs. ——
lives, and whereof my old schoolfellow Elborough is parson,
taken fire in the very top, and there burned till it fell down;
I to White Hall, with a gentleman with me, who desired to
go off from the Tower, to see the fire, in my boat; and there
up to the King's closet in the Chapel, where people come
about me, and I did give them an account dismayed them all,
and word was carried in to the King.   So I was called for,
and did tell the King and Duke of York what I saw; and
that, unless his Majesty did command houses to be pulled
down, nothing could stop the fire.   They seemed much
troubled, and the King commanded me to go to my Lord
Mayor[2] from him, and command him to spare no houses, but to
pull down before the fire every way.   The Duke of York bid
me tell him, that if he would have any more soldiers, he shall;
and so did my Lord Arlington afterwards, as a great secret.
Here meeting with Captain Cocke, I in his coach, which he
lent me, and Creed with me to Paul's; and there walked
along Watling Street, as well as I could, every creature coming away loaden with goods to save, and, here and there, sick

---

[1] St. Lawrence Poultney, of which Thomas Elborough was curate.
[2] Sir Thomas Bludworth.   See 30th June, 1666, ante.

people carried away in beds.   Extraordinary good goods carried in carts and on backs.   At last met my Lord Mayor in
Canning Street, like a man spent, with a handkercher about
his neck.   To the King's message, he cried, like a fainting
woman, "Lord! what can I do? I am spent: people will not
obey me.   I have been pulling down houses; but the fire
overtakes us faster than we can do it."   That he needed no
more soldiers; and that, for himself, he must go and refresh
himself, having been up all night.   So he left me, and I him,
and walked home; seeing people all almost distracted, and no
manner of means used to quench the fire.   The houses, too,
so very thick thereabouts, and full of matter for burning, as
pitch and tar, in Thames Street; and warehouses of oyle, and
wines, and brandy, and other things.   Here I saw Mr. Isaac
Houblon, the handsome man, prettily dressed and dirty at his
door at Dowgate, receiving some of his brother's things, whose
houses were on fire; and, as he says, have been removed
twice already; and he doubts, as it soon proved, that they
must be, in a little time, removed from his house also, which
was a sad consideration.   And to see the churches all filling
with goods by people who themselves should have been quietly
there at this time.   By this time, it was about twelve o'clock;
and so home, and there find my guests, who were Mr. Wood
and his wife Barbary Shelden, and also Mr. Moone: she
mighty fine, and her husband, for aught I see, a likely man.
But Mr. Moone's design and mine, which was to look over
my closet, and please him with the sight thereof, which he
hath long desired, was wholly disappointed; for we were in
great trouble and disturbance at this fire, not knowing what
to think of it.   However, we had an extraordinary good
dinner, and as merry as at this time we could be.   While at
dinner, Mrs. Batelier come to enquire after Mr. Woolfe and
Stanes, who, it seems, are related to them, whose houses in
Fish Street are all burned, and they in a sad condition.   She
would not stay in the fright.   Soon as dined, I and Moone
away, and walked through the City, the streets full of nothing
but people; and horses and carts loaden with goods, ready to
run over one another, and removing goods from one burned

house to another. They now removing out of Canning Street,
which received goods in the morning, into Lumbard Street,
and further: and, among others, I now saw my little goldsmith Stokes'[1] receiving some friend's goods, whose house itself
was burned the day after. We parted at Paul's; he home,
and I to Paul's Wharf, where I had appointed a boat to
attend me, and took in Mr. Carcasse[2] and his brother, whom
I met in the street, and carried them below and above bridge
too. And again to see the fire, which was now got further,
both below and above, and no likelihood of stopping it. Met
with the King and Duke of York in their barge, and with
them to Queenhithe, and there called Sir Richard Browne to
them. Their order was only to pull down houses apace, and
so below bridge at the water-side; but little was or could be
done, the fire coming upon them so fast. Good hopes there
was of stopping it at the Three Cranes above, and at Buttulph's
Wharf below bridge, if care be used; but the wind carries it
into the City, so as we know not, by the water-side, what it
do there. River full of lighters and boats taking in goods,
and good goods swimming in the water; and only I observed
that hardly one lighter or boat in three that had the goods of
a house in, but there was a pair of Virginalls[3] in it. Having
seen as much as I could now, I away to White Hall by ap-

---

[1] Humphrey Stocks, at the Black Horse in Lombard Street.

[2] James Carcasse, who is again frequently mentioned, was a clerk in the office
for issuing tickets to the seamen. He published a 4to volume of poems in 1679,
called "*Lucida Intervalla*," the following extract from which strongly reflecting
upon Pepys, has been printed in *Notes and Queries*, vol. ii., p. 87:—

> "Get thee behind me, then, dumb devil, begone,
> The Lord hath Ephthatha said to my tongue.
> Him I must praise who open'd hath my lips,
> Sent me from Navy to the Ark by Pepys;
> By Mr. Pepys, who hath my rival been
> For the Duke's favour, more than years thirteen;
> But I excluded, he high and fortunate,
> This Secretary I could never mate.
> But Clerk of th' Acts, if I'm a parson, then
> I shall prevail, the voice outdoes the pen;
> Though in a gown, the challenge I may make,
> And wager win, save, if you can, your stake.
> To th' Admiral I all submit, and vail———"

The concluding line cut off and imperfect.

[3] A sort of spinet, so called from young women playing upon it.

pointment, and there walked to St. James's Park; and there met my wife, and Creed, and Wood, and his wife, and walked to my boat; and there upon the water again, and to the fire up and down, it still encreasing, and the wind great. So near the fire as we could for smoke; and all over the Thames, with one's faces in the wind, you were almost burned with a shower of fire-drops. This is very true: so as houses were burned by these drops and flakes of fire, three or four, nay, five or six houses, one from another. When we could endure no more upon the water, we to a little ale-house on the Bankside, over against the Three Cranes, and there staid till it was dark almost, and saw the fire grow; and, as it grew darker, appeared more and more; and in corners and upon steeples, and between churches and houses, as far as we could see up the hill of the City, in a most horrid, malicious, bloody flame, not like the fine flame of an ordinary fire. Barbary and her husband away before us. We staid till, it being darkish, we saw the fire as only one entire arch of fire from this to the other side the bridge, and in a bow up the hill for an arch of above a mile long: it made me weep to see it. The churches, houses, and all on fire, and flaming at once; and a horrid noise the flames made, and the cracking of houses at their ruine. So home with a sad heart, and there find every body discoursing and lamenting the fire; and poor Tom Hater come with some few of his goods saved out of his house, which was burned upon Fish Street Hill. I invited him to lie at my house, and did receive his goods; but was deceived in his lying there, the news coming every moment of the growth of the fire; so as we were forced to begin to pack up our own goods, and prepare for their removal; and did by moonshine, it being brave, dry, and moonshine and warm weather, carry much of my goods into the garden; and Mr. Hater and I did remove my money and iron chests into my cellar, as thinking that the safest place. And got my bags of gold into my office, ready to carry away, and my chief papers of accounts also there, and my tallies into a box by themselves. So great was our fear, as Sir W. Batten hath carts come out of the country to fetch away his goods this night. We did put Mr. Hater, poor man! to bed a little; but he got but very little rest, so much noise being in my house, taking down of goods.

3d. About four o'clock in the morning, my Lady Batten sent me a cart to carry away all my money, and plate, and best things, to Sir W. Rider's, at Bednall Greene, which I did, riding myself in my night-gown, in the cart; and, Lord! to see how the streets and the highways are crowded with people running and riding, and getting of carts at any rate to fetch away things. I find Sir W. Rider tired with being called up all night, and receiving things from several friends. His house full of goods, and much of Sir W. Batten's and Sir W. Pen's. I am eased at my heart to have my treasure so well secured. Then home, and with much ado to find a way, nor any sleep all this night to me nor my poor wife. But then all this day she and I and all my people labouring to get away the rest of our things, and did get Mr. Tooker to get me a lighter to take them in, and we did carry them, myself some, over Tower Hill, which was by this time full of people's goods, bringing their goods thither; and down to the lighter, which lay at the next quay, above the Tower Dock. And here was my neighbour's wife, Mrs. ———, with her pretty child, and some few of her things, which I did willingly give way to be saved with mine; but there was no passing with any thing through the postern, the crowd was so great. The Duke of York come this day by the office, and spoke to us, and did ride with his guard up and down the City to keep all quiet, he being now General, and having the care of all. This day, Mercer being not at home, but against her mistress's order gone to her mother's, and my wife going thither to speak with W. Hewer, beat her there, and was angry; and her mother saying that she was not a 'prentice girl, to ask leave every time she goes abroad, my wife with good reason was angry; and, when she come home, did bid her be gone again. And so she went away, which troubled me, but yet less than it would, because of the condition we are in, in fear of coming in a little time to being less able to keep one in her quality. At night, lay down a little upon a quilt of W. Hewer's in the office, all my

own things being packed up or gone ; and, after me, my poor
wife did the like, we having fed upon the remains of yesterday's dinner, having no fire nor dishes, nor any opportunity
of dressing any thing.

4th. Up by break of day, to get away the remainder of my
things ; which I did by a lighter at the Iron gate:¹ and my
hands so full, that it was the afternoon before we could get
them all away.   Sir W. Pen and I to the Tower Street, and
there met the fire burning, three or four doors beyond Mr.
Howell's, whose goods, poor man, his trayes, and dishes,
shovells, &c., were flung all along Tower Street in the kennels,
and people working therewith from one end to the other ; the
fire coming on in that narrow street, on both sides, with infinite fury.   Sir W. Batten not knowing how to remove his
wine, did dig a pit in the garden, and laid it in there ; and I
took the opportunity of laying all the papers of my office that
I could not otherwise dispose of.   And in the evening Sir
W. Pen and I did dig another, and put our wine in it ; and I
my parmazan cheese, as well as my wine and some other
things.   The Duke of York was at the office this day, at Sir
W. Pen's ; but I happened not to be within.   This afternoon,
sitting melancholy with Sir W. Pen in our garden, and thinking of the certain burning of this office, without extraordinary
means, I did propose for the sending up of all our workmen
from the Woolwich and Deptford yards, none whereof yet
appeared, and to write to Sir W. Coventry to have the Duke
of York's permission to pull down houses, rather than lose
this office, which would much hinder the King's business.
So Sir W. Pen went down this night, in order to the sending
them up to-morrow morning ; and I wrote to Sir W. Coventry
about the business,² but received no answer.   This night,

---

¹ Irongate Stairs, Lower Thames Street.

² The letter, among the *Pepys MSS.*, was as follows :—

Sir, — The fire is now very neere us, as well on Tower Streete as Fanchurch
Street side, and we little hope of our escape but by that remedy, to yᵉ want
whereof we doo certainly owe yᵉ loss of yᵉ City, namely, yᵉ pulling down of
houses in yᵉ way of yᵉ fire.   This way Sir W. Pen and myself have so far concluded upon yᵉ practising, that he is gone to Woolwich and Deptford to supply
himself with men and necessarys in order to the doeing thereof ; in case, at his
returne, our condition be not bettered, and that he meets with his R. H. appro

Mrs. Turner, who, poor woman, was removing her goods all
this day, good goods, into the garden, and knows not how to
dispose of them, and her husband supped with my wife and
me at night, in the office, upon a shoulder of mutton from the
cook's without any napkin, or any thing, in a sad manner, but
were merry.   Only now and then, walking into the garden,
saw how horribly the sky looks, all on a fire in the night, was
enough to put us out of our wits; and, indeed, it was
extremely dreadful, for it looks just as if it was at us, and the
whole heaven on fire.   I after supper walked in the dark down
to Tower Street, and there saw it all on fire, at the Trinity
House on that side, and the Dolphin Tavern on this side,
which was very near us; and the fire with extraordinary
vehemence.   Now begins the practice of blowing up of
houses in Tower Street, those next the Tower, which at first
did frighten people more than any thing; but it stopped the
fire where it was done, it bringing down the houses to the
ground in the same places they stood, and then it was easy to
quench what little fire was in it, though it kindled nothing
almost.   W. Hewer this day went to see how his mother did,
and comes late home, telling us how he hath been forced to
remove her to Islington, her house in Pye Corner being
burned; so that the fire is got so far that way, and to the
Old Bayly, and was running down to Fleet Street; and
Paul's is burned, and all Cheapside.   I wrote to my father
this night, but the post-house being burned, the letter could
not go.

5th. I lay down in the office again upon W. Hewer's quilt,
being mighty weary, and sore in my feet with going till I was
hardly able to stand.   About two in the morning my wife
calls me up, and tells me of new cryes of fire, it being come
to Barking Church, which is the bottom of our lane.[1]   I up;

---

bation, which I have thus undertaken to learn of you. Pray please to let me
have this night, at whatever hour it is, what his R. H* directions are in this
particular.   Sir J. Minnes and Sir W. Batten having left us, we cannot add,
though we are well assured of their, as well as all y* neighbourhood's con-
currence.

                                                      Y' obedient Serv*.
Sir W. Coventry,   S. P.
      Sept*. 4, 1666.
[1] Seething Lane.

and finding it so, resolved presently to take her away, and
did, and took my gold, which was about 2350l., W. Hewer
and Jane down by Proundy's boat to Woolwich; but, Lord!
what a sad sight it was by moone-light, to see the whole City
almost on fire, that you might see it as plain at Woolwich, as
if you were by it. There, when I come, I find the gates
shut, but no guard kept at all; which troubled me, because
of discourses now begun, that there is a plot in it, and that
the French had done it. I got the gates open, and to Mr.
Shelden's, where I locked up my gold, and charged my wife
and W. Hewer never to leave the room without one of them
in it, night or day. So back again, by the way seeing my
goods well in the lighters at Deptford, and watched well by
people. Home, and whereas I expected to have seen our
house on fire, it being now about seven o'clock, it was not.
But to the fire, and there find greater hopes than I expected;
for my confidence of finding our Office on fire was such, that
I durst not ask any body how it was with us, till I come and
saw it was not burned. But, going to the fire, I find, by the
blowing up of houses, and the great help given by the workmen out of the King's yards, sent up by Sir W. Pen, there is
a good stop given to it, as well at Marke Lane end as ours;
it having only burned the dyall of Barking Church, and part
of the porch, and was there quenched. I up to the top of
Barking steeple, and there saw the saddest sight of desolation
that ever I saw; every where great fires, oyle-cellars, and
brimstone, and other things burning. I became afraid to
stay there long, and therefore down again as fast as I could,
the fire being spread as far as I could see; and to Sir W.
Pen's, and there eat a piece of cold meat, having eaten[1]
nothing since Sunday, but the remains of Sunday's dinner.
Here I met with Mr. Young and Whistler; and, having
removed all my things, and received good hopes that the fire
at our end is stopped, they and I walked into the town, and
find Fenchurch Street, Gracious Street, and Lumbard Street
all in dust. The Exchange a sad sight, nothing standing
there, of all the statues or pillars, but Sir Thomas Gresham's

---

[1] He forgot the shoulder of mutton from the cook's the day before.

picture in the corner. Into Moore-fields, our feet ready to
burn, walking through the town among the hot coles, and
find that full of people, and poor wretches carrying their goods
there, and every body keeping his goods together by themselves; and a great blessing it is to them that it is fair
weather for them to keep abroad night and day; drunk there,
and paid twopence for a plain penny loaf. Thence homeward, having passed through Cheapside, and Newgate market,
all burned; and seen Anthony Joyce's house in fire; and
took up, which I keep by me, a piece of glass of the Mercers'
chapel in the street, where much more was, so melted and
buckled[1] with the heat of the fire like parchment. I also did
see a poor cat taken out of a hole in a chimney, joyning to
the wall of the Exchange, with the hair all burned off the
body, and yet alive. So home at night, and find there good
hopes of saving our office; but great endeavours of watching
all night, and having men ready; and so we lodged them in
the office, and had drink and bread and cheese for them.
And I lay down and slept a good night about midnight:
though, when I rose, I heard that there had been a great
alarme of French and Dutch being risen, which proved
nothing. But it is a strange thing to see how long this time
did look since Sunday, having been always full of variety of
actions, and little sleep, that it looked like a week or more,
and I had forgot almost the day of the week.

6th. Up about five o'clock, and met Mr. Gauden at the
gate of the office, I intending to go out, as I used, every now
and then, to-day, to see how the fire is, to call our men to
Bishop's-gate, where no fire had yet been near, and there is
now one broke out: which did give great grounds to people,
and to me too, to think that there is some kind of plot in
this, on which many by this time have been taken, and it
hath been dangerous for any stranger to walk in the streets,
but I went with the men, and we did put it out in a little
time; so that that was well again. It was pretty to see how
hard the women did work in the cannells, sweeping of water;

---

[1] Buckled, i. e., bent; in which sense it is used by Shakespeare, *Henry IV*
part II., act i., scene 3.

but then they would scold for drink, and be as drunk as
devils. I saw good butts of sugar broke open in the street,
and people give and take handfuls out, and put into beer, and
drink it. And now all being pretty well, I took boat, and
over to Southwarke, and took boat on the other side the
bridge, and so to Westminster, thinking to shift myself,
being all in dirt from top to bottom ; but could not there find
any place to buy a shirt or a pair of gloves, Westminster Hall
being full of people's goods, those in Westminster having removed all their goods, and the Exchequer money put into
vessels to carry to Nonsuch ;[1] but to the Swan, and there was
trimmed : and then to White Hall, but saw nobody ; and so
home. A sad sight to see how the river looks : no houses
nor church near it, to the Temple, where it stopped. At home,
did go with Sir W. Batten, and our neighbour, Knightly, who,
with one more, was the only man of any fashion left in all the
neighbourhood thereabouts, they all removing their goods, and
leaving their houses to the mercy of the fire ; to Sir R. Ford's,
and there dined in an earthen platter — a fried breast of
mutton ; a great many of us, but very merry, and indeed as
good a meal, though as ugly a one, as ever I had in my life.
Thence down to Deptford, and there with great satisfaction
landed all my goods at Sir G. Carteret's safe, and nothing
missed I could see or hear. This being done to my great
content, I home, and to Sir W. Batten's, and there, with Sir
R. Ford, Mr. Knightly, and one Withers, a professed lying
rogue, supped well, and mighty merry, and our fears over.
From them to the office, and there slept with the office full of
labourers, who talked, and slept, and walked all night long
there. But strange it is to see Clothworkers' Hall on fire
these three days and nights in one body of flame, it being the
cellar full of oyle.

7th. Up by five o'clock ; and, blessed be God ! find all
well ; and by water to Pane's[2] Wharfe. Walked thence, and
saw all the towne burned, and a miserable sight of Paul's
church, with all the roofs fallen, and the body of the quire

---

[1] At which house the Exchequer had been kept during the plague.
[2] Paul's Wharf?

fallen into St. Fayth's; Paul's school also, Ludgate and Fleet
Street. My father's house, and the church, and a good part
of the Temple the like. So to Creed's lodging, near the New
Exchange, and there find him laid down upon a bed; the
house all unfurnished, there being fears of the fire's coming
to them. There borrowed a shirt of him, and washed. To
Sir W. Coventry at St. James's, who lay without curtains,
having removed all his goods; as the King at White Hall,
and every body had done, and was doing. He hopes we shall
have no public distractions upon this fire, which is what every
body fears, because of the talk of the French having a hand
in it. And it is a proper time for discontents; but all men's
minds are full of care to protect themselves and save their
goods: the Militia is in arms every where. Our fleetes, he
tells me, have been in sight one of another, and most un-
happily by fowle weather were parted, to our great loss, as in
reason they do conclude; the Dutch being come out only to
make a shew, and please their people; but in very bad condition as to stores, victuals, and men. They are at Boulougne,
and our fleete come to St. Ellen's. We have got nothing,
but have lost one ship, but he knows not what. Thence to
the Swan, and there drank; and so home, and find all well.
My Lord Brouncker, at Sir W. Batten's, tells us the Generall[1]
is sent for up, to come to advise with the King about business
at this juncture, and to keep all quiet; which is great honour
to him, but I am sure is but a piece of dissimulation. So
home, and did give orders for my house to be made clean;
and then down to Woolwich, and there find all well. Dined,
and Mrs. Markham come to see my wife. This day our
Merchants first met at Gresham College, which, by proclamation, is to be their Exchange. Strange to hear what is
bid for houses all up and down here; a friend of Sir W.
Rider's having 150*l.* for what he used to let for 40*l.* per
annum. Much dispute where the Custome House shall be;
thereby the growth of the City again to be foreseen. My
Lord Treasurer, they say, and others, would have it at the
other end of the town. I home late to Sir W. Pen's, who

---

[1] The Duke of Albemarle.

did give me a bed, but without curtains or hangings, all being down. So here I went the first time into a naked bed, only my drawers on; and did sleep pretty well: but still both sleeping and waking had a fear of fire in my heart, that I took little rest. People do all the world over cry out of the simplicity of my Lord Mayor in generall; and more particularly in this business of the fire, laying it all upon him. A proclamation is come out for markets to be kept at Leadenhall and Mile-end Greene, and several other places about the town; and Tower Hill, and all churches to be set open to receive poor people.

8th. I stopped with Sir G. Carteret to desire him to go with us, and to enquire after money. But the first he cannot do, and the other as little, or says, " when we can get any, or what shall we do for it?" He, it seems, is employed in the correspondence between the City and the King every day, in settling of things. I find him full of trouble, to think how things will go. I left him, and to St. James's, where we met first at Sir W. Coventry's chamber, and there did what business we could, without any books. Our discourse, as every thing else, was confused. The fleete is at Portsmouth, there staying a wind to carry them to the Downes, or towards Boulogne, where they say the Dutch fleete is gone, and stays. We concluded upon private meetings for a while, not having any money to satisfy any people that may come to us. I bought two eeles upon the Thames, cost me six shillings. Thence with Sir W. Batten to the Cock-pit, whither the Duke of Albemarle is come. It seems the King holds him so necessary at this time, that he hath sent for him, and will keep him here. Indeed, his interest in the City, being acquainted, and his care in keeping things quiet, is reckoned that, wherein he will be very serviceable. We to him: he is courted in appearance by every body. He is very kind to us; and I perceive he lays by all business of the fleete at present, and minds the City, and is now hastening to Gresham College, to discourse with the Aldermen. Sir W. Batten and I home, where met my brother John, come to town to see how things are done with us, and then presently he with me to Gresham College; where infinity of people, partly through novelty to see the new place, and partly to find out and hear what is become one man of another. I met with many people undone, and more that have extraordinary great losses. People speaking their thoughts variously about the beginning of the fire, and the rebuilding of the City. Then to Sir W. Batten's, and took my brother with me, and there dined with a great company of neighbours, and much good discourse; among others, of the low spirits of some rich men in the City, in sparing any encouragement to the poor people that wrought for the saving their houses. Among others, Alderman Starling, a very rich man, without children, the fire at next door to him in our lane, after our men had saved his house, did give 2s. 6d. among thirty of them, and did quarrel with some that would remove the rubbish out of the way of the fire, saying that they come to steal. Sir W. Coventry told me of another this morning in Holborne, which he showed the King: that when it was offered to stop the fire near his house for such a reward that come to but 2s. 6d. a man, among the neighbours, he would give but 18d. Thence to Bednall Green by coach, my brother with me, and saw all well there, and fetched away my journall-book, to enter for five days past. I was much frighted and kept awake in my bed, by some noise I heard a great while below stairs; and the boy's not coming up to me when I knocked. It was by their discovery of some people stealing of some neighbours' wine that lay in vessels in the streets. So to sleep; and all well all night.

9th. (Sunday.) Up; and was trimmed, and sent my brother to Woolwich to my wife, to dine with her. I to church, where our parson made a melancholy but good sermon; and many and most in the church cried, specially the women. The church mighty full; but few of fashion, and most strangers. I walked to Bednall Green, and there dined well, but a bad venison pasty, at Sir W. Rider's. Good people they are, and good discourse; and his daughter, Middleton, a fine woman, discreet. Thence home, and to church

again, and there preached Dean Harding; out, methinks, a
bad, poor sermon, though proper for the time; nor eloquent,
in saying at this time that the City is reduced from a large
folio to a decimo-tertio. So to my office, there to write
down my journall, and take leave of my brother, whom I send
back this afternoon, though raining, which it hath not done a
good while before. But I had no room or convenience for
him here till my house was fitted; but I was very kind to
him, and do take very well of him his journey. I did give
him 40s. for his pocket, and so, he being gone, and it presently raining, I was troubled for him, though it is good for
the fyre. Anon to Sir W. Pen's to bed, and made my boy
Tom to read me asleep.

10th. All the morning clearing our cellars, and breaking
in pieces all my old lumber, to make room, and to prevent
fire. And then to Sir W. Batten's, and dined; and there
hear that Sir W. Rider says that the town is full of the
report of the wealth that is in his house, and he would be
glad that his friends would provide for the safety of their
goods there. This made me get a cart; and thither, and
there brought my money all away. Took a hackney-coach
myself, the hackney-coaches now standing at Allgate. Much
wealth, indeed, there is at his house. Blessed be God! I got
all mine well thence, and lodged it in my office; but vexed
to have all the world see it, and with Sir W. Batten, who
would have taken away my hands before they were stowed.
By and by comes brother Balty from sea, which I was glad
of; and so got him and Mr. Tooker, and the boy, to watch
with them all in the office all night, while I went down to
my wife, to Woolwich.

11th. By water, with my gold, and laid it with the rest in
my office. In the evening at Sir W. Pen's, at supper: he
in a mad, ridiculous, drunken humour; and it seems there
have been some late distances between his lady and him, as
my wife tells me. After supper, I home, and with Mr. Hater,
Gibson,[2] and Tom alone, got all my chests and money into

---

[1] Nathaniel Hardy, Dean of Rochester.
[2] Probably Clerk of the Cheque at Deptford, in 1688.

the further cellar with much pains, but great content to me
when done. So very late and weary to bed.

12th. Up, and with Sir W. Batten and Sir W. Pen to St.
James's by water, and there did our usual business with the
Duke of York.

13th. Up, and down to Tower Wharfe; and there, with
Balty and labourers from Deptford, did get my goods housed
well at home. So down to Deptford again, to fetch the rest,
and there eat a bit of dinner at the Globe, with the master
of the Bezan with me, while the labourers went to dinner.
Here I hear that this poor town do bury still of the plague
seven or eight in a day. So to Sir G. Carteret's to work,
and there did, to my content, ship off in the Bezan all the
rest of my goods, saving my pictures and fine things, that I
will bring home in wherrys, when the house is fit to receive
them: and so home, and unload them by carts and hands
before night, to my exceeding satisfaction: and so, after
supper, to bed in my house, the first time I have lain there;
and lay with my wife in my old closet upon the ground, and
Balty and his wife in the best chamber, upon the ground
also.

14th. Up, and to work, having carpenters come to help in
setting up bedsteads and hangings; and at that trade my
people and I all the morning, till pressed by publick business
to leave them against my will in the afternoon; and yet I
was troubled at being at home, to see all my goods lie up
and down in the house in a bad condition; and strange
workmen, going to and fro, might take what they would
almost. All the afternoon busy; and Sir W. Coventry come
to me, and found me, as God would have it, in my office,
and people about me setting my papers to rights; and there
discoursed about getting an account ready against the Parliament, and thereby did create me infinity of business, and to
be done on a sudden; which troubled me: but, however, he
being gone, I about it late, and to good purpose. And so
home, having this day, also, got my wine out of the ground
again, and set it in my cellar; but with great pain to keep the
porters that carried it in from observing the money-chests there.

This day, poor Tom Pepys, the turner, was with me, and Kate Joyce, to bespeak places—one for himself, the other for her husband. She tells me he hath lost 140*l.* per annum, but have seven houses left.

15th. Captain Cocke says he hath computed that the rents of the houses lost by this fire in the City comes to 600,000*l.* per annum; that this will make the Parliament more quiet than otherwise they would have been, and give the King a more ready supply; that the supply must be by excise, as it is in Holland; that the Parliament will see it necessary to carry on the war; that the late storm hindered our beating the Dutch fleete, who were gone out only to satisfy the people, having no business to do but to avoid us; that the French, as late in the year as it is, are coming; that the Dutch are really in bad condition, but that this unhappiness of ours do give them heart; that there was a late difference between my Lord Arlington and Sir W. Coventry about neglect in the latter to send away an express of the other's in time; that it come before the King, and the Duke of York concerned himself in it; but this fire hath stopped it. The Dutch fleete is not gone home, but rather to the North, and so dangerous to our Gottenburgh fleete. That the Parliament is likely to fall foul upon some persons; and, among others, on the Vice-chamberlaine;[1] though, we both believe, with little ground. That certainly never so great a loss as this was borne so well by citizens in the world; he believing that not one merchant upon the 'Change will break upon it. That he do not apprehend there will be any disturbance in State upon it; for that all men are busy in looking after their own business to save themselves. He gone, I to finish my letters, and home to bed: and find, to my infinite joy, many rooms clean: and myself and wife lie in our own chamber again. But much terrified in the nights, now-a-days, with dreams of fire, and falling down of houses.

16th. (Lord's day.) At noon, with my wife, against her will, all undressed and dirty, dined at Sir W. Pen's, where was all the company of our families in town: but, Lord!

---

[1] Sir G. Carteret.

so sorry a dinner—venison baked in pans, that the dinner I have had for his lady alone hath been worth four of it.

17th. Up betimes, and shaved myself after a week's growth: but, Lord! how ugly I was yesterday, and how fine to-day! By water, seeing the City all the way—a sad sight indeed, much fire being still in. Sir W. Coventry was in great pain lest the French fleete should be passed by our fleete, who had notice of them on Saturday, and were preparing to go meet them; but their minds altered, and judged them merchant-men; when, the same day, the Success, Captain Ball, made their whole fleete, and come to Brighthelmstone, and thence at five o'clock afternoon, Saturday, wrote Sir W. Coventry news thereof; so that we do much fear our missing them. Here come in and talked with him Sir Thomas Clifford,[1] who appears a very fine gentleman, and much set by at Court for his activity in going to sea, and stoutness every where, and stirring up and down.

18th. It was a sad rainy and tempestuous night. I did my business in the afternoon, in forwarding the settling of my house, very well. Troubled at my wife's hair coming off so much. This day the Parliament met, and adjourned till Friday, when the King will be with them.

19th. To St. James's, and did our usual business before the Duke of York; which signified little, our business being only complaints of lack of money. Here I saw a bastard of the late King of Sweden's come to kiss his hands; a mighty modish, French-like gentleman. Thence to White Hall, with Sir W. Batten and Sir W. Pen, to Wilkes's: and there did hear many stories of Sir Henry Wood,[2] about Lord Norwich drawing a tooth at a health. Another time, he, and Pinchbacke, and Dr. Goffe,[3] now a religious man, Pinchbacke did

[1] Eldest son of Hugh Clifford, of Ugbrooke, M.P. for Totness, 1661, and knighted for his conduct in the sea-fight of 1665. After filling several high offices, he was, in 1672, created Baron Clifford, of Chudleigh, and constituted High Treasurer; which place he resigned the following year, a few months before his death.

[2] Clerk of the Spicery to Charles I.; and, after the Restoration, Clerk to the Board of Green Cloth.

[3] Dr. Stephen Goffe, Clerk of the Queen's Closet, and her Assistant Confessor. He had been Chaplain to Colonel Goring; but became, in 1641, a Roman Catholic. Evelyn's *Diary*, vol. i., p. 19, edit. 1850.

begin a frolick to drink out of a glass with a toad in it:[1] he
did it without harm.   Goffe, who knew sacke would kill the
toad, called for sack : and, when he saw it dead, says he, "I
will have a quick toad, and will not drink from a dead toad."
By that means, no other being to be found, he escaped the
health.   To Deptford, and got all my pictures put into
wherries, and my other fine things, and landed them all very
well, and brought them home, and got Symson to set them
all up to-night.   I and the boy to finish and set up my books
and everything else in my house till two in the morning, and
then to bed ; but mightily troubled, even in my sleep, by
missing four or five of my biggest books, Speed's Chronicle
and Maps, and the two parts of Waggoner,[2] and a book of
cards.   Two little pictures of sea and ships, and a little gilt
frame belonging to my plate of the River, I want; but my
books do heartily trouble me.   Most of my gilt frames are
hurt.   This day I put on two shirts, the first time this year,
and do grow well upon it ; so that my disease is nothing but
wind.

20th.   The fleete is come into the Downes.   Nothing done
nor French fleete seen : we drove all from our anchors.   But
Sir G. Carteret says news is come that De Ruyter is dead, or
very near it, of a hurt in his mouth, upon the discharge of
one of his own guns ; which put him into a fever, and he
likely to die, if not already dead.   In the afternoon, out by
coach, my wife with me through all the ruins, to show her
them, which frets her much, and it is a sad sight indeed.   To
the office, to even my journal, and then home.

21st.   W. Hewer tells me that Sir W. Pen hath a hamper
more than his own, which he took for a hamper of bottles of
wine, but they were carried into a wine-cellar.   I sent for
Harry, and he brought me, by and by, my hamper, to my
great joy, with the same books I missed, and three more great
ones, and I did give him 5s. for his pains.   The Parliament

---

[1] They swallow their own contradictions as easily as a hector can drink a frog
in a glass of wine.   *Bentivoglio and Urania*, book v., p. 92, 3rd edit.

[2] Apparently Wagenaer's *Speculum Nauticum*, published at Leyden in 1585; and
translated into English, by Anthony Ashley, about the year 1588.

meet to-day, and the King to be with them.   At the office, about our accounts, which now draw near the time they should be ready, the House having ordered Sir G. Carteret, upon his ordering them, to bring them in on Saturday next.   Home, and there, with great pleasure, very late new setting all my books; and now I am in as good condition as I desire to be in all worldly respects.   The Lord of Heaven make me thankful, and continue me therein !

22d. My house is so clean as I never saw it, or any other house, in my life, and every thing in as good condition as ever before the fire; but with about 20*l.* cost, one way or other, besides about 20*l.* charge, in removing my goods, and do not find that I have lost anything but two little pictures of ships and sea, and a little gold frame for one of my sea-cards. My glazier, indeed, is so full of work, that I cannot get him to come to perfect my house.   In the afternoon I paid for the two lighters that carried my goods to Deptford, and they cost me 8*l.*

23d. (Lord's day.) Mr. Wayth and I by water to White Hall, and there at Sir G. Carteret's lodgings Sir W. Coventry met, and we did debate the whole business of our accounts to the Parliament; where it appears to us that the charge of the war from September 1st, 1664, to this Michaelmas, will have been but 3,200,000*l.*; and we have paid, in that time, somewhat about 2,200,000*l.*; so that we owe above 900,000*l.*: but our method of accounting, though it cannot, I believe, be far wide from the mark, yet will not abide a strict examination if the Parliament should be troublesome.   Here happened a pretty question of Sir W. Coventry, whether this account of ours will not put my Lord Treasurer to a difficulty to tell what is become of all the money the Parliament have given in this time for the war, which hath amounted to about 4,000,000*l.*, which nobody there could answer; but I perceive they did doubt what his answer could be.   My wife and I for pleasure to Fox-hall, and there eat and drank, and so back home.

24th. Up, and down to look for Sir W. Coventry; and at last found him and Sir G. Carteret with the Lord Treasurer at White Hall, consulting how to make up my Lord Trea-

surer's general account, as well as that of the Navy particularly. Found that Sir G. Carteret had altered his account
since he did give me the abstract of it: so all my letter must
be writ over again. So to Sir G. Carteret, to speak a little
about the alteration; and there, looking over the book Sir
G. Carteret intends to deliver to the Parliament of his payments since September 1st, 1664, I find my name the very
second for flags, which I had bought for the Navy, of calico,
once, about 500 and odd pounds, which vexed me mightily.
At last, I concluded of scraping out my name, and putting in
Mr. Tooker's, which eased me; though the price was such as
I should have had glory by. Here I saw my Lady Carteret
lately come to town, who, good lady! is mighty kind, and I
must make much of her.

25th. With all my people to get the letter writ over about
the Navy's accounts; and by coach to my Lord Brouncker's,
and got his hand to it; and then to the Parliament House,
and got it signed by the rest, and then delivered it at the
House-door to Sir Philip Warwick; Sir G. Carteret being
gone into the House with his books of accounts under his
arme, to present to the House. With Ned Pickering, who
continues still a lying, bragging coxcomb, telling me that my
Lord Sandwich may thank himself for all his misfortune; for
not suffering him and two or three good honest fellows more
to take them by the throats that spoke ill of him, and told
me how basely Lionell Walden[1] hath carried himself towards
my Lord, by speaking slightly of him, which I shall remember.
All night still mightily troubled in my sleep, with fires and
houses pulling down.

26th. By coach home, calling at Bennet's, our late mercer,
who is come into Covent Garden to a fine house, looking down
upon the Exchange; and I perceive many Londoners every
day come; and Mr. Pierce hath let his wife's closet, and the
little blind bedchamber, and a garret, to a silk-man for 50*l*.
fine, and 30*l*. per annum, and 40*l*. per annum more for dieting

---

[1] M.P. for Huntingdon.

[2] John Dugdale, Chief Gentleman of the Chamber to Lord Chancellor Clarendon, and afterwards Windsor Herald. He died in 1700.

the master and two prentices. By Mr. Dugdale[2] I hear the great loss of books in St. Paul's Churchyard, and at their Hall also, which they value at about 150,000*l.*; some booksellers being wholly undone, and among others, they say, my poor Kirton. And Mr. Crumlum, all his books and household stuff burned : they trusting to St. Fayth's, and, the roof of the church falling, broke the arch down into the lower church, and so all the goods burned. A very great loss. His father[1] hath lost above 1000*l.* in books; one book newly printed, a Discourse, it seems, of Courts. Here I had the hap to see my Lady Denham : and at night went into the dining-room, and saw several fine ladies ; among others, Castlemaine, but chiefly Denham again : and the Duke of York, taking her aside and talking to her in the sight of all the world, all alone ; which was strange, and what I also did not like. Here I met with good Mr. Evelyn, who cries out against it, and calls it bickering : for the Duke of York talks a little to her, and then she goes away, and then he follows her again like a dog. He observes that none of the nobility come out of the country at all, to help the King, or comfort him, or prevent commotions at this fire, but do as if the King were nobody : nor ne'er a priest comes to give the King and Court good council, or to comfort the poor people that suffer : but all is dead, nothing of good in any of their minds : he bemoans it, and says he fears more ruin hangs over our heads. My wife tells me she hath bought a gown of 15*s.* a yard ; the same, before her face, my Lady Castlemaine this day bought also, which I seemed vexed for, though I do not grudge it her, but to incline her to have Mercer again. Our business was tendered to the House to-day, and a Committee of the whole House chosen to examine our accounts, and a great many Hotspurs enquiring into it. Sir W. Pen proposes his and my looking out into Scotland about timber, and to use Pett there ; for timber will be a good commodity this time of building the City. Our fleete abroad, and the Dutch too, for all we know — the weather very bad, and under the command of an unlucky man, I fear. God bless him, and the fleete under him !

---

[1] William Dugdale, then Norroy Herald, knighted in 1676-7, and made Garter King at Arms. The work alluded to was the *Origines Juridiciales.*

27th. A very furious blowing night all the night ; and my mind still mightily perplexed with dreams, and burning the rest of the town ; and waking in much pain for the fleete. I to look out Penny, my tailor, to speak for a cloak and cassock for my brother, who is coming to town : and I will have him in a canonical dress, that he may be the fitter to go abroad with me.   To Sir W. Coventry's, and there dined with him and Sir W. Batten, the Lieutenant of the Tower, and Mr. Thin,[1] a pretty gentleman, going to Gottenburgh.   No news of the fleete yet, but that they went by Dover on the 25th towards the Gun-fleete : but whether the Dutch be yet abroad or no, we hear not.   De Ruyter is not dead, but like to do well.   Most think that the gross of the French fleete are gone home again.

28th. Comes the bookbinder to gild the backs of my books. Sir W. Pen broke to me a proposition of his and my joining in a design of fetching timber and deals from Scotland, by the help of Mr. Pett upon the place : which, while London is building, will yield good money.   I approve it.

29th. Sir W. Coventry and I find, to our great joy, that the wages, victuals, wear and tear, cast by the medium of the men, will come to above 3,000,000*l.* ; and that the extra-ordinaries, which all the world will allow us, will arise to more than will justify the expence we have declared to have been at since the war ; viz. 320,000*l.*

30th. (Lord's day.)   Up, and to church, where I have not been a good while : and there the church infinitely thronged with strangers, since the fire come into our parish ; but not one handsome face in all of them, as if, indeed, there was a curse, as Bishop Fuller heretofore said, upon our parish. Here I saw Mercer come into the church, but she avoided looking up.   Home, and a good dinner ; and then to have my hair cut against winter close to my head, and then to church again.   A sorry sermon, and away home.   This month

---

[1] Thomas Thynne, Envoy extraordinary to Sweden. He was the eldest son of Sir Thomas Thynne, Bart., of Kempsford, by Mary, daughter of Thomas, first Lord Coventry ; and on the murder of his cousin, Thomas Thynne, of Longleato, succeeded to all his possessions. In 1692 he was created Viscount Weymouth, and died in 1714, æt. 74.

ends with my mind full of business and concernment how this office will speed with the Parliament, which begins to be mighty severe in the examining our accounts, and the expence of the Navy this war.

October 1st. All the morning at the office, getting the list of all the ships and vessels employed since the war, for the Committee of Parliament.

2d. Sir G. Carteret tells me how our lists are referred to a Sub-committee to consider and examine, and that I am ordered to be there. With Mr. Slingsby, of the Tower, who did inform me mightily in several things—among others, that the heightening or lowering of money is only a cheat, and do good to some particular men, which, if I can but remember how, I am now by him fully convinced of. Into the Committee-chamber before the Committee sat, and there heard Birch discourse highly and understandingly about the Navy business, and a proposal made heretofore to form the Navy; but Sir W. Coventry did abundantly answer him, and is a most excellent person. By and by, the Committee met, and appointed me to attend them to-morrow, to examine our lists. This put me into a mighty fear and trouble—they doing it in a very ill-humour, methought. When come home, I to Sir W. Pen's, to his boy, for my book, and there find he hath it not; but delivered it to the door-keeper of the Committee for me. This, added to my former disquiet, made me stark mad, considering all the nakedness of the office lay open, in papers within those covers. But, coming to our rendezvous at the Swan tavern, in King Street, I found they have found the housekeeper, and the book simply locked up in the Court.

3d. Waked betimes, mightily troubled in mind, and in the most true trouble that I ever was in my life, saving in the business last year of the East India prizes. So up; and, by and by, by eight o'clock comes Birch the first, with the list and books of accounts delivered in. He calls me to work, and there he and I begun; when, by and by, comes Garraway,[1]

[1] He was an M.P., and appointed by the House to confer with Lord Shaftes-
bury respecting the charge against Pepys being popishly affected. See note to
the *Life*, vol. i.; and for his character, 6th August, 1666.

the first time I ever saw him, and Sir W. Thompson, and Mr
Boscawen.   They to it, and I did make shift to answer them
better than I expected.   Sir W. Batten, Lord Brouncker,
and W. Pen, come in, but presently went out : and J. Minnes
come in, and said two or three words from the purpose but to
do hurt; and so away he went also, and left me all the morning with them alone to stand or fall.   After dinner to work
again, only the Committee and I, till dark night; and it ended
with good peace and much seeming satisfaction : but I find
them wise and reserved, and instructed to hit all our blots.
To White Hall, and there among the ladies, and saw my Lady
Castlemaine never looked so ill, nor Mrs. Stewart neither, as
in this plain natural dress.   I was not pleased with either of
them.   Find my father and my brother come to town — my
father, without my expectation, but glad I am to see him.
Home, to set up all my folio books, which are come home gilt
on the backs, very handsome to the eye.   This night, W. Pen
told me W. Batten swears he will have nothing to do with
the Privateer, if his son do not go Lieutenant, which angers
me and him ; but we will be even with him, one way or
other.

4th.   Up, and mighty betimes to Sir W. Coventry, to give
him an account of yesterday's work, which do give him good
content.   He did then tell me his speech lately to the House
in his own vindication about the report of his selling of places,
he having a small occasion offered him by chance ; which he
did desire, and took, and did it to his content, and, he says, to
the House's seeming to approve of it, by their hum.   He
confessed how long he had done it, and how he desired to have
something else : and, since then, he had taken nothing, and
challenged all the world.   To Sir G. Carteret, and there discoursed much of the want of money, and our being designed
for destruction.   How the King hath lost his power, by sub-
mitting himself to this way of examining his accounts, and is
become but as a private man.   He says the King is troubled
at it, but they talk an entry[1] shall be made ; that it is not to
be brought into example; that the King must, if they do not

---

[1] In the Journals of the House of Commons.

agree presently, make them a courageous speech, which, he
says, he may do, the City of London being now burned, and
himself master of an army, better than any prince before him.
After dinner the bookbinder come, and I sent by him some
more books to gild.

5th. The Sub-committee have made their report to the
Grand Committee, and in pretty kind terms. Captain Cocke
told me of a wild motion made in the House of Lords by the
Duke of Buckingham, for all men that have cheated the King
to be declared traitors and felons; and that my Lord Sandwich was named. This had put me into great pain: so the
Vice-chamberlain. who had heard nothing of it, having been
all day in the city, away with me to White Hall; and there
told me that, upon my Lord Ashly's asking their direction
whether, being a peer, he should bring in his accounts to the
Commons, which they did give way to, the Duke of Buckingham did move that, for the time to come, what I have
written above might be declared by some fuller law than heretofore. Lord Ashly answered, that it was not the fault of
present laws, but want of proper ones; and the Lord Chancellor said, that a better law he thought might be made: so,
the House laughing, did refer it to him to bring in a bill for
that purpose. Mr. Kirton's kinsman, my bookseller, come
in my way; and so I am told by him that Mr. Kirton is
utterly undone, and made 2 or 3000*l.* worse than nothing,
from being worth 7 or 8000*l.* That the goods laid in the
Church-yard fired through the windows those in St. Fayth's
church: and those coming to the warehouses' doors fired
them, and burned all the books and pillars of the church,
so as the roof, falling down, broke quite down; which it did
not do in the other places of the church, which is alike pil-
lared, which I knew not before; but, being not burned, they
stood still. He do believe there is above 150,000*l.* of books
burned; all the great booksellers almost undone: not only
these, but their warehouses at their Hall and under Christ-
church, and elsewhere, being all burned. A great want therefore there will be of books, specially Latin books and foreign

books; and, among others, the Polyglottes[1] and new Bible, which he believes will be presently worth 40*l*. a-piece.

6th. Up, and having seen my brother in his cassocke, which I am not the most satisfied in, being doubtful at this time what courses to have him profess too soon; Sir W. Coventry and I discoursed of our sad condition by want of a Comptroller:[2] and it was his words, that he believes, besides all the shame and trouble he hath brought on the office, tho King had better have given 100,000*l*. than ever have had him there. He did discourse about some of these discontented Parliament-men, and says that Birch is a false rogue: but that Garraway is a man that hath not been well used by the Court, though very stout to death, and hath suffered all that is possible for the King from the beginning. But, discontented as he is, yet he never knew a Session of Parliament but that he hath done some good deed for the King before it rose. I told him the passage Cocke told me of — his having begged a brace of bucks of the Lord Arlington for him: and, when they come to him, he sent them back again. Sir W. Coventry told me, it is much to be pitied that the King should lose the service of a man so able and faithful: and that he ought to be brought over, but that it is always observed, that, by bringing over one discontented man, you raise up three in his room: which is a state lesson I never knew before. But when others discover your fear, and that discontent procures fear, they will be discontented too, and impose on you. This morning my wife told me of a fine gentlewoman my Lady Pen tells her of, for 20*l*. per annum, that sings, dances, plays on four or five instruments and many other fine things, which pleases me mightily: and she sent to have her see her, which she did this afternoon, but sings

---

[1] Bishop Walton's great work, published in 1657, entitled, *Biblia Sacra Polyglotta*, in six large folio volumes. Nine languages are used in it, though no one book of the Bible is printed in so many. It was printed by subscription, under the patronage of Oliver Cromwell: but the Protector dying before it was finished, the Bishop cancelled two leaves of the Preface commendatory of his patron, and others were printed complimentary to Charles II. Hence the distinction of *republican* and *loyal* copies. The former are the most valued.

[2] Sir John Minnes performing the duties inefficiently.

basely and is a tawdry wench that would take 8*l*.—but [neither] my wife nor I think her fit to come.

7th (Lord's day.) To White Hall, where met by Sir W. Batten and Lord Brouncker, to attend the King and Duke of York at the Cabinet; but nobody had determined what to speak of, but only in general to ask for money. So I was forced immediately to prepare in my mind a method of discoursing. And anon we were called in to the Green Room, where the King, Duke of York, Prince Rupert, Lord Chancellor, Lord Treasurer, Duke of Albemarle, Sirs G. Carteret, W. Coventry, Morrice. Nobody beginning, I did, and made a current, and, I thought, a good speech, laying open the ill state of the Navy: by the greatness of the debt; greatness of the work to do against next year; the time and materials it would take: and our incapacity, through a total want of money. I had no sooner done, but Prince Rupert rose up, and told the King, in a heat, that whatever the gentleman had said, he had brought home his fleete in as good a condition as ever any fleete was brought home: that twenty boats would be as many as the fleete would want: and all the anchors and cables left in the storm might be taken up again. This arose from my saying, among other things we had to do, that the fleete was come in,—the greatest fleete that ever his Majesty had yet together, and that in as bad condition as the enemy or weather could put it: and to use Sir W. Pen's words, who is upon the place taking a survey, he dreads the reports he is to receive from the Surveyors of its defects. I therefore did only answer, that I was sorry for his Highness's offence, but that what I said was but the report we received from those entrusted in the fleete to inform us. He muttered and repeated what he had said; and so, after a long silence on all hands, nobody, not so much as the Duke of Albemarle, seconding the Prince, nor taking notice of what he said, we withdrew. I was not a little troubled at this passage, and the more when speaking with Jacke Fenn about it, he told me that the Prince will be asking who this Pepys is, and find him to be a creature of my Lord Sandwich's, and therefore this was done only to disparage him. Anon they broke up, and Sir W. Coventry come out: so I asked his advice. He told me, he had said something to salve it, which was, that his Highness had, he believed, rightly informed the King, that the fleete is come in good condition to have staid out yet longer, and have fought the enemy, but yet that Mr. Pepys his meaning might be that, though in so good condition, if they should come in and lie all the winter, we shall be very loth to send them to sea for another year's service without great repairs. He said it would be no hurt if I went to him, and showed him the report himself brought up from the fleete, where every ship, by the Commander's report, do need more or less, and not to mention more of Sir W. Pen for doing him a mischief. So I said I would, but do not think that all this will redound to my hurt, because the truth of what I said will soon appear. Thence having been informed that, after all this pains, the King hath found out how to supply us with 5 or 6000*l.*, when 100,000*l.* were at this time but absolutely necessary, and we mention 50,000*l.* This is every day a greater and greater omen of ruine. God fit us for it! I made my brother, in his cassocke, to say his grace this day, but I like his voice so ill, that I begin to be sorry he hath taken orders.

8th. Towards noon by water to Westminster Hall, and there, by several, hear that the Parliament do resolve to do something to retrench Sir G. Carteret's great salary; but cannot hear of any thing bad they can lay to his charge. The House did this day order to be engrossed the Bill against importing Irish cattle: a thing, it seems, carried on by the Western Parliament-men, wholly against the sense of most of the rest of the House; who think, if you do this, you give the Irish again cause to rebel. Mr. Pierce says, the Duke of York and Duke of Albemarle do not agree. The Duke of York is wholly given up to his Lady Denham. The Duke of Albemarle and Prince Rupert do less agree. The King hath yesterday, in Council, declared his resolution of setting a fashion[1] for clothes, which he will never alter. It will be a vest, I know not well how; but it is to teach the nobility

---

[1] See 13th and 15th of this month, *post.*

thrift, and will do good. By and by comes down from the Committee Sir W. Coventry, and I find him troubled at several things happened this afternoon, which vexes me also; our businesses looking worse and worse, and our work growing on our hands. Time spending, and no money to set anything in hand with; the end thereof must be speedy ruin. The Dutch insult and have taken off Bruant's head, which they had not dared do, though found guilty of the fault he did die for, of something of the Prince of Orange's faction, till just now, which speaks more confidence in our being worse than before. Alderman Maynell, I hear, is dead. Thence returned in the dark by coach all alone, full of thoughts of the consequences of this ill complexion of affairs, and how to save the little I have, which, of I can do, I have cause to bless God that I am so well, and shall be well contented to retreat to Brampton, and spend the rest of my days there. So to my office, and finished my Journal, with resolutions, if God bless me, to apply myself soberly to settle all matters myself, and expect the event of all with comfort.

9th. To the office, where we sat the first day since the fire, I think. Home, and my uncle Thomas was there, and dined with my brother and I.

10th. (Fast-day for the fire.) With Sir W. Batten, by water to White Hall, and anon had a meeting before the Duke of York, where pretty to see how Sir W. Batten, that carried the surveys of all the fleete with him, to show their ill condition to the Duke of York, when he found the Prince there, did not speak one word, though the meeting was of his asking, for nothing else; and when I asked him, he told me he knew the Prince too well to anger him, so that he was afraid to do it. Thence with him to Westminster, to the parish church,[1] where the Parliament-men; and Stillingfleete in the pulpit. So full, no standing there; so he and I to eat herrings at the Dog Tavern; and then to church again, and

---

[1] St. Margaret's. Dr. Sancroft, Dean of St. Paul's, preached before His Majesty at the Cathedral; Seth Ward, Bishop of Exeter, before the House of Lords, in Westminster Abbey; and Dr. Stillingfleet and Dr. Frampton, before the House of Commons, at St. Margaret's, Westminster—*The London Gazette*, No. 94.

there was Mr. Frampton[1] in the pulpit, whom they cry up so
much, a young man, and of a mighty ready tongue. I heard
a little of his sermon, and liked it, but the crowd so great I
could not stay. Captain Cocke, who is mighty conversant
with Garraway and those people, tells me what they object as
to the mal-administration of things as to money. But that
they mean well and will do well; but their reckonings are
very good, and show great faults, as I will insert here. They
say the King hath had towards this war expressly thus
much : —

Royal Ayde..	£2,450,000
More..	1,250,000
Three months' tax given the King by a power of raising a month's tax of 70,000l. every year for three years......	0,210,000
Customes, out of which the King did promise to pay 240,000l., which, for two years, come to	0,480,000
Prizes, which they moderately reckon at................	0,300,000
A debt declared by the Navy, by us......................... ...	0,900,000
	5,590,000
The whole charge of the Navy, as we state it for two years and a month, hath been but.............................	3,200,000
So what has become of all this sum?[2]............	$2,390,000

He and I did bemoan our public condition. He tells me the
Duke of Albemarle is under a cloud, and they have a mind
at Court to lay him aside. This I know not; but all things
are not right with him: and I am glad of it, but sorry for
the time. So home to supper, it being my wedding night,[3]
but how many years I cannot tell; but my wife says ten.[4]

11th. *Memorandum.* I had taken my Journall, during the
fire, and the disorders following, in loose papers, until this
very day, and could not get time to enter them in my book
till January 18, in the morning, having made my eyes sore
by frequent attempts this winter to do it. But now it is

---

[1] Robert Frampton, a native of Pimpern, in Dorsetshire, educated at Corpus Christi College, Oxford, and afterwards a student of Christ Church, and Chaplain to a man-of-war. In 1673, he became Dean of Gloucester, and in 1681, Bishop of that See: but refusing to take the oaths of allegiance to William and Mary, he was deprived, and retired into private life. Ob. 25th May, 1708.

[2] The remainder of the receipts.

[3] See on this subject, a note in the *Life,* vol. I.

[4] It was eleven years.

done: for which I thank God! and pray never the like occasion may happen.

12th. Taking leave of my poor father, who is setting out this day for Brampton, in the Cambridge coach, he having taken a journey to see the city burned, and to bring my brother to town. To St. James's, and there, from Sir W. Coventry, do hear how the House have cut us off 150,000*l.* of our wear and tear, for that which was saved by the King while the fleete lay in harbour in winter. However, he seems pleased, and so am I, that they have abated no more; and do intend to allow of 28,000 men for the next year; and this day have appointed to declare the sum they will give the King,[1] and to propose the way of raising it; so that this is likely to be the great day. My wife come home, and hath brought her new girle I have helped her to, of Mr. Falconbridge's. She is wretched poor, and but ordinary favoured; and we fain to lay out seven or eight pounds worth of clothes upon her back, which, methinks, do go against my heart; and do not think I can ever esteem her as I could have done another, that had come fine and handsome; and, which is more, her voice, for want of use, is so furred, that it do not at present please me; but her manner of singing is such, that I shall, I think, take great pleasure in it. Well, she is come, and I wish us good fortune in her. Notice of a meeting of the Commissioners of Tangier to-morrow, and so I must have my accounts ready for them.

13th. My accounts cost me till four o'clock in the morning, and, which was pretty to think, I was above an hour, after I had made all right, in casting up of about twenty sums, being dozed with much work, and had for forty times together forgot to carry the 60 which I had in my mind, in one denomination which exceeded 60: and this did confound me for above an hour together. To my Lord Bellassis, whom I find kind, but he had drawn some new proposal to deliver to the Lords' Commissioners to-day; wherein one was, that the garrison would not be well paid without some goldsmith's undertaking the paying of the bills of exchange for tallies He professing so much kindness for me, and saying, that he would not bo

---

[1] The parliament voted this day a supply of 1,800,000*l.* sterling.

concerned in the garrison without me; and that, if he continued in the employment, no man should have to do with
the money but myself, I did ask his Lordship's meaning of
the proposition in his paper.   He told me, he had not much
considered it, but that he meant no harm to me.   I told him,
I thought it would render me useless; whereupon he did very
frankly, after my seeming denials for a good while, cause it to
be writ over again, and that clause left out, which did satisfy me
abundantly.   To White Hall, and there the Duke of York,
who is gone over to all his pleasures again, and leaves off care
of business, what with his woman, my Lady Denham, and his
hunting three times a week, was just come in from hunting.
So I stood and saw him dress himself, and try on his vest,
which is the King's new fashion, and he will be in it for good
and all on Monday next, and the whole Court: it is a fashion,
the King says, he will never change.   He being ready, he and
my Lord Chancellor, and Duke of Albemarle, and Prince
Rupert, Lord Bellassis, Sir H. Cholmly, Povy and myself,
met at a Committee for Tangier.   My Lord Bellassis's propositions were read and discoursed of, about reducing the garrison to less charge; and, indeed, I am mad in love with my
Lord Chancellor, for he do comprehend and speak out well, and
with the greatest easiness and authority that ever I saw man in
my life.   I did never observe how much easier a man do speak,
when he knows all the company to be below him, than in him;
for, though he spoke, indeed, excellent well, yet his manner
and freedom of doing it, as if he played with it, and was
informing only all the rest of the company, was mighty pretty.
He did call again and again upon Mr. Povy for his accounts.
I did think fit to make the solemn tender of my accounts that
I intended.   I said something that was liked, touching the
want of money, and the bad credit of our tallies.   My Lord
Chancellor moved, that, without any trouble to any of the
rest of the Lords, I might alone attend the King, when he
was with his private Council, and open the state of the garrison's want of credit; and all that could be done, should.
Most things moved were referred to Committees, and so we
broke up; and, at the end, Sir W. Coventry come; so I away

40 *

with him, and he discoursed with me something of the Parliament's business. They have voted giving the King for the next year 1,800,000*l.*; which, were it not for his debts, were a great sum. He says, he thinks the House may say no more to us for the present, but that we must mend our manners against the next trial, and mend them we will. Sir J. Minnes most certainly must be removed, or made a Commissioner, and somebody else Comptroller.

14th. (Lord's day.) To church, which was mighty full: and my beauties, Mrs. Lethulier [1] and fair Batelier, both there. A very foul morning, and rained. Sent for my cloak to go out of the church with. To Westminster Abbey. Here I met with Sir Stephen Fox, who told me how much right I had done myself, and how well it is represented by the Committee to the House my readiness to give them satisfaction in every thing, when they were at the office. I was glad of this. He did further discourse of Sir W. Coventry's great abilities, and how necessary it were that I were of the House to assist him. I did not own it, but do myself think it were not unnecessary, if either he should die, or be removed to the Lords, or any thing happen to hinder his doing the like service the next trial; which makes me think that it were not a thing very unfit; but I will not move in it.

15th. Colvill tells me of the viciousness of the Court: the contempt the King brings himself into thereby; his minding nothing, but doing all things just as his people about him will have it! the Duke of York becoming a slave to this Lady Denham, and wholly minds her. That there really were amours between the Duchess and Sidney; that there is reason to fear that, as soon as the Parliament have raised this money, the King will see that he hath got all that he can get, and then make up a peace; that Sir W. Coventry is of the caball with the Duke of York, and Brouncker, with this Lady Denham: which is a shame, and I am sorry for it, and that Sir W. Coventry do make her visits; but yet I hope it is not so. Pierce tells me, that as little agreement as there is between the Prince [2] and Duke of Albemarle, yet they are likely to go

---

[1] See note to Dec. 13, 1665, *ante*.   [2] Rupert.

to sea again; for the first will not be trusted alone, and nobody will go with him but this Duke of Albemarle. He tells me much how all the commanders of the fleete and officers that are sober men do cry out upon their bad discipline, and the ruine that must follow if it continued. But that which I wonder most at—it seems their secretaries have been the most exorbitant in their fees to all sorts of the people, that it is not to be believed that they durst do it, so as it is believed they have got 800l. a-piece by the very vacancies in the fleete. He tells me that Lady Castlemaine is concluded to be with child again; and that all the people about the King do make no scruple of saying that the King do intrigue with Mrs. Stewart, who, he says, is a most excellent-natured lady. This day the King begins to put on his vest, and I did see several persons of the House of Lords and Commons too, great courtiers, who are in it; being a long cassocke close to the body, of black cloth, and pinked with white silk under it, and a coat over it, and the legs ruffled with black riband like a pigeon's leg; and, upon the whole, I wish the King may keep it, for it is a very fine and handsome garment.[1] I fear that Pen will be Comptroller, which I shall grudge a little. The Duke of Buckingham called Sir W. Coventry aside, and spoke a good while with him. I did presently fear it might be to discourse something of his design to blemish my Lord of Sandwich, in pursuance of the wild motion he made the other day in the House. Sir W. Coventry, when he come to me

---

[1] Rugge, in his *Diurnal*, thus describes the new Court costume:—"1666, Oct. 11. In this month His Majestie and whole Court changed the fashion of their clothes—viz., a close coat of cloth pinkt, with a white taffety under the cutts. This in length reached the calf of the leg, and upon that a sercoat cutt at the breast, which hung loose and shorter than the vest six inches. The breeches the Spanish cut, and buskins some of cloth, some of leather, but of the same colour as the vest or garment; of never the like fashion since William the Conqueror." Evelyn says, "It was a comely and manly habit, too good to hold, it being impossible for us, in good earnest, to leave the *Monsieur's* vanities long." See also his *Diary*, Oct. 18, 1666. Charles resolved never to alter it, and "to leave the French mode, which had hitherto obtained, to our great expence and reproach." But his inconsistency was so well known, that "divers gentlemen and courtiers gave him gold, by way of wagers, that he would not persist in his resolution."—*Quar. Review*, vol. xix., p. 41. It is represented in a portrait of Lord Arlington, by Sir P. Lely, formerly belonging to Lord de Clifford, and engraved in Lodge's *Illus. Persons*. Louis XIV. ordered his servants to wear the dress: see Nov. 22, 1666 post.

again, told me that he had wrought a miracle, which was the convincing the Duke of Buckingham that something, he did not name what, that he had intended to do was not fit to be done, and that the Duke is gone away of that opinion. By and by the House rose; and then I, with Sir G. Carteret, and walked in the Exchequer Court. I observing to him how friendly Sir W. Coventry carried himself to him in these late inquiries, when, if he had borne him a spleen, he could have had what occasion he pleased offered him, he did confess he found the same thing, and would thank him for it. Away with him to his lodgings at White Hall to dinner, where my Lady Carteret is, and mighty kind, both of them, to me. Their son and my Lady Jemimah will be here very speedily. She tells me the ladies are to go into a new fashion shortly, and that is, to wear short coats above their ancles; which she and I do not like; but conclude this long trayne to be mighty graceful. But she cries out of the vices of the Court, and how they are going to set up plays already; and how, the next day after the late great fast, the Duchess of York did give the King and Queen a play. Nay, she told me that they have heretofore had plays at Court, the very nights before the fast for the death of the late King. She do much cry out upon these things, and that which she believes will undo the whole nation; and I fear so too. This day the great debate was in Parliament, the manner of raising the 1,800,000*l.* they voted the King on Friday: and, at last, after many proposals, one moved that the chimney-money might be taken from the King, and an equal revenue of something else might be found for the King: and people be enjoyned to buy off this tax of Chimney-money for ever at eight years' purchase, which will raise present money, as they think, 1,600,000*l.*, and the State be eased of an ill burthen, and the King be supplied of something as good or better for his use. The House seems to like this, and put off the debate to to-morrow.

16th. To the office, where set to do little business, but hear clamours for money. Hearing my brother play a little upon the Lyra viall, which he do so as to show that he hath a love to musique, and a spirit for it.

17th. To dinner alone with my brother, with whom I had now the first private talk I have had, and find he hath preached but twice in his life. I did give him some advice to study pronunciation, but I do fear he will never make a good speaker, nor, I fear, any general good scholar; for I do not see that he minds optickes or mathematiques of any sort, nor anything else that I can find. I know not what he may be at divinity and ordinary school-learning. However, he seems sober, and that pleases me. To White Hall, and there heard the Duke discourse, which he did mighty scurrilously, of the French, and with reason, that they should give Beaufort[1] orders when he was to bring, and did bring his fleete hither, that his rendezvous for his fleete, and for all sluggs to come to, should be between Calais and Dover; which did prove the taking of La Roche, who, among other slugs, behind, did, by their instructions, make for that place, to rendezvous with the fleete; and Beaufort, seeing them as he was returning, took them for the English fleete, and wrote word to the King of France that he had passed by the English fleete, and the English fleete durst not meddle with him. The Court is all full of vests, only my Lord St. Albans not pinked, but plain black; and they say the King says the pinking upon whites makes them look too much like magpies, and, therefore, hath bespoke one of plain velvet.

18th. The waters so high in the roads, by the late rains, that our letters come not in till to-day. Towards Lovett's, in the way wondering at what a good pretty wench our Barker makes, being now put into good clothes, and fashionable, at my charge; but it becomes her so that I do not now think much of it, and is an example of the power of good clothes and dress. To Lovett's house, where I stood godfather. But it was pretty, that, being a Protestant, a man stood by and was my Proxy to answer for me. A priest christened it,

---

[1] François de Vendôme, Duc de Beaufort, well known in the annals of France, was born in 1616, and in 1664 and 1665 commanded a naval expedition against the African corsairs. (See 11th October, 1664, ante.) The following year he had the charge of a fleet intended to act, in concert with the Dutch, against England, but which was merely sent out as a political demonstration. He was killed at the siege of Candia, in 1669.

and the boy's name is Samuel. The ceremonies many, and some foolish. The priest in a gentleman's-dress, more than my own; but is a Capuchin, one of the Queen-mother's priests. He did give my proxy and the woman proxy, my Lady Bills,' absent, had a proxy also, good advice to bring up the child: and, at the end, that he ought never to marry the child nor the godmother, nor the godmother the child or the godfather: but, which is strange, they say the mother of the child and the godfather may marry. By and by the Lady Bills comes in, a well-bred but crooked woman. The poor people of the house had good wine, and a good cake; and she a pretty woman in her lying-in dress. It cost me near 40s. the whole christening: to midwife 20s., nurse 10s., maid 2s. 6d., and the coach 5s. The business of buying off the Chimney-money is passed in the House: and so the King to be satisfied some other way, and the King supplied with the money raised by this purchasing off of the chimnies.

19th. To Povy's, who continues as much confounded in all his business as ever he was; and would have had me paid money as like a fool as himself, which I troubled him in refusing, but I did persist in it. Sir Robert Viner told me a little of what, in going home, I had seen: also a little of the disorder and mutiny among the seamen at the Treasurer's office, which did trouble me, considering how many more seamen will come to town every day, and no money for them. A Parliament sitting, and the Exchange close by, and an enemy to hear of, and laugh at it.[2] Viner, too, and Bakewell were sent for this afternoon; and was before the King and his cabinet about money. They declaring they would advance no more, it being discoursed of in the House of Parliament for the King to issue out his privy-seals to them to command them to trust him, which gives them reason to decline trusting. We do not do the King any service, but rather abuse and betray his service by being here, and seeming to do something

[1] Lady Diana Fane, daughter of Mildmay Fane, second Earl of Westmoreland, widow of Edward Pelham, Esq., of Brocklesby, in Lincolnshire, re-married John Bills, Esq., of Caen Wood, Highgate. Her only child, Diana, by her second husband, died the widow of Captain Francis D'Arcy Savage, 23d May, 1726, and is buried at Barnes. Lady Diana Bills was at this time in her 36th year.

[2] War was declared against Denmark this day.

while we do not.   Sir G. Carteret asked me whether 50l. or
60l. would do us any good; and when I told him the very
women must have 200l., he held up his eyes as if we had asked
a million.   The Duke of York did confess that he did not see
how we could do anything without a present supply of
20,000l., and so we broke up, and all parted.   Nothing but
distraction and confusion in the affairs of the Navy; which
makes me wish, with all my heart, that I were well and quietly
settled, with what little I have got, at Brampton, where I might
live peaceably, and study, and pray for the good of the King
and my country.

20th.   Commissioner Middleton[1] says, that the fleete was in
such a condition as to discipline, as if the Devil had commanded it; so much wickedness of all sorts.   Enquiring how
it come to pass that so many ships had miscarried this year, he
tells me that he enquired: and the pilots do say, that they dare
not do nor go but as the Captains will have them; and, if
they offer to do otherwise, the Captains swear they will run
them through.   He says that he heard Captain Digby,[2] my
Lord of Bristoll's son, a young fellow that never was but one
year, if that, in the fleete. say that he did hope he should not
see a tarpawlin[3] have the command of a ship within this
twelve months.   He observed, while he was on board the
Admirall, when the fleete was at Portsmouth, that there was
a faction there.   Holmes commanded all on the Prince's side,
and Sir Jeremy Smith on the Duke's; and every body that
come did apply themselves to one side or other; and when
the Duke of Albemarle was gone away to come hither, then
Sir Jeremy Smith did hang his head, and walked in the
General's ship but like a private commander.   He says he was
on board the Prince, when the news come of the burning of
London : and all the Prince said was, that now Shipton's prophecy was out;[4] and he heard a young commander presently

---

[1] Thomas Middleton, who had been made a Commissioner of the Navy in
1664.

[2] Francis Digby, afterwards Colonel.   He was killed in the sea-fight at Solebay.

[3] A sailor.

[4] Evidently the concluding passage of "Mother Shipton's Prophecies,"—viz.,
"A ship come sayling up the Thames to London, and the master of the ship
shall weepe, and the marriners shall aske him why he weepeth, being he hath

swear, that a citizen's wife that would not take under half-a-piece before, would be contented with half-a-crowne: and made mighty sport of it. My Lord Chancellor, the other day, did ask Sir G. Carteret how it came to pass that his friend Pepys do so much magnify the bad condition of the fleete. Sir G. Carteret tells me that he answered him, that I was but the mouth of the rest, and spoke what they have dictated to me: which did, as he says, presently take off his displeasure. With Sir G. Carteret home to dinner, with him my lady, and Mr. [William] Ashburnham, the Cofferer. They talk that the Queen hath a great mind to alter her fashion, and to have the feet seen; which she loves mightily. I met with the King's declaration about his proceedings with the King of Denmarke, and particularly the business of Bergen: but it is so well writ, that, if it be true, the King of Denmarke is one of the most absolute wickednesse in the world for a person of his quality. Met Mr. Povy by appointment, and he and I till late at night, evening of all accounts between us; but that which troubles me most is, that I am to refund to the ignoble Lord Peterborough what he had given us six months ago, because we did not supply him with money.

21st. (Lord's-day.) To White Hall, and there attended the Cabinet, and was called in before the King, and then to give an account of our want of money for Tangier, and that which is no welcome thing to be the solicitor for, and to see how like an image the King sat, and could not speak one word when I had delivered myself, was very strange: only my Lord Chancellor did ask me whether I thought it was in nature at this time to help us to anything. So I was referred to another meeting of the Lords' Commissioners for Tangier, and my Lord Treasurer. Walking with Sir H. Cholmly long in the gallery, he told me, among many other things, how young Harry Killigrew [1] is banished the Court lately, for saying that

---

made so good a voyage, and he shall say, ' Ah, what a goodlie citie this was, none in the world comparable to it, and now there is scarcely left any house that can let us have drinke for our money.' "— Quoted from the edition of 1641, which Prince Rupert might have seen.

[1] Son of Tom Killigrew by his first wife, Mrs. Cecilia Crofts. He was baptized in St. Martin's-in-the-Fields, 16th April, 1637, and is called " young," to distinguish him from his uncle of the same name, who was Master of the Savoy.

my Lady Castlemaine was a little wanton when she was young. This she complained to the King of; and he sent to the Duke of York, whose servant he is, to turn him away. The Duke of York hath done it, but takes it ill of my Lady that he was not complained to first. She attended him to excuse it; but ill blood is made by it. Sir H. Cholmly tells me how Mr. Williamson stood in a little place to have come into the House of Commons, and they would not choose him: they said, "No courtier." And, which is worse, Bab May went down in great state to Winchelsea with the Duke of York's letters, not doubting to be chosen: and there the people chose a private gentleman in spite of him, and cried out they would have no Court pimp to be their burgesse; which are things that bode very ill.

22d. At the Temple Church, looking with pleasure on the monuments and epitaphs.

23d. Sir W. Batten told me Sir R. Ford would accept of one-third of my profit of our private man-of-war, and bear one-third of the charge, and be bound in the Admiralty, which I did like mightily of, and did draw up a writing as well as I could to that purpose. After dinner, down by water to Shadwell, to see Betty Mitchell, the first time I was ever in their new dwelling, since the fire.

24th. Holmes did last Sunday deliver in his articles to the King and Cabinet against [Sir Jeremy] Smith, and Smith has given in his answer, and lays his not accompanying the fleete to his pilot, who would not undertake to carry the ship further: which the pilot acknowledges. The thing is not accommodated, but only taken up, and both sides commanded to be quiet, but no peace like to be. The Duke of Albemarle is Smith's friend, and hath publickly swore that he would never go to sea again, unless Holmes's commission were taken from him. I find by Hayes,[1] that they did expect great glory in coming home in so good condition as they did with the fleete; and therefore I the less wonder that the Prince was distasted with my discourse the other day about the sad state of the fleete. But it pleases me to hear that he did expect

---

[1] Prince Rupert's Secretary.

great thanks, and lays the fault of the want of it upon the
fire, which deadened everything, and the glory of his services.
Called my wife, and, it being moonshine, took her into the
garden, and there layed open our condition as to our estate, and
the danger of my having it all ' in the house at once, in case
of any disorder or troubles in the State, and therefore resolved
to remove part of it to Brampton, and part some whither
else, and part in my own house, which is very necessary, and
will tend to our safety, though I shall not think it safe out of
my own sight.

25th. To Mrs. Pierce's, where she was making herself
mighty fine to go to a great ball to-night at Court, being the
Queen's birthday ; so the ladies for this one day wear laces,
but are to put them off again to-morrow. To Mrs. Williams's,
where we met Knipp. I was glad to see the jade. Made
her sing ; and she told us they begin at both houses to act on
Monday next. But I fear, after all this sorrow, their gains
will be but little. Mrs. Williams says, the Duke's house will
now be much the better of the two, because of their women ;
which I was glad to hear. The House of Parliament makes
mighty little haste in settling the money ; but they fall into
faction, and libells have been found in the house. Among
others, one yesterday, wherein they reckon up divers great
sums to be given away by the King — 10,000l. to Sir W.
Coventry, for weare and teare, the point he stood upon to
advance that sum by, for them to give the King : Sir G. Carteret 50,000l. for something else — I think supernumerarys ;
and so to Matt. Wren 5000l. for passing the Canary Company's patent ; and so a great many other sums to other
persons.

26th. Up, and all the morning within doors, beginning to
set my accounts in order from before this fire, I being behind-
hand with them ever since ; and this day I got most of my
tradesmen to bring in their bills, and paid them. Nothing
done in the house yet, as to finishing the bill for money,
which is a mighty sad thing, all lying at stake for it.

27th. Up, and there comes to see me my Lord Bellassis,

---

i. e., his money. See 12th Nov., post.

which was a great honour. He tells me great news, yet but
what I suspected—that Vernatty is fled, and so hath cheated
him, and twenty more, but most of all I doubt Mr. Povy. He
tells me how the two Houses begin to be troublesome; the Lords
to have quarrels one with another. My Lord Duke of Buckingham having said to the Lord Chancellor, who is against
the passing of the Bill for prohibiting the bringing over of
Irish cattle, that whoever was against the Bill, was there led
to it by an Irish interest, or an Irish understanding, which is
as much as to say he is a fool; this bred heat from my Lord
Chancellor, and something he [Buckingham] said did offend
my Lord of Ossory, my Lord Duke of Ormond's son,[1] and
they two had hard words, upon which the latter sends a challenge to the former; of which the former complains to the
House, and so the business is to be heard on Monday next.[2]
Then, as to the Commons: some ugly knives, like poignards,
to stab people with, about two or three hundred of them, were
brought in yesterday to the House, found in one of the
house's rubbish that was burned, and said to be the house of
a Catholique. This and several letters out of the country,
saying how high the Catholiques are every where, and bold in
the owning their religion, have made the Commons mad, and
they presently voted that the King be desired to put all
Catholiques out of employment, and other high things; while
the business of money hangs in the hedge. Home to dinner,
where Mrs. Pierce and her boy and Knipp, who sings as well,
and is the best company in the world, dined with us, and
infinite merry. The playhouses begin to play next week.
Towards evening, I took them out to the New Exchange, and

---

[1] On the 14th Sept., 1665, the Earl of Ossory had been created an English
Peer, as *Lord Butler of Morepark.*

[2] The proceedings on the 27th are not clearly stated. According to Clarendon,
this Bill was urgently pressed forward in the House of Lords by the Duke of
Buckingham. The debate became most disorderly, especially on the part of its
promoters. On the Duke making the remark above quoted, Lord Ossory, not
trusting himself with a reply in the House, challenged Buckingham privately.
This the Duke endeavoured to avoid, and was found in a place not fixed for the
meeting. On the following morning, he informed the House of the affair.
Clarendon regards the whole as a "gross shift" on the part of the Duke. Both
parties were sent to the Tower. The Bill was subsequently passed. See Lord
Arlington's account of the quarrel in Brown's *Miscellanea Aulica,* p. 423, &c.

there my wife bought things, and I did give each of them a pair of jesimy[1] plain gloves, and another of white. Here Knipp and I walked up and down to see handsome faces, and did see several. Then carried each of them home, and, with great pleasure and content, home myself.

28th. (Lord's day.) Captain Guy to dine with me, and he and I much talk together. He cries out of the discipline of the fleete, and confesses really that the true English valour we talk of is almost spent and worn out; few of the commanders doing what they should do, and he much fears we shall therefore be beaten the next year. He assures me we were beaten home the last June fight, and that the whole fleete was ashamed to hear of our bonfires. He commends Smith, and cries out of Holmes for an idle, proud, conceited, though stout fellow. He tells me we are to owe the loss of so many ships on the sands, not to any fault of the pilots, but to the weather; but in this I have good authority to fear there was something more. He says the Dutch do fight in very good order, and we in none at all. He says that in the July fight, both the Prince and Holmes had their belly-fulls, and were fain to go aside; though, if the wind had continued, we had utterly beaten them. He do confess the whole to be governed by a company of fools, and fears our ruine. The Revenge having her forecastle blown up with powder, to the killing of some men in the River, and the Dyamond's being overset in the careening at Sheernese, are further marks of the method all the King's work is now done in. The Foresight, also, and another come to disasters in the same place this week, in the cleaning; which is strange.

29th. Up, and to the office to do business, and thither comes to me Sir Thomas Teddiman, and he and I walked a good while in the garden together, discoursing of the disorder

---

[1] Jessemin (*Jasminum*), the flowers of which are of a delicate sweet smell, and often used to perfume gloves. Edmund Howes, Stow's continuator, informs us, that sweet or perfumed gloves were first brought into England by the Earl of Oxford, on his return from Italy, in the fifteenth year of Queen Elizabeth, during whose reign, and long afterwards, they were very fashionable. They are frequently mentioned by Shakspeare. Autolycus, in the *Winter's Tale*, has among his wares —

" Gloves as sweet as damask roses."

and discipline of the fleete, wherein he told me how bad
every thing is; but was very wary in speaking any thing to
the dishonour of the Prince or Duke of Albemarle, but do
magnify my Lord Sandwich much before them both, for
ability to serve the King, and do heartily wish for him here;
for he fears that we shall be undone the next year, but that
he will, however, see an end of it.   To Westminster; and I
find the new Lord Mayor Bolton[1] a-swearing at the Exchequer, with some of the Aldermen and Livery; but, Lord!
to see how meanely they now look, who upon this day used
to be all little lords, is a sad sight, and worthy consideration;
and every body did reflect with pity upon the poor City, to
which they are now coming to choose and swear their Lord
Mayor, compared with what it heretofore was.   To my goldsmith, to bid him look out for some gold for me; and he tells
me that ginnys, which I bought 2000 of not long ago, and
cost me but 18½d. change, will now cost me 22d.; and but
very few to be had at any price.   However, some more I will
have, for they are very convenient, and of easy disposal.   To
White Hall, and into the new playhouse there, the first time
I ever was there, and the first play I have seen since before
the great plague.   By and by, Mr. Pierce comes, bringing my
wife and his, and Knipp.   By and by, the King and Queen,
Duke and Duchess, and all the great ladies of the Court;
which, indeed, was a fine sight.   But the play being "Love
in a Tub," a silly play, and though done by the Duke's
people, yet having neither Betterton nor his wife,[2] and the
whole thing done ill, and being ill also, I had no manner of
pleasure in the play.   Besides, the House, though very fine,
yet bad for the voice for hearing.   The sight of the ladies,
indeed, was exceeding noble; and, above all, my Lady Castlemaine.   The play done by ten o'clock.

30th. Mr. Hater staying most of the afternoon abroad, he
come to me, poor man, to make excuse, and it was that he
had been looking out for a little house for his family.   His

---

[1] Sir William Bolton, Merchant-Tail.
[2] See note, Feb. 1, 1663-4.

wife being much frightened in the country with the discourses of troubles and disorders like to be, and therefore durst not be from him, he is forced to bring her to town. This is now the general apprehension of all people : particulars I do not know, but my own fears are also great, and I do think it time to look out to save something, if a storm should come.

END OF VOL. II.